THE MEMOIRS OF A PENNY-A-LINER

James 'Jack' Vincent was a Chartist writer whose name is now as obscure as it was once famous, his popular fiction from the first half of the 19th century quickly eclipsed by the next generation of literary authors. Described by Dickens as a 'Manichean novelist' and designated the 'last of the Romantics' by W.H. Ainsworth, Vincent was the product of a culture in transition, no longer Regency but not quite yet Victorian. His work was equally mercurial; although fashionable in the 1830s little of it has survived, while his descent into the murky world of penny dreadful publishing also makes much of this material difficult to identify and attribute. Even less is known of his life, and Malcolm Elwin does not even consider him worthy of a mention in his book on forgotten 19th century novelists, *Victorian Wallflowers*. Jack Vincent has always been a mystery, at least until now.

Lost for over a century, and rescued from a dead hoarder's collection, the Jack Vincent Papers comprise letters, fiction and a series of memoirs, all written by hand and never before published. This work is now being painstakingly edited by Dr. Stephen Carver, who also located the original manuscripts. The present volume is the first of these memoirs.

Stephen Carver is a writer and academic. For sixteen years he taught literature and creative writing at the University of East Anglia (where he also took his doctorate), spending three years in Japan as an associate-professor of English at the University of Fukui. He is presently Head of Online Courses at the Unthank School of Writing, the Senior Editor at Green Door Design for Publishing, and a Reader for The Literary Consultancy. He is the biographer of the Victorian novelist William Harrison Ainsworth, and has published extensively on gothic film and fiction. He lives in Norfolk with his wife and son, and far too many books and motorcycles.

JACK VINCENT

SHARK ALLEY

THE MEMOIRS OF A PENNY-A-LINER

From
The Jack Vincent Papers
Volume I
1852

STEPHEN CARVER

GREEN DOOR PRESS

First Published in Great Britain in 2016
By Green Door Press, UK

www.greendoordp.com

ISBN: 978-1523935451

Cover Design by Rachael Gracie Carver
Typeset in Adobe Garamond Pro & Ivory
by Green Door Design for Publishing

Cover Image © Rachael Gracie Carver

FOR MY WIFE AND SON

NOTE ON THE TEXT

Jack Vincent's private papers came to light three years ago. As a literary historian specialising in this period, I have no doubt as to the authenticity of this material. The paper on which it is written, the ink used, and the entire external aspect of the documents put their date beyond the reach of question. Even allowing for the inevitable issues surrounding truth and memory in life writing, when Vincent refers to the historical record he is consistently accurate and easily cross-referenced.

Shark Alley: The Memoirs of a Penny-a-Liner (Vincent's original title) is the first volume of the autobiographical papers, although it might be more adequately described as a 'bio-novel,' foreshadowing as it does the New Journalism of the 1960s as much as it reflects the more conventional Victorian 'triple-decker' serial romance. Vincent's memoirs therefore eschew the more traditional form of autobiography in favour of the devices of literary fiction. The present narrative is also of particular historical significance as it includes the most complete eyewitness account of the final voyage of the troopship *Birkenhead* ever discovered, and equally because of Vincent's close association with many of the major writers and artists of his day, most notably Thackeray, Cruikshank, Mayhew, and Dickens.

Aside from the correction of a few minor spelling and grammatical errors, I have left the manuscript as I found it. I have therefore restricted myself to the appended account of its discovery, and a few explanatory notes when the passage of time has rendered the reference obscure and the context fails to clarify.

S.J.C.

CONTENTS

'I can fancy a future Author taking for his story the glorious action off Cape Danger, when, striking only to the Powers above, the *Birkenhead* went down; and when, with heroic courage and endurance, the men kept to their duty on deck.'

— William Makepeace Thackeray, speech to the anniversary meeting of the Royal Literary Fund Society, reported in *The Morning Herald,* May 13, 1852.

'How do you like Forster's *Life of Dickens*? I see he only tells half the story.'

— William Harrison Ainsworth, letter to Jack Vincent, January 25, 1872.

BOOK ONE

- The Shivering of the Timbers -

CHAPTER I

We were approaching the islands of Madeira, about midway in our journey, the day we lost a man and a horse. The animal belonged to Sheldon-Bond, and he was considerably more put out by its passing than he was that of the human being that accompanied it into the void. The young subaltern remained in a foul humour for the rest of that miserable and ill-omened day, his unfortunate man, Private Dodd, getting the worst of it. I tried to avoid him, as there was already bad blood between us, but this was difficult given the confines of the ship. As he stormed around the deck like a vengeful wraith in a graveyard, I could read the message in his eyes when they connected with my own quite clearly.

My suppositions were verified when our paths finally collided in the corridor that led to the wardroom later that evening. 'Do not dare to write about today's events, you Chartist swine,' he had said, his voice soft yet pregnant with menace, 'or things might go very badly with you before we reach our destination.'

But I did, of course, damn him, for that was my job.

The accident happened towards the end of the forenoon watch. It was a calm, clear morning, and not unpleasant to be above deck. The air was far too still for the ship to go under sail; and, as was not uncommon, we were therefore becalmed while Whyham and his engineers made repairs to the engines. These were, like several of the ship's company if truth be told, prone to seizures, as well as other mechanical ailments too various and incomprehensible to innumerate. Whyman, the Chief Engineer, was a good sort, and fancied he had found in me a mouthpiece by which he could share his passion for marine engines with the empire. He had therefore explained the working of this great machine to me at length, although I must privately confess that I had not the wit or wisdom to truly appreciate the functional beauty of the thirty foot connecting rod which was currently being straightened on deck by the ship's blacksmith, an ancient and spark-scored creature who would obviously have preferred to work unhindered by Whyman's constant and nervous interruptions. Although such delays drove our Captain to despair and distraction, they were a welcome break for the rest of us, when the weather was fine at least, affording a tranquil respite from the constant drone of those Tartarean engines.

It was at these times that Herbert Briscoe, a stoker from Liverpool, took it upon himself to provide us with some light entertainment. When the drift anchor was deployed and the ship relatively static, several blinking soot-stained stokers would emerge on deck to take the air; and if Speer, rather than Davis, had the deck, Briscoe was given leave to do his popular *mélange* act. He would begin by taking a running dive off the bow, after first hesitating to indicate mock apprehension like a Harlequin in a low opera, before expertly plunging into the depthless dark. He would then swim the length of the hull underwater, before surfacing astern to a muddle of Flash obscenities and enthusiastic applause, much of either stripe on account of the wagers placed upon the length of time it had taken him to run the keel, the winners dropping ropes that he might re-embark, temporarily cleansed of engine room filth and several shillings the richer. We would all count together in order that the timing be accurate, bellowing the numbers aloud as one. He usually did it in about two minutes.

I declined an offer from Private Moran to place a bet. A man of my means should never gamble. His countenance, in reply, was a strange combination of obsequiousness and contempt, suggesting that he imagined me a swell or a cheese screamer: either too full of myself to game with common soldiers, or opposed on ecumenical grounds. The reality was that with all his wheeling and dealing he was likely much wealthier than I, and that God was as dead to me as to him. I liked Moran though, and through his patronage I had been able to interview many of his companions. I therefore did something that would have appalled my dear wife, and responded by turning out my trouser pockets with an exaggerated shrug and a winsome smile. I doubt he believed me, but the old pirate rewarded me with a sympathetic grin before darting off into the mass of men crowding the rails in search of Briscoe.

I rejoined the count at sixty-five. Briscoe should now have been about halfway, just past the huge steam driven paddle-wheels on either side of the hull that would, were they in motion, have ground him to pie filling in an instant, like the victims of the demon barber of Fleet Street himself. I swear the old bake head was more fish than man. I knew many seamen did not swim, but Briscoe was not of that kidney. He loved the water as much as I feared it, for I could barely swim a stroke. I knew that this was a skill I should acquire in order to swim with my son, but I had thus far declined Briscoe's offer of 'a few pointers.' He expected me to practice in the open water and I could not bear the thought of entering such a vast expanse of nothingness. To my mind, Milton would have done better to imagine the hellish void through which Satan travelled as the black Atlantic rather than some frozen wasteland. At least on land a man might have a chance, but consider the horror of being lost at sea, with no land in sight or beneath your feet, no cognisance of what moved beneath save your worst imaginings, and the odds of rescue so long that even Moran's most reckless customer would shake his head and keep his money in his pocket. This was why many seamen to whom I had spoken would not learn to swim, a stance that might have surprised many but not me. No, I would not swim, especially in that God cursed ocean.

The count had now passed eighty, which was close to Briscoe's best time on the voyage thus far (which was ninety-six seconds). While the count continued, I was distantly aware that Cornet Bond and his man were attending to the young officer's horse, which like the other animals on board was corralled in a temporary but well-constructed stable on the upper deck. When the ship was not violently in motion, Bond liked to walk his horse so that it remained in good fettle throughout the arduous journey. He was a Lancer, and those men valued their mount above all else in the world; but as one of only two cavalrymen on board, Bond's fellow officers obviously viewed his relationship with his horse as somewhat obsessive. I could sympathise, though I did not care for the man. I knew his type, and he, it would seem, knew mine. Nonetheless, he possessed a very fine horse, a young solid white gelding, and his attention to its care was admirable. If only he afforded his human subordinates the same level of kindness I would have been glad to have counted him an ally, despite his social rank. I could not hear him from my position, but I could tell he was berating his orderly, the long suffering Dodd, a gentle soul of twice the years of his master. I could see the petulance in Bond's features (when he lost his temper he revealed his true face, which was that of a spiteful youth several years shy of twenty), while, similarly, he was always shouting at poor old Private Dodd.

The count approached two minutes. No one else was watching Bond, but I could see through the open stable gate that his horse was becoming agitated, like a child, by his mood. Dodd was hanging on to the frightened animal's bridle as if his life depended upon his very grip, which looking at his officer it may well have done, while Bond, to give him his due, attempted to calm the creature by whispering in its ear. Between them they guided the nervous animal onto the deck, Bond now taking the bridle, to Dodd's obvious relief. The upper deck was perhaps thirty yards in length, and was cluttered with lashed down military equipment and a complex web of rigging. Mindful of obstacles, Bond carefully walked his horse through that decidedly unsuitable paddock.

Would that we could communicate with the lower forms, for how could such a creature possibly have comprehended the point and purpose of sea travel? I was reminded of the feelings of helplessness attendant in the care of the very young, when one cannot explain to a baby yet to acquire language why she or he must be cold or sick or hungry. Perhaps, I thought, Bond communed with his horse as I did my son, by means of a kind of desperate kindness, a non-verbal reassurance made of soft sounds and gentle gestures.

When I saw my boy again he would probably be talking in quite complex sentences. How I hated to miss such a significant development. I also feared that this thinking, speaking child would not remember his father, despite our early attachment. I banished the thought as best I could. In that environment, I could ill-afford the kind of black mood that such ideas engendered. His mother would not let him forget me, I decided, and when the *Morning Chronicle* paid me I would be better placed to raise a family. My present situation was, as my friend Reynolds put it, 'a tour of duty,' much like that of the soldiers and seamen about whom I was charged to write. It was a necessary means to an end, and at least I was still working, albeit in the face of my original promise to Grace that I would never allow my career to remove me from my family. No, that was another train I must let pass me by. We needed the money, and there was no decent work for me in London anymore.

The count was by then becoming decidedly less enthusiastic. How long may a man hold his breath under water, I wondered; two, perhaps three minutes? If our collective enumeration was accurate, then Briscoe was now approaching three minutes without air. Speer, the Second Master, was looking decidedly queasy. The mood of the men on deck had changed as well, and they looked to the officer in charge for guidance, for a clear sign from above. No one counted after the fourth minute has passed. We stood in helpless silence while Speer weighed up his options. Even Bond had come to a halt.

'Man overboard!' screamed Speer. The spell was broken, and the seamen exploded into activity. Aldridge sounded the alarm from the poop, hammering on the great bell as if the French were attacking. Speer bellowed the order to lower a boat, putting Able Seaman Blake in charge of the rescue. There was a deafening babel of competing voices. Everywhere seamen were shouting, mostly trying to clear the rest of us from their way.

It was clear that Bond and his horse were a serious obstruction. 'Mr. Bond,' yelled Speer above the general cacophony, 'will you please remove that animal.'

It was my guess that Bond was so taken aback at being thus addressed that he slightly relaxed his grip on the bridle. In that instant, the horse, already panicked by the general alarm, bolted. Seamen scattered like churchgoers menaced by a vagrant, and, as if to confirm his master's frequent boasts that he could have been a steeplechase champion, the horse cleared the port rail like a five bar gate. Bond screamed like a woman and ran to the bar, followed by several of the men, myself included. The hapless animal had survived the drop and was swimming, quite adeptly, in an uneven circle about five yards from the ship. Blake had steered his boat in the direction of the commotion, hoping no doubt that someone had spotted Briscoe. Bond was shouting at Blake in the gig, but the latter was signalling with his hands that there was nothing he could do. Bond ran off to request the deployment of the windlass.

'This is better than the penny theatre,' said Private Moran.

All the senior officers were now on deck; Major Seton looking nervous, Brodie, the Acting Master, looking annoyed, and Salmond, our Captain, looking drunk. Drake, the marine Colour Sergeant, was ushering the women and children below deck, while Lakeman, the mercenary, struck a long match and lit a cigar. There was still no sign of Herbert Briscoe.

It looked as if Bond had managed to convince Speer to save the horse, and the ship's huge cargo winch was now swinging seaward with the aid of half-a-dozen ordinary seamen. The plan, it appeared, was that Blake would send a couple of men into the water to get the harness under the horse, but before the winch could be lowered to retrieve the terrified animal, a shout went up from the masthead.

'What the devil's that?' said a man next to me, shading his eyes with the flat of his hand, 'a whale perhaps?' We all strained to follow his gaze. A dark shape in the azure waters lay.

An animal fear came over me, and I suddenly wanted to back away from the rail. That was no whale. We had seen such creatures on the voyage, and despite their immense size they had none of the menace that this shadow conveyed. Everywhere men began to bellow, 'Shark!' at Blake and his crew, who in their turn looked around in obvious panic.

The great fish approached Bond's helpless mount and the horse began to swim frantically back towards the ship. The shark pursued unhurriedly, surfacing as it passed its prey, dwarfing it in size as it did the small open boat. It must have been fifteen feet long at least, if not more.

'Christ and all his holy angels,' said Moran.

I had read of sharks, and also written of them, but even the most lurid accounts of the illustrated press or my own imagination had not prepared me for this terrible apparition. There was something ancient in the simplicity of the beast. It was a flat, implacable grey with no features save dead, black eyes, like a doll or a devil. Bond watched the enormous animal glide through the clear water in total horror. I saw him call to a nearby marine, who unslung his rifle and handed it to the young officer. Bond raised it at once, sighted carefully and shot his beloved horse a fraction above its left eye. He hung his head, and offered the musket back to the shocked leatherneck. We became aware of more shots then, as the other marines fired on the shark, which was still close to the surface and circling the twitching carcass of the horse. Comparing the animal with the now limp body of the horse, I inwardly increased my original assessment of its length. I saw four shells strike it around its huge dorsal fin. Blood flowed from the broad grey back, but the shark did not even slow its pace or bother to dive. Then its huge triangular head seemed to hinge back, and its terrible mouth fastened onto the horse`s flank, shaking from side to side as it tore away a great chunk of marble flesh. Fascinated and appalled, I watched as the water turned to blood.

Lakeman, who had thus far taken no part in proceedings, called for his man. The steadfast Private McIntyre was immediately at his side. Words were exchanged, and McIntyre scurried off as Lakeman strode purposely towards us, still casually smoking. The men parted as he approached the rail, leaving the two of us together. Lakeman nodded in greeting but said nothing, watching the monster feeding below. McIntyre returned carrying a long rifle.

'Loaded?' said Lakeman.

'Of course, sir,' said his batman.

Lakeman held the rifle in the crook of his arm and inserted cork earplugs. 'You might want to cover your ears,' he told me, a trifle loudly, raising the rifle.

There was a crack of thunder and a split second later the shark's great head exploded in a shower of blood and bone. Shuddering, it fell away from our horrified eyes, disappearing beneath the flat red surface of the water like a sinking ship.

'Will sir take nuts or a cigar!' cried Lakeman, delighted with his shot. A cheer went up from the deck, and Blake and his crew visibly relaxed.

'Brute,' whispered Bond, who had joined us at the rail. 'Rotten filthy brute.'

The air around us was muddy with foul tasting smoke. Lakeman tossed the gun back to McIntyre and threw me a wink through the murk. He removed the earplugs and dropped them into McIntyre's waiting palm. My ears were ringing like a man in a bell. 'Elephant gun,' he announced, '2 bore: half-pound ball. Hard on the arm and a devil to load in a hurry, but it'll pretty much stop anything.'[1]

'You might want to start reloading now then,' I said, as, God help us, there were more of them, three, at least, tearing into the body of the horse.

Lakeman, however, had lost interest. I received the impression that he had been conducting an experiment and, satisfied with the result, he saw no reason to repeat it. 'It'd just be shooting fish in a barrel,' said he, strolling away with the nonchalance of a winner at a faro table, McIntyre trotting dutifully behind.

Bond and I were left alone. I awkwardly tried to express my sympathy.

'What would you know about it?' he said vituperatively.

I shrugged and kept my own counsel as he took his leave. Needless to say he was right. I really didn't care how he felt about anything, and as the probable fate of poor old Herbert Briscoe, forgotten in all the excitement, occurred to me, I ceased to concern myself with Bond or his bloody horse.

There was nothing for it but to finish the repairs, and when we were once more under weigh the sharks followed. Over dinner there was talk of some sort of memorial service for Briscoe, but during the discussion I found myself suddenly distracted and preoccupied by a curious childhood memory. The more I tried not to think of it, the more vividly I recalled an incident with a cat I had once owned. One spring, a baby sparrow fell from its nest in an elm in my parents' garden, and my little cat was on it before I could help the unfortunate bird. She sat under the same tree every day for the rest of the month, waiting for another fledgling to fall.

CHAPTER II

A FEW PASSENGERS, including myself, had embarked at Portsmouth a month earlier, on the first day of January, 1852. This gave us a day or so of relative peace in which to become acclimated to the ship and to each other, before she took on the bulk of her human cargo at Cork. The 12th Foot (the East Suffolks) were already on board, seventy-odd men and their officers, Granger and Fairtlough, as well as the mercenary Lakeman and his contingent, the Lancers Rolt and Sheldon-Bond, and about a hundred Highlanders from the 73rd, 74th, and 91st Regiments, including Major (soon to be Lieutenant-Colonel) Seton and Captain Wright, the senior military officers on the ship.

With the beginning of the New Year our journey also commenced, with a brief, uneventful jaunt around the south west coast and into the Western Approaches. As I had anticipated this adventure with a cold, sick dread for several weeks by that point, I was relieved that modern sea travel notionally appeared much less arduous than my research and limited personal experience had led me to surmise. On the contrary, I supposed that my initial concerns were groundless, and that sea legs were much more easily acquired than I had previously thought. Looking back, I was as a man receiving the first stroke of a surgeon's blade or a sergeant's lash, naively believing that such a short sharp shock could be endured, and not at all considering the duration of the torture. I recall my wife making a similar error of judgement regarding the pain of labour, assuming the initial stage to represent the whole, and wondering aloud to the attending midwife, with her usual sunny wit, why there was so much fuss and screaming normally associated with the miracle of birth. This misplaced bravado occurred a while before the true contractions commenced, turning her inside out with agony for the next five hours or so. And this was a remarkably short labour, I am told.

Despite her reassuringly gentle passage through the smooth waters of the Solent, the ship possessed an eldritch aspect, at least to me, from the beginning. There was something ancient and foreboding about her, the paradox being that she was a relatively new vessel, built only a dozen years or so before. As a steam powered ship of iron, she could not, in fact, have been more modern. I should note here that I tended towards Luddism as a general rule in those days, although if pushed I would concede that some of the new technology was not without a certain merit. I was grateful, for example, for rail travel over those interminable coach journeys, while pulp mills and steam driven paper making machines were a definite boon to my profession, bringing printed knowledge to the common man for the first time in history. Nonetheless, I feared that the savage pace of change, as Mr. Marx and Mr. Engels had so persuasively written, was of little benefit to my class.

My nostalgia for less complicated times did not, however, extend to matters maritime, and I found the political and popular arguments in favour of conventional wooden warships over iron and steam to be ill-informed, backward looking and ridiculous. I expressed these views to Captain Salmond upon our first meeting, and was invited to dine at his table thereafter. This was a fortuitous turn of events for me, given that the salty old cove liked a drink and bled freely, while my personal supplies were far from endless. (The fact that my sea chest audibly clinked was a source of much ill-disguised amusement to the bluejackets who had conveyed it to my quarters.) He also had coffee, which was a rare treat.

To be a journalist, one must be able to get the measure of a man very quickly and, in doing so, gain his trust whether he be of high or low estate. This was a facility I had always possessed, which I took to come from my youth, when I had to learn quickly how to adapt to very different social environments. Robert Salmond R.N., Master and Commander, was reasonably easy to read. He was a disappointed man. I had the hairy old spud hooked and landed as soon as I asked him where his guns should have been placed. In an impossibly low voice that seemed to rise from the very depths above which we precariously sat, he solemnly described the two 96-pounders mounted on pivots fore and aft, and the four 68-pounders, paired each broadside, imaginary guns that had been originally intended by her designer, commissioned, as he was, to build a warship not, said Captain Salmond, 'a damn troopship.'

The ship and her architect were the victims of political expediency. John Laird was a visionary, who staked his reputation and his business on iron over oak. Cockburn, the First Sea Lord, was of a similar opinion, convincing Peel, then in his second term, that the future of England's undisputed mastery of the waves was cast in iron. The frigate *Vulcan* was therefore commissioned by the Admiralty to be built by Laird as part of a proposed new fleet of iron vessels. Such armadas do not come cheap however, and not everyone in government approved of such unproven, they said, extravagance. Wooden ships had been good enough to best the Spanish and the French, argued the traditionalists. Would Nelson have triumphed at Trafalgar were he in command of a fleet of kettles, they demanded, did Raleigh assault Cadiz in a bathtub? It was a collision between the old world and the new, and for once the industrialists were routed. I covered parts of the story myself, although while most papers, whether for or against, were keen to support the Royal Navy in its on-going maintenance of world peace, we at the *Northern Star* continued to argue that the planet was, in reality, in a constant state of turmoil, much of it engendered by us.

The change from wood to iron thus proved much more contentious than the relatively smooth progression from sail to steam. Lobbyists for the timber shipbuilding industry argued that ships built of iron could not possibly float, despite the re-invention and refinement of the watertight bulkhead by maritime architects such as Laird. It was also widely believed that iron hulls were more easily subject to catastrophic damage than wooden ships, and there were also issues raised regarding the effect of the iron on magnetic compasses, a constant deviation, easily corrected, but presented in the popular press as damning evidence for the prosecution. As I reported at the time, many of these critics also had their own interests and investments to protect. I thus collected a few new enemies along the way, but it was not the first time and, in any event, that is always the nature of my profession.

By the time Laird had won his contract, Peel's administration was on its last legs, battered by recession and deficit, and rotted from within. In my opinion, he gave ground on the naval budget in order to hold out long enough to repeal the Corn Laws. Cockburn's building programme was cancelled, and Peel went out the following year. When Laird finally launched what was to have been the frigate *Vulcan*, completed only because she had been too advanced to scrap, she hit the water a hastily redesigned troopship. Just as Juno had cast her infant son off Mount Olympus, the Admiralty had rejected their Vulcan, pulled her teeth and prosaically re-named her *Birkenhead* after the city of her birth. The presence of the god of fire and iron was now marked only by an incongruous effigy of him as the ship's figurehead, either left in defiance by Laird or not considered worth the bother of changing.

'I have often felt that Mr. Laird and myself have much in common,' Salmond confessed, 'although we've never actually met.'

'In what way?' I said, wondering but not asking if Laird also had a beard like a wild hedgerow in winter.

'In the manner of life seeming to promise one thing, and then delivering quite another,' he said.

In that sense the Captain and I were also of a similar stripe. This affinity was more than I felt able to volunteer at that juncture, although no doubt he privately knew full well that Mr. Dickens and Mr. Ainsworth had no need to leave their families and supplement their incomes by freelancing as special correspondents, despite my mask of professional respectability. So natural was my performance by then that I sometimes almost fell for it myself.

Salmond loved his ship though, but it was obvious to me that he could never quite master that nagging feeling that he was no more than the driver of a sea-going omnibus, having previously seen active service on the *Retribution* and the *Vengeance*. Nowadays he carried passengers, always anathema to a sea captain of the old school, men and their families away to wars in which he would take no part. A man can justify his place in the world in many ways, and Salmond knew that ships such as his own were as much an organ of empire as the fast frigates, but, said he, again in confidence, 'There are captains of warships, and then there are captains of troopships.'

He could trace his seafaring lineage all the way back to the reign of Elizabeth, with all that means to any navy man. He knew that he could have been more than he was, and you could see in his salt blasted eyes that this intelligence gnawed at his very soul. It was equally obvious that this frustration at his own sense of failure was not easily kept at bay by any intoxicant he knew of, and as a well-travelled man he knew of quite a few.

Having no military laurels to gain, Salmond had determined to distinguish his command by virtue of speed and efficiency. He therefore promised me that we would make the Cape in forty-five days, as against the naval and mercantile average, which was sixty-four. This was music to my ears, for every day spent away from my family was torture. If Salmond was as good as his word, I would spend about three months at sea, there and back again, while another three at the most should garner more than enough material from the regiments garrisoned around Port Elizabeth and in country for a decent series of articles. With a bit of luck I would be home before my son's third birthday.

I did not share these thoughts with the good Captain, but when I first spied his ship, she seemed an awkward marriage of sail and steam and wood and iron. She was rigged as a brigantine, but carried a tall funnel between fore- and main-masts, combined with a pair of paddle-wheels set on the outside of the hull, each a good half-dozen yards in diameter. Her hull was constructed of riveted iron plating, while her decks, paddle-boxes and masts were made of wood, the contrast made sharper by the paintwork, which was black on the iron and white on the woodwork. The ship was small by the standards of modern liners like the *Oceanic*, but back then she dwarfed all other vessels in the harbor, being a good seventy yards from stem to stern, and displacing a couple of thousand tons. The surrounding cutters, gigs and fishing boats were toys in her presence, fit for nothing but the bathtub or the boating lake.

Silent, lonely and sublime she was. Against the fading light of a brittle winter day the men in the triple-masted rigging reminded me of spiders, while the miserable looking figurehead glared balefully down with a look in his eye that I generally associate with management and magistrates rather than celestial metalwork. Child Rowland to the dark tower came, I had thought as I mounted the gangplank.

To my considerable relief I was accorded a private berth. The icy grey walls recalled the box of a stone jug, yet for all the unpleasant associations that this brought forth, I remained grateful to have a place to myself in which to retire and write. The men in the troop decks had naught but eighteen inches of hammock space to claim as their own, buried in low bulkhead compartments so airless that lamps and candles barely burned. When I paid a visit to the lower decks I felt like a miner, bent over and making my way to the coal face through ghostly lamplight; half crawling through low, jagged openings that snagged and scratched, cut as an afterthought into the ship's bulkheads to improve the movement of the troops.

It was all too easy to lose one's way, and to my shame I did just that the first time I descended into the blackness with the intention of documenting the layout of the ship for my readers. I collected a similarly bemused ranker along the way who had been sent on an errand from the troop deck and was now lost in the labyrinth. The man was a private in the 12th Foot name of Edward Moran, who, like me, had come aboard at Portsmouth. It was well worth my while to engage him in conversation. I needed a conduit to the soldiers in order to do my job, and I was much more likely to gain their trust if presented by one of their own rather than an officer. Upon making his acquaintance, I was gratified to learn that the private had read my work, and was particularly fond of *The Darkman's Budge* (my life of Joseph Blake, or 'Blueskin'), and *The Black Grunger of Hounslow*, which had both been serialized by Edward Lloyd.

He was a typical London Irishman, possessed of hair even darker than my own, and keen, intelligent eyes. 'Love and murder suit me best, sir,' said he, 'but your stories set me a thinking too.' I took from this that he had radical leanings, but politics aside I was absurdly flattered, especially when he went on to describe my fair weather friend Dickens as a jawbreaker and an anthem cackler of which he could make neither end nor side. 'I'd like Mr. Dickens fine,' he said, 'if only he'd kept to being funny like he was in the Pickwick Club.' I was compelled to agree, and had given up after *Dombey and Son*, a turning point in English letters so I've been told, but damned hard reading.

My new found friend had never seen the inside of an iron ship either, and had no more idea of where to go than I. An orange glow in the distance suggested lamplight, so we decided to head for that, in the manner of moths to a flame. But when the sepulchral light expanded, instead of arriving at the troops' quarters we suddenly found ourselves at a dead end, face to face with two unblinking marines, armed and at attention, at either side of a great iron door. Oil lamps hung overhead, casting long shadows that gave the guards a similar aspect to that of the ship's figurehead, as if they too were cast in heavy metal.

'Halt! Who goes there?' demanded one of the frozen leathernecks, his musket suddenly rampant in the most alarming manner.

'Friends,' said my companion, gently diverting the long barrel of the gun with his index finger. Behind him, I shuffled around like a schoolboy, too nervous to appreciate that at least I could stand up straight for a moment. The marine growled at us. 'I take it this ain't the soldiers' billet?' ventured Moran.

'This is the magazine, private,' replied the marine, with danger in his eye, 'there's nothing for you here.' He ignored me completely. This was insulting, but also a profound relief. I made a mental note that the magazine was physically guarded, instead of simply locked, which seemed unusual.

His comrade had been of a more understanding disposition. 'Ain't you got a guide then, mate?' he asked gently, although he moved not a muscle below the neck as he spoke.

'No, your worship, we have not,' said Moran, 'it's more of a case of the blind leading the blind.'

'So I see,' said the second marine, dismissing me with a glance no doubt reserved for civilian males, which had no relevance in his world whatsoever.

'I am The Press,' said I, feeling the need for validation.

'Then God help us,' he said, with not a trace of humour. 'There's supposed to be bluejackets showing you lot where to go,' he continued, in the overly measured tone of one permanently exasperated. 'Take yourselves back where you came from until you see a set of steps. You came down one deck too many.' He nodded towards the dark passageway behind us. 'Now shake your trotters and don't come back, and we'll say no more about it.'

'That's very kind of you,' said Moran, with a lick of the Blarney about him. The first marine then dismissed us with a dreadful oath, and we beat a hasty yet, I hope, dignified retreat; a manoeuvre to which I, in common with the British Army, was not unaccustomed.

A distant thunder, initially suggesting the movement and speech of a large body of men below decks had next led us along another narrow, dimly-lit passageway. As the sound became more unearthly and cacophonous, this new section of freezing maze coughed us out into the nave of a vast cathedral raised in praise of the new science. It was not soldiers we had heard but engines, unfeasibly large engines, their howl weirdly distorted by the acoustics below deck, and all being primed for our imminent departure.

My companion swore for several seconds, never, I noted, once repeating his self. He was in need of a berth not, as he put it, a frimicking manufactory. A dozen trains seemed crammed into the belly of the ship. Shimmering waves of heat from massive boilers and condensers seared our faces, while gigantic cranks spun storms of deafening volume to burst the eardrums and rattle the bones. Engineers swarmed around the machinery. Some dripped oil on exposed levers and cogs; some listened, with the benefit of ear trumpets, to shafts spinning in highly polished bushes, and yet more checked chronometric dials and screamed the readings to each other. Half naked beings, corded muscles blacked by soot, fed the insatiable furnaces. We stood there like tourists who do not speak the language, gazing uselessly into a cavern as tall as the ship herself, until a stocky man with a miner's face looked up from the huge dial it was seemingly his sole task to carefully monitor, and waved us out with his slate, as if swatting flies.

Once more we entered the gloomy passages, miserably retracing our steps. The ship seemed to have no end. 'We are as Jonah, my friend,' I observed, 'trapped within the belly of a whale.'

'Mark that place we've just been well, sir,' he had shouted back, 'for that's where we'll go when we die.'

More by luck than judgement, we found the troop section on the third attempt, forward of the engine room. By this point I would not have been surprised to have emerged under water. Those that knew Moran hooted from their hammocks.

'Get lost did you?' said an immaculately turned out marine who was obviously in charge, and whose features were distinguished by an ugly, livid scar beneath his chin. Like his fellow leathernecks at the magazine, he did not spare me the time of day.

'Tour of the ship, Colour Sergeant,' said Moran cheerily.

These early arrivals had already chosen their spots and stowed their kit, keeping to a vague regimental order with the Cockneys at one end of the troop deck and the Scots at the other, separated, I later discovered, by a tight huddle of labouring lads from East Anglia and the Home Counties. I followed Moran around the long mess tables running the length of the vast compartment, and along the narrow gangway down the middle of the deck. Everywhere men were netting their gear or lounging in hammocks slung from the low beams overhead. Like a cat, Moran had chosen a corner, up against a bulkhead and quite private by local standards.

'Here we are, sir,' he had said, 'the finest room in the hotel.'

It was like climbing into a kitchen range, and not a large one either, but this tight little cranny was to become as much of a home from home as my own berth over the next few days. It was here that I came to know many of the future heroes of the *Birkenhead*, and a fair few of the villains as well, not that the company of thieves and murderers was in any way remarkable to my experience by then. But whether good, bad or, like me, somewhere in-between, I cared little for their moral disposition as long as they talked to me. And in that way something of these young men is preserved, for in under two months most of them would be dead.

CHAPTER III

To the main, I preferred the company of the lower ranks to that of their officers, although in truth I fit no better with the former than the latter. Like the ship, I was an awkward hybrid: too educated to feel comfortable with most working men, yet lacking the breeding to move freely among the so-called upper classes, despite wasting several years in a foolish and ultimately disastrous attempt to do so when I was young. I had more recently come to understand that my place in the world was with my family.

I rather liked Lakeman, the *condottiere*. He was of my kind, although he would likely not have admitted this, being considerably richer than I (though how he came by this conspicuous wealth was a secret he was not willing to disclose). His rank was even more ambivalent than my own, for he travelled as an officer in charge of a large body of men, in common with the other senior military commanders on board, but he was of no army save his own.

When Lakeman and his party joined our little charabanc, there was obviously some confusion among the ship's officers concerning what, precisely, to do with him. He was, like me, an outsider. Having failed to gain a commission on the terms that he wished, he had, in the great tradition of the East India Company, raised his own regiment. As an officer and a gentleman, it seemed appropriate that he should dine with the other senior ranks at the Captain's table, although Major Seton had privately made it known that he considered Lakeman to be at best a deluded fop and at worst a vulgar adventurer, a soldier of fortune whose national affiliations were far from clear (his mother was French). As the Major had also made his views about warrant officers more than plain, I think the old dog Salmond, whose rank was by warrant rather than commission, kept Lakeman close because he knew that this irritated Seton. He did much the same with me, a known radical and iconoclast, presenting me to his military counterparts as a *fait accompli*, 'Mr.

Vincent: author and scholar.' Lakeman seemed oblivious, and was possessed of an enviable self-confidence, although I would not have put his age at much more than twenty-five. I had no doubt when I made his acquaintance that he would go far, in whatever army he ended up serving.

Lakeman came aboard with a beautiful chestnut mare called Élise, his mount since the late-40s, when, as he never tired of telling us, he was attached to the French staff in Algeria. During this time, he fought in several campaigns against the Arabs and the Kabyles, when he was presumably no older than the teenaged subalterns presently under Seton. In addition to this fine Arabian charger, Lakeman was the proud owner of his very own hobby horse, also acquired in Northern Africa. While slaughtering the locals, Lakeman had become deeply impressed with the superiority of the new French Minié rifle over the old Brown Bess smooth-bore. Upon his return to England, he therefore took it upon himself to enforce on the military authorities the advantages of this new weapon, which he knew, from personal experience at the sharp end, to outstrip the range of the British Army Land Pattern musket at least six fold.

He somehow managed to arrange an audience with Wellington. The Commander-in-Chief's response was that in the British Army it was not the weapon that counted but the man behind it, while also arguing that the rapid twist of the rifling in the Minié would so increase recoil as to render it useless to a true marksman, because, he said, 'Englishmen take aim, while Frenchmen fire anyhow.' His Grace then delegated the matter to his adjutant, who conceded that the Minié might be of some use for taking long shots from ramparts, but he was certain that it had no other practical application in the field. (The implication being that a rifle best suited to sniping was a coward's weapon, and entirely what one would expect from a French designer.) Lakeman was then unceremoniously passed to a colonel at the Board of Ordinance, who expressed his surprise at the Duke having displayed so much patience with his outlandish and foreign ideas, before bringing the interview to a close.

'I made him uncomfortable,' Lakeman told me, 'for, unlike him, I knew which end of the rifle the ball came out of.' Shortly afterwards, the war broke out at the Cape, and while the British Lion slowly shook the cobwebs from its ears and set about gathering fresh food for spear and powder, Lakeman saw his chance and promptly volunteered his services, under the condition that the men that served under him should be issued with Minié rifles. 'There is no such thing as luck,' he liked to say. 'One must simply be prepared when an opportunity arises.'

Such was the need for manpower that some lunatic at the War Office gave him leave to enlist up to two hundred volunteers, the government offering rations and pay, although no staff, with Lakeman expected to provide uniforms, weapons, and barracks at his own expense. Should Lakeman manage a force of at least a hundred and fifty strong (which he had), the military authorities had guaranteed this contingent free passage to the Cape, to go and shoot, and be shot at by the Basuto tribesmen presently harrying the settlers. Thus was formed the notorious Shoreditch Rangers, so named because of the area in which recruitment was most enthusiastic, who now travelled with us to the Cape. It was rumoured that upon learning this intelligence Wellington was heard to remark that this was as good a way as any for Lakeman to commit suicide. I heard Seton and his staff privately referring to Lakeman's people as the 'Newgate Rangers,' which did not seem to me to be far short of the case. To further paraphrase the Iron Duke to the point of cliché, I did not know what the enemy would make of them, but they scared the browns and whistlers out of me.

Dining in the presence of that company was therefore reminiscent of being placed at the worst table in the wedding party, with the mad aunts, the ex-lovers, and the ginger step-children. This was meat and drink to me, though, in more ways than one. As those sons of empire struck sparks off one another, I marked their stories well; those they told, and those they did not.

The Captain held court in his cabin below the poop deck, where we repaired that first night, the senior ranks and I (less Fairtlough, who was already feeling seasick, and Granger, who was on duty). This was after a surprisingly acceptable meal in the recently redecorated wardroom, although the damn place had still reeked of paint. The old bene cove was usually sailing with Admiral Lushington by the sixth bell of the dog's watch, much to the obvious discomfiture and disapproval of Seton. The Major was a son of the manse, and his commitment to the pledge was obvious. As for myself, I loved a good comedy drunk, as did Lakeman, it would seem. He kept catching my eye and grinning as our Master and Commander meandered through one of his interminable anecdotes concerning his certain belief that mermaids were not only quite real (he had, he confessed, been intimate with females of the species on more than one occasion), but that they were another branch of the human family tree that had taken to the water millennia ago in accordance with Maupertuis' theory of natural selection and Erasmus Darwin's concept of common descent.

'To see one of these creatures, in the flesh,' said Salmond, after the table was cleared, the bingo served and the stinkers lit, 'is to know that they are, in fact, quite human.'

They were, he said, of a like appearance to us, only perfectly adapted for the life aquatic, being physically streamlined and in possession not of a fish's tail, as was the legend, but a great leathery paddle where once were legs and feet, in the manner of the other great ocean-going mammals.

Seton was attempting to engage in a polite and balanced manner with his host that one could not help but admire. The Major was tall man from the Granite City, although he did not look it on account of his soft, almost androgynous features. He was a little younger than me, no more than forty, and he spoke like an academic (with the added gravitas that a refined Scots accent always seems to convey). He had thus stoically fastened onto Darwin's name, and his thesis that all warm-blooded animals had arisen from one living filament, which, he said, the great First Cause endued with animality, with the power of acquiring new parts attended with new propensities, directed by irritations, sensations, volitions, and associations.

'The First Cause,' he said, 'of course refers to Aquinas' proofs of the Lord Our Father as the primary generator of all things material, regardless of how much they may alter through either random or selective breeding across the centuries.'

'And whatsoever passeth through the paths of the seas,' added Captain Wright, the highest ranking army officer on board after Seton. They were of a similar age, but there any resemblance ceased, even though Wright, too, was a Scot. Behind whiskers of great ferocity, upon features as sharp as a sabre, Wright had the look of a soldier about him. He was confident, and comfortable with his own authority in a way that Seton was not. Wright, I had heard, had already been in the thick of it. Of all the army officers on board, only Wright and Lakeman had ever fired a shot in anger.

'The Eighth Psalm,' muttered Seton in absentminded reply.

'Exactly so, sir,' said Sheldon-Bond, nodding with exaggerated interest. I noticed Ensign Rolt kept his own counsel, but he probably knew that no one gave a bobstick for his opinions one way or another. Bond was more ambitious, and had weighed Seton up as a bit of an anthem cackler, which was a fair assessment, at least in provisional terms. I had arrived at a similar conclusion having watched him quaff nothing but rainwater the entire dinner.

Salmond motioned to his man to charge his glass and fixed Seton in a pernicious gaze, his ancient face horribly underlit by a squat glimstick that threatened to ignite his beard like a roman candle. 'Balderdash,' he said, in that low tone of his, like the echo within some great iron bell. Seton looked embarrassed, and for a moment no one spoke.

Salmond had quite a pronounced scar on his forehead, and although I later heard Bond and Rolt nervously joshing in private that he had probably fallen down some steps while in his cups, I wondered if this wound, however it may have been come by (more likely by ball and shot given his past), was the crack in his head by which a little bit of the dark world had crept in and found easy purchase in his disappointed soul. I had seen this sort of thing happen before, and I had lately began to wonder, as I slid past the middle age myself, if once all the hopes and dreams of youth were certain not to come true, and the demons and eidola of one's heart had reached a particular density, with every missed opportunity, failed love, betrayal and defeat logged, stored and reviewed, that most of us simply went mad.

It was a quiet night, windless and calm but very, very dark. The cloud was low and thick, and what moon there was cast no light whatsoever. There was only the constant vibration of the ship's great engines, that distant hammering, coupled with the sounds of the twin paddles slapping the sea. But now another sound interrupted Salmond's increasingly deranged monologues, a booming, doom laden howl, which shuddered through us like the sounding of the seven trumpets.

'What in God's name was that?' said Wright.

The echoing lamentation sounded again, long and mournful in the night. I felt it travel the length of my spine and then ruffle my hair like a troublesome spirit. I beckoned for more drink and took a cigar, for I could feel a familiar sense of building panic, the cold, hopeless dread that crawls over me when I look too closely at my station and my circumstances, like a man on a precipice who suddenly and foolishly looks down. And I had looked down. I was suddenly aware of the icy vastness of the black Atlantic upon which we presently balanced, bobbing atop the waves with no more presence than the floats my father once fashioned with cork to fish for pike. My fancy then turned to the huge creatures I knew to glide beneath, unseen yet ever present, as the siren song outside clearly evidenced. The fauna of a thousand childhood nightmares began to swim upwards towards me, and I imagined, too, the agony of drowning, of taking that final breath of freezing water until your lungs burst and your eyes popped. And contrary to polite and popular opinion, I was confident that you would feel every second of it. My chest tightened and my hands trembled, neither symptom connected, I knew, to the cheap cheroot between my teeth. I hoped that my companions had not noticed, and continued to draw upon the cigar.

'Perhaps whale song,' Salmond was saying, 'perhaps something else.'

'What exactly do you mean by "something else"?' I asked him.

Salmond just stared, past me and into the heart, I fancied, of some fantastic and terrible memory which my own imagination was happy to embellish. 'I have heard the mermaids singing,' he said, 'when there are sharks close by.'

'And do the sharks join in?' said Lakeman, his fine features twisted by a facetious mirth, ill-disguised yet, apparently, unmarked by the Captain.

'Sharks,' said Salmond, 'snort like swine.'

I had no desire to think on that, so while the Captain continued his soliloquy about sea monsters, both real and illusory, I attempted to follow some common advice from my wife and to 'think of something nice.' Yet despite my finest efforts, I was swiftly swamped by a wave of my own anxieties. I had heard tales of ships stove in by sharks and whales, like the *Essex* out of Nantucket, and I shuddered anew at the thought of entering the water myself.

I recalled then the river sharks of my childhood, the ugly pike with the thin snouts, vicious teeth and mirthless smiles that my father loved to fish, first for sport, later for food, though the damn things tasted muddy and were as full of bones as an eel. For an English coarse fish, Pike were powerful fierce, and would bite clean through anything but a wire line. I even saw one take a moorhen once. She was in the reeds when the big fish grabbed her and pulled her down, leaving nought but a few feathers and a cold ripple slobbering about the bank. Where I had grown up, folk said that a hungry pike would go as far as to grab a horse's snout when it dipped its head to drink from the river, but I never witnessed that myself.

My father told tall tales of a giant pike that the labourers that worked the fields by the river called 'Razorhead,' that, local legend had it, was over a century old and a good two yards in length, if not more. My father dreamed of catching this creature, and carved elegant lures and tied beautiful flies to entice the beast. I remembered with a bittersweet pleasure those dawn trips we took to the river that snaked through the fields of lazy cows and bad tempered horses beyond our cottage to hunt the great fish, before everything went to hell.

We never caught the pike, but I was swimming once (for I swam quite happily as a boy), when I saw it, gliding beneath me on the sandy bottom. The thing was huge, easily as long as my father was tall, maybe six, even seven feet long. I froze, treading water like a ghost, my heart hammering and my eyes locked on the predator below. To my profound relief the brute continued on its solitary course, seemingly unconcerned by my presence in its domain. I could see it was approaching a bend in the river, and as soon as it was out of sight I raced for the bank.

I had my arms on dry land when the bastard grabbed me and dragged me under. There was no pain, but I could feel that the animal had a good hold on my right foot so I kicked as hard as I could with my left, my hands scrabbling uselessly for purchase and finding only liquid. I screamed and was rewarded with a burning lung full of water, and I knew then that soon I would be dead. I thrashed about wildly in the monster's shredding grip, until finally my heel connected with something solid and it let me go. I had the presence of mind to do what my father had taught me when I was learning to swim, and I followed the path of the bubbles upwards to fresh air and safety. When I dragged myself out of the water I realised that two of my toes were missing. Some farm hands found me later, shivering from shock and grasping my ruined foot in horror. They gathered me up gently and took me home, and after that day I swam no more.

I returned my attention to the present company. The mysterious song outside was receding, and when the orderly replaced the candle the atmosphere in the cabin became lighter. The Captain had concluded his discourse upon the subject of mermaids, and Lakeman's features were contorting into fantastic expressions as he struggled manfully to suppress the gales of laughter screaming for release. He took a reckless drag on his cigar and commenced to snort and cough convulsively. I bashed his back and he spluttered as if drowning.

'By God, sir!' he finally exploded, addressing the Captain, 'that was a damn fine story.'

The party relaxed, with the exception of Salmond, who glowered at Lakeman with eyes like a brace of blown lamps. 'There's them that laughs,' said he, 'and them that know better.' He nodded sagely and indicated to his man that his glass was once more empty. Fortified by a generous balloon of brandy he regarded us all with a baleful eye. It was interesting to me that the soldiers were wary of passing comment. The younger men were waiting for Seton to speak, I was sure, but he kept his opinions to himself. I had noticed that keeping even a normal conversation in train with him was quite difficult. His protracted silences tended to cause one to babble. I said nothing, because, at that moment, I believed the Captain's chimerical stories of mermaids, or at least I wanted to believe, but I was equally reticent about declaring for his side, especially so soon in the collective acquaintance of the group there assembled. I doubted he cared what I thought anyway. He had the look of a man familiar with ridicule, and it was difficult not to concede that this particular yarn was ripe for parody if presented as anything other than a colourful fantasy. I wanted to believe him, though, because there was no magic left in the world, and what use is a world like that?

Wright was the first to crack. 'I think,' said he, leaning conspiratorially towards me, 'that perhaps you might get a story out of this, Mr. Vincent.' I took this in good part, and was beginning to feel quite flattered until he followed this with, 'Even better, come to think on it, you could call upon your friend Mr. Dickens to write of this matter in *Household Words*.'

'Yes,' I said flatly.

''Sdeath, sir,' said Lakeman. 'Do you mean to say that you know Dickens personally?'

I nodded glumly, fabulous nautical beings forgotten in an instant. Dickens. They always wanted to know about bloody Dickens. You would think sometimes that there was not another writer active in England at the time. Even Seton was looking on hopefully, and from the expression on his face that old fool Salmond thought he was already halfway to a cover story illustrated by Knight Browne or Cruikshank. If he had read Dickens' recent comments on the new American spirit mediums he'd not have been so keen. Dickens would have torn him apart for breakfast, and then tossed the bones to Thackeray, Forster and Hengist Horne to gnaw upon like dogs beneath his table.[2]

'Perhaps I can get you a headline in the *Illustrated London News*,' I offered, although he looked less than impressed at this, and returned a bulldog stare, chewing his cigar and expelling smoke as if he were his own ship's funnel. The illustrated press was a much better home for tales of madmen, monsters and mermaids though. Those things were *de rigueur* in New Grub Street.

But they had me outflanked. Like the rest of the world and his brother, they all wanted to know about Dickens. Well, I knew all about Mr. Dickens. We went a very long way back indeed. I knew him so long ago in fact that he had by then almost managed to convince himself that the young man he had once been was not him at all.

Now me, I knew exactly who I was and where I came from, as assuredly as I knew exactly where I was going. I had a gift for dramatic narrative, it was true, but I knew my limitations. I was no great novelist (although my work had sometimes sold well), and I had long since given up trying to be so. Dickens, of course, was great, if a trifle melodramatic and sanctimonious, and Thackeray, the insufferable son of a whore, was probably a genius, although I would be laughing in my grave before I ever told him so to his face. I was a good all-rounder, but only in the second eleven. I was not a great philosopher, a brilliant social critic, or a sophisticated literary stylist. I was, and had always been, a simple storyteller, and I wrote to live rather than the other way around. I was a penny-a-liner—

CHAPTER IV

LAKEMAN HAD GOT me wrong. The world which I inhabited was far from glamorous. The literary life is rarely the path to wealth and celebrity of which ambitious young authors eternally dream, despite all our public protestations to the ideals of art and philosophy. We write because we feel we have something to say, at least in the beginning, but beyond this romantic desire to fashion something beautiful and true out of nothing more than ink and paper lays the longing for recognition, preferably critical and popular, for what use is literature if it does not sell? It is fame we crave, do not be fooled, fame and fortune, for the other dream of the writer is to be financially secure, to be untroubled by the landlord's agent and the bailiff, to have no other line of work to distract him, and to simply write. It is, however, far from a wise path to take, at least for those who have any other before them. Nonetheless, it is a course to which men will obsessively devote themselves, as they might to a perverse marriage, contrary to other men's warnings, and even to their own legible experiences of a life spent entirely within a dream.

In this regard I was my father's son. My father was a consummate dreamer, and as it was with my politics and my religion, I had also inherited his dreams. He was a child of the Romantic era, and its values never really deserted him, no matter how much they were assimilated and polluted by the world of the profit and the loss. When news of the drowning of Shelley reached England, my father wept with a passion I had not witnessed since the passing of my mother. Would that he had lived to see me walk out with Mrs. Shelley, albeit quite briefly, for I was one of many young men with stars in their eyes with whom she dallied and soon discarded. My father would have been very proud, and, I'd warrant, not a little jealous, for she was a handsome woman, a brilliant thinker, and damn fine sport, even though her heart lay with a corpse.

Father took the *Examiner* when he could spare the coin. He loved to read to us, my mother and me, and could recite from memory many lines by Mr. Keats, Mr. Shelley and Lord Byron (all doomed of course, although we did not know it then), just as he could long passages from his beloved gothic romances, old friends all that had sustained him throughout his lonely life. He had an equal passion for Sir Walter Scott, especially his poetry, and how my spine thrilled when blood rained from the sky in 'Lord Ronald's Coronach,' and during the punishment of Constance in *Marmion* (a mad poem published the year I was born). Entombed alive within convent walls, her wailing torment compelled her executioners to order the chapel bells tolled to drown out the horrific screams. This terrible lament caused the hair of the most powerful highland creatures to stand on end, as it did my own every time my father spoke the lines, as ever doing so from memory.[3] I did not so much share his enthusiasm for Mr. Wordsworth, but was stunned by the fancies of Mr. Coleridge. I still carried my father's copy of *Lyrical Ballads* about me on the *Birkenhead*, a first edition I had managed to save from the bailiffs. When I later met the Ancient Mariner himself, at the *Fraser's Magazine* inaugural banquet, it was as much as I could do to refrain from falling at his feet and proclaiming my unworthiness to be in his presence, the irony being that the poor old soul was so out of his mind by that point that he would have neither known nor cared.

I spent my early years in a small cottage that seemed built of books, and I took to the printed word so fast that it seemed I was remembering rather than reading. Thus was my education conducted, for there was no formal provision in those days; much as it is now, it would seem that our masters prefer to keep the laboring classes ignorant as well as poor. There cannot have been as many books as my memory has embroidered, for my parents were never that prosperous, even in the best of times. But, as my mother would say in the lean months, when my father despaired of raising a child in poverty and his voice travelled further than he intended, it was love and common sense that raised decent children, not money.

Our private library was, like me, the result of the coming together of my mother and my father. Both were inveterate bookworms, although she came from the better family, so more shelf space originally belonged to her than to him. His collection was mostly the result of diligent purchasing at fire auctions in town. He was an autodidactic master of restoration, and could stitch and rebind damaged pages in beautiful hand fashioned leather covers. He was a tailor by trade, but I think he would have loved to have been a bookbinder's apprentice. As it was, he sewed paper as much as he did cloth. The books were always the last things to go when it was time to visit the pawnbroker's shop in town, and I soon came to understand that to my father the significance of these volumes went far beyond the wit and wisdom contained therein. For my father these poems, tales, histories, dissenting tracts, and philosophical treatises represented an intellectual and emotional freedom that it was not his lot in life to achieve in the physical world. Further to this meaning, it was also his constant, yearning hope that these books were the path by which his only child would ascend to some sort of respectable and secure profession, perhaps in education, or even the law. He imagined me a schoolmaster or an articled clerk, while all the time filling my head with tales of mad monks, animated skeletons, and the shades of bleeding nuns.

It was my father's literacy that had attracted Sarah, my mother. Her father had done business with him, and she had been quite taken with his soft, well-spoken and slightly old fashioned manners. She could see he had a disenchanted soul, yet felt sure she detected a warm hearted and fine man under that nervous countenance and made it her mission to have him for her own. This was much to the chagrin of her family, who were of the mercantile class and, although far from rich, believed themselves to be considerably better heeled than the object of her affections, although at this point in the proceedings he knew not that she was, as he later used to joke when he told me the story, 'trying to hook him.' She countered that he was an honest, God-fearing and hardworking man, with his own shop and therefore prospects. She was also keenly aware that her father would not live forever, and she had no means of survival without him save relying on her brother. Moreover, she did so desperately desire a family of her own. At more years past thirty than she cared to admit, she was fast running out of time.

It was always, on the face of it, an unlikely match. She had been a beautiful, if delicate, flower of the fields in her day, but she was no longer young, and this was a factor in my father's favour in the eyes of her own. Her brother, however, opposed the match to the end, being particularly appalled that my father was several years my mother's junior. My father was also useless around women. Although he was a good looking specimen in his own way, tall, with thick black hair and vivid blue eyes (both features I have inherited), he was bookish, introspective and painfully shy around the opposite sex. His parents were long dead and he had no surviving siblings, and although distantly polite in public he much preferred his own society to that of his neighbours, so was in consequence completely lacking in the social abilities prerequisite in the ritual of courtship.

'You always think of such things at other folks' weddings,' my mother used to say. Everyone in the small market town turned out for such events, and when George Leggett wed Daisy Holmes in the spring, my mother made her move. She was helping the other women with the outdoor party after, and made sure it was always her that served my father. He nervously accepted brimming plates of bacon and greens, bread, cheese and cake from this equally brimming beauty, while the other men at his long table grinned and winked and muttered, with Samuel McGuire, the butcher, whose capacity for the drink was a mystery to medical science, asking in the most audible whisper how it was that my father's mug was always filled first and fullest, and always by the same girl. My father made a big thing of cleaning, filling and lighting his pipe, and then drank his beer deliberately to hide his embarrassment. This did not help him, for he was not by nature a drinking man and every time he drained his pint, my mother appeared as if summonsed by ring or lamp and filled it again.

'So how is it you never married, Joseph?' McGuire was asking, 'a big fine fellow like yourself.'

'Too busy,' my father mumbled, 'the shop—'

'And sure what use is a big old shop with no one to keep you warm in the winter?' said the butcher, who was secretly of the old faith and had a plump wife and ten children, 'Just wet the bottom of the glass girl,' he said then, for my mother was back again. 'And with all these grass widdys, staid damsels and young and blooming maidens in the world,' he continued, looking slyly up at my mother to signal in which category she was placed and draining his tankard. She bent to top him off again from a big stoneware jug, and McGuire gave her a boozy wink. 'More's the shame and pity,' he went on, 'that a fine big man like this, with the ball at his foot so to speak, don't just give it a kick and send it straight into the chapel.' He appealed to the surrounding company, half of which were in suits made by my father and were taking immense delight in his discomfiture. 'Now why is that do you think?' He looked my father in the eye interrogatively.

My father became acutely aware that my mother was also watching him. He took in her fine figure, agreeably presented in her best frock, and finally met her steady grey-eyed gaze.

'I never, I mean I didn't really, I suppose—'

'Spit it out man,' said McGuire, and he laughed.

'I never met the right girl,' my father finally confessed, looking for all the world as if he had been caught stealing apples from the tree in the vicar's garden. My mother just smiled, and waltzed away to attend to her father's glass (he was the guest of honour), of which she had been uncharacteristically neglectful.

She sang 'The Knight and the Shepherd's Daughter' that evening, in the candlelight after the new Mr. and Mrs. Leggett had slipped away. My father's eyes never left my mother's after that, not until the night he killed her.

It was a laborious courtship though, observed with great amusement by my father's customers, while their wives secretly lamented that they had never been wooed with such delicacy. My mother was satisfied that my father's intensions were amorous, and so she waited upon his proposal. Usually a patient woman, she finally convinced her father to invite his tailor to the front door for once, and after an awkward Sunday dinner at which her brother glowered silently throughout every course, she bade my father stay a while and take the air in the garden. They were married in the autumn, the year the French occupied Portugal, with Sam McGuire sagely remarking that, 'The pitcher which goeth often to the well getteth broken at last.'

My grandfather would not see his daughter live above a shop, and purchased a modest cottage for her on the outskirts of town from a local farmer. He died quite suddenly soon after, finally joining his wife, who had been taken giving birth to his only son twenty-odd years since. My parents were fortunate to have been given the cottage, for he left his daughter not a penny. Her brother sold the family home and business and left for London. After the funeral he exchanged not a word more with his sister. Although my mother was not young, or in the best of health, truth be told, love and life found their way, and I was born the following year. It was a difficult birth, and my mother knew she'd not have another. By common agreement I was named in honour of her father, James.

The reclusive Joseph had not expected to become either husband or father, but he took to his new role as if he had been made and was waiting all along just for us. He thanked the Lord every day for granting him a son, and spent as much time with me as his work would allow; reading, playing and teaching me everything he could. Our Sunday trips to the river to fish were as sacred to me as the morning service. I adored my father, and much to the amusement of my mother I would follow him around like a puppy, and he always had time to stop and ask after the nature of my day, regardless of how busy his own. Best of all he would promise, and always deliver, a story before bed. My mother he taught to sew, and together they ran a modest business. The work was hard, and there was never much money, but my father watched his small family flourish with pleasure and pride. Despite his characteristic sense of caution, he had no idea how precariously balanced was this new found happiness. You never do, do you?

CHAPTER V

EIGHT HAPPY YEARS passed.

I cannot precisely recall when Grimstone and O'Neil took over the town. Their coming was insidious, like the cholera a few years past, a slow pestilence that eventually became a plague. It was an open secret that they had had a good war, and I later discovered that their oft repeated philosophy that good business was where you found it was manifest in their company variously supplying the British Army, the Prussians, the Spanish, and the French. But nobody seemed to care. To hell with morality, loyalty, and honesty, does it make any money? That was and is the whole of the law. I swear to God that if the Great Tribulation began in the present age, all that would concern the City would be how the opening of the seven seals would affect the next quarter's profits.

Why these men of business should choose our little provincial backwater was originally a mystery, but looking back later I realised that they were not particularly big fish, at least initially, and were most likely out of their depth among the brokers of London. It was also rumoured that Grimstone had family in the area, and might even have been a native of our little town, a prodigal son with some sort of chip on his shoulder, back to throw his weight around and show his people how important he had become. One thing was certain, big fish in small ponds tended to stink.

They contrived to buy up much of the property in the high street. Grimstone was rarely seen outside his office, which was headquartered in the house where my mother had been born, and I only ever glimpsed him by pure accident, usually getting in or out of a coach. He was quite a small man, with sharp features, honed all the more by a small beard, which, in combination with the most penetrating gaze, gave him a vaguely satanic appearance.

O'Neil, on the other hand, was often out and about. He was quite the physical opposite of his business partner, being a big, bluff northerner. My father's first impression of him was positive. O'Neil had visited the shop, to personally explain that he was now the landlord, but that my father need have no concerns over the new arrangement, which O'Neil insisted would remain unchanged from the old. He also promised restoration, and complimented the quality of my father's work. Father bought the news to my mother that evening with a cautious optimism. She knew the type better, and was inwardly sceptical, despite her essentially sunny disposition. I was too young to follow their discussion, and was more concerned with the adventures of Captain Singleton that evening, having discovered the novel nestling at the top of the tall bookcase in the parlour earlier in the day.

Shortly after this first meeting, O'Neil called upon my father again, only this time with a proposition. I was helping in the shop that day, so I overheard the conversation.

'As the town is growing,' he said, 'Mr. Grimstone and I are considering diversification.'

'Oh aye?' said my father.

'Yes,' said O'Neil, mopping his greasy brow with a handkerchief almost as red as his hair, 'in point of fact, we're after establishing a haberdashery right here on the high street, perhaps also offering clothes off the peg, manufactured offsite through subcontracts to local weavers.' (Many of these folk were on the parish, and would work for next to nothing.) 'Would you consider selling, at all?' he continued. 'Would you take thirty pounds, Joseph?'

The offer was absurdly low. My father was a sitting tenant, and in no hurry to relinquish either lease or business. 'That's very kind, sir,' he said diplomatically, 'but I'm happy where I am just now.'

'You could stay on if you liked,' said O'Neil, ignoring what my father had said, 'perhaps making simple alterations, cleaning, and managing the till.'

My father parried again. 'I thank you for your interest, sir,' he said, 'but this business was my old dad's, and it's my intention to apprentice the boy here, should he wish it, and then pass the shop over.'

'I quite understand,' said O'Neil, going as far as to ruffle my hair like a favourite uncle. 'Don't you worry, Joseph,' said he, 'they'll always be a place for your business here, whatever progressive changes we might make. I'm confident it'll grow with the town.'

'I'm glad to hear it, sir,' said my father, 'thank you again.'

'They'll be prosperity for all, Joseph,' said O'Neil, as he took his leave, 'now the railway's coming.'

What in fact happened was that the rent was raised, shortly after my mother realised that she was once more with child. The annexation of the high street continued, with more and more business falling under the control of the two men. Those of which they did not approve, could not acquire, or had no interest in one way or the other, were forced out by a process of attrition. McGuire soon found himself under siege, his rents raised and his business undermined by vicious rumours. He was not clean. There were rats in the kitchen, cats in the pies. Apparently Grimstone and O'Neil had no time for left footers. Grimstone, meanwhile, took to affecting the title of 'Captain,' although he had served in no regiment we had ever heard of, the arrogant, unbloodied bastard. He courted the local gentry through the provincial social circuit, and was soon a regular guest at the manor. It was clear he had political ambitions.

It would seem that neither were the men of business too keen on Methodists, for when my parents worked harder and economised at home in order to meet the rent on the first of each month, now double what it had been a year before, O'Neil next let out the room above the shop. The new tenant was a vile and uncouth man name of Slaughter, who was in the employ of O'Neil, although what he actually did for his living was unclear. He came with an ugly dog, some sort of bull terrier, which barked day and night and whose filth Slaughter took to flinging out of the front upstairs window so that prospective customers had to gingerly step around it in order to enter the shop. My poor father spent as much time removing that dog's shit from the front of his shop as he did tailoring. I was pretty certain the cur killed our cat as well, for it was never seen again. Slaughter was a drunk and a blackguard, and revelled in intimidating and insulting my father's clients whenever their paths crossed. Trade began to drop off.

'You must talk to him,' my mother would say. But my father loathed confrontation. He simply had no idea how to cope with someone of such an unwholesome disposition. My father was no coward, mind, but neither was he a fool. By the look of Slaughter, who was built like a brick privy, he could quite easily break my poor father in two.

'Some people cannot be reasoned with,' my father would answer, looking miserably at the floor. He did this more and more. His gaze always seemed to be cast downward, and he would sit by the mostly unlit fireplace late into the night staring into space, inwardly computating his options with increasing despair. Like physical pain without the hope of recovery, my father knew that there was no way out of the current situation. There was nothing illegal occurring, and even if there were my father had no way of affording representation. Grimstone had become the local magistrate by then anyway. What was required was capital, but less was coming in while more was going out and now there was another child on the way. My mother was always hopeful that somehow our fortunes would improve, that the business would pick up or some grand commission would fall into their laps, but my father shared no such illusions. He kept working, more and more giving the outward appearance of a somnambulist as he mechanically went about his professional and domestic business. We stopped fishing, for he now worked on Sunday, although this decision went much against my mother's wishes.

'Was not the Lord a carpenter,' he would say by way of explanation and apology, 'he will understand.' The land now belonged to Grimstone in any event, and he was already prosecuting any poor fool caught with rod and line for a poacher. As the bespoke side of the business was in decline, my father had compromised his standards and was producing shirts and waistcoats of generic size that my mother would then attempt to sell on market day in the neighbouring town, twelve miles to the west, along with dolls and doilies of her own design and manufacture.

O'Neil controlled our market, and one day my Mother, with me in tow, sought him out there in order to apply for a local pitch.

'I'm terribly sorry, my dear lady' he intoned, making a great show of his apology by bowing in the manner of a bad tragedian, 'but we have no spaces available at this time.'

Even I could see that this was a nonsense. 'What about those?' said my mother, gesturing towards several empty vending stations between nearby stalls, like gaps in a row of teeth.

O'Neil breathed in sharply. 'I'm afraid those pitches are all spoken for,' said he, adding, 'by traders from out of town.'

'In that case,' replied my mother, 'perhaps you could have a polite word with your tenant Mr. Slaughter. His uncouth behaviour is alienating custom in my husband's primary place of business.'

'I'm shocked that anyone could possibly think ill of such a fine, upstanding man as Mr. Slaughter,' said O'Neil, 'but for you, Mrs. Vincent, I will look into the matter.'

'You are very kind,' said my mother, and in reply he took her hand and kissed it wetly, the way a lizard might commence to eat a piece of fruit.

*

I never knew precisely what happened to my mother at the shop. She had gone there in my father's stead one Saturday as he was abed with a fever. Saturday was still the best day of the week for sales and they could ill-afford not to open. I wanted to go to, but my mother bade me remain at home to tend to my father. She was beginning to show at that point, but was still able to get around and work. I gathered soon enough that Slaughter had been about, and was delighted at this unexpected opportunity to have it out with my mother regarding the 'dreadful slanders' she had recently made against his good character.

She staggered home some ninety minutes after she had left. Her hair and clothes were in some disarray, and she had obviously been crying. She evaded my childish concerns and asked after my father, who was then asleep. She told me not to wake him, and to tell him nothing of the morning. She was going to wash, she said, and have a little rest. She had decided not to open the shop that day, and did not want me to go there. She told me not to worry, that she and my little brother or sister were fine, and that I should go and read or play. This suited me, as I had by then discovered Swift and was eager to return to the Country of the Houyhnhnms.

Later in the day I heard raised voices, and then my father stormed out of the house, my mother screaming in his wake, 'It doesn't matter, Joseph.'

'What doesn't matter, Mum?' I asked, but she spoke not and simply sunk to the floor in tears. I was frightened and helpless, unsure whether I should stay with her or run after my dad.

My inclination was to fetch my father, who I assumed had gone to the shop. I could never match his stride though, and by the time I arrived there he had already been arrested. I quickly learned that he had attacked Slaughter, for no reason said the neighbours, and had struck a glancing blow to the big man's ear. Slaughter had broken my father's nose, dislocated his shoulder, and set the dog upon him before calling for the watch. My father would give no account of his reasons for swinging for Slaughter, and was prosecuted for common assault and disturbing the King's peace at the next assizes. Grimstone was the beak. My father was fined five pounds, and was forced to put up the business to raise the money and avoid gaol. O'Neil bought him out for a pittance, and he made up the rest by selling the majority of his books. He promised me that this did not matter much, for he had his favourites by heart, but I knew that this loss was almost as soul destroying as that of the shop. His face was one terrible bruise for weeks afterwards, while his nose, which had been imperfectly set, gave him the look of a well-milled loser from the Prize Ring. This was probably not so far from the reality; that Slaughter had the look of the Fancy about him.

Slaughter's name, I soon realised, was never to be spoken. I was too young by far to comprehend exactly what the mention of the brute, even the merest thought of him, could trigger in the minds of my poor parents. Yet I knew in my heart that something terrible had now been planted in theirs, a dungeon spiral of frustration, rage and regret within each of their gentle souls that, once entered, was utterly self-annihilating. It was not just my father's body that had been broken, or the business, it was the spirit of the family itself.

My parents became withdrawn. The constant, easy conversation that had always existed between them ceased. Their carefree shows of affection, the way they had always so casually touched, likewise stopped. They seemed awkward around one another now, cautious, as if the oak boards upon which they walked had suddenly transmuted into the thinnest sheets of mica, a glass floor atop some terrible abyss that might, at any moment, crack. Ordinary and innocuous conversations could at any point ignite into the most violent of arguments, inevitably concluding with my father storming from the cottage and my mother retiring to bed, whatever the hour. To their credit, neither turned on me, but I bore witness to some dreadful rows. There was now, it would seem, but a step between the quotidian and the horrible, a situation in life of which my childish self had not been previously aware.

I began to feel unsettled at night; not yet afeared of the dark, but aware of it, and increasingly wary. Alone at night, the curtains by my bed when animated by a sullen draft now appeared to me as wights and visitants poised to fall upon me the moment I succumbed to exhaustion and slumbered. A shadow was falling across my young life, and in this new dark world my parents were as strangers. To one such as myself, an imaginative, bookish child who already saw all life as structured like a fantastic narrative, it felt as if my parents had been kidnapped by some malevolent being, replicated, and then replaced by these sinister automatons. The manufacture of these beings was expert, I gave the makers their due, but not exact. The creature that was supposed to be my mother looked a good ten years older, and thinner than the original, while my replacement father's eyes were not right at all. The playful, mercurial shine that I had associated with my father's countenance since I was a babe in arms was completely absent in this new model. All I could see behind these eyes was a terrible darkness. I could not even detect the clockwork gears that I assumed provided animation. My new father appeared quite empty. All the stories were gone.

CHAPTER VI

THE MACHINE PEOPLE continued, nevertheless, to toil. They had rescued what assets they could from the shop without arousing suspicion, and they set about working from home. My father now took the long walk to the market, and I began my apprenticeship. The work was hard on the eyes and the fingers, but I took to it readily enough for I had watched my father labour for years. I enjoyed the precision of measuring, cutting, felling and hand stitching, and loved losing myself making buttonholes or embroidering, hours passing without my notice as I sewed. This was a calm, meditative state that I have rarely, if ever, achieved since as an author. It felt good to be active within the process of mending the family. As we all worked, day and night, we began to stitch the family back together. As the arrival of the new baby approached, the machine people grew softer again, and I knew that my parents had returned, changed, it was true, by their experiences, wherever they had been (I was not going to ask), but fundamentally themselves again. For a while at least, the shadow receded.

My father still made time for me as well, even if our elementary entertainments cost him dear in terms of the extra hours he had to work before dawn to catch up. His love of stories appeared returned, and I had contrived the plan of enacting a simple play to celebrate my mother's forthcoming birthday, which fell upon All Hallows' Eve. My father thought this a capital idea, and agreed to not only assist with costumes but to act alongside me.

Given the influence I was later to have on the popular stage, it was in every way appropriate that I begin my authorial career in my twelfth year with a little gothic melodrama called 'The Gold Tooth.' We were compelled to rehearse out of doors in the biting cold, but after a few turns we had quite got the thing down.

We set up behind the curtains dividing the parlour from the kitchen. For a backdrop, we had painted the silhouettes of gravestones on an old sheet, using dyes from the shop to simulate a night sky. A plank borrowed from the woodshed propped upon its leading edge in the foreground served as the side of a coffin, my father lying behind it playing the corpse, and a pile of sacks sprinkled with dirt from the garden implied a mound of freshly turned earth. I took the leading role of 'Fulgentius,' a common country sexton by day, but by night a notorious resurrection man known only as the 'Snorter' on account of his huge nose, and his habit of taking snuff ground from coffins and human bones. I was armed with the garden spade, and wearing a scarlet cloak made from an old curtain. Long lank hair was fashioned from floured wool, my face rendered sharp and wicked by virtue of a cardboard snout of exaggerated length and girth, more flour, and a grinning mouth drawn roughly in rouge pinched from my mother's dresser. By candlelight the effect was striking. My mother was our sole audience, seated upon a dining chair at the far end of the parlour.

The story opened with a thunderstorm, establishing mood and symbolising the inner processes of the villain. In my later 'Newgate' period, the apocalyptic storm became something of a trademark, and that insufferable prick Thackeray used to lampoon me about it something chronic. In this case, the dramatic affect was achieved by my father wobbling a wood saw before the curtain was raised, while I whacked a partially shielded lantern hung out of sight above my head during the performance.

In the opening scene, Fulgentius digs by lantern light, exhuming the corpse of the investment banker 'Magnus,' recently deceased from shock upon being presented with a bill from his wife's dressmaker. 'When did any man's heir feel sympathy for his decease?' he soliloquises. 'When did his widow mourn? When doth any man regret his fellow? Never! He rejoiceth. He maketh glad in his inmost heart. He cannot help it, for it is in our nature. We all delight in each other's destruction. We were created to do so; or why else should we act thus? I never wept for any man's death, but I have often laughed.' At this point he raps his shovel on the top of the coffin (the floor) and exclaims, 'By the old gods of England that's pay dirt! Here is a coffin in an exquisite state of decay. It'll scarcely require any grinding to make excellent snuff.'

He pauses to produce a snuffbox (my father had a tin one full of pins in a workbench drawer which he had generously loaned), and I made comic play of snorting a huge pinch, followed by a long-builded, harlequinesque sneeze.

'My heavens, but that's strong stuff,' says he, 'this must be the batch I made up from the judge. He needed no embalming; he was pickled and preserved long since.' He examines the corpse, lowering the plank to its side, revealing my father lying in state in his best clothes, his face made cadaverous with ash from the fireplace and trying not to laugh. 'Ah, Mr. Magnus. You once refused me a loan, but what's that you say?' He leans close, 'You've reconsidered. A wise and generous choice, sir! No need for paperwork I'll be bound, I'll just take it now if I may.' He begins to rifle the corpse's pockets. 'What's this? You didn't take it with you? Mr. Magnus I am shocked! Was it that pretty young wife of yours? You left it all to her? Egad sir! She's left you nothing but the fillings in your teeth. You'll never pay the ferryman at this rate, but what banker ever pays his way like an honest man? You'll have some speculation in mind I expect, a sound investment overseas, if only Charon will put up some modest collateral, his little house in the Styxx perhaps. Well, no matter, I'll take these handsome gold caps upon your choppers, and the surgeon will make up the rest.'

He tries to remove the front teeth, allowing for several seconds of slapstick as he attempts different methods of extraction, bracing his foot on the banker's chest and pulling. At last, breathing heavily, he produces a large pair of pliers from a poacher's pocket and removes the offending ivories. I had motes of gravel in my palms and appeared to scrutinise extracted teeth, before pocketing a couple and discarding the rest, which rattled very satisfactorily along the floor.

The shock of this injury wakes the corpse, who was not dead at all but in a cataleptic trance. (We had in advance blackened out my father's front teeth with boot polish.) He sits up and addresses the body snatcher in a state of some confusion. 'Are you angel or devil?' says he.

'I am neither, sir,' says Fulgentius, 'I am merely an honest tradesmen going about his business. Now kindly resume your place that I might continue in my work.' He tries to push the banker back into the coffin with his booted foot.

'Oh unhappy happenstance,' moans the banker, 'it is clear to me that I am in the abode of the Unholy One.'

'And what did you expect?' rejoins Fulgentius. 'You grow rich with neither talent nor trade, you contribute nothing to society, yet you reward yourself with a king's ransom in wages, and if your bank should fail you still turn a profit. Then you presume upon the shareholders of your next venture to bestow upon you a bonus, for your business experience is such a valuable asset to the corporation, and must be rewarded according to scale that you and your fellows set yourselves. Surely the last truly fine idea the Devil had after the seven deadly sins was speculative finance!'

'But the empire requires a strong economy,' says the banker, 'which my colleagues and I underwrite. To be in financial services is truly a patriotic calling.'

'Such insouciance,' says Fulgentius. 'You make me feel a clean and decent man in comparison! Now I'll to my patriotic exertions. I provide a true public service, you old usurer, for how could surgeons study anatomy if they could not dissect the likes of you? How could they perform operations on the living? They'll find no heart in there, I'll be bound, but I'm sure the other bits'll be of some interest.'

He raises his shovel to strike a fatal blow, but the corpse springs up, pushes him aside and legs it stage left. Fulgentius calls after him: 'Stop, ghost! Stop, body! Watch! Watch!' He appeals to the audience for support. 'The natural order of life, death and commerce has been transgressed. That man is my property. I am natural guardian of the churchyard, and he must come back and be sold and dissected like an honest Christian, or I'll get a warrant.' He shakes his head sadly. 'I shall be ruined. If the other bodies should learn this trick, and walk off too, what shall I do? I shall never have any more business.' He becomes more agitated, appealing now to the heavens. 'I'll be hanged if I'll be bilked in this manner. I'll after him, and claim him wherever I find him. I'll get a search warrant, and an officer.' He too runs off stage crying, 'Watch!' as the curtain falls.

In the shorter second act, the banker has made his way home (the backdrop was now a plain sheet with a window painted on it), only to discover his supposedly grief-stricken wife already in the arms of his best friend. This is done in the form of a diegesis, the revenant emoting in the direction of events only he can see. He dives offstage and loudly murders both wife and lover, flinging body parts of my father's manufacture across the stage, decorated with red silk to affect torn and bloody skin.

Fulgentius then arrives declaring, 'Zombi bankers I doubly hate!' before braining Magnus with his shovel. The curtain falls as the sexton sings a variation of an old pewter woggler's bangling song, celebrating his new found fortune of three corpses and all their cash and jewellery:

'How merrily lives a grave digger.
He sings as he shovels away!
His purse was light, but his spade was bright.
Now he cavorts both night and day!'

The cast then took the curtain call to enthusiastic applause, after which there was cake.

For a pious woman, my mother loved a good gothic tale as much as my father and myself, and she subsequently bade me transcribe my little play in the form of a short story. I was delighted to oblige, and felt it came out fairly well. I have never really been one for drama to be honest (poetry neither), and much prefer the ebb and flow of narrative prose, as anyone who has experienced my attempts at the latter classes will no doubt attest. But we cannot all be good at everything, and it is a wise man indeed, I have always felt, who is mindful of his limitations.

*

In a cruel inversion of life and nature that I have nowadays come to expect, Christmas that year was as terrible as Halloween had been grand. Whereas Dickens always delighted in pushing this tiresome ritual down everyone's throat, it has always infused my soul with the most profound sorrow, for if something bad happens on a red letter day then you must re-live it annually while the general population celebrates idiotically around you. The Yuletide festival does not, therefore, represent the Nativity of our Lord and Saviour or goodwill to all men in my heart so much as it does the agonising death of my mother in childbirth.

The memory haunts me still. The labour seemed to have no end; and while she pushed and sobbed and prayed and screamed and panted through the limitless night, I repeatedly and mechanically dampened and applied a flannel to my poor mother's brow in between her body's violent contractions as if in a trance. The midwife alternately cooed in encouragement or bellowed orders, periodically listening for the infant's heartbeat with a small ear trumpet. My father, meanwhile, gripped his wife's hand and silently mouthed a continuous and hopeless prayer.

The child would not come. After the worst night I had ever lived (God alone knew what torture it was for my dear mother, if God there was), the midwife finally took my father aside and asked, 'Might I at least save the child?'

He wept and raged until my mother stared him down and pleaded without words that she be set free and the baby delivered safely. He finally acquiesced, and I was sent from the room. Although I blocked my ears with my balled fists I still heard the sliding scrape of a blade on stone, and then her animal screams as they killed her. Next there came a new-born's cries, soon to be drowned by the desolate howls of my father. Time paused, as I have heard it does the instant before a cannon shell explodes amongst a group of unlucky soldiers, then he burst from the charnel room like an assassin discovered and fled into the frozen dawn, growling obscenities as if possessed by some demon.

The gory fingersmith followed, carrying my tiny sister in a bloodied rag. 'You'll need a wet nurse,' she said, casually handing me this little dab of humanity. 'Mrs. McGuire'll probably oblige,' she advised, 'if the money's right.' She spoke not a word of condolence, the old bitch, for in the spirit of the times she was all business.

She quickly took her leave, registering in no uncertain terms her irritation at the fact that my father had quit the cottage without leaving her fee. 'If he does away with himself,' said she, 'I'll still expect reparation.'

I numbly agreed that I would see her all right, and showed her to the door. And that was how my sister Sarah entered the world.

I knew not what to do with the shivering, screaming thing in my hands, but placing a finger in her tiny mouth seemed to placate her. I wrapped her in a spare shirt and made my way across the muddy fields to the McGuire's cottage. The butcher had become a farm labourer, so I knew the family would be awake even at that godforsaken hour. Mrs. McGuire was a deal more sympathetic than the midwife, and insisted I take a drop of the creature to soothe my shattered nerves while she attended to the baby behind a curtain. She gave me some gin and hot water, with a few drops of laudanum in it. I was too exhausted to protest on religious grounds and past caring anyway, and this was in consequence my first taste of strong drink and the peace that it temporarily brings to the soul. I have heard tell of youngsters who spewed their insides out after a single swig and never touched another splash, but I was not so fortunate. I took to that liquid darkness from the first, with a pleasure for the bottle matched only by my sister's lust for Mrs. McGuire's pendulous dugs.

I was drunk by the time I returned home, having left the baby with that goodly woman until some sort of nursing arrangement could be formalised. She assured me that after ten of her own, all still kicking, she knew what she was doing, and that she further knew that my father would be good for the reckoning when things settled down. I should be brave, she said, attend to my mother, and try not to worry. I was not so intoxicated as to believe that things would ever settle down again, but I had nowhere else to go but back to the cottage.

My father had not returned. The low winter sun suggested it was the afternoon, but I was not exactly sure for the clock had wound down. I wanted more drink, but had to settle for icy well water, which to a certain extent at least restored me to my senses. It was as cold as the grave, so I made up a fire and boiled water for tea, not yet quite able to banish the routine by which I would normally prepare a cup for my mother. That was when the nerveless shock of the morning finally gave way to a profound grief and I sat and cried out my heart like the child I still was. I know not what, but something within must have broken then, for I have not shed a tear since, neither in pain, rage, sadness or passion. I believe that the dark world got in that day, for when I composed myself my first thought was to go to my mother. God help me, I wish it were true that I wanted to clean her and lay her out before my father's return, but in my soul I knew that more than anything else I wanted to see the corpse. I had to see the corpse.

The room stank. I knew not until that moment that a human being was no more than blood and shit, a putrid sludge that had not only soaked into the horsehair of the mattress but had sweated its way into the very walls. No attempt had been made to cover her in her murderers' indecent haste to quit the scene. It had obviously been an inexpert operation, and she looked as if she had died trying to scramble uselessly away from the pain. Her head was flung back, and the language of her body still told a tale of unimaginable agonies endured for the sake of her child, because there was no other way, and because no one could undertake that final trial but she. Her nightdress had been raised and her swollen belly had been slit from the centre of her breasts to her private parts, and the flesh and fat pulled aside that the child could be snatched from the uterus, leaving an obscene crimson cavity. Her skinny white legs were splayed wetly like those of some grossly violated rag doll, while her delicate hands were as claws, locked in a final, fatal grip upon sodden and twisted sheets. She looked more like a butchered sow than a human woman, save for her face, which was not in repose, as I had been told the dead looked, but instead frozen in her last moments of pain and horror, her wild eyes staring blindly, her mouth wide and her teeth barred in mute protest at such an ugly, pointless, and untimely death.

I stared deep into those dry, dead eyes and I saw no God there, no final, fleeting glance that denoted any recognition of salvation in my mother's final breath. All I saw was darkness.

CHAPTER VII

All told, after my mother died it took about eighteen months for things to fall apart. My sister survived, thanks to the priceless ministrations of Mrs. McGuire, who was as a mother to the child for the first year of her life, after which she was weaned and I tentatively assumed the duty. It was unanimously agreed that the baby should be named for her mother, whom she uncannily resembled, especially about the eyes. She was thus called Sarah, with the second name of Frances appended in honour of Mrs. McGuire, despite her protestations. The tribute was well deserved. In saving little Sarah this fine working woman saved my father and I as well.

My mother was not buried in her family's plot, for Grimstone now owned the land along with the rest of my late grandfather's estate, and he denied permission for the interment. Still he toyed with my father, like a child that has already torn the wings off a fly yet cannot resist playing with the unfortunate creature in its death throes. I did not understand why Grimstone hated my family so much. At first I thought we were just in the way, unwanted tenants in a high street property that the new owner wished to develop, but I realised the animosity was more personal when the note came from O'Neil concerning my mother's funeral and my father crushed it in his fist and uttered a stream of curses and obscenities that seemed to have no end, the bitter monologue growing in violence until there was nothing left but the vile words echoing through an impenetrable darkness.

There had never been any thought given to an alternative burial site, although in hindsight I wonder why my father had not considered the possibility that there would not be access to the ground, given how many other things had changed since the town and its provinces had become the fiefdom of Grimstone and his agents. He was not himself, though. The automaton had returned, but this time it was broken.

I do not think that either of my parents had anticipated death coming so swiftly. They had made no plans, while the scant documents left by my mother that did concern this matter presupposed the continued use of the family plot, with a naive faith in the essential goodness of human beings that remained with her to the end despite overwhelming evidence to the contrary. The last offices therefore overran by several days. Even in the December air the heavy scent of wreathes and candles (and the bloody mattress that we had burned), did not disguise the miasma of decay emanating from the closed coffin that my father had made, and which clung ever after to the cottage like the breath of a tomb.

I began to suspect that my father was not going to give up my mother, and that she was to remain in her box in the parlour, the curtains closed, the clock stopped, and the mirror veiled to prevent her spirit from becoming trapped in the glass forever. His heart simply would not let her go, so he just left her where she was, in a liminal realm between the living and the dead.

It was clear that Mrs. McGuire was of the same opinion. 'You must put her in the ground, Joseph,' she would say, on her daily visits, when she would feed me and try to feed my father.

'Not yet,' he would reply, before returning to a hopeless silence, slumped in his chair by the unlit grate, staring at the space where my mother was not. He had once indicated that he was waiting for a reply from her brother, to whom he had written informing him of the birth and the death. No word was thus forthcoming, although how this would have affected the arrangements was unclear.

After almost a week Mrs. McGuire took charge. She arranged what she called 'a respectable funeral,' raising the fee, she said, among the immediate community. Very few of these mysterious neighbours subsequently attended the service. She most likely funded the whole event from her own purse, supplemented by the money my father was managing to pay her to wet nurse my sister. This was in the days before garden cemeteries and municipal graveyards, and a spot was found for my mother in the local church yard, for she was not, like my father, a non-conformist, although the grave was not marked, the cost of a stonemason being beyond the scope of even Mrs. McGuire's efforts.

It was a modest affair, and there were no feathermen, pages and mutes, or any other of the theatrics that now characterise the middle class funeral, a morbid celebration matched only by the pharaohs of Egypt. Death, nowadays, is very big business, and there are different qualities of grief available according to price. For a couple of quid the regard is very small, but a fiver buys sighs that are deep and audible; for seven pounds ten shillings the woe is profound, but properly controlled, and for a tenner the despair bursts through all restraint, and the mourners water the ground with their tears.

On that morning though, no hearse was engaged, and my mother was conveyed to her last rest in a borrowed cart, with Mr. McGuire and some of his fellow labourers good enough to act as pallbearers. My father and I followed the coffin, and Mrs. McGuire carried Sarah because, she said, she will not understand now but her presence here will mean much to her in later life.

The sober country service passed off for me as if in a dream. Like my father I was exhausted by grief. My parents had always kept themselves to themselves, and without any surviving family beyond my uncle (who had chosen not to be there, despite another letter, this time from Mrs. McGuire), the service was not well attended. My mother had been well liked by those that did business with her, and had I been of sounder mind that day I would have marked the absence of mourners beyond the kindly McGuires, all of whom were in attendance, and missing work to do so. We had become pariahs, as least as far as those in power were concerned, and our neighbours feared to show support for the sake of their own continued and fragile security. This mattered not to the McGuires, who were already beyond the pale by virtue of their faith. More came to the wake than the funeral, perhaps because it was private and therefore a safe environment in which to pay their respects, but probably more for the free ale, pies and cakes that Mrs. McGuire had so generously provided.

I was greatly troubled that the grave bore no marker, and fearful lest I forget its exact location after the grass grew back. In consequence I returned later that afternoon, confident that the sexton would have done his work by then, and resolved to make my own sign upon the ground for future reference, having vowed that one day I would purchase a headstone so that my dear mother's name should not disappear so absolutely from the world. As this was a decision made upon the spur of the moment, I was not exactly sure what I might use to serve as a permanent marker. Like most boys I had a magpie's instinct for interesting yet useless objects, and had in my possession a few treasured items that I thought durable enough to do the job without looking too obvious and out of place. I thus carefully embedded at each corner of the oblong of freshly turned earth a flint arrowhead, a small belemnite fossil, a polished cockle shell, and a chunk of black obsidian glass, confident in the knowledge that these could be located at a later date. Innocently reassured, I made my way home to another silent and saturnine evening in the morose company of my father. When I was drawn once more to the grave the next day to lay a few more wild flowers all my markers had gone.

There were a dozen or so years to go until the Anatomy Act gave up the bodies of the unclaimed poor for dissection, and grave robbing was then quite common, although not yet epidemic. It would be a while before Hare was blinded and Burke went to the scragging post, but I already knew enough from rumour to have written a satire upon the subject that had then seemed so delightfully gothic yet so remote. In the end I resolved to leave the matter ambivalent. For all I knew, the sexton had cleaned the ground because, I convinced myself, he was a diligent and conscientious worker. Or perhaps the minister had absent-mindedly removed the items. Who could say? I said nothing to my father, and years later, when I found myself famous, I returned to my hometown and had a marble stone placed over the grave, although to this day I have no idea whether or not this memorial covers my mother's remains or an empty coffin, like the grave of a mariner lost at sea. Sometimes it is better not to know.

*

Time passed, and my father and I struggled through the remainder of that miserable winter, working together but rarely speaking. He sewed mechanically, turning his hand to lacework, which had always been my mother's job. This was a reasonably guaranteed earner, although, as I later discovered was similarly the case with literary work, there was little correspondence between the effort involved in its production and the eventual remuneration. I, meanwhile, kept house as best I could, and slogged through the rain or snow to market to hawk that bloody lace like a woman, silently resenting the customers, who could afford such frippery, and who often still haggled me down, and my father, for my young and uncomplicated mind harboured a persecuting echo that muttered darkly that it was he who had destroyed my mother and was thus the author of our misfortune. He had aged terribly. He took little food and frequently worked through the night, not because he needed to, though the more stock he generated the better, but because he could not sleep and found the thoughts that came with inactivity unbearable. Only my sister prospered, but then she was not with us.

Eventually the spring came, and with the rebirth of the land a certain hope returned, for we both felt once more the hand of my mother, her gentle touch borne upon the warm March air like a gift from Heaven.

Her intervention was as unexpected as the letter by which it was conveyed. It is always unpleasant when correspondence arrives addressed to someone you love who has recently died, and it hit my father with some force when a letter was delivered bearing my mother's name. He had been coping slightly better with his grief of late, and some of his old self was breaking through the cold ground like the green shoots of our little garden. The name on the letter was a crushing reminder of the great silence left behind by my mother, and this was a setback that I inwardly cursed. The surface of his composure was as thin as a single atom, fragile and easily disturbed, exposing a dark and depthless ocean of despair beneath. He accepted delivery like a mute simpleton, but this incomprehension quickly turned to rage and he cast it from him, commanding that I throw it upon the fire. I hesitated, and in the time it took for me to gawp like an idiot he had changed his mind and snatched it back. He did not, however, open the missive. Instead he placed it upon the mantle, unable to either read or destroy it.

This went on for days. Every time his eyes or thoughts were drawn to the letter his insidious fatalism would intervene. 'It can be nothing good,' he would say, and the matter would again be temporarily closed.

'But what if it's a bill?' I finally asked him. A look of panic animated his dejected features, then he snatched the baleful thing from its resting place and thrust it into my hand. The deadlock was broken.

It was not a bill. The letter was from someone called John Scott, who introduced himself as the editor of the *London Magazine.* He wrote with great enthusiasm about a short story my mother had submitted to Leigh Hunt at the *Indicator* on behalf of its youthful author, her only son, entitled 'The Gold Tooth.' Scott explained, briefly, that his good friend Mr. Hunt had received the story and read it with great interest. We knew of Leigh Hunt from his time at the *Examiner.* He had apparently felt that although the *Indicator* may not be the natural home of such fiction, it might well serve Scott to meet what he called his 'quota of grim stories' and he had thus forwarded it with a personal endorsement.[4] Scott loved it, and the story was to appear in a forthcoming edition of his magazine. He enclosed a money order for five shillings as a fixed fee for the work, concluding that he would look favourably on further contributions of a similar length, tone and content, and that he looked forward to hearing from the author, whom he felt showed 'strong potential,' or his agent (my mother) by return of post.

I have never missed her so much as I did at that moment. I handed it to my father without a word. He read it quickly and collapsed into his chair. 'Well done, son,' he finally said.

I mumbled my thanks and then suggested tea. I needed to get away in order to master my emotions, and all I could think of was a trip to the well. I was certain that my father would also require a moment or so alone. While drawing the water I looked to the sky and silently blessed my dear mother.

We both regained our composure in our own ways and then took stock over a brew. Neither said it, but we both knew that there was a potential here to greatly improve our material circumstances, assuming that I could produce further stories in a similar vein, which I was quietly confident that I could. We both knew that in 'The Gold Tooth' I had merely been replicating a formula that was then still greatly popular in the literary magazines and annuals, that of the Tale of Terror.

My father had raised me on the things, reading me stories by Lewis, Beckford, Dr. Drake, and Francis Lathom (who he had met), and a variety of anonymous meditations on the mad and the macabre, our favourites, I recall, being 'The Conclave of Corpses,' 'The Midnight Groan,' and 'The Dance of the Dead.' But the best of the best were always published by *Blackwood's*, like Sir Walter Scott's 'Narrative of a Fatal Event,' an account of a strangely protracted death by water, 'Extracts from Gosschen's Diary' by 'B.W.,' a confession of obsession, murder and necrophilia, and 'A Night in the Catacombs' by 'E.,' in which an unidentified tourist recounts the terror of being lost in the vaults beneath Paris. Back then my father's love of a good gothic tale had always transcended the true horror of the Edinburgh magazine, which was its politics. The management were Tory scum to a man.

With the careful cashing of the cheque my father authorised some research, so I purchased recent numbers of several popular magazines, including Mr. Scott's, in which we discovered that, during the period in which the low family income had precluded the possibility of new reading, the sensational story had continued to flourish and had, indeed, become even more extreme. 'The Vampyre,' in the *New Monthly* (which some attributed to Byron but was actually written by Dr. Polidori of Norwich), Leigh Hunt's 'Tale for a Chimney Corner' in the *Indicator*, and the anonymous *Blackwood's* story 'The Early Grave' confirmed this thesis and showed me the path by which I must proceed. Many of these tales seemed to thrive on sensational physical and psychologic violence. The characteristic style was increasingly one of grotesque and clinical reportage, the narrative constructed to convey exaggerated emotional intensity. The point of view was usually first person, and the observational detail (like the voice of a disembowelled surgeon naming each organ as it plopped out on the ground before him), placed the reader behind the horrified eyes of the protagonist. 'The Early Grave' was a particularly fine example, and I made it my model. As the narcoleptic narrator is presumed dead and sealed in his coffin, he reports that: 'I remained voiceless and paralysed within that terrible frozen darkness, yet I could still feel, and hear, and suffer.'[5]

So it was, then, that I commenced my career as a professional author. I had nothing to send the *London Magazine*, so set about wracking my brains for a gothic tale. Drawing upon a recurring nightmare I penned a new story in a single sitting between dusk and dawn. When I was satisfied with the draft I copied it again without corrections and sent it to Mr. Scott, appending a letter thanking him for his patronage, apologising for the lateness of the reply, and requesting that he further pass on my warmest regards to Mr. Hunt. Scott had not indicated in his original correspondence that my mother had made him aware of my young age, so I gambled that she had not and made no mention of my years, which were barely thirteen in number. I entitled my story 'The Final Entry in the Journal of the Late Leviticus Lovecraft,' which I presented as a found manuscript dated October 31, 18—, assuming the voice of the deranged diarist and telling the following tale—

> My reason fails me this night. Already, I have seen the shadows moving in the darkness beyond the glass. And yet, they tell me that I am ill. Ill I am, but I know that I be not mad. 0 curs'd flame that flickers but for the briefest instant! Yes, I am not mad although, in truth, I am yet afflicted with a dread-filled acuteness of the senses common to the male lineage of my family. Nay the less, I know what I have seen: things beyond the most vile imaginings of the minds of mortal man. What hellspawn awaits me, eager at the funerary scent of my most shameful degradation? 0 Bless'd Saviour, wherefore hast Thou abandoned me so?

The nightmare began but a year ago. Grenville and I had taken it upon ourselves to traverse the Swiss Alps for the duration of the summer months, it being the occasion of the mutual completion of our respective courses of study at Cambridge. Both in our twenty-first years, our European sojourn had passed without noteworthy incident, let or hindrance until we came upon the village of Karldstadt in the fading embers of an unnaturally becalm'd day. Almost beslumber'd after our day's constitutional, we sought lodgings at a humble inn, thinking to stay but for the night before striking forth for the cathedral at Inglestadt the following morn. Grenville, a scholar of theology, was desirous of viewing the triptych of the famed Swiss master guild's man Feidelstein housed within that great temple of our Lord, and I was happy to accompany my good friend on such a noble quest. Would that we had completed that simple task! But cruel Fate intervened as Grenville, that night, was overcome by a nervous exhaustion, no doubt engendered by the vagaries of such a foreign clime. We were thus compelled to remain in Karldstadt while I nursed my companion.

It was during this enforced hold in our expedition that I experienced my first sublime taste of that which men call love, beautiful yet perverted by the disastrous events that I may yet, God willing, relate.

Being a stranger of not unimpressive bearing, I was fortunate, or so it appeared to an innocent such as I, to court the attentions of the beautiful Isobella, a girl of but eighteen summers and the daughter of a local shepherd. Our youthful passion was withal but painfully brief, for her fair countenance, of such delicate, pallid complexion, foreshadow'd a consumption to which she would soon tragically succumb. After three months of divine exile, while my friend gradually recovered and my passion for Isobella flower'd into most perfect consummation, the Lord took her from me. The last word upon her exquisite lips, pale in mortification, was my name. With this, the breath left her body and my dearest love was gone.

Beyond consolation, I saw fit only to drown my fevered ravings in ever larger doses of laudanum, while the worthy Grenville supported me as best he could despite his weakened condition. Neither priest nor physician could restore my enfeebled spirits and, in despair, Grenville returned to England, unable to longer bear witness to my determined self-destruction.

No man has ever been closer to me in this life, yet I could not tell even he, my most benevolent brother, the true nature of the torment that enshrouded my very existence like the veil of the tomb. My beloved did come to me in my dreams each night; and the excesses of my fancied depravity wore heavily upon my heart, draining the life from my body. Unable to confront that which my mind could not comprehend, an animal lust did consume me. I thought of nothing but our one night of love together and this once glorious, yet now painful, recollection did burn me to my very soul. No longer sensible of my actions, I took to wandering the bleak cemetery in which my love was entombed. Finally, one terrible night some weeks after Isobella's demise, I did enter her sepulchral boudoir and there, in that blighted vault, I gave myself to my beloved once again.

With the coming of the dawn, I realised the full import of this most heinous of crimes against Nature. Tortured to the very edge of madness, a fit of self-loathing came upon me and I hurled myself off the face of the mountain side. Memory of the vile deed which I alone had perpetrated had left me weary of this mortal coil and longing, in that final blasphemous act, for nothing more than the merciful oblivion of death. Yet God had deserted me utterly, denying any such relief from my agony. Instead I lay broken and bleeding beneath a precipice for two days and two nights, before my shattered body was recovered and returned to the keeping of that self-same humble swain who had sired my Lady Isobella. Inwardly I begged for death, but this good and gentle man did save my worthless life by applying balms made from the roots and herbs of the forest. And as I write, some nine months hence from that awful night, my health has all but returned to me; returned to face one final horror before Satan will, as I have no doubt, claim me for his very own.

So now, this night, they tell me that the balance of my mind is disturbed. 0 ye men that call me mad! Could ye but know what I know, have seen what I have seen within the shadows of Lucifer's dark domain, that which numbs my very heart with the most unspeakable terror. For I have heard it, screaming like a feral cat in the night; I have heard it, my most loathsome progeny, wailing from within that ghastly mausoleum. A thing so hideous that I scarcely dare give its frightful form utterance. Yet I know, I am in no doubt, that a monstrous child was conceived that abominable night, within the dead womb of my beloved. And now that foul creature, neither living nor dead, comes to exact most bitter retribution upon the unworthy father that so callously created it.

As the church clock sounds the hour of midnight, I see again the shadows beyond the door and I am cognisant that no earthly lock will protect me from this dæmon. My blood chills, for I hear the creak upon the stair, the ghastly, laboured, preternatural breathing. My prodigal child is without the room. May Christ have mercy upon my tainted soul.

They say that childhood ends when you realise that you must die. Looking back, it is clear that the gothic sensibility of my childhood fancy was now infected by a gallows humour that had come upon me as a way of coping with the miserable reality of grief and loss, but which did not conceal a newly rooted fear of the mysterious processes of childbirth. In all honesty, I knew little of the mechanics of procreation, so the morbid sexuality of the piece was largely extrapolated from 'Gosschen's Diary' and *Marmion*, crossed with the talk of the McGuire boys and their sister, Molly, who would show you for a penny.

Discounting 'The Gold Tooth,' which was nought but a sketch, this was my first serious attempt to put my mind into that of another, and to find his voice. I was reasonably pleased with the resulting dramatic monologue, although reviewing it now the lack of reported speech is an embarrassment. The structure of the tale was, nevertheless, very tidy. It began *in medias res*, as Horace would have it, with a decent frame and overall premise. There was a 'primary generator' by which the engine of the tale was set in motion, and a short first act in which the point of view narrator was introduced, the scene set, and romance initiated. The death of the lover set the narrative upon a different trajectory, concluding the opening act and establishing the longer second, which closed upon another turn of the plot, in which the protagonist entered the tomb and violated the corpse. The story then concluded in a short third act containing a very nasty epiphany. Mark that structure well, because if you can master the form it can be worth to you up to a guinea a sheet.

Scott accepted my story enthusiastically. This time I received ten shillings and a request for a longer piece. Christopher North wrote in *Blackwood's* that 'The Final Entry' represented 'the most obscene depravity of late to originate from the sewers upon which the Cockney School is founded,' while the vituperative 'Z' (his fellow columnist John Gibson Lockhart), pronounced me an idiot and a scoundrel. Hunt countered in the *Indicator* that it was a 'damn fine grim story,' and that he expected 'great things' from its young author, noting that he hoped to hear more soon. John Scott cited my story in a long editorial that denounced the duplicity of Blackwood, North, Lockhart & co as the originators of the short sharp shocker who, when bested at their own game, squawked for a ruling from the umpire like a poor batsman bowled for a duck, while pretending a pompous piety that indicated a level of hypocrisy that even he had hitherto hesitated to expect of his rivals.

'I wonder if there is any depth to which they will not sink?' wrote

Scott, concluding that, 'I probably better not answer that.' He and Lockhart continued to bicker in the black print throughout the year, in a dialogue that was vicious even by Regency magazine standards.

Scott's dispute with Lockhart, however, was no concern of mine. I was now on a roll. I wrote freely and prolifically, relieved by my father of all stitching and hawking duties, which would now have made considerably less money than my stories. I barely noticed as the seasons changed, so engrossed was I in my imaginary realm. I had developed a writing schedule whereby I wrote around the routine of my baby sister, who obligingly slept for two hours each afternoon, and mostly through the night unless ill or scared (and even then she was soon soothed back to sleep). Mrs. McGuire had lavished much love upon her, and my father and I had continued in kind for she was a bright, even-tempered and beautiful child, with golden hair and her mother's eyes. Thus secure in our affection, Sarah was always a good sleeper.

I had followed 'The Final Entry' with 'The Vivissected,' wherein a highwayman's spirit survives hanging, leaving the unfortunate toby-gloak to experience the full agony of surgical dissection, which he duly relates in anatomically precise and disgusting detail. 'T.H.' (William Ainsworth of Manchester) was good enough to give this story a very positive review in *Arliss's Pocket Magazine*, and Scott was well pleased with his sales that month. I then penned 'The Labyrinth,' in which an archaeologist exploring the ruins of Knossos drops corn as a marker in the manner of Theseus' skein, blissfully unaware that it is being consumed by rats in his wake. He wanders lost, starving and increasingly fevered in the infinite darkness until the rats finally fall upon him and eat him alive, whereupon it must be supposed that he produced tinder and tablet, for he gave a full record of his sensations. This I followed with 'The Wail in the Windows,' the tale of the lone occupant of an isolated farmhouse who is slowly driven insane by the sound of a wild wind whistling through the ancient and ill-fitting casements, which he supposes to be the voices of demons calling upon him to join them. Whether or not his supernatural conjecture is accurate, or the product of a demented imagination, is never made clear, but the protagonist's descent into madness is carefully recorded.

By now I was earning a guinea a story, and although my father insisted on continuing to keep busy, as he put it, I was confident that our ship had come in, and that we need not fear poverty again. I therefore suggested that if my father wished to continue plying his own trade that he might like to dress us in the manner of gentlemen, which he set about doing with great enthusiasm. I next wrote 'The Shivering of the Timbers,' a tale of a haunted ship, the *Venus*, built out of wood harvested from the demolition of the 'chronic' wing of the original New Bethlehem Hospital (known more commonly as Bedlam), and infused with a murderous consciousness born of the tortured souls of a hundred dead maniacs. The timbers were capable of dreadful animation, and creaking limbs sprouted in the lower decks to strangle unsuspecting seamen in the dark. I always liked that one.

My final piece for Scott was entitled 'Wilhelmina the Werewolf Woman.' This was the tale of an unfortunate Eastern European aristocrat who received a lycanthropic curse from gypsies she had caused to be evicted from her husband's land. Exiled and destitute after the death of her husband, Wilhelmina is forced to enter the oldest profession, but she is doomed to always transform during congress, consuming her lover in a frenzied passion, as she had her husband on the first full moon after the hex had been cast. I confess that I did try to be more salacious and violent with every story, and I made it my mission to up the ante against *Blackwood's* whenever possible, not for the reasons that the radicals Scott and Hunt hated the 'Maga,' but because their Tales of Terror represented the yardstick by which all others must be reckoned. I was very innocent in those days.

'Wilhelmina' was duly dispatched, but this time no payment was forthcoming. I waited several weeks, and eventually decided to locate the latest issue of the *London Magazine* to see if my story had been published. No copy could be found. I consulted the town booksellers, one of whom directed me to the latest edition of *Blackwood's*, which proudly proclaimed itself to be 'wet with the blood of the Cockneys.'

'Why, didn't you know?' he said.

'I've been writing,' I said miserably. 'I don't get out much.'

Scott, it transpired, was dead, killed in a duel by Lockhart's London agent, the bastard Henry Christie. He had apparently insulted Scott in the street and my hot-headed employer had called him out. They met at a farm between Camden and Hampstead, and Scott took a ball in the gut on the second round, dying a couple of weeks later in the most dreadful agony. By the time the news reached me, Lockhart's man and his second had already been acquitted.[6]

Shortly thereafter my latest manuscript was returned, with a note from the new editor, one John Taylor, rejecting the story and explaining that there was to be a new direction in the magazine, based upon critical writing, poetry, and satire rather than sensation and violence. He wished me luck in my future endeavours, and suggested I try *Blackwood's*.

The luckless Scott had been my only connection with literary London, and without him I was helpless. I tried to contact Hunt, but the *Indicator* had folded suddenly and its editor had left the capital in a hurry, *en route* to Italy and completely incommunicado. I had the wit to try my other positive reviewer, Ainsworth, though he was then almost as young and unknown as I. He eventually wrote back, briefly explaining that my story had been returned to him from the editor of *Arliss's* with 'No thank you!' scrawled across the first page in blue pencil. Ainsworth said that he planned to begin his own literary journal, which was to be called the *Boeotian*. He offered me half a bar, upon publication, for 'Wilhelmina,' and promised to let me know when he was up and running.

'Take heart and have patience, son,' counselled my father. 'You might yet thrive as a gentleman of letters if you can but wait until you're old enough to meet a prospective publisher in person.'

That was then still far from the case, but he suggested that I continue to write every day, advice I have followed ever since, aside from a couple of deeply regretted periods of inactivity when I fancied I was in love. He also tactfully suggested that we return to our more conventional labours, for the money I had lately earned was not going to support us forever. I therefore concluded that the experience had been fun while it lasted, and returned with a heavy heart to my needle and thread, scribbling random thoughts each night in a recently purchased journal in the hope of finding another story. I was suddenly bereft of ideas, being ill-prepared for such a sudden failure after the promise of success.

As it turned out my father's prediction was more apposite than either of us could possibly have realised at the time, for soon after we lost not only our new income but our home.

While I was writing silly stories, dark forces had been slowly and stealthily marshalling against us, like pieces carefully arranged upon a chessboard. The request to lay my poor mother to rest in what had formally been her family burial plot had, unbeknown to us, been another sort of primary generator, such as that which begins a story, and this initiated a process that was to inextricably lead to our final dissolution.

When my father had contacted Grimstone's agent regarding the land, the contents of his letter must have settled with the spiders at the back of O'Neil's mind, quickly dismissed after his master had spoken upon the matter, but now quietly in residence. There was something aporic about the request, but O'Neil had not immediately grasped what it might be, although he must have sensed that something was amiss. Because of the time that elapsed between my mother's demise and the dreadful repercussions, it is to be assumed that each time the thought rose in O'Neil's head it was quickly eclipsed by another, so the path that it might have illuminated remained impassable. Finally, a little over a year hence, almost to the hour, as it turned out, that Scott lay bleeding in a frozen field with his belly ruptured and his hopes and dreams as shattered as his spinal cord, O'Neil had a revelation. He communicated this to his employer, who called for his lawyer and the deeds to his local properties.

With that there came fast on the heels of my correspondence with Ainsworth a letter to my father from a certain Mr. Powis, of Carroway, Byng, and Powis, Solicitors, explaining that we illegally occupied a residence owned by Mr. Grimstone which we must quit forthwith. He generously suggested that forty-eight hours upon receipt of his communication would be adequate. The long and the short of it was that my mother had not ever owned our little cottage. It had remained the property of her father, and upon his death it had passed to her brother, my uncle, with the rest of the estate. When he had sold out to Grimstone, he had also, presumably unwittingly, sold our cottage.

My father's immediate response was unexpected. He neither swore nor shed any tears, no walls were punched, as had lately become his custom when displeased, and nothing was broken. Instead he began to laugh, at first in a low cackle that seemed to originate from far away, but which soon grew in volume and intensity to a howling guffaw that was both infectious and insane. That laugh rained down upon us like shards of ice. I first heard it some thirty years ago, but at night sometimes I hear it still, screaming out of some terrible dream that rips me from my slumber so I know not whether the hysterical cries originate in the darkness around or within me.

It thus fell upon me to investigate. It is a truth well remembered that one should never put one's life in the hands of the law. I engaged my own solicitor, Slourup, who never missed an opportunity to patronise me on the grounds of age, profession, and social class, while setting me to do all his work for him by researching the history and ownership of the property, while he wrote the same letter over and over again for a shilling a line. Would that my form of writing paid so well! A stay of eviction had been negotiated, but like my savings this was fast reaching its end. Salvation, of a kind, arrived in the form of a note from my uncle, to whom I had written begging for some sort of statement in my father's favour. This was not forthcoming, but he did offer to take Sarah in rather than see her on the street, out of respect, he wrote, for his dear dead sister. Whether or not my father and I were also welcome was unclear, but as our deadline loomed, with all hope lost, it was mutually decided that we should quietly leave for London.

We had not had enough money left for a coach, so we walked all the way. We had been provisioned by the McGuires, to whom we gave our furniture, and we travelled by necessity very light, carrying nought but a few shillings, the essential and most portable tools of our trade, and the clothes in which we stood up. It was a miserable journey of some seventy or so miles, which took us the better part of a fortnight, although it felt at the time like years. We took turns to carry Sarah, then about eighteen months old, and whenever we saw a farm we would try to buy milk for her and bread, eggs, and cheese for ourselves. I kept her clean as best I could, mostly from streams and, if needs must, puddles, but a horrible rash was creeping all over her body and causing her terrible distress. She only slept when worn out from her constant and deafening lamentations, and we would try to nap when she did, often continuing to walk in our sleep. But it was not the exhaustion, the numbing cold, the incessant, pissing rain, the stabbing pain across my neck and shoulders as I carried my sister, her ceaseless crying, or the burning sores that covered my bleeding feet that I hated the most on that awful march. It was, instead, the shame of being reduced to the status of vagrants. Our clothes were ruined after the first night spent in the open, and we might as well have been begging for food as paying for it for all the respect accorded us by the farmers. Even their servants and labourers looked down upon us.

As I automatically put one foot in front of the other, my body instinctively knowing that to stop would be to die on that terrible road, my conscious mind seemed to contract until it acquired a purity of focus that I had never previously experienced. As I stared through the rain and the darkening sky, I was concentrating upon a fixed point in the future that was not our destination, not the city, my uncle, his house, his table, a bed, nor even the books I knew I would one day write. All I saw were the unctuous features of that son of a whore Grimstone, the author of my family's despair, our Nemesis. One day, I vowed upon my mother's bones, I knew not when, or how, I would have my revenge.

My father had wanted to torch the house, saying that he would leave that blackguard Grimstone nothing, but I managed to calm him enough to see reason. I felt much the same as he, but I was more aware of the legal repercussions for incendiaries, being in a somewhat sounder state of mind. It was a Pyrrhic victory, for we were inside soon anyway. By the time we arrived at my uncle's residence a couple of weeks hence, the bailiffs were already waiting with a warrant. Grimstone was suing my father for years of back rent on the cottage, while Slourup was after me for the balance of our account based upon another series of useless letters. And so it was that we came, at last, to the Marshalsea Debtor's Prison.

CHAPTER VIII

I WAS BARELY fourteen years old when my father and I were arrested for the crime of destitution. The long walk to London had enfeebled us to the point of near insensibility, and that we found my uncle's house at all was close to miraculous, just as inebriates often seem to be guided safely to their beds by angels, having subsequently no memory of the journey. There our luck had ended. We were received at the side entrance like particularly poor applicants for a vacancy below stairs. A vinegar-lipped housekeeper bade us wait for the master in the kitchen, but it was not my uncle who came but the traps. We were carried to the Sponging-house immediately, without the opportunity of either rest or sustenance.

I have little recollection of my uncle's dwelling, other than a vague impression of affluence, but the Sponging-house I remember clearly. It was a terraced house fortified, I knew not where at the time, with heavy locks on the doors and bars on the windows. We were conveyed to an unfurnished upstairs room by a bailiff and advised to send for money, as there was rent to pay on our new lodgings. Having nowhere else to turn, my father requested that word be sent to his brother-in-law, although under the circumstances any assistance from that quarter seemed highly unlikely. My father preferred to give my uncle the benefit of the doubt, speculating that we must have been followed from home by Grimstone's agents. It was my private belief that he was most likely in collusion with our enemy, and had dobbed us in himself.

My conjecture was largely confirmed when my uncle deigned to visit a couple of days later, in the company of the equally traitorous housekeeper. He shared my mother's eyes, but there any resemblance ceased. He had about him the same pinched look of arrogance and abstinence as his woman, in the way that dogs often resemble their masters, and to my fevered eyes they appeared as a pair of darkly accoutred weasels.

No one shook hands and my uncle did not bother to remove his hat. 'I knew you would come to this in the end,' he said, addressing my father. 'Did you think to outrun your creditors by coming to me?'

'I thought you might help my children,' replied my father, with admirable control. 'But I see now that I was mistaken.'

My uncle then briefly directed his attention to me. 'You look like your father,' he said, in the manner of the foreman of a jury delivering a verdict of 'Guilty.'

I was too weak to respond, but he had already turned away. I was evidently considered well beyond redemption by virtue of nothing more than my countenance. They both seemed more interested in my sister, who the housekeeper had swept up in her skeletal arms without invitation or consent. Sarah was horrified, and was twisting and screaming like a child of the fairy mounds. That's my girl, I thought.

Undeterred by this obvious hostility, the woman looked knowingly at my uncle, although she said not a word. 'We will take the girl,' he said.

'No!' I cried, forgetting myself.

'Be quiet, boy,' said my uncle, fetching me a powerful blow across the face. I did as I was told and shut up. He turned to my father. 'She will be safe from the gaol fever with us,' he said, as if nothing untoward had happened, 'as well as the pernicious influence and perverted attentions of other prisoners.'

'We will see that she is well established in Society,' added the housekeeper, keeping a tight hold on my still protesting sister.

My uncle's face seemed to soften at the sound of the woman's voice. 'She will have a much better lot in life in our care,' he said.

My father did not even pause to consider the offer. 'Jack,' he said, in an uncharacteristically authoritative voice that was, just for that instant, more than the equal of my uncle's hectoring tone, 'your sister is upset, please attend to her.' I rose quickly and took possession of Sarah before the woman could react. She stopped crying and settled contentedly in my arms. I moved to my father's side. 'I will leave no child of mine under such a bleak roof as yours,' he told my uncle.

The woman seemed to hiss, but said nothing coherent, and my father continued. 'It seems safe enough, I grant you,' he said, 'but it looks to me a joyless home in which to grow, and Sarah is such a bright and happy child.'

'Then the Devil take you, sir,' said my uncle, 'for I'll have no more of you.' And with that, the austere couple took their leave.

'The Devil take you too, Judas,' I whispered in his wake.

My father slumped against the wall and slid slowly to the bare wood floor. 'I know I'm selfish, son,' he said quietly, 'but I couldn't do without her.'

I sat down beside him and managed a smile, letting Sarah crawl between us. 'It's like Mum used to say,' I told him, 'love will always hold much more value in our family than money.'

'Then I am rich indeed,' said he, doing his best to return my lopsided grin, 'but I fear our creditors will not accept it.'

*

Soon after, we moved from the Sponging-house to the main prison with very little ceremony, there being no way to settle our debts, which, in my father's case, were huge. My lawyer's bill was not so extreme, amounting only to a pound, but it was a quid more than we had, and our debts increased daily by virtue of our continued habit of breathing, like a tax upon fresh air.

As Dickens has written, at considerable length, and in finer terms than I ever could, the paradox of debtor's prison was that you could not earn the money you so desperately needed in order to pay off your creditors from the inside. This penny plain yet devastating reality was another of those great and terrible jokes played upon the poor and vulnerable of our society by those that did and still do own and control it, just as the Great Architect torments us all with endless toil to no avail, incurable disease, old age, deformity, lost love, dead children, and an individual consciousness aware at all times of its inevitable demise. I would not have invented such things were I creating the universe, nor lawyers, politicians, or publishers neither. I would have left all that out of the grand celestial scheme of things, along with Newgate, the Fleet, and the bloody Marshalsea.

Like souls passing through the gates of Hell, those that entered the Marshalsea left all hope behind, although not all immediately realised that they had done so, or the desperate nature of their new situation. There were those, usually relatively young men, reasonably dressed and well spoken, who genuinely believed that the likely duration of their stay was to be so brief as to be hardly worth the bother of unpacking. These tragic optimists had not yet learned that in addition to meeting their creditor's demands they must also pay for the privilege of incarceration, and that now denied access to the labour market, their initially modest debts would thus soon increase to small fortunes as unpaid prison fees accumulated alongside the interest on their debts, like the grains of wheat doubled upon each square of Ferdowsi's chessboard. The only possibility of release from this grim spiral of debt, and therefore the prison, was to come into a large sum of money, which from the look of the majority of the inmates was about as likely as being twice struck by lightning on a clear summer day.

For those who still managed to obtain some sort of income, usually from family or friends, there was a thriving black economy that could provide anything from basic needs to comparative luxury. Rent on a good cell ranged from twenty to five hundred pounds per annum, and food, tobacco, whores, and strong drink were all available in house via the tap room (or 'snuggery'), which functioned as a shop, bar and restaurant. Those that could afford to pay the turnkeys also received the best commodity of all, freedom, at least during the day, whereby they might work, although most earned only enough to meet their gaol costs rather than repay their creditors, so the vicious circle remained both intact and unbreakable.

Like all prisons, this one was dark, dank and overcrowded. When we were led through the great iron doors set in a high, spiked wall, we might as well have been entering Newgate. There was a small turnkey's lodge by the entrance, and a dusty yard beyond it in front of the debtor's section of the prison, which was a brick barracks built around a square, or 'airing yard,' with the look of a modern manufactory about it, the only difference being the bars on the windows.

That said, it could have been worse. The head turnkey, whose name I am ashamed to say I do not remember (Porter, possibly), provided us with a private room on the second floor which was quite light and almost airy by local standards, charging us only the most minimal of rents when, by rights, we could have been cast to the poor side of the barracks and left to rot in the meanest and most overcrowded of cells. This good man even waived the 'garnish,' a charge of five shillings and sixpence levied on all new prisoners. When news travelled that we had a motherless child, gifts of furniture, clothes, money, and even a few toys began to arrive from the generous people of Southwark. Because of the charity of the decent working poor, and the goodwill of our fellow insolvents, we were able to create quite a pleasant living space, albeit in a cell. The more we attempted to make things feel like home, though, the more we missed it. But our little cottage in the country was now lost to us forever, and with no hope of clearing my father's debts beyond a miracle, we settled in for the long haul.

Little Sarah charmed everyone. She was then learning to walk and talk, and would hurtle around the courtyard unsteadily proclaiming wonder and fascination at the most quotidian of objects in a language known only to herself. Her burbling enthusiasm was infectious, and when she interacted with a fellow inmate you could see that invisible yoke of hopelessness that we all carried, like a wraith upon our shoulders, momentarily ease. Even the most hardened of cases, the ones who seemed born ugly, scarred and old, would pause to talk to her or even play. They called her the Child of the Marshalsea, and even though she was not born within those walls she might as well have been for the reverence in which she was held by the prison community.

The story that she had, indeed, been delivered there soon circulated and stuck in any case, as did the wink of the word from the senior members of the club, the real denizens of the London underworld with whom we shared the prison, that any man who harmed a single golden hair on her head would be cut in ways that would make him thereafter worthless to a woman. My father and I, meanwhile, were blessed by association. Dad became the Father of the Marshalsea, and he and I were similarly protected. And thus we gradually adapted to our new environment and community.

I tried to wear a brave face, and I put a singular amount of effort into concealing the secret agony of my soul from my poor father. None of these trials were of his own devising, after all; he was as innocent as my sister and myself. Like most of our fellow prisoners, we were merely victims of the free market. Memories of my happier childhood faded, and I felt my hopes of becoming a writer, a learned and distinguished man, crushed in my breast. My whole being was so penetrated by such rage, grief and humiliation that even years later, during the height of my literary celebrity, or even in the loving arms of my wife and child, my soul would always wander desolately back to that time in my life. My nature, my very essence, was formed within that blighted place, and I have never been truly free since.

I have heard tell that shipwrecked mariners often live or die in the water based upon the effort of their own will, and that at least in the first few hours it is not the cold or exhaustion that causes them to slip beneath the water and silently drown, but a conscious decision to surrender to despair. Others, no fitter or stronger, will equally resolve to stay alive for as long as possible in the hope of finding land or rescue. So it was with me. I chose to survive.

*

There were many classes of person in the Marshalsea, from unemployed labourers and artisans to redundant clerks and bankrupt swells, all in clothes that were out at the knees, arse and elbows. Eventually, my father set about repairing these raggedy men for food or a few pennies while I minded Sarah. Caring for her quickly became my reason to keep on kicking. Looking after such a gorgeous, vulnerable little bit of a person provided a routine that I had to follow, regardless of how I was feeling, and when I heard her little voice in the morning she became my motive for rising and getting through the day. Feeding, entertaining and chasing after a toddler from dawn to dusk, in the hope of tiring her enough for a peaceful night, as well as the endless changing and boiling of soiled napkins, also left me sufficiently exhausted to sleep, whatever the tempest within my head. I had resolved that no matter how angry, depressed or hopeless I might feel I would never display an ugly emotion in front of her (a rule I have also lately followed with my own child), and so I at least affected the appearance of a good humour and an even temper around the prison. This tended to count in my favour with the general population, some of whom were nutty enough upon me to make a gift of the odd penny or bit of bread.

Sarah was still not yet two years old, and the benevolent influence of Mrs. McGuire had forged in her an easy going and adaptable temperament. She was, in a word, a joy. She could amuse herself for hours investigating odds and ends about the room, or communing with a wooden soldier that some kind soul had donated. She was fit and strong, and determined to live; she would eat whatever was available without fuss, and she slept deeply and regularly unless troubled by her teeth, some of which were then still coming through. The easiest way to soothe her was always to tell her a story, and her afternoon nap and evening bedtime were always prefaced by about half an hour of readings and recitations. This ritual became as central to my emotional wellbeing as it was that of my little sister, always a moment of perfect peace, the eye of my storm.

In happier days, my mother had owned the first volume of *Kinder und Hausmärchen* by the Brothers Grimm, and I recalled enough to improvise basic versions of the German folk tales I had heard in my youth, my favourite being 'The Valiant Little Tailor,' in which the hero tricks two evil giants into fighting each other. I could also offer fair renditions of 'Cinderella,' 'Hansel and Gretel,' 'Little Red Cap,' and 'Snow White,' and as all these things kept to a very precise structure it was a straightforward task to invent others. When I became bored with fairy tales, I would take to declaiming poems I had learned with my father, and on a good night he might even join in as I chanted lines from Scott, Coleridge, Byron, or Shelley while Sarah nestled in my arms like a kitten, calming me as I calmed her. We only had the one book, my father's first edition of *Lyrical Ballads*, but I was determined to teach Sarah to read, so whatever story or verse was actually coming out of my mouth I had the book in my hand where she could see it, turning the pages regularly. She must have thought that slim volume to be the most magical book in the world, for its contents would have seemed to her infinite.

Seasoned knucks in quod will discourse at length on the horrors of incarceration; bewailing the mordant cold and the foul air within the cramped, overcrowded and filthy cells, gaol fever, the constant battle to cheat starvation, the rats, the rapes, the beatings— But the real torture is the boredom, all those frozen hours by which you measure out the passage of your life. The inmates of the Marshalsea were thus as aimless as apparitions, and they lingered in great numbers about the courtyard and the staircases, restless and miserable, for their cells were too hot or too cold, or too crowded or too lonely, and not a one of them really possessed the secret of knowing what the hell to do with all the time on their hands.

After we had been in residence some six months or so, one such wraith nervously appeared at our open door at the approximate hour of Sarah's afternoon rest. Freddie was an orphan and only a couple of years older than I, although he acted as if he were younger, and appeared to have moved seamlessly from the workhouse to the debtor's prison. I had not, at that point in my life, ever seen a more pathetic urchin; only the filth that encrusted him from his wild hair to his bare feet seemed to hold his bones together. He leaned unsteadily upon the heavy wooden frame and in a shy, soft and surprisingly polite voice he asked, 'Might I sit quietly and hear the story?' I had not the heart to send this broken boy away, so I beckoned him in and he positioned himself on the opposite side of the fireplace to my chair, crossing his spidery legs underneath himself.

Sarah was already upon my lap. She looked the boy over, sniffed like a puppy, and then returned her attention to the ubiquitous book. 'Once upon a time,' I began, 'a little tailor was sitting at his table near the window—' One story would take about five minutes to tell, and it usually took four or five to knock Sarah out enough to get her into her bed. I could then relax for the next hour or so. After the little tailor became king, Rapunzel had let down her hair, and the wolf's belly was filled with rocks, I ended with a dash of Byron, carrying my drowsy charge to her cot while whispering the final lines, 'A mind at peace with all below, a heart whose love is innocent.'

When I had finished and the child was down, Freddie rose without a word, and reaching into his rags withdrew a piece of greasy bread which he forced into my hands.

'Thank you,' he said in a whisper, before silently taking his leave.

'What a strange boy,' said my father.

Freddie returned the following day. Once more he spoke but little, other than to ask if he might listen, and to thank me when he rose to leave. This time he gave me some tea in a twist of newspaper. I urged him to keep it. 'No,' said he, cupping my hands in his own so I could not return the wrap, 'I want you to have it.' My father cleared his throat and told Freddie that we were very grateful. The young man let my hands drop, and looked not at me but somewhere past my right shoulder. I attempted to catch his eye but he looked away like a girl. 'Same time tomorrow?' he asked quietly.

'Why not,' said my father. I nodded in mute agreement and Freddie grinned back like an idiot. 'What in God's name is that child doing in here?' he said when Freddie had taken his leave.

'What are we doing in here? I said.

There was no answer to this, beyond the obvious, and my father did not reply. He shrugged and returned to his labours. I had chores to attend to, but instead I sunk back into my chair and could not move. To talk of the walls closing in would be a horrible cliché, and I will not use it (Lytton began *Paul Clifford* with, 'It was a dark and stormy night,' and has been rightly mocked for doing so ever since), but the room certainly became darker and more oppressive at that moment, and suddenly appeared to me flooded, the prison part of some vast submerged metropolis. The inner and outer worlds fused, as if I inhaled water that then froze, leaving me dead and buried in an ocean of ice. I could still see my father, though he appeared a great distance away. This had been happening to me more and more of late. I was caught in the grip of a monstrous and paralysing anxiety. While my body was useless my mind surged like a galvanic current. I was as a spirit trapped within its own rigid corpse, cursed to experience itself rotting to nothing with no possibility of either cure or oblivion. Then Sarah awoke. I rose without thinking to comfort her, and the attack passed.

The next day Freddie bought another gift of bread and a friend of about the same age that he introduced as Sid. 'Well,' said my father, 'the more the merrier.'

I was far from sure about this new audience intruding upon my special time with Sarah, but in the Marshalsea you lived from meal to meal so I acquiesced. For her part, Sarah had no anxieties involving strangers; she enjoyed interacting with new people, so I decided to accept the extra scran and be grateful for it. We might be a novelty now, with our sweet little mouse and her gentile ways, but children soon grew and I had no desire to be beholden to the mercy of the dubsmen. Regardless of their kindness, they were still my gaolers, and I hated them accordingly. It also seemed to me that I was at least in some small way starting to earn my bread, while there was also an increasing sense of family about the place, Freddie and Sid beginning to occupy in my small world the roles of older but more artless siblings.

My not-quite-family now grew so fast you would have thought us Catholic, and within the month I was reading to a dozen or so children between the ages of about five and ten every afternoon, and receiving a penny a pop from the parents which Freddie dutifully collected and passed on. Then one day an older man knocked upon our door who was not a parent, and who had no clothes in need of repair.

He introduced himself simply as 'Bill.' In common with most prisoners incarcerated for any length of time it was difficult to judge the man's age; he might have been anywhere between thirty years old and fifty. Bill was not a small man, and a dilapidated top hat worn in mockery of better days gave him an extra eight inches or so, but he was still lost within a mouldy fustian coat obviously cut for a giant. He had the voice of working class London, born and raised, and a Cockney's tendency to leer when he spoke. In round and rough tones, he explained that he had heard that I was a reader, and he was wondering if I might read a bit to him and his mates of an evening, for they knew not how to read themselves.

'For a small remuneration, naturally,' he growled.

I asked him what I might read, and he produced a small, fragile and coverless volume entitled *The Lives of the Pirates, Being a True and Genuine Account of the Robberies and Exploits of Brigands, Buccaneers, Privateers, Corsairs, and Marine Freebooters from the Notorious Kidd and Teach who was also called Blackbeard to Long Ben Every the King of the Pirates & co.*

'It's not Shakespeare, then?' said my father, examining the book, his old sense of humour surfacing briefly, like a nervous goldfish.

He assented surprisingly quickly, though, declaring that he was all in favour of literature for the working man. It was agreed that I would read in the snuggery of a Sunday evening, after Sarah went down, for an initial fee of five pence per night raised by those there assembled, food and drink to be provided.

And that was how I became the Storyteller of the Marshalsea.

CHAPTER IX

I HAD THUS far avoided the tap room for it was intimidating to me, full of rough men and rougher women. I had no experience of such places beyond reading of them in picaresque novels. I was well out of my depths and I knew it. Although I had fooled Scott and Ainsworth by strongly implying that I was fully grown in our correspondence, there was no faking adulthood in the real world, the universe outside the text. My father, meanwhile, had a Methodist's disdain for the drink, although it was practical rather than evangelical, as even though our cause was futile he tried to save as much money as he could towards our debts.

'I might at least settle your accounts,' he would say, 'in a couple of years or so.' There was also the matter of the rent on our cell. I was reasonably certain that it was our constantly pressing need for cash without the possibility of real work that had purchased his permission for this queer venture so easily, for both of us knew, without speaking out, that my poor mother would have been appalled.

The boy Sid was dispatched to collect me on my first night on the job, and although I felt quite awkward around him I was grateful for a familiar face. Such ceremony was hardly necessary; the Marshalsea was really no more than a small brick barracks, though the walk still felt long and terrible to me. Public speaking was a good way outside my area of comfort, and a deal more frightening in prospect than writing for a living, which was odd given that my first publisher had been killed by a rival reviewer.

Henry Mayhew told me once, years later, that he had conducted a survey of this subject among readers of the *Morning Chronicle*, and had discovered that the majority would, they said, rather die than speak in public. 'That would mean,' he had said, with that yawning great grin of his, 'that at any given funeral in the city, the majority of mourners would prefer to be the corpse over the gentleman that delivers the eulogy.'

By the time we reached the great green door I might as well have been climbing the steps to the triple tree. The atmosphere beyond was solid with smoke, beer, and human grease, and although I later grew to love this foul miasma, at that moment it felt to me like the vapours of a killing jar. 'Just remember they're all bastards,' said Sid, and then he shoved me across the threshold.

The snuggery was no more than another cell, different only in that it was larger than most and included a bar and kegs along with the usual decor. It was about thirty feet long, but quite narrow, no more than ten or twelve feet at the most, with the oak bar at one end, backing on to the communal kitchen, and a large fireplace in the centre of the long inside wall of much the same location and design as the one in our cell. The head turnkey's son, who was not much older than I, was stationed behind the bar, where, Sid had told me, one might purchase a pint of ale or a measure of gin for five pence, which rather put my fee in perspective.

The room was lit by multiple candles stuck upon various surfaces, casting a vaguely orange light, refracted by thick tobacco smoke, upon the plain wooden benches, stools and tables scattered about the place, about half of which were presently occupied by the unsophisticated sons and daughters of the Marshalsea. The men outnumbered the women (who were quartered above the tap room), by about four to one. Bill was leaning by the fireplace smoking a long pipe, and when he spied me he waved me over, shoved a warm glass into my hand and raised his arms to quiet the company. I nervously sluiced my ivories and was rewarded with the comforting burn of sugared gin and hot water, a drink I had not tasted since the day my mother died.

Bill attempted to work the crowd, such as it was, explaining that I was the young gentlemen of whom he had spoken, and that I was here to entertain them all with a reading.

'What from?' moaned a wretched northern voice from the floor, 'the bloody Bible?'

Bill sought the speaker out with a menacing eye and stared him down. 'Oh no,' said he, 'we'll have none of that in here.'

A woman at the next table similarly took up my cause, and I received the distinct impression that everyone there present was down on the first speaker, on account of his evident inability to see the bright side of any given situation.

'Shut your hole, Mournful, you miserable old cadger,' said she, 'and give the boy a chance.' She wore a black damask robe *à l'anglaise*, tight at the waist and adorned with spidery feathers that would have been the height of fashion at the end of the last century. Like Bill, she could have been in her thirties or much older. As with many in the Marshalsea it was impossible to tell, although she was in possession of a full set of teeth so was perhaps younger than she looked. 'He don't look like no cheese screamer,' she concluded, addressing her final remark to me.

I replied that a cheese screamer, whatever that might be, sounded most disagreeable, and I assured all present that I was certainly no such thing.

'He don't patter the Flash, Nanse,' said a big, bewhiskered badger of a man, leaving me none the wiser for the remark. He had thick black hair shot through to the mutton chops on either side of his broad face with a dirty grey streak. He propped up the bar and regarded the woman with devouring eyes.

'Leave him be,' she said, slyly catching me in the arc of her vision as she turned towards the big man, 'he'll learn it soon enough.' She had the look of a raven about her, eying up a field mouse.

'Thank you very much,' said I, artificially emboldened by the drink. 'That's one friend there, anyway.'

The man called Mournful regarded me desolately but several others laughed, including the woman. Mournful muttered that he did not cadge, which apparently meant beg, causing the company to laugh all the louder, for by the look of him he surely did.

I was unsure how to proceed, but Bill saved me by furnishing me with the chosen text of the evening and telling me to get on with it.

'I just stand here and read this, then?' I asked him, and he affirmed with a nod, after which he took a long match, already spent, from a pot on the fireplace, thrust it into the fire and then lit his pipe.

I regarded the booklet, which was my first full Newgate Calendar.

There was a crude woodcut of a billowing black flag bearing a skull and cross'd bones beneath the bold title in the form of a frontispiece, and a note at the bottom of the title page acknowledged that the work was printed in Seven Dials, although author, publisher and printer were not identified. There was no date upon the thing, and for all I knew it could have either been printed in the last century, or last year.

'While we're still young, son,' said Bill, taking a seat by the once fine woman in black.

I positioned myself to the side of the fire, availing myself to the light of a candle stuck in a mound of ancient tallow cascading in fantastic shapes down the brickwork. The book was printed in tiny text laid out in two tight columns, its legibility made worse by the ancient stains on the delicate paper. I tossed off my drink and cleared my throat theatrically, then, squinting desperately at the infinitesimal print, I began to read the first entry, which was entitled 'The True and Accurate Account of the Vile Crimes of Captain William Kidd, Who Suffered for Piracy at Execution Dock, May 23, 1701.'

'Piracy,' I read out carefully, enunciating every single syllable, 'is an offence committed on the high seas, by villains who man and arm a vessel for the purpose of robbing fair traders.'

'Speak up,' called a male voice, not the badger, from the back of the room.

'Piracy,' I bellowed, 'is an offence committed on the high seas, by villains who man and arm a vessel for the purpose of robbing fair traders. It is also piracy to rob a vessel lying in shore at anchor, or at a wharf.'

'That's better,' said the unidentified man at the back.

'Piracy,' I continued, *voce di petto*, 'is a capital offence by civil law.' Bill nodded sagely from the floor, as if this was an obscure legislative point and he wished to signal his expertise on the matter. I paused respectfully for a moment (it was his shilling after all), and then carried on. 'The life of Captain Kidd,' I read, beginning to catch the flow of the thing, 'while in agitation, engaged the attention of the public in a very eminent degree, though the man himself was one of the most contemptible of the human race—'

William (or John, the chronicler was unclear) Kidd (or Kyd) was born in Greenock (or possibly Dundee) in or around 1645, I read, and was the son of a sailor lost at sea. Like many Scotsmen he found himself more in sympathy with the French than the English, and ran away to sea on board the French privateer *Sainte Rose*, serving his seaman's apprenticeship among Caribbean buccaneers in a mixed crew that included one Robert Culliford, later a notorious pirate in his own right. Patriotism eventually got the better of the British sailors, and they took the ship by mutiny. They renamed her *Blessed William*, probably after the King rather than the Catholic martyr. Kidd was elected captain, but he was later deposed by Culliford. The crew surrendered to the English colony of Nevis in the West Indies, whereby the governor engaged them as privateers to defend the island from her enemies, declaring that they must take their pay from the French. Kidd was once again made captain, and he harried the French across the Caribbean until Culliford stole the ship at Antigua.

Kidd fruitlessly pursued the *Blessed William* to New York, where he married a rich widow and set himself up in business as a sea trader, undercutting the legitimate competition by secretly dealing with pirates and smugglers, who tended not to bother with import and export duties. 'He was neither remarkable for the excess of his courage, nor for the want of it,' wrote his anonymous biographer, 'but his ruling passion appeared to be avarice.'

While in the company of pirates Kidd would converse and act as they did; to the mercantile middle classes he appeared as they were. He was a natural raconteur and would often discourse with authority upon the subject of pirates. Impressed, the town fathers recommended Kidd to Lord Bellamont, the Governor of the Province, as a 'wizard of the seas' who could rid the West Indies of the piratical menace. Bellamont agreed, as did the King, and Kidd was asked in a way that could not be easily refused to accept a commission to seize pirates and their assets, along with any French ships he might happen to encounter.

The account at that point became vague, convoluted, and, to be frank, boring, as the author explained the funding of the expedition. Although supported by the Admiralty, the venture was a private one patronised by a long list of English and colonial noblemen who expected a major share of the profits against their investment. I gritted my teeth and kept reading, aware that I was losing the crowd.

I prayed for a good bit, which came at last when Kidd, at the helm of his new thirty-four gun man o' war *Adventure Galley*, made prize of two French ships off Madagascar and then turned pirate. He refused to attack British ships, a stance which led to an altercation with his gunner, William Moore, over the decision to let an East India Company ship pass unmolested. Kidd beat him to death with the first object that came to hand, which was a bucket.

Kidd then took the *Quedah Merchant*, an Indian ship under a French passport. He inexplicably burned the *Adventure Galley* at Hispaniola and divided the profits from the *Quedah Merchant* cargo with his crew, taking forty shares for himself. He then sailed for the West Indies in a sloop bought off an Englishman name of Bolton, leaving the *Quedah Merchant* in his charge. Kidd disposed of a great part of his treasure at a secret location, and then steered for Boston. Bolton sold the *Quedah Merchant* and also sailed for Boston, where he arrived before Kidd. He then sold Kidd as well, turning evidence against him. Kidd was arrested on his arrival, and charged with numerous acts of piracy, including the murder of William Moore.

Kidd argued that he thought the *Quedah Merchant* was a lawful prize, but Bellamont sent him to England in chains. Such was the public and political clamour surrounding the case that Members of Parliament debated an emergency opposition motion that 'The letters-patent granted to the Earl of Bellamont and others respecting the goods taken from pirates were dishonourable to the King.' The motion was defeated, yet Kidd's principle English backers continued to face public accusations that they were giving countenance to pirates and no less culpable than the actual offenders. Kidd, by then in Newgate, was examined at the bar of the House of Commons, with a view to fix part of his guilt on his noble business partners, but he was too pissed to give a good account of himself. His original letters of commission had also mysteriously vanished.

Kidd protested his innocence to the last, but nothing came of the political inquiry, and he was hanged in chains at Execution Dock. He reportedly refused the exhortations of the attending ordinary to repent of his sins and prepare himself for this important change, and went to the gallows in silence. He did not die well. Such was the weight of his chains that on the first drop the rope that was to hang him broke, depositing him upon his arse. According to the biographer, the preacher then seized the opportunity to speak with the condemned man once more. This entreaty appeared to have the desired effect, and Kidd supposedly cut his last fling 'professing his charity to all the world, and his hopes of salvation through the merits of his Redeemer.' (Of course he did, I thought.) His body hung in a gibbet at Tilbury for three years as a warning to those that would be pirates.

The inhabitants of the snuggery were by now completely entranced by the narrative once more, and a silence so profound had fallen that I could hear each tap of the legs of the huge spider slowly perambulating across the top of the mantelpiece. Fortunately, the beast was moving away from me, but I kept a weather eye on the bastard nonetheless. At that moment, I owned that crowd.

I took a long breath and delivered the author's closing remarks. 'Thus ended the life of Captain Kidd,' I said in a stage whisper that was, if I say so myself, most effective. 'A man, who, if he had entertained a proper regard to the welfare of the public, or even to his own advantage, might have become a useful member of society, instead of a disgrace to it. Hence we may learn the destructive nature of avarice, which generally counteracts all its own purposes. The story of this wretched malefactor will effectually impress on the mind of the reader the truth of the old observation, that honesty is the best policy.'

'Bollocks,' muttered someone from the back.

As the former conclusion was not the message that I had extrapolated from the account either, I felt emboldened enough to embellish: 'Or,' I concluded, 'to put not your trust in princes.'

The room exploded with applause. Bill rose, clapping, and then elbowed his way to the bar, from which he presently returned with two very large flashes of lightening, one of which he thrust into my hand. 'Well done, son,' said he, causing me to flush with pride, or gin, or both. It can be difficult to tell in these situations.

My audience was now talking enthusiastically upon matters literary and piratical, while ordering up brimming pots of baptised beer or tall measures of the blue ruin, several of which came my way. The night, it would appear, was yet young, so when my dark congregation had returned to their seats and looked towards me with expectation, I took up once more *The Lives of the Pirates.* That night I also read the other two pieces that related to Kidd, one on his treasure, which was never recovered (if it ever existed), the other on the unfortunate Darby Mullins, an Irish waterman who fell in with Kidd and consequently joined him at Wapping in the dance without music. 'From the fate of this offender,' concluded his biographer, delivering the final sermon that I soon learned characterised the form (a muddle of morality, voyeurism and sensationalism), 'we may learn the sin and danger of quitting an honest employment to engage in a business of a contrary nature.'

So that was us telt.

I returned to our room late. 'Have you been drinking?' said my father, sniffing the air suspiciously.

'No,' I said, hurriedly taking to my bed and turning to the wall.

My first performance was deemed a great success, and on the subsequent month of Sundays I refined my technique by also reading the histories of Samuel Burgess, who was peached by Robert Culliford (proving, said Bill, there was no cure for a cunt); Henry Every, the 'King of Pirates,' who vanished with his treasure; Walter Kennedy, cretin, whose navigation skills were such that he confused Scotland for Ireland and then wrecked his ship anyway; Henry Morgan, who occupied Panama but was killed by his doctor; Israel Hands, who served under Edward Teach, the most terrible of all pirates ever to embark upon a pillaging spree, Blackbeard himself. 'A very great man,' said Bill, with a heartfelt solemnity that could not easily be gainsaid.

He was not present on the following Sunday, although Flashy Nanse was in her usual position. That night I read of the female buccaneers Anne Bonny and Mary Read, who sailed the Caribbean with Captain Jack Rackham. The presence of women and boys in a band of brigands was, said their chronicler, generally forbidden in ship's articles, the so-called 'Pirate's Code,' because the men would fight to obtain their favours. Anne and Mary, who wore dresses and finery when not in battle, were excepted as they made themselves available to the entire crew. 'They were both very profligate,' said a witness at their trial, 'cursing and swearing much, and very ready and willing to do anything.' They pleaded their bellies and got off, although Captain Jack and his men all went to the scragging post.

Three Newgate biographies, each two or three thousand words long and in the most visually taxing script, were usually enough (especially given the attention span of the listeners), so I called it a night, bowed out, and approached the bar.

'Give it a name, Jack,' said a voice behind me that was, being feminine in origin, both beguiling and disconcertingly deep.

As with Bill, I had become quite close to Nanse over the intervening weeks, and although incarcerated like the rest of us they were certainly the master and mistress of the snuggery or, in the Flash tongue, which I was at that point learning, the cove and covess of the ken, Freddie and Sid at their feet like dogs. She was standing close by me, so when I turned I inhaled the warm and heavy scent that came off her hair and clothes, an alchemical blend of tobacco, gin, and human odours.

I shyly requested a drop of the creature.

Bertie the Badger was by my other side and he laughed. 'By God, the boy's gammon,' said he, 'better make it a large one, Nanse.'

In reply she wrapped an arm around the both of us and began to sing quite sweetly:

'How happy could I be with either
Were t'other dear charmer away
But while you thus tease me together
To neither a word will I say.'

She had what my mother would have called a filthy laugh. I had initially made sport of this attribute in my own mind, filing it away as an interesting character trait that might one day be applied in a work of fiction, but just then the sound was ineluctably thrilling.

She leant on the bar and flirted with the tap-man, and was rewarded with a complimentary brace of jackeys. She guided me back to her usual table and we talked for hours, the barman inexplicably bleeding quite freely, and that wonderful liquid darkness warming our thoughts and our bodies. By the light of the candle her greying hair, worn loosely up, regained its lustre, her slightly skull-like countenance softened, and the folds of her flesh testing the seams of her dress became as alluring as they were sometimes repellent. What was different that evening was that Bill and the boys were absent. Bill, attended by Freddie and Sid, had been in a card game for two days and two nights that was showing no signs of quitting, but Nanse had needed to deliver to me the precious book, and she had, she informed me, not wanted to miss the girl pirates.

She was particularly taken with Bonny and Read, and quizzed me in detail although in truth I knew no more than she, having never heard of them before I opened the tatty volume that night. 'I am also very profligate,' she said huskily, 'and ready and willing to do anything.' There was no answer to that, so I stared at her dumbly and could think of nothing better to do than finish my drink. She gently brushed my hand from my face and leaned forward, mashing her wet mouth into mine. She tasted sharp and bitter; her hair smelt of bear, whiskey and wine. 'Walk me home,' she whispered.

I had never had a woman before, and were I not drunk to a merry pin I would have been laughably flustered by the subsequent encounter. As it was, she took me in her mouth in the dark, deserted courtyard by the stairs to the women's rooms. It was all over pretty quickly. Afterwards she spat on the gravel, gave me a warm and final kiss, and then charged me a shilling.

I told my father I had lost the money. The effect upon him was as a naked flame applied to black powder.

'*You did what?*' he cried, leaping from his chair with uncharacteristic energy.

'I'm sorry, Dad,' I stammered, instinctively backing away. 'I didn't mean to.'

'Liar!' he bellowed, clearly losing all mastery of his passions. 'You witless, selfish boy! Don't you realise how much we need that money?'

He was severely agitated by this point, pacing the cell and waving his arms violently as he berated my general incompetence, as if he meant to batter the very words he spoke with his fists. I was too young and too shocked to understand that I had fired a train of thought within him that, once set, could not be easily extinguished.

His voice rose to a constant bark as he accused me of spending the money on my new friends as he called them. He raved and he ranted, and I pleaded and apologised and denied. He seemed possessed by some terrible force that could not be calmed or controlled until it had tasted blood. He denounced me as a drunk and a whoremaster and struck me repeatedly about the head and face. He had never beaten me before, and the shock of the act itself was much worse than the pain it engendered. I finally managed to push him from me, but he continued to shout, lamenting his lot and repeating over and over again the need for us to make and save as much as we could, wasting nothing, so as to pay off our creditors and be free.

It was a hopeless argument. He owed hundreds of pounds, with interest accruing. 'But Dad,' I said in desperation, shouting to get above him and giving voice to that which we both knew, but of which we never spoke. 'We will never be free. Can you not see that? It makes no difference what we do. This is a life sentence.'

He froze then, turned to stone in the glow of the fire, and from the contortions of his face I would not have been surprised at rage, tears or laughter. The anger did not stay in check for long though. He re-ignited quickly and damned me for a rake and a cur, raising his fist once more.

At this point, a tiny voice from the corner of the room very distinctly cried, 'No.' My little sister was standing, wide awake, in her cot and regarding my father with a look of absolute horror. He staggered back as if shot, and fell into a chair. It was soon apparent that he was quietly weeping.

I left him to it and took little Sarah in my arms, eventually calming her, although I very much doubted she would sleep. She was trembling and unnaturally quiet, and I stayed by her for an age, stroking her hair and soothing her as best as I could until she finally drifted off. I had nowhere else to go, so I went to my bed, cursing quietly, for I was now horribly sober and there was thus no possibility of slumber. Whether my swollen eyes were tightly shut or staring miserably at the skylight, I could not burn the image of my father's fury from the front of my mind, where it howled around the equally powerful memory of Nanse's lips, like a banshee screaming and clawing about a well. In an epiphany of both shame and elation I knew then that I must have her again, whatever the cost. As I had hitherto grimly suspected, there was apparently an implicit connection in life between sex and violence.

CHAPTER X

I HAD NOW run out of pirates. Bill had not been forthcoming with any other books or broadsheets, and there was not a single line of print to be found anywhere in the damn prison. It seemed to me that my father and I were the only literate occupants of the entire place, but between us we had but one book. I lobbied the turnkey for literature, and he promised me that he would see what he could do, as long as I could pay him up front, which just then I could not. I was desperate not to lose my spot in the snuggery on Sundays, for this seemed to me the most likely path to Nanse's further affections.

On the following Sunday I therefore returned to the pages of the enchanted book, confidently producing the Wordsworth and Coleridge, which I claimed was a lately acquired miscellany of grotesque and phantasmagorical tales by a fashionable author. I affected to carefully select a story, and then began to recite and extemporise, while blindly turning the pages of the *The Rime of the Ancyent Marinere.* I started with an extended version of my old story 'The Shivering of the Timbers,' in the hope of hanging it out as long as possible while also providing some sort of bridge between the piratical histories of the previous month and my own gothic tales. I would have loved to have read out the Coleridge, but my listeners didn't strike me as the metaphysical type.

The story seemed to go down well, especially a new episode that I had made up on the spot in which the captain's beautiful daughter was threatened by the creeping tendrils of the mad ship, leaving little doubt as to the danger which they represented or their intended destination. The original story had ended with the usual revelation and twist, in which the hero finally discovered the truth from the dying words of the ship's carpenter, before firing the haunted vessel and escaping in a gig that sprouted uncanny limbs and ripped him to pieces in the final line. This I now embroidered.

The captain's beautiful daughter, it turned out, was a spirit medium who was rescued at the last moment from a fate worse than death by the hero. The pair escape to a lifeboat, upon which the medium performs a séance intended to invoke the spirits of the ship in order to cast them out. As the insane phantoms manifest themselves across the boiling surface of the ocean, the medium casts an arcane enchantment to create a rip in the fabric of time and space that will banish the evil ghosts forever. The portal opens in the form of a giant whirlpool, but the small boat is possessed and murderous wooden arms tear the unfortunate enchantress apart before she can complete the incantation. The hero jumps from the writhing boat as it is drawn into the maelstrom, but he is caught in the wake of the imperfect spell, and is sucked through the terrifying vortex as if pulled under by a sinking ship.

'For the love of God,' he cries, as he is dragged into the darkness along with the screaming dead, 'how do you stop it?' I left it there, with scope, I felt, for a sequel the following week.

My audience applauded and stamped their feet. I leaned back against the wall, spent. I caught Nanse's eye and she smiled so I made my way over. Bill and the lads were back at their usual places, unfortunately, and were engaged in a heated discussion with the men at the next table concerning the fate of the hero. Sid reckoned he was drowned, but this was shouted down quickly on the grounds that there was obviously more to come. I would not be drawn, although I did suggest that to kill the hero would surely be to kill the tale. Bill agreed. He felt strongly that the hero had been transported back through time, and that he would continue to fight the malevolent shades in the age of the pirates, while Freddie was sure he was on the moon. These were both pretty good ideas, so I made a mental note.

Bill lurched up to buy drinks, and Nanse shuffled up next to me. 'That medium looked a lot like me,' she said. I felt my face colour, but I laughed it off as a coincidence. She casually dropped her hand into my lap. 'Tell me,' she demanded.

'I can't stop thinking about you, Nanse,' I confessed, 'I fancy I am bewitched.'

'I know, darling,' she replied, at which point her husband, like her hands, returned to the table with a long bottle of the heart's ease, a pewter jug of hot water and a handful of sugar. I started drinking heavily, and affected to make merry, continuing to take part in the discussion upon the fate of the hero from my story, although I did not let on that I was the author.

The party disbanded some hours later. As Nanse took her leave she kissed me on the cheek and whispered that I should wait until midnight then come to her room. I felt quite lightheaded as I regained my seat. I took up the short clay pipe I had lately acquired, filled it from a small leather pouch of tobacco that I could ill-afford and lit it off the candle upon the table. Smoking deeply, I regarded the clock above the fire. I was at once impatient, excited, and terrified.

At about ten to midnight, a boy I did not recognise, but of whom I had been indistinctly aware during the reading, cautiously approached my table. He was quite neatly dressed by local standards, with a white cap failing to contain unruly brown curls, a short blue jacket and corduroy trousers, leading me to surmise, correctly, that he was recently arrived. 'That was a very fine story, sir,' he said shyly.

I was too spoony and preoccupied to be civil. 'I wouldn't know,' I said sharply, 'I just read them for a bob a go.' His facial response to my crude indifference reminded me of Sarah on the brink of tears. I immediately felt ashamed. Had I not once been exactly as he was now, in a state of fear and shock, and hopelessly lost in this terrible dungeon? I began to appreciate that my father was right to be concerned. I had changed. Was I not now in my cups, smoking, drinking and waiting upon a whore?

I softened my tone and tried to make contact. 'You're new here, aren't you?' I asked, in a voice that I hoped would communicate kindness, rather than the advanced condition of intoxication I was presently experiencing.

His looked utterly crestfallen. 'I'm not here, as such sir,' he said, and thus the dam broke. 'My poor father has recently arrived,' he continued, beginning to babble, 'and I was sent to visit today and he didn't wish to see me and then I was locked in and I didn't know what to do and the man at the gate he said I should come here.' He was stammering, weeping, and clearly in a profound state of agitation.

When he paused momentarily for breath, I noticed that he was trembling with the effort to compose himself. The brave little chap sucked all that emotion back up before my eyes, and then continued in a much more measured tone. He had not dared to approach the common men and women in the tap, and had ended up cowering in a dark corner, taking some solace, it would appear, from my silly story. Now the bar was all but empty, he had summoned the nerve to approach me, the storyteller, in the hope that a reader might be a little way out of the gutter. I must have been a profound disappointment.

I tried to pour him a drink but he politely refused. 'Oh I couldn't possibly do that, sir,' he said. I bade him drop the formalities given our circumstances and call me Jack, and he replied that I may in that case address him informally as David.

'How old are you, David?' I asked him gently.

'I am just twelve,' he replied. That reminded me of the hour and I swore quietly. I could not leave this small, frail and wretched child to the mercy of the Marshalsea at midnight.

'Come on,' I said, rising unsteadily, 'I have somewhere you can stay.'

We quit the snuggery and walked briskly across the courtyard, for the air was powerful sharp, and I had an appointment to keep. It was late-February, I think. (It is an easy matter to lose track of time in prison.) I tried to point out areas of interest, but my companion preferred to talk about my story and had already sniffed me out.

'You don't just read the stories, do you, Jack?' said he. 'You write them as well.'

I bade him lower his voice. 'How did you know?' I hissed.

'I could tell,' said he, quite matter-of-factually. He then offered a brief critique, in which he praised plot, pace and premise, but confessed that he felt the characters were insubstantial, the setting vague, and the resolution confusing.

I told him he should be a literary critic and he returned a brittle laugh. I realised I had hit a nerve, so I hastily set myself to explaining the history of the story, its original publication, the magic book, and my current intention to make it into a serial. He thought the latter a very fine idea, but expressed surprise at meeting a published author in such a place.

'From what I know of the literary life so far,' I replied, 'I am surprised that there are so few.'

'You are a philosopher, Jack,' said David.

'I'm drunk,' said I, 'now be quiet for we must not wake my sister.' We had arrived at the stairs to the family room, which we cautiously ascended.

My father was still awake, sitting by a paltry fire and staring morosely into the embers.

'This is David, Dad,' I explained. 'He's been locked in. I thought he could take my bed for the night.' My father looked up slowly, as if it were he and not I that were at lush. He said nothing, but shrugged his shoulders and nodded, before returning his attention to the ashes. 'Don't mind the Governor,' I told David, 'he's not been himself of late.' He tried to thank my father, but I lit a candle from the fire and steered him towards my bed, which was by Sarah's cot. 'Whatever you do,' I whispered, 'do not wake the little one.'

He nodded, and then looked suddenly worried. 'I have work in the morning,' he said. I promised him that I would rouse him in good time, and then left him to his rest, although I doubted the poor child would sleep.

'And where are you spending your night, boy?' said my father as I took my leave. He had the same look in his eye that he now had when forced to exchange words with Bill, a kind of mixture of fear and disgust, as one might have for some giant, tropical spider that has invaded your quarters but which is too big to safely squash.

'With friends,' I said, closing the heavy door behind me.

I was late, very late, but I still made my way quietly across the courtyard to the stairs to Nanse's room. I was armed with half a bottle of gin, I had no bed for the night, and I was willing to talk myself inside if she were still awake, even if I had no idea what to do once I crossed her threshold.

I need not have worried, for she was obviously waiting. Candles and fire still burned, although she was prepared for bed, wrapped as she was in a long night gown of faded black silk. She kept me outside freezing, just to let me know who was in charge, and regarded me from behind the door with dark, indecorous eyes.

'You took your fucking time,' she finally said, and then she let me in.

This time there was no charge.

CHAPTER XI

THE BUILDINGS AND courtyard of the Marshalsea had a much more pleasant aspect than usual the morning after the first night I spent in the bed of Flashy Nanse. Even though I had not slept, my senses seemed strangely acute as I quit her room and walked softly into the frozen dawn. I had left my lover sleeping heavily, and had taken leave of her soft warm body only by a tremendous effort of will, based upon duty to my sister, my promise to David, and my fear of being surprised in Nanse's bed by Bill, the man I took to be her husband. Despite the latter trepidation, I left in a state of elation that I had not known before, exceeding, as it did, even the feeling of triumph and excitement I had experienced when my first story had seen pay and print. I had travelled far and learned much in the space of that short and single night, and I was deliciously aware that I was returning to the world changed. My life, I was sure, would never be the same again.

Snow had fallen during the night, and lay thick, glowing and undisturbed on the external staircases, the slate roofs of the barracks, and the courtyard square. I paused to take in its virgin beauty, but wary of leaving an obvious trail from Nanse's door as much as disturbing the purity of the scene, I kept to the edge of the steps, and then hugged the wall as I made my way home. Snow was not black in those days, as it is in London now, and this soft white shroud, that made even the Marshalsea glorious, was perfectly pure, like a fresh sheet of expensive stationary. The air was sharp and silent, and it felt to me just then as if I were the only conscious being in the great city, whether within or without the high spiked walls that contained me. At that hour, everything around me, whether man, beast or insect, was dreaming, dying or dead.

I let myself into our cell silently. I had learned to move about the room as a phantom, for the brief period when only I was awake was an essential and sacred moment of peace before my long day began.

In my present state, a spiritual and sensual alchemy of alcohol, love and lost sleep that I have since found no drug to match, I particularly wished the night to have no end. I prayed for the chance to briefly re-live the last few hours in secret and solitude, before my return to the grind of prison life and my duties as my sister's keeper.

Sarah was now just past three years old, and knew nothing but the Marshalsea. Her pleasing features, framed by long golden hair, suggested that she had retained her originally angelic nature, but I fear she had learned from her elders. She was now easily frustrated and subject to fits of terrible rage, while at other times she was unusually quiet and withdrawn, although when she did talk she was remarkably articulate. She also affected an imaginary friend called 'Carol,' who, she explained, also lived in the prison. It seemed a harmless bit of fun, and at least Carol could get a few words out of Sarah, which was usually more than we could.

I had a ritual of domestic tasks every morning that began as soon as I rose with the lighting of the fire. I would then boil water for the preparation of Sarah's breakfast (usually porridge, or bread mashed with warm water on a bad day, and some dried fruit if I could get it). This I followed by washing and dressing. Sarah would usually wake the instant I moved from my bed, which was why her food always came first (for patience is not a virtue among infants), and if she surfaced in a good humour I would leave her in her cot to babble away to Carol while I made a brew, sometimes placating her with a knuckle of bread. If, on the other hand, she awoke discomposed and complaining, which was more usual nowadays, then I would have to get her up, fed, changed and entertained immediately. Were I lucky, she would sleep through all the stages of the ritual, and I would be left in peace to take tea by myself. When she snapped into consciousness before me, whether happy or sad, I would be most put out. The ritual would then be rushed or broken and I would spend the rest of that day feeling as if I were losing a race. More recently, I also needed to compose myself each morning before facing the increasingly awkward interactions with my father, as we broke our own fast on dry bread and black tea.

But today was different. We had a guest.

Asleep the boy looked younger, the inadequate blanket pulled up about his face to mask him from the cold, his dark curls wild and girlish. I shook him awake as gently as I could and his expression went from tranquillity to panic in an instant. 'It's Jack, mate,' I said, 'I'm a friend, remember?' He relaxed and sat up in the bed rubbing his eyes.

Then the panic returned. 'What is the hour?' he said.

'Not much past dawn,' I told him, 'no more than six.' At this statement he became again agitated, and untangled himself from his blankets as if trapped in a net.

'I must be at work at seven,' he said in an anxious whisper, at least mindful that my sister was still, miraculously, asleep.

What job, I wondered, could instil such fear in one so young? This was hardly a deep insight, for at that stage in my life my experience of the lot of the urban poor was extremely limited. As I later discovered, children much younger than this worked, if they were lucky, otherwise they begged and starved on the streets, or worse.

The boy had at least three miles to cover, in his estimation, and his face fell when I told him of the snow, for he was woefully underdressed for winter walking. He fretted about the time that the adverse weather conditions would most likely cost him, but I managed to convince him to at least stay long enough to take some tea and a bit of dry toast to fortify him upon his journey back into the mysterious world beyond the walls of the prison, which was, he explained, just off Borough High Street. He must then, he said, walk north along the high street, then up Southwark Street, over Waterloo Bridge, and then along the Embankment, until he must enter the dark, labyrinthine rookeries that lay hidden and filthy behind the Strand, all names that were common cultural currency about the prison, but which meant nothing to me. London was then to me a shadow, a smudge within the blur of my memory of arrival and incarceration. I might as well have been living upon the surface of the moon for all I knew of it. Finally, the boy must descend to the very edge of the foul water of the Thames by the Hungerford Stairs, where stood his place of employment, a rotten and rat-infested factory that avoided falling into the river itself, he told me, with genuine horror in his eyes, only by the intervention of great bars of wood reared against its walls.

'It sounds worse than this place,' I said, and then wished I had kept my opinion to myself, for the poor creature looked so forlorn I was sure that tears would soon be forthcoming.

'It is, Jack,' he finally said, with an accent so refined that it was difficult to associate anyone speaking thus, especially a child, with manual labour, 'much, much worse.' His family must have fallen very far indeed, I thought, although he volunteered no more on the subject and I did not push him. He carefully finished his toast, and prepared to go. Sarah was stirring so I dare not walk him to the gate, although he promised me that he would find his own way. This was fair enough, for you could see it from our door. I found him a spare jacket and insisted that he wore it. It buried the poor thing, but at least the weight of it would warm him up, if it did nothing else. He shook my hand at the door and thanked me very formally. 'I do hope I shall hear more of your fine story,' he said.

'Then you must visit me again,' said I, 'if you've a mind to.'

'I would like that very much,' he said, and then he was gone.

I wondered what would become of him out there in the cold. I considered seeking out the strange boy's father later, but then thought better of it. I had my own problems.

Then Sarah woke, in good humour, and my working day began. 'Hullo gorgeous,' said I, sweeping her up out of her cot. She snuggled in my shoulder and I enjoyed the feel of her soft hair and warm skin on my face as she pointed at the wall and named things that only she could see.

'Doggie,' she said, emphatically, for she had lately encountered a mongrel at the Gate House Lodge and was now fascinated by the things. To Sarah, all animals, real, represented, or imagined, were dogs, including the vermin we often saw in the courtyard.

'Carol's mummy,' she had recently told me, 'said they was all puppies, and I mustn't be scared.'

I had assumed this originated from one of the women in the prison, for what else could you tell a child who might be afraid of the rats? 'I don't think I've met Carol's mummy,' I said.

'Don't be silly,' Sarah had earnestly replied. 'Carol's mummy's gone to Heaven.'

I thus looked about for a rat, but saw none. The bloody things have probably all frozen to death, I thought, setting Sarah down upon my lap to feed her. Shortly thereafter I became uncomfortably aware that her night time napkin was leaking.

'Merciful heavens,' said my father, rising at last, 'but there's a stench in the air this morning and no mistake.' He approached the fire cautiously, but smiling.

I nodded in reply.

'Morning Daddy,' said Sarah enthusiastically.

Apparently we were to pretend nothing out of the ordinary had happened the night before, as was now often our way on Sunday nights and Monday mornings. It was a familiar pattern. My father was a morning person by nature, and tended to wake in a reasonable humour, but as the day progressed the black depression that now ruled him would slowly annex his soul, until by the evening he was either silent and desolate or excitable and violent.

'Mayhap the Fleet Ditch has overflowed again,' he said, pouring himself some tea while I attended to Sarah. 'God's trousers,' he continued, peering at the filthy napkin and wrinkling his nose theatrically in an approximation of a good humour I knew to be artificial and temporary, 'it's a wonder you have any bones left, my girl.'

Sarah giggled and stuck both her hands in her own bodily waste. My lack of sleep suddenly caught up with me. Between my father's barometric mood swings and my sister's on-going toilet training, this had 'long day' written all over it.

*

Sunday evenings now became my reason for doing anything, and much of the time that I snatched while Sarah slept was devoted to scripting the next instalment of my serial, either in my head or on paper when I could get it. I wrote around my little sister and the other domestic tasks that my father expected of me, which included all the duties traditionally associated with the lady of the house. I acquired food, by a variety of means in which non-circuitous purchase was but one option (there was also begging, bartering and theft), I cooked, and I cleaned, and when not skivvying I was often obliged to help my father tailor. I was thus, like working class women, doubly exploited under capitalism, for I kept house and also worked. My writing in that period was therefore rather episodic in structure, the text a series of brief, incremental units of narrative constructed around childcare and basic survival.

The problem of paper was finally solved by a female enthusiast in her middle years, who visited the prison attended by a strapping servant with the intention of distributing bibles by which we poor sinners and fallen souls might learn the error of our ways, and be lifted up once more to the bosom of our Lord and Saviour.

'God bless you, madam,' I said, when I received my copy, with genuine feeling, for I really needed that book. I grasped her frail hands in heartfelt thanks and obviously disconcerted both lady and servant, for the former appeared suddenly quite flustered while the latter pulled me away roughly and called me a 'dirty fucking beggar' under his breath.

'That wasn't very Christian,' I told him.

Those bibles were of inexpressible aid to myself and my fellow sufferers. The pages were soft, strong and absorbent, and the good book therefore became a source of great solace for anyone visiting the long-drops at the back of the yard for months afterward. Equally, paper stuffed between layers of ragged clothing was a wonderful insulating agent against the ravages of the endless cold. You could read it too, although, as I had learned to my advantage, that was quite a rare skill in these parts.

In my case, after much experiment on single sheets, I developed a system of deinking based upon soaking the pages, by means of personal micturition, until the print was reasonably faded, then rinsing them thoroughly in rainwater and pegging them on string across a corner of the room to dry. (That's a technique you will not find in any guide to literary composition.) My father said I would most likely be damned, but I replied that we already were. Try not to judge too harshly though, but instead reflect on the user and commodity value of paper in the subterranean regions. That good lady did indeed do the Lord's work by easing the suffering of the poorest of the poor, and is not that, in the end, what Christ urges us all to do? It is more to the pity that we could not eat the things, for that would have saved many back gate paroles that winter.

Ink I made from rainwater and soot, and my quills were cut from pigeon feathers gathered in the courtyard or traded with other prisoners, once the word was out that I needed such things. Sometimes I would be presented with an entire bird, which we would eat if it did not seem too game. The consensus of opinion in the snuggery was that I was building a machine for the purpose of self-pollution. While I stammered out my protestations and explanations, my Nanse would just smile.

The Shivering of the Timbers therefore continued, getting sillier with every passing instalment. My protagonist fell through time and was found by pirates adrift in the Indian Ocean, having spent the next and linking part of the narrative upon a raft fashioned from driftwood and fighting a giant shark. After a long battle of wits, he eventually bested the beast with a harpoon improvised from a shattered mast. Fortunately, the debris of his ship, which had similarly travelled through the magical portal, was no longer possessed. That was a bit of a yawning plot hole, but I managed to get away with it because everyone loves stories about sharks.

He and I then embarked upon a complex spiritual and physical journey, locked in a war of attrition with the evil ghosts, who had possessed a ship and its sailors, and in quest of a legendary grimoire. This was an ancient book of spells reputed to hold the power to exile the undead scourge and return the hero to his own time. Captain Kidd had saved the hero, and they frequently fought together, alongside other famous pirates of the day, although who they sided with was often unclear. Mary Read and Anne Bonny formed two sides of an interesting romantic triangle, much in the manner of the real-life relationship between Jack Sheppard, Edgeworth Bess and Poll Maggot, and which, had it ever seen print in the form that it was originally penned, would have seen me prosecuted for obscenity, forgetting all the other stuff that later got me into so much trouble.

My new friend David never missed an episode, or the opportunity to afterwards explain its many structural and figurative shortcomings. 'The point of all this blood and thunder,' I would tell him, 'is that if you must write for the mob then you must not write too weak.'

He tended to damn with faint praise, suggesting that my talents might be better employed in more serious literary endeavours. 'But why, my dear Jack,' he would say, 'do you insist on writing about nothing but pirates?' That was a good question, and it has been asked since, repeatedly, and with considerably more judgement, derision and downright venom behind it that when first raised by my young friend all those years ago.

'For money, of course, you needy-mizzler!' I would reply. What did he think we were in here for, the pillock?

There was also my outcast's natural affinity for the outlaw, or at least the romantic image of the outlaw, who I always saw as a rebel and a class warrior, never just a thief and a murderer, which was invariably the truth of the thing. I was also writing for love, for the thought of losing my special night, and therefore Nanse's affections (for the two things had become inextricably linked in my young mind), was a constant source of anxiety. I already knew, you see, even back then, that a writer is only ever as good as his last story. The patrons of the snuggery could tire of me very easily, and the last thing they wanted was the kind of contemporary social realism that was the bee in our Davey's bonnet. This was a subject that we also discussed as much as we were able between my readings, my family, my love life, and the demands of his day job.

'Why do your manuscripts always smell funny?' he asked me once. I dare not tell him, because there was enough circumstantial evidence to suggest that he was a true believer, and I was in no mood for a sermon. I sniffed my papers and stuffed them quickly into a poacher's pocket, muttering something about 'bloody cats,' although there were, to my certain knowledge, no such animals located anywhere within these walls. Even though the turnkeys frequently introduced stray cats to take care of the rat infestation, the inmates just kept eating them. They ate the rats too, and if there were no dubsmen about the place to keep the peace then I'd not have ruled out cannibalism either.

'It would be my object, were I you,' said my young companion, 'to present little pictures of life and manners as they really are, not in some melodramatic fantasy in which every character has a clearly defined sphere of action—hero, villain, damsel in distress—and everything is resolved with such neat simplicity.'

'Thank you, Dr. Johnson,' said I, more than a little put out of humour by this remark. 'Have you any idea at all how difficult it is to maintain so many story lines at one time,' I continued, moved to defend my art in the face of its critics (a habit I have not lost), 'half of which take place in different centuries and, indeed, astral dimensions, while obliged to tell jokes and get in a fight or a fornication every five pages or so, because you'll lose your audience otherwise, and then come up with an ending each time that satisfactorily closes one episode while setting up another? Do you know how taxing it is to invent a character, to give him a life and a distinct voice?' I was quite carrying the keg by then, as the locals would say of a man greatly tested and unable to conceal his chagrin. I spat on the floor and summed up: 'It was an easier matter by far for Wellington to organise his forces at Waterloo, or for Ajax to lay waste to the Thracians. I would sooner unravel the skein of my family's debts, or yours for that matter, than embark upon another God cursed serial romance!'

'But could not you at least set the story in the present?' he persisted, 'in London, perhaps?'

'No,' said I, determined to be difficult. The pitiful truth was that I knew nothing of London beyond roughly where it was located on a map of England.

'When I walk to work,' he persisted still further, for he was a stubborn cove, even back then, 'I see such things on the streets.'

'What things?' I demanded, aware that my pitch was rising in the wake of my little artistic tantrum. I was momentarily blessed with the insight that, unlike my sister, I was supposed to have mastery of my emotions. I was waiting on Nanse, who was significant by her absence, and beginning to crash like a dipsomaniac deprived too long of the drink.

'Wonderful and terrible things, Jack,' said he, 'there is tragedy and comedy everywhere.'

'Even at the factory?' I said. That was a low blow, but it not deter him.

'Yes,' he said, quietly, 'even at the factory.'

I knew all about that factory by then. In terms of my blindness to the world outside the walls, he was my eyes. I thus often saw the city as he did, with all its humour and horror, and his own sense of self-worth in relation to it. When he spoke uninhibited, which was not often then, he could already paint pictures with his words. It was a talent he told me he had inherited from his mother and his grandmother, both consummate storytellers.

It was his mother who had betrayed him though, as much if not more than his father, of whom he still saw nothing. He would receive his daughter in his cell on Sundays, but not his son, whether because of pride or indifference my friend did not know. He seemed even more alienated than I, for at least I had Sarah, and, sometimes, Nanse, providing me with some kind of rudimentary human validation. It is no wonder that the poor child had therefore attached himself to me, for his mother sent him to visit his father every week, regardless of the boy's protestations that he was obviously not wanted. I wondered who the mother had calling that required such a need for privacy.

The factory on the Hungerford Stairs haunted us both, for I saw it as clearly as he: as crooked as an old man, rotten, damp, cold as a witch's slit, and swarming with rats made fat off the filth of the river it abutted, the drowned, the murdered, and the suicides, always in the foul mud and dark water that lapped at the piles and posts like a hungry whore at a cock. It was into this blighted place that the boy's parents sent him to work, for ten hours a day, two days after his twelfth birthday. As his father was useless with money and his mother had, he told me, resolved to 'do something,' it was clear that it was she that had been the architect of his despair, transforming his young life at a stroke from that of a promising and ambitious scholar to a manual labourer.

Shortly after that his father went into the Marshalsea as an insolvent debtor, leaving David in much the same position as I, although I was coming to realise that he had the worst of it. It was true that he did have the notional freedom to walk out of the main gate during daylight hours, and was not obliged to return in the evening, but he was at liberty only to travel between an unhappy and neglectful home, and a loathsome house of miserable toil that was no less of a dungeon to him than my own place of incarceration. We were both of us in chains forged by our elders.

Likewise in common with me, my friend would protect himself by withdrawing into the realm of his own imagination, although whereas I tended towards the fantastic he favoured a kind of embellished realism, by which he created biographical sketches of those around him through a blend of conjecture and often staggeringly acute observation. His flair for describing places was matched by his eye for people, and through our conversations I felt as if I knew the staff of the factory as well as he, from the avaricious and falsely benign owner, to the ambitious charge hands that harried him constantly to work faster, and his fellow labourers, who quickly ostracized him on account of his 'airs.'

We did the same thing with the clientele of the snuggery, looking at mannerisms, inventing histories, and drawing grotesque caricatures with words. 'See that one—' one of us would begin, looking discreetly towards a likely victim, sometimes known to us, and sometimes not. We would then extemporise a character study between us, taking turns at the crease, until we eventually collapsed into helpless and ill-disguised giggles, our ages betrayed, just for that moment, by a youthful joy that could still resist the creeping cynicism of our circumstances.

Bertie the Badger wrote himself. 'We are quiet here, my friends,' he was fond of saying, to any new arrivals, and plenty of old ones as well, although we'd heard it all before. 'We don't get badgered here. There's no knocker, sir, to be hammered at by creditors and bring a man's heart into his mouth. Nobody comes here to ask if a man's at home, and to say he'll stand on the door mat till he is. Nobody writes threatening letters about money to this place. It is freedom, sir, it is freedom!' Bertie's thesis was simple: 'We have got to the bottom,' he would say, 'we can't fall no further, and what have we found? Peace. That's the word for it,' he would triumphantly conclude. 'Peace.'

This, I recall, particularly got under my friend's skin. 'Are we really at the bottom, Jack?' he asked.

'I'd probably better not answer that,' I said.

There was a serious point to all this though. We were both, after our own fashion, turning to the idea of somehow writing *politically*, although neither gave it a name at that point.

Our original experiments were primitive, to say the least. There was no real satire in my early stories, and I tended to see factions in society that oppressed my class in terms of personal vendetta, so did not get much further initially than naming villainous characters after my enemies. Traitors, turncoats, corrupt politicians, and wicked noblemen tended to be either physically modelled upon or named after my family's landlords and solicitors over and over again. David was much the same. Although he had a natural eye for detail, his observations seemed more to the purpose of aiding and easing his own understanding of his revised position in the world. He would invent alternative versions of his own life, he admitted, which he would adopt when between factory and prison. So to tradesmen along the route with whom he conversed, he remained a middle class schoolboy with prospects.

On one visit he was particularly excited, not to say slightly pissed, having just spun a convincing yarn to a publican and his wife on Parliament Street about it being his birthday.

'They asked me a good many questions,' he reported, 'what my name was, how old I was, where I lived, and how I was employed. To all of which, that I might conceal my true station, I invented appropriate answers.'

'And they fell for it?'

'They made me a gift of a glass of their very best ale,' said he.

'You're learning,' I said.

Inevitably, David pointed out Bill and Nancy quite early on. They did stand out somewhat. 'Let's do them,' he said.

'Can we not,' I said, 'they're me mates.'

He looked to another subject instead, Penelope, a naturally morose woman who had some kind of connection with Bertie and who I assumed to be on the bash, only lower down the local hierarchy than Nancy. 'Nelly, then,' he began, 'not a natural blond, of course—'

But I could have done Bill and Nancy. I was beginning to grasp the complexity of their relationship, and a sense of myself in relation to it that was far from reassuring, for I did love her, in my way, in much the same way that I would later love opium.

My insights began one night as I lay with her, our sweat cooling as we drank gin in bed and shared a long pipe. 'I have a son about your age,' she had said.

It crossed my mind that she might be referring to Freddie, the obedient puppy, or Sid, who looked like a miniature version of Bill, complete with battered topper. I was wrong on both counts. She had not seen her son for years, she said, not since the death of her husband, who had been a greengrocer in Wapping. It was a familiar story. The business had failed, and Nanse, by degrees, was driven to the street to support herself and her boy. He had not understood, and in the rage that comes of adversity and a childhood lost he had denounced her as a low whore and left to make his own way in the world. She knew not whether he had lived or died, although she carried with her his youthful likeness in a pewter spinner about her neck, purchased in better days, with her own miniature portrait, as fresh as it was foreign, on the opposite face. He looked a bit like me, the same sharp features, dark hair and eyes. She had been stunning.

'I do like my young men.' She would say, while toying with my hair or stroking my skin.

She had a way of talking about other men that was both disconcerting and exciting, especially the pretty boys, whom she preferred, but soon discarded. Our foreplay would often involve anecdotes about previous lovers and clients, and I would hate her for it and want her more than ever. She would start to breathe deeply and tell me that I was the best, and, like an idiot, I would believe her, secretly thrilling at the thought of all the dirty things that she had done, and at what a fine young buck I was for stealing her heart away.

Needless to say, I knew what she did, and often with whom, but I also knew that I was special, for no money ever passed between us. It was Bill, who I had cast in my own mind as the cuckold, who popped that particular bubble one night in the snuggery, when I asked him for a modest raise. I had gathered from Nanse that he was charging the audience considerably more than he had admitted to me when we entered into our partnership.

'Aren't you getting more than enough already, son?' said he, with an evil leer, nodding casually in the direction of my lover.

I withdrew, humiliated, and took my leave as soon as I had finished my reading. My heart had not been in it, and my words felt witless and leaden, as befitting, I realised, something effectively written upon toilet paper. Since that night, pimps and publishers have always been linked in my mind.

I sulkily avoided Nanse, until she sought me out in the family cell, fully aware that my father was engaged for the evening as chair of the debtor's committee. It was only Wednesday night, but those three days had been eternal. I did not rise, and remained awkwardly seated at the table where I had been sewing for my father.

She arrived quickly at the point. 'I have something in need of maintenance, my valiant little tailor,' she said, coming to me and placing a high-booted foot upon the table in front of my face, raising her skirts. 'Look,' she demanded, 'I have a velvet purse that requires immediate attention.'

I could no more reject her than I could have turned down a drink and a smoke. I buried my face between her thighs and forget about everything, until, that is, I noticed the bruises concealed beneath her clothes. 'What did you expect?' she said quietly, 'he knew it was me that blew the gaff.'

I did not discuss such things with David, although I suspect that he knew, and character studies of Bill and Nancy remained taboo, as did comments concerning our own families. We both still did it, of course, only we did not admit it to each other, for writers use everything.

Like many of my friendships, the one with David was intense but short-lived. Times must have become harder, for with the coming of the spring my friend's entire family moved into the prison, setting up house in a similar room to that occupied by my own folk. Either the head turnkey was turning soft in his old age, or he was easily swayed by a posh accent. I think he fancied David's sister as a match for his own boy too, which, from what I could see of her parents, was as likely to come to pass as gold raining from the heavens or an honest man entering government or the law. My friend continued to leave the prison to work in the dreaded factory, but his people wanted no association with the Father of the Marshalsea or his children, and David was forbidden to see me or to venture anywhere near 'Book Night' in the snuggery. Once more his mother was 'doing something.'

Our continued contact therefore became as clandestine as my early relationship with Flashy Nanse, with snatched and secret meetings, out of sight of watchful eyes. This was a small barracks however, and there was no way to avoid each other in reality. The trick was in how one might contrive the meeting to appear accidental, so that David might avoid a beating from his father while his mother drummed into him with equal if not more force her maxim that although his family was in the Marshalsea, they were not of the Marshalsea. I was touched that my friendship meant so much to him, but I needed him as well. Writers are for each other. No other bugger understands us.

CHAPTER XII

In addition to reformers and evangelisers, another species from the outside well known to us was the tourist; dandies in the underworld who treated a visit to Bedlam, Newgate, or the Marshalsea as a social occasion.

Sometimes they would even turn up with hampers and make a day of it. And if prisoners were willing to be observed in their natural habitat then boons might be bestowed upon them, in the form of food, drink or money. My dad was apt to indulge the voyeuristic swine for the latter reason, playing the Father of the Marshalsea and then leaving it to their honour to tip him for an audience. If food were offered I would take it and hold my tongue, but inwardly I smouldered with a special kind of hatred reserved for the idle rich, those who viewed the lives of ordinary people as some form of entertainment (as long as we stayed out of their part of town), and had neither the wit nor the wisdom to realise that it was luck, not rank or birth, that separated them from us. They lorded it over the rest of us as if they had some God-given right to wealth, comfort and social superiority, when all they did was be born in the right place and the right time. It made as much sense to me as a man waking up on a fine, sunny morn and then taking credit for the weather. At least the evangelists and anthem quavers believed in something, no matter how implausible or misguided, and came to us to offer help, no matter how implausible or misguided.

I was in the snuggery one night, preparing for a recitation, when such a shower of bastards descended upon us. There were three of them, obviously blunted, that is in funds, wearing the flashiest toggery, and with their hair all faked in the newest twig. When the most rakish of the trio removed his tall silk hat, so powerful was the waft of macassar oil that it momentarily masked the common miasma of the room, that of sour sweat, smoke and strong drink.

'Beautiful ladies,' he intoned, addressing Nelly and her

companion, a fading ginger known only as The Bat, so called because of her habit of only emerging in the dusk of the evening, and for the kind of suck she might offer when she slipped out her wooden teeth.

They simpered and giggled like drains, and the man took one in each arm and headed for the bar. His companions appeared older and younger than he. The younger looked embarrassed, the older good humouredly drunk. The regulars looked on in a collective and resentful silence, which allowed the older man's voice to carry quite clearly across the entire room as he polished his tinted spectacles and addressed his youthful escort.

'This is a fine sketch of real life,' he was saying, in a rich Irish brogue. 'Our good friend Tom is already sluicing his ivories with a brace of unfortunate heroines of the blue ruin, by the look of 'em.' The man with the oiled hair, oozing over poor old Nelly and Batty, looked up and returned a lascivious leer. 'Tom is in Tip Street upon this occasion,' explained the older man, meaning that his friend was flush, 'and the mollishers are all nutty upon him as you can plainly see, putting it about, one to another, that he is a well-breeched swell.'

'Oi,' said Nelly, 'who are you calling a mollisher?' This meant a prostitute in the vulgar tongue.

'My dear lady,' said the bespectacled man, cutting an exaggerated bow, 'I assure you that I meant no offense.' He called to his friend at the bar. 'Tom, the lady is dry. Give her one from me, old man.'

'Delighted,' said the one called Tom, calling for a bottle of the good stuff. This seemed to mollify the mollishers, so the loud one carried on with his lecture.

'This fine sluicery,' said he, continuing to set the scene, 'contains a rich bit of low life for our observations, my friend, and also points out the depravity of human nature. Feast your eyes upon them and rub off a little of the rust.'

The youth attended with exaggerated ear, for seeing life was apparently his goal, and this curious fellow with the shades was obviously playing Virgil to his Dante.

'They are all resident within this grey bar hotel, my lad,' counselled his guide, 'for want of the blunt.' The boy nodded in sage agreement, although whether or not he understood a single word in twenty was open to question. 'And blunt, my dear boy,' said the older man, pausing for theatrical effect, 'in short what is it not?' This was clearly a rhetorical question for he ploughed on without catching a breath. 'It is everything now o' days. To be able to flash the screens, sport the rhino, show the needful, post the pony, nap the rent, stump the pewter, tip the brads, and down with the dust, is to be once good, great, handsome, accomplished, and everything that's desirable. Money! Money is your universal God, and these poor folk are fallen angels.'

He put that quite well, I thought.

'They are down,' said the oratorical bellowser, who was obviously building up to a big finish, 'they are out, but they are, my dear boy, inevitably, invariably, indubitably life in London!'

'Hear! Hear!' shouted Tom from the bar, while Nelly beamed desperately and The Bat sucked at her glass like a piglet at a sow's tit. 'I am quite satisfied in my mind,' he began, 'that it is the lower orders of society who really enjoy themselves—'

I had heard enough, and my time around Bill and his boys had given me the mettle to back up my simmering indignation. I rose to my feet and bellowed across the room. 'Oh shut your fucking bone box, you sack of shit!' said I, approaching the one called Tom. He closed his hole in shock, as if suddenly slapped, but the colour quit his face in silent fury.

'Such a parade of mediocrity,' I continued, 'such a cavalcade of nothing!' There was a murmur of approval around the room, although Nelly was glaring at me, for she was a forward girl, a *Quicunque Vult* as they say, and ever ready to oblige whosoever wished it. 'Are we to be observed for sport,' I said, appealing to my fellow inmates, 'like the poor mad fools of Bedlam, by this bloody bingo club?' I turned my aggressive attention to each in turn, starting with the bantling chav: 'A quockerwodger in rank bounce,' (I indicated that I was referring to the young man with a loud sniff, then I directed my gaze towards the Irishman), 'a bog trotting cheesecake steamer, and, most importantly,' I continued, looking Tom clear in the eye, 'a beau-nasty, woolly bird's beard splitter like this.'

He rose from his stool with his fists clenched and murder in his eyes. His nose, hooked and prominent, gave his long face a raptor-like appearance. I was far from sure I could take him.

'Do you dare—?' he began, before he was interrupted again, all-a-mort, this time by the Irishman, who was slowly applauding.

'Bravo, sir,' said he, coming over and clapping me on the shoulder like a long lost friend. 'Well said, my dear young fellow, you patter the Flash like a family man.'

'On occasion,' I said, caught on the back foot by this unexpected amicability.

'You are perverted by language, my young friend,' he said, with something like respect.

'As, sir, are you,' I replied. He beamed widely in return. It was very difficult not to immediately like the man.

'And what, may I ask,' said he, 'did you just call my friend?'

'A slovenly fop who prefers to shag sheep,' I said, translating casually.

Tom again erupted, and his two friends were forced, with some difficulty, to hold him onto his stool.

''Tis like trying to keep a dog in a bath,' observed the Irishman.

'I bet that's what you say to all the boys,' said a rich, cloying voice from the rear of the room. The trio stopped playing with themselves, and turned toward the speaker.

'My God,' said the young one, in an awed whisper, 'what a fabulous voice.' The speaker remained in the shadows, but I knew exactly who it was.

I was not alone. 'As I live and breathe,' said the Irishman, 'would that be Flashy Nanse of All Max?'[7] He turned to his young charge. 'You are privileged to witness a living legend, for this one has gammoned more seamen out of their vills and power than the ingenuity or palaver of twenty of the most knowing of the frail sisterhood could effect.'

Tom was likewise enchanted. Perhaps he and I had something in common after all. 'Give us a touch girl,' he said, advancing towards her, Nelly and Batty forgotten in an instant, 'for old time's sake.'

A naked blade flashed through the air in reply, and embedded itself at his feet.

'You come near me, Corinthian Tom,' said Nanse, 'and I'll cut it off.'

The Irishman roared with laughter, removing the stiletto from the floor and handing it back to its rightful owner. 'Not since the days of Wilhelmina the Werewolf Woman,' said he, 'have the concepts of pain and pleasure been so beautifully entwined.'

At these words I was thrown into a state of confused agitation. Everyone was laughing now, even Corinthian Tom, but for me the floor was pitching and reeling like a deck plate in a gale. I wanted to sit down. 'How did you know about Wilhelmina the Werewolf Woman?' I managed at last, choked and panicking.

'My dear sir,' said the Irishmen, 'they are bringing her out in half the theatres in London.'

I knew not whether to laugh or cry. Ainsworth had obviously found a publisher, but this was the first I had heard of it, being stuck in here like a dog.

'But I wrote that,' I whispered, crestfallen, 'it's mine.'

The Irishman wrapped a brawny arm around my shoulder and blasted me with his beery breath. 'Then we must have you,' he said.

'Avast and belay,' said Tom, coming over, 'this one's a liar and a scroof, plain and simple. He's half-flash and half-foolish, and good for nothing but the sea lawyers I'll be bound.'

'Nonsense,' said the Irishman, with clear authority, 'this young man is a quill driver and a brother, and that's as plain as the formidable nose upon your face.'

'I'll not support it,' said Tom.

'Noted, but overruled,' said the Irishman, pulling out a huge watch upon a heavy fob. 'Now,' he continued, 'unless we wish to spend the night in this charming place, I suggest we go to the bolt-in-tun.'

Tom responded by taking Nelly in his arms, sweeping her off her feet and kissing her deeply. The Bat, meanwhile, surreptitiously removed the bottle they had been sharing, as, unlike her friend, she could see that the bit of a spree was obviously at an end, at least as far as these ladies were concerned. 'Parting is such sweet sorrow,' he said, before dropping her on her arse and taking his leave, laughing.

As he reached the door, Nelly, looking flushed and breathing heavily, addressed him from the floor with a most unfeminine imprecation.

'Madam, I am *shocked*,' said Tom, in pantomimic horror. He shoved the young man through the door in front of him, and then followed him into the courtyard, leaving only the grand orator in the room.

'Do you feel that, my young friend?' the Irishman called to me with a gleam in his eye. 'The dice are rolling.' The trio then left, singing 'Come list ye all ye fighting Gills,' a popular boxing song back then.

I fell into a seat next to Nanse. Bill was not in evidence. 'What just happened?' I asked her.

'Something bad,' she said, looking balefully towards the door. 'Why the Christ did I make myself known to them?'

'I thought you were helping me,' I said.

She looked surprised. 'Yes,' she said, 'I suppose I was.'

We had, I later gathered, been blessed with a visit by the predatory rake Corinthian Tom Hawthorne, his country cousin Jerry, and their mate and mentor Bob Logic, a cheerful middle-aged scholar with a razor-sharp wit and a taste for wine and women, who everybody knew were, in reality, the brother artists George and Robert Cruikshank, and the journalist Pierce Egan. These silly sods were regulars of the Fancy, the finishes, the penny gaffs, barrel houses and brothels of the East End. Egan published their supposedly fictional adventures every week under the title of *Life in London*. Nanse said she reckoned their true identities were the worst kept secret in the city.

'How do you know them?' I asked her carefully.

'From bitter experience,' said she. 'Egan means well, but don't trust that Cruikshank further than you could shoot shit from your hopper.' I assured her that if our paths ever crossed again I most certainly would not. She let the matter rest at that, and left soon after. 'I need to find Bill,' was all she said, distractedly, when I attempted to kiss her goodnight. 'If that old fool writes that he saw me here then the jig's up for sure,' she added cryptically, 'and if the jig's up with me, it might be up with a good many more besides.' Then she was gone. There was no invitation to her room that night, and I retired miserable, confused, and alone.

I saw little of her after that night, and a couple of days later, without a word, she was gone. The word was that all claims against Bill, Nanse and Sid had suddenly been dropped, and they had left on Wednesday morning as soon as the great gate was opened. The feeble minded boy Freddie and I were left to mourn their absence together. I was bereft on a level I had not experienced since the death of my poor mother. I cared for my sister in a daze, reacting to the most minor domestic demands and calamities with disproportionate fits of rage or despair. I slept not, haunted by the image of my lover.

So, it would seem, was Freddie. By and by, his story came out. 'She was nice to me, too,' he confessed, fidgeting, 'until she got bored.'

'How do you mean "nice"?' I asked, with an increasing sense of unease. Was she kind? Did she feed him? Did she take care of him? Why did that guileless adjective, even on such childish lips, sound so lascivious?

He hugged himself, and grotesquely mimed the act of kissing. 'You know,' he said, 'nice.'

'Was she nice to Sid, too?'

'Oh yes, sometimes at the same time as she was being nice to me.' I had heard enough, but the idiot kept talking. 'She wasn't so nice after you came along,' said he, 'not very often anyhow.'

'Did Bill know?'

'Oh yes, he liked to watch. Sometimes he'd be nice too.' He looked at me pleadingly then, and I presumed that his simple mind was relieved to have shared its burden. I was wrong. 'Perhaps,' he said, reaching tentatively towards me, 'we could be nice to each other instead.'

'Jesus Christ, Freddie!' I avoided his hand like a wasp. I had not the heart to hurt him though, so I added, 'Let's just be mates, same as ever.'

'Same as ever,' he said, with an asinine grin.

What could I do? We were both of us victims of the same crime, after all, although I knew I was not so innocent as he. Had she appeared again at that moment I would still have followed her to the place where the worm never dies and the fire is never quenched just for one more touch.

David had more concrete intelligence. I knew he would. Nanse, he had discovered, was a 'hempen widow,' that is her husband had been hanged, while Bill was an 'area diver,' a housebreaker, and Sid, who was presumed to be Bill's son, was a 'buzgloak,' or pickpocket, and sometimes also a 'standing budge,' meaning he would act as a scout or spy for thieves. The three of them formed part of a notorious crew from Saffron Hill, who had been boned the previous year. Bill had contrived to hide in plain sight, and had bribed some associates to take the role of creditors and have the 'family' incarcerated for entirely fictitious debts until the whole affair blew over. Egan's identification of Nancy, if publicised, would therefore be fatal, at least for her men folk, for both were wanted for capital crimes. With the game likely up, Bill had got word to his counterfeit creditors, and they had immediately affected to waive all monies owing. Freddie, it would appear, was not of this gang, and had been picked up for a bit of sport and easily discarded, as had I.

'How do you know all this?' I asked him.

'People talk,' he said, casually citing the simple credo of the born journalist. He saw right through me as well, even then, and even though I had told him nothing of my relationship with Nancy. 'Chin up, Jack,' he said, 'you still have me.'

That was not true, but it was kind of him to say so. Something turned up not long after. His father came into some money and the family were released. David promised to visit, but I assumed after a while that his parents forbade this, because he never came.

*

I now hungered for release, with a passion I had not felt since resigning myself to an endless incarceration. Time froze, creeping down the walls like the black mould mottling the plaster about the skylight in my cell. If only I could get out, I thought, then I could find her. I was sure that in the end I had meant more to her than the others, and that some expressions of love could not be easily forged, even on the lips of one as artful as her.

Having no other role, I continued to read in the snuggery. I dallied briefly with Nelly, but it wasn't the same. She was a miserable cow, and she always charged, and without Bill to act as my agent I made much less from my readings. The Bat would have popped her teeth out for a large gin, but just as Buckingham drew the line at the murder of the princes in the tower even I had my boundaries.

I had stopped writing my own material, for my heart was no longer in it now that my work was stolen and my muse had taken flight. Instead I relied largely on broadsheets and papers discarded by visitors and diligently collected by Freddie. He could not read, so could not assess the content and quality of the literature he procured, but he did his best. In return for his labour my father and I allowed him to reside in our room, where he also proved to be invaluable in the care of little Sarah.

In the snuggery, the crowd-pleasers remained accounts of crime and retribution. The prisoners, unable to enjoy a good hanging themselves, were reduced to consuming their pleasures vicariously through the medium of print. I personally found the contemporary reports to be much less fun than the Newgate Calendars, which rendered pirates and highwaymen romantic, while the distance of centuries made their last ends noble and historic, rather than uncomfortably real. Reading the last words of children publically executed the week before for stealing food appalled me. But the law was vindictive, cowardly, mean spirited and ignorant, and cared not for my opinion.

Freddie could not be blamed for the last broadsheet I read out in the snuggery. He had no idea what it said, while I was in a hurry to get it over with when he pressed it into my hand, and more than a little pissed. It was a classic study in scarlet, topped by two woodcut illustrations. The first depicted a rough, wild-eyed man cudgelling a woman at his feet, her hands raised as if in prayer; the second was of the same man decapitated at the end of a rope, his spurting corpse falling from the roof of an unkempt building into a crowd of horrified spectators. The headline read 'Horrible Murder and Accidental Suicide in Saffron Hill!'

One William Sikes (or Sykes), I read, had beaten his *sui juris* wife to death in a rented room, for reasons that remained unclear to the authorities. He had then tried to escape across the rooftops after a young man, believed to be his son, raised the alarm. The murderer was attempting to swing from one building to another by means of a rope around a chimney stack, when he lost his footing and accidently hanged himself. As hanging, the article explained, was an exact science by which the length of the drop must be calculated according to the weight of the condemned, Sikes' impromptu self-execution had taken his head clean off. The couple were part of a local gang of housebreakers and pickpockets that had been broken up the previous year, and were believed by police to have left the city. The son was suspected of acting as an accomplice in several robberies and was on remand in Newgate. The murdered woman, I read, was a well-known local prostitute known as Nancy or Flashy Nanse.

A deathly silence descended upon the room. I stared numbly at the document in my hand, noticing as if in a dream that Freddie had slumped down in a corner and was quietly weeping. 'Well, fuck me,' said Nelly, finally.

Still, no one else uttered a word. Was this, then, I wondered, the only epitaph my first love deserved? I dare not speak, for fear that the grief that now congested my soul would surge out of my mouth in a wailing lamentation that I would be unable to contain. I wanted to claw at my flesh, rip my own teeth from my jaw, and slam my head into a wall. I wanted to be dead, too. I didn't know what I wanted. Finally, I stopped looking at the broadsheet.

It was Bertie the Badger that broke the silence. He stood slowly and raised his glass with great solemnity. 'Bill and Nanse,' he said.

'Bill and Nanse,' agreed the regulars, lifting their glasses in turn.

'May they sleep well,' said Bertie, his voice faltering.

He drained his glass and rushed from the room. The crowd closed in his wake and began once more to drink and talk. Someone, the barman I think, given the generosity of the measure, shoved a half pint glass of neat gin into my trembling hand, and I drained the burning bastard in a single draught, before following Bertie out of the room. For all the good it did me it might as well have been water.

I passed the night on the stairs that had led to her room, which was now occupied by a stranger, self-murder on my mind. But I had not the nerve, and still do not, although the comforting thought of suicide has since carried me through many another bad night. Having nowhere else to go, I eventually returned to my cell, and mechanically began my morning ritual. There was no sign of Freddie, who had likely drunk himself into oblivion in the snuggery.

Sarah was already awake and talking about Carol and dogs. I tried to interact with her as best I could, but my mind kept returning to memories of my lover, the image of the woman in the picture, and the terror and pain of her final moments. I thought of the death of Bill, too, and wished his immortal essence well on its final journey, because I do pray for the souls of my enemies. I pray they go to Hell.

'Doggie!' said Sarah from her cot.

'There's no dog, darling,' I whispered, attempting to start a fire. The smoke made my eyes smart and I sniffed violently.

'You ill or something?' said my father, rising from his bed.

'I just heard Bill and Nanse died,' I said, knowing that the intelligence would mean little to him. When they had left he had not disguised his delight at the removal of their influence.

He was gentle enough to ask what had happened, but all he could say by way of reply was that they had brought it upon themselves. I felt my blood begin to boil. I realised that I wanted a fight, so I turned on him with a low growl, poised to pounce and just then more animal than man.

'You sanctimonious cunt,' I rasped through clenched teeth, aping Bill at his most ferocious. This had the desired effect. My father backed away.

He did not, for all that, have the good sense to hold his tongue.

'She was a whore, son,' he said quietly, 'and twice as old as you at least,' as if the latter point was somehow worse than the former.

'I don't care,' I said, trembling with rage, 'I loved her.'

And however idiotic, self-destructive, shameful or downright absurd that statement must have sounded to him, what I needed at that moment was his love, his sympathy, and his support. If my son ever comes to me with such a grieving heart, no matter how inwardly relieved I might be that his latest mistake has now been rectified, I will give him that love without question.

But my father was no longer that way inclined, at least not to me. 'You won't believe me now,' he said, 'but this is the best thing that could have happened.'

'But she's dead, Dad.'

'Good,' he said, at which point I swung for him. It was an inexpert punch, a glancing blow at best, but I could see in his horrified eyes that I had done more damage than any prize fighter could have.

'Doggie,' said Sarah emphatically.

'There's no fucking dog!' I bellowed, turning my fury on her. She looked shocked, and then began to cry.

'Get out,' said my father, in a voice that suggested to me that he meant it, but should I refuse he was unsure as to whether or not he could enforce the injunction.

'Doggie!' my sister again repeated. This time I looked. There was a huge rat nestling in the corner of her cot, the kind you normally only see in graveyards. 'Doggie, doggie, doggie,' said Sarah, prodding at the hideous thing with her tiny hand.

In the time it took me to get to her, the monster had already struck. Sarah screamed and withdrew her ruined hand, her blood splashing across the wall. The rat sprang from the cot and disappeared under my father's bed. I ignored it and grabbed my sister, examining the damage while my father got in the way.

It could have been worse, I suppose, but the brute had taken off the top joint of her right index finger. And she had possessed such beautiful hands. She sobbed and shrieked as I wrapped her hand in a sheet to staunch the bleeding. I had no idea what to do, so I just held her as she screamed. Eventually it occurred to me that we might distract her, so I placed a heel of dry bread in her good hand and she began to gnaw at it. In want of anything useful to do, my father searched the room in vain for the rat, until I managed to convince him to go to the lodge and request a doctor be sent for. I gave him all the money I had for this purpose.

'This is all your fault,' he said, as he left the room, and he was right.

We spoke little upon his return, by which point Sarah had fallen into a deep sleep. I marvelled at her resilience. She could, so it seemed, bear the loss of a finger bravely, whereas if I ever sneezed loudly in her presence she would scream and sob as if tortured.

The sawbones arrived in the early part of the afternoon, accompanied by the head turnkey and a sour-faced man I did not recognise. The latter pair kept to themselves while the doctor attended to Sarah. He told me to keep the hand clean and apply an ointment that smelled of paraffin each time I changed the dressing. For this foul concoction, a bandage and his learned opinion he charged us a guinea and took his leave, assuring us that sleep was nature's balm and that there was little harm done, a diagnosis I did not share given that my perfect sister was now scarred for life.

The man of mystery now stepped forward, removing his hat and absentmindedly rubbing his head, which was as bare and pitted as a gunstone ball. 'Mr. Vincent,' he said, in a voice that was authoritarian yet oddly common, 'I am here by order of the court to inform you that your debt has been paid in full. You are free to go.'

My father leapt up and grabbed the stranger's hand, shaking it furiously.

The man looked ill at ease, and regained possession of his hand firmly. He looked at the turnkey appealingly.

'He doesn't mean you, Joseph,' said the gaoler quietly. 'He means Jack.' The colour drained from my father's face like the blood leaving a butchered pig. He swore violently.

'There's no need for profanity,' said the stranger.

'He's right, Joe,' said the turnkey, 'this is good news, surely.'

I said nothing. If I had any more news that day, of any colour, I did not think I would be able to stand it. At that moment, though, I would have done anything to exchange places with my father. I was past caring now, but the humiliation and disappointment on his face was truly terrible to behold. I wanted to go to him, but was too ashamed at my own good fortune to make such a feeble gesture. It was clear that that brief moment of hope had cost him more than the years of despair. He looked at me then, with a darkness in his eyes that has haunted me ever since. It was an expression of pure hatred.

'Take him,' he said flatly, addressing the two men before turning his attention to me. 'Collect your belongings,' he instructed me coldly, 'and get out.'

'Dad—' I pleaded, uselessly.

'Get out,' he said levelly, in a voice I did not know. 'Get out, and don't you dare to ever come back.'

'Joseph—' the turnkey began, but the desolation written upon the face of my father strangled his appeal at its birth. 'I'll leave you to your business, then,' he finally said, before beating a hasty retreat, closely followed by the clerk of the courts.

I had nothing to collect save the clothes I stood up in, and a destroyed bible containing between its covers the loose leafs of my incomplete serial. My father's *Lyrical Ballads*, my magic book, stood on top of this profane manuscript, and I took that too, for he had turned his back on me and saw not what I did. Sarah still slept, so I left without saying goodbye.

I next sought out Freddie, who was sleeping like a dog before the embers of the fire in the snuggery. I shook him awake, and, with a terrible weight upon my heart, I explained that I too must leave him. It was a miserable farewell, for he wept and said that I was the last true friend that he had, and that like Bill, Sid and Nanse he knew he'd not see me again.

'That's not true,' I pleaded, taking his hands in my own and looking him firmly in the eye. 'You stay close to Dad and Sarah and take care of them for me, for we are all family now.' He wiped the snot from his nose with his sleeve and nodded enthusiastically. 'And I swear,' said I, 'that somehow I will find a way to get you all out of here.'

We embraced then, and I left without another word. I had not a penny to my name and nowhere to go. I made no further farewells, and trudged towards the gate and the alien city beyond with no more idea of what was to happen than I did regarding my stalled and unfinished serial. When Nanse left and I stopped writing, my hero was walking the plank in shark infested waters and anticipating Valhalla on the noon tide. It occurred to me that we had an allegorically common dilemma, in the manner of the oriental story about the tiger, the cliff, and the strawberry. I could no more retreat than could my hero, and the city, from what I had heard of it, consumed the likes of me in a single bite. As far as I could see we were both buggered, but with revenant pirates at his back, vicious fish beneath, and not a strawberry in sight, I suddenly heard his voice in my head (which is always the sign of a good character).

'Any man that fears the unknown,' said he, 'will one day take fright at his own arsehole.'

The fact that he was a figment of my imagination notwithstanding, he had a point. I made a mental note to use this line somewhere, took a deep, purifying breath, and struck out for the city.

CHAPTER XIII

MY MYSTERIOUS BENEFACTOR had, of course, been Egan; Bob bloody Logic himself. Having built up all my courage to walk through that Plutonian gate and face the Modern Babylon on my own, he was waiting for me across the street, learning against a knacker's wall and smoking a long cheroot.

'Well if it isn't London's latest literary sensation,' he said, revealing both rows of his glittering teeth in a broad grin, and thereby saving me from the indignity of offering myself up to the mercy of my uncle, which had been the only plan I had thus far formulated.

I did not know it then, but he had recently left the *Weekly Dispatch* to publish his own Sunday newspaper, *Pierce Egan's Life in London and Sporting Guide*, and he was desperate for cheap copy. I was tailor-made for his needs. My apprenticeship in the Marshalsea had made me, in his words, 'street wise,' while 'Wilhelmina' had proved that I could write, and for peanuts at that.

I offered him my hand and said no more than, 'Thank you.' He wrapped his arm about my shoulder and gently led me away. I have not returned since, and ten years ago the damned place was finally closed by Act of Parliament. They call it Angel Court now.

Like most writers, Egan did not shut up. His idea of conversation was to monologue in the manner of Socrates, leaving one only the space to occasionally affirm or deny before he launched into a new topic. He would only pause if something struck him as worth recording, in which case a small moleskin notebook would appear in his hand, into which he scratched hieroglyphics with a stub of pencil.

'Shorthand,' he explained, 'invaluable in our line of work. I can teach you, if you've a mind to learn.' I assured him that I was most eager to do so, and he took me at my word and over the next few months pretty much taught me everything that I know about journalism, although not, as he was fond of saying, everything he knew.

'Well,' said Cruikshank, when next we met, 'you cannot legislate against wrongful encouragement.'

On that first day I learned two important things. The first was that Egan had not paid my debts, merely acted as my agent with Ainsworth (who was now relocated to London), and obtained my ten bob for 'Wilhelmina,' which had now made several publishers and theatricals rich through unlicensed adaptation. Ainsworth had not done too badly either, and whereas those that had knocked off the story were under no legal obligation to me whatsoever, Ainsworth, with whom I had a contract that he had discharged to the letter, was decent enough to also offer me a share of his profits. Egan had used this to pay my debt in full, and after a modest deduction for expenses he passed the balance onto me. It was a couple of shillings shy of ten pounds, which was a small fortune in those days, and easily enough to live well off for a year. It could have also made a modest yet significant dent in my father's debts.

'You are returned to your rightful station in the world, my young friend,' said Egan, 'now come and write for me!' Under the circumstances, this was hardly an offer I could refuse. His enthusiasm, like his long laugh, was also infectious. After half an hour in his company I was convinced his newspaper would shortly be bigger than the *Times.*

The other thing I learned that day was my new employer's philosophy of what is nowadays called social investigation, and which I was expected to assimilate and apply. 'The Metropolis,' he liked to say, 'is a complete cyclopædia, where every man of the most religious or moral habits, attached to any sect, may find something to please his palate, regulate his taste, suit his pocket, enlarge his mind, and make him happy and comfortable!'

I caught on straight away. This was what David and I had been trying to do with our childish character studies, and was also obviously what had brought Egan to the Marshalsea in the first place. 'And it is our job,' I conjectured, 'to read the city, and report upon it.'

'Exactly so,' said he, 'for there is not a street also in London, but what may be compared to a large or small volume of intelligence, abounding with anecdote, incident, and peculiarities. A court or alley must be obscure indeed, if it does not afford some remarks, and even the poorest cellar contains some trait or other, in unison with the manners and feelings of this great city, that may be put down in the note book, reviewed at an after period, and then reported for the edification, pleasure and satisfaction of our readership.' This he called 'seeing life,' which, he noted, was what his readers also wished to do, but without being seen themselves.

'But I don't know London,' I conceded.

'I know,' said he, smirking like a slightly unhinged ten-year-old, 'isn't it wonderful?'

And thus began my rambles and sprees through the metropolis, my very own rake's progress. This was exactly what I needed, or so I thought, to drown out all the memories that were trying so aggressively to drown me. If I stopped moving, watching, writing, and drinking, even for a moment, they would rise up from the depths to consume me.

I fought hard to control and conceal these dangerous emotions in public, while affecting a devil-may-care attitude which I largely copied from the more confident Cruikshank, George, who paradoxically turned out to be the younger brother. You would not have thought so to look at the pair together: Bob fresh faced and innocent, George debased, decadent and debauched. Inwardly, I perversely longed for my former life in the Marshalsea, another home to which I knew I could never return, for the people that had made it so were either gone, against me or dead. I believed myself abandoned by my young friend from the Hungerford Steps, despite all the support I had given so freely; I was betrayed by my father, while towards Sarah and Freddie I felt a crippling sense of guilt. Nanse I loved as much as I hated. I was furious with her for using me, leaving me, and, most of all, for dying, the silly bitch. Worst of all, my father's parting words would not leave me: *This is all your fault.*

But unlike Egan I was no left-footer. There was no absolution available to me, only the endless derangement of the senses that my new job afforded me, for Egan had made me his apprentice in all things, including the Irish custom of drinking oneself blind every night.

These were still the times of the bucks, blades, bloods and bruisers. I did not know it then, but I was in at the death of that era. George IV was still on the throne, and London in those days was a colourful and dynamic place to be, the throbbing heart of a country intoxicated with victory and basking in the afterglow of Waterloo. Boroughs were expanding, the population was in flux, and although no longer quite the bawdy Augustan pantomime chronicled by Boswell, the capital was far from the puritanical Pandemonium presently presided over by that sanctimonious cow, Victoria. Industry, trade and sobriety were not yet in fashion, and in the fast set to which I now belonged, idling, gaming, drinking and whoring were the sport in view. Corinthians, plungers and dandies were still abroad most nights, staking their fortunes on the turn of a card in the hells around Hanover Square, drinking cross-ways in the clubs of St. James', wrecking the wenches of Waterloo and Piccadilly and then slumming it in the brothels and gin palaces of the East End.

'It is never too late,' Egan would say, 'to have a happy childhood.'

I confess that it is all a bit of a blur now, but then the articles remember that period for me, although the so-called 'Victorians' burn *Life in London* nowadays, alongside Mrs. Wilson's memoirs. I still have copies of both, however, along with some of my own memories of Mrs. Wilson, whose favours I once shared, though they never knew it, with the Prince of Wales, the Lord Chancellor, the Governor of the Bank of England, and four future Prime Ministers.[8]

I had quickly revised my opinion of the present company. George Cruikshank took some winning over. He had a fast temper and never forgot a slight; he was also fiercely possessive of his friendship with Egan. I got on his good side by deferring to him in all things pertaining to the life of the city. He loved to lead and guide, and already his brother was tiring of this and straining at the leash. I therefore assumed the role of 'Jerry' when Robert was otherwise engaged and let Cruikshank act as my mentor just as much as Egan, the latter in journalism, the former in hell-raising. Cruikshank was a true Corinthian back then, although you would not think it these days, with all his fine preaching on abstinence and temperance (while everyone knows he keeps a mistress and a small army of bastards hidden in Hampstead).[9] It was also an easy matter to flatter his illustrative skills, which were, and remain, stunning. Egan had it right when he called him 'the Gillray of the day.' Nowadays he is more like Hogarth, an even better graphic artist, but more puritanical and much less funny.

Egan, then about fifty, was more of a kindred spirit, being the son of an Irish road-mender who, like me, had received little formal education. He became a printer's apprentice at the age of twelve, acquiring a love of the written word and a flair for linguistic experimentalism that I have never since seen matched. Also like me, he had soaked himself in English literature, as well as some more popular sources, such as broadsheets, Newgate calendars and gothic romances. Upon completion of his apprenticeship, at about the same age as I was now (sixteen), he had thus entered the cut-throat world of popular printing, publishing and bookselling, starting out as a copy-editor and proof-reader, but quickly advancing to hack writer and catchpenny broadsheet-monger. Not exactly Jane Austen, our Bob Logic, but he was widely read and he made money.

After the war he crossed over into sporting journalism for the *Weekly Despatch*, covering the Turf and the Chase, and, most importantly, the Prize Ring, or 'Fancy,' illegal bare-knuckle boxing matches that could last for dozens of irregularly timed rounds. His serial *Boxiana or Sketches of Ancient and Modern Pugilism* was still running when we met, and I was expected to assist by covering bouts he was unable to attend. The 'Sweet Science,' as he called it, was his passion, and the Fancy the temple in which he came to worship, presenting this insane milling house to me as something magical and sacred, although it scared the hell out of me.

By hanging around with the clientele—working men, gypsies, whores, swells, half-swells, nib sprigs and tidy ones, hard cases, head cases, drag fiddlers, bookies, buggers, bucks, bloods and thieves—I was gaining a knowledge of the London underworld that would serve me very well for several years to come, until the New Age dawned and it was no longer good to be bad. (The scales had fallen from my eyes by then in any event.) I was also rubbing shoulders ringside with quality. Courtiers, courtesans, and plungers (army officers who had purchased their commissions and never left London or fired a shot in anger) gamed and drank with dandies and Corinthians. It was rumoured that the King himself sometimes still attended a bout in disguise, as he had done when Prince Regent. To Egan and Cruikshank, the so-called 'Canting Crew,' the truly terrifying villains that not only patronised but ran the Prize Ring, were not representative of the collectively menacing underclass that already so troubled politicians, but characters to be cultivated, and with whom one might have a bit of a spree. It was, however, notable that the honest poor interested them but little.

I was accepted into this fraternity surprisingly quickly, on account of Egan letting slip to the right people that I had 'worked for Bill and Nancy, late of Saffron Hill.' I confess that I found this quite upsetting at first, but this reputation was certainly the passport I required, for although Egan was evidently regarded with great affection by the followers of the Fancy, it was apparent that they were much more guarded around Cruikshank. I, on the other hand, was granted much more privileged access.

I was even graced with an audience by Ikey Solomon himself, the so-called 'Prince of Thieves,' then at the height of his power and at the head of a criminal empire that dwarfed even that of the legendary Jonathan Wild in the last century. I found him to be an intelligent and erudite man, and nothing like his later grotesque depictions in popular literature, wherein every Jew is a ridiculous devil. He was sharp featured, but no more so than Cruikshank, well turned out, and very well spoken. His only real concession to the fashions common to his race was an obvious love for rings, of which he sported several on each hand. He had sent for me with a different kind of trinket in mind, which, with a fence's instinct, he felt sure would be of interest.[10]

We met in a candlelit tent in Stanfield Park, in which Solomon held court like a general on the eve of a battle, which was exactly what he was, only the battle was a championship bout between Jem

Ward, the 'Black Diamond,' and Tom Cannon, the 'Great Gun of Windsor.' I was ushered in with great solemnity by a well-dressed bodyguard, no less terrifying for the cut of his coat, who took up a sentry's position between me and the exit. Solomon was on an ornate chair and attended by a servant, who at a glance from his master silently provided me with a straight backed chair and a glass of very fine sherry.

Solomon addressed me imperiously, but not without grace. 'So you are the last of the notorious Sikes gang,' he said, regarding me with his deep, dark eyes.

'I have that honour, sir,' I replied, meeting his gaze with a bravado I did not feel.

'You read for them, I believe,' he said. He had me there. He knew I was no criminal. I nodded awkwardly but said nothing. 'Don't worry,' my dear,' he said with a smile, 'your secret is safe with me.' I returned his benevolent smirk and took a large pull on the sherry. 'I have something,' he continued, 'that I think might appeal to you.'

He reached into the pocket of his elegant waistcoat and withdrew something on a chain that was not a watch. He held the object up before my eyes by its chain, the light of the candles reflecting dully off its sides. It was Nancy's locket.

'My God,' said I, taken by surprise, 'where did you come by that?'

He looked suddenly serious. 'I come by many things, my dear, and where and by whom is of no concern of yours.'

I recovered my composure quickly. 'Forgive me,' I said, 'I meant no disrespect.'

'If I thought that you did, my dear,' said he, with another disarming smile, 'then Mr. Smith would have handed you your liver by now.'

'That is true, sir,' agreed the bodyguard, 'although I would have taken no pleasure in doing so.'

I assured him that neither would I. The butler coughed discreetly, indicating that bearing silent witness to such horrors was included in his job description.

Solomon, meanwhile, had sprung the locket. 'I had it in my

mind that you might be the young man depicted herein,' he said.

I shook my head sadly. 'That was her son. I know not his name or his whereabouts.'

'I see,' said Solomon. He thought for a moment, turning the cheap bauble in his fingers.

'May I ask you something?' I said, carefully.

'You may.'

'Do you know why Bill did it?'

'All I heard,' said he, 'was that it was a crime of passion. A foolish reason, for there is no profit in it.'

'Must there always be profit?' I asked him quietly.

'You are an idealist, Mr. Vincent, but you are young,' he said, 'it will pass.' I knew better than to push him further. 'I fancied,' he said, finally, 'that this item might be worth something to you, beyond its usual exchange value.' He lingered on the word 'usual,' for the locket was a worthless piece of tin.

'It would mean a lot to me, sir,' I admitted.

'You loved her, of course.'

I nodded, mutely.

'As did we all,' said he.

'She was my first love,' I confessed.

'And first love never dies,' said Solomon sadly. He tossed me the locket and bade me farewell. 'You can pay my man on the way out,' he said.

I had no idea to what I had just agreed, but knew better than to argue. Fortunately, Smith only tapped me for five bob, which was cheap at the price. I fastened the locket about my neck and trudged off in search of Egan and a large gin. I wore the thing for years after, until I fell in love again, or so I thought at the time, and was only allowed to retain possession of it by claiming that the portraits were of myself and my late mother.

My mentor was impressed. 'It took me years to see that one close up,' he said.

Egan's ticket had been his gift for language. Just as I had done in the Marshalsea, Egan had, by necessity, mastered the Flash tongue at the Fancy, the deliberately obscure and exclusive anti-language of the punters. Had he not become quickly bi-lingual around that lot, he might have been taken for a beak, a peeler or a maw-worm and never been heard of again. And if accused of using a little too much of the slang in his writing, he would reply that he purely employed 'the strong language of real life' because his intention was 'to report, without embellishment, living manners as they arose.' This he described as 'New Journalism.'

It was my ability to likewise converse in St. Giles's Greek, combined with my capacity to write to a deadline, which made me so appealing to Egan. The brothers Cruikshank were not writers, and the original *Life in London* had been envisioned by them as a series of engravings with Egan hired to provide a modest accompanying text. The billowing and highly successful serial that it had become was all down to Egan, an easy-going picaresque journey down the dark side of the street, all written entirely in the vulgar tongue. Reading Egan was an exhilarating experience, and I was immensely flattered when I realised that he saw in me himself as a young writer, or 'fresh meat,' as he put it, because he took nothing seriously save deadlines.

Needless to say, I was never able to approach his level of sheer Blarney, but I could still act as a suitable ghost to keep the story running on time, as well as covering a fair few fights under Egan's own byline, 'By one of the Fancy.' (As these events were entirely illegal it was prudent not to report under one's own name.) The money was good, and through a solicitor recommended by Egan I set about anonymously repaying my father's debts, a process that would still take many years at my current level of income. Freddie I could have bought out immediately, but I needed him where he was. Having witnessed how he cared for my sister, I trusted this gentle soul more than I did my father to keep her healthy and safe. My father meant well, but like most men he was worse than useless around small children. I also arranged that every week a parcel of food should be anonymously sent to my family. I knew my father would not speak to me, so this was the best I could do for Sarah and Freddie. When I had dreamed of achieving moderately good fortune through the labours of my pen, this was not what I had envisioned. The gesture helped with the guilt though, but it did little to ease the grief.

As 'The Author of "Wilhelmina" & co' I was also allowed to return to my romantic roots in the paper, although it was Egan's belief that the mixed reviews of the late Reverent Maturin's *Melmoth the Wanderer* indicated that gothic fiction, although fun while it lasted, had largely shot its commercial bolt. I still wrote several new Tales of Terror for Egan, although it soon became clear that what he was really after was a gothic *Life in London*, sensational reportage given an additional macabre dimension by its association with my fictional credentials, but essentially factual and contemporary. Egan always knew what sold, and had covered the trial of Thurtell, Probert and Hunt. There the Prize Ring and the gothic had met as the ringleader, John Thurtell, was a trainer well known at the Fancy. It was a popular murder, and I still recall the verse written upon it by Will Webb:

His throat the cut from ear to ear
His brains they punched in;
His name was Mr. William Weare,
Wot lived in Lyon's Inn.[11]

This was hardly a challenge, for beneath the fashionably façade that Egan and Cruikshank had constructed, the rookeries of the East End were already downright infernal. I think he wanted a murder a day, which was almost but not quite feasible, although I suspected (wrongly as it turned out), that the same story so often repeated would hardly fly off the newsstands. I have since learned that what audiences mostly want is something reassuringly familiar, in which their own view of the world and attendant opinions are essentially ladled back to them.

This work did not sit so well with me as reports from the Fancy and the Daffy Clubs, and smacked rather too much of the new broadsheets that had so appalled me in the Marshalsea. But I was in want of money and eager to please, so I fooled myself into believing this to be an opportunity, as has since often been my wont when it comes to a new penny-a-lining position. Egan said that I was merely moving from the theory to the practice, and

I am ashamed to say that I had a gift for such grim business as well.

Looking back, the formula that we arrived at, as a result of observation and experiment, very much anticipated the later fodder of the *Illustrated Police News* and its imitators. Our staple was reporting on horrible murders, suicides, violent accidents, discovered corpses, apparitions, animal attacks, and, my least favourite category, executions, most of which were true, unless it was a particularly slow news day. Egan employed a variety of informers, from street folk to policemen, and a productive working day would usually commence when some chit or chick-a-biddy would turn up at the office in Great Marlborough Street to tell us that a body had been found at such and such a place and in such and such a state. After a while I learned who was more likely to be telling the truth, and to never pay in advance.

It was gruesome work. In the first six months I reported on dozens of accidents and atrocities, too numerous to cite in full. I particularly recall the strange case of a woman incarcerated and starved to death by her parents in a boarding house in Penge; a spate of garrottings in Lewisham; a somnambulist decapitated by a carriage wheel on Shooter's Hill; a vagrant eaten by dogs on Chadwell Heath; grave robbing in Shoreditch; a deadly display of elephant teasing during a parade along the Strand; baby farming in Brixton; a self-crucifixion in Croydon (not uncommon, I discovered, although they could never manage the final nail); a fatal affray at a gaming table in Holborn; a clergyman killed by a cricket ball at a charity match in Hyde Park (left hand drive to mid off); a lethal encounter between a mail-sorter and a lunatic at the post office in Lombard Street; a badger on the rampage in Twickenham; a young wife in Deptford restrained and driven insane by her husband's relentless tickling; an idiot boy thrown upon an open fire in Fulham; a little girl in Whitechapel blinded by her parents to make her a more effective beggar (again not an uncommon practice); and a nun raped and strangled on the steps of St. Anne's in Limehouse.

You could not measure the human misery on those streets. Corpses sprouted like weeds. I saw as much rotten death as any diener or coroner, from bodies dumped on waste ground by their killers to those who simply died on the street of poverty or drink, gnawed upon by rats and, in one case, pigs, to skeletons walled up or buried in cellars and discovered by plasterers and builders in private and public buildings all over the city. The Thames, meanwhile, was as awash with carcasses as the Ganges. There were the stupid drowned, like the broken-hearted suicides that leapt from every bridge in London on an almost daily basis, and those too inebriated to watch their step. Then there were the victims; men robbed and killed to keep them quiet, women stabbed and beaten, sometimes for love, mostly for sport, and the children, so many children, unwanted and drowned like kittens. Very few of those responsible were ever brought to justice, and most of the hangings I had the misfortune to witness were for minor crimes against property.

I swear to you that not a single one of these stories was an invention. 'Such intelligence,' Egan was fond of saying, 'is more than enough to keep a man at home with the curtains closed, and reading nought but The Holy Book.'

This was an uneasy jest, for I have noticed that few indeed, who have seen such things as I, will allow themselves the full insight into the true nature of the human experience that accompanies the vision: the certain knowledge that there can be no God, and that the only meaning to life is that it ends, farcically, violently, and without dignity, point or purpose.

To find my way back from the dark places was a problem; not physically, but spiritually, although I confess I often found myself lost in the rookeries of London, surviving only because I could lapse into the Flash and generally talk my way out of trouble. At these times the drink was not my friend. I never knew which way it might take me, whether into comedy or tragedy, and a bingo-fuelled depression could cost me dear, rendering me incapable of writing a word for days. I therefore started to occasionally purchase laudanum, which could be had for a penny a bottle at any street apothecary's, in order that I might sleep after reporting upon a particularly unpleasant demise.

The ghost stories were much less frightening. These were reported like any other news story, and I wanted so much to believe in them. I was still a very young man, and Solomon was right, I was an idealist. Having rejected religion, I immediately replaced it with a different delusion. I still yearned for magic, and longed to witness proof of some sort of afterlife. It was at best a childish stance, and at worse hypocritical. Rest assured that I knew it was so, and that I was falling into the trap of many an author of the literary fantastic by coming perilously close to believing in his own bollocks. The sightings and accounts related to me by the most earnest of witnesses, who I am sure believed every word they said, were often very eerie and enchanting, but I never personally saw anything that led me to conclude beyond any doubt that there was enough evidence to support a supernatural interpretation. Who has not seen an old dark house, closed up and fallen into decay, from which after midnight weird sounds have been heard to issue: aerial rappings, the rattling of chains and the moaning of perturbed spirits; a house where apparitions are seen at windows, and which locals believe is unsafe to pass after dark, and which no tenant would occupy, even if he were paid to do so? There are hundreds of such houses in London, and every one has its own particular legend, tales of hauntings that seem more thrillingly plausible with every advancing second towards dusk, once you have taken up your position like a hunter in his hide. But when a man avers that he has seen a ghost he is passing far beyond the limits of the visible and into the realm of inference. He in fact sees something which he supposes to be a ghost. I witnessed this optical alchemy many times, in which the simplest trick of the moonlight became dreadful figures in the shadows. It is my belief that the events recently reported in New York will turn out to be much the same; those people will fall for anything.

My own phantasms were not so easily explained away, although I knew that they were no more real than the ones I reported upon. They would nonetheless come to me, out of the dark, the noiseless ones, the dead and the not dead, to gather about my bed: my mother, naked and obscenely wet, my sister reaching out grotesquely from the ragged cavern of her belly; my father, pointing, accusing, a silent scream unhinging his jaw; Freddie at his feet, starving, too weak to rise, his hand in his breeches, his sunken eyes imploring; and

Flashy Nanse, dearest Nancy, her head stove-in and distorted like a melted candle. Her damp skirts up, she would straddle me, and I would taste her blood until I awoke in shameful security and slept no more. And they whispered to my heart to join them, and asked why I was still here. Were they not my family, they said, should I not be reunited with them all?

And, God help me, they were tempting. I felt their lack dreadfully, and thus far no amount of drink or doxies had relieved the constant longing so leaden in my soul. I knew that one must beware the view back, but still I would fret away the hours before the dawn, smoking heavily and internally debating whether or not to oblige these nightly visitations, to become one of my own stories: self-murdered, like Chatterton or Polidori, just another putrefying corpse with delusions of romance in a cheap garret with the rats at it. 'Horrible discovery of a writer found poisoned in his rooms,' would be the headline, accompanied by a suitably lurid illustration by Cruikshank.

But every night, just as it had been in the Marshalsea, I had not the courage. I would die soon enough, I would convince myself, at the conclusion of each nocturnal battle, probably from insomnia. My visits to the apothecary therefore became, by necessity, more frequent, just for a tincture that might help me pass a night in peace.

On one such occasion, quite late in the evening, a small, dark man with an unhealthy sheen about his features, who I assumed was waiting to be served after me, tapped me gently on the shoulder when I had made my purchase.

'Perhaps you could spare a drop, sir,' said he, for I've a terrible toothache and find myself temporarily financially embarrassed.' He tried to press a filthy card into my hand. 'You'll take a note, won't you, sir,' he pleaded. He was visibly shaking, and his pupils were so dilated it appeared that his eyes were quite black.

He had played his hand too soon. 'Away with you,' said the druggist, placing a long cosh upon the counter for added emphasis. 'Stop bothering my paying customers and go and grin in a glass case, for you'll get nothing else from me.'

The little man slunk away, and I made sure that I took my

leave in the opposite direction. He doubled back and followed me all the same, quickening his pace when the street became deserted and once more tapping me upon the shoulder, this time with considerable force.

'I am the antichrist,' he declared, 'will you deny me?'

I raised my arm to strike him, but instead of drawing back he began to laugh. It was forced at first, but his howls of mirth quickly became utterly deranged. I bolted, but could still hear him when I turned the corner into Camden High Street, where I then lodged, shrieking behind me like a soul in torment.

That night I doubled my usual soporific dose to forty drops in absinthe and slept surprisingly well. I soon forgot about the strange little man, and took a most agreeable breakfast with Egan and Cruikshank the next morning. My working day began at about ten, with a tip from a reliable source that the mutilated body of a butcher's wife had been discovered in Barnet.

CHAPTER XIV

YEARS PASSED. And so, as they say, I grew to manhood. By the early part of next decade, I was quite the man about town, and as in love with the city as is any Londoner who was not born there but came in from the provinces.

I was in the prime of my life, and fancied that I cut quite a dash. I dressed well, and like Cruikshank I was a bit of a dandy. My dramatic blue eyes and wild black hair, which I wore rather long and romantic, were always popular with the ladies. Affairs tended to be brief, which suited me perfectly well. This was mostly on account of my moods, which were better than they had been when I left the Marshalsea, but were nonetheless still quite erratic. I could disguise this tendency to swing between reckless optimism and hopeless despair to the casual or professional acquaintance, but anyone with whom I became intimate was likely to encounter my dark side, which was not particularly pleasant, especially if I were on a deadline. Neither had I ever experienced again the same feeling during physical love as I had with Nancy, which was more like the relief of a craving for laudanum (which I had also managed to do without for some years), so I bored easily. People who fancy they love you will also always stop you writing, and that I could not afford.

Egan's *Life in London and Sporting Guide* had merged with *Bell's Life in London* in 1827. I maintained a freelance association with *Bell's*, but the pay was nowhere near as decent or reliable as it had been under Egan's stewardship. The fashion for jolly journeys to the underworld appeared to have passed, and like many others Egan was no longer the hell-raiser he had been during the Regency. I had also returned to the *London Magazine* under the editorship of John Taylor, but the man was an idiot and the magazine ceased publication in 1829.

Ainsworth, with whom I had become quite tight, had also put

me onto *Arliss's Pocket Magazine* and the *European*, but these were tuppenny-ha'penny outfits which had a poor circulation and paid a pittance. I threw a few gothic tales their way, but could have made more money tailoring. Unfortunately, nothing fired the public imagination in the same way as 'Wilhelmina the Werewolf Woman.' The thought of that story still made me very angry; very few experiences feel quite as hideous as that of another stealing your work and then making a fortune out of your labours, although, to be honest, the publishers were almost as bad in this regard as the plagiarists. Egan and Ainsworth had both attempted to be ethical publishers, always a recipe for disaster, and their liberal and gentlemanly principles had made them very little in the way of profit. In commerce, one has to be ruthless, which was the undoing of us all, because we were dreamers by nature, and fundamentally honest, which was a terrible handicap in business.

I was on a better wicket making regular contributions of short fiction, articles and reviews to the *New Monthly Magazine* and the *Quarterly Review*. I could also always sell my 'Horrible Discovery' articles to the press, and I made quite a bit of money out of Burke and Hare and the Murder at the Red Barn. The *Morning Chronicle* would always take 'em, and I even managed to flog a few to the 'Thunderer.' I was also one of the original 'Fraserians,' and regularly attended the literary club which formed itself around the Regent Street premises of *Fraser's Magazine for Town and Country*.

I could thus never bring myself to write for *Blackwood's*, although I doubt they would have given me the time of day on account of my affiliations with their professional rivals, especially Hugh Fraser himself, but also Henry Colburn at the *New Monthly*. Then there was my association with the *European*, which was considered positively seditious because of its support of the Catholic cause. I was nevertheless presented to William Blackwood at Prince's Street by Ainsworth during a visit to Edinburgh, but the encounter was not an agreeable one. I got on much better with Archie Constable at the *Edinburgh Magazine*, and was soon getting regular work from him, which further made me *persona non grata* with *Blackwood's*.

I also made the acquaintance of Thomas De Quincey in

Edinburgh, a small, nervous, rat-like man with a shockingly keen intelligence. 'We have met before, I fancy,' said he, taking my hand limply and looking me over with eyes like foxholes in long fallen snow.

'I have a similar sense of *déjà vu*, sir,' I confessed, although we got no further and thus politely concluded that we had formed visual impressions based upon the reading of each other's work.

Only later did I place him as the opiated imp that had chased me down Camden High Street in 1826. In consequence of this unlikely reunion, I fell off the wagon for a week of which I have no recollection whatsoever. When I recovered my senses I found myself alone in a wrecked hotel room, my body stripped and covered in inexplicable cuts and bruises. De Quincey was long gone, and had left me with the bill, subsequently denying all knowledge of this mysterious sojourn. He was a good friend, and a brilliant man, but a dangerous bastard for all that.

What eluded me now was the achievement of a novel. The financial necessity of producing a near constant stream of short articles left no space to hold a long narrative complete within my mind, or the time to physically write it. This was a frustration, as I was reasonably confident that with my professional connections I could find a good publisher, if only I could apply myself to the task. A book-length romance, if it was taken up by the public, which was, admittedly, largely a matter of luck, also had the potential to make a lot more money than the journalism. A literary success could also get me out of Grub Street and into somewhat better social circles than the ones in which I presently moved.

I was finally inspired to put my pen to a large pile of paper through a combination of genuine inspiration and friendly rivalry.

I had remained in touch with Ainsworth, who had married the first girl that came along, and was now saddled with a family in Old Bond Street. He had kept the faith, and had already collaborated on a novel, although no one seemed to have read it, or heard of it, which was largely because he had let his father-in-law act as publisher. I had read the novel though, and thought it fairly good, for a first attempt. Ainsworth was hinting now that he had begun another, this time all of his own creation.

'This is the one, Jack,' he would say, but otherwise he quite sensibly kept the subject matter to himself. I did not blame him and took no offence, for there were (and remain) many rogues out there who will steal your idea as soon as look at you, and then swear blind it was theirs all along.

Like me, some of my friend's short stories had attracted a moderate amount of favourable critical attention, but he had yet to break through professionally. He was desperately ambitious, and reasonably talented, and I must confess that I had no desire to be left behind in this matter. I was equally aware that if Ainsworth was capable of writing a major project around the demands of his nervous wife, her weak and profligate father, and three young daughters, while also practising law (which he loathed), then there was really no excuse for my present state of inertia. I had no such commitments or impediments, and had nought to do when all was said and done but bang out a few column inches every day and a couple of short stories each month.

Despite feeling both shamed and motivated by the industriousness of the local competition, it was Lord Lytton's *Paul Clifford* that really set fire to my haystack. The novel was a revelation, and well worth the fiver it cost me for the three volumes. The hero of the title was a chivalrous highwayman (more than a little influenced, I thought, by Schiller), who was driven to a life of crime through poverty. But underneath all the *Sturm und Drang*, the novel was genuinely revolutionary. Lytton's tortured protagonist was a radical spokesman who quoted William Godwin from the dock, looking his judge (and us) straight in the eye and proclaiming, 'I come into the world friendless and poor; I find a body of laws hostile to the friendless and the poor! To those laws hostile to me, then, I acknowledge hostility in my turn. Between us are the conditions of war.'

This was marvellous stuff! I had felt just the same in debtor's prison, although I had never expressed myself so clearly. But it was not the flash and dash of it all, or even the politics, that so enchanted me. What I loved the most about *Paul Clifford* was what the author had done with his sources. Like my own reference material during the Marshalsea readings, these had clearly been the chapbooks and broadsheets. Lytton had created a composite fictional highwayman from the pages of the Newgate Calendars, made up of bits of Dick Turpin, Tom King, Claude Duval and the like, but he had parted company with the traditional blend of sanctimony and sensation in favour of the more daring flamboyance of legend. He had dropped his bottle in the third act, however, and Paul Clifford was drearily rehabilitated through love. I would have given him a glorious and unrepentant death. Despite the survival of his protagonist, Lytton's fundamental formula, I realised, might be adapted and applied to present the outlaws of the last two centuries in a romance, not as the thieves and cutthroats that the originals undoubtedly were, but as heroes of whom Englishmen of all classes might be proud.

It had been eight years since I had allowed myself to think of the Marshalsea, but I realised now that by doing my level best to consciously erase the experience from my memory I had also thrown out the baby with the bathwater, and forgotten all about my old serial. My thoughts turned upon it once more in light of Lytton's latest, and I began to realise that I might have the novel I so needed half written already.

No writer will ever discard an unpublished piece if he or she can help it, no matter how imperfectly realised it might be, for it may later be required to fill the lacunae of inspiration when the original ideas have dried up and the money run out. I thus began to ransack my lodgings in a feverish excitement, intent on locating my ancient manuscript, which I felt certain was still in my possession somewhere. I was right, for it turned out to be stuffed in a small sack beneath the bed, still in the remains of my prison bible.

I am all in favour of leaving a manuscript to mature. If you are able to resist looking at a piece for a reasonable interval you will, upon your return, surprise yourself with material you had forgotten that you wrote. Horace recommended ten years for a piece to age, which is rarely practical, but I took it to be a good omen as I was only two years off. Although it was well past midnight, I went to my writing table and immediately began to read, straining to interpret the faded handwriting upon the filthy pages by the light of single candle, my body tense with anticipation and anxiety.

After the first few pages I began to relax. From time to time I still inwardly winced at some terrible simile and made a correction with a square pencil, or hissed aloud in pain and embarrassment and struck out entire passages. But on several occasions I also felt more or less satisfied with what my younger self had written, impressed even, at its energy and originality. I even laughed at a few of the jokes, and when the story abruptly ceased I was struck by an overwhelming desire to know what would happen next. It was hardly *Waverley*, but as incomplete first drafts went, this was far from terrible, and I slept very little that night for planning how it might be improved and speedily completed. Like Leviathan, *The Shivering of the Timbers* was about to rise from the depths.

Having resolved upon a plot, I first set about transcribing the original manuscript, revising as I went along. I had invested in a couple of reams of very good paper for the purpose, and it was a pleasure to feel the nib of a new Mitchell pen scratching and whispering across the page. I had developed an efficient and practical system of production for this project, which was a resolution to work upon it every night, without exception, for a minimum of three hours, upon the conclusion of my daily business, the writing and delivery of short articles and stories.

This was a debt of honour, maintained with a similar fervour to the one I had imposed upon myself a few years previously in order to relieve myself of the pains of opium. The copying of the original manuscript, which translated to about a hundred and fifty printed pages, took me about two months to complete, after which my pace slackened with the grinding commencement of a long literary composition. Some nights it went very well, and I blackened dozens of pages, while others were a slow and tortuous slog to the next scene. But whether the muse was with me or not, I required of myself at least a thousand new words in a sitting before I was allowed to rest. If I had any spare time around the business of life, I worked on my novel, and in six months I had a full first draft. This I then polished for another month, re-copying the final manuscript neatly for two more months after that.

You will remember the story. I retained the original premise, and once more sent the hero, now named 'Bannockburn' in honour of my admiration for Sir Walter Scott (I had just read *Tales of a Grandfather*), and the savage presence from the haunted ship back to the end of the seventeenth century, the golden age of pirates. I took a few minor historical liberties in order to place the likes of Morgan and Kidd in the same period as Blackbeard and Rackham. While there was, in reality, a generation between them, I wanted them all.

I employed a very straightforward plot, inasmuch as the buccaneers either aided Bannockburn (after a few initial misunderstandings), or became adversaries through the possession of the evil spirits. Apart from what I hoped were improvements in setting, character development, pacing, and overall style, I pretty much retained the first half of the tale as it had been originally written and read out in the snuggery.

Captain Kidd was still the hero's saviour, their paths criss-crossing throughout the narrative, until he saved the day at the end of the second act. 'Calico' Jack Rackham, Mary Read and Anne Bonney were Bannockburn's fellow adventurers, with both the women acting as love interests, often together. The adversary was the possessed revenant of Edward Teach, Blackbeard turned Rottenbeard, and the horribly reanimated crew of the *Queen Anne's Revenge*. The main body of the story mostly involved Bannockburn charging about the Caribbean in search of an ancient book of spells, and meeting various famous freebooters along the way. The grimoire was reputedly authored by Zosimos of Panopolis in the third century, and according to a gypsy mystic whose life he had saved, this mythical book held the key to destroying the evil pirate ghosts and returning Bannockburn to his own time. Blackbeard, meanwhile, also desired the book, which he had learned of from a traitor in Kidd's crew who had jumped ship at Haiti, the undead pirate king's base of operations. He planned to use the book to raise an armada of drowned souls, bringing about Hell on earth, before destroying it to guarantee the preservation of his unholy existence. Bannockburn finally locates the book in an ancient temple in Imerina, but loses it to Blackbeard soon after in a classic reversal of fortune. The climax of the novel is a prolonged sea battle between the *Queen Anne's Revenge* and Rackham's smaller ship, the *Kingston*, as Calico Jack fights to save Bannockburn and the ladies, who are imprisoned aboard Blackbeard's forty-gun galley, and retrieve Zosimos' book. When all seems hopeless, Kidd arrives in the *Adventure Galley* and carries the day like Nelson at Trafalgar. The mysterious gypsy is travelling with Kidd, and after Bannockburn has bested Blackbeard on the burning deck of the *Queen Anne's Revenge*, he employs the book to deport the maleficent dead to an empty dimension.

I wrote the final battle, which is fifty-odd pages in length, in a single, breathless sitting that went on all night and into the better part of the next day. I, too, was possessed. The book concludes with Captain Jack and the ever-ready Mary Read finally pairing off, and Bannockburn and Anne Bonney returned to the present day and wed.

To apply a Classical archetype, the narrative was one of 'Voyage and Return,' in which the protagonist had to undertake a difficult and dangerous journey, facing obstacles and forces arranged against him, and ultimately gaining a deeper understanding of himself and the world. I certainly put Bannockburn through some trials, while also humorously playing upon his anachronistic qualities by having him apply his modern intelligence and experience to seventeenth century problems. I was not clever enough at that point to write the kind of political allegory that Lytton had in *Paul Clifford*, but I felt that I had surpassed His Lordship in terms of social realism, especially in my depiction of the criminal classes. Drawing on my experiences of the Marshalsea and the Fancy, I made liberal use of the slang in dialogue, so whereas Lytton's outlaws tended to speak like Oxford debaters, my characters really did swear like wounded pirates.

With the manuscript completed, redrafted and copied, the easy part of the process was now concluded. The real work then began. Now I had to sell the bastard.

Colburn and Bentley had published *Paul Clifford*, but they were no longer in partnership. As I had a previous association with Colburn through the *New Monthly*, I took my manuscript to his office at Great Marlborough Street in the hope of making a deal. He and Bentley had done well out of Lytton's highwayman after all, so why not my pirates?

'I have written a romance,' said I, trying to sound casual about it.

'Oh aye,' says Colburn, equally if not more coolly, 'what's it about?'

'Pirates,' said I, 'it is a piratical romance.'

'Is it, by God,' said he, for pirates were still popular in the theatres just then, although what I had written was a far cry from nautical melodramas like *Black Ralph*. 'Leave it with me, and I'll see what I can do.'

This was good. This was not a rejection. I was past the first gatekeeper, as it were, having not been immediately told that my work did not fit the publisher's needs at the present time. A week later I received a note from him which said: 'I read your novel in one sitting. It is utterly chuckle-headed and preposterous from start to finish, and impossible to put down. Let us talk terms at the earliest opportunity.'

Colburn could always smell a bestseller, and his nose was definitely twitching in anticipation when next we met. I should have been wary of how quickly he produced a contract, especially after the 'Wilhelmina' fiasco, but I was young and hungry and he was offering me five hundred quid, which was a king's ransom as far as I was concerned. (In those days I did not realise that fixed-fee contracts were just a long way of saying, 'Close your eyes and bend over.') For this he required all rights to my novel, with a further undertaking that I would produce two more romances within the next five years. I did not know it then, but he was also in a hurry because his spies had brought him word of Bentley's latest project, and he was desperate to publish first. Cruikshank was engaged to illustrate, and the only conditions imposed upon me were the removal of a scene in which a captured civil servant is forced to eat his own toes, and a subplot in which Teach uses the book of spells to open up a portal to the infernal regions between Anne Bonney's legs. (The latter episode was later restored in full in the French edition of 1835.)

Cruikshank worked at astonishing speed, and within two months he had produced a set of twelve beautiful engravings, his style by then much darker than it had been in *Life in London*, and perfectly suited the gothic tone of the novel. My favourite illustrations are of the two women, Bonney and Read, who he depicts as gorgeous Restoration beauties in plate five, and, in plate eight, wild warrior women. I fondly remembered the Whitechapel girls on whom he based these portraits, and the fine time we had together in the days of Tom and Jerry.

Whether through *zeitgeist* or simple coincidence, Bentley's secret weapon turned out to be Ainsworth's *Rookwood*, which was destined to re-launch heavily romanticised highwaymen in much the same way as I was pirates and parrots, through his canny inclusion of Dick Turpin as a central character in a gothic romance. Lytton may have got there first, but *Rookwood* was just so much more fun to read, a mad and energetic page-turner that included thirty-odd Flash songs of great jauntiness. (I wished that I had thought of that, although Ainsworth cribbed all his slang from Vaux's *Memoirs of a Transport* and his plot, *sans* the Turpin episodes, from Scott's *St. Ronan's Well.* But nothing's new these days, is it?) While our publishers raced to the presses like suicidal squires on a steeplechase, we remained the firmest of friends, and it was Ainsworth rather than Colburn who first told me how well my novel was actually doing when the reviews began to appear.

'I awoke one morning,' he later liked to joke at banquets, 'and found Jack and I both famous.'

As was to be expected, the Fraserians supported us both to the hilt, while also taking a fair few shots at Lytton, who had depicted the *Fraser's* editor William Maginn as the intellectual charlatan 'MacGrawler' in *Paul Clifford.* 'With Mr. Ainsworth and Mr. Vincent, all is natural, free, and joyous,' wrote Jack Churchill, while, 'with Mr. Lytton all is forced, constrained and cold. Ainsworth and Vincent are always thinking of their heroes and their readers, while Lytton is always thinking only of himself.' Ainsworth's songs were quoted and hailed as the most original feature of his book, while I was praised for my linguistic verisimilitude, again at poor old Lytton's expense. Thackeray celebrated the return of the 'true picaresque' in my novel, and called me 'the new Defoe,' while Ainsworth was 'the English Victor Hugo.' Lytton, he said, 'had no sense of humour.'

Daniel Maclise drew our portraits in *Fraser's* 'Gallery of Illustrious Literary Characters' (Numbers fifty and fifty-one), putting Ainsworth on horseback in the rig of an eighteenth century highwayman, and dressing me as a pirate with the Jolly Rodger (reputedly designed by Calico Jack Rackham) fluttering behind me. The accompanying caption, written by Maginn, said, 'You see what pretty fellows are the young Novelists of the Season, and we commend Mrs. Ainsworth for her choice of such a dashing husband. Mr. Vincent, we gather, is as yet unattached, and given how exactly, it must be said, he resembles one of the most classically handsome and brilliant lady-killers of our age' (he meant Byron, who I supposedly looked like), 'that if he escapes scot-free during the first month of the blaze of his romance, he is a lucky as well as a well-grown lad.'

The Shivering of the Timbers was doing famously across the board for that matter. Even the reviews in the Tory rags were surprisingly favourable. 'This story is one that never flags,' wrote Southey in the *Quarterly Review*, for example, adding, 'we expect much from this writer.' There was even a Bon Gaultier Ballad devoted to me in *Tait's* which began, 'Kidd! Thou should'st be living at this hour: England hath need of thee,' while Lockhart, in a review for *Blackwood's*, begrudgingly admitted that, 'Some of the later scenes at sea are quite engaging.' I had respectfully dedicated the book to the memory of Sir Walter Scott, then not long passed, so it would have been disrespectful to ignore or criticise, especially as Lockhart was the son-in-law of the late Enchanter of the North.

All these lovely critical accolades were not quite unanimous. That insufferable and sanctimonious ass John Forster could not resist protesting the success of his contemporaries—he never could—and thus gave us a right kicking in the *Examiner.*

'Turpin, Rackham, and Kidd,' he wrote, 'whom the writers are pleased with loving familiarity to call "Dick, Jack and Will," are the heroes of these tales. Doubtless we shall soon see Thurtell and Corder presented in sublime guise, and the drive to Gad's Hill or the interior of the Red Barn described with all pomp and circumstance. These young authors have, we suspect, been misled by the example of more worthy literary outlaws. But while the words and deeds of Karl von Moor and Rob Roy serve for moral instruction, in *Rookwood* and *The Shivering of the Timbers* the highwayman, the pirate and their vulgar, if not obscene, talk are presented as if in themselves they had some claim to admiration.' He concluded that, 'There are people who may like this sort of thing, but we are not of that number.'

But this did us no harm. As Ainsworth was fond of saying, there was no such thing as bad publicity, or so it seemed back then, and despite the very occasional suggestions of vulgarity from the likes of Forster, our books outsold everything else published that year, aside from each other.

Even though the Fraserians had used my work as an excuse to fire several broadsides at Lytton, he was extremely gracious in his praise in return. He edited Colburn's magazine, the *New Monthly*, so he was hardly likely to undermine a fellow contributor, but he seemed to genuinely like the book. Neither had I in any way stolen his thunder, as had Ainsworth, by writing about highwaymen, and when interviewed by the popular press, I was also free with my praise of *Paul Clifford*, which I cited as an influence. This naiveté cost me later, for my stated 'support' for Lytton put me on the wrong side of his many enemies, most notably Thackeray. I was still very innocent in those days, and thought literary talk was about literature, whereas I now know that it is all about personality, politics and profits.

Lytton also sent me a most flattering letter, and it was his patronage rather than my sales or the quality of my writing that really launched me into the exclusive world of London Letters, because through him I was introduced to Lady Blessington, and thus admitted to her famous literary *soirées* at Seamore Place on Park Lane, which was, as Nancy would have put it, where all the big nobs hung out.

I was out of my depth, and I knew it, and in that knowledge I should have been safe, but I wanted access to that world very much, and was thus willing to do anything, which is always far more than one should ever be willing to do under any circumstances.

'They eat their own young up there,' said Egan of the d'Orsay set, on one of the last occasions I saw him.

I assured him I would be very careful, and thus walked up the scaffold of my own volition, with the invitation to my new friends implicit. Any one of them could pull the lever whenever they chose.

CHAPTER XV

IT WAS STRANGE to think that a domestic withdrawing room, even one as ostentatiously furnished as Lady Blessington's, was the acknowledged centre of all that was considered brilliant in literature and art in those days. But it was, and to be seen there was worth a thousand copies shifted in a week.

Ainsworth seemed quite comfortable in this new environment, although his stentorian Lancashire accent was as foreign there as my own by then fluent Cockney. I had long ago shed my original country voice, but that which had replaced it was just as coarse to the collective ear of the present company. But Ainsworth was a lawyer, and from money, albeit new money, and he understood the cultural codes in ways that I did not and never could. When I was first presented to *miladi*, I distinctly heard a foppish Frenchified voice, which I correctly identified as the famous (for being famous) Count d'Orsay himself, enquire if I were 'properly housetrained.'

Lady Marguerite's expression was enough to drown this discourtesy at birth. 'More than you,' my dear Alfred,' said she, her Irish accent just breaking the surface of her words, a sparkle in her eye for me.

She was in her forties then, and quite magnificent, even more impressive in middle age than in the lovely splendour of her youth, judging by the portrait on the far wall. Like every other man in that room, I fell madly in love, but she was as unobtainable as any goddess, having eyes, I soon learned, only for d'Orsay. I was aware of him through his connections with *Fraser's*, though I swear the man never wrote a word. I have heard it said that he contributed to the spirit of the magazine, but I remain unconvinced. He was supposedly a sculptor, but whether or not he was an artist he fancied himself a work of art, for his creativity was manifest mostly through his apparel. He was the undisputed king of the dandies now Brummell was in exile. I always thought he dressed like a Parisian pox doctor's clerk.

That evening Lytton also presented me to Charles Lamb, 'Elia' himself, who Ainsworth already knew. He was not long for this world then, and I am glad I got to shake his hand. Leigh Hunt and his circle were there: Barry Cornwall, the artist Ben Haydon, the academic Cowden Clarke, Wentworth Dilke (who later gave me a terrible review in the *Athenaeum*), Walter Coulson of the *Morning Chronicle*, Sir Thomas Noon Talfourd, John Reynolds, and his brother-in-law Tom Hood. Despite the fact that Hunt, Hood and Talfourd had all been closely associated with the *London Magazine* under John Scott, they obviously did not recall my name, although all were civil enough to pretend that they did. Coleridge was in attendance too, and by the look of it under the influence of at least one psychotropic drug. I had met him at the *Fraser's* inaugural banquet, but he did not recall me either.

I spoke briefly with Walter Savage Landor, who was visiting from Florence. He was well named, for I found him to be both brilliant and incredibly volatile. Fortunately, I had done nothing in print or in person that had offended him, so I just let him rant about his publishers, pouncing on the very occasional gap in his diatribe to moan about my own, for I was beginning to suspect that Colburn had royally robbed me.

'They always do, son,' said Landor.

Then there was the author of *Vivian Grey* and *The Young Duke*, the Jew, Benjamin Disraeli, who, like me, did not seem to be part of the in-crowd. We got on well, largely through our shared dislike of John Gibson Lockhart, who was fortunately not in attendance. I still viewed him as John Scott's murderer, even if he did not pull the trigger himself.

And, finally, there were the Garwoods, Mr. And Mrs., patrons of the arts. Garwood was an investment banker, and had made a fortune on the Stock Exchange, enough to buy his wife a place in London Society, and to bankroll half the writers and artists in the room. Mrs. Garwood was the only other woman present, not counting the servants. She looked to me slightly younger than Lady Marguerite, and although not as immediately charismatic as our hostess, she remained a striking woman in her own right, her dark hair, pale skin and full figure all perfectly complimented by a red satin gown. Mr. Garwood was notably older, but did not seem as attentive to his woman as husbands with younger wives usually are. I gathered they were long married, so complacency and familiarity had no doubt set in. He was obviously enjoying being in company, although apparently not mine, and was soon in another part of the room animatedly discussing business and politics with Coulson and Talfourd.

Mrs. Garwood though, was quite taken with me. 'You must call me Wilhelmina,' she said huskily, when I took her hand and bowed awkwardly. Rest assured that the irony did not escape me.

After the social preliminaries, there was a sumptuous buffet, the like of which I would formally have only associated with royalty, before an evening of literary readings commenced, beginning with Ainsworth and myself. He chose an atmospheric chapter from the fourth book of *Rookwood* entitled 'The Phantom Steed,' in which, during the Ride to York, Dick Turpin becomes aware of a spectral horseman riding by his side in the midnight mist. Eventually, the apparition resolves itself into the figure of Luke Rookwood, the half-brother and rival of the novel's hero, Ranulph. They ride together for a while, and then Luke vanishes into the night to resume his by then near-demented and ultimately fatal pursuit of the fair Eleanor Mowbray. It was a fine piece of writing, positively balletic in its breathless and beautiful descriptions of horsemanship, yet also dark and gothic. He was nervous though, and did not do the extract justice. I, on the other hand, had faced much tougher crowds than this.

I had taken a gamble in my choice of readings, based on my knowledge that Lady Blessington's salons were all-male affairs, with the exception of the lovely hostess herself. Society women tended to shun Lady Marguerite, supposedly on account of her scandalous relationship with d'Orsay, who was the estranged husband of her step-daughter. Having now seen her myself, my analysis was that they were simply jealous, for she was more brilliant and beautiful than the rest of them put together. (They destroyed her in the end of course, but that came later.) It was fair to say, however, that she did have a reputation for being quite broad-minded. I had thus boldly elected to read the chapter that Colburn had made me cut, the one concerning the haunting of Anne Bonney's private places, and the novel form of exorcism employed by the hero. I had not banked on the presence of Mrs. Garwood, but having no other reading material to hand (it did not occur to me to ask the hostess to borrow a copy of my book), I was committed to the handwritten manuscript in my pocket.

It was subtler than it sounds, for I was no pornographer, at least not in those days. I cleared my throat ostentatiously, as if upon a stage, and began my reading—

> Cursing and stumbling, Anne and Bannockburn fled blindly from Blackbeard's fortress in stolen boots. Every step was a symphony of agony, but despite the ravages of their starved and tortured frames, they ran as if the Great Adversary himself was upon their heels, and, given the Stygian dungeon from which they had lately been liberated, who could say he was not? The local inhabitants of the island, they had learned, believed the dreadful pirate Edward Teach to be a demon, and there was no doubt in Bannockburn's mind that something alien and terrible now possessed the spirit of the already brutal buccaneer. He gripped the hilt of the sword that he had taken from a poisoned guard, along with his boots, and ran on, following the boy who had aided their escape as he crashed through the leathery jungle foliage that concealed paths which, he claimed, were known only to his family.
>
> The insane flight seemed to have no end to it, until the fugitives knew nothing but the fire in their lungs and the need to keep moving. The boy cut the way forward with a short cutlass, hacking mechanically at branches and vines that flew back like knotted whips and lashed savagely at exposed flesh, but Anne and Bannockburn were past caring.
>
> Eventually, the boy stopped.
>
> Bannockburn was shattered to the point of near

insensibility, but as he sunk to the ground he was dimly conscious that they had reached some sort of clearing, for the break in the trees allowed the moonlight to penetrate. So dense was the jungle canopy that he had not realised that night had fallen.

Anne similarly collapsed on the dank and sodden jungle floor, exhausted, and heedless of the loathsome creatures which crawled about her. The boy remained alert, and bid them be silent while he listened intently for the sounds of pursuit above the natural life of the jungle. He stood frozen for several minutes, poised like a gun dog, before he finally relaxed. He took a sip of water from an elaborately carved gourd and then passed it to Anne, who sucked upon it hungrily.

'Don't take so much,' warned Bannockburn, lifting the flask gently from her hands and putting to his own lips.

'They will not follow us here,' said the boy, speaking reasonably good, if heavily accented English, learned while serving Blackbeard's gaolers.

'You seem very sure,' said Bannockburn, pushing a hank of his filthy black hair from his eyes. He regarded the young man sceptically. 'This wouldn't be a trap would it?'

The boy looked worried and appealed with his eyes to Anne, who was now engaged in shortening her skirt with a long blade in order that she might walk more freely. She tore off the last of the fabric and rose, her pale thighs glistening with mud and sweat above leather boots made long on her. She sidled up to the boy and began toying with his hair. 'Leave the lad be,' said she. 'He knows that if he plays right by us he'll be well rewarded.' The boy trembled beneath her touch. 'Don't you darling?' she added, addressing the young man.

'Madame is right,' he said, nodding enthusiastically. 'I help you, for money, yes, and a passage on your ship. We agreed!'

'That we did,' said Anne, giving the boy an affectionate

pat on the rump.

Bannockburn snorted. It had been the young servant's liking for Anne that had turned him to their cause, and it was clear what manner of recompense he really desired in return for drugging their guards and leading them to safety. 'So are we safe now?' he finally demanded.

'Oh yes,' said the boy. 'They fear this place.' He gestured towards the clearing ahead, in which a derelict church now became visible, its form distinct from the surrounding jungle by virtue of a strange luminous mist, which hung about the surrounding graveyard reflecting the rays of the moon. 'Now no more talk,' he said. 'You follow.'

Anne crossed herself, and fell into step behind the young man as he entered the ancient cemetery.

'The tropics, damn them,' muttered Bannockburn, scanning the surrounding shadows once more before walking into the mist, 'murderous yet strangely magnetic.'

Lost in the quiet of a forgotten conquistador cemetery and long since abandoned to the jungle, the church had originally been built by the Spanish. The place was shunned by superstitious locals, the boy explained, to the extent that even Blackbeard's men gave it a wide berth. 'My grandmother live here,' he said, opening a heavy wooden door no longer adequately supported by its hinges. 'No one bother her.'

Except for various undocumented tree frogs and tarantulas, thought Bannockburn with a shudder, as something hard and hairy scuttled into the shadows beyond the door.

'You are safe here,' said the boy. 'Come, I fetch my Grandmother.'

'In for a penny,' said Anne cheerfully, disappearing within.

Bannockburn drew his sword and followed her inside. 'All right,' he proclaimed to the assassins he remained convinced were lurking in the corners, 'who dies first?'

At that moment a light was struck, and a voice as dry and ancient as conquistador bones demanded their business. After the darkness of the jungle, the lamp was blinding, but as his eyes adjusted Bannockburn saw no assailants, merely a frail looking woman supported by the young man. The room they were in must once have been the atrium, but it now more closely resembled a barn, strewn, as it was, with straw and palm leaves.

Anne intervened before her companion could formulate one of his customarily inappropriate replies. 'Two humble fugitives from the castle, madam,' she said, speaking in French, the language of the old woman, 'in search of a safe place to lay our heads. Your grandson aided us and brought us hither.'

'If you are friends of Selvandieu and enemies of the pirate then you are welcome here,' replied the old woman. 'Now do you desire rest or sustenance?'

Bannockburn dropped his guard, and his body answered with a great wave of weariness. He could not recall when he had last slept. 'Rest, please,' he whispered, leaning heavily against the rough plaster of a cool stone wall.

The old woman directed her grandson to fetch blankets, and he returned with an armful of discoloured linen augmented with sackcloth. He fashioned makeshift beds in the two corners furthest from the door, where he took up station, leaning against the wall with his weapon at the ready. 'The boy will keep watch,' said the old woman, taking her leave through the narthex. 'It is late, sleep now, we will talk later.'

Bannockburn muttered his thanks and made himself a nest in the blankets and straw. He thought it the most comfortable bed he had ever known and, enfeebled by days of torture, he was soon asleep and snoring loudly, as was the old woman, who could clearly be heard rattling the windows of the nave.

Anne was wide awake in the opposite corner. Swearing

quietly, she found herself in a heightened state of excitement, incited by the flight through the fleshy jungle, and perpetuated by constant fear of recapture. Unable to sleep in the heat, she cast the damp covers from her body and shivered in the cooling touch of the darkness. It was a deliberately provocative act, for she was aware that the young servant could see her in the moonlight from his position by the door. Anne looked once towards the unconscious Bannockburn, and then beckoned the boy with her finger to come to her. The boy moved to her as silently as a spider, and then shyly, gently and noiselessly, they began to make love.

Their companion did not stir, so the lovers quickly become bolder, more passionate, until Anne approached the moment of ecstasy. She was on the point of surrender when the boy started shouting. Anne raked his skin with her nails in delighted response, all else forgotten, not caring whether Bannockburn heard or not. But it had been a cry of pain not pleasure. As Anne arched her body to receive him further, her lover assumed the most unnatural angle. His shriek of horror was cut short by a sound resembling the rending of damp timber. Blood sprayed from the boy's mouth, showering the horrified woman. Then he folded the wrong way in half as easily as a dry twig snapping, and was instantly drawn into her nether regions by a monstrous invisible force, like a swimmer suddenly taken by a shark.

Anne screamed, and the wasted Bannockburn was immediately at her side, his sword in his hand. 'Is Blackbeard among us?' said he, his eyes searching the dark corners of the room.

'I fear that he may be,' whispered Anne, shaking with terror, and pointing to her belly, '*in here—*'

Bannockburn lowered his weapon and smiled kindly. 'You are dreaming, my girl,' said he, 'and it's no surprise in such a place as this that you would be beset by nightmares.'

'You don't believe me,' she said, quietly weeping.

'Where is Selvandieu?' whispered the old woman, joining them. 'What have you done with my grandson?'

Anne took the old woman's claw-like hand and stroked it down across her stomach to her mound. 'He wanted me,' she said, 'and he took me, and suddenly he was gone.' The old woman nodded sagaciously but said nothing. She felt between Annie's legs like a midwife, bringing her glistening fingers to her face and sniffing.

'I understand,' she said.

Preposterous,' said Bannockburn, a twist to his long features that almost suggested levity. 'The boy's just run off, and he won't be the first you've scared away, 'ay milady?'

Anne sat up, her eyes as hard as knapped flint. 'Do you doubt me, sir? You, who have travelled through time and fought with demons.'

'Enough!' said he, once more drawing his sword. 'It is true that I have seen men and ships possessed by terrible, insane spirits, but never once,' he continued, pointing the tip of his blade towards her private places, 'have I seen any such devils residing in *there*.'

'Perhaps,' said the old woman, 'but I have heard of such things, and I fancy I have fought with many more demons than you.'

Bannockburn returned a petulant sneer, but he held his tongue while the two women conversed in hushed tones, the older of the two carrying out further physical examinations. Being a man of reasonably good breeding, Bannockburn turned his eyes to the far wall throughout the procedure. Finally, the unfortunate boy's grandmother spoke. 'It is my belief,' said she, 'that this young woman has been cursed, most likely by the vile Blackbeard, who is rumoured to be in possession of Zosimos' book of magic.'

'I can confirm that rumour,' said Bannockburn, 'for I have seen the vexatious tome with my own eyes.'

'I had feared it was so,' said the old woman, 'look ye here.' She beckoned Anne lie back and open her legs, indicating also that Bannockburn should pay close attention. No candle was required, for a shimmering universe of distant stars and planets was clearly visible between Anne's thighs, like a night sky observed through a porthole.

'Good God,' said Bannockburn.

'No, not God,' said the old woman, 'something much older. *Regardez vous!*' She took his trembling hand, rolled back his sleeve, and inserted his hand, slowly guiding his arm inside up to the elbow. The young woman moaned and writhed in the strangest fashion until, horrified, Bannockburn withdrew his hand as if from a fire.

'It is deep, no?' said the old woman.

Shivering violently, Bannockburn held his wrist and flexed his hand, which was coated in a thick layer of freezing slime.

'More,' cried Annie.

Bannockburn swore hopelessly. 'Even she's not usually this bad,' he told the old woman.

'She is possessed,' said the old woman. 'Come, there is but little time.'

They tied Annie at her wrists and ankles, and withdrew to a separate room fashioned of coconut wood like a hut built within the nave. The room contained a rustic bed, but the space was dominated by a large sea chest that functioned as a table, bearing a brace of black candles, a weathered Latin bible, and strewn with ancient and arcane objects.

'You are a witch,' said Bannockburn.

'No witch,' she replied, '*bokor*. I am a healer, you understand, a priestess of the old ways.'

'Can you heal my friend?'

'For Selvandieu's soul I will try,' she said. 'The altar still stands,' she continued, you will know where.' Bannockburn nodded, for in his experience one church, consecrated or otherwise, was much the same as another. 'Collect the girl and meet me there,' commanded the woman, gathering various items from the top of the chest. Bannockburn reached for one of the black candles, but the woman stayed his hand. 'No,' said she, lighting a crude oil lamp, 'take this instead.'

They left the room together. Bannockburn found Anne where he had left her, moaning and writhing on the earth floor. 'Give us a touch darlin', I'm dying for it,' said she, regarding him with unnaturally bright eyes.

He ignored her with difficulty, and keeping her bound he hoisted her over his shoulder. It was not her curses that troubled him as he carried her to the altar, but her unholy laughter.

The *bokor* was waiting, now clad in a long robe of dark silk and illuminated from behind by the black candles from her room, which now adorned the altar. 'If the girl will not keep silent,' she told Bannockburn, 'then gag her.' Anne adopted the look of an ill-tempered child, but she held her tongue. 'You must keep her away from me while I perform the ritual,' said the *bokor*, letting the robe fall from her shoulders to reveal a cadaverous physique, her bare skin like ancient leather. Anne snorted but said nothing. Bannockburn looked around until he located a solid pew among the rotten wood of the nave; there he deposited his prisoner, slumping down beside her with a complicated and obscene oath that at once conveyed anxiety, rage, and complete confusion. Trussed and snake-like, Anne attempted to rub her body against him, but he pushed her away and moved to another seat, kicking a path through the rubble of fallen masonry and animal bones that littered the floor of the nave in mockery of its original function.

Alone on the bema, the old woman began the performance of an elaborate ritual dance, moving to a rhythm known only to her and displaying an athleticism impressive for her years. As she spun crazily around the altar, Bannockburn fancied he was dreaming, for he perceived a much younger woman now before him. Her form had grown taller, and was now as smooth and tight as oiled ebony. Her lips were full, her dark eyes clear and vivid, and her wild hair as black as midnight. As she continued her gyrations, Bannockburn was aware that he was becoming somewhat invigorated by the spectacle, and he shifted uncomfortably upon his seat, coughing to conceal his embarrassment.

'Bitch,' muttered Anne from behind him.

All at once the dancer stopped, and walked towards Bannockburn. He did not feel able to stand, so he found his face level with her belly, from which radiated a tremendous heat. '*Bokar*?' he ventured, looking up shyly.

'Not *bokar*,' said the goddess before him, '*loa*,' as if that explained everything. Bannockburn swallowed dryly. 'I am Erzulie,' said the mysterious young woman, 'a spirit of love called forth to aid your friend.'

'Thank Christ for that,' muttered Bannockburn.

'Oh no,' said Erzulie, coyly, 'I come not from him.' Bannockburn decided not to ask, and the spirit continued, her hands on her hips and as naked as polished stone. Bannockburn was having trouble meeting her gaze, but Anne looked on with hungry eyes. The *loa* smiled at her but spoke to Bannockburn. 'The Devil Pirate,' she said, 'has used the book to open a portal to a realm of ancient and mad gods who claw at the boundaries of your world, and will bring about Armageddon should they ever break through in force. One such demon, I assume, was close enough to the mystic orifice to grab the unfortunate boy.'

'That sounds plausible,' agreed Bannockburn.

Erzulie's expression was, for a moment, confused. 'I must confess some puzzlement,' she conceded, 'as to the location of the rift. It is more conventional among wizards and witches to employ magic doors or mirrors.'

'Yes, I was wondering about that myself,' said Bannockburn.

'Withal, her salvation may well be in the location of the rift,' concluded Erzulie, selecting a long bone from the ground and using it to draw a wide circle upon the altar, marking a star within it with five straight strokes, and placing a candle at the points which Bannockburn guessed were north and south. She bade Bannockburn lift Anne into the circle, and then snapped the girl's bonds with her fingers as if they were cotton. 'Don't move,' she commanded. Anne complied without a sound, lying back on the cool granite and letting her legs fall open, her eyes moving between the man and the goddess before her.

'What now?' said Bannockburn.

'We close the portal,' replied Erzulie.

'How?'

In reply Erzulie grabbed Bannockburn between his legs. He felt himself stirring once more, but, being at heart a gentleman, he tried to think of things from his own time that would always dampen his ardour, such as pastoral verse, the rules of cricket, the novels of Mrs. Radcliff, and Pitt's strategy for reducing the National Debt. But nothing worked, and when the *loa* squeezed him harder a sigh of pleasure escaped his lips, which was then echoed by Anne. 'Impressive,' said Erzulie, 'for a human.' Bannockburn decided to take this as a compliment while there was still some ambiguity in the statement and grinned proudly. 'But not quite enough for demons,' continued the *loa*, gesturing mesmerically with long fingers while murmuring mysterious incantations in a language that made no sense to him.

Bannockburn became uncomfortably aware that part of him was growing, and pushing against his garments with the most exquisitely intolerable pleasure.

'Now you are ready,' said the *loa*, tearing away Bannockburn's breeches as if removing the wings from an insect, and tapping his monstrously engorged member with a long index finger. 'Take her now!' she commanded.

With difficulty, Bannockburn regained his composure, as much as was possible under the present circumstances. 'Madam,' he said, in faltering tones, 'I will do no such thing.'

The *loa* raised an eyebrow.

'Miss Bonney and I have never been intimate,' continued Bannockburn in desperation. 'And neither is it seemly to perform an act of such gross indecency in a holy place, and in the presence of an elder, especially a woman, even if she is a foreigner.'

'You would prefer that I was male?' asked Erzulie, quizzically.

'No I would not!' bellowed Bannockburn, backing away, appalled.

But Anne could wait no longer. She disobeyed the *loa* by jumping down from the altar and giving pursuit, chasing the helpless Englishman around the church until she grabbed him by the vestibule. She led him back to the altar like a dog, by means of his most prominent appendage.

'Her only hope,' explained the *loa* patiently, 'is to reach of frenzy of passion of such intensity that it will shake the fabric of time and space and, hopefully, collapse the portal before Satan's legions are unleashed.'

Anne climbed back onto the altar, keeping a tight grip on her man. She lay back and pulled him on top her, holding on with both hands.

'If you fail,' said Erzulie, addressing the prostrate Bannockburn, 'demons will come forth like an infinite army of deformed and bastard babies.' He staredback over his shoulder in horror. 'Needless to say,' she continued, 'your friend will not survive the birth in this case, and neither will you.'

'As a gentleman, then,' he replied, 'I cannot in good conscience refuse.'

'Good boy,' said the *loa*, giving him a hard slap across his raised buttocks.

As Anne took him inside, the *loa* began to chant in a strange and extrinsic tongue before the altar.

It was an epic copulation, and as the couple built to a frenzied climax, the dead conquistadors rose reeking from their graves, and entered the church, surrounding the altar in silence. The lovers paid no heed, and as Bannockburn thrust deeper into the terrible black hole, the walls of the church itself began to shake as if in the grip of an earthquake. Ancient plaster and giant spiders fell from the roof upon the careless lovers, and the skeletal conquistadors began to crowd around the *loa*, caressing her at first, but then clawing and rending. She began to laugh madly, and at the point when the revenants ripped the body she had possessed limb from limb the lovers exploded into one another. The bloody conquistadors fell as if shot, corpses once more, and Bannockburn and Anne were suddenly alone in the church, thirsty, out of breath, a touch peckish and surrounded by body parts. The spell had been broken.

Bannockburn rose, brushing dust from his hair and shoulders, and looking for his clothes. 'We must leave this dreadful place at once,' he said.

'Shut up,' replied Anne, pulling him back, 'and do it to me again.'

On reflection, perhaps the episode was not *that* subtle. My audience was quite hot and bothered by the end of my reading, but the majority had laughed in the right places, and been suitably horrified by the violence, although I would argue that there are passages in *Rookwood* that are worse, such as the scene in which someone brings Luke Rookwood's dead mother to his wedding. Blessington and d'Orsay both looked at one another and roared with obscene laughter at the end, while Mrs. Garwood just stared at me in a most unseemly manner. She was quite flushed, and in the tight red satin she resembled a large and exotic fruit, fleshy and slightly over-ripe. I met her gaze, briefly, and she did not look away. It would seem that she was not, perhaps, quite as unattainable as *miladi.*

'Who says history is boring?' said Ainsworth, getting a good laugh.

Best of all, Coleridge began to applaud with great enthusiasm. 'Follow that, my friend' he said to Hunt, whose turn it was next to read, 'if you can.' Everyone laughed with him, including, thankfully, Hunt.

'I would rather face a regiment of French cannon,' said he, causing d'Orsay to look quite put out. 'Let's have a toast before I try.' Our glasses were hastily charged and raised. 'To Jack and Will,' cried Hunt, and all said, 'Aye!'

I had arrived. And in damn fine style, I thought.

BOOK TWO

- The Death Hunter -

CHAPTER XVI

After a couple of days spent rattling around a relatively empty vessel while she chugged around the Western Approaches, the *Birkenhead* docked off Queenstown in the precincts of Cork Harbour on the fifth of January. It was a miserable morning; wet, and as hard and cold as flint, while the terraces of ugly slated houses in view beyond the quay stuck out like rows of monstrous teeth. I felt equally wretched, and I thus did not reject Captain Lakeman's offer to 'Irish up' the mug of tea around which I wrapped my numb fingers from a silver hip flask when our paths crossed on deck. I inwardly blessed him for a saint in soldier's clothing, for I desperately needed a dare of the hog. I was shivering within the shabby grandeur of a much loved topcoat cut in Saville Row that had been the height of practical fashion for any young blood a quarter of a century since but which, like me, was now showing its age. This had been pressed back into service after the distressing loss of a newer garment a few years ago that I never had the means to replace. Even with all my tender loving care (for I could still patch and sew with ease, and always had a needle and thread about me), it had to be admitted that this old coat had seen much better days, its black wool turned to a deep grey, much as my once raven hair was similarly beginning to fade. In terms of costume, my act as a man of reasonable and stable means was no longer convincing.

Lakeman looked me over with a critical yet concerned eye. 'If you will forgive me for saying so, old chap,' said he, 'I fear you are not best dressed for the coming journey.'

This was perfectly true, but his remark stung all the same. In my youth I had been something of a dandy, and when I later found myself famous I always took pleasure in dressing well. My present wardrobe mostly dated from that period, which was almost half a lifetime ago. When I lamented this situation, my dear wife would gently tease that there were few men of my age who could still comfortably wear garments purchased in their twenties. As I knew that my tendency to self-deprecation upset her, I would always try to refrain from replying that my svelte frame was more to do with the fact that we were half-starved than a youthful physical demeanour. Grace saw me through eyes clouded by a love that I treasured but never really understood, but however I looked I felt every second of every one of my forty-three years that morning.

'I'll be too hot when we cross the Equator,' I said, trying to conceal my embarrassment with something like wit. I did this a lot around people who were better off than I was. I would normally have been burning with resentment and contempt by that point, but I could not help but like this fellow. Brandy always made me magnanimous.

My companion had another healthy pull on his flask, and then took my arm conspiratorially. 'Step into my office,' he said, guiding me in front of him and indicating that we should make our way below deck to our neighbouring quarters.

Seaman Bewhill, a man with the misfortune to possess a face that resembled a rat that had recently taken a punch, leered at us suggestively as we made our way towards the bulkhead door. I was suddenly taken with the horrid feeling that Lakeman and I must look like illicit lovers, sneaking off for some filthy assignation. I had previously made the acquaintance of Seaman Bewhill, so he may have just been attempting civility, his strange countenance warping a perfectly innocent look into something twisted. His duties on board included having charge of the ship's poultry, under the supervision of the Quartermaster, which made him, in naval parlance, a 'duck fucker.' My discomfiture was fleeting, however, for the sensation in my breast at that moment was more akin to that of a schoolboy on an adventure. Lakeman's general exuberance had a way of generating that effect, I was finding, although whether this was natural or intentional I had yet to discover.

Lakeman must have had a similar thought regarding Bewhill's interpretation of our intentions, for he beamed at the young seaman as he passed and then slapped him on the shoulder convivially.

'For shame, man,' said he, 'it's not all rum, sodomy and the lash!' He bellowed with laughter at his own joke, and the poor bemused seaman looked quite worried, before deciding that the prudent course of action was to return, with exaggerated attention, to his running bowline, or whatever the hell it was that he was supposed to be doing.

Although adjacent to my quarters, Lakeman's cabin was at least twice the size. 'Yours is bigger than mine,' I said. He grinned but said nothing.

His berth had the appearance of a gentleman's outfitters. There were fancy military clothes hanging from every bulkhead. There were also two huge trunks left casually open and bursting with finery, as well as several crates marked Fortnum & Mason. I considered copping up that I'd once been a tailor's apprentice, but thought better of it and took a polite interest. Lakeman was particularly proud of the uniform he had commissioned for the rangers, and was showing me a beautiful leather storm coat that had been designed especially for himself and his officers. The thing was cut from quarter inch cowhide and lined with black silk. It was very long, and very black, vented, buckled, and about half a ton in weight.

'I'll wager this'd stop the bite of a lion or a spear from a Basuto warrior,' said Lakeman, 'so I reckon it'll do well enough against sea and storm.' I agreed that this would certainly be the case. 'How tall are you?' said he. I told him I was an inch or two above six feet, and he proceeded to rummage through one of the trunks, which contained several of these coats, examining the labels stitched beneath the inside pockets. He eventually found what he was looking for, and tossed the chosen item to me. 'Try this on,' he said. It fit as if bespoke. The leather was surprisingly supple given its newness, and wonderfully warming. 'Marvellous!' said Lakeman. 'Consider it yours.'

I was dumbfounded. 'I can't accept this,' I said, feeling more than a little foolish.

'Of course you can. I'll not have your freezing to death on my conscience.' He appeared quite genuine, but I am always wary of such outwardly spontaneous generosity, not that I've encountered it very often, because there is invariably a price to be paid later. That said, I was equally aware of the vacillating eccentricities of the rich and shameless. This fine garment, the value of which could probably support my family for a year, meant absolutely nothing to him. He had purchased half a dozen or so, in addition to kitting out his own private army.

'Fair enough,' said I, 'thank you.'

'Just give me a good puff in the *Chronicle*,' said he.

I assured him that I would. He was exactly the kind of character that would capture the imagination of the readers: exotic, heroic, reckless, and probably mad; a compelling protagonist as we say in the trade.

I was thus comfortable in the fresh and freezing air for the first time since embarking at Portsmouth as I watched the main contingent of redcoats boarding later that morning. 'Have you joined the rangers, Mr. Vincent?' Captain Wright had inquired, regarding my new toggery with affected curiosity.

I took his jest in good part and returned a self-conscious grin. 'I fear I'll never make a soldier, sir,' I said.

Wright gestured vaguely towards a huge marching column, slowly coming into view in the distance. 'That's what they all say,' he said.

I had elected not to go ashore to view the barracks earlier, as Seton, Wright and Salmond were all in agreement that the men should be embarked and quartered as soon as was reasonably possible, and it was obvious that the last thing they needed was me getting in the way. I thought it prudent to keep on Major Seton's right side as much as I was able, at least so soon into my assignment. Although Salmond and Lakeman were perfectly happy to grant interviews, both having axes to well and truly grind and thus desirous of some free publicity, Seton and his staff were going to be much more difficult to get on the record. And the thing with army barracks, in any event, is that when you have seen one you have pretty much seen them all. I had visited several in and around London for Henry Mayhew a couple of years back. I think Lakeman would have liked the guided tour, but he had his hands full keeping his rangers from jumping ship and making for the nearest public house.

Despite Wright's joshing, I felt quite up in the stirrups. I stood upon the main deck looking every inch a gentleman again, although probably in the manner of Varney the Vampire given all the black leather, and observed the approaching column. The soldiers were, I noted, in less than perfect formation as they marched through the town in the relentless rain to the steady beat of drum and fife. The local yahoos were out in force as well, many brandishing small, crudely fashioned union flags with which to wave the young soldiers away to war. Rough looking working men were cheering with an alarming fervour, while their women blew kisses and, in many cases, screamed with almost equal passion. Which were friends, family or deserted lovers I could not tell.

Some raggedy arsed street children had broken from the crowds lining the streets, and were marching alongside the troops, their exaggerated goosesteps a grotesque reflection of the movements of the brightly dressed rankers, mostly raw recruits, and the majority not much older than the shabby doubles that ran beside them. After what we've done to them, why any Irish man, woman or child, whether Protestant or Catholic, should want to hold a British flag with any intention other than to wipe their arse with the thing, let alone take the Queen's shilling, was and remains a constant source of mystery to me. I am not sure that it is exactly patriotism, but the economy of garrison towns depends on the military at every level. The relationship is symbiotic and parasitic, and about as healthy.

The column, which was about four hundred men strong, marched on along the slippery cobblestones, until it finally started to dribble onto the quayside, where boats and barges were waiting to ferry the soldiers across to our vessel. Non-commissioned officers were screaming at the bemused and bedraggled young men as they arrived, and I inwardly recoiled at the emotional violence of it all. The rocking of the barges caused many of their occupants to evacuate over the sides, and it must have been a profound relief to the passengers when the seamen struck their oars and the tiny boats came alongside. Looking down, I could see the redcoats rise to their feet unsteadily to face their next ordeal. When I had come aboard it was via a broad and steady gangplank, but these poor devils had to grab hold of scramble-nets and scale the ship's implacable hull, which rose sixty-odd feet above their heads with nothing but unforgiving water below, its surface as hard as a cement pavement if encountered from that height. Indifferent marines waited at the rails to haul the exhausted soldiers aboard, while many of those that had embarked as I had in Portsmouth hung around on deck shouting encouragement or abuse (it could have been either). Miraculously no one fell, and soon the first contingent of soldiers stood shivering on the deck, while the grim seamen pulled back towards the quay for the next batch. For them this was going to be a very long day, their incremental trips amounting very probably to several miles when taken collectively. As I always do among such hard men, I marvelled at their stamina.

The soldiers were lining up and stealing glances along the deck, trying to get the measure of their new location and circumstances. The old hands among them were immediately obvious, for they were the men who looked neither nervous nor curious, but merely bored. I saw rather than heard Sheldon-Bond barking at a sergeant I did not recognise. He pointed with his swagger stick towards the absurdly small open hatch in front of the great funnel by which the swoddies presently stood, and the sergeant saluted smartly and turned to give the order. I loathed that hatch, and my heart went out to those about to be thus extruded. In full pack, the soldiers could barely fit. I could see them awkwardly clutching their tall muskets to their bodies in order to scrape through, as one by one the ship swallowed them up.

And so it went on. To give Seton his due, the embarkation was a masterpiece of organisation. Administration was, by reputation, his true gift, and before this promotion he had been an Assistant Quartermaster General. As far as I could ascertain from my research, he had recently been promoted without purchase to the rank of Lieutenant-Colonel in the 74th without ever seeing battle.[12] And now he was in absolute command of all the five hundred or so redcoats on board, a mongrel force of mostly raw recruits under the age of twenty from ten different regiments, and heading out to reinforce the Cape.

I was no tactician, but I found the War Office's choice confusing, as did Lakeman, who, although young and easily dazzled, it would seem, by killing technology, was decidedly of the old school when it came to notions of leadership. It was possible, on the other hand, I thought, that Seton's appointment was a sign of things to come, when wars would be viewed not in terms of valour and glory, but in human resource management. Blue Books and over-promoted desk clerks seemed to be the spirit of the age. Lakeman did not comprehend what he called the 'half-military, half-civilian' existence of the British officer, and doubted the abilities of many of them to successfully undertake a campaign against any form of serious opposition or, as he put it, organise a nun shoot in a convent. His ill-disguised yearning to belong to a class he despised was a familiar sentiment to me, although I kept this insight well to myself. I still felt much the same about the literary lions of London.

He thus took it upon himself to test his theory that evening, as we dined once more with Salmond, Seton and his staff. Several new faces had appeared at the table. There was Ensign Russell of the 74th, a slight young man who kept himself to himself but attended to Seton like a personal assistant. Lieutenant Granger was a mealy looking boy, and still rather green around the gills; like Cornets Rolt and Bond, he looked no more than twenty years old. He had attached himself to the Lancers, and although the cavalrymen were inclined to look down upon the ground pounders, the trio shared the culture and language of the English public school system and were chattering inanely about the coming fight against the formidable (and thus far undefeated) Basuto Chiefs Sandili and Mosesh as if it were a game of cricket. I wondered if the African rebels knew the rules.

The other junior officers, Giradot of the 43rd and Lucas of the 73rd, had embarked at Cork, and although most likely the same age as their fellows, they had a yeastier look about them for having at least been posted outside London for the first few months of their first commissions. Surgeon Bowen was an older man, and I presumed from his conversation that he was of the same generation as Seton and myself, although he had not worn quite so well, having very little hair upon his small, round head besides a carefully clipped beard. I suspected that his somewhat boyish face had gone down well with the ladies in his youth, but in the middle age his appearance was not dissimilar to that of an ornamental gnome. Like most medical men he knew how to drink.

Seton and Wright were discussing the new intake. Seton looked nervous, but as that was his permanent expression it was difficult to read. I fancied I knew that look, which had more to do with an active mind turning upon many issues at once, and leaving the features to settle as they may. I am often likewise accused of looking either worried or stern, when all I am doing is concentrating upon the thesis of an essay or the plot of a story. My suspicion was that Seton's faraway look had a similar origin, although what exercised his intellect was military logistics.

Wright was certainly taking Seton to be concerned, and as the decanter was sent again upon its rounds he set about doing his best to reassure his superior. 'Soldiers are not dissimilar to children,' he was saying. 'They require discipline and routine, and will kick up something rotten when the ordinary pattern of their lives is disturbed.'

The British fighting man, Captain Wright was firmly convinced, from his personal experience, he assured the present party, was the finest soldier on God's green earth, but these men did like their routines. They were like dogs, he reflected, so must similarly be kept well fed and watered, not spared the rod, and let loose the leash every now and again.

'Treated thus,' he maintained, 'they will follow you anywhere, but, conversely, let them become too unsettled and any officer will have a surly, disorganised rabble on his hands.'

Wright's point was essentially that the secret to a straightforward and effective command was to keep your men busy. Salmond did not comment, but a measured nod indicated his assent to this opinion.

Bowen was more direct. 'What you have here,' said he, swigging hungrily at his glass, 'is a monstrous regiment of bog trotters and

Papists. Most of the poor devils have made their mark because they're starving, and I doubt if one among them could write his own name, or name his own father.'

Wright smiled. 'I want them to shoot, not write,' he said. I considered raising Lord Lytton's essay upon the subject of the pen being mightier than the sword, but decided to hold my tongue. This was not the right crowd.

Bowen assured us that he spoke from the position of one who had lately observed theses young man as they had assembled at the barracks over the last few weeks. 'These new boys are farm labourers, gentlemen, not soldiers,' he said. 'They are undisciplined, and slow to learn on the square.'

'It sounds to me,' said Lakeman suddenly, hacking his way into the conversation, as was his wont, for the professional soldiers would not discourse with him otherwise, 'that these fellows will not last twenty minutes against the Basuto horsemen.'

Granger was brave enough to venture an opinion. He had forlorn hope written all over him, that one. He would either rocket through the ranks like that idiot Cardigan or get his brains blown out for Britain as soon as he went up country. 'But they're just savages,' he said.

Lakeman looked the young lieutenant straight in his Etonian eyes. 'The Basuto warrior,' said he, with a tone that was intended to convey authority, but which struck me as a touch melodramatic, 'is a well-trained, self-disciplined and highly motivated soldier. These "savages" gave your Colonel Somerset a run for his money in '46, and swept away your so-called Warden Line at Viervoet last summer, which is why your men, and mine, are now *en route* to the Cape to shore up Harry Smith's defences.'

Granger turned as scarlet as his dress tunic. 'By God, sir, you'll take that back,' said he, in a sort of strangulated squeak. Had he a gauntlet to hand, I have no doubt he would have thrown it down. The other officers scowled.

Unlike Somerset at Burns Hill and Hobbes Drift, however, Lakeman held his ground.[13] 'Calm down, Lieutenant,' said he, in a measured tone, 'we are all on the same side. I am merely enumerating the facts as I understand them.'

'I would venture, sir,' returned Granger,' that you are on no man's side but your own, and further more I resent the comparison you have the temerity to draw between your motley crew of sots, beggars and thieves, and the soldiers of Her Majesty's Armed Forces.'

I perceived that the man was trembling, either with rage or nerves, but most likely both. He was as tense as a pane of glass when warped and twisted, and I suspected that like most Englishmen, myself included, Granger detested a scene in public.

'Hear, hear,' muttered Wright. His junior officers all nodded in agreement. The atmosphere felt suddenly galvanic, like the September air before a storm breaks upon it. The entire wardroom had fallen silent, and all eyes, soldiers and sailors too, were on my new friend.

Lakeman was as cool as a riverboat gambler. 'I'll wager my passage,' said he, 'against ten guineas from each of you gentleman, that my motley crew could best an equal number of your farm labourers on the square or in the field on any day of the week.'

Salmond positively bellowed with laughter, thankfully breaking the unbearable, key-bending pressure of the moment. 'God strike me blind, sir,' he roared at Lakeman, causing Seton to wince, 'but you're a devil's card! I'll take that wager, what say you, Major?'

The final remark was addressed to Seton, who was now in an impossible position. The honour of not only his but all regiments represented on board was now at stake. Even though all his charges were safely squared away, he was going to be forced to unpack, rendering the entire day's business redundant.

Lakeman regarded him coolly, and Seton acted as he knew he must. 'Very well,' he finally said, 'I accept your challenge.'

'Bravo, sir!' said Salmond.

Granger was ordered to confer with Giradot and Lucas, who had a working knowledge of the men newly boarded, and to select a force of the best of them equal in number to Lakeman's contingent. Salmond, meanwhile, called for Mr. Brodie, Master of the ship, to go ashore with a note for the commanding officer at Cork Barracks, that he might liaise with the local civic authorities in the hope of arranging some sort of field day in which Lakeman's rangers could compete with Seton's infantrymen on the square and in a skirmish. Our good Captain appeared considerably more excited at the prospect than did his opposite number, who looked decidedly uneasy.

Lakeman was obviously delighted. 'If it please you gentleman,' said he, 'we will exempt Mr. Vincent from our little wager, for he is not a soldier.'

The others agreed. It had not occurred to me that I had ever been included, and inwardly my nerves quivered like a taut wire that had just been struck. This would have been a debt I could not pay. Captain Salmond was similarly excused, and instead offered the role of senior arbiter, which he cheerily accepted. That much arranged to his satisfaction, Lakeman then excused himself to begin preparations immediately. I considered following him, but he was right, I was no soldier, so what, really, would have been the point? Of equal consideration was the fact that it was undoubtedly in my best interests to appear as impartial as possible in the present company, although I was already surreptitiously willing Lakeman to win, for it would be a tedious journey indeed without his companionship. In any event, the real story, which it was now my unspoken task to record, was to be the physical act itself, not the foreplay.

'Cry "Havoc," and let slip the dogs of war,' said Salmond, laughing like an undertaker going through the Society obituaries in the *Times*.

Major Seton did not offer a reply.

CHAPTER XVII

IN THE LONG summer of 1834, I became the success story of the season, at least in literary terms, leaving poor old Ainsworth behind in the end, for his family soon spoiled his fun. But I was yet young, and unblessed by either wife or children as far as I knew. I would like to claim that it was the quality of my work that caused my star to rise so far and so fast, but the truth, at least in part, was that the public enthusiasm for Ainsworth and myself was more of an indication of the state of English letters in those days, in particular the yawning void left by Walter Scott, who had died two years since. This was a situation that both Bentley and Colburn understood, and were able to exploit commercially. This was what all those comparisons to Defoe and Hugo were about. The Romantics were all dead, and the only serious commercial novelist on the scene was Lytton, and he had already made far too many powerful enemies in publishing. *Life in London* had run its course, and 'Boz' was not particularly active as yet. So more by luck than judgement, I was quite the classic 'Rags to Riches' hero. The popularity of my first novel had propelled me, like a cheap firework, from the relative obscurity of the penny press to fame and, by my standards, fortune. As Ainsworth had said, this really had all happened virtually overnight. My social stock had greatly increased through my association with Lady Blessington's set, I was a bestselling author, and I had five hundred quid in the bank. At sales in the tens of thousands, and at a fiver a pop, Colburn had probably already made a hundred times that amount, but I tried not to think about that.

'If I had a dog that could count,' Egan had said, 'he'd howl with laughter at a deal like that.'

I did, however, think about my own security, in a way that only those who have experienced true poverty can, regardless of their age, for do not doubt that part of me was just as eager to dress well and shag everything in sight as any other man in his mid-twenties who has come into money. Ainsworth was already spending his profits from *Rookwood* recklessly, under the assumption that he would now remain on Tip Street forever. I, on the other hand, understood my archetypes better than he, and knew full well that any character in a story who achieves success so rapidly invariably loses everything in the second act.

Much to the amusement of my friends and professional contemporaries, I therefore set about buying myself a house while I was in a financial position to do so. I settled upon one of Allason's new stuccoed brick houses, and left my attic room in Paddington for a terrace on the Ladbroke Estate. This turned out to be one of the best decisions I ever made, and I have managed to hang on to the place to this day, although it is rather run down in comparison to its neighbours, as, to be honest, am I.

Maginn teased me about this dreadfully in *Fraser's*. 'Such a wise head does Mr. Vincent have,' he wrote, 'and still on such young shoulders.' In an accompanying illustration Maclise drew me again as a pirate, but this time in a bath chair and blankets, brandishing a huge ear trumpet.

I was an object of remark whenever and wherever I stepped out, and the pasteboard invitations to receptions and soirées fell thick upon the doormat. Mrs. Garwood made her move quite quickly, establishing the groundwork common to bored, over-privileged women who live off their husband's money. We met and conversed at a variety of social functions, and during that period she slowly revealed a personal narrative in which she was the victim of a loveless and abusive marriage, into which she had been forced far too young, and from which she yearned to escape.

I fell for it, naturally, and confess that the anticipation alone was nothing short of sublime. Although I met several uncomplicated and unattached young ladies that summer, who were more than interested, I felt not the least attraction to any of them, whereas even the thought of the voluptuous Mrs. Garwood was enough to cause a rush of physical reactions that would have so unnerved a man of her own class that he would have commanded his valet burn feathers beneath his nose in order to restore him to his senses. The problem was how to get her alone.

There were other parts of my life, however, about which I now had more control, principal among them the liberation of my family. Grove, my lawyer, a brilliant but dour gentleman with teeth like mossy tombstones and a refined Edinburgh accent, had been managing my financial affairs for years, deploying a percentage of my earnings to the eradication of my father's debts. This was a process not unlike the construction of my novel, only in pennies rather than words, and some months were considerably more profitable than others. There was, nevertheless, always some sort of modest progress, and I was now in a position where this process of financial attrition could finally and emphatically come to an end. On a whim, I also asked him to look into the affairs of my other old friends in quod, Bertie the Badger, Nelly, and the old Bat.

The redoubtable Grove made discreet inquiries, and ascertained that Bertie and Nelly were as I had left them, only now married, whereas The Bat had quit the prison feet first during an outbreak of Typhoid fever two summers past. It turned out her given name had been Martha Randall. I ordered Miss Randall a decent headstone, and bought out Bertie and Nelly, for, as was not uncommon, they had wasted half their lives in debtor's prison for want of a couple of quid. Even with interest, a tenner was more than sufficient to settle for both of them, and I threw in another as a late wedding gift. It took a little more than that to finally clear my father's slate, but as I had been whittling away at his debts for the better part of ten years already the damage was not so great, and, as with my other old friends, Freddie's liabilities turned out to be negligible. I instructed Grove to find them lodgings and to give them some money, while I tried to raise the courage to face them.

Bertie and Nelly were a much less fraught opening bet. Like me, the Marshalsea had knocked some financial sense into the pair of them (though I suspected the wife was the driving force), and they had used the money I gave them to buy a leasehold on a public house in Whitechapel. I resolved to pay them a visit as soon as they were established in their new business.

The Horn of Plenty stood on the north corner of Crispen Street and Dorset Street. It was the usual East End shithole, a low den frequented by low people, of the type that had seemed so glamorous when I was cavorting with Egan and Cruikshank all those years ago. I could smell the old trades a mile off: buzgloaks and bit fakers rubbed shoulders with bat fowlers, blowsabellas and body snatchers. I obviously still fit right in, for they paid me no heed whatsoever. The muted ambiance, as of a tomb, also reminded me of the snuggery, which was no doubt the appeal of the place to the new proprietors, the cove and covess of the ken as we used to say.

'I see you've got The Horn' said I, approaching a familiar figure behind the bar.

'Always,' said Bertie, for it was he, leering at a couple of old girls propping up the bar and each other, one of whom returned his gaze knowingly. He topped off her glass, but I noticed that no money changed hands.

Age had enhanced the badger-like qualities of Bertie's countenance. The grey mutton chops were now as dense and white as a snow covered Rhododendron, while the remainder of his thick, coarse hair was still quite black. The man's head was positively striped, while small, sharp features and eyes like polished onyx completed the effect.

'It's atmospheric,' I lied, 'I like it. Now how the devil are you?'

The intervening years had not moderated the force of his handshake. 'I was doing perfectly well,' he said, all beams and bristles, 'until some young fool of an author bought me out.'

The lady of the house was quickly summoned from her kitchen to see me grown to manhood. Her long face, never a picture of happiness, now bore a fair few deep lines, and she was much broader in the beam, thereby managing to look gaunt and fat at the same time. Her breasts were more impressive than I remembered though, and were straining for release from a grey apron, like two bald convicts at the window of their cell. I told her she was as beautiful as the day that we had parted, and was rewarded with a salty embrace that crushed me to that monster chest, briefly recalling to my mind the inconclusive tumbles we had shared at the prison, with the accompanying, icy and familiar breath of old guilt and self-loathing.

By way of 'catching up,' she then commenced a long monologue on the subject of her many physical ailments, personal and professional grievances, and the deplorable state of the premises.

As Nelly moaned away I was gripped with a terrible urge to laugh. I fought hard to control the wayward muscles of my mouth, but fortunately my expression was interpreted as the joy of meeting old friends after a long absence, so I got away with it. 'It is good to find you so unchanged,' I finally managed, smirking like an imbecile.

We talked while they continued to work, Bertie plying the heavy wet and the gin and water while Nelly bustled about in the back frying fish. For an early evening in the midweek, business appeared to be buoyant, with tradesmen stopping for a pint on their way home, and then leaving with a woman, who would return a few minutes later for another shilling measure of gin. Obvious denizens of the Black Economy, meanwhile, conducted their business in curtained booths, usually buying bottles rather than glasses of spirits.

Bertie confirmed that the bathtub gin business was booming. 'You should come in with us,' said he, 'it's all done with your money anyhow.' I assured him that it was no more than a little starting capital that I was glad to offer a good friend, and that I was doing all right in the book business just then. He looked a bit emotional, which was unsurprising given how much he was drinking. 'Your old dad would be proud of you,' he said, brushing a tear from a cheek livid with broken veins.

'Do you think so? Some are already calling it a Newgate Novel.' (Forster had used this catchy little term first, and it had clung to Ainsworth and I like shit to an army blanket.)

'It's a fine book, Jack,' said Bertie, which was initially perplexing, for as far as I knew he could not read. 'Fred read it out to us all in the snug. Young Porter gave it him.'

'Freddie can read?' I was nonplussed, as they say. The boy had been an idiot in my day.

'Yes,' said he, 'I believe your dad taught him. Ain't that right dear?' he bellowed over his shoulder.

'What?' said Nelly, barking from the hole in the wall that passed for a serving hatch.

'Joe taught Fred to read.'

'That's right, five years or so back.'

Well bloody hell, I thought.

'So does Dad know about me then?' Needless to say, this was why I was there in the first place, the charm of the present reunion notwithstanding. Bertie looked a trifle disconcerted by the question, the way my father used to when, as a child, I asked him if there was a God.

'Well,' said he, 'in a manner of speaking, that is to say, he does and he doesn't.' I looked at him blankly, forcing him to keep talking in order that the sudden and awkward silence might be filled, for I knew Bertie to be a sociable soul who abhorred a conversational vacuum. He was a wily old buffer though, so tried to change the subject instead. 'That Mr. Grove's a queer old sort,' said he. 'He don't give much away, do he?'

'He made it clear he acted on my behalf though, I hope.'

'Well, he did to us, but your old dad, he got it into his head, you see, that this lawyer was an emissary from some long lost brother-in-law or other, and once he had the idea set in his mind, well, there were no shifting it.' This was news to me. Grove had reported only that the matter had been attended to, and that the parties concerned were now at liberty, although lodged, by choice, close to the prison. Bertie placed a consolatory hand upon my arm. 'The thing with your dad, Jack,' he said, 'is that he gets a little confused sometimes.'

'How confused, exactly?'

'I would have to say a bit more than somewhat.'

'Would he know me?' I said, crestfallen, although I do not know why I should have expected anything other than bad news, for my poor father had always been a delicate soul, and I had left him incarcerated in that terrible dungeon for almost ten years.

'Why don't we have another drink, son,' said Bertie, uncorking a bottle of halfway decent brandy.

My recollections of the remainder of that evening are hazy, to say the least. When my reason returned it was clear that I must see my father, and it was only the blinding intensity of my hangover that prevented me from visiting the next day. I swore off the drink forever, and struck out for my family's lodgings the following morning.

Grove had furnished me with an address, and when pushed admitted that he had not been able to persuade my father to better quarters, which he had been charged to arrange. His assessment was that my father was a very stubborn and a very frightened man; fearful of the world beyond the walls, he had insisted on remaining in Southwark. Even thus prepared, I was appalled at the location, a low boarding house that ended a row of ancient and ruinous buildings known as Mawley's Rents, the area perhaps a few degrees less chthonic than the rookeries of Saint Giles's and Saffron Hill that had furnished me with so many ghastly stories when I worked for Egan.

A toothless old woman carrying a blind cat under her arm conducted me to my father's rooms, which were on the top floor where, she proudly informed me, the air was freshest, on account of the wind across the Surrey hills. I can only assume that the poor old soul's olfactory organ functioned as well as her cat's vision, for it reeked of mould, smoke and piss to me, the same as all the other landings.

A spidery man of about my age in a black frock coat opened the door. 'Can I help you,' he said. For an instant I feared that the undertaker had beaten me to my big reconciliation scene, until I realised who it was that addressed me.

I seized his skinny hand and pumped it as if drawing water. 'My dear Freddie,' I began, 'I barely recognised you.' Presumably I was equally changed, for he jerked his hand away and stared at me like a mad fellow, his long, bony body barring entry to the room.

'Do I know you, sir?' he said coldly.

'It's Jack,' I said, pathetically, 'your old friend Jack.' He surveyed me carefully but spoke no more, as if investigating something on the sole of his boot, as yet unidentified but with bits of grass sticking to it.

A voice I had not heard in a decade but recognised immediately broke this unpleasant and unexpected strand-off. 'Would that be the worthy Mr. Grove?' said my father, from the interior of the apartment. I seized upon this opportunity and shoved my way past the doorkeeper, who had been momentarily distracted and foolishly looked over his shoulder. He clearly did not know that you should never take your eyes off a journalist. I had jammed my foot in doors all over London.

'Not Mr. Grove, sir,' said I, removing my hat and tossing it carelessly to the cadaverous Freddie as I approached my father, who was sitting by a meagre fire, a young girl at his feet, 'but his employer.' There was no heavenly fanfare, so I just stood there, waiting for the embrace that I confidently anticipated. My father had aged terribly, well beyond his true years, which did not even number fifty, and the chiselled features that had once turned the head of a rich man's daughter now looked as if they were melting. He appeared lost in a faded twill suit as he rose from a burst armchair to offer his hand. I wanted to crush him to my chest as Nelly had me the night before last, because that is what you are supposed to do in these situations, but I followed his lead and took his shrunken hand instead. I was so overcome with emotion that it was all I could do to whisper, 'Father.'

The prodigal son had returned. I felt like the hero of a stage melodrama, until I saw in my father's eyes that he had not the remotest idea who I was.

I let go of his hand and tried another tack, addressing myself to the quiet little girl in a blue apron dress who sat on the floor beside him. 'And you must be little Sarah,' I said, 'now a beautiful young woman.' She was the mirror of our mother, the same soulful eyes, golden hair and alabaster skin. There could be no doubt as to her identity, anyway, for the top of her right index finger was missing, and this was her only imperfection. She looked at our father, worried, and he indicated without words that she should greet me.

She rose slowly and curtsied. 'I am very pleased to make your acquaintance, sir,' she said, directing he gaze at my shoes.

I smiled. 'You will not remember me,' I said, 'for we have not seen each other these ten years, but I used to take care of you in—' I faltered, but then decided on, 'the other place.'

She looked confused, as did my father. Freddie, meanwhile, loomed behind me. 'We do not speak of the other place,' he said, 'do we, Father?'

I was too shocked to respond. That familiar feeling of doom was creeping down my spine and numbing my limbs like a subtle poison.

My father shook his head sadly. 'Indeed, we do not,' he said, still standing awkwardly. I realised that he was waiting for me to sit. I moved to a dining chair in the middle of the small room and he nodded enthusiastically before taking his own chair with obvious relief. It was clear he could barely stand. Freddie continued to hover, ordering Sarah to bring tea. 'My son is ashamed of the other place,' said my father, in a stage whisper, 'but we all have you to thank for our deliverance, and, of course, your employer.'

'I have no employer, sir—' I began, but he cut me off.

'I understand,' he said, 'some names should not be mentioned, and I respect that.'

'No, really, Mr. Vincent,' there is only me. Mr. Grove represents me, and I represent no one.'

'Understood,' said my father, tapping the side of his nose conspiratorially.

'Do you not know me at all?' I said, pleading with my eyes for him to stop this silly game.

'I must confess, my dear sir,' said he, 'that I cannot for the life of me place you.'

'He is Mr. Grove's associate,' said Freddie, 'now come away Father, you must rest.' He took my father's arm and assisted him to once more stand. The poor old soul was up and down like a jack in the box.

'Good day to you, kind sir,' he said, 'I hope we will meet again.' Then Freddie led him from the room as if he were the parent and my father the child.

'If there's anything you need, don't hesitate to ask,' I said feebly in his wake.

'Leave the tea,' Freddie called to Sarah, who was fiddling about at a small stove in the corner, 'the gentleman is just leaving.' Sarah turned to me, curtsied again, and then followed her father to an adjoining room. I was left alone with Freddie.

'What's all this about, Freddie?' I demanded.

'We are very grateful for all your help,' he said, as if butter wouldn't melt, 'but I'm sure that we can manage by ourselves from now on.' He handed me my hat and showed me the door. He obviously was not going to let me past him again.

'But you're not his son,' I said defiantly, 'you know perfectly well that I am.'

'Prove it,' said he, slamming the door in my face, the insidious bastard.

It was apparent that I had not simply been replaced, but utterly erased from my own family. I cannot adequately describe quite how hideous was this revelation. I wanted to kick the door down, which I could have, quite effortlessly, for it was very rotten, and then make a start on the imposter; there was nothing to him either, and it would have been an easy matter to break his scrawny neck for him. Yet despite my passion, I knew that this would achieve nought but my arrest, incarceration and execution, unless it was decided that all this raving about being replaced indicated insanity, in which case I might get off with life in the madhouse instead. And what, I further considered, would my father and sister think if I assaulted the man they genuinely believed to be son and brother? Sarah was too young to remember, and the balance of my father's mind was obviously disturbed, probably permanently. Even if Freddie suddenly came clean it would likely have made no difference. The game was blocked at both ends, plain and simple.

That night I raged about my house, drinking and dwelling obsessively, until I finally resolved to turn off the tap. But by the time I saw Grove again I had relented, for the sake of my poor father and sister. To protect them meant subsidising the serpent; there was nothing, for the moment, to be done about that.

'Just do what you can for them,' I told him, and then left the matter open.

'As you wish, sir,' he had replied, making no judgement one way or the other. Like God, I imagine, he was largely indifferent as long as all fees were paid.

CHAPTER XVIII

Already being in possession of a husband and a good fortune, and what with the fashionable summer season drawing to a close, Mrs. Garwood decided that what she was most in want of was culture, in the form of a personal tutor, an expert, she said, in literary history and composition, someone, in fact, very much like me. Now, never let it be said that I do not know an invitation when I hear one. Her husband was happy to consent, and I was engaged, on two hundred pounds a year no less, to minister to all of Mrs. Garwood's creative needs, of which she apparently had many.

In light of recent events, which were polarised and extreme, I was hardly thinking clearly when I made my way to the Garwood's town house in Mayfair in my capacity as a very expensive private tutor. I was, to say the least, emotionally vulnerable. But my life was so intense just then, good and bad, that excess had become quite normal, as had the wild swings between success and failure and pleasure and pain. This is not to say that had I been in a more stable state of mind I would have done anything differently, but there might at least have been some rational thought expended upon the matter first.

This was not the first time I had visited this luxurious crib, but it might as well have been as far as my nerves were concerned. I had never ventured there before without the society of a dozen or so writers and artists to protect my neck. The attendant physical and emotional feelings were not unfamiliar either. I still vividly recalled the first night I had visited Flashy Nance. My instinct was to approach by the tradesman's entrance, but at the last moment I corrected my trajectory and called at the front door like a proper gentleman. As I was known at the house already, the servants seemed genuinely civil, and as usual I tried to talk to them, and as usual they managed to evade. Surely they must have realised I was one of them, or, at least, had been, but they gave no sign of it as I was shown to the library.

It was a vast and beautiful space, with elaborately carved cabinets shelving thousands of books, floor to ceiling, a highly polished reading table, and a stately suite of black leather. There was a large portrait of the master and mistress of the house above a Georgian fireplace, and ancestral busts studded about the place on marble plinths. The reading rooms of the British Museum at Montagu House were no less lavish, and, as one always is in the face of real money, I had a vision of my own exchange value in comparison to such casual opulence. I was similarly struck by how pointless and poxy were my own efforts to turn the unused servant's quarters on the third floor of my little house in Ladbroke Grove into a library and study. Unlike my old friend Ainsworth, who was lording it up in a big house on Kensal Rise (with an even bigger mortgage), I felt very middle class.

All the same, I was heartened by an examination of some of the collections, for I began to suspect that I carried within me much more of the intelligence contained in these volumes than did the owners. Thus did the illusion of self-worth return, for whatever people say knowledge is not power.

She kept me waiting, naturally, which made the anticipation of fear and desire all the more sweet. We both knew what was coming. She played it perfectly as well. After an imperious entry, for bejewelled in a low cut gown of black and gold she was hardly dressed for scholarship, she dismissed her maid and instantly adopted a charming and uncharacteristic informality, instructing me to call her 'Mina,' and summoning me to sit beside her on the deep leather couch while she poured us both iced punch from an enormous jug. I watched her dainty hands, which were covered in rings, and breathed her in. My body, which was rigid with anxiety, instantly relaxed as if I inhaled raw opium. There was, I later came to understand, a scent about her which, though delicate and indefinable, was utterly hypnotic, at least to my sex for women did not like her. This was why she had not forsaken Lady Blessington in common with the majority of Society women. They were of a kind those two, and loved each other for it.

She smoked too, which was terribly daring and incredibly exciting. 'You are contractually obligated not to reveal my secret,' she drawled, lighting a cheroot with a long match, 'for I don't see why physical pleasure should be a male preserve.' I promptly pledged myself to her honour, like a knight in a fairy tale. 'Good boy,' she said.

I wondered if I should at least try to talk about English literature. I had even prepared something on close reading, just in case I had completely misread the signals. It always pays to be prepared, but she wanted, she said, pouring another drink, to get to know me better first. The punch must have been stronger than it seemed, for I told her far too much, but with every revelation of my past she became more attentive, and when I got to the death of my first love she was positively flushed, and started waving a dirty great fan about.

'My God,' she finally said, 'your life sounds like one of your stories.'

'I have often thought that myself,' I confessed, which was true. Freddie flashed before my eyes and I shuddered. You could not make such things up, could you?

Her autobiography was somewhat less sensational. She was the oldest daughter of a landed family in Surrey, and her future husband hunted with her father. When Mr. Garwood, already a very wealthy man, plighted his troth her parents deemed it a most satisfactory match and he had her up the aisle just after her sixteenth birthday. They had been married for nearly twenty years and had a small army of children, the youngest two, a boy and a girl, were still at home, although managed by a tutor and a governess so neither seen nor heard as far as I was concerned. There were four other boys, away at a boarding school somewhere in Warwickshire. I cannot recall the names.

I told her more of myself, and of my time with the Fancy. She charged my glass again, and used the act of handing it to me as an excuse to move even closer.

'I rather fancied from your readings,' she said, 'that you had done much of what you wrote about, and now I am convinced.'

'Well,' said I, stealing a furtive look at her heaving bosom, 'it's all grist to the mill you know.' She was breathing quite heavily now, and I could feel the warmth of her next to me.

'Show me,' she said.

*

It was around this time that it occurred to me that I had better write another romance. *The Shivering of the Timbers* had gone through three editions already, but I was under contract for two more novels, and I had nothing else half written under the bed to get me rolling. I also had Ainsworth and his beloved highwaymen to compete with, but I did not just wish to best him in the literary marketplace, I wanted to be better than myself.

Mina found it all terribly thrilling, and we discussed many ideas and potential projects, for her love of literature was insatiable and she had me in that library every chance she could. She made me feel as if I could achieve anything, and while we lay together on the big black couch or the snowy white rug by the fire, drinking and smoking and playing, we planned an epic narrative. The book-to-be belonged to us both, but for myself I was quickly bewitched and increasingly unbothered by the outside world. There was such peace to be found in her arms that I thought not of my publisher, my enemy, or his hold over my family. Neither did it concern me overmuch that I was falling desperately in love with another man's wife.

It was Mina's assessment that the popularity of my first novel had been founded largely on the pirates rather than the protagonist. She cited *Rookwood* as a precedent, for the Dick Turpin sections were already being published separately and reputedly out-selling the original novel. Ainsworth, meanwhile, was now courting literary respectability by writing a much more conventional historical romance than his breakthrough novel. His stated subject was James ('the admirable') Crichton and his adventures at the court of Henri III of France. By the sound of it there was nary a highwayman, a vengeful spook, or an amorous gypsy in it, for Ainsworth fancied himself the successor to Sir Walter Scott and the 'Newgate' label obviously troubled him.

Mina was certain my friend was making a serious commercial blunder. 'It is not heroes that will sell your next book, my love,' she had counselled, 'but anti-heroes.' I felt much the same myself, so whereas Ainsworth had rejected the obvious next move I embraced it. Was I not, after all, something of an expert on pirates?

I did not, however, wish to simply re-write my first novel, although I suspect I could have gotten away with doing just that if I wished, for many popular authors do. I still wanted to entertain, but this time I also wished to edify and challenge. I wanted to transcend Lytton's *Paul Clifford*, and write a political novel that was also authentic and engaging, and to show those damned critics my mettle. Most of all, I wanted to impress my lover.

In order to achieve this goal, I returned to my roots, and the first story I ever read aloud at the Marshalsea, the life of William Kidd.

I had admittedly used Kidd as a secondary character in my first novel, but it had been a primitive portrait, with little attention paid to historical verisimilitude. As Ainsworth had done with Turpin, I had made Kidd heroic, in a bluff, straightforward sort of way, while casting him in a fictional drama that was supposed to have taken place a good quarter of a century after the original had died. I still believed that the real Captain Kidd had been a brilliant and resourceful naval tactician, rather than the avaricious braggart portrayed by the Newgate Calendars. I saw him as exploited and betrayed by politicians, just as Guy Fawkes was more likely an agent of the Crown than the papist terrorist of popular legend, both men conveniently silenced by execution.

I resolved to write the true account of the life of Kidd, in the manner of an epic tragedy crossed with a political satire. There would be genuine emotional and philosophic depth, combined with an attention to *mise-en-scènic* detail worthy of Hogarth and Defoe. My intension was to recreate the reality of the life of a privateer, against a late-seventeenth century colonial backdrop that was politically complex and culturally accurate. Furthermore, as both Mina and Colburn were quick to point out, that there was also a direct link between this novel and my first would not hurt the sales either.

I researched my project obsessively, and did nothing for half a year save collect, read and annotate primary and secondary sources. I immersed myself in contemporary accounts of the period and the biographies of Kidd and his cronies, effectively becoming an expert in Restoration England and her colonies, as well as maritime law, legend, and practice. Once I felt I had absolute intellectual mastery of this material, I began to plot my book. This is the secret of good historical romance, for you cannot adapt a factual account literally and expect it to function successfully as a novel. The trick is to craft a good story based upon the historical sources, but never ruled or constrained by them. You must try to honour the spirit of your subject, but make the history your own.

This still left me with the problem of the ending. There are some truths that cannot be otherwise, even in a historical romance, and it was a matter of public record that, rightly or wrongly, my hero met his end at Execution Dock. I considered, briefly, the options of concluding my narrative before his fall, or employing a theatrical device common at the time and simply changing the story so that Kidd escaped the gallows. (They were even giving *Romeo and Juliet* a happy ending on the Haymarket in those days.) These contingencies were quickly discounted, as the first robbed me of my main political allegory (the betrayal and show trial), while the second trivialised the subject. I finally overcame the problem of historical determinism through the application of the central tenet of Classical tragedy, *inevitability*. I made my Captain Kidd a tragic hero, and went so far as to have him forewarned by Cassandra in her many guises (witches, mediums, heathen priestesses, itinerant fortune tellers and the like). In the manner of the Trojans he of course paid no heed, and was thus destroyed by his own destiny. Finally, just in case the application of Aristotle's *Poetics* to privateers was insufficient to guarantee success, I also plundered *Rookwood* and threw in a few pirate songs this time, some authentic sea shanties, others pure invention.

Once I was ready, I began to write like a steam engine. My pen flew across the page as if possessed. I barely paused to eat, sleep and wash, and stopped only to call upon Mina. The book became, in my mind, a way to consolidate my rank and status, so that I might make her more fully mine. With her implicit encouragement, I dreamed of spiriting her away from her husband forever, and for that I needed money. Her tastes were expensive.

I called the book *Blessed William*, playing upon the name of the first ship Kidd took and captained, and making the connection between his monarch, William III, after whom he named his vessel, and my own, William IV, to whom I expansively dedicated the book. The King let it be known in the right circles that he was delighted at this, and considered my book to be 'a bloody good yarn.' This right royal endorsement (which Colburn seriously considered using in advertisements until I reminded him about the Tower of London), suggested to me that His Majesty had skipped over the hegemonic critiques and conspiracy theories in favour of the jokes, the love scenes, and the fighting, which is pretty much what everyone else did. His famous hatred of the French was probably also a factor, as Kidd harried them something rotten. I was hoping for a knighthood, but he died the following year and was replaced by Victoria, who would not have given me the drippings off her snout.

Colburn again published as a three-decker, once more illustrated by Cruikshank, although the trend for serials was growing by that point. *Blessed William* blew all opposition out of the water like so many French merchantman, establishing the legend of Captain Kidd in much the same way that Ainsworth had done with Dick Turpin. (Whatever you think you know about these men is most likely to have originated in the pages of our books.) Mina was terribly proud, and decided that she would use one of what she termed her 'little literary soirées' to celebrate the launch.

The Garwood salons were, in reality, far from modest occasions, and she spent more on one of these things than I was earning for this book, the one before, and the one not yet written combined. I should have been appalled at such extravagance. But I was utterly dazzled by love, and as it was theoretically for my benefit I was nought but pathetically grateful for the opportunity to shine in the face of London Society, an elite social set to which I now so desperately wished to belong. With another bestseller under my belt, I was beginning to believe that some dreams might really come true, as my secret lover took me by the arm and led me into the light, having paused only to whisper that a room had been prepared for me and that she wore nothing beneath her gown but perfume.

As we entered the ballroom a great cheer went up, followed by a positive earthquake of applause.

'Happy birthday, my love,' she whispered.

I was twenty-seven years old, and the world was at my feet.

Ainsworth was there, looking tired. He was always generous in his praise of my achievements, in public and in private, and my heart went out to him, for *Crichton* was not a success and I knew he was stretched for cash. Mina had been right; the central character was too remote, clean-cut, aristocratic, perfect and invulnerable to appeal to fans of Dick Turpin. He had also lost his wife after *Rookwood*, some said to *Rookwood*, for she did not cope well with her husband's newfound notoriety, and the more he grew the more she had seemed to wither. Her family had taken Ainsworth's girls, and the lawyers had bled him white getting them back. He was there with 'Phiz' (Knight Browne, who had illustrated *Crichton*), the young publisher John Macrone, and Cruikshank, the latter talking animatedly to a slight, dark-headed man with his back to me as we approached. I guessed from the company that this must be the inimitable 'Boz,' who was quite the sensation that year.

I had not been paying close attention and we had yet to meet, but I had read him and been, like everyone else, deeply impressed. His sketches of London life and manners in *Bell's* and the *Morning* and the *Evening Chronicle* were most entertaining. He reminded me a lot of Egan. The style was totally different, but there was that same sense of the *mouvement perpétuel* of the city, with a similar eye for detail and a dark humour about them, the common root, I suppose, being the urban chroniclers of the last century. A collected edition was known to be in the offing, backed by Cruikshank, who had agreed to illustrate, and published by Macrone, who had met Dickens at one of Ainsworth's lavish parties at Kensal Lodge.

Good luck to him, thought I.

Cruikshank waved cheerfully when he spotted me, and his companion turned. He smiled warmly and extended his hand without formal introduction.

'I see you're still writing about pirates, Jack,' he said.

'Good God, Dickens,' roared Cruikshank, 'but you know everybody!'

And know me he did, for there before me stood little David of the Marshalsea, my biggest fan and fiercest critic, grown now to manhood and quite the rising star in his own right.

It had occurred to me long since that the reason he had so emphatically severed all ties was nothing against me, but purely a desire, if not a necessity, to put the shame of the prison behind him. (The false name had obviously been a similar defence, and from what I recalled of the shabby snobbery of his parents they would have done everything to separate us.) I had never held it against him, and saw no reason to do so now, for it is an easy thing to be magnanimous when one is at the top of one's profession, as I was that night.

'We were childhood friends,' I explained to the company, 'isn't that right, Charles?'

'The best,' said he, 'until my family moved away.' I nodded in voiceless agreement. They do not know, I thought.[14]

'How charming,' said Mina, playfully, for I had told her everything of my own youth, and she was always devilishly quick on the uptake, 'did you boys school together?'

'Eh, yes,' said I, hurriedly, having no idea where bloody Boz had gone to school.

He was fast, though, he always had been. 'Dear old Chatham,' he said, obligingly, 'and the worthy Mr. Giles.'

'A mentor to us both,' I agreed, 'a very great man.'

I could see that everyone was loving this. Ainsworth was beaming, and a small crowd had collected to witness the meeting of what one reviewer subsequently described as 'the three most popular writers in England.'

We all praised each other's work at great and sentimental length, and Cruikshank made a speech about the 'rising generation of English letters' that went on for at least an hour after dinner. Dickens and I made plans to dine and catch up properly, and at dawn I let Mina take me to bed. The entire night was magical, and after all these years I can still hardly bear to think of it, given what came later.

CHAPTER XIX

It was decided that Spike Island, a fortified islet within the lower harbour of some hundred acres and, according to our political masters, of great strategic significance, would serve Lakeman and Granger as a most efficacious pitch for a war game. Fort Westmoreland, a star fort built in the previous century, provided a square, while the beaches of the small, green skerry might be assaulted and defended. The location was also far enough away from the town for the discharge of blank cartridges to cause no inconvenience to the local civilian population, while also ensuring that the battle might be conducted with as much martial authenticity as possible. The fort was both garrison and convict depot. I had heard of the place before. To the eternal shame of my nation, John Mitchel, the founding editor of the *United Irishman*, had been incarcerated there four years since, prior to his transportation to the prison hulks of Bermuda (for on British justice the sun never sets).[15]

A coin was tossed, and it was agreed that Lakeman's force would defend while the redcoats would conduct an amphibious landing. The field of honour was to be a wild stretch of beach on the south east edge of the island that served as a small cemetery for the transports who did not survive the holding cells. Before the main event, both units would drill upon the Westmorland square, and receive an inspection by the prison's Governor, Mr. Grace, and the garrison commander, Colonel Camden.

The miserable edifice sat atop a moderate hill in the centre of the island, surrounded by a dry moat. It was long, low and grey, with squat bastions connected by ramparts, and a battery commanding the harbour. Although less than a century old, it recalled to my mind the castles of King William, constructed by the Normans to oppress native Englishmen. The penal fortress was under some sort of expansion or renovation, and vaporous tarpaulins flapped and howled around flimsy looking wooden scaffolds clinging to the pitiless grey walls.

Camden thought the field day a capital idea, and he had persuaded Grace to suspend building work for twenty-four hours, much to the relief, I imagined, of the convict labourers who slaved in the island's quarry or built with its slate. In consequence we saw no prisoners during our visit, although you could sense their presence. Their collective despair hung in the air like the stench of a week old battlefield. I gathered that when Lakemen's people realised that the island was also a prison a sense of panic had gripped them to a man, much as it had my own heart, for I was no more a stranger to the inside of a cell than were many of the Shoreditch Rangers. It must have been a hard sale to make, but Lakeman and his junior officers somehow managed to drive the bargain. The trick, I learned, was to cajole and persuade the men's unofficial spokesman and spiritual leader, who would in turn convince his companions. Samuel Barker had been one of the first to be recruited by Lakeman, who signed him up after a savage drinking bout in a low public house on the Whitechapel Road. The Brick Horse thereby became the unofficial headquarters of the recruitment drive, which Barker in part oversaw while Lakeman arranged temporary accommodation for his soldiers and staff at the infantry barracks in St John's Wood. Barker had later turned down Lakeman's offer to act as corporal, preferring, he said, the simple life of the rank and file, but he had informally retained his original role, that of liaison between the private soldiers and their officers.

'They will learn soon enough that this company is no more a democracy than the United Kingdom of Great Britain and Ireland,' Lakemen had told me, 'but for now an *entente cordiale* is best suited to my purpose.'

Barker wove his rhetorical magic, and so it was that on a raw Tuesday morning the rival forces met. It had been decided by both commanders that fifty men apiece would be enough for a practical test of comparative skill, and Seton had kept to the spirit of the wager by assembling a force comprising only those lately boarded (so there were no professionals from the Black Watch or the Highlanders on his team), and all freshly recruited. Seton's company was thus a hybrid born of the 2nd, 6th, 43rd, and 60th Regiments of Foot, the famous green jackets of the latter sprouting like a grassy knoll among the traditional red coats of the Warwickshires, Monmouthshires, and the Queen's Own; the War Office then still being of the opinion that bright red marked with a large white belted cross was the best design choice for a field uniform.

This clash of colours immediately set Seton at a semiologic disadvantage when compared with the neat black leather tunics and forage caps of Lakeman's rangers, who marched from the small dock with pride and precision. They had all bet heavily upon themselves and had no intention of losing. Further to the spirit of the wager, Seton had delegated the role of drill commander to Granger whereas Lakeman took that honour himself. Granger's formation took the lead, with the lieutenant's sabre presented while the soldiers were at right shoulder arms. Lakemen's men followed suit, while those of us observing ambled along at the tail. The infantrymen were tight, but Lakemen's rangers were tighter.

The fort rose before us all the way. We soon crossed the drawbridge and walked past several bored looking sentries, passing through a number of gratings, each of which had to be first unlocked and then relocked in our wake, and at last into a large open central court. The men came to attention in three dressed ranks, both companies standing side by side.

As was the custom, the parade began with an inspection. Mr. Grace, attended by Colonel Camden and Captain Salmond, passed a review of the men, who were likely as freezing as I, even in my fine coat, for there was a hard frost on the ground and the threat of snow in the low, bruised clouds. Both companies looked very well in line, and although of approximately equal inexperience, all seemed to know enough of the standard infantry rifle drill to take open orders for inspection.

This first part of the programme passed successfully for all parties concerned, until upon the conclusion of the inspection Mr. Grace, with a civilian's disregard for the order book, launched into an impromptu speech addressed to the men in praise of their gallant appearance. No sooner had he finished than the low, viscous

Cockney voice of Private Barker was heard, begging permission to speak. Lakeman warily responded that permission was granted, and Barker boldly addressed himself to the Governor.

'As your honour is so pleased with our trim,' said he, as brazen as alabaster, 'and as the air is so sharp this morning, perhaps you might give the order for a mug of grog all round, man-o'-war fashion so to speak.'

The Governor, whose kindly, paternal oration had indicated a certain gentleness of spirit which was surprising, given his occupation, appeared rather bewildered by this unorthodox request. 'You had better ask your captain,' he finally said.

'If it pleases your worship,' said Barker obsequiously, 'I'll not ask the skipper when the admiral is on the bridge.'

The Governor looked helplessly at Camden, who turned his gaze to Lakeman who responded with an almost imperceptible shrug. Salmond, meanwhile, was doing his damnedest to suppress his mirth, and his hard visage was going through the most extraordinary contortions.

There was no obvious way out without the Governor losing face. Barker, meanwhile, remained silently at attention, beaming like an imbecile. On his dark countenance, leathery and prematurely lined, and in which angry eyes appeared as twin markers upon a Hachure map of the Himalayas, the effect was decidedly sinister. The Governor and Commandant conferred for a moment, and then the word was given and a harassed looking commissariat officer was dispatched to make the arrangements. The soldiers were ordered to stand easy, and Lakeman approached Barker for a quiet word. From my position at the eastern edge of the square I could not tell the nature of the exchange, but Barker was no longer smiling when Lakeman walked away.

The commissariat officer returned in about ten minutes, along with two soldiers struggling with a handcart that looked not dissimilar to a fire engine, carrying a huge tapped barrel. Two great earthenware jugs were filled, and one given to the first man in each squad while glasses were charged and passed to all the spectators. When all were supplied with a brimming tumbler of rum, the

Governor drank to the success of both companies, and Lakeman and Granger raised their glasses to him and returned thanks. The men cheered, and then Lakemen's company broke out with 'We won't go home till morning.' The rum was wonderfully warming, and about half an hour passed in this most agreeable manner, before the men once more fell into the ranks and the rifle drill began.

Lakemen went first, while Granger and his men remained at attention. The open order right dress was once more given, and on the word 'Dress' the front rank came to attention, paused, and then took one pace forward, the soldiers turning their heads and eyes to the right and taking up the correct dressing. The rear rank followed suit, and then the centre. The men were as one, their movements instinctive, oiled and fluid, their muscles already trained to remember the actions and their order. I marvelled at such a display of autonomic prowess, given the state I knew I was in after whetting my whistle until the rum had run dry, as had Lakeman's boys. The regular army soldiers had been much more restrained as far as I could tell, even the Celts among them, and each had taken only a small sip from the jug for show before passing it on. I am pretty certain that Lakeman's company got hold of the second jug and finished that off as well. Some were silently calling out the time, the speechless movement of their lips the only sign that the drill was in any way a conscious process. Lakeman confidently marched his men around the square in quick and slow time, paying compliments to the Governor and Commandant, saluting to the right flank on the march. The display concluded with arms drill at the halt, ending with a flourish at port arm. It was a superb last turn. To my admittedly untutored eye the parade had been flawless.

I had contrived to get close to Seton and Wright during the toast, and was thus now in a position to hear Wright's expression of amazement, breathed *sotto voce* to his superior. 'By the living Jingo,' said he, 'those laggers were powerful good.'

Seton did not immediately reply, but his eyes betrayed his anxiety. 'There were always going to be a few able amateurs among them,' he finally conceded. The rangers, meanwhile, fell out proudly, alert and obedient; their collective discipline an unspoken but nevertheless loud statement, appealing, I felt, to the regular army infantrymen and their officers to read 'em and weep as they say in the low gaming houses.

Granger did his best, but he was as an unknown tragedian treading the boards in the wake of Mr. Kean or Mrs. Keeley. Lakeman was simply an impossible act to follow. His men initially appeared competent on the open order, but when they began to move things fell apart, and the more each tried to compensate, the more extreme the collective errors became. On the close order march, the distance between the ranks was unequal, and dressing was not maintained. Many of the soldiers' eyes were not front but down, and even when the feet were thus examined there was still some audible scraping of boots along the ground. A good third seemed incapable of remaining stationary when marking time, they swayed on the halt, and their muskets were rarely fully vertical but instead waved like reeds in a gale.

On the right wheel, files in the rear swung out and away from the wheeling point, and judging by the wild glances around the quod few indeed looked the Governor in the eye when paying compliments, like guilty costers unable to meet the gaze of a peeler. The final indignity came in the arms drill, where on the command to fix swords several bayonets clattered to the ground, causing Seton to visibly wince. Granger's composure was admirable, but his humiliation radiated across the square in waves that, like the rays of the sun, could not been seen but were nonetheless felt.

It was a relief to all when the interminable display of square bashing came to an end, although we all applauded like good sports, albeit in a somewhat desultory fashion that bore little relation to the enthusiastic ovation that Lakeman and his men had received. Granger was joined by the subaltern Metford of the 6th and Sergeant Moore of the 2nd, and the trio hastily organised their company and quit the square in order to begin the next stage of the tournament: the mock battle.

Lakeman did not yet possess a full staff, and this detail probably went a fair way to explaining why he felt my company worth cultivating, given that the professional foot wabblers and donkey wallopers would not give him the time of day. His plan was to recruit officers at the Cape, where he felt he would find a better class of freelancer among those experienced yet somehow superfluous men that one only seems to encounter in the colonies. His present staff therefore amounted only to Sergeant Major Herridge, an ex-policeman; the volatile Sergeant Waine, who had once been a non-commissioned officer in the 44th but who had been broken and discharged for improper conduct of an unspecified nature; the more steady Sergeant Beaufort, also known as 'Handsome George' (for his disconcertingly good looks and his dandy's attention to their maintenance); and the mysterious Lieutenant Graves, who for reasons that remained obscure chose to take his meals privately below decks, rather than dining with the other officers as did his captain. Religious enthusiasm was rumoured, but as Seton's staff viewed Graves as another mercenary there was no terrible breach of protocol in this absence, and Lakeman did not appear to care.

For the field day, Lakeman had selected Herridge and Beaufort as his seconds, leaving Graves and Waine to maintain order on the ship, where the balance of his force remained confined, much to the increasing irritation of the soldiers. These placements struck me as a very well-considered use of resources. Herridge's apparent disdain for his fellow man, manifest mostly in an ill-disguised contempt easily provoked to wrath, made him a leader to be feared, while Beaufort's charm and charisma had the men as obedient as hounds to a huntsman. With the triumvirate completed by the Byronic Lakeman, who, including myself, I had to admit, would not blindly follow?

It came to me at that moment that there was something quite mythic about these men, and that perhaps this was where the true source of the tension lay with Seton and his subordinates. I suddenly felt, too, an affinity with the ordinary soldiers of Lakeman's rangers who, by the look of them, were by nature even more rebellious and obstreperous than was I. Yet we had all so easily fallen under the influence of this golden-headed, aristocratic maverick. I laughed aloud at this revelation, and inwardly felt both strangely elated and thoroughly ashamed.

Herridge fell the men in, and, having been released through the labyrinth of cage doors, they proceeded in a spirited manner towards the position assigned them in the forthcoming engagement, the potter's field wherein so many forgotten prisoners slumbered known as Cemetery Beach. Once again, the observers followed. It had begun to snow quite heavily while we were inside the fort, but the walls surrounding the quod had kept the worse of it off us; outside it was already settling and the cold was corrosive. I felt for Granger's unfortunate charges, which were tasked with approaching from the sea, and were likely already upon the frozen waters in open boats. The defenders were at least warmed by their brisk march across the island, if not the inward glow of victory in the first round, for there was no doubt the judgement would go in their favour. Now all they had to do was stand fast and hold the bone garden.

It was a miserable place, lost among the dunes at the base of a rocky cliff some thirty yards high with a narrow diagonal path the only passage landward. The painting of snow, to my eyes, made the scene even more gothic than it already was, like a canvas by Friedrich depicting medieval ruins in midwinter.

My group, which consisted of Seton, Wright, Salmond, Camden, Giradot and Lucas, remained concealed atop the cliff, which offered a clear, if bracing point of vantage from which to observe both the beach and the burial ground. Mr. Grace had cried off, citing pressing administrative affairs, which I took to mean that he had realised that he was expected to lie upon the snow covered scrub as were the rest of our party. With my arse in the grass, I was once more grateful for the gift of the waterproof greatcoat. The icy damp, which would have been soaking through the army officers' tunics and coating their bellies like frozen sweat, must have been most unpleasant. They all bore it well, and their collective stoicism was doubly impressive given that I was reasonably certain that Wright was the only one that had actually seen active service, and therefore experienced any such level of physical discomfort.

To Salmond, who had navigated wooden ships through the North East Passage, this was as a balmy spring afternoon. The old pirate was having a fine time, and while the three senior officers looked through field glasses at the events unfolding below, and the rest of us squinted down as best we could, he wielded a brass telescope as long as a javelin and as thick as a baby's arm.

'You could have someone's eye out with that,' I said, and he laughed.

While watching Lakeman deploy I began to grasp the Spanish concept of guerrilla tactics, and that there was another type of war that had nothing to do with cavalry charges and vast formations upon a field, but was more akin to a deadly game of hide and seek; a war of reconnaissance, patrols, ambushes, and surprise raids fought out across broken ground. Based upon his experiences in Algeria, it was Lakeman's expectation that the Basuto war was likely to be fought on such terms, with small, irregular forces striking at vulnerable targets and then melting away almost immediately. These were terms, he felt, that the British military plainly failed to appreciate.

Neither side knew the exact location of the other. Granger had a map reference, assuming he could keep his bearings, and the choice of how best to approach his target. Further assuming that he had the sense to land further up the beach (which he did), Lakeman could only presume the direction of attack and reinforce accordingly. His position was in a natural impression, so he posted concealed lookouts forward, left and right supported by runners. I imagined he did not anticipate a frontal assault, for he relied on the rock at his back and the exposed stretch of beach before him to preclude attack, and fortified on either side using hastily dug redoubts which he packed with riflemen, scattering snipers further down the beach that hid among the freezing rocks and dunes like Alpine bandits. The remainder of his force, I guessed, were firemen, held back by the cliff face to reinforce any weaknesses in his defences. Satisfied, he gave the order to stand to with stealth, and his men dropped to the ground. We could still see most of them, but at ground level they would have been quite invisible, even in the snow.

Granger was clever. He had sent half his force one way around the island and the rest the other, co-ordinating an impressively timed twin landing out of Lakeman's likely line of sight. His forces approached on each flank, feeling their way through the Marram grass and taking all due precautions, probing the ground left and right, with an advance and a rear guard, the men first bent low with their firelocks at their sides, then upon their bellies like snakes. A smaller sacrificial force, meanwhile, also crawling, slithered across the beach to approach from the direction of the sea in a calculated feint.

The first contact occurred on the right flank, when one of Granger's scouts met one of Lakeman's forward observers. The ranger swung his rifle at the elbow and knocked the unfortunate redcoat senseless in one fluid movement.

'That's first blood, by God,' said Salmond in a delighted undertone.

Seton was less impressed. 'This is supposed to be an enactment,' he said indignantly. The same scene was then repeated on the left flank. The rangers were clearly planning to remove the opposition by silent degrees, as if incapacitating guards during a bank robbery or a prison break. 'For heaven's sake,' said Seton.

The rangers closest to the advancing redcoats and greenjackets were now creeping through the dunes and quietly disarming the soldiers by approaching from behind and then swiftly holding evil looking bush knives to their throats. The soldiers were then led back to Lakeman's lines as prisoners, where they were directed to lie face down upon the snow covered graves, with their hands clasped behind their heads. In addition to the two knockouts, this noiseless skirmish did for another eight of them. Now obviously cogent of the directions and time of attack, the rangers withdrew to their fortified positions and waited, completely ignoring the forward platoon, who seemed unsure what to do when not fired upon. Moore was at their head, and he had the good sense to disperse his half dozen charges amongst the rocks and dunes. Granger and Metford were less patient, and elected to storm the defences of both flanks together. The order to fire was given and these brave but misguided invaders received a peppering volley from both of Lakeman's redoubts.

As the pungent smoke rose to our nostrils, Salmond bellowed down to Granger's wasted forces, many of whom, Ensign Metford included, were writhing on the ground checking their bodies as if really shot. 'You men there,' he intoned, 'are all dead.'

The remainder of the force, including Moore's contingent, sprang up and bolted for the boats down the beach, sliding about the snow like particularly inexpert skiers. Lakeman's men were clearly most anxious to prove their capacity for combat beyond the opportunity presented by the failed assault, so with loud and exulting cries they jumped up from their positions and started off in pursuit of the scuttling foe.

Private Barker was particularly conspicuous in the melee that followed, fetching the butt of his rifle upon the heads and shoulders of his foes until, like Achilles in pursuit of Hector, he faced the defeated Granger, sword drawn and pistol in hand. The battle was done, and all eyes (the living and the dead) were now on these two men. Like Broughton and Slack in the Prize Ring they circled one another for what seemed like an age, their eyes locked in a burning hatred apparent even at our distance. Granger, his blood up, finally swung his sword with the finesse of a man cutting wood, only to have it expertly blocked by Barker's rifle, which continued its arc upward until its heavy stock connected with the young officer's chin. Granger went down, stunned, and Barker kicked the weapons from his hands. He then raised his rifle and sighted down the long barrel of the Minié into Granger's face, his lips moving in words obviously meant only for his vanquished enemy.

Just as Lakeman called, 'Enough!' he fired.

*

Granger complained all the way back to the boats. Lakeman's team, he argued, should be disqualified on the grounds of unnecessary and excessive force. The whole affair, he asserted, had gone off in a most unsportsmanlike fashion, which entirely proved his point regarding the inferiority of Lakeman's men. His, he said, was the moral victory. He had pulled himself together and scrambled up the cliff path to demand adjudication, although I do not imagine that his hopes were very high. The young lieutenant was looking much the worse for wear, and was obviously flustered, if not dazed, for an angry bruise was flowering the line of his jaw, which was swelling in a most alarming manner. When our referee and judge, the formidable Master and Commander, had directed him to shake hands with his victorious opponent, he had first tried to do so with Salmond himself, who registered his contempt with a long growl.

'I rather think, sir,' Lakeman had replied, 'that your decisive defeat has vindicated my position.'

It goes without saying that Lakeman had carried the day and won the bet. He had also joined the judges' party, and left the fair and fragrant Sergeant Beaufort to release the dishevelled and traumatised prisoners and organise the triumphant rangers, who needed to be marched along the beach to the pier and then conveyed back to the ship sharpish, before they realised that there was to be no celebratory shore leave granted. To these victors there would be no spoils, although Lakeman had promised a share of the profits from the wager. That these funds would not be immediately transferred to the ale houses and brothels of Cork was, I am sure, a source of profound disappointment to all parties concerned.

The ferocious Herridge had charge of Private Barker, who Granger wanted on company punishment. 'I'm not sure we do that,' said Lakeman, who had offered various excuses for the behaviour of his men. The temperature of their blood, he said, had been raised by the heat of battle. Barker had lowered his rifle at the last second, and discharged the weapon between the splayed, frog-like legs of his prostrate foe, destroying both pride and breeches, but nothing else. This symbolic unmanning was so humiliating that it would have been more humane by far to have blown out Granger's brains upon the sand, which at that range would have been as easily achieved with a blank charge as a loaded one. Disgrace at the crease or a white feather would have been mere bags of shells by comparison.

Not for the first time that day Seton had visibly winced. 'The mercenary is right,' he said, as Barker blasted away at Granger's bollocks below. 'Our men are not ready for war. If we send them up country it will be murder.'

His face was as set as a plaster death mask, and deep in thought he spoke no more after receiving Granger's report and conceding the wager. He and Wright then trudged disconsolately back to the fort in silence, accompanied by Colonel Camden. Giradot and Lucas did their best to consol Granger, whose excruciating embarrassment was manifest in a rambling monologue interrupted only by swigs from a silver flask.

Lakeman and Salmond walked together enthusiastically discussing the battle. As ever, I hung back and observed. It was still snowing heavily, in great irregular flakes that had quickly coated the entire island, bleaching sand and shore. In the lee of the cliffs, snow danced and flurried about the forlorn churchyard where Granger's honour, like the luckless convicts, was now crudely interred, drifting against the meagre and twisted crosses. Dickens would have no doubt found the scene sublime, poetic and beautiful, but all I saw was the colour of bone.

CHAPTER XX

DICKENS HAD NOT changed much. In common with MacBeth he was possessed of a vaulting ambition, and although by nature still taciturn, he remained remarkably confident in his own talent. I envied his self-assurance. However well I was doing, I never felt the like, and was confident only in the coming of the next personal catastrophe. I learned later that he was not so different regarding many areas of his life, only he hid it better than I; but in his own faith in his abilities as a writer he was always supremely secure, and with good reason. He really was quite brilliant. I suppose I should have viewed him as a rival, but I was doing very well myself, and for all his aspirations he was a long way from being an established novelist then, while I was riding high on a three book deal with two in the bank. I was pretty sure there was room for us both, and anticipated no more than an amiable competition, in much the same manner as my relationship with Ainsworth. I was delighted to have my old friend returned to me, and looked forward to the resumption of our old debates about literary composition.

We dined together at the Athenaeum Club, shortly after renewing our friendship at the *Blessed William* banquet. After a fine meal we killed a couple of bottles of very good claret and then got started on the brandy. The talk was of life, love, and, most importantly, literature. If he knew of my affair with Mina he was too polite to show it, although he did ask what had become of my friends and family at the Marshalsea, so I told him of the deaths of Bill and Nancy, the marriage of Bertie and Nelly, and the strange story of my father, my sister, and Freddie, who was still going to Grove to tap me for money.

'You are not paying, surely?' said Dickens.

'What choice do I have?' I answered mournfully. This subject, coupled with memories of Nancy and stoked by the booze, always caused me a severe melancholic reaction, unless I was with Mina and thus able to lose myself in her. 'I have to support my family.'

'I do not envy you, my friend,' said he, 'it is a horrible dilemma.'

'Perhaps I will write about it one day.'

'Someone should,' he said.

He was desperate to escape what he called the 'little world of journalism,' and we talked much of my own transition from journalist to novelist. His energy was impressive, although I wondered if he might be spreading himself too thinly, for he was still writing for the *Chronicle*, while also under contract to Macrone to edit his 'Sketches.' William Hall was also after him to write the text for a series of humorous illustrations by Robert Seymour, and Bentley was chatting him up as a potential editor for a new miscellany.

'You toil harder than a beaver with Puritan leanings,' I told him.

I was joking, but he looked at me in deadly earnest. 'We both know better than most what happens if you do not earn enough money in this world,' he said.

'Fair enough,' said I, 'now drink up you needy-mizzler!'

He smiled at this, despite himself, for this had been his affectionate nickname within the Marshalsea. It meant a poor ragged object. 'Thank you,' he said, 'for not giving me up the other night.'

'I could tell at once that you did not want it known.'

'Do you?'

To be honest, this was not really something I had considered, for it was such a long time ago. When I wrote of the Fancy, time spent inside had actually aided my credibility, though I had not since advertised this part of my childhood, except in confidence to Mina. I decided not to mention that. 'I am not ashamed of my past,' I finally conceded, 'but I see no reason why it should be common knowledge either.'

'I agree,' he said. 'In the wrong hands, this information could be very damaging to us both.' I was not entirely convinced, which shows how far my finger already was from the pulse of the new moral age that was coming.

'Let it always be a secret between us, then,' said I, and he seemed very satisfied, if not relieved, although he did insist on shaking upon the agreement. I also received the distinct impression that were there a bible to hand he would have sworn me to silence upon that as well.

I left the meal in need of a woman, but calling on Mina at that hour was not appropriate or allowed, while a whore would be an act of betrayal. This was no fault of my guest, for he had been very pleasant company, but rather the return of the repressed, you might say, for it was still difficult to talk of my family, while the memory of Bill and Nancy was an old wound that had never really healed. The clubs of St. James' and Mayfair beckoned, or I could slum it for a while round The Horn, but I decided instead to take a leaf out of Dickens' book, and therefore returned to my house with the intention of writing. A plot was forming in my mind concerning fraud and the theft of identity. I supposed that if I could explore Freddie's actions and motivations in a dramatic narrative, because for me there never really was a world outside the text, then I might, perhaps, discover his true purpose, and find a way by which I might defeat him. I had realised, you see, in the course of my conversation with Dickens that evasion was the weakest and worst strategy that I could have adopted. As we had both seen many times over in the prison, inactivity was death.

I had not taken any servants, so I made my own coffee, and carried it up the dark stairs to my study, balancing a candle next to the pot on a silver tray that cost more than my father and I used to earn in a year. I sat at my desk, lit a cigar and looked out of the window, past the heavy velvet drapes and out across the moonlit fields and rooftops of Notting Hill, thinking. After a while I began to create Freddie in my head as a character in a fiction.

As any author worth his salt will tell you, the essence of a good character is to be found in his or her primary motivation, the central, dramatic longing that pulls them through the story like a horse before a cart. So what did Freddie most desire? I thought back to our childhoods. As far as I could discern he was an orphan, and after Bill and Nancy had discarded him he was piteously thankful at being admitted to our family, destitute and dysfunctional though we all undoubtedly were. Would he not, I realised, have thought my departure another betrayal? He would have cleaved himself even more to my family after that, for fear of losing them too, clinging to them like a limpet in a whale's crack. If my father then became weak-minded enough to believe him his son, Freddie would have seized upon the chance to become, in effect, blood. Sarah would have been too young to know the difference.

I had initially wondered if Freddie harboured designs upon my sister, like some melodramatic villain, but his subterfuge would not suit seduction, for he had made them both siblings, although his actions could equally suggest some sort of need for control. He was also taking my money, it was true, and relying on my honour not to withhold it for the sake of my kin, but I was far from making him rich. Freddie, I reasoned, wanted love, not money, and not even physical love, just the simple warmth and affection of a close family.

I must have been channelling my mother's good nature that night, for I began to feel quite sorry for the man. I therefore resolved to call upon him at the earliest opportunity, confident that he could be persuaded that there was room enough for us both in the family.

Mina was not of a like mind, and counselled that I have Freddie prosecuted for fraud. 'Surely it is of little matter to a man of your professional standing to have the scoundrel returned to His Majesty's pleasure at the earliest opportunity,' she said, adding a further suggestion involving a horsewhip.

I had asked a copper about this once, in fact, and he had told me that if he arrested all the impostors in London, half the population would be in prison. I was not really concentrating just then though, for she was doing things to me on the library couch that would shame a Shoreditch whore. Having teased me for a glorious eternity, she finally allowed me release. Just as I spent, the door opened.

It was the husband. I was well and truly boned.

You have to admire the composure of the upper classes, for he said not a word, although neither did he withdraw. I started to pull on my clothes but Mina bade me hold. Although naked but for a black French corset, she rose imperiously and moved towards him, rubbing her hand across her gleaming face and chest and then through her hair.

'You see this, you old fool,' she said, smiling wickedly, 'this is what you're missing. Now get out.' And damn me if he didn't just leave us to it. 'Now, you dirty boy' said she, pouring two large gins at an occasional table and then returning to the couch, 'fuck me again.'

A wiser lover, especially one that aspired to wedlock, would have found such open contempt for a husband disconcerting, but who is rational under such a spell? I was young and naive, and believed myself loved, so the display was to me exciting. I pleasured her every way I knew that night, and at the end of the month Mr. Garwood still paid me for the private tuition.

I did not find Freddie quite so accommodating. In an attempt to resolve the very unsatisfactory state of affairs in which I presently found myself, I had sent him my card with an informal message suggesting that we talk in private. I knew he could read, for Bertie had told me, and he also communicated with Grove by letter. This was ignored, as were two further requests for a meeting. I finally ambushed him by having Grove arrange a consultation in which Freddie expected to see only my solicitor, and to receive some money. When an obliging clerk showed Freddie to Grove's office at Gray's Inn, he found me waiting for him instead.

He hesitated at the door, avarice and curiosity struggling with a very obvious desire to bolt. I managed to lure him in with gentle words, as one might a stray dog. This was not entirely without conviction either. Perhaps against my better judgement, I still retained my original hypothesis concerning the man's essential vulnerability.

Once more I took his hand. 'My dear friend,' I said, 'how good it is to see you.'

The look in his eyes was difficult to read. It seemed to signal both fear and defiance. I gestured that he should sit, and positioned myself on Mr. Grove's side of the desk. He carefully removed his hat and placed it upon his bony knees, looking around the room, rather than at me, but saying nothing.

When I rang for tea he visibly flinched. Upon its arrival I clapped my hands and he jumped again. 'Well,' said I, 'shall I be mother?'

He looked bemused. I poured the tea.

Finally, he spoke. 'Is this a legal matter, sir?'

'I don't know,' I said, 'do you think it should be?'

He really did appear on the verge of tugging his forelock, and I realised, with a touch more satisfaction than was seemly for a gentleman, that I had taken exactly the right tone with him. He might have me on animal cunning, but I was the dominant male, or so I thought, blessed with higher reasoning, wealth and social status. Why I had let this insignificant little shit play me for a fool for so long was, quite frankly, embarrassing.

He bowed his head. 'Please,' he said, quietly.

'Very well,' says I, all business, 'why don't you tell your big brother all about it.'

'I'm sorry,' he said.

'So am I,' I said sternly.

'I meant no harm,' he said.

'But you have caused plenty,' I said, my sermon already prepared. 'I thought you my friend, Freddie. I looked out for you. I left my family in your care—' I had more, but he cut me off.

'You left us,' he said, his voice growing in strength.

'I had no choice.'

'We were all fine,' he said, almost hysterically, 'everything was fine, and then those men came and you talked to them and suddenly everyone was gone.'

'But can you not see, Freddie?' I said, my original feeling of helpless frustration returning. 'Those men got us out. It took me a while, but because of them I earned enough money to secure your freedom, and that of Father.' I carefully kept it neutral, and avoided the possessive form of the personal pronoun, implying no ownership of my father either way.

But it was a clear case of pearls before swine. My grammatical subtlety was wasted on the bastard. When it comes to the correct use of English, I don't know why I bother sometimes.

'You talked to those men,' he said, speaking more quietly now, 'and Bill and Nancy left me on my own.' I started to say that he was never alone, for he had my family and me, but he again interrupted. 'They left,' he repeated, his eyes now varnished with tears, 'and then they died.' He suddenly appeared very young, wiping his sleeve across his nose, his expression so disconsolate that I wished for a second that I had a sweet about my person that I could offer him. But just as I dropped my guard, he struck: '*She* died,' he whispered.

So how, you may wonder, did protagonist address antagonist, now that all the cards were finally face up? Did I confess how much I had loved her, too; how she still often stole, unbidden, into my thoughts, and how I would have done anything to have saved her? I even wrote crackbrained stories about travelling through time, so much did I yearn to go back to then and change it all.

None of the above.

'It was a tragedy,' I said, weakly, having no way to express such profound and deep rooted emotions. It is funny that when we are at the height of our passions, good and bad, we become so utterly inarticulate. It was an ineffectual answer. I knew it, he knew it, and he treated it with the contempt it deserved.

'You,' said he, pointing a cadaverous finger accusingly, 'you killed her.'

'Oh Christ,' I said, slumping back in Grove's chair, all the wind suddenly removed from my sails. And the conversation had started so well, I thought miserably.

'I hated you after that,' he said. 'I wanted to hurt you.'

'So you stole my family.'

'Yes,' he said, simply.

The air between us seemed suddenly charged. So the true reason had been revenge, and he had not even had to leave the prison to mark me forever. I could never, I realised, convince Sarah and my father that I was the real brother and son, and Freddie the imposture, the *doppelgänger*. After all these years, no legal proof would sway them, and I doubted even Freddie's word, should he give it (which looked increasingly unlikely), would carry any weight in the matter. It was hopeless, but I felt compelled to play out the remainder of the scene regardless. There are rules to these things, after all.

'Do you still hate me, Freddie?' I asked slowly.

'I don't know,' he said, looking at the floor. And that was that. We sat in awkward and oppressive silence for a while, perhaps only for seconds but it felt like hours at the time.

Finally, he said, 'Can I go now?'

'You know we have more to discuss,' I told him, although my heart was not really in it. I wanted him out of there just as much as he did himself.

'Yes,' he said, 'but not today, 'ay Jack?'

'All right, Freddie. No more today.'

'And the money?'

Don't push it, I thought, but I had a fiver about me which I ended up giving him, anyway, stuffing it into his hand inelegantly as I showed him to the door. 'You know where I am,' I told him, 'come and see me soon.'

He offered that crooked smile of his, and promised me that he would, and then he was gone, lost in the crowd.

So much for bloody character studies, I thought.

I decided to call upon Mina. We were not scheduled to meet that day, and I knew that calling unannounced was a dreadful breach of etiquette in her world, like passing the port the wrong way or buggering the governess, but I needed her very much just then. I wanted to kill all those fears and frustrations and pathless paths, and I knew of no better place to exorcise these demons than beneath her skirts, but more than that I wanted to feel loved. If she cared for me as deeply as I did her, which she appeared to do, then she would see me, I reasoned, even if just to talk.

I was confident and desperate enough to barge past the maid when I arrived, tossing my card into my hat and presenting both to her as a *fait accompli.*

'I'll wait for the mistress in the library,' said I, swaggering towards our inner sanctum, the poor servant gawping after me and babbling away that the lady was entertaining and not to be disturbed. 'She always has time for me,' I told her, knocking confidently and then swinging open the great door, for I fancied I had heard an invitation to come inside.

It was immediately and painfully apparent that the remark had not been addressed to me. Mina was upon the couch (our couch) kneeling on all fours with her skirts up and d'Orsay hanging out of the back of her in his shirt tails. At the same time, she pleasured the impressively naked Lady Marguerite with her tongue. (It was a big couch.)

'My dear Jack,' purred *miladi*, 'don't just stand there letting out the heat, come and join us.'

Now, if I said that I did not consider this proposal I would be lying, but what I wanted just then was not on offer, and, although I am not morally opposed to orgies, the thought of cavorting anywhere near that French fop was appalling. By the look of things, the two women were doing perfectly well without the need for more men anyway, and could probably have quite easily dispensed with the frog. (He was a terrible artist too, no technique whatsoever.) I am pretty certain that if I had pitched in all would have been fine between us, and by the look of it I would have had a rare old time with Lady Marguerite, but I could not bear to share Mina any more than I already did. The cuckold husband and the children were more than enough.

'No thanks,' I said, utterly crestfallen. I must have been looking quite put out, for only then did Mina acknowledge or address me. The Count, meanwhile, did not stop going in and out like a fiddler's elbow.

'Darling,' she said, as if admonishing a sullen and slightly slow child, the affect rendered even more unreal by the rocking motion caused by d'Orsay doing his business, 'you didn't think you were my only boy did you?'

It was not the betrayal so much as her casual indifference that enraged me. 'Damn you!' I cried uselessly, struggling for the right insult. 'You degenerate, you filthy fornicator.'

This was the best I could manage on the spot, although I later wished that I had denounced her as a whore as well, for all the good it would have done. She evidently did not care for my opinions one way or another and, as you will recall, it was she, or at least her husband, who had been paying me.

'Well I certainly won't be fornicating filthily with you anymore,' she said, and by her voice I knew she meant it. Whatever it was that we had had was categorically and incontrovertibly over. 'Now get out,' she ordered, 'before I call my husband.'

She would have, too, and the idiot would have come to her aid as if she were being hounded by a tramp outside a fashionable restaurant, not getting shagged silly on the settee by some French ponce and his doxy.

'Yes, do go away Jack,' said Lady Marguerite, 'don't be a bore.'

Then d'Orsay stuck his oar in as well. 'Bugger off, old boy,' he said, wearily, 'and shut the door behind you.'

It was on the back of that last remark that I finally broke. I swore and I stamped and I railed, until one of the ancestors went over and shattered upon the floor, at which point Mina rang a bell and two brawny footmen escorted me off the premises. One of the bastards punched me in the stomach before he shoved me through the tradesmen's entrance and onto the street, where I writhed and gasped on the ground like a fish that had just been caught and landed.

'You want to know your place,' said the big servant that had thumped me, 'now sling your hook and don't come back, or it'll be the dogs you'll be meeting next time.'

A coster hawking cold pies over the road left his barrow with his boy and helped me up. 'That taught him a lesson,' he said, patting the dust off my jacket. He obviously thought me one of his class, given my route of exit. 'Fucking toffs,' he added, as he bade me farewell, 'fuck 'em.'

'Yeah,' I said, 'fuck 'em all.'

I ended up at The Horn of Plenty, where I effectively took up residence for the better part of a fortnight, although much of the memory of doing so escapes me. It was the best place for me just then. It required no patronage, a card of admission was not necessary, and no inquiries were made. All were welcome, and parties paired off according to fancy. The eye was pleased in the choice, and nothing thought of about birth and distinction.

The crew down there were motley indeed, and all my ain folk. There were lascars, blacks, soldiers and sailors, coal-heavers, dustmen, costermongers, fences, fakers, and shapers, all laughing over their exploits, and planning fresh depredations. Then there were the women, a fair sprinkling of the remnants of once fine girls, all of whom could be had for the price of a glass, and to hell with the high class whores of Pall Mall and Mayfair.

I vaguely remember a plan to drink myself to death in the company of a beautiful young whore name of African Sally, but Bertie and Nelly took charge of me in the end. Their motives, I was sure, were essentially philanthropic, although the cove of the ken had put a block on my slate. 'You're not that bloody rich, Jack,' he had said.

Bertie was also in possession of a letter addressed to me, delivered in person, he said, by a mere scrap of a girl the night before last. The letter (or to be more precise note), plucked me from the arms of Bacchus good and quick. It was from my sister.

'Mr Vincent,' it began, 'as we share the same name I pray that you are the benevolent relative of whom my father often speaks.' This made my black heart beat again, until it occurred to me that she was probably confusing me with something she had heard about my uncle, for she obviously knew not that I was her brother. 'We have not seen you lately,' the note continued, 'and I am greatly concerned for my poor father's welfare. My brother, as you know, is a good man,' (my body went as tense as a cobra at this), 'and I believe that he has our best interests always at heart, but he has of late changed, and acts like a man hunted. I pray, sir, that you use your influence to calm him, for the recent violence of his moods is causing my dear father great distress. Please forgive this inelegant missive,' she concluded, 'for I write in stealth and haste.'

'Why didn't you bring her to me?' I asked Bertie.

'You were too far gone to see her,' he said.

I arose unsteadily from my pit with the intention of doing something chivalrous, and then my head spun and I was forced to lie back down again. It took a couple of pints of the black sludge Nelly passed off as coffee to get me on my feet, but I was determined to go to my sister's aid. My badgerly friend insisted on accompanying me to Southwark, for, he said, I'd not last five minutes on my own in the state I was in. I was grateful for the support, but when we arrived at Mawley's Rents we were already too late. My family had gone.

CHAPTER XXI

Making life on the ship a deal more complicated than it had been, women and children had now boarded. The presence of more civilians at least made my position more tenable and less isolated, but the young families in particular made my heart ache for my own. I had managed thus far to not dwell upon this lack by immersing myself in the company of military men by day, while tapping the admiral and then writing at night, so as to have something halfway decent to dispatch to the *Chronicle* before we sailed. Thus far all these activities and attendant mental states (observer, reporter, and drunk) had served as albeit very different distractions from a loneliness upon which I did not dare to fixate. Now, however, I was to be tormented by other peoples' wives and children, and thus constantly reminded of my own family and our extended separation.

'Tell me you're coming back to me,' Grace had said when we parted, 'for I cannot live without you.' That was not at all the case, but I thanked her in my heart for saying so. At almost half my age, attractive, talented and resourceful, the reality was that she would be a deal better off without me.

My little man had wobbled up upon my chair by the window to wave enthusiastically when I took my leave, as he always did when I went out to work or run an errand, only this time I had not come back. I wondered how he had coped with my absence. I fretted about his sleep. A disturbance in his routine invariably resulted in troubled nights for at least a week, and if I was detained by work and unable to read him to sleep he would be less than impressed at my replacement by his mother. I wondered if he had become used to her telling bedtime stories already, wanting him to have adapted for her sake and his, but in equal part hoping that he missed our time together so that I would not easily be forgotten. And I had barely been away a week of an expedition that would at the very least take six months to complete.

I marvelled at how military families survived. It was not uncommon in those days for regiments to be posted to the colonies for years at a time, sometimes decades. In response, the British Army had learned to create familiar little domestic enclaves across the empire, at least for its officer class, so a version of English suburbia could now be found in the heart of deserts and jungles, all as transient and fake as the sets in a theatre. The gentlewomen presently taking the bracing morning air on the upper deck attended by their servants (some with golden headed toddlers tottering around their feet that were breaking my heart), were the wives of officers who were brave or determined or desperate enough to join their husbands at the Cape, all taking their places in the imperial harlequinade.

While I was thus taking stock of the new passengers and pining for my wife and son, our good Captain approached and slapped me on the back with such force that my teeth rattled in my head. 'Let us consider the words of the late Reverend Knox, Mr. Vincent,' said he, quoting from memory: '"the first blast of the trumpet against this monstrous regiment of women."' He roared with laughter, and then notably lowered his voice. 'Only these foppish army prigs would take their womenfolk to war, Mr. Vincent. It is to your credit, sir, that you left your family where it is.'

I thanked him for his generous praise of my conduct, and managed to hold my tongue beyond that. I would have lost all credibility in his eyes by confessing how much I already missed them, and that the only reason that my family did not accompany me was that Doyle, my editor, would not spring for the extra passage and I had not the blunt to fund it myself.

Salmond, meanwhile, was continuing his complaint against women and children travelling on a troop carrier. Culhane, the ship's surgeon, had, he said, just informed him that six of these women were with child. '*Six*,' he repeated, in a kind of apoplectic amazement. One was one too many in his opinion, and as it turned out he was entirely in the right in this assertion, for within a fortnight half of them were dead.

A small boy in a blue sailor suit on the lower deck was now

pointing at us and waving for some reason. It was possible his mother had identified the Captain, or perhaps he just found us amusing, Salmond in his towering stovepipe hat and me in my huge overcoat, both of us resembling villains in a play. I doubt he knew who I was, for he seemed a trifle young to be a fan of the penny dreadfuls. I cheerfully returned the greeting without thought, but Salmond just glowered.

'The rod has evidently been spared with that one,' he said, with a fearsome, Palmerstonian expression on his face, like a bulldog chewing a wasp. 'I would rather face typhoons and tidal waves, Mr. Vincent, or sunken reefs and sea monsters,' said he, 'than exchange hollow pleasantries with an army officer's wife or her offspring, hectoring me with silly requests for tours of the ship, and asking endless, ignorant, and impertinent questions.' He paused then, and we both smiled, for we each knew that I had been doing precisely that ever since I had come aboard. 'Don't take that wrong, my friend,' he said, 'I am always delighted to talk to the press.'

I reassured him that nothing untoward had been inferred at my end, and he removed himself, with an easier heart no doubt, in the direction of his cabin, with the intention, he said, of taking a cigar and consulting his charts. If he remained in the open, after all, one of the women might have the temerity to engage him in conversation. 'Mark my words, Mr. Vincent,' he said over his shoulder, this is going to be a long voyage.'

With the likes of you at the helm, I thought, that may well be the case.

Brodie, the Master of the ship, managed to head him off while still in earshot. 'Report, Mr. Brodie,' said the Captain, suddenly all business.

'We're ahead of schedule, sir,' said Brodie, another older man who had, like his commander, also seen action. Unlike his superior, I received the distinct impression that Mr. Brodie was perfectly content to serve on a troop carrier rather than a warship. 'Will we be swinging the ship, sir?' he said.

I confess that upon hearing this term I eavesdropped as nonchalantly as was possible. I was vaguely interested in compass calibration, for the effect that iron hulls had upon the instrument was the primary complaint from the oak lobby regarding safe navigation. To write about this ship I needed to understand such things. There was a deviation, apparently, but it was a standard one and could therefore be determined and compensated by placing the vessel on various headings and comparing compass readings with corresponding but previously determined magnetic directions. This practice was more usually known as 'swinging.'

'I am perfectly satisfied with the correctness of the compass, Mr. Brodie,' said Salmond. 'Now carry on.' Brodie excused himself and returned to his duties, while Salmond made purposefully for the greatly desired privacy of his cabin, like a shot off a shovel.

'He can move when he wants to,' said Lakeman, joining me at the rail.

He offered me one of his weird French cigarettes, which are over and done with in less than half a dozen drags but which leave you immediately wanting another. We smoked in silence for a while, each privately assimilating the alteration in social circumstances now inflicted upon us, and trying not to be too obvious about our mutual observation of the ladies.

Officer's wives have to keep up appearances, and it had to be said that there were some handsome women gliding along the deck in their fashionable crinolettes. I confess that I used to find the bodice and the bustle about broad hips and a solid waist extremely alluring, but I have learned from experience that what lies beneath is generally far less attractive, and thus treat any social interaction with extreme caution. As my old partner in crime Reynolds liked to joke, there were only two types of women in my life, anyway: my wife and everyone else. To all the other women of the world I attempted to be chivalrous at all times, yet guarded and defensive, like a medieval knight facing a queen or a dragon. Although in my case, I thought, as I regarded these bourgeois women circling below, a more honest analogy might be that of an exorcist facing a legion of devils and uppity revenants that continued to torment him but which one of more faith would have defeated years since. By the look of Captain Lakeman, conversely,

I fancied I might have spied a different kind of chink in his armour.

I asked him if he was married.

'Heaven forfend!' said he, 'Do I look as if I'm married?'

I had to admit that he did not. He looked neither worn down or cared for, trapped, content, resentful or guilty. Neither did his features bear the pride or worry of a father.

As his occupation suggested, I replied, he seemed to me a free agent.

'Exactly so,' said he, 'I take great pleasure in the society of women, but on my own terms, which do not involve marriage, at least not to me.' He left that final clause hanging in the air for a moment before he continued. 'Can you think of anything,' he said, 'quite frankly more inhumane than subjecting someone you love to the life of a soldier?'

I could, in point of fact, though I did not answer. I had subjected someone I loved to the life of a writer, which was arguably worse.

That evening the wardroom took on the air of the main restaurant at Mivart's of Mayfair, which seemed to suit some of our party more than others. Rolt and Bond were in their element, and conversed with great enthusiasm upon Society matters with the elegant women whose husbands were of such a senior rank that the Captain had no choice but to invite them to dine at his table. It was nevertheless notable that Salmond, Wright, and Seton, the latter closely followed by Russell, all excused themselves swiftly after dinner in order to attend to pressing matters concerning our imminent departure. The slightly more worldly subalterns Lucas and Giderot were actively attempting to flirt with a brace of quite glamorous older women, the comely brunette Mrs. Spruce and the statuesque redhead Mrs. Montgomery, but both men were being hopelessly outclassed by Lakeman, against whose French blood and genuine war stories they stood no chance.

Lieutenant Fairtlough was again significant by his absence, being once more down with the seasickness. The other infantryman, Granger, had also elected to keep himself to himself, having received what we used to call in the Flash tongue a chancery suit upon the nob, courtesy of the soft end of Private Barker's rifle, and his lower jaw had swollen to the shape and proportions of an oriental chamber pot. His subordinate in the ill-fated landing party, Ensign Metford, was, on the other hand, in attendance, and paying the most shy but intimate attention to a pale young Irish beauty who looked considerably out of her depth in the present company. This was the newly wedded Mrs. Metford, although when I first set eyes on her I had assumed the poor dear to be a servant. She was a Galway girl, and the two had been married the week before after a mutual *coup de foudre.* It was all very romantic, but she would be the death of her husband's fledgling career. It was plain to me that she was Catholic. I wondered if he knew he was doomed, or at that moment even cared.

The Granger business had been carried off with a certain amount of grace on all sides, although I suspected that his prospects for military advancement might now be as dick in the green and generally dingable as the career of Ensign Metford, unless there was a world war coming. Lakeman had formally and publically apologised for the conduct of Private Barker, who had escaped a flogging only because of the conditions of the exercise, which had been simulated combat. Barker had argued that it was a perfectly sound military tactic to 'take out the enemy chief,' as he put it, and even Seton had been forced to partially concede the point. His late tackle had nonetheless cost Barker his pay for the duration of the voyage, as well as extra duties and forfeiture of his share of the prize money. As he considered himself the victor of the skirmish he was not best pleased, but he did, upon Lakeman's order, mutter an apology to Granger and Seton that was begrudgingly accepted. Judging from the murderous look in his eye ever since, I think Private Barker would have taken to the lash with more pleasure. As he was not bound by oath like a soldier of the Crown, it was a mystery to me why he did not simply desert, for I was sure a man of his obvious talents could have easily found a way off the ship.

Lakeman still relieved the officers of the fifty guineas, but in return he had then given more ground by suggesting that the battle had been a close run thing, and that the outcome would have no doubt been very different had he not known the landing party was coming. This was all pure balloon juice, but still a magnanimous gesture for all that, and a needful one. Lakemen knew as well as any there present that for the chain of command to continue to function on board Granger had to save some face. We had therefore constructed a narrative in which neither the drilling competition nor the subsequent scrap had been quite so one-sided.

My contribution to this necessary fiction had required a certain compromise of my professional ethics, although I had long since learned that eating dry bread on one's principles was not so much noble as reckless and suicidal, both traits, admittedly, often associated with heroism, but no way to feed one's family. I had started my career as a journalist armed with a simple code taught to me by that wise old Irish quill driver, Egan, which ran: *Report what you see, be sure of your facts, never miss a deadline, and write it well.*

'For once you've gone to press,' he would say, 'you're going to have to live with it.'

It had been by my communication of this notionally straightforward doctrine to the pencil pushers of Pall Mall that the War Office had let me anywhere near Her Majesty's Armed Forces in the first place. Given my well known political affiliations, this acquiescence was still something of a surprise, although I suspect that it was not my stated commitment to verisimilitude, efficiency and quality that carried the application so much as my hastily scrawled endorsement from Dickens. I had not given him a choice on this matter. He owed me.

My articles were to be carried with military dispatches, my first series going from Queenstown before we set sail. These covered the details of the ship, a brief biographical sketch of senior personnel, and an account of the Spike Island debacle. There was no point trying to censor the latter subject. It was already a topic of discussion and great amusement in every bar in which soldiers drank all across the province of Munster. The story, however, that is the events as they actually happened that day, could be arranged by the expedient of simple plotting into any number of different yet equally valid accounts. It was a matter of basic *narratologie*, I had explained to Seton. Stories are stories at the end of the day, whether literary fiction, journalism, science, religion, or the so-called historical record; but once the official version is in print and circulated in a respected published source it becomes, to all intents and purposes, the 'truth,' the history of the thing. It was not in my interests to humiliate the British Army. I desperately needed this job, and to do it I needed the co-operation of Seton and his staff. I had therefore written what everyone wanted, my Editor, Seton, Granger, and no doubt Wellington, the Prime Minister and Queen bloody Victoria herself.

My account of the exercises, as they were presented, was, I confess, somewhat economical with the *actualité.* As a compromise with my own standards, for the sake of professional and physical survival, I had indeed reported what I saw, just not all of it. But what else could I do? In my experience people do not want the truth. It is invariably either so absurd that they would not give it credence, or utterly dreadful, or both; and those that attempt to tell it are discredited or otherwise silenced through a variety of means, ranging from black balls and slander to being publically flayed, burned or crucified. I was too old for martyrdom (again), and the dustbin men would never take me. I had thus decided that in the present circumstances, at least, the emperor's new clothes looked perfectly all right to me.

Having already written on the new recruits and Lakeman's private soldiers, I kept the rivalry between them in my narrative, but made it temperate and sportsmanlike, while the bet became a gentleman's wager where no money changed hands. I described the drill in terms of pageantry and military precision, making much of the gloomy gothic splendour of the setting, but playing it up as a fort and down as a prison. No bayonets were dropped, and I essentially presented the outcome as a draw. As Lakeman was going to win the mock battle whatever, this concession returned some honour to the professionals. The toast was presented in humorous colours, in the manner of a scene from *Life in London* or *The Pickwick Papers*, and I painted such a fine portrait of Mr. Grace that I can only hope that should I ever join the increasing ranks of radical journalists under his care that he will look upon me kindly.

I was pretty honest about the actual engagement at the graveyard, only Lakeman's sentries overwhelmed Granger's probes in a more chivalrous way in my version, the redcoats were bested but not completely routed, and the incident with Barker was entirely omitted. Lakeman's men were presented as no better than Granger's, just slightly more seasoned, while also having the natural advantage of a defending force. I concluded that the entire affair had been an excellent training event, morale booster, and bonding experience for the floating population of the ship. I called the piece 'The Graveyard Rangers.'

When it was done, I shared the fruits of my labours with Lakeman. 'You have found the perfect name for the company,' he declared, hooting with delight.

I inwardly prayed that when Reynolds and Grace saw this obviously gross and cynical misrepresentation in the *Chronicle* they would read between the lines and realise that I was compelled by circumstances to thus coat with sugar. I might once have been able to claim that I was working undercover, subverting from within and all that, but that wouldn't wash these days. I had well and truly sold out.

Lakeman's man, Private McIntyre, delivered my dispatches to Seton, and I returned to my cabin with the intention of drinking myself to sleep. A drowsy ocean of ink black water washed up to meet me. I closed my eyes, fell in and was gone.

CHAPTER XXII

I SEARCHED FOR MY family for months, but found not a trace. I had Grove hire agents to investigate; that, too, was all to no good purpose. Even in those days it was estimated that there were already almost two million people living in London, and anyone not wishing to be found could effortlessly disappear into the labyrinth, as Freddie had done, evidently dragging my family along with him into the shadows.

When I returned my attention to the literary life, I discovered that I was no longer welcome at most Society functions.

'The thing of it is, Jack,' Ainsworth tried to explain, 'is that it's very bad form to get all possessive about another chap's wife like that.'

He had taken me aside for a heart to heart at one of his Kensal Lodge parties, where I knew I would always be welcome. He was not really helping though, but I was safe in his home as the d'Orsay set had tired of him quite quickly as well, especially after *Crichton* fell stillborn from the presses.

Cruikshank was not helping either. 'The trouble with you common people,' he was saying, 'is that you don't know how to have an affair.'

'Pray do enlighten me,' I said.

'First off, you have to punch your weight,' he said, helping himself to the claret and pouring about half the bottle into a huge glass. 'Your Lady Abbess, see,' he continued, 'she's a definite heavyweight, if you take my meaning.'

'That's true enough,' said Ainsworth, 'she has tremendous wealth and status.'

'Exactly,' said Cruikshank, warming to his subject, 'and I mean no offence by it, my dear fellow, but you're at best a middleweight.'

'A welterweight,' agreed Ainsworth.

'If not a featherweight,' said Cruikshank, exploding with laughter.

'Enough! You sons of bachelors!' I cried, though he was right, damn him.

'You should find a pretty shop girl, Jack,' Cruikshank advised. 'Set her up in a nice crib, give her an allowance, and she'll let you do whatever you want to her, I guarantee it.'

Well, you should know, I thought, keeping my own counsel.

'I fear our Jack's the last Romantic,' said Ainsworth affectionately, 'he's looking for true love, not an easy tumble.'

'Same thing,' said Cruikshank, belching like a bag of nails. 'More tea, Vicar!' he exclaimed, helping himself to another reservoir of claret. 'Jack's trouble,' he continued, 'is that women make him stupid.'

He had insinuated himself into our conversation because he wanted to complain about Dickens without Forster or Thackeray hearing. They were on the veranda arguing about the novels of Henry Fielding. I would not have given this pair the run of my privy, let alone my house, but Dickens adored them, and as Ainsworth loved Dickens like a brother he accepted the entourage.

Thackeray was a clever man but he did not care for most things, and appeared to exist in a permanent state of explosive frustration. This was largely engendered by his lack of any real commercial success, 'While the idiots and the charlatans prospered,' as he would have it, usually adding, 'present company excepted, of course.'

Forster, the Unitarian Geordie, had attached himself to Dickens like a barnacle. Ainsworth may have pardoned him, but I had neither forgive nor forgot the mauling he had given us both in the *Examiner*. Personally, I would not have cut him down if I found him hanging.

Cruikshank's grievance concerned the collected 'Sketches by Boz' that were presently coming together. He felt himself to be the senior partner in the venture, and was doing Dickens and Macrone a huge favour by attaching his name to it, but Dickens kept finding fault with his drawings or rejecting them all together. The result was that the illustrations that were agreed upon were stunning, and Cruikshank knew that, but he was loath to admit that it was the young writer who was setting the standard.

Dickens was not in attendance, and was presumed to be working.

'You heard about Bob Seymour?' he said.

'Heard what?' I said, although I did not really care. Seymour was working with Dickens on the Nimrod Club series for Chapman & Hall. Dickens was doing the letterpress around Seymour's comic illustrations. 'Are they bickering an' all?'

'Blew his head off with a fowling piece, day before yesterday,' said Cruikshank. He paused for dramatic effect, and then added, 'Dickens was the last person to see him alive, they say.'

'Good God,' said Ainsworth, 'his poor wife.'

'She blames Dickens, naturally,' said Cruikshank.

'That's not on,' said Ainsworth. 'He'll need another artist,' he added.

'Phiz says he's up for it,' said Cruikshank. 'He'll have to start again though, the delay will cost him.'

'How very unfortunate,' said Ainsworth, shaking his head sadly, 'I do feel for Charles.'

'Indeed,' I agreed flatly, 'poor Charles.'

Seymour had always been too sensitive for his own good, and too many years in our game had made him bitter and fatalistic. His first publishers had gone under, owing him a lot of money, and Gilbert à Beckett had recently given him the push from *Figaro in London*. If Dickens was cutting up rough as well (and he and à Beckett were close), then my guess was that Bob could not be bothered with going through it all again.[16]

If I knew one thing that Bob Seymour seemingly had not, it was that when your entire world is collapsing around you it is best to focus on what you do well. I owed Colburn a third novel, so I got on with that.

I had abandoned the story about identify theft, as for the life of me I could not think of an ending. What came out of me instead was *The Death Hunter*, at once a change of direction and a return to source. Dickens described it as a 'Manichean novel,' which I suppose it is, although there is little doubt in the text which side is winning in my dualistic cosmology. The title comes from the old Flash term for an undertaker. It is also the common name given to freelance journalists who, as I once had, cover horrible murders, and my protagonist, referred to throughout only by his journalistic pseudonym, 'J,' is one of that profession. He is a hard-drinking, godless and cynical man who haunts the rookeries and thieves' kitchens of contemporary London in search of a murder a day, his story thereby flying in the face of the conventional gothic narrative, my own included, which were in those days always set abroad and in the distant past, which was supposedly more barbaric. Also in common with his creator, 'J' was raised in a debtor's prison, and I made much use of my own childhood memories in forming his hard, ruthless and embittered persona. (Even Bill and Nancy put in an appearance, although under different names.) I equally plundered my days in Grub Street, retelling many of the terrible deaths I had reported in order to depict an urban nightmare at the heart of the empire, in which the most obscene luxury is often only separated from the most appalling misery by a couple of streets. I portrayed the denizens of this fallen city as selfish, brutish and ignorant, regardless of gender and social class. Except for the victims of poverty and crime, no one was innocent.

The main plot concerns 'J''s relationship with Millicent, or 'Millie,' an older, sensual and financially independent widow he meets while investigating a death at St. Katharine Docks. Millie makes a living as an agent placing poor children in the colonies as servants, labourers and apprentices. The couple are fiercely attracted to each other physically, and embark upon a passionate affair. Whether or not they love each other is unclear, but as Millie is a woman of means and property, as well as an energetic lover, 'J' believes that his ship has come in and proposes. He moves into Millie's rambling house in Tower Hamlets following a modest wedding, after which a series of mysterious and troubling occurrences lead 'J' to suspect that his new bride might not be quite what she seems.

The punch line is that 'J''s wife has been killing her charges, and then passing forged letters to the families to maintain the illusion that their children not only live but prosper in India, Africa, and Australia. Having grown up an East End beggar, and later prostitute, Millie has learned to waste nothing. In addition to her fee and the expenses for sea voyages that the children never take, she is also turning an extra profit by eating them, and selling what she does not consume herself to a local butcher. 'J' discovers the truth when he breaks into a mysterious locked room in the cellar. There he finds a young girl on the floor who has been rendered immobile by having her spinal cord expertly severed at the neck, and silenced by having her tongue cut out. The girl is being kept alive so that the meat stays fresh, and is missing both legs, which have been carefully tied-off to prevent her bleeding out. 'J' is violently sick as he realises that his wife must have been feeding him the flesh of living children. He attempts to rescue the suffering child, but misinterprets her agitated, animal grunts as signs of gratitude rather than a warning and is struck from behind and rendered insensible. The novel ends when 'J' awakens in the cellar next to the now dead girl, unable to move or speak, as his wife calmly amputates his leg. As she goes about her work she tells him of her life and crimes with a ghoulish pride. Before leaving him in the dark, she also removes his manhood, explaining that she had always liked this part, but, as was the case with her previous five husbands, the pity was that he had been attached to it.

The Death Hunter is bleak, disturbing and unpleasant throughout, which is exactly as I intended it to be. The novel's principal killer remains at large at the conclusion of the narrative, with no suggestion that she is being investigated or that she or her accomplice will stop. No one is saved, there is neither message nor moral, and the hero's journey means nothing.

Cruikshank was then working on two serials for *Bentley's Miscellany*, which Dickens was now editing, so my illustrations were drawn and engraved by George Stiff, whose dark, menacing and grotesque style perfectly complemented the overall tone of my narrative. Although my story may sound quite fanciful, it was actually based around what we nowadays call 'baby farming,' which I had witnessed many times as a death hunter myself. The unwanted children of the poor were placed in the care of (mostly) women who contracted with the parish at four bob a head, and then kept them in appalling and frequently fatal conditions in order to maximise profits. A brisk turnover was most desirable, meaning that these kids were quite literally worth more dead than alive.

When I showed Dickens the completed manuscript he pronounced it brilliant but impossible to market.

The latter opinion was shared by Colburn, but not the former. 'Where are the jokes and the bloody pirates?' he demanded, furious.

'T'aint none,' said I, 'but there's romance.'

'There's pornography!' he snapped back. 'The honeymoon scenes are scandalous.'

'But true to life, as is the rest of the book.'

'True to life be damned,' said he, 'I can't sell true to life.'

'Try.'

'There's no hero,' he pleaded.

'There's the journalist.'

'He's a bastardly gullion who gets what he deserves,' said Colburn. 'How is a drunk, a lecher, a hack, and an atheist to be presented to the public as a hero? He marries a tart who castrates and eats him for God's sake.'

'Captain Kidd was hanged, as was Dick Turpin,' I countered.

'But they died *heroically*,' he said, emphasising the last word to ensure that his argument was got across.

'Have you ever been to a hanging?'

'That's not the point,' he said, looking away.

'That's exactly the point,' I said, 'now take it or leave it for I'll not write you another.'

I had him there, for he had paid for this manuscript, a pittance given how successful I had become, but good money as far as he was concerned, and our contract had not specified a subject. Had he suppressed the book I would have been buggered. Although I had done all the work it belonged to him and not me. I had gambled upon his business acumen (he was as tight as a gnat's chuff), and I was right to do so. He eventually published the novel, and puffed it as a 'Shocking New Gothic Romance.'

'Shocking' was right. Ainsworth, who was then writing his what he called his 'Hogarthian serial,' *Jack Sheppard*, for *Bentley's*, told me that he found the experience of reading *The Death Hunter* extremely distressing. 'When I finished the damn thing,' he said, 'I felt quite dirty.'

'But what did you think of it, Will?' I had asked.

'It'll be tricky to market.'

After *Crichton*, Ainsworth had sensibly returned to the Newgate Calendars for inspiration, and had fictionalised the exploits of the dashing prig John 'Jack' Sheppard, who was briefly famous in the days of Defoe for several daring prison escapes before his luck ran out and he went up the ladder to bed. You all know *Oliver Twist*, but *Jack Sheppard* is not so well remembered nowadays. The basic plot and premise closely followed Hogarth's *Industry and Idleness*, being the story of two apprentices, one good, one bad, but with just enough of *The Beggar's Opera* thrown in to make it clear that it was the 'Idle 'Prentice' that was Ainsworth's favourite, not the industrious one. The novel covers the adolescent Jack's fall from grace and into the clutches of the evil thief-taker and criminal mastermind Jonathan Wild (and the beds of Edgeworth Bess and Poll Maggot), his career as a housebreaker, his escape from the condemned hold at Newgate, and his eventual execution at the ripe old age of twenty-two. Ainsworth gives it all a redemptive veneer, having Jack turn against Wild in support of the titular hero (Thames Darrell), but these episodes are much less fun to read.

Jack Sheppard had begun its serial run in *Bentley's Miscellany* in January 1839, and it overlapped with Dickens' latest, *Oliver Twist*, until the spring. Because of a certain amount of prevarication on the part of Colburn with regard to *The Death Hunter*, all three novels appeared at roughly the same time, even though mine had been written first, and the 'three most popular writers in England' all fought it out in the marketplace.

We all sold well, albeit to very different audiences, but those who remember that year will have to admit that it was *Jack Sheppard* that carried the day, and for a while at least Dickens' star paled. Bentley reckoned he was shifting three thousand copies a week, and Ainsworth was rewarded by the sincerest form of flattery from the penny-a-liners, who rushed out plagiarised versions faster than the original Jack Sheppard could pick a lock. Ainsworth thought this tremendous sport, and he loved the inevitable theatrical adaptations, though he never saw a farthing in royalties.

When the same thing happened to Dickens he did not see the funny side, and flew into a rage in which he pronounced himself robbed every time a third party was reckless enough to mention the various stage versions of *Oliver Twist*.[17] *The Death Hunter*, on the other hand, appeared to be inviolate, probably because nobody, not even an old crook like Moncrieff at the Surrey, would dare put it on, although there were soon several theatrical revivals of my piratical romances doing the rounds on the back of my new book.

It was clear from the reviews that Dickens had attracted the respectable middle class audience, while, as that old pirate Edward Lloyd told me, I was picking up his readers, the penny dreadful crowd, the literate costermongers and other working folk. Groups of them would club together to buy my book, and then pay one of their educated brethren to read it out aloud to them in the factory or the pub. Lloyd also reckoned that *The Death Hunter* was unusually popular with the ladies. Colburn's relief was palpable, but he did not offer me another contract, not that I would have accepted one anyway. I had a feeling that, like Dickens, who seemed to write his own ticket with his publishers nowadays, I could do better next time. I fancied it might be time to go after an editorship myself. I knew that Dickens was privately keen to get out of his contract with *Bentley's Miscellany*, and was considering putting myself forward. Ainsworth, meanwhile, was thrashing the pair of us, at least in terms of sales, by attracting readers from both classes.

That I was now reaching my own class was a source of great pride. There were more of 'em than there were middle and upper class fools in the country as well, so business was booming, even if there was only one book between half a dozen or so readers. I was on a fixed fee rather than a royalty, anyway, so it made no difference to me. After such an *annus horribilis*, it was nice to be shifting so much copy again.

As the Wheel of History teaches us, however, such periods of satisfaction and success are inevitably brief. The downturn began quietly and slowly. A few months after *The Death Hunter* was launched, the first part of a mysterious serial called *Catherine* appeared in *Fraser's*, credited to the pen of 'Ikey Solomons Esq. Jr.' It was based on the life of the eighteenth century murderess Catherine Hayes, and was lifted from the original Newgate Calendar, *The Malefactor's Bloody Register*. As I had met the notorious fence Ikey Solomon Esq. Snr., I doubted that any kin of his were writing for the literary journals. Instead it had Thackeray's paw prints all over it.

I knew the original story. Well, I would, wouldn't I? Catherine Hayes had talked her lover and her son into murdering her husband with an axe. They dismembered the body and dumped it in a pond in Marylebone Fields, with the exception of the head, which they threw in the Thames in the hope of making identification impossible. The head turned up though, as heads often do, and some bright spark in the local Watch decided to display it in the hope someone might recognise it, first on a pole in a churchyard, and later preserved in a glass of spirits. Mrs. Hayes claimed her husband was in Portugal, but his friends were suspicious. Eventually the killers confessed and the trio were executed at Tyburn a couple of years after Jack Sheppard. The men were hanged in chains and Catherine was burnt at the stake, as a wife killing her husband was petty treason under law. The flames caught so quickly that the executioner was not able to strangle the condemned as was customary, and the unfortunate woman was roasted alive. I have heard it takes several minutes for the nerves of the skin to be destroyed by fire, before which you feel everything.

Catherine was indeed the work of Thackeray. His intention was to savagely shame and satirise the whole of the so-called 'Newgate School' of writers and their audience, in which he included Lytton, Ainsworth, Dickens, and myself. 'The public will hear of nothing but rogues,' he lamented in print, continuing, 'The only way in which poor authors can act honestly by the public and themselves is to paint such thieves as they are: not dandy, poetical, rosewater thieves, but real downright scoundrels. They don't grow up in the Marshalsea quoting Byron, like that unbelievable author and carnal maniac "Jay," or live like gentlemen like Kidd, Turpin or Jolly Jack Sheppard. Neither do they prate eternally about the Rights of Man like Paul Clifford, or die white-washed saints like poor "Biss Dadsy" in *Oliver Twist*. Men of genius have no business making these characters interesting or agreeable, and should stop feeding your morbid fancies—or indulging their own—with such monstrous food.'

When the serial ended, there was also a companion article in the same issue devoted to *Jack Sheppard* and *The Death Hunter* that suggested that the novels could turn impressionable boys, and, worse, girls to a life of crime. Dickens and Lytton escaped this accusation, but were instead attacked for sentimentalising crime.

Generally speaking, nobody got the joke. *Catherine* was not well received, being neither fish nor fowl. This just made Thackeray even angrier with everyone, but mostly at what he saw as his own failure to succeed as a novelist, while what he believed to be simple-minded books for simple-minded people made their authors both rich and famous, present company, it appeared, no longer excepted. I, in turn, tried not to mention my own continued good fortune in his presence, and could go as long as a minute without doing so.

The dinner parties at Ainsworth's house became somewhat strained after this, but still we all tried to be pals, and although the half-cocked *Catherine* failed to find popular favour either as a satire or a romance, I remember it still, for it was to be the first shot of a very long war of words indeed.

'Biss Dadsy' had caused a grumble in my gizzard as well, but not for the same reason as Thackeray. At least I had had the tact to change the names in my book. Dickens had just sucked the king and queen of the snuggery into his text and then made out they were a complete invention, whereas only the dog was actually a fiction. That she ultimately became such a literary icon would have tickled Nanse, as would Dickens' portrayal of her as the fallen woman redeemed. Were her spirit to manifest at one of the author's famous readings, she would have called this a fine piece of cheese screaming.

She would not have thought much of Cruikshank's illustrations either. Even though he had known her during the Regency he drew a fairly large lass, and Nancy was always proud of her figure. 'I'm damned if I can remember what the woman looked like,' he told me, when I asked him why. (His depictions of Bill Sikes, however, are the dead spit of the bastard.) The rendition of Flashy Nance in Egan's *Life in London* is much more true to life, if you can find a copy these days.

The next critical salvo was harder to ignore. This one was launched from the pages of the *Athenaeum,* which ran a long piece on the declining moral standards of the nation. Ainsworth brought it over one morning, and I read it while he paced about my kitchen. The author was unidentified, but we suspected it was the editor, Wentworth Dilke.[18]

'The problem in the present age,' I read, 'is that writers take their tone from the readers, instead of giving it; and thus pains are taken to write down to the mediocrity of the purchasing multitude.'

'Does he mean us, do you think?' I asked my friend.

Ainsworth looked positively seasick. 'Keep reading,' he said.

'If we consider Mr. Ainsworth and Mr. Vincent in the usual light of mere caterers for the public appetite, and as devoting their talents to a popular work either at their own or their publisher's suggestion,' wrote the anonymous dandy prat, 'then we must freely admit their books to be on a level with the usual specimens of the class, and at least as good as the occasion required. It is not their fault that they have fallen upon evil days, and that, like other tradesmen, they must subordinate their own tastes to those of their customers.'

'Shit,' I said.

'That's exactly what I said. Keep reading, I'm afraid it gets worse.'

'These books then,' I read aloud, 'are simply bad books got up for a bad public; and should an ambassador from some far distant country arrive on our shores for the purpose of overreaching us in a convention, we know not where he could find a better clue to the infirmities of the national character than in the columns of our book advertisements.' He didn't like the pictures either. 'In these hideous representations,' he continued, 'are embodied all the inherent coarseness and vulgarity of the subject, and all the unnatural excitement which the public requires to awaken sensation.'

'The Georges will not be best pleased,' said Ainsworth, 'although I suppose Stiff's used to this sort of thing.' He was alluding to the fact that my artist mostly drew for the penny magazines. I let this go for I am sure he meant nothing by it.

'Does he mention Dickens?' I asked, in all honestly hopefully, for the sinking ship is not quite so terrible if one is among friends.

He did indeed mention Dickens, but only as a shining contrast to peddlers of filth and perversion such as myself. 'In thus introducing Mr. Dickens's name,' I read, 'we are far from classing him with his imitators, or ranging his works with the Death Hunters and the Jack Sheppards, —in external appearance so similar. If Boz has depicted scenes of hardened vice, and displayed the peculiar phases of degradation which poverty impresses on the human character, he is guided in his career by a high moral object; for, instead of sullying the mind of an intelligent reader, he leaves him wiser and better for the perusal of his tale.'

'High moral object my arse,' said I.

The problem, apparently, lie not with Dickens (although Ainsworth and I were as guilty as sin), but with his readers, who were too thick to appreciate the difference between our 'criminal romances' and the sermons of the great and powerful Boz.

'Without a familiarity with the noble and the beautiful,' the article concluded, 'the irony is lost, the spirit is overlooked, and *The Beggar's Opera* becomes a mere "Tom and Jerry."'

'The sanctimonious hog's pizzle,' I said, screwing up the paper and throwing it into the fire. Ainsworth looked aggrieved; it was his copy, after all. 'They'll be wrapping fish in it next week,' I assured him.

He appeared far from convinced. 'What should we do, Jack?'

'Fancy a drink?'

A show of strength was, I felt, required. So, protesting all the way, I managed to get Ainsworth into the Athenaeum Club for an apéritif. Upon our arrival, brother members that we had always called friends turned their backs and muttered, 'Shame.' We held our nerve and enjoyed a very good breakfast, until an embarrassed looking waiter came over and discretely handed us both black balls.

Ainsworth took it like a proper gentleman. He rose, a little stiffly perhaps, and then bade the onlookers, 'Good Morning,' before making his exit with a quiet dignity.

'And may rabid dogs copulate upon your mothers' graves,' I added, following my friend out onto the Mall.

Sensing blood in the water, Forster struck a couple of days later in the *Examiner.* My novel, he wrote, was 'in every sense of the word bad,' and 'the very worst specimen of rank garbage thus stewed up in the sewers of the popular press,' while *Jack Sheppard* had been 'recommended to circulation by disreputable means,' by which he meant the stage versions for the working folk. Ainsworth, he argued, in the tone of a disappointed headmaster, was capable of far better things. It was notable that he did not say the same of me. What lay behind all this, I reckoned, was that Ainsworth and I were out-selling his beloved Dickens.

Ainsworth remained damned decent about the whole thing. 'Forster's article has been perfectly innocuous, and has done no harm whatever,' he reassured guests still prepared to dine with him at the Lodge that weekend. 'In fact,' he continued, throwing me a Grimaldian wink, 'both the Jacks are carrying everything before them.' That was true. We were getting more press between us than the Bedchamber Crisis.[19]

'And what, pray, of the affair at the Athenaeum, Jack?' said Cruikshank, turning his formidable attention to me, his face a mask of severity. 'Did you really tell Wellington, twice Prime Minister, and Commander-in-Chief of the British Army—'

'The Iron Duke,' chimed in Ainsworth.

'That,' Cruikshank continued, 'his mother was known carnally by dogs in Hell?' By end of the question he was positively quaking with merriment.

'Not exactly,' I stammered.

'He did, he did!' Ainsworth was saying, his eyes tormented by tears of mirth.

Sam Blanchard was quick to join in. 'I heard it was Lord Haddo,' he said, 'and that your words were to the effect that he fornicated with his mother on a regular basis.'

'Wasn't it Palmerstone?' said Dick Barham, 'something about his wife?'

'Oh Christ,' I said, 'was he there?'[20]

The whole table was now howling with laughter. 'I'd say that's your knighthood out the window, Jack,' said Thackeray, almost choking on the port.

He was the only one of the so-called 'Anti-Newgate' crowd who still maintained a presence in our circle. Dickens, although thus far keeping his opinions to himself, was giving us a wide berth. Forster was similarly significant by his absence, perhaps on account of a rumour currently circulating, that I had not bothered to contradict, that I had vowed to shoot him on sight. But Thackeray's way was more insidious. He would play your friend, eat at your table, and then stab you in the back while you slept with another damning article in the name of Mr. Punch or whomever.

I thought it best to brazen things out, and to make the most of my new reputation as a bit of a wild one. 'If you can't sell it,' said I, of the Most Noble Order of the Garter, 'drink it, smoke it, or shag it then it's of no damn use to me.'

'Well said, old boy,' said Thackeray, thumping me on the back to prove to those there assembled that he was my one true friend.

His touch made me squirm. And although I took it all in good humour and had another drink, I inwardly realised I was doomed. I was making some very powerful enemies.

CHAPTER XXIII

I WAS REASONABLY twisted on the laudanum I had packed in case of seasickness, washed down with gin and water, when a relentless hammering on the door of my cabin recalled me from the depths. It was McIntyre, bearing an enamel mug of steaming black coffee and a request from Captain Lakeman to join him for a conference in Major Seton's private quarters in fifteen minutes. I accepted the coffee with bleary-eyed thanks. Lakeman had obviously got the measure of me already, and it was disconcerting to accept that I was so transparent: the tortured and self-destructive artist, the doomed romantic. It had been a stylish affectation in my youth, but now, like Coleridge and De Quincey, I was just another pathetic inebriate.

'Any idea what's in the wind?' I said.

'I really couldn't say, sir,' said he, 'but if I were to guess I would suggest that your recent dispatch concerning the rangers has either found favour with the Major, or caused him great offence.'

'That's what I was thinking.'

Both options were equally credible, but I was pleasantly numb enough just then to be temporarily free of my natural state of near-crippling anxiety, so cared not particularly one way or the other. I set about making myself as presentable as possible, cooling the coffee with a splash of the blue ruin.

Seton's cabin was at the stern end of the upper deck. I knocked politely and entered with exaggerated sobriety. It was a relatively roomy cabin, arranged as an office, with a desk and blotter, an irregular selection of chairs and even a well-stocked bookcase; a curtain behind the desk divided the space and partially concealed a crude bunk much like my own. Lakeman was already there, conversing in friendly terms with Seton and Wright, while Ensign Russell hovered silently in the background. All three senior officers were standing and drinking tea, although the sun was by then well past the yard arm. Seton greeted me formally but pleasantly and offered me a brew. I would have preferred strong drink or a cigar, but any sort of stage prop suited me in such challenging social situations so tea it was. Judging by the general air of conviviality I was not there to receive a dressing down.

The symposium now assembled, Seton invited us to sit and took his place behind the desk. 'I'll just fill Mr. Vincent in, if I may,' he said. Wright and Lakeman nodded their assent and Seton addressed himself to me while Russell minuted. 'I am as Saul on the road to Damascus, Mr. Vincent,' said he, 'if you take my meaning.'

'You have had a revelation,' I ventured.

'Indeed I have, Mr. Vincent,' he said, 'although not a pleasant one.'

'You mean a sort of dark epiphany,' I said.

'Quite,' said he, thoughtfully. 'Having recently witnessed the military acumen of the supposedly best of the young men now in my charge,' he continued, 'I am forced to confront the very plain fact that the majority of the soldiers on board are inexperienced, undertrained, and therefore woefully ill-prepared for the tasks and trials ahead.'

'In a word,' said I, 'they are all doomed.'

Seton did not immediately speak, but he nodded sadly. 'As I have been explaining to Captains Wright and Lakeman,' he finally said, 'I feel most strongly that these issues must be addressed, and quickly, and the only chance to do so is while at sea.'

I began to see where this conversation was leading. Seton was an intelligent man and a born administrator, and it was clear to him that this task was best served through the mutual co-operation of all the disparate contingents on board, regimental and otherwise. His grand vision, he soon explained, was that the entire voyage be turned into an elaborate training course, comprising intensive drilling and gunnery instruction, but also offering a comprehensive series of improving lectures. To achieve this marvel of organisation, he needed to make the best use of all the resources at his disposal, and these included Lakeman and myself. He was too polite to say it, but he had obviously also revised his opinions regarding our general and mutual worth, given that we had both acquitted ourselves decently over the Granger fiasco, and had thus proved ourselves to be gentlemen; or, as Lakeman had put it, 'He may be an idiot, but he's our idiot.'

Seton's suggestion was that the Graveyard Rangers, though he did not call them such, should be more fully assimilated and welcomed into the bosom of Her Majesty's Armed Forces, at least for the duration of the voyage, treated equally with all the other British Army squads on board, and subject to Queen's Regulations. There would therefore take full part in the training, while Lakeman and his staff would volunteer their expertise as instructors as, intriguingly, would I. While Lakeman taught skirmish tactics, Wright lectured on Africa (being the only officer on board to have served there), and each senior company officer acquainted his men with regimental history, I would be edifying the troops with lessons on English language and literature.

'You might also offer a few classes to the ladies on board,' said Seton, 'separately of course.'

'Of course,' I said.

'Perhaps including a little literary composition,' he continued, 'to ease the tedium of the voyage.'

'And keep 'em out of trouble,' added Wright.

Seton would naturally be the chancellor of our floating academy, also drilling, and teaching something he called the 'art of war.' He was also a natural linguist, and hoped to school the men in some of the South African dialects they would need to function in any useful way up country, which he had been diligently studying with Wright's help. It was an ambitious and remarkably progressive approach to military management, and Seton's commitment to the education of his men impressed me greatly. I therefore agreed to help in any way I could, also mindful of what a fine story this would make for the *Chronicle*.

'There's just one thing, Mr. Vincent,' said Seton, casually, as I was taking my leave. 'No Marx, Engels, or O'Connor if you please.'

I assured him that I would restrict my remarks to gentlemen of letters and he appeared quite reassured, although I was already constructing a lecture upon the 'Condition of England' novel in my mind that might have made him quite nervous.[21]

'Well that's a turn up for the bloody books,' said Lakeman, when we were safely out of earshot.

I returned to my berth inwardly planning lectures on the philosophy of literary form, and a variety of subjects and authors that I felt I could either discourse on from memory or to which I had access on the ship. Seton travelled with a small private library, and had offered to lend me the complete works of Shakespeare, while I always had my father's copy of *Lyrical Ballads* about me, although I pretty much had that off by heart anyway. I thus had Shakespeare and the early Romantics covered, both areas I knew I could extemporise around further, while my own role in the development of the contemporary English novel certainly gave me much to talk about, especially with regard to the popular authors of the day, whose work I knew as well as the men, and, occasionally, the women, themselves.

I must confess that I felt quite elated at the prospect. It had been a while since I had been accorded any such respect as a literary scholar, and my spirits were pitifully lifted. Were my dear wife present she would have pointed out that Seton had known exactly the right line to take with me, which was intellectual flattery, and that thus buttered I had essentially blundered into a lot of extra and unpaid work. But despite overwhelming experience to the contrary (which Grace would have also reminded me), I felt that naive sense of hopefulness returning to my shrivelled soul, as it always did when I was presented with a literary project; a feeling that suggested that this work, although voluntary and transitory, might actually lead somewhere, perhaps to some sort of academic appointment in the military that might finally give my family a few hundred a year. It is this type of idiot optimism that keeps men like me writing, grinding away every day at the wheel of fortune, and tricking ourselves and our loved ones into believing that a life devoted to literature is never wasted.

The Articles of War had now been read, and after our eventful sojourn in the precincts of Cork Harbour, it was finally time to get under weigh. While the military and the press had been playing silly buggers, Salmond and his crew had been ceaselessly toiling to prepare the ship for her voyage, taking on and stowing fresh water, meat, and coal. It was incredible to me to think that it was now only the end of the first week of the New Year. So much had already come to pass. There were now almost seven hundred souls on board, five hundred-odd of them military personnel, then about fifty civilians, with the balance comprising the ship's company. Lakeman said that the ship was now reminiscent of Waterloo Station on the May Day bank holiday. The cramped and crowded conditions put me more in mind of prison, but I kept that to myself and mumbled some apposite comparison with the crowds attending the Great Exhibition.

The colours were hoisted at eight bells on the Wednesday morning, and 'Hands to station for leaving harbour' was piped. The hands had, as ever, fallen in at five bells and had thus been cleaning for the last hour and a half. The ship was positively gleaming in the low winter sun, the decks swabbed and polished, and the copper and brass burnished like gold. The mooring parties fore and aft singled up, pushing the great capstans as if on a treadmill. I had managed to talk my way onto the Bridge beneath the poop awning, and was there when Brodie reported to Salmond that the ship was ready to proceed. The word was given, and with the pilot boat ahead of her the great ship edged outwards from the quay and gathered way, with Richards, the Master's Assistant, at the wheel. Ship and boat soon parted, upon which the company took up a rousing and spontaneous cheer. With the ship now under her own power we soon left the Lee and steamed into the Celtic Sea, thrusting, like destiny's tool, into the black Atlantic.

CHAPTER XXIV

I WAS FORCED to withdraw my candidacy for the editorship of *Bentley's Miscellany*. Ainsworth got the job instead. This was much less bitter medicine for me than it could have been, but by the end of the year the moral panic inaugurated by the *Examiner* had, like our characters, acquired a life of its own. Although this initially did sales more good than harm, our names were becoming alarmingly linked to the contemporary debate on the supposedly rising crime rate among the ever increasing urban population. We were also blamed for the popularity of unlicensed theatrical adaptations of our work, over which we had no control whatever. These cheap and cheerful melodramas were believed to be disseminating moral corruption to the masses, inciting the young men of the labouring classes to choose the left hand path rather than taking the Queen's shilling or embracing a life of backbreaking toil for a pittance in field or manufactory like an honest Christian.

It seemed to me that the causes of crime were considerably more complicated than the consumption of escapist romance, and might be perhaps connected with the appalling social deprivation that one saw everywhere; that obscene divide between wealth and poverty, with the one class motivated by the basic desire for survival, the other avarice.

Not so, said the bourgeois critics.

Forster once more took the lead in the *Examiner.* 'In the adaptations of Ainsworth and Vincent that are alike rife in the penny theatres that abound in the poor and populous districts of London,' he wrote, 'tales of thieves and murderers are more admired than any other species of representation. The pirate, the highwayman, and the assassin are portrayed in their natural colours, and give pleasant lessons in crime for the amusement of those who will one day become their imitators.'

Clearly, the cause of the revolution in France could be traced not to the excesses of the *Ancien Régime*, but to the pernicious influence of Harlequin, Columbine and Pantaloon (*Comédie-Française* aside, but that's another argument).

Speaking personally, I always adored the penny gaffs, the dingy shops and smoking rooms that became temporary theatres by night. When the sun went down, the miserable grey façades were transformed into something wonderful, with extravagant pictures of the performers displayed outside and illuminated by coloured lamps. Tragedy, comedy, music, and dance could be had on any night of the week, the price of admission a penny. Given the awful lives anyone in the audience not slumming it led, how could we begrudge them such a simple pleasure?

Looking back, I think the problem was that neither Ainsworth nor I had realised how much and how fast times had changed under the new Queen. We were both of us, after all, children of the Regency. The newly styled 'Victorians,' on the other hand, who had only a few years before exhibited a passion for heroes in fetters, now discovered that pirates, highwaymen and prostitutes were disreputable characters, although they remained enraptured with the more established brigands of legend. They could embrace Robin Hood as fondly as ever, and dwell with unhurt morals on the little peccadilloes of William Wallace. The outlaws of Schiller, Scott and Byron were similarly spared any charges of the corruption of public morals, but they shook their heads in horror at our brand of hero, because the low people began to run after them at the music halls.

We still might have ridden out the storm, if only the former Member for Surrey, the legendarily eccentric Lord William Russell, had not had his throat slit by a servant while he slept. I knew there was going to be trouble as soon as the news broke. It was a depressingly stupid story, for the assassin, the valet François Courvoisier (whose name would live ever after in infamy alongside the likes of Thurtell, Corder, Greenacre, and Burke and Hare), attempted to stage a robbery to misdirect the authorities, but then left all the loot poorly concealed in his master's house, including a tenner stuffed behind the wainscoting. It was clear to the peelers that this was unlikely behaviour for a burglar, and it came out soon after that Russell had caught his man nicking the plate, and demanded his immediate resignation. Courvoisier had decided to resolve the matter by permanently silencing his master, rather than giving up his position without a reference. If further evidence of the man's idiocy was required, Courvoisier soon confessed, but then instructed his barrister to continue to defend him based on his original plea of 'not guilty.' That'll be one less moron in the world when they hang him, thought I, but then the silly bastard had to go and say that he had got the idea after reading our books.

'If ever there were publications that deserved to be burnt by the common hangman,' thundered Forster in the *Examiner*, 'they are *Jack Sheppard* and *The Death Hunter.*'

It was unfortunate that we were both on fixed fees and not royalties, because you couldn't buy publicity like that. Our books sold better than ever, but we were blackballed again, this time at the Trinity Club. The bells of St Sepulchre's had tolled, and the drop had fallen on the Newgate novel. A common man had killed a gentleman, and although the truth of the matter was more avaricious than political, the press saw it as another sign of the coming revolution, incited by idealised working class heroes like Ainsworth's highwaymen and my pirates. 'All the Chartists in the land,' wrote Mary Mitford, 'are less dangerous than these terrible books.'

Thackeray took this opportunity to loose another shot at Dickens. This time he fired from the gates of Newgate itself, in a piece for *Fraser's* entitled 'Going to See a Man Hanged,' in which he continued to rant about the 'unrealistic' portrayal of Nancy. 'Boz, who knows life well,' he wrote, 'knows that his Miss Nancy is the most unreal fantastical personage possible; no more like a thief's mistress than one of Gessner's shepherdesses resembles a real country wench.'

This was of course true, although my own attempt at a more honest realism in *The Death Hunter* had come as much of a critical cropper as Ainsworth's Cockney Aphrodites in *Jack Sheppard* and Dickens' tart with a heart.

'He dare not tell the truth concerning such young ladies,' Thackeray had continued, concluding that, 'Not being able to paint the whole portrait, he has no right to present one or two favourable points as characterising the whole, and therefore had better leave the picture alone altogether.'

As far as I understood it, he was demanding accurate reportage, while at the same time arguing that it would be quite improper to represent anything nasty. With Thackeray you could never win. The man getting hanged, incidentally, was François Courvoisier. When the drop fell, Thackeray admitted that he could not look.

Dickens was privately livid, but he kept his powder dry and let Ainsworth and me draw the fire. While the rest of us bickered, he had moved on from *Oliver Twist* and already finished *Nicholas Nickleby*. The man wrote with the speed and precision of a well-oiled machine, and each new serial was more confident and sophisticated than the last. It was by now very apparent that as a stylist he was better than the rest of us put together.

When Dickens finally broke cover he was devastating. He did it in print, naturally.

'The greater part of this Tale was originally published in a magazine,' he wrote, in a preface added to the new edition of *Oliver Twist*, continuing that, 'when I completed it, it was objected to on some high moral grounds in some high moral quarters. It was, it seemed, a coarse and shocking circumstance that some of the characters in these pages are chosen from the most criminal and degraded in London's population, that Sikes is a thief and the girl is a prostitute.'

He then went on to make his agenda very clear, staking a claim to social realism in defiance of Thackeray's calls for censorship, Ainsworth's romantic criminals, and even his good friend Forster's arguments about the corrupting effects of popular narratives upon the masses.

'What manner of life is that which is described in these pages, as the everyday existence of a Thief?' he countered. 'What charms has it for the young and ill-disposed? Here are no canterings on moonlit heaths, none of the dash and freedom with which "the road" has been invested.' This was a clear nod towards Ainsworth, but presumably in deference to our little secret, I noted that there was no reference to pirates, cannibals, or the activities of Grub Street death hunters.

Dickens made the popular tales of Turpin and Sheppard sound trivial. They suddenly seemed to have no point beyond generating the debate he was about to win. 'I have read of thieves by the score,' he continued, 'seductive fellows (amiable for the most part), faultless in dress, bold in bearing, great at a song, and fit companions for the bravest. But I had never met with the miserable reality.'

This was the heart of it. Dickens was telling Thackeray that he refused to look away; instead he twisted the heads of his middle class audience towards the squalor and depravation that surrounded them, and demanded that they look, and, if at all possible, that they try and do something to alleviate all this bloody misery.

It was an impassioned and persuasive manifesto. Dickens knew he was walking a tightrope, and that literary reputations had already been destroyed, nonetheless 'Truth' remained his watchword. He positively bellowed the word at his detractors, frustrated at having to explain the obvious, and hammering the point home through his justification of his much criticised depiction of Nancy.

'It is useless to discuss whether the conduct and character of the girl seems natural or unnatural, probable or improbable, right or wrong,' he wrote, 'IT IS TRUE. From the first introduction of that poor wretch, to her laying her bloody head upon the robber's breast, there is not one word exaggerated or overwrought. It is emphatically God's truth, for it is the truth. It involves the best and worst shades of our common nature, its ugliest hues and its most beautiful; it is a contradiction, but it is a truth.'

It wasn't true at all though, any more than his sugared version of Nancy reflected the complexities of the original model. He was so full of moral fervour just then though, that he almost had me convinced.

'I am glad to have had it doubted,' he concluded, 'for in that circumstance I find a sufficient assurance that it needed to be told.'

Dickens had in one stroke marked out his pitch and moved the goalposts. If he was to be believed (and he was), then the controversy offered no reason for novelists to abandon the subject of crime and social deprivation. Indeed, at least for Dickens, the reverse was closer to the case. The moral panic that had knackered the rest of us had actually consolidated his career.

'Having dealt with the gainsayers,' he told me, 'I can now go about my business.'

As I was still selling, despite the critical cat whipping, I let them all get on with it. It was plain that my audience had ceased to be the one that read Dickens and Thackeray in any event. My work was increasingly disregarded as 'popular' rather than 'literary,' and I dropped out of the headlines soon enough. After a certain amount of soul-searching, I realised that this was a distinction I could live with. As long as I kept well away from the Athenaeum Club I reckoned I was in the clear. My real challenge was what to write next.

I had discussed this with Ainsworth, who was now doing more conventional histories, and was working on *The Tower of London* and *Guy Fawkes* simultaneously. He was keeping his historical romances gory though, which I admired, but the politics were a touch superficial. This was not for me. I had vented a lot of personal spleen in the last book, but what I wanted now was to retain the social realism of *The Death Hunter*, but without the sensational story, and bugger Thackeray's public modesty argument and Dickens' appeals to Christian Brotherhood. What I needed was some sort of third path. The whole 'Newgate Controversy,' as it became known, had certainly given me pause for reflection, although not on account of the ridiculous arguments of Forster and Thackeray. Reviewing my travels in the underworld, especially during my period with Egan, I was forced to face the fact that I had been worse than the tourists I had once despised in the Marshalsea. Like Ainsworth, I had glamorised the whole thing, and never once said a true word about the wretched reality of it all.

I could have done something different in *The Death Hunter*, but instead I was as feckless, cynical, and opportunist as the novel's protagonist, turning the narrative into a crowd pleasing horror story, while deceiving myself that I was making some sort of profound philosophic statement. As anyone that knew me well might have privately observed, as I'm sure they all did, all I was really doing was indulging my own self-pity after an unhappy love affair. I was thoroughly ashamed, and eager to somehow make amends with my own class by doing what no other living English novelist so far had, including Dickens, whatever he claimed, by accurately reflecting the plight of the urban poor.

As I was already out on my ear as far as London Society was concerned, I re-aligned myself with the local artisan radicals, and joined the London Working Men's Association. This was much to the horror of Ainsworth and the amusement of Cruikshank. The latter banged off a sketch of me for *Punch* in which he suggested that the Chartist orator Henry Vincent and I were the same person, and that I maintained the deception by sporting a huge fake beard at rallies. My namesake's trademark was a vast thicket of facial hair, and the caption read: 'There's a notorious pirate lurking behind that great old bush.'

I immediately found a kindred spirit in Henry Hetherington, the radical publisher who, like me, was the son of a tailor. Also like me, he had seen the inside of a prison, having been prosecuted under England's ancient blasphemy laws after publishing a cheap edition of Haslam's *Letters to the Clergy of All Denominations* ('showing the errors, absurdities and irrationalities of their doctrines'). Hetherington, like Milton in the *Areopagitica*, had enthusiastically defended the right to freedom of religious expression, but the Whigs were afeared of the Chartists after Newport, and were locking up the leaders under any pretence. William Lovett was still doing twelve months in Warwick for seditious libel, having supposedly described the Birmingham police, who had violently broken up a tiny assembly, as 'a bloodthirsty and unconstitutional force' (which was probably quite an accurate representation), while Henry Vincent seemed to be permanently on baked dinners.

Hetherington, like Lovett, believed in education, and urged me to re-explore the streets of London, now that, he said, 'Your eyes have been opened,' and to write about what I saw for the unstamped press.

As Ainsworth had taken me on as a regular contributor to *Bentley's*, I had to keep my head down (having declared for the Six Points of the People's Charter), so I took the byline 'Jay' when I wrote for Hetherington's *Halfpenny Magazine* or Feargus O'Connor's *Northern Star*. I doubt this fooled anybody, but the deception allowed Ainsworth to plausibly look the other way, which was needful to me, because no one ever made any money writing for the radical newspapers.

Once again, I was back amongst my own class.

CHAPTER XXV

It was Hetherington who asked me to look out for the French journalist Flora Tristan on her 'Promenades dans Londres.' This plucky little Judy immediately struck me as more than tough enough in her own right though, and from the obvious force of her will I certainly would not have wished to get on her bad side. She was surveying life in London in a very different way to either Egan or Boz, and studying the effects of the new industries on the lives of the working poor, especially women. Hetherington admired her socialist principles, while I was quite taken by her quick wit and Andalusian beauty.

She had long black tresses and fervent, dusky eyes, and in character she reminded me of Mrs. Shelley, only louder. We were initially chaperoned by Hetherington, but soon I became both guide and bodyguard, and we walked out alone together most nights for several weeks, in order to encounter what she called the 'Monster City.'[22]

By Christ she was a handful. She was frequently moved to explosive indignation, in a Babel of linguistic virtuosity, at the many injustices she observed. And woe betide any man who advised me to, 'Control your woman,' as several did, for she would fly at 'em like a soldier's doxy defending her pitch outside the barracks. She carried a stiletto concealed in a high silk boot, and on a full moon I feared for their lives.

She had been raised in South America, and detested the English climate. 'In London,' she would say, 'there are eight months of winter followed by four months of rain.'

'In England,' I told her, as we set forth upon another evening reconnaissance in a freezing and torrential downpour, 'one must never be deterred from an activity on account of the weather.'

Having ascertained quite early in our acquaintance that she preferred, shall we say, the society of women to that of men, I was released from the usual burdens attendant on friendships between members of the opposite sex. I was thus able to engage reasonably equally (for she was considerably more intelligent than I), with one of the most stimulating and fascinating intellects it has ever been my pleasure to encounter. She had some respect for the Chartists, who were then making such outrageous and terrorist demands against democracy as universal suffrage, a secret ballot, no property qualification for M.P.s, payment for Members (so poor men could serve), constituencies of equal size, and annual elections. She was particularly taken with my governor at the *Northern Star*, the Irishman, O'Connor, who, unlike the London Chartists, had a mind to make a fight of it.

'Put your trust in God,' he would tell his followers, 'but keep your powder dry.'

I was more Moral Force than Physical Force in those days, but she lapped it up. 'I see a good augury,' she told me, 'in the talent, sincerity and devotion of the men whom the Lord has brought forth to lead your people.'

I was not so sure. Most of the good ones were in the box or the floating academy, and the rest were already splitting into bickering factions. And in the time it took for them to fall out, make up, and elect new leaders, Parliament had granted itself a whole new swathe of powers to combat sedition and revolution. Mademoiselle had a different issue with the six-pointers though, which was that they were not yet radical enough.

'Radicals, Reformers, Chartists, Whigs,' she said, pausing to spit on the street, 'and Tories, are all at war with one another.'

'But?' Like Socrates, she wanted me to ask.

'But,' she smiled, 'the Great Struggle, the struggle which is destined to transform the social order, is yet to come.'

'And that would be?

She took a deep breath and continued. 'The struggle which pits property owners and capitalists, who control everything, and for whose benefit the country is governed, against the workers, who have nothing, neither land, nor capital nor political power, yet who pay two-thirds of the taxes, furnish recruits for army and navy, and whom the rich keep on the verge of starvation to get them to work for cheaper wages.'

'Oh, that struggle.'

'There is no war,' said she, 'but class war.'

'Can't you keep that woman under control?' said a passing toff, for this conversation took place on the Haymarket just before the spell was broken up and the saloon's turned out.

'Va te faire foutre, trouduc!' said my companion, delivering a crippling kick to the basket-making equipment.

'Bloody foreigners,' said the man, in a low hiss, as he dropped to his knees in a state of some discomfort.

He'll feel that in the morning, I thought.

We were in the West End at that hour because my fiery escort had been interviewing members of the oldest profession, and had heard tell of the 'Finishes,' the taverns and public houses where a gentleman might finish off the night after dinner and a show. We had been talking recently to some of the girls who worked the theatres, and Mademoiselle's blood was up over the chance to see some of those 'damned aristos' openly cavorting with common prostitutes, who they picked up after the curtain fell and took off to the Finishes around the Haymarket and the Strand. From what I had observed, these were the victims of poverty with which she felt the most sympathy.

'Never have I been able to see a prostitute,' she had told me, 'without being moved by a feeling of compassion for the woman, and of contempt and hatred for her clients, who reduce her whom the Lord created to the lowest degree of debasement.'

'You view this as a moral issue, then?' I was foolish enough to ask. I could immediately sense that I had fallen in her estimation for asking such an idiotic question.

'You are a poor disciple, Jack,' she chided. 'I keep pointing, and you keep staring at my finger. You are no use to the cause unless you appreciate the very simple fact that *everything* is political.'

I assured her that I did, but she gave me the lecture anyway.

'Prostitution is the ugliest of all the sores produced by the unequal distribution of wealth,' she said, 'which, much more damningly than crime, bears witness against the organisation of society. Prejudice, poverty, and serfdom all combine their pernicious effects to produce this revolting degradation.' She spoke, as ever, with a fervour that would have given any hirsute Chartist orator a run for his money, although while they were calling for reform what she wanted was revolution.

Given what had happened in France I was less than convinced, although that did not mean that I did not agree with her social diagnosis. Where we differed was that she was still an idealist, whereas I was tending increasingly towards cynicism. As far as I could see of human history, evil empires periodically replaced themselves, but they never truly fell, and if you stripped away one uniform, there was like enough another one beneath. Mademoiselle, bless her, still believed in the Glorious Day.

Buckstone's *Jack Sheppard* was still packing them in at the Adelphi, and this was the first to chuck out, the Strand filling with theatre goers enthusiastically belting out the play's concluding song, a rousing rendition of Ainsworth's 'Nix My Dolly Pals' grafted on to the production from *Rookwood*. That bloody song travelled everywhere, and made the Flash patter of thieves and burglars as familiar in our mouths as household words. It deafened us in the streets, once the organ-grinders got hold of it, and it was whistled by every dirty guttersnipe you passed. It was similarly chanted in drawing-rooms by much fairer lips, little knowing the meaning of the words they sang. 'Nix my dolly pals, fake away!' translated as, 'Never mind, my friends, carry on stealing!'

We attached ourselves to a likely group of young warbling swells and their common lady-birds, and followed them into an establishment trading under the sign of The Fiddler's Elbow, an outwardly respectable tavern off the Strand, and one of the most notorious of the Finishes.

'Stay quiet and close,' I told Flora, 'and try to look like a working girl.'

Without hesitation she undid more than a couple of top buttons and thrust out her chest like a true Haymarket Hussar. 'I look the part now?' she said. It was more of a statement than a question.

'Très bien,' I said.

You had to go up a flight of external stairs to the Finish, presumably to shield the middle class diners on the ground floor from the sight of the more clapped out old blowens that shuffled up those steps as if they led to the gallows. The pretty young things did not work the Finishes, which were waiting for them in their middle years, if they lived so long. In the Finishes a woman had to be prepared to do anything.

The Finishes always reminded me of a bastard hybrid born of the gentleman's clubs of St. James' and the gambling hells of Hanover Square. Flora described this one as, 'A temple raised by English materialism to the false idols of gold and debauchery,' which is a fine example of what we call in the trade 'showing and not telling.' I always quite liked them personally, but I decided to keep that observation to myself, and hoped to Christ that no one recognised me and called us over. These places were as exclusive as the clubs as well, and only my celebrity status got me through the door. It was not every night that they received a visit by Charles Dickens, after all.

My only complaint at the time would have concerned the illumination, which was dazzling. I liked dark and intimate spaces lit by candles and bathed in smoke myself; the gas lights here were far too bright and unforgiving. The second floor of the tavern was a huge saloon, or 'long room,' divided in two lengthwise. On one side there was, as in most restaurants, a row of tables separated by low wooden partitions and loaded with cold meats, pastries, and a variety of wines and cordials. There were sofa-like benches lined with red leather on either side of the tables, while opposite there was a raised platform that looked like a narrow stage. This part was less like a restaurant, unless it were one in which you chose the beefs in advance. This was where the house girls paraded, displaying themselves to the customers.

We took a table and waited. I had to pay an extra fee for bringing a woman in with me, on top of the small fortune it had cost me to get us through the door. I was running out of money now, and the expenses incurred thus far on this expedition were beginning to hurt. The real habitués began to arrive around midnight, and I spotted several familiar faces from the literary salons. There were noble scions, a fair few captains of industry, and a murder of parliamentarians, all doffing their coats, popping their collars and lounging about as if in their private boudoirs. Some brought their own doxies; others chose women from the catwalk.

The orgy began sometime around two o'clock, by which point the clientele were well and truly in their cups, and what we saw that night, well, you would not give it credence. These places had certainly livened up of late. My previous experience of the Finishes had been more akin to that of the classier brothels of Waterloo, in which there was a certain amount of privacy involved. Here, the rutting was mostly happening in the booths, the public exhibition, worthy of Ancient Rome, evidently all part and parcel of the gratification. There were girls spread across tables and taken at both ends at once; others were kneeling down and pleasuring men on the sofas, or being shagged on floorboards made muddy by dropped food and spilled drink. Those men not actively involved watched and cheered, often fiddling with themselves as they did so. Several were pouring drink onto their fellow fornicators, and the women, in particular, were becoming so covered in filth that it was often difficult to judge the original colour of their dresses or undergarments. The atmosphere reeked of cigar smoke, strong drink, sweat and, above all, sex, and the glistening red faces of the elite of England puffing and blowing towards their little deaths rendered the whole scene utterly malefic.

It was impossible to hide under those damn lights, so we affected to canoodle in our little booth, until I got a touch too much into the role, at which point Flora sprung off my lap as if stabbed and started babbling at me in her native tongue.

I tried to explain that I must have had one small sherry too many.

'Have another,' said she, pouring me a drink and looking a trifle flushed herself. 'We will take a break, n'est-ce pas?'

'Fair enough,' I said, nervously lighting a cheroot and feeling, once more, somewhat ridiculous. I was not Orpheus, nor she Eurydice, and as a guide to the underworld I was no Pierce Egan either.

It was difficult to know where to look. I had therefore not noticed how much the crowd had grown while we were fumbling about like farmhands at a dance. As I squinted at the new arrivals my eyes met those of a small man with the face of a pantomime villain a couple of tables down. He froze for a second, as if he beheld the corpse of his best friend at the banquet, then recovered and resumed his activities.

It was Grimstone. I knew him at once, aged though he was, and although he was busy at the tradesman's entrance of some poor old ginger bat, he had most certainly clocked me as well, for I was the dead spit of my father.

I continued to regard him, enjoying his obvious discomposure, and in consequence he quite lost his stroke. Furious, he grabbed a wine bottle and finished the job with that while his companions held the woman down. Her screams provoked nothing but laughter.

Flora rose to intervene, but I grabbed her arm and pulled her back down. 'Make a scene and we're dead,' I said urgently.

She sulkily resumed her seat, staring in horror at the continuing rape. 'Why doesn't somebody stop him?' she pleaded.

'Look around you,' I said, 'everyone is enjoying this.'

The faces reminded me of the expressions you saw at a hanging. Even the other women were laughing. I suspected they saw worse most nights. I felt frightened, weak and useless. If only I had the mettle of one of my fictional creations, I thought, not for the first time. Bannockburn or Kidd would have flown across the room and settled matters by fist, boot and steel (the real Captain Kidd would probably have joined in though), but all I had were words. The best I could do, I realised, was expose the bastard in print. I suggested this to Flora, and she concurred. This was also the purpose of her investigations, after all.

'What noble use these English lords make of their wealth and power!' she spat.

Grimstone finally stopped, and when his companions let go the woman she rolled off the table and onto the floor, where she lay gasping and sobbing. A man I did not recognise threw some coins at her, and then gave her a kick for good measure. Grimstone adjusted his garments with care, and then waved over an attendant.

Words were exchanged while both looked in our direction.

I took Flora's arm, grabbing the heaviest bottle I could find with my free hand. 'Time to go,' I said.

I shoved my way through the drunken rabble towards the exit, dragging poor Flora behind me like a sack of spuds. Someone was shouting, but we made it to the door and clattered down the stairs as if the Arch Fiend himself was after us, rather than a couple of South London boys most likely equipped with razor and cosh.

'Run! Get a cab and go!' I shouted when we reached the street. She lingered, unwilling to leave me, so I swore at her and this time she bolted. I withdrew into a convenient doorway and waited. I saw her hail a cab and get in, but it was too far away to do me any good.

When our pursuers rounded the corner, I struck the first as hard as I could in the face with my bottle. It was a magnum of champagne, so it held and did a deal of damage. He went down spitting blood and teeth, and I set about the other. He was a big man, but was obviously thinking about it in light of current events. Instinct took advantage of his hesitation, and I bashed him brutally and then I ran.

Flora had kept the cab waiting, God bless her. I fell inside, breathing hard and still clutching my trusty bottle. 'My hero!' she laughed, then whacked me with her fan. 'That was very foolish, Jack,' she said. She was trying to brazen it out, but I could see that she was trembling.

I thumped the roof of the cab and called out her address, and then I opened the champagne. It was as warm as living blood, but a very good year.

We arrived at her lodgings drunk and excited. She did not invite me in, and I did not ask.

CHAPTER XXVI

OUR VOYAGE WAS ill-omened from the start. I had long since come to expect a hard and sorrowful life, and this fatalistic perception of the waking world was equalled and, indeed, exceeded by that of my professional dreaming: a dark realm as crammed full of horrors as Victor Frankenstein's hotpot. The real and the unreal had both engendered within me a natural state of spiritual dread that had rarely disappointed, but I was nonetheless to shortly learn that whatever atrocities I may have previously experienced or imagined, I had never truly known mortal terror, that purest of animal fears, until I had experienced the full force of an Atlantic storm.

We were not a day clear of the harbour and into the open ocean when the tempest fell upon us with the elemental ferocity of the Last Judgement. It was a savage westerly and Captain Salmond had little option but to steam into the jagged, hellish teeth of the apocalyptic gale. So affronted was the storm, it seemed, by this gesture, that it increased in unremitting fury with every passing day, as if possessed of a malevolent consciousness driven to a blind rage, all of its force directed against our defiant little ship as she fought a fantastic battle for her life and the lives of her children.

Monstrous waves, miles from crest to crest, roared down upon us, and the ship screamed and shuddered as hundreds of tons of dark water crashed like a swollen river from her stem to her stern. I witnessed men washed away so fast that they might never have existed at all, yet still the ship rode these giant waves with a ridiculous tenacity that recalled to me some of the bare knuckle bouts I had reported during the Regency, when men fought on for dozens of rounds beyond any reasonable measure of human endurance. Like the great pugilists Molineux and Cribb, our ship would simply not stay down. And the blows were relentless, causing her iron hull to resound like some ancient and colossal bell, prognosticating our doom. We knew what Hell was then, a ship of the damned and we her crew. And as befitted the true horror of eternal damnation, the torture could have no end. There was no reality beyond the relentless violence of the ocean, a constant rising and falling that turned your stomach, robbed you of your wits, and felt like death at every roll. When the ship was born up by the unimaginable force of each new wave you became momentarily weightless as she hung suspended between sea and sky, before commencing a thunderous and terrifying descent that each time might continue indefinitely, becoming the final death plunge into the crushing deep. The sublime and savage cycle would then repeat. Wind and rain howled and clawed about rails and rigging, lashing canvas covers to ribbons resembling flayed flesh, and turning deck gear into lethal projectiles. There could be no accurate navigation in such a terrible and unholy maelstrom, yet still the Captain ground grimly forward, clamped to the poop rail with arms of iron, his oil-skinned form fused to his ship, as much a part of her as the great grey figurehead of Vulcan at her prow.

A few channel crossings and the paintings of Mr. Turner had not prepared me for this terrible reality, and there was no relief to be found in gauging the duration of the thing. It would take as long as it took, said any crewman I asked. The storm would either pass or blow itself out, or we would capsize and sink and know no more about it one way or the other, for in the unlikely event of escaping the stricken ship there would be no surviving the freezing and wild water.

'Them that drowned the fastest would be the lucky ones,' Brodie had told me, when we had briefly discussed the drill for abandoning the ship in the event of a catastrophic emergency.

This had not really been the answer I had been seeking, but I duly recorded it for my readers; the act of writing, as ever, providing me with a necessary escape from the horrible circumstances in which I frequently found myself. I had been initially ignorant of the likely duration or intensity of the storm as well, and had been attempting to move independently about all parts of the ship until the Captain chased me below with a terrible oath. As our plight worsened, it became even more important to me to observe and report, no matter how futile this act most likely was, for I was soon convinced that the ship must break apart. When the sky is falling in upon you, it is best to concentrate your attention upon your work.

The situation was arguably worse below decks, where those of us not concerned with the running of the ship cowered, permanently cold and damp, and hanging onto whatever we could. Unsecured debris of every sort assaulted us. Tools, bales and barrels flew, mixed with an infernal baptism of frozen sea water, shit, piss, blood and vomit that the men constantly toiling upon the chain pumps could never fully disperse. The galley fires had all been extinguished by sea water pouring down the vents, so there was nought to eat but fruit, if you could get it, and cold tinned meat, if you could face it. Either way, whatever you attempted to eat would most likely fly from your hands and then back into your face and clothes as the ship violently pitched and villainously rolled.

Sleep was impossible, and many of those that succumbed to exhaustion without securing themselves to their bunks in some way were hurled against the bulkheads and broken like birds hitting a window. Culhane, the ship's surgeon, and the army doctors Bowen, Robertson and Laing, toiled around the clock treating cuts and gashes, setting bones, and doing what little they could for men, women and children so drained and dehydrated by endless seasickness that they had lost all will to live. Worse of all, the pregnant women on board all went into premature labour. Their screams haunted the lower decks for days and nights without end, while some of the tougher officer's wives attended to them. Three of them eventually delivered, and three of them died, along with their babies. There was nothing to prescribe but brackish rainwater for the sickness and rum for everything else; although I cannot imagine that there was enough strong drink on board to dull the agony of some of the injuries I observed: compound fractures that left the surgeons no choice but to remove the shattered limbs, a futile operation in every case for the patients always died.

In a fortuitous turn of physical events, which I ascribe largely to heroic doses of laudanum, I was not afflicted with the terrible seasickness that crippled hundreds of the soldiers and civilian passengers. I was thus soon deputised by Culhane to assist below decks, and, as he put it, become part of my own story.

'You have the heart of a poet,' I told him.

'I would profoundly hope that I possess no such organ, sir,' he replied, 'for poets are invariably dreamers and fools.'

It was exhausting and frequently revolting work, mostly spent delivering food and water, and then cleaning it up once it was regurgitated. The civilian passengers had been ordered to remain in their cabins, where stewards and volunteers such as I attended them as best as we were able. Reynolds would have no doubt found the rapid collapse of social divisions fascinating, while I pondered issues of etiquette such as how to address a gentlewoman and colonel's wife as I held her hair out of her own vomit because her maid was too weak to rise from her bunk. Miss Martineau had left that out of *How to Observe Morals and Manners*. I made a mental note to drop her a line should I survive.

The troop decks were even more Avernal. Culhane had sent me struggling down, laden with as many canteens as I could carry, but it was nowhere near enough. Men were packed in with little more space than that accorded to slaves by the brutal traders that still moved between Africa and America in those days (and to England too, not so long before). Rows of filth-encrusted men with faces as colourless and drawn as inexpertly embalmed skulls sat stoically on the long, heavy benches, their fingers clamped to the base and their bodies jammed together for safety. Others huddled in shadowy nooks and crannies like spiders. The presently useless and potentially lethal hammocks had been unslung, and those too sick to support themselves lay upon the deck in several inches of foul water. Each presumably took turns to breathe, and were wedged in place by the booted feet of their comrades, the iron columns supporting the ceiling, any furniture screwed to the deck, and each other. It appeared that they were all too far gone to care when someone above evacuated upon them. If the sea does not get us, I thought, then the cholera surely will.

There was a low sound around them that was not the ocean, and in moments of quiet suspension I began to discern that it was a murmur of voices; some praying, and some cursing continuously, like privateers cut down but not yet dead. The storm had darkened what little natural light there was down there to an eternal dusk, while the air, what there was of it, had the stench of the tannery, the sewer, and the charnel house about it. It was too damp to keep a cigar burning, and the handkerchief soaked in *Eau de Cologne* that I had taken to wearing about my face to mask and filter this pestilential miasma did not prevent me from adding my last meal to the muck that sloshed about my borrowed sea boots.

Drake, the marine Colour Sergeant, spotted me through the gloom and came to my aid. 'Generally speaking,' he said, as he relieved me of my burden, 'when I've eaten something I have no desire to see it again.'

I wiped my mouth and accepted the offer of one of my own canteens. He passed the others to some NCOs he had managed to gather about him, instructing them to give each man a capful of the precious water. These men looked as dishevelled as I, but Drake, by means I can only conclude were in some way supernatural, was as immaculately turned out as usual. When I later bumped into Seton and Wright doing the rounds they were similarly fit for the parade ground, and to this day I have no idea how this was achieved.

I asked Drake how the soldiers were coping.

'They're not happy, sir, but they'll live,' said he, adding, 'most of 'em, anyway.'

'Bloody weather,' I observed uselessly, as if we had been attending a cricket match together and rain had stopped play.

'Bloody weather indeed, sir,' he replied, before fading back into the false twilight.

He was proud of his men, you could tell. They were enduring the unendurable, while a large proportion of them were new to the life, and had likely never been ten miles beyond their place of birth, let alone upon an Atlantic crossing. Yet these unruly, under-educated costermongers and farm labourers did what they were told, and bore every new horror with a kind of working class nobility. As I stood there watching the soldiers, jammed into the hatchway like a finger in a dyke, I found myself constructing romantic and heroic narratives around them as a result, as I had once done with the Chartists and Communists.

Moran was in particularly good spirits, and was certain that all would be well for us in the end. 'We won't sink, sir,' he told me, his confidence and general good humour incongruous to say the least.

'You seem very sure, my friend,' I said, 'I wish I had your faith.'

'We'll be all right,' he said, 'Colour Sergeant says so.'

Lakeman's party were similarly beleaguered when I later called upon them. They had a little more space than the redcoats, and the rangers appeared in slightly better spirits than their counterparts as their officers were not sparing the rum. Motivational singing was also encouraged, and I arrived to the final bars of 'Finnegan's Wake,' slightly re-worded to suit the current situation: 'And when the Devil comes to call me to his kingdom, I'll take all you bastards with me when I go.'

Again, I was carrying water, and this set me in good stead with the men. They crowded about me as eager for news from above as they were for my canteens. 'Give him room, boys,' said Lakeman, who was staying with his men like a concerned parent.

I lied through my teeth and told them that that the Captain expected a break in the weather soon, and that the ship remained as sound as a bell. What else could I say? Their guess was as good as mine, but I had learned from my time in prison that a little hope, however false or farcical, really could mean the difference between life and death.

When too exhausted to act the Samaritan, I did what everyone else was doing and kept to my cabin, in which I was thrown around like a cat in a barrel going over the Falls of Glomach. Regardless of how hard I had tried to secure my possessions, I was met by various personal items flying about as if animated by a poltergeist every time I returned to the room. I eventually crammed everything loose into my trunk, which I had long-since lashed to my cot by its fastening straps in order to protect its fragile contents. I likewise tied myself down each night by means of belt and braces and knocked myself out with the laudanum.

Such dreams I had. My mind was free to fly while my physical frame was tethered and tormented. My visions were epic, sublime and terrible. I dreamed of infinite glittering deserts in which metal insects the size and form of men fought immense, intricate and savage battles that had neither end or reason; of vast vaulted caverns deep beneath the earth in which slumbered great and ancient beings far superior to man; and of endless seas shimmering with diamond encrusted creatures of impossible size that could devour entire fleets of ships in a single breach. Beings from another world visited the earth in great silver flying machines in order to damn and save us with magical and terrible science, teaching that life is an illusion, that there is no God and no such thing as death, and that we are all part of the same consciousness, experiencing itself subjectively and eternally. I lived through the rise and fall of great civilisations in a single night, and with the coming of each new dawn I watched the sun explode. I saw the dead give up their graves and dance, and my mother, reanimated and ghastly, crawling towards me with a long blade between her teeth. I knew my own death, which came by water night after night, my living corpse silently travelling forever on the dark tides of the world, my soul returning thence every time I slumbered.

Sometimes I returned to my family, taking my place in a chair by the fire in the parlour, reading stories to my son while Grace would sit and sew. Sometimes I journeyed to our bed. Sometimes I dreamed that I wrote, although upon waking very little remained and I was once more inside my own coffin, a green sheet on one side, an iron bulkhead on the other, curving above in a low and oppressive ceiling.

I loved the opium as much as I hated it, and every morning I awoke in a cold sweat feeling scared, sick, and ashamed. I had long since promised Grace that I was free of it, and although I had purchased my present supply in secret, it had genuinely been intended only for medicinal purposes, specifically relating to the nausea caused by the motion of the sea. Every day I would swear off it forever, while every night I took it still. And having once more started I could not stop. I had been using laudanum and opium on and off since I left the Marshalsea, and had been an addict for more than half my life. Grace had saved me, but away from her I was useless and weak, and the expectation that we would not survive the storm had made it all too easy to break my promise.

The assault continued, with every dawn as violent as the last, and Chaos our only god. We had no choice but to suffer and endure, and to direct our prayers and curses where we may. I continued to stubbornly traverse the ship, aiding Culhane as best I could, and visiting the troop decks to deliver supplies and swap a few rather strained and desperate pleasantries. Formality still ruled among the officer classes, and neither army nor navy would go on the record in any way that might indicate the dread or hopelessness that they must all have privately felt. If I asked a seaman when the storm might end the most usual reply was, 'When it's ready.'

The storm's final joke was at my expense. On the tenth day there was a suggestion of respite, and the drunken motion of the ship began to slowly subside. I was therefore able to make the return journey from below to my cabin with more ease than of late. But upon my arrival at the door I heard a disquieting sound from within, that of a large object pounding about the cabin. This was accompanied by the unmistakable crunch of broken glass in motion and crushed to powder, like a crate of bottles thrown without care from a dustcart and then stomped by the draught horse.

When I opened the door, the demolished cabin reeked of the flash ken and the looted apothecary's. My trunk had broken loose, and all its precious contents were destroyed.

CHAPTER XXVII

HAD I MET Old Scratch himself at the Finish that night, in sulphurous evening dress with horns protruding from a collapsible Gibus, I could not have been more horrified than I was to once more encounter John Grimstone in the flesh. It would appear that he was of a similar mind, and clearly age had not made him any less of a stranger to decency. I was in no doubt that our assailants were either his agents, or sent by the Master of the Finish at his command. Had they caught us I was equally sure that it would have been all up with the both of us.

Grimstone had marked me as an enemy at once. He knew exactly who I was; and although the habitués of the low taverns were as free around each other as they were in front of their mistresses and servants, there was an implicit covenant that what occurred within the Finish remained there, and that names were never mentioned. Journalists and known radicals were certainly not on the guest list, and even if he did not know me for an old victim who might exploit the situation, he knew me right enough as a reporter. My guess was that his instinct was to have me silenced, along with my companion, just to be on the safe side.

Needless to say, I was still aware of Grimstone, but who in London was not in those days? Hero of the French Wars, property developer, investment and merchant banker, patron of the arts and the sciences, and soon to be Conservative Member of Parliament for my home town. He was truly a man of prestigious enterprise, a King of Phrygia in modern dress in whose hands everything in which he speculated turned to gold. His personal wealth was widely rumoured to be on a par with minor royalty, and it will be remembered that my family had contributed a morsel to the feast in the form of our little house, a fief paid twice over, for I also had to buy my father out of the debtor's gaol in which Grimstone had left him to rot. I did not care to think on it too often, but most of the profits from my literary exertions to date had actually found their way into the Grimstone corporate coffers.

But this time I had the bastard. Naming and shaming him in popular print would destroy him. I was confident I could sell the story to a major newspaper that had no love for the Tories, such as the *Observer* or the *New Monthly*; and if they would not run it, the *Northern Star* surely would. No one would care that Grimstone had raped a whore with a bottle, but the intelligence that he had been consorting with a common woman, and, worse, been spied in the act by the press, would annihilate his reputation in Fashionable Society. He would still be immensely rich of course, but at least I would have thoroughly scuppered his political aspirations well before the swine got a chance to climb to the top of the greasy pole. I would have preferred his head on a spike, but this was a pretty fair second best.

I burned the midnight oil and wrote a devastating article on Grimstone's antics at the Finish, full of lurid description and righteous moral indignation. I decided this was best delivered by hand, and as it was a fine morning, I struck out on foot for the offices of the *Observer* on Tudor Street, in the hope of cornering Doxat, the editor, and cutting a deal; although it goes without saying that I would have happily handed him the copy for nothing. As I strode along Fleet Street, I was as full of myself as Leonidas after the first skirmish at Thermopylae, and just as doomed.

Doxat returned my card, as did, inexplicably, Giffard of the *Standard*, and, most puzzlingly, Colburn at the *New Monthly*. Somewhere someone was walking over my grave.

I hastened to Hetherington's press in Holborn in a state of much confusion and not a little trepidation. As soon as I knocked I was ushered inside as though I had just escaped from Newgate. 'Something's in the wind, Jack,' said Hetherington, obviously shaken. 'What on earth have you been up to?'

He had not seen Flora yet, so I gave him a quick, summary account of our recent adventures, adding some contextual history concerning my family's dealings with Grimstone.

'He's a nasty piece of work, right enough,' said he, 'with some very powerful friends. Does he have anything he could use against you? You said you assaulted his men.'

'They were low ruffians,' I told him. 'I doubt a case could be made against a gentleman on their account. My guess is that they were no strangers to a street fight, and any injuries I inflicted would be easily forgotten after the second or third drink.'

'I hope you're right, Jack. All I know is that your name is travelling around London in a less than favourable light this morning. My advice is that you go home and prepare for some sort of a siege.'

I knew he was speaking from experience; the law and the press had been harassing him for years. He gathered some provisions for me from about his office, some bread and cheese, tea, and half a bottle of brandy (in case it was not safe for me to leave my house for a while), and then went outside and hailed a cab.

'Watch yourself,' he said, as I took my leave.

'Do you want the story?' I asked him.

'Good God, no!' said he, 'I doubt even O'Connor would touch it.'

By the time we reached Ladbroke Grove my porch was already livid with journalists, swarming about the door like maggots at an open wound. They were easily identified by pad and pencil, a level of obvious intoxication ill-advised for the hour, and the fact that I would have counted several of them friends the day before. I told the driver to head for The Horn of Plenty and kept my head down the whole way.

''Ay up, it's the son of the dawn,' said Bertie, cryptically, when I knocked him up, for it was still only about ten o'clock in the morning.

'Yeah, get thee behind me, Satan,' added Nelly, laughing.

I was ready for a drink and a smoke. 'Can somebody please tell me what the bloody hell is going on?' I demanded.

Bertie tossed me the early edition of the *Times*. 'There's something about you in here, mate,' he said.

Not that you'd be able to read it, I thought petulantly.

It was not good news. Like my father before me, I had fatally underestimated my opponent. Grimstone had struck first, and with lethal force. As we say in the trade, I was the front page.

'The so-called author, Jack Vincent,' I read, 'if filth mongering deserves the title, has been seen in the company of a common prostitute in the area of Westminster, fleeing the scene of a drunken brawl in which he seriously injured a coachman and a valet in a frenzied and unprovoked attack.' It was reported that I was presently sought by the police, who could not have been looking very hard for I had been at home all night.

'Coachman and valet my arse!' I snorted, reading on.

The tirade did not stop with my alleged assault of a cabbie and a gentleman's gentleman. An additional warrant had also been issued, I read, with a creeping sense of dread shot through with basic incredulity, on the charge of blasphemy, it having come to light that I was a known defacer of The Holy Book, which I used in performance of certain satanic rites.

'The obscene drivel which this enemy of all that is decent passes off as entertainment,' wrote my unnamed accuser, 'is now known to have been written upon the most foully desecrated pages of The Bible of Our Lord.' This unholy practice, the article continued, could be dated back to my early life as a defaulter in the Marshalsea, further suggesting that I was long overdue for a box in the stone jug again. It concluded by calling for all my books to be burnt in the street.

'Oh shit,' I said, which, so I've heard, is also the most common phrase uttered upon the moment of death.

I realised that Mina must have talked to someone, for no one else knew of my unorthodox homemade papermaking activities as a youth. Nor did I boast of my time in debtor's prison. Dickens was right; it was easy for decent folk and publishers to get the wrong impression. When the pennies dropped from my eyes, I also knew, with the absolute certainty of the truly damned, that for the second time in my life John Grimstone had ruined me. It could have been no other, for the coincidence of our meeting and the immediate assassination of my character, by my own profession at that, would have tested even the most irresponsible of gamers.

I knew that the law, and probably the press, would find me soon enough, for my haunts and habits were hardly mysterious at the best of times, so Bertie sent his pot-boy for Grove and we set about constructing a defence. Fortunately, I had destroyed the original manuscript of *The Shivering of the Timbers* years before (the thing was, after all, revolting), so I decided that my best strategy as far as that part of the story was concerned was just to stubbornly deny everything and hope that it eventually went away. Mina was hardly likely to reveal herself as the ex-mistress of a devil worshipper, or worse, a member of the labouring classes. There was a lesson to be learned here, I realised, concerning pillow talk.

Grove's view was that the situation was mostly made of smoke and mirrors, and more of a *Congregatio de Propaganda Fide* than a serious attempt at legal action. No one from the Finish, either punter or proprietor, would want to peach me for fear of exposing himself, while there was little doubt, said Grove, that Miss Tristan would bear witness to my chivalrous defence of her virtue. Similarly, there was no evidence of this supposed 'blasphemy,' aside from unverified newspaper accounts and unnamed sources, although I would have to cop up, he advised, to my time in the Marshalsea as that was a matter of public record.

As Freddie Biles was still presumably passing himself off as the old version of me, I suggested that perhaps we could claim that the papers had confused us.

'That could work,' said Bertie.

'Don't be silly, Mr. Vincent,' said Grove, 'this is not one of your novels.'

I have heard armour-plated fellows by the score, politicians mostly, dismissing such smears, and the papers that carry them, as no more than hack-rags fit for nothing but the wrapping of fried cod. So saying, as Ainsworth and I had recently discovered, once the press got hold of you on a supposedly 'moral' issue the taint of it would cling to your reputation ever after, like bloodstains on your tie. Furthermore, as I had heard many editors exclaim over the years myself, who cared if it were true or not?

These types of stories also had a nasty habit of finding ways to perpetuate themselves. In my case, when the momentum appeared to be lessening, an enterprising journalist at the 'Thunderer' started talking to members of the Athenaeum Club, many of whom could 'keep silent no longer.' They thus told many tales (some of them, unfortunately, accurate), of my loutish behaviour at that establishment, until I was, as one put it, justly seen off the premises. Much to Bertie's ill-concealed amusement, I was even outed as 'a major shareholder in a low tavern in Whitechapel.'

The long and the short of it was that this story buried me, although no charges were ever brought, and no evidence uncovered. The word alone was more than enough to destroy my reputation as a gentleman of letters. Sales of my books actually increased in that dreadful period, but people were buying them just to burn them, and there would be no further editions. Thackeray wrote a notice in *Punch* announcing the death of my career, with the fitting epitaph, 'Early to ripen, and early to rot.'

My closest friends deserted me. At the time I felt betrayed, but looking back I do not blame them, especially Ainsworth; he had suffered enough at the hands of the press already, and he had three motherless children to support. He was decent enough about it all though, and explained by letter that he could not, 'under the present disquieting circumstances,' accept any more contributions to the *Miscellany.* Cruikshank was blunter, although his signals could equally be described as 'mixed.' He sent me a case of very good brandy, accompanied by a hastily scrawled note requesting that I give him a wide berth until 'all this blows over.' Colburn upbraided me for scaring away all the money, and even Egan ducked below the parapet. Forster wrote another one of those editorials in the *Examiner* that essentially said 'I told you so,' and strongly urged me to repent of my sins and accept Jesus Christ as my Lord and personal saviour.

I did better in the radical press. Hetherington, in particular, was a trump. He had also experienced spurious blasphemy charges, and lost no time in championing my cause as an example of an honest working man who had dared to rise through the social ranks by dint of his own talent, and who had thus been broken by the ruling elite, who felt their security challenged when one such as I scrambled through into their world.

'His was a voice that had to be silenced!' he wrote, making me sound quite heroic, and placing my name upon the growing list of Chartist activists who were constantly harried by both police and press. I never had the heart to tell him that I really did piss on a prison bible in order to write stories about pirates on the paper.

Although I never got to publish my piece about Grimstone in the Finish, Flora Tristan subsequently wrote a savage description of that night in her *London Journal*, though she was prudent enough not to name names. She suggested that I might find a more favourable audience if I relocated to Paris, and I later did just that. Our association was not a long one, alas. She was not as strong in body as in mind, and she died at the age of forty-one. But that is another story. Poor old Hetherington did not see out the decade either, and was carried off by the cholera epidemic of '49.

I issued a denial of all accusations through Grove, but as I did not sue for libel no one believed a word of it. After that I just tried to keep my head down, and eventually the journalist stopped camping in the front garden of the 'Wickedest Man in England,' and drifted away to poison some other poor bugger's well.

I was thus surprised to receive a caller late one weekday evening shortly after the pack had withdrawn. It was Dickens, wearing a great coat with the collar up, and a large cap pulled low upon his brow. He was sporting glasses with tinted lenses, and hiding behind a ridiculous counterfeit beard.

'Are you still acting in those bloody awful plays?' I asked him at the door.

'Let me in,' he cried urgently, 'and be sharp about it.' I steered him into the parlour and put the kettle upon the fire. He accepted a chair, but did not beat about the bush, as was his way. 'Is it true, Jack, about the bible?' he said, looking around nervously, as if a reporter might be concealed in a cupboard.

It was always impossible to lie to him. 'You know how hard it was to get paper in that place,' I said, by way of a confession. 'And I was there a lot longer than you.'

'When did you lose your faith, Jack?' he said sadly.

'You know when.'

'But the desecration of The Holy Book!' he said, in a wounded tone, ignoring my final point.

'Right,' said I, my blood already warming, 'the two thousand-year-old myths and politics of an oppressed people that we are supposed to somehow apply to life in the present.'

'But it is an ideal to which we all must aspire, Jack,' he said piously.

'Oh course it is,' I said, clasping my hands in an affectation of prayer that was probably asking for trouble. 'And on the sixth day, the Lord created 300,000 varieties of beetle,' I intoned in mock solemnity, 'all of them slightly different.'

'It is the word of God!'

'It is a fiction, man, like any other,' I countered. 'Beautifully written, I grant you, even if the plot is full of contradictions and the style is all over the place, but you must see all of the tricks of the trade as well as I.'

'It is obvious,' he said frostily, 'that you are incapable of discussing this matter either reasonably or rationally.'

If there is one thing I detest, it's a bloody anthem cackler. 'Did you just come here to deliver a sermon?' I demanded. 'You're good at that these days, aren't you?'

He looked quite fierce, but he quickly mastered his temper and held his tongue. We both of us knew exactly why he was there. He was quite clearly terrified of exposure, and had thus to treat me very warily. I felt hurt and insulted, but, like Ainsworth, I could not, in all honestly, blame him. I cannot say that I would not have reacted in exactly the same way had the tables been reversed.

'Don't worry,' I finally said quietly. 'I've said nothing, and I never will.'

He relaxed a little, but not much. 'And Mrs. Garwood?' he said, because one did not have to be a master of deductive reasoning to know that she was the source of the corruption.

'Knows nothing,' I said, 'other than I was friendly with a young boy called David, who also liked to tell stories, and whose family quit the place after only a few months.'

'And I have your word you said no more.'

'On my mother's grave,' I said.

He seemed satisfied, and his tightly wound wrapping seemed to loosen a little more. He met my eye then and I saw my old friend. 'I have worked too hard to lose everything again now, Jack.'

'I know,' I said with a sigh. 'I understand.'

'Thank you,' he said simply.

There was nothing else to discuss. When we parted, shortly thereafter, he assured me that he would do what he could for me, just not in public.

Once Dickens had replaced his disguise and departed, I decided that it was time to open another bottle of Cruikshank's bingo. It was best to drink myself to sleep, as although my address was thankfully not widely known, I was still being harassed by outraged members of the public. They would shout through my letterbox at all hours, or smear the excrement of animals across my door and sometimes break a window or two, to the extent that I had now spent money I could ill-afford installing wooden shutters. I later wrote a story inspired by this period in my life called 'Necrotic Eyes,' about a man who had secured himself in his house after the Great Tribulation, and who was nightly under siege by a legion of brainless, bloodthirsty revenants.

My neighbours turned their backs on me in the street, but I was determined that neither they nor my nocturnal tormentors would drive me from my home. My stubbornness was rewarded in the end, for idiots are easily bored, and soon drift away if you show them nothing but indifference. There were also rumours growing that unspeakable occult rituals regularly took place in my house, which was also increasingly reckoned to be haunted by the more credulous and superstitious locals.

I saw off the last of them in person. This funny little fellow had stalked me for months, brandishing wooden crosses and muttering nonsense from the Revelations of St. John as he followed me down the street. He was some sort of minister, by the look of his rather greasy apparel, but I could not say of what denomination. My normal strategy of pretending that he was not there as I went about my business had not worked, and he shadowed me like a relentless and inconvenient *doppelgänger*. I finally confronted him outside The Horn of Plenty one night, having turned down the offer of a foreign gentleman with whom I had been drinking to stab the silly sod and drop him in the river.

'Be gone, foolish and reckless mortal!' said I, swaying slightly and gesturing theatrically. He looked worried, but raised his cross defiantly. I snatched his talisman from his hand and flung it to the ground. 'If you do not get thee gone, never to return,' I intoned, 'I will curse you forever, along with your family, your descendants, and all of your friends.'

'Can you really do that?' he stammered.

'As far as you know,' said I, 'now fuck off.'

Stories concerning my Faustian activities suited me fine, and my privacy by degrees returned, although these tales did sometimes attract a different class of visitor. I was, for instance, approached in all seriousness by the Rosicrucians, as if I did not have enough problems, under circumstances which I will not document here. I also became a lodestone for Romantics, gothicists, and mediums of every stripe, strange young men and women dressed entirely in black who were searching for answers I did not possess, but was happy to discuss if they had a bottle about them.

I continued to write for Hetherington and O'Connor, under the new byline of 'Churchman,' but the fees were minimal. No major publishing house would have touched me with a bargepole dipped in dog dirt, so I was forced back upon the world of the penny dreadful in order to survive, in particular Edward Lloyd's popular periodicals the *Penny Weekly* and the *Penny Atlas*. Lloyd knew full well that even though I was tarnished I was still a bargain, but he also knew I was desperate, so he paid me a penny a line, the same as everyone else. I thus found myself in a sub-literary sweatshop in Salisbury Square, one of a stable of irregular and easily replaced contributors, all younger than me, and expected to produce original copy to ridiculous deadlines. Lloyd mostly had me anonymously writing stories about pirates, ghosts and outlaws, chopping and changing (sometimes in mid-sentence) with the best of his team, Jim Rymer and Tom Prest, who later came up with *Sweeney Todd* and *Varney the*

Vampire. Our little triumvirate also imitated Dickens, writing under the collective pseudonym of 'Bos.' Lloyd was a rich man even then, but many of the writers that made him so lived, and sometimes died, in terrible poverty.

I hated the work, which was poorly paid and uncredited (although my name was so toxic that the latter point was moot anyway). At the same time, I felt compelled to still write as well as I could; although insane deadlines and the need to make sentences as short as possible, in order to grab those extra pennies, were definite impediments when it came to quality control. Sometimes it was a relief to be writing under another name, or no name at all.

Rymer and Prest were the same, and we all took a perverse pride in the standard of a good plagiarism of Dickens, or early Ainsworth, for stories about highwaymen still sold. I authored three cheaply produced Newgate novels for Lloyd in the early-40s, under the pen name of 'William Harrison,' because consumers really were (and remain) that brainless. *The Darkman's Budge* was a heavily fictionalised account of the life of Joseph Blake, more commonly known as 'Blueskin,' a minor name from the Newgate Calendars enlivened by his friendship with Jack Sheppard; *The Black Grunger of Hounslow* was a load of nonsense about a phantom highwayman; and *Jack Sheppard in Space* was a failed attempt to reinvigorate the genre that sank without a trace but which I maintain was ahead of its time.

It was industrial writing, and a long way from the world of Dickens and his friends. Even so, the penny authors, like any other struggling artists, worked hard for very little gain in the forlorn hope of success, blind to the evidence that although their path ran parallel to that of the literary celebrities, it never crossed. I maintained no such illusion. The most I could wish for was redemption. Rymer, Prest and I all respected one another though, and got on quite well all things considered, like lost souls in the lake of fire cracking jokes and generally trying to make the best of it.

Gin and opium also dulled the despair, for I was tortured by the memory of what I had once been. 'At least you were famous for a time,' Prest had once wistfully remarked.

'But that just makes it worse,' I told him wretchedly.

I cannot remember exactly how long I slaved in Lloyd's publishing manufactory, because one tends to lose track of the time during periods of thankless toil and crippling depression, but I remember noticing that the work I was being given was beginning to tail off. No one in the firm would tell me what was going on, but I knew my employer's methods well enough, and I had seen him ruthlessly cut the mooring line with several of his writers, if he gauged that popular tastes were changing. In my case, public interest in stories about pirates and highwaymen was definitely on the wane.

The thought that I might have to return to my apprenticed trade to survive brought me to my knees. I had no idea how to be a tailor anymore, and no capital to start a business anyway. I had already re-mortgaged my house to half its value at 4% and was struggling to maintain the payments. I did not dare mortgage it all. At best, I realised, I might find employment in a rag trade sweatshop in the East End, and I would frequently become frustrated to the point of violence at the prospect of finally abandoning my career and calling; although, in truth, I was now no more part of 'English literature' than a man who shovelled elephant dung for a travelling circus could be said to be in what the theatricals called 'show business.'

The most sensible choice increasingly seemed to be self-murder, before I lost my books, then the house and, finally, returned to the Marshalsea, this time without any hope or possibility of release until I starved or the fever carried me off.

The only issue left was how the act should be done. I thought that a bullet to the brain would be the most painless option, but I had never possessed a firearm and had no money to buy one now. The other choices were fraught with the possibility of partial failure, and thus a lingering death (an overdose of opium was disqualified on these grounds, as was jumping off a roof); and although hanging, drowning, severing an artery, or a glass of arsenic or prussic acid would certainly do the job, any and all of these methods would mostly likely hurt like buggery. Thus, even though the thought of spending another day on earth was becoming more disturbing than the prospect of my own demise, I was too much of a coward to take any of the available paths to oblivion.

Looking back, the absence of a barking iron amongst my possessions was my salvation. I would have eaten the barrel of a pistol without compunction on the day that Lloyd finally dropped me, for the only thing worse than being a penny-a-liner was to fail at it.

It would be a dramatic plot point to say that the call which ultimately saved me came as I was touching my wrist with a razor, but as I am resolved to restrict myself utterly to the legitimacy of the facts, as far as I know them, in this and all other memoirs, I will not make that rather obvious move. I was drunk, probably, or sleeping one off, for I remember being roused from a clammy doze on the couch in my study one morning by a messenger from my old illustrator, George Stiff, requesting the pleasure of my company for lunch at a tavern not far from my home. As one should never turn down a free meal, I cleaned myself up and went along, trying not to look too much like the walking disaster that I had in reality become.

Stiff was looking well. He was at a table in a booth with a somewhat dandified companion that I did not recognise. Stiff rose to greet me and shook my hand warmly, introducing the other man as George Reynolds, or 'G.W.M.'

'It is an honour and a pleasure,' said Reynolds, with all appearance of sincerity, 'to meet the author of *The Death Hunter* at last.'

'You are too kind, sir,' said I, flattered but already desperate for a drink. Reynolds, it turned out, had signed the pledge, but as he seemed genuinely in awe of me I reckoned that I could get away with ordering a bottle of something. Stiff, I recalled, had always been a hard drinker.

Stiff had done well for himself. He had been an artist and engraver for the *Illustrated London News* (a relatively recent publishing phenomenon to which I had singularly failed to flog a single story), and he was now going it alone, as the proprietor of a new penny magazine he proposed to call the *London Journal and Weekly Record of Literature, Science and Art.*

'Catchy,' I said.

He had a publisher in the bag (George Vickers, who I had heard of but did not know), and Reynolds was to be his editor, while he proposed to illustrate as much as possible himself. Reynolds was no beginner, it transpired, and turned out to be the man who had written *Pickwick Abroad* for the *Monthly Magazine*, batting away Dickens' protests by countering that, 'If Boz has not chosen to enact the part of Mr. Pickwick's biographer in his continental tour, it is not my fault.' He had more recently knocked off *Master Humphrey's Clock* as *Master Timothy's Bookcase*. I liked him immediately.

Reynolds was passionate about the new project, which he assured me was to be no penny dreadful. 'It will be a true miscellany of the arts and the sciences,' he said, his eyes all aglow behind his spectacles, 'intended solely for the working man.'

'And run according to socialist principles,' chimed in Stiff, adding, 'we will look after all our staff.'

'Obviously,' Reynolds was saying, 'we will need a certain amount of sensational content,'

'But that will just be to draw our readers in,' said Stiff.

'Because our aim,' said Reynolds, 'is to edify as well as entertain, in accordance with the central tenets of the People's Charter.'

'And that is why—' said Stiff, shovelling mutton into his pie hole and almost choking before he could finish the sentence.

I patted him on the back while Reynolds finished it for him. 'That is why we want you to write for us, my dear fellow,' he said, beaming at me like a lunatic. He reminded me of Egan; not quite bereft of all his marbles, but definitely a hole in the bag.

'For an equitable remuneration, naturally,' concluded Stiff, noisily blowing his nose.

It sounded like another penny-a-line operation to me, but as far as I was concerned this was the only game in town. 'Gentleman,' said I, raising my glass, 'I will be proud to be a part of this project.'

'Splendid!' said Reynolds, clapping his hands and then tapping my glass with his teacup. 'Can you start tomorrow?'

CHAPTER XXVIII

The storm blew itself out as quickly as it had come in. By the afternoon watch the sea was as soft as milk, the ship moving gently forward under sail not steam while the repairs began. I was the first passenger to seek out the light and the space of the main deck, and Salmond let me hang around the poop as an observer, as long as I kept out of the way.

I was quietly taking notes and making rough sketches of the men working around me when Hare, one of the Master's Assistants, sighted what appeared to be a small open boat on the horizon. It was almost dead ahead, and on an identical course to us. The Captain produced that formidable telescope of his, and as we closed on the vessel he described a small sloop with a single mast and a fore-and-aft rig, with, it appeared, a single occupant at the tiller.

'She's a bit beaten about,' said he, his tone mildly perplexed.

As we bore down on the tiny boat, I saw what he meant. The black paint of the hull was blistered in places, and salt blasted away in others, while the sail was grey and ragged. That she had survived the storm, for she must, like us, have passed right through it, was miraculous.

'Fisherman?' suggested Hare.

'Not all the way out here,' said Salmond.

'Possibly a lifeboat then,' said Hare. 'Shall I alert Dr. Culhane?'

'I wouldn't bother the good doctor just yet,' said the Captain. Then, turning to his helmsman, he said, 'See if you can't get us alongside.'

Hare began hailing the little boat as we approached. 'He'll have to shout louder than that,' said Salmond.

As we came alongside and matched our speed, I realised what he meant. Looking down into the boat I saw several apparently sleeping figures lying beneath the wasted sail. The helmsman, dressed in faded oilskins, remained hunched over his tiller, resolutely holding his course, his face screwed against the wind and the spray, his eyes dark with exhaustion.

'The beggar must be asleep as well,' said Hare, calling again, 'Ahoy!'

The man at the tiller ignored him. 'Get a line on him,' said the Captain.

Hare called to a seaman on the main deck, and a heavy line was thrown while the young midshipman again hailed the boat. The line slid into the water, untouched, and Hare damned the man in the boat for a fool and a lubber.

'They look sick, sir,' cried the seaman.

'Try the boathooks,' commanded Salmond.

At last the boat was drawn alongside, and Hare climbed down to investigate. I watched him approach the helmsman with a look of mild irritation on his face, which rapidly turned to horror. He tried to call up to Salmond, but his nausea overcame him and instead he vomited over the side of the sloop.

'Pull yourself together, man,' bellowed Salmond, 'and see if you can find some sort of identification.'

Hare apologised, and gave the boat a very cursory examination, which was more than enough to confirm what Salmond had known all along. As I looked down on the man at the tiller and his slumbering companions I knew it, too. What had at first appeared eyes heavily shadowed by fatigue were nought but empty sockets, and the hand that gripped the tiller a desiccated talon. The entire crew were the same, with bones protruding from tears in their clothes, and any skin left by the gulls as dry as parchment or as tanned as leather. If there was a name on the boat the sea and the sun had burned it off, and Hare found no log, charts, chronometer, or compass. Neither did he find any evidence of food or water.

'I wonder how long they've been out here,' I found myself saying.

'Too long,' said Salmond. 'Hare! Get out of there!'

'With pleasure,' said Hare, his face still ashen with disgust.

I wondered, too, how long it had taken them all to die, and who had lasted the longest? The helmsman, I presumed, the last man with the strength to sail the boat, navigating as best he could, praying for land or help, his crewmates too weak to move, unable or unwilling to turn the dead over the side. And so they had kept dying; withering away, unburied, in this obscene tableau.

'Shouldn't we bury them, sir?' said Hare.

'No,' said Salmond, 'let them loose.'

So that is what they did. Set free, the wind caught the tattered sail and the phantom helmsman resumed his original course southward.

'It's bad luck just seeing something like that,' said Hare, as we pulled away from the sloop, and watched it recede to nothing behind us.

CHAPTER XXIX

REYNOLDS WORKED AT such a speed that he might as well have been powered by coal. I swear the man never slept, and if there was ever an advertisement for temperance then it was he, at least in terms of productivity. I have seen him have three sets of papers open upon his desk, each a separate article or story for a different publication, and be working on all of them simultaneously, fuelled by nothing but tea.

He was about thirty when we met, making him a couple of years younger than Dickens, although I learned quite quickly that this was not a name to drop in his company, just as my collaboration with him was to sorely test what remained of my friendship with Boz. Generally speaking, the fact that I had once been identified with the so-called 'Dickens Circle' was my primary qualification when looking for work, but with Reynolds, and indeed Stiff, who had been a friend of Bob Seymour, the opposite was more to the purpose. What the rest of the world viewed as my vices, they considered virtues. That I was a friend of Flora Tristan carried an enormous amount of weight, as Reynolds, who had lived and worked in Paris, held her in the highest esteem as a journalist, a political activist, and a fine example of the fair sex (in that order). My close association with the *Halfpenny Magazine* and the *Northern Star* was also to my advantage (although Hetherington and O'Connor did not trust Reynolds), as was my experience on Lloyd's penny bloods. My early days as one of the Fancy, and my pedigree as an accomplished death hunter, not to mention my supposed occult practices and my time inside, all counted in my favour, whereas my *Curriculum Vitae* would have made any other London publisher chase me out of his office brandishing either a cross or some sort of weapon.

Reynolds admired my fiction in general, but he loved *The Death Hunter*, and it was my work on that novel which had ultimately led him to approach me, through Stiff, to assist on the great *roman feuilleton* that he had been planning ever since his time in France. It was to be a gothic serial of epic proportions, he said, set in the present time, and with a serious political purpose, tentatively entitled *The Mysteries of London.*

There was likely not much money in it, as ever, but from the start we were definitely singing from the same hymn sheet when it came to our views on the representation of the modern urban experience, and the shortcomings of popular fiction on the subject to date, our own included. What was most interesting about Reynolds, though, was his intended readership, which was the mass market that Lloyd had so successfully tapped: lower middle class at best, with the majority of consumers (either reading or paying a halfpenny to have it read to them), being working men and women. I was all part of the plan, for my byline, he calculated, should attract what he called the 'radical crowd,' who tended to shun the usual penny dreadfuls as either trivial or downright offensive, given their sensational reportage of the low life of the lugubrious areas in which the honest labouring classes also resided.

I knew many Chartists who thought, and still think, that Reynolds was nothing more than commercially motivated, exploiting the cause in order to corner a new and growing market, but if that was the case then it was a performance that never ceased, a mask that never slipped, and I always marked the same fury at injustice in him that had animated Flora Tristan. He simply understood his clientele.

'To educate the proletariat,' he would say, 'you must first grab the buggers' attention.'

As I had expected, I earned little more than I had under Lloyd, but the difference was in my slowly returning sense of value. I liked working with Reynolds. He would listen to any idea, no matter how unorthodox, and support every member of his crew, from writers and subs, to typesetters, engravers, and charwomen, running the paper like a New Lanark cotton mill.

The *London Journal* blazed a trail from the start, and for the most part our publishers just let us get on with it, Stiff drawing the pictures and Vickers taking the money. There were firebrand editorials extolling the virtues of Chartism addressed 'To The

Industrious Classes,' essays on the arts and the sciences (which I knew were getting through when I heard a coster explaining *ekphrasis* in literature to his son as they set out the barrow), and a series of touchingly paternal articles penned by Reynolds intended to educate our rough and ready readers, such as 'Etiquette for the Millions' in which he advised that one should not just eat with a knife at a polite table, ever dip bread in the gravy, swear and blaspheme in company, or spit food back onto the plate. And in tandem with the improving articles, there was the same kind of material that I used to write for Egan: a bit of sport, a murder a day, and some sensational fiction. Once more I was death hunting and telling tales of terror, only this time, as Flora Tristan would have said, everything was political.

I therefore resolved not to sulk about what could have been perceived as a continuing professional reversal. Instead I looked to the future as an agent of change—if luridly reporting on bodies half eaten by rats or something bigger, dead of the cholera and dumped in basements, and then blaming the government, could be viewed as revolutionary. Seemingly it could, given the enthusiastic reception of our readers, and the outrage expressed by the middle class magazines, which frequently depicted the pair of us as 'The Pirate and the Parrot.' I was drawn as a foul and grizzled buccaneer, with Reynolds, who unfortunately did resemble a parrot, perched upon my shoulder. There was even a direct challenge, in the form of the *Working Man's Friend and Family Instructor*, which took us on in a battle for the hearts and minds of the people, and which we quickly exposed as an organ of the government and saw off the field.

The really exciting project was *The Mysteries of London*. This was an illustrated eight-page serial which Vickers put out once a week for a penny, initially inspired by Eugene Sue's *Les Mystères de Paris*, which we both loved. But we were not just stepping on frogs. It was at once a political romance, a radical melodrama, and a penny blood that bellowed like a Chartist orator at Hyde Park Corner. Next to our serial, Dickens' social critiques looked trite and naïve, and he hated Reynolds even more than he had as a plagiarist, attacking him in open letters in the press, while sending me a private missive warning that I consorted with a devil in human form.

'This is surely a fitting collaboration,' I replied, 'for the wickedest man in England.'

The central plot involved two brothers, Richard and Eugene Markham, one of whom followed the path of rectitude and virtue, the other chicanery, dissipation, and vice. Eugene was the wrong'un, rising from corrupt property developer and financier to Member of Parliament, until he was mortally stabbed by one of the many he had cheated. Richard was the hero, and he travelled through all strata of the Modern Babylon, falling foul of a terrible villain along the way. He ultimately becomes a champion of the republic in the struggle for independence of a fictional Italian state called 'Castelcicala.' Reynolds saw this climactic plot line as an allegory of a just revolution. I could not personally see why we could not set the class war in our own country, which was why Reynolds was the editor and not I. They would have locked us in the Tower and buried the key.

Within this unambiguous moral dialectic there existed a positive legion of ancillary characters, and a vast maze of sub-plots of the sort that grow in long and hastily composed serials. We were both insomniacs, and would remain at the *London Journal* office late into the night talking through possible plot points, story lines and characters, before one or other of us would tear through that week's instalment, usually in one sitting, with enough time to spare for Stiff to come up with an illustration and cut the block.

New characters were improvised as we went. The dissolute Marquis of Holmesford, our primary symbol of the aristocracy in decline, was founded upon the Marquis of Hertford, a notorious rake who had recently had his bucket kicked during an orgy in a brothel, and I steered Eugene Markham towards a pretty fair representation of that bastard Grimstone, an alpha dog in the new breed replacing the aristocracy as the natural enemy of the people. Our primary antagonist, the villain that terrorises Richard Markham, was based on a series of notable monsters, real and imagined, as well as rumours of a Lord of the Underworld, a terrible criminal genius that had been co-ordinating gangs across the East End for years. The legend was that this man, whose identity remained the best kept secret in

London, had started out Burking in the late-20s, so we called him 'The Resurrection Man.'

We also had a strong female protagonist to balance Richard Markham called Ellen Monroe, a seamstress ruined by the wicked brother Eugene. Through Ellen's adventures, we sought to subvert the conventional tale of the 'fallen woman,' so instead of having her repent and then die (in the manner of such women in Dickens' fiction), we celebrated her spirit of survival and independence. Even Queen Victoria, Prince Albert and several prominent members of Her Majesty's Government were cast as characters in our drama. The prominent authorial voice, which was an amalgam of Reynolds' and my own, was also effectively a character in its own right, offering a polemical commentary repeatedly returning to the social divide between rich and poor. 'There are but two words known in the moral alphabet of this great city,' we wrote in the prologue to the first volume, summing up the essence of our entire philosophy, 'for all virtues are summed up in the one, and all vices in the other: and those words are WEALTH and POVERTY!'

Like many of the early social investigators, however, Reynolds could not resist the lure of the sensational, especially when writing about the criminal underworld; thus his politics, and indeed his plots, did not always make sense. I soon tired of arguing the matter though, for it was his name on the thing each week, not mine. I was the ghost, and his answer was invariably the same in any account.

'London,' he would say, 'does not make sense! Why, then, should I?'

I was compelled to admit that he had a point.

Stiff was less convinced. In common with many other radicals, he was increasingly of the opinion that Reynolds' ratiocinations were at best one-dimensional and at worse an affectation, while he found much of the gothic and Newgate aspects of the serial vulgar and distasteful. He was also a political moderate (a 'moral force' rather than a 'physical force' Chartist), and he disliked our revolutionary rhetoric and obvious republicanism. It had been a genuine struggle to convince him to illustrate the Buckingham Palace episode, although I think the sales of that number did much to salve his conscience in the end.[23] I was aware that he and Reynolds regularly argued, and that there was also increasingly bad blood between Reynolds and George Vickers, our publisher, mostly over the disposition of the profits. Like all publishers, Vickers was making a pound to every shilling Reynolds earned, out of which he also had to pay his staff. Even on a royalty, Reynolds was far from the rich man that *The Mysteries of London* should have made him, and we would often discuss the avarice and uselessness of publishers into the small hours.

We lasted about two years, and with the ink still drying on the concluding part of the second volume of *The Mysteries of London* (Chapter CCLIX), Reynolds was on my doorstep all smiles telling me that we were going it alone.

'You've got a lot of room here, Jack,' said he, waving his tea about in my parlour to vaguely indicate the size and disposition of my home, 'do you mind if I set up shop here for a bit?'

'Why would you want to do that, George?' I said, my heart already sinking.

'Because Stiff has changed the locks at the office.'

'You're not having the study,' I told him.

'Fair enough,' said he, in that annoyingly sunny way of his. I could have guiltlessly strangled him, for he was obviously set on taking me down with him. I could hardly stay on with Stiff if my home address was to be Reynolds' new business premises. He was my friend though, and he was confident that he had enough capital to establish his own magazine, so off I went again, nailing my colours to the wrong mast as ever.

Reynolds had no money to fight Vickers and Stiff for *The Mysteries of London*, and would likely have lost anyway as it is the publishers not the authors who own all the copyrights. The serial therefore continued without us, and it is not without satisfaction that I note that it has never sold as well since.

Reynolds managed to persuade one of Vickers' clerks, John Dicks, to throw in with him, and together they put everything they owned into forming their own publishing house. I had no funds to invest lest I mortgaged the rest of my home, which I dare not do, so I remained a writer, freelance rather than staff because Reynolds and Dicks had not the cash to pay any salaries. It was penny-a-lining again, but at least it was among friends. This time I was writing for *Reynolds's Miscellany of Romance, General Interest, Science and Art* (another catchy title), and *The Mysteries of the Court of London.*

The latter title lacked the bite of the original serial in my view, the Georgian setting Reynolds had chosen diluting the social commentary. He said it was 'allegorical,' but I reckoned it was outdated. I never liked it quite as much as a result, but a job's a job when all's said and done.

*

It was, however, money not political conviction that led me to start freelancing for Henry Mayhew and his big project at the *Morning Chronicle.* This came about when some idiot journalist tried to interview me in the street one day when I was conducting some business in Clerkenwell. He offered me a tanner for my trouble, which was a drink with a penny over, so I strung him along for a bit just to see what he was about. He was a young fellow, quite fashionably dressed, which meant check trousers and an elaborately printed silk shirt depicting sea monsters or dragons or some such nonsense, giving him the appearance of a particularly extravagant Harlequin. He did not have much presence about him, apart from the togs, but he was quite full of himself when he announced that he was with the *Chronicle.*

'That's nice,' I said, 'now what exactly is it that you want?'

'I'm working on a very important new series of articles,' he said.

'I'm sure you are,' I said.

'For Mr. Mayhew,' he added, as if that explained everything.

I was well off the beaten track as far as the middle class press was concerned by then though, so this was not particularly informative. My first thought was Thomas Mayhew, who had edited the *Poor Man's Guardian* for Hetherington, but I then remembered that he had killed himself so it was unlikely to be him.

'Henry Mayhew,' the youth helpfully appended. I recognised the name then, which I associated with *Punch* and, more recently, a couple of unremarkable novels that had been illustrated by Cruikshank, indicating that he was part of that crowd. The last I had heard of him he was going bankrupt. Business was now clearly looking up. I did not let on that I knew any of this, so the young man continued, going into what I imagined was a well-rehearsed little speech. 'Mr. Mayhew is writing a major series on the city,' he said, 'and the real people that live here.'

'Like Mr. Egan,' I said, interrupting facetiously.

He looked very earnest. 'Oh no,' he said, 'it's nothing like that. It is an objective and detailed social study of the lives, habits, trades, and habitations of ordinary working folk.'

'And what do you people call this worthy epic?'

'Labour and the Poor,' he said proudly.

'What a terrible title,' I said.

I must have looked unintentionally severe when I spoke, for instead of defending his editor's vision the young man hurriedly added, 'Not that I'm suggesting that you are poor, of course.'

I should note here that as I drifted towards my fortieth year the natural cast of my features had become downright fierce. I was usually quite unaware of this expression, which essentially signalled my permanent preoccupation with my own sense of professional failure, an equally constant concern over the dismal state of my personal finances, and a general air of hopeless rage. Reynolds said that whenever a name from my former life was mentioned in my hearing I looked like a gypsy preparing to attack a gamekeeper.

'Heaven forefend!' said I, trying to soften my bracket-faced exterior. 'Now why don't we conduct this interview of yours in yonder tavern? You have expenses, naturally?'

He fell for it, and I guided him towards The Coach and Horses in Ray Street. My other business could wait. Plainly the afternoon had to be written off, for sometimes one simply has to give the Devil his due.

My youthful inquisitor, whose name was Binny, confided after the second round that no one was talking to him, anyway, hence his desperate gambit of offering me a small fee for my time.

'Do you think they took me for a policeman?' he said.

I looked him up and down and gave him the benefit of my professional opinion. 'Not in those clothes,' I said.

I decided to do him a favour, and proceeded to explain, as one would to a child, that in this part of town strangers did not talk to strangers, especially middling posh ones dressed like clowns.

'To be a good street reporter takes patience and perseverance,' I told him, 'and more front than Brighton. You have to build up contacts, and round here that requires the same level of caution and confidence required to win the trust of a wild animal.'

'How do you know so much about journalism?' he said.

'Because I've been doing it longer than you've been breathing,' I said, 'have you never heard of Jack Vincent?'

'But you're dead,' he said.

'Not quite,' said I, which just about covered it. Well, I thought, I may be a shade of departed talent as far as this one's concerned, but at least the bugger's heard of me.

He looked quite crestfallen, and not at all pleased to find himself in the presence of a literary legend. 'So you're not a street labourer or trader then,' he said, obviously disappointed.

'You'd have me in an earth bath or knocking apples, you Grub Street scribbler,' said I, becoming increasingly exasperated, and thus lapsing into the vernacular, as Egan would have put it. 'Do you not know a dog in a doublet when you see one, you bookseller's hack?'

'That's another thing,' he said despondently, 'I can't understand a word that any of you people are saying.'

I restrained myself, and refilled my glass from the half-bottle of frog's wine that I had just talked him into buying. I topped it off with water and sugar, lit a cheap stinker and looked at him levelly.

'If you want to talk to the street folk,' I told him, 'then what you need is a guide—'

CHAPTER XXX

THE UNRELENTING FEROCITY of the elements was such that the dead not lost overboard had lain unburied for the duration of the storm (inasmuch as interment in the ocean can be considered a burial), and their corpses were rank indeed when finally laid to rest. One of the women that had died in childbirth was of the Old Faith, and although her friends did their best to disguise her condition, and that of her travelling companions, by burning copious quantities of a foul, popish incense, even this did little to disguise the stench rising from the canvas packages that were once the young wives of soldiers at the Cape. The babies, I noted, were not buried separately, but were unceremoniously bundled up with their mothers, having not been deemed to have existed without the benefit of baptism. The Irish boys were unhappy about this, as they believed that the children's souls had gone to Purgatory.

One subsequently told me he no longer believed in the existence of Heaven, but he was confident that there was a Hell.

'How do you know?' I asked him.

'Because I am convinced that we inhabit it now,' he had replied.

I was inclined to agree just then, being as much in mourning for my drugs as for the unfortunate souls going over the side with a plop. I was heedful enough of my own self-respect not to badger Culhane for laudanum with fraudulent tales of ague and neuralgia. He would have seen through me in a second in any event. Not for the first time in my life, I was going to have to ride it out. While all my fellow passengers were slowly recovering from the sickness, mine was about to begin.

The restoration of the ship had commenced as soon as the storm blew itself out, and the hastily organised mass funeral was just another part of the process, like the pumping of the bilge. Activity had been respectfully suspended while the bodies were committed to the deep, and all who could stand (and were not required to keep us afloat), were in attendance. This strange congregation was a sorry sight, myself included. My clothes had yet to dry, and were also infused with gin and laudanum. I was acutely aware throughout the service that I stank like a wet dog that was also drunk. Only the officers were well turned out, their neatness and preternatural cleanliness as incongruous as it had been below decks in the teeth of the gale, like roses sprouting upon a dung heap. The women that had dragged themselves up on deck had done their best. There was Mrs. Darkin, the Drum-Major's wife, her friend Mrs. Zwyker, and another I knew only by sight. These ladies had been spared the sickness, and had spent much of the storm tending the pregnant women in shifts. I had seen them with Culhane but we had not spoken. They all looked quite shattered, but bore the ceremony with the kind of stoicism one would expect from the wives of soldiers, so no tears in public, although they were the closest to the dead. I was sorry for the women, but they had been and gone so quickly that I could not tell you what they looked like. It was the thought of those tiny, cold children that affected me the most. Perhaps this is where the winged *putti* so popular in Baroque art come from, I thought: dead babies.

Lakeman's rangers appeared surprisingly undamaged. This was also the word concerning the ship, which was only in need of superficial repairs. The rangers had a collective demeanour which was instantly recognisable to anyone familiar with the Prize Ring, and which I had first marked when they bested the redcoats on the field day. It was a look reserved for an enemy, whosoever or whatsoever it may be. In this case they had met the gaze of the storm, as they would the eye of any man, and, with exactly the same level of contempt that they had displayed for Granger and his soldiers, they had asked without words: *Is that the best you can do?*

There were, it must be admitted, soldiers of the Queen on deck who also possessed that look, as if they were carved from oak or cast in iron, but most did not. These hard faced men were the lifers, the laggers, the old survivors, veterans of Africa, India, Afghanistan, and God knows where else, for whom this was just another transit between stations, worse than some, perhaps, yet not so bad as others. But the rest, the majority of the swaddies on board in fact, were new to this game and it showed. The Irish boys, who made up the bulk of the raw recruits, had looked none too healthy when they had initially come aboard, half-starved by years of famine and hopeless toil as they were. In the wake of the storm they appeared wraithlike. Enfeebled by sickness and exhaustion to the point of collapse, they desperately propped one another up at attention. Many looked in little better condition than those being dropped into the ocean.

We were none of us there assembled much warmer either, I fancied, for the storm's abatement had done little to make the atmosphere any less freezing, and I noted several of those closest to me were shivering feverishly. Even my new coat, the leather already weathered as ancient armour, could neither heat my bones nor fully disguise the periodic shudders of opium withdrawal. The corrosive morning cold thus soon counteracted the relief of breathing clean air, even after a week and a half confined in the poisonous environment below decks, and I repaired to the dubious comfort of my shattered cabin as soon as the service was concluded.

I could not be bothered with formal cleaning protocols, not that I knew them, and I restored my berth to order by disposing of much of the contents of my trunk out of the solitary porthole. This was a technique I had already developed in order to avoid visiting the lavatories at the head of the ship, which were essentially holes above the ocean, without even the delicacy of a canvas partition between them, about which the less said the better.

Everywhere the ship was being returned to order, with teams of seamen and soldiers working together to remove refuse and square away equipment that in its unfastened state had been as deadly as chain-shot. The upper deck was scoured and swabbed, the masts re-rigged, and the brass polished until it once more gleamed. Seton also set his men to work on the troop decks, scrubbing the long wooden tables and benches. The great disorganised mass of kit strewn across the deck was collected, cleaned and repaired, after which the men were ordered to clean and repair themselves. I felt for them. All I wanted to do was sleep, but only those demonstrably half-dead escaped the heavy lifting, and most of them were still expected to undertake light duties. Even though I fancied myself a grafter,

I reckoned the regime would have killed me in under a week, and if lack of sleep and hard labour did not do for me my issues with authority probably would.

With the elements seemingly satisfied with their recent exertions and keen to rest, and normality thus superficially restored, I returned to my job. I continued to work on profiles of the officers, based chiefly on my own observations as most of them were wary of going on the record. Even Lakeman was reticent. Although I had established a rapport with him quickly, he gave me little personal information beyond what I learned of him on first meeting. He was, however, perfectly content to gossip about the other officers on board, which was how I found out that Girardot was the son of a vicar, that all Seton's promotions were by purchase bar the last, that Rolt and Sheldon-Bond were rich, and that Wright was a genuine hero of the frontier, having been mentioned in dispatches and general orders for conspicuous gallantry.

'There's a man of steel behind all those whiskers,' said he. Along with Drake, the marine, Wright was the only army officer on board to whom Lakeman would have given the time of day.

The ordinary ranks were more forthcoming, and often downright keen to share their biographies. Even so, I still had to tread carefully. The army was also a fine place to hide for men wanted under their own names, and those that did so were naturally suspicious, and more than willing to cover their tracks in the most extreme of ways.

'What's one Hackney writer, more or less, over the side,' remarked Private Barker to his fellows, for example, when I was reckless enough to enquire as to his origins.

The job was much the same as it had been when I worked as a social investigator, combining personal histories with professional details, although in the latter regard one young private was much the same as another, with a few minor differences in uniform and kit depending on the regiment. Most wore the black shako and the red coat, cut to the waist in front, skirted at the back, and fastened with pewter buttons, dark grey trousers, and square-toed black boots. Much to the chagrin of technological reformers like Lakemen, they all carried the Brown Bess smooth bore musket. There was a feral scent about them made worse by the privations of the recent storm, but different to ordinary working men. There was the usual sweat, shit, and smoke, but mixed with various and mysterious odours that I soon learned were associated with common soldiering: pipe clay to whiten belts, brick dust to polish brass and gunmetal, while there lingered always the clinging, rotten egg stink of black powder.

Some of them were literate, a few surprisingly so, most were not. But if they knew one thing it was that a British soldier's duty was to obey every order, without ever wondering why it was given or whether it was right.

Individuality was thus not encouraged, but individuals there were. Sometimes you could catch a glimpse of the human being inside the fighting unit, if they'd a mind to show you, like the two Irishmen who had no previous history but had both volunteered together for the Queen's Royal Regiment in a recruitment drive in Cork a couple of weeks before, and who must have known little more of soldiering than did I. The younger one, Lavery, would not meet my gaze and told me nothing other than his Christian name, which he whispered was Patrick, while the other, Quinn, who was as protective of Lavery as an older brother, said only one thing to me: 'Do you know what it is to truly love?'

Then there was William Butler, the son of a Nottinghamshire farmer, who had talked his way into the 11th Hussars, the Cherry Pickers themselves, but had so detested Cardigan that he volunteered for the Cape just to get away from him and was now a corporal in the 12th Lancers.

'So like the fabled fish you have jumped out of the frying pan and into the fire,' I ventured, for I assumed there was not much in it when it came to the caliber of the officers in the two regiments. Cavalrymen always fancied themselves.

Butler took my drift, but although he did not disguise his contempt for Cardigan's airs and graces, he would not speak ill of his present superior, who was Sheldon-Bond. Cornet Bond was an ambitious young man from the privileged classes who made no secret of his hatred of Chartists, Radicals and Communists, and we had detested one another since our first meeting. His brother Lancer,

Cornet Rolt, was much more backward in coming forward, and was subordinate to Bond because his commission was a couple of weeks younger. Rolt seemed decent enough from what I had observed, although I found it difficult not to resent the rich on principle, regardless of their personal conduct.

I told Butler what I thought of Bond and he smiled. 'Well, he does come across a touch high and mighty,' said he, 'but I reckon he's all right.'

'How so?' I asked him.

'Well, he's here, sir, with us,' said Butler, 'while most of his mates are strutting around Knightsbridge on half-pay playing the hero.'

'He means to make a reputation for himself,' I suggested.

'I'd say he has something to prove,' said Butler, 'him and the quiet one from the East Suffolks, Mr. Granger, though for different reasons of course.'

I nodded my assent, feeling quite sorry for the disgraced young officer, even though, like Bond, he had always exhibited a similarly ill-disguised disdain for me and my affiliations, political, professional and personal. 'You heard about Lieutenant Granger, then?' I said.

'Who hasn't?' he replied.

The non-commissioned officers were, like me, *in medias res*, and those of us in the middle of things, whether socially or professionally, I am convinced, have a certain connection. I therefore also got halfway decent interviews out of Corporal Smith of the 12th, Sergeant Teale of the 6th, Sergeant Kilkeary of the 73rd, and Corporals Laird and Matheson, who were both in Seton's regiment, the 74th. My prize, though, was Drake, the marine Colour Sergeant, who had once had his throat cut by Spanish slavers and was delighted to regale me with the anecdote.

Drake had enlisted in 1843, he told me, and his first ship was the *HMS Waterwitch*. Early in his career, the *Waterwitch* had taken a Brazilian slaver, the *Romeo Primero*, and Drake, along with a young officer, three bluejackets, and six of the captured Spanish crew were charged with sailing this prize back to England. The prisoners attempted to re-take the ship a couple of days into the journey, while Drake was off-duty and asleep below deck with another British sailor. The Spaniards took the upper deck quickly, and then attacked Drake and his companion as they slept, killing the latter outright and bludgeoning Drake with a handspike before cutting his throat. Miraculously, the wounds were not fatal and Drake set about the Spanish slavers with his bare hands, killing two and rendering the other four unconscious. The ship and the other British seamen were saved, and Drake was subsequently promoted to the rank of corporal for his actions.

I think Drake had decided I was worth the time of day after my recent charity work during the storm. In theory they all had to talk to me, for Seton had ordered it, but how they talked to me was not specified, and many could clearly not be bothered, offering very little beyond name, rank and number.

I did not need all of them in any event. The younger ones were the easiest to reach, although less interesting as soldiers, for they had seen no action yet. As they were so new to this life though, they still clung on to their previous one, which for the older soldiers was a half-remembered dream at best, and these life stories yielded some surprising insights into why so many young men were willing to take the shilling. I tended to assume that the driving force was poverty to the point of exposure and starvation, and in the case of many of the new recruits from Ireland I was not far wrong, but there were also working class adventurers who thought to test themselves in battle, heads often turned by old soldiers in the family; although why someone with pieces missing (as was often described) could be taken as a positive advertisement for the way of the warrior was beyond me.

The recruits were mostly no more than sixteen or seventeen years old, with NCOs and junior officers barely in their twenties. They therefore all possessed that misconception common to the young men of all classes, which was that it could never happen to them. I remembered the feeling but dimly, not that one among them would have listened to me had I tried to set him straight. However we choose to evade it, reality is generally far too much to bear.

Moran remained my passport to the lower ranks. He liked a bet and in common with most men who kept book in closed communities he seemed to know everyone. He had taken quite a shine to me, too, his friend the celebrity author.

Moran was 12th Foot, who were apple knockers and hedge monkeys the lot of them, mostly men from the south east who did not want to live off the land, or had simply failed at it, all born in bleak market towns or bleaker villages in the middle of God's own rural nowhere, like the place I came from myself. To Londoners like Moran they were 'yokels' and 'country clowns,' while the Scots called them 'teuchters' and the Irish called them 'bugs,' but some of the most baffling accents of East Anglia were alarmingly intelligible to my ears. If I remained too long in their company, in fact, my original dialect would begin to make its long hidden presence felt. And it was not one of the good ones. I swear half of them thought they were being interviewed by George Borrow by the end of the day.[24]

Ernest Jeffries of the East Suffolks was a mentor to many, including Moran. Jeffries deigned to speak with me in Moran's corner one evening before lights out, as long as I provided a smoke. Lakeman had been kind enough to replenish my spoiled cigars, and I had begrudgingly stuck a handful in my pockets for the interview. Jeffries was a great crag of a man, with intelligent blue eyes set in a face as scarred as weathered granite. He was about ten years my senior, and spoke with casual authority in the accent of the Cambridgeshire Fens. He had been quite content in Ireland and was far from thrilled at the prospect of going up country from the Cape.

'The colonies,' said he, 'are nought but sand, shit, and snakes. If the fever don't get you then the locals will. There's a thousand ways to die out there, and ain't none of them pleasant.'

'My editor called this a grocery run,' I told him.

'Well I suppose they take deliveries in the infernal regions as well, sir,' he said.

'You've been around then?' I said, using a typical journalist's trick to further draw him out.

He puffed thoughtfully on one of my stinkers and replied, 'I've been here, sir, I've been there, I've been fucking everywhere.'

'Africa?' I asked, hopefully, for I still knew precious little about our destination myself.

'India, mostly, but it's the same difference,' said he. 'I was garrisoned in Gibraltar for a time as well, and later Mauritius.'

'Places with a bit of sun at least.'

'Gibraltar was crawling with some evil foreign plague that killed half the regiment,' he said, 'and there were a lot of planters in Mauritius who didn't take to abolition at all well. All in all, sir, those were terrible holiday destinations.'

'Have you seen much action?' I asked, still fishing.

This time he bit. 'Oh yes,' he said, in a low tone that strangely combined a sense of pride with complete contempt. Then he told me his story, which of all those I heard on the troop decks was by far the most memorable—

'I was just a boy when I ran away to war,' he began. 'In those days they'd take anyone who had two arms and two legs, and cared not much for your age, as long as you could lift a musket and hated the French more than you feared death. I wanted adventure, and I never saw myself a farmer. If that meant fighting the French then that was fine by me, and it was fine by the recruiting sergeant an' all. "They die just as well aged fourteen as forty," he said, although in God's truth I was even younger, barely twelve summers on me. I was a tall lad though, and passed for older. Enlistment was for life, which meant twenty-five years give or take. I didn't much care. I reported to my major in Cambridge, and he sent me to the camp doctor, in the care of a sergeant name of Thorpe. The old butcher pronounced me fit for service without bothering to look, for he needed to keep the new war well fed. Then the same sergeant took me and some other scrawny boys to the town hall, to swear us in before some drunken magistrate. They called us gentleman soldiers until we took the oath, after that they called us the scum of the earth and a parcel of devils and such like. Some of the boys sobered up and began to fret, but I felt good. I was on my way.

'They gave me a scratchy uniform that didn't fit proper, gave me a musket too, taught me how to march and how to kill. I was put in Wellington's army, Wellesley he was in those days. I was in the Cambridgers then, the 30th Foot, the Triple X. They were the finest men I ever knew. I shipped for the Peninsular in a wooden ship name of *Samaritan*, but there weren't nothing good about it, mind. She carried more rats than bayonets, and the devils devoured not only half our provisions but nearly ourselves as well. One mate of mine, Charlie Bridgewater, had his big toe chewed clean off while he was laid low with seasickness, and some young officer lost the end of his pretty nose. When we finally berthed at Lisbon, I were already half dead, and had the leeches put on me more than once before we went anywhere near the sight of a French gun. I had my first woman there, an old Spanish whore. She were older than my mother, I reckon, but I did it anyway.

'The new boys, who'd seen no more of the world than me, wondered what manner of hell they'd blundered into, and many cried for their mothers on the first long march. When it was realised I was no older than thirteen, the officer in charge made me a drummer boy. He was a good man, Lieutenant Mansfield, fell storming the defences at Badajoz, where we did the business with cold iron. I played that bloody drum through Badajoz and Salamanca and all the way to Waterloo, where I took my first ball for the King.'

'You were at Waterloo?' I said, with genuine reverence, before blundering in with a really stupid question. 'What was it like?'

'It was like fucking,' he said, 'only cheaper.'

'Can I quote you on that?'

'Off the record,' said he, and he laughed darkly and continued his story. 'They were all of them bad, but that particular God cursed battle seemed to have no end to it. All I remember was smoke and screaming, and slowly advancing, stepping over dead and dying, just following the boy in front and praying not to be blown to atoms. Bloody cavalry charging at everything, men and horses falling like grass before a scythe. I saw the whole of the Enniskillen boys lying dead from a canister shot, but still in the square, like their ghosts were still holding.[25] Then something slammed into my arm and spun me around like a whirligig, and I fell and saw no more.

'It were Colour Sergeant Thorpe found me after, and carried me half a mile or so on his back to the surgeon. I couldn't tell how or why I lived through that, except for William Thorpe of Colchester, and this mad old Irish sawbones name of Quill, who had some odd ideas concerning musket wounds and wanted plenty of meat to practice on.[26] I was lucky though, for I was strong then and although the ball lodged in my shoulder, it broke no bones. And when I begged the surgeon not to take me arm, he took pity on me and removed the ball, what had driven part of my tunic in with it, and cleaned me up proper careful. I've never known pain like it, but they gave me strong drink, and left me outside the tent, by the mass graves.

'I suffered, I suffered terrible, but I did not die, so they stuck me in the field hospital. And old Thorpy, he found an excuse to come and see me every day, bringing bread and grog and tobaccy. "I didn't carry you all that way to have you up and die on me now, Private," said he. He was a good man. Dead now though, a Pindari spike in his back, God rest him. Then infection set in and I knew I was done, but old Thorpy he brought Captain Reed over and he ordered me not to die. I'd seen Reed flog so many boys for bugger all, I was terrified. So I didn't dare die, but I was off duty for months, and couldn't move my arm right for years after. When it's cold, my shoulder still hurts something chronic. No one wants an invalid after the war's won either, so they discharged me as unfit and I found myself in London.

'When I went up before the Chelsea Board, one of them Lords Commissioners looked me up and down, asked me nothing, then said how I was a young man and would easily get a living. So I was knocked off with a shilling a day for my part in Napoleon's downfall. I bought myself a suit of plain clothes, and entered the world of normal folk a cripple, aged no more than eighteen. If ever you see a poor lame soldier on the street, sir, remember what I've told you here and never pass him coldly by.'

(I assured him that I would do the right thing should the situation ever arise.)

'A lot of discharged soldiers take to begging,' he continued, 'but I'd sooner strike my colours to a Frenchman, so I bought a patch and barrow off this old boy from Belfast, and tried my luck selling dried herrings and salt cod, starting at six in the morning, and working till ten or eleven at night. I would've rather worked on the railways, but what could I do with but one good arm? Pushing that stinking barrow damn near killed me as it was, although I reckon the work helped me in the end, as the feeling started to come back into my hand after a while, although I could not lift with it.

'I never did take to the civilian life though, sir,' he concluded, 'and when I fancied I'd recovered enough to re-enlist, I joined the 12th and Her Majesty was glad to have me. The rest you know. I've been fucking about on some frontier or other ever since, and now it's to be Africa.'

He swore and spat on the floor by way of a *denouement*. I didn't know if this was all balloon juice, but Moran and his mates had fallen for it and so would my readers.

'So we'll be fighting the blacks then?' said one of Moran's entourage, Kelcher I think it was. Jeffries nodded wisely by way of an answer.

'Shouldn't be too difficult,' chipped in another. 'We're better than a bunch of savages right enough. We'll see 'em off sharpish, then I'll take myself a fine, dusky girl, start a family and settle down.'

'You wouldn't go with a black woman, would you?' said Moran, oddly horrified, given his own station in life.

'Christ Almighty,' said Jeffries, 'and what do you think we are if we're not bloody black?'

'Black Irish,' said Kelcher, nudging Moran and laughing.

'Yeah,' said Moran, morosely, as if this was a profound revelation.

I fancied I knew the feeling.

It had to be said that Jeffries' story was exceptional. Such resonant and detailed accounts were rare. For the most part it was slow and uninspiring work, especially sober, and not all that I would want on my tombstone. But, I reasoned, if it got me back into respectable journalism then it was a price worth paying. I also felt an increasing sense of kinship with these men. This sympathy particularly applied to those that, like me, had tried to improve the bloody awful hand that they had been dealt at birth. Also in common with me, they were evidently still trying, in the hope of avoiding poverty, mediocrity and an early grave. And as we thus collectively toiled, we were all of us, of course, forgetting the old rule: *On ren-*

contre sa destine souvent par des chemins qu'on prend pour l'éviter.[27] And at the end of our path, something truly terrible was waiting.

CHAPTER XXXI

Reynolds thought I was mad, but he did not begrudge me a bit of extra work as long as I got him the latest instalment of *Wagner the Wehrwolf* on time (the *Miscellany's* answer to *Varney the Vampire*). He was mostly concentrating on *The Mysteries of the Court*. I had also calculated that I could cannily combine my regular street reporting for Reynolds and Dicks with my work for Binny, as long as I kept my eyes and ears open while I walked the low neighbourhoods with him like some Cockney Pathfinder.

It was money for jam really, for I was well known in the East End, and if I said that the clown was all right then that was more than enough to convince a reasonable selection of street people to talk to him for half an hour, especially if he threw them a couple of pence for their time and trouble, while I received a quid a week from the *Chronicle* for mine.

Binny's results soon spoke for themselves, and Mayhew was reportedly more than pleased. I introduced him to a wide variety of packmen, hawkers and costers, sellers of everything from flowers and fried fish to the dog shit that the pure finders collected to flog to the tanneries. (It's a living, and everyone has to sell something.) Bertie and Nelly also let us set up shop in The Horn of Plenty, where we bought a drink for anyone prepared to talk to us, and to tell us about their lives, habits, trades, and habitations. We often worked, and drank, around the clock, with young Binny left to take his rest wherever he fell.

It made obvious sense in the end for me to start writing copy as well. I contributed quite a lot to the section on the habits and amusements of costermongers, taking great pleasure in one particular interview I conducted in which a very literate costermonger told me how popular Reynolds' periodicals were in comparison those of both Lloyd and Dickens. Not that I was bitter.

It goes without saying that Mayhew got all the credit, but my work on the literature of costermongers resulted in a summons from the chief himself at the offices of the *Morning Chronicle*. These were on the Strand, just around the corner from Reynolds' and Dicks' office on Wellington Street, and as far away as Persia in terms of industry standing. It had been so long since I had moved in such circles that I felt on the one hand as mithered as a farm hand before a magistrate, while on the other there was that familiar resentment at having to beg for another dead end position, and from someone in authority who I did not particularly esteem.

Mayhew was about the same age as I, although not wearing as well. He was a big man, tall, broad shouldered, long-limbed, horse faced and bald, with a voice like thunder in the autumn. He occupied all the space in his office, his chair pushed far back from his cluttered desk in order to accommodate his massive form. He nodded at an unoccupied chair piled high with papers when I entered, but did not rise. I carefully put the stack on the floor and took a seat, regarding him warily.

'Didn't you used to be Jack Vincent?' he said, without wasting words on an introduction.

I knew his type at once. He had that seedy look that all middle aged journalists share, intelligent but unrefined, a bit frayed and dog-eared, pickled and preserved. They tend to look hungry, desperate, arrogant, or complacent, depending on the level of job security. He looked quite ravaged, but also rather pleased with himself. And why should he not? His so-called investigative reporting was a publishing sensation. Yes, I knew the type, for, God help me, I was one of the bastards myself.

'Oh, I'm still here,' said I.

'*The Mysteries of London*, wasn't it?' he said offhandedly, adding, 'Uncredited, of course.'

'True,' I conceded, 'but *The Mysteries of London's* just been picked up in America, and translations have been published in France, Spain, Italy, and Germany. I hear even the serfs are reading it in Russia.'

'But you just received a penny a line for the original, I'll be bound,' he said, seemingly determined to put me in my place.

I shrugged. 'It's a living,' I said, for I had no better answer than that to offer. For all my labours, I was still much closer to Bushy Park than Tip Street, and we both knew it. Hackney writers like me made money for our publishers, not ourselves.

'But not much of one,' he said.

'I've had better.'

'What if,' he said, leaning forward, 'you could have better again?'

I had long ago realised that this was never going to happen, and that particular insight scratched away at my soul constantly, like a man buried alive clawing at the lid of his coffin. Yet still my heart sighed to be anointed once more with a small ray of the sunshine of public favour, and this kept me writing as much as the requirements of basic survival, which was all my scribbling provided in actuality.

'I'm listening,' I said, for it is certainly true that hope can torture with more keenness than despair.

He did not immediately answer, but instead picked up a sheaf of papers casually scattered, it would seem, across his desk. 'Mr. Binny's latest,' he said, by way of explanation. I nodded. He peered at the first page for a minute, affecting to read. 'It's very good,' he finally said.

'John is an extremely talented young man,' I agreed.

He snorted and tossed the packet into my lap. 'Mr. Binny's latest,' he repeated, 'which we both know was written almost entirely by your good self.'

He had me there, but I was unsure what was now expected of me. This was, after all, hardly an unusual practice. I knew from his weekly articles that he did not write all of it himself. I often recognised my own choice of words for a start, and it was as sure as sixpence that I was not the only spectre at the table. Although writers whose very names were brands, such as Egan, Dickens, and, indeed, Reynolds, liked to claim that every word was their own, they were in point of fact supported by a team of assistant writers. It was simply the way with daily deadlines, and Mayhew was no different from the rest.

'I think we've already established that I am a ghost, Mr. Mayhew,' I finally said.

His hooded eyes softened, giving his countenance the impression of a benevolent schoolmaster. 'And now it would seem that you are haunting my column,' he said. 'Why is that, exactly?'

That was a good question. I was not sub-contracting to Binny as a reporter but as a guide, and the payment would have been exactly the same if I had never written a word. I could see that Mayhew was thinking the same thing.

'I'm contributing because I want to be part of this,' I said, slowly, getting to the truth of it in my head as the words were formed and uttered, 'because it is a project for which I have the deepest respect. I was hoping that *The Mysteries* would be like this, but in the end it was not—' I trailed off, realising that the Chartists had been right. We were walking shadows, Reynolds and I. What we had been selling was all just gammon and patter, nothing more, and no different to Egan's *Life in London*, with sensation quickly overwriting social physics.

'Aha!' he said, beaming and pointing at me as if he had just beaten me at three card brag. 'I always knew there was more to you than met the eye, my friend! You're not all pirates and penny polemics are you? There's a heart of oak in there as well. I knew it! I knew it all along!' He was babbling now, clearly delighted at my apparent breakthrough.

'You're thinking of sailors,' I said.

'Nonsense, my dear fellow,' he said, looking slightly perplexed but then once more excited. 'Now let us get down to business shall we? How would you like to officially be part of this project as you so charmingly call it?'

'In what capacity?'

'You would be a staff writer, specifically attached to my team.'

'So I would be employed by the paper, not by you?' I said guardedly.

'Something like that,' he said, smiling broadly and flashing those great equine teeth of his.

'And the byline?'

'Anonymous, I would think, my dear fellow,' he said, frowning like a child frustrated. The expression was bizarrely endearing, although

I felt at the same time the familiar bite of my bad reputation.

'Forever?' I said, weakly.

'For now,' he replied kindly. 'Now come and work for me! What say you, man?'

It was a foot in the door at the *Chronicle*, the paper that had made Dickens' name, and only an idiot would have refused. I was very nearly that idiot. 'Might I give Reynolds some notice before we shake hands?' I said.

'Indeed you may, my dear fellow,' he said, 'as long as your mind is already made up.'

'It is.'

'Capital!' he said, in that explosive way of his, and that was the deal done.

I had been well and truly headhunted, as I have heard some people speak of that kind of aggressive recruitment, and I walked back to Reynolds' office slowly, fearing the confrontation that I knew must come. He had a pool of very good writers he could draw on when needed, but I was undoubtedly his right hand.

The meeting did not start well.

'You turncoat!' said Reynolds, as soon as I had said my piece. 'You whited sepulchre!'

'Yeah,' said Dicks from his desk, growling like a terrier, 'and after all we've done for you.'

An icy rage rose in me, causing my hands to tremble as if suddenly frostbit. My jaw tightened, and I did not immediately respond.

'Oh no,' said Reynolds, his knuckles pressed to his teeth in mock horror, 'he's channelling the black-hearted gypsy!'

'Please don't hurt us, mister,' Dicks pleaded, theatrically cowering behind a large porcelain inkwell, 'we meant no 'arm.'

I looked on in confusion, not for the first time that day, unsure as to whether to laugh, cry or swing. The world had turned upside down, and I suddenly craved sugary tea, that being my late-mother's prescription for moments of severe stress. A little lie down would have been most pleasant as well. My soon-to-be previous employers, meanwhile, caught each other's eye and roared with laughter

'My dear chap,' said Reynolds, tears streaming, 'your face is a picture.' He was beside himself with glee.

Why, I wondered, were all these bloody editors laughing at me today?

'Congratulations, Jack,' said Dicks. 'It's about time you got a proper job.'

'I think we can just about spare him,' agreed Reynolds, regaining some sort of composure, 'although the werewolves will miss him.'

'To be sure,' said Dicks.

'Bastards,' I said.

'You'll still be at the meeting though, won't you, Jack?' said Reynolds, turning to matters more serious.

'I would not miss it for the world, George,' I assured him.

'Quite right, too,' said he, with a long grin.

As Reynolds was so pleased with himself, I suggested a round of tea. He immediately agreed and flew to the door to bellow across the shop floor for Mrs. Burick, our tea lady and thus the cornerstone of the business as far as Reynolds was concerned.

'White and eight sugars, please' I said, when the worthy woman arrived with her mighty urn. It had been that kind of day.

*

The meeting Reynolds had mentioned was to be held the following Monday in Trafalgar Square, and was to be a demonstration against the raising of the new income tax. The organiser was a man I did not know name of Cochrane. As it was an open secret that the latest Chartist petition was to be presented to Parliament the next month, Reynolds had it in mind that this event would constitute a kind of preliminary rally. He had put the word out that the 'Workers of London' should gather beneath the monocular and no doubt disapproving gaze of Lord Nelson, even though not a man jack of them, including us, earned anywhere near enough to be liable for income tax, the threshold then being a hundred and fifty a year.

Reynolds was positively intoxicated with radical fervour, and had learned German just so that he could read the *Manifest der Kommunistischen Partei*. You will remember the time. Continental

Europe was experiencing the greatest upheaval since Napoleon. The year had begun with a revolution in the Two Sicilies, by February the French had declared another republic, and now there were barricades in Berlin. The Hapsburgs were looking decidedly insecure as well, the Danes were acting up, and so were the Irish. It was Reynolds' belief that the working men of all countries were uniting, having nothing to lose but their chains.

It was the same rousing call that we had both heard before, but I was by now old enough to be sceptical. This was, after all, England, and we had already had our revolution, for all the good it had done us. Nonetheless, as red flags went up all over the old empires, it seemed the case to many English radicals that the time was ripe for a Chartist revival. My instinct was that we were doomed, but I could not bring myself to do the sensible thing, which would have been to stay at home and then read about it in the papers on the morrow. As with all my other vices (strong drink, tobacco, opium, women of easy virtue, and writing), I was unable to give up my politics.

Trafalgar Square was still a building site, although the Vice-Admiral himself had been up in the air for the last five years. The surrounding roads were freshly laid, and there were still wooden hoardings around the pedestal at the base of Railton's great column. As a venue for a demonstration it left a lot to be desired, other than in its centrality and its proximity to the heart of government.

The day did not begin well, with Cochran publishing notices that the meeting was cancelled, as he had been informed by the Home Office that large public gatherings were prohibited within one mile of Parliament when it was in session. Reynolds was having none of this, and he dragged me along anyway. The workers of London were of similarly like mind, and a good ten thousand of them, by my estimation, had turned up by lunchtime expecting a speech.

Reynolds saw his chance, and shoved his way to the plinth, where he declared himself Chair to a rousing cheer from the crowd. I did not fancy myself an orator, and elected to remain where I was, which was relatively front and centre, about ten heads back. Reynolds, on the other hand, was born to it. He said nothing at first; he merely held his arms aloft and absorbed the applause and adulation. I am not certain how many there even knew who he was at that point, other than one of their own taking charge. After a minute or so, Reynolds gestured for quiet with his hands, as if soothing a child. As a hush spread through the crowd like mist on a spring morning he spoke.

'The history of all hitherto existing societies,' he began, 'is the history of class struggle—'

There were coppers everywhere, but the crowd was behaving itself so they let him speak, which he did, for upwards of two hours, unscripted, unrehearsed, and utterly voltaic. When he concluded with, 'Let the ruling classes tremble, for the voice of the people is the voice of God!' I would have followed him anywhere, and as the huge crowd exploded into a rapturous ovation that lasted for a good ten minutes I shouted myself hoarse along with the rest.

Reynolds declared the meeting closed at about three, and the crowd began to peacefully disperse. I sought him out, but he was so thronged by well-wishers and hero worshippers that I could not get to him, although he did catch my eye from the centre of the group and offer a cheery wave. I decided not to wait, and to instead meet up with him again later at the office. In the meantime, I had a burning need to relieve myself, and a thirst on me that I would not have sold for half a bar, so I allowed the crowd to carry me out of the Square and along the Strand.

I felt quite intoxicated by the whole experience, and could almost have believed that I was part of some righteous people's army, marching amid the True Levellers with Gerrard Winstanley at its head. But opinions on the street that day were just as divided as they were in the age of the New Model Army. In the case of the Chartists, the middle classes were not with them, and neither were many of the workers. Although the crowd to which I belonged was imposing, if not downright intimidating, there were still passers-by who thought it prudent to air their contrary views in no uncertain terms. There was one group in particular whose voices certainly travelled. They were well-dressed and well-watered fellows, and had elevated themselves on steps and lampposts around The Coal Hole Tavern. I could quite clearly hear an obvious ringleader colourfully asserting that the people leaving the meeting were lazy and would not work, while his companions maintained a supporting chant of 'Jobless scum!'

The police made no attempt to discourage this clear provocation, indeed I noticed a fair few joining in with this idiotic braying. The effect on the demonstrators was slow, but catastrophic, as if one of Professor Owen's *dinosauria* had been lumbering down the Strand minding its own business when it was suddenly struck upon the tail by some manner of troglodyte. Those who were close enough to hear themselves thus addressed resented the charge with some emphasis, and the word then began to ripple through the rest of the crowd and back to the Square until all assembled felt greatly insulted. All it took then was a single word (I know not whence, only that it was given), and the crowd roared as one and rose up against its tormentors. The peelers had no doubt been waiting for this moment, too, for they charged with truncheons rampant, precipitating a riot and thus confirming the old adage that no situation, however desperate, has ever been improved by the arrival of officers of the law.

I now found myself in a pitched battle in which I wanted no part, but from which I could not easily flee. Like many, I was trapped within the crowd, which became more constrictive as it was slowly driven back by the police. My primary preoccupation was remaining on my feet for fear of falling and being trampled to death. Like everyone else I was screaming at the coppers.

The fight proliferated itself in skirmishes between police and demonstrators along every street within a mile radius, for by the time the sun was low in the sky they had closed off all means of exit and had us once more contained within the Square.

Reynolds once more took control, regaining the plinth and urging the multitude to break out. Some of the harder members now started to tear down the wooden hording around the column to fashion clubs, while granite blocks from the new roads were uprooted and smashed, providing handy missiles. Soon the crowd surged forward alarmingly once more, and the police were forced back under a hail of rough projectiles, while those tooled up with improvised cudgels fought the front line hand to hand. It was still impossible to escape, or to move in any direction or at any pace not dictated by the throng, so I kept my head down and was borne south west along the Mall accompanied by the sounds of windows being put out and shouts of 'To the Palace!'

Having no desire to be tried for treason I finally managed to contrive an escape from both sides by sneaking through St. James' Park under cover of darkness, so I know not exactly what happened at the Palace Gates, while witness accounts vary wildly. All I can say for sure is that the Crown was still in control the next day, while a hundred or so men went to the stepper for thirty days for riotous conduct.

As all the fighting was concentrated at the western end of the Mall, I managed to make my way back towards the Strand. Being well-dressed, most of the coppers I saw either tipped their hats or ignored me, and the pair that did take me for a person of interest were quickly mollified by my notebook and my confident assertion that I was with the *Chronicle.* They warned me to avoid the Strand, but I explained that I must return to my office so they let me pass. That I meant Reynolds' office and not that of the *Morning Chronicle* I kept to myself. I needed to see for myself that my friend was all right, and if all was well he would be back at his headquarters with the kettle on writing up the riot. If he had gone to the Palace though, then God help him, I thought.

I need not have worried. I could not get to the office, for Wellington Street was packed wall to wall with a heaving mass of working men, Chartists and Communists mostly I would say, whom Reynolds was addressing from an upstairs window, like Napoleon rallying the *Grande Armée* from a balcony at Austerlitz.

I left him to it and staggered off in search of a cab. I sat out the rest of the proceedings, but the following morning I heard that the crowd had reformed and had erected a barricade in Charing Cross next to the statue of Charles I. The fighting continued all that day and into Wednesday, by which time every copper in London was on duty and the Met was slowly regaining control. By Friday, the *Times* reckoned it was all over, although at the premises of *Reynolds' Miscellany* Chartism's latest star speechifier was already making plans for the presentation of the movement's third and greatest petition to Parliament the following month, because, as he said, we had a world to win.

CHAPTER XXXII

WHEN NOT WORKING for the *Chronicle* on board ship, I worked for Major Seton. The latter toil was entirely philanthropic, as no wages were exchanged for my labour. My second employer had my academic services for hope and duty alone. I think Seton often genuinely forgot that the whole world was not in the army. I was also ripe for exploitation as a writer, being accustomed to working for nothing or next to nothing, driven always by that vital spark of idiot optimism that still believed that something good must ultimately come of all that solitary effort. When I have succeeded in print, it has not been me that has made the serious money but the publishers and their agents.

Suffice it to say that my intention was to gently encourage my son to enter a more secure profession. I desperately wanted him to have a formal education, and to know none of the privations I had experienced as a child or an adult. Grace and I could educate him to a reasonable level ourselves, but it was not the knowledge that saw the Old Wykehamists and Etonians through life, but the prestige of their *alma maters* and the social connections they made there. (Truth be told, most of these people are as dim as toast.) After a lifetime spent despising the ruling classes, I wanted nothing more than for my son to join them. If I had confessed this to Reynolds he would have denounced me as a hypocrite and a class traitor and he would have been absolutely right. But inner conflicts aside, and heedless of my own self-respect, I was on this damn ship to begin the process of earning the money required to make this dream a reality. God help me, I was becoming a member of the aspirational middle class.

Teaching working men on the hoof was not a new experience for me. I had been involved in William Lovett's National Association for Promoting the Political and Social Improvement of the People, a commitment that had not done me any favours at the *Northern Star*, for Lovett and O'Connor despised one another in much the same way as Dickens and Reynolds. Like most writers I adore the sound of my own voice, and you need to talk steady to bring a lecture to life, especially to a captive audience.

The teaching passed the time. The journey was already becoming tedious, and life on board a ship was uncomfortably close to my memories of incarceration. Roberts, the ship's carpenter knocked me up a portable blackboard, and Heming, the Quartermaster, provided me with chalk. I wrote several lectures on the mongrel history of the English Language, which allowed me to dramatically describe the Roman conquest of Britain, the Vikings, and the Norman invasion, 1066 and all that.

I was not so sure how to approach literature without becoming immediately soporific. I therefore adopted the Socratic method, and worked in small seminar groups in which I tried to get the soldiers to talk about their favourite stories; what they read, or had read to them, and what they saw at the penny theatres. I had enough narrative junk in my head to keep up with most of their interests, and attempted to steer discussions towards the way stories were actually structured. I also answered vital literary questions of the day, such as—

* Would the molten core of Vesuvius have really destroyed Sir Francis Varney, and why did he jump in there in the first place? (Yes, and low self-esteem.)
* Was there really cannibalism in Fleet Street in 1785? (I was not sure but suggested that there certainly was now.)
* Could the Lancashire Witches really fly? (Probably not, but with the right kind of mushrooms they might have thought so.)
* Was time travel possible? (Theoretically.)
* Who would win in a fight, Captain Kidd, Jack Sheppard or Dick Turpin? (Captain Kidd without a doubt, even if the other two ganged up on him.)
* Could a drowned man be revived with a tobacco enema? (No.)

The soldiers seemed quite engaged by it all, probably because my classes punctuated the daily drilling and inspections Seton and his staff were putting them through on deck. And in this manner we steamed into warmer waters, hardly noticing the heavens changing above us as we chugged towards the Equator.

In addition to me dragooning it, the soldiers also had stories of their own, and by the beginning of February I started to hear rumours in my classes and around the troop decks about the ship secretly transporting a fortune in gold. This was by no means as farfetched as it sounded. It was not unusual for the navy to convey vast 'war-chests' to overseas armies, for the purposes of everything from paying troops on active service to building roads and bribing foreign potentates. It had, for example, been the reduction of the gold subsidies to the Ghilzai chiefs that had led to the Afghan uprising of '41. Estimates of value varied, while officers would neither confirm nor deny, but the booty was believed to be held in the magazine, which it occurred to me would explain the constant presence of the leatherneck guards.

Moran had also made this connection, and the gold became a constant topic of conversation with him. 'They say there's a cool quarter of a million down there,' he would say, when off duty and apt to gather wool, 'all minted in two pound bars.'

'I always imagined a gold bar would be worth more than that,' I replied in sport.

'Two pound in weight, you dozy scribbler!'

When I asked its value in coin his eyes veritably glowed with avarice. 'A hundred and fifty,' he said, 'give or take. It depends on the exchange rate, don't it?'

It was an increasingly dull conversation, but it perversely passed the time, torturing us both with the reminder of our own relative penury. Each time there would be some new detail. Moran had received his most recent intelligence from a private in the 12th who knew a private in the Sherwood Foresters who had been on the detail that restored the magazine to order after the storm, and had seen several cases of gold bars spilled out upon the deck like a brick wall clipped by a horse and cart.

'Them bloody bootnecks had to account for every last one,' said Moran, unconsciously licking his broken teeth and daydreaming of pocketing a handful of army blunt in all the chaos and confusion.

In deeper dreams he further imagined what he might do with the contents of an entire strongbox, oblivious to the logistics. I could just about countenance the idea of pilfering a couple of the smaller two pound bars and then bolting, but there were apparently thirty carefully packed in a single box, and I could not envisage running while carrying sixty-odd pounds, especially with a brace of stout and heavily armed marines closing in pursuit. Moran, on the other hand, knew no such limits once his fancy overcame him. In fact, he reckoned he could carry a couple.

He had calculated that each box was worth about four and a half thousand. 'Nine grand would set a simple man up for life,' said he.

'Nine grand, my friend, would get a simple man hanged,' I told him.

'But not a clever man, Jack,' he said, all cutty-eyed. 'A clever man would find a way.'

I patted him on the shoulder as I took my leave. 'Good luck with that,' I said.

'What would your man Bannockburn do?' he called after me, like the voice of temptation in the wilderness.

That was a good question, I thought, but one I best not answer. What would the hero of my first piratical romance do, the time travelling buccaneer who fought side by side with Rackham and Kidd? He would go for the gold without question, battle overwhelming odds and dreadful peril, and, thus tested, come through victorious with a witty remark upon his lips, a fortune in the bank and a girl on each arm. But that was fiction. Fantastic tales of likable rogues who were always brave, handsome and funny were all very well, but the only reward for a picaresque scapegrace in reality was the dance without music followed by the cold kiss of the surgeon's knife.

There were truly no more heroes anymore.

CHAPTER XXXIII

IN THE WAKE of the Trafalgar Square riots, the Duke of Wellington himself, then in his seventy-ninth year, was called upon by his government to protect the nation once again. This time the Iron Duke was tasked with defending London against the dangerous radicals that were intent on marching *en masse* to Westminster to present a third petition once more calling for the adoption of the People's Charter, that terrible document that gnawed at the very bones of our great democracy by daring to suggest that perhaps more than five percent of the adult male population should have the right to vote. The politicians need not have worried though, for the day of the proposed mass procession, Monday the tenth of April, was not, as many had genuinely feared or desired, the beginning of a revolution so much as the end of one.

Much as I loved the ideals of the Chartists, it was obvious to me that even if they did have the five and a half million signatures on the thing that Feargus O'Connor claimed, it would not make a damn bit of difference to the government of the day unless it was backed up by a revolutionary army. This we did not have. The petition was a symbolic gesture, nothing more, a public protest against the obscene divide between the unbounded wealth and the hideous poverty that unevenly fractured the nation. We would certainly make some noise, but unless there was a spontaneous uprising of support in the capital, nothing would change.

Those of us with long memories could recall the tortuous passage of the previous reform bills, which were fought tooth and nail by the establishment, when all the damn act did in the end was to clear away a few rotten boroughs which were laughably corrupt, even by contemporary standards, and give a few rights to property owners. The Chartists wanted every man over the age of twenty-one to have the vote, with secret ballots and working class M.P.s. They might as well have been asking for a free dinner on Mars. I recall suggesting to

Reynolds that he should also ask for votes for women, wage reform, affordable housing, cheap medicine, and free education, but he thought I was serious so my point fell rather flat.

I went along anyway, against my better judgement given the Trafalgar Square fiasco, because some events are just too momentous to miss, especially if you call yourself a journalist, and also because, like everyone else in London that day, I wanted to know what was going to happen.

Reynolds was a delegate, which gave me a reasonably privileged view of the proceedings. Feelings were mixed and uneasy at the rallying point, the Literary and Scientific Institution in Fitzroy Square, an independent library and meeting place for working men. It was a fine day, and by nine o'clock there was a large crowd gathered around the entrance, many wearing tri-colour rosettes of red, green and white, the colours of the National Chartist Convention. Some were ready for a fight, some feared one. No one seemed quite sure whether or not the march would happen at all, because every copper in London was on duty, supported by a legion of special constables, while it was known that all the public buildings and bridges were fortified and invested with soldiery. O'Connor was late, and rumours abounded that the traps had nabbed him already. The delegates and their aids (including me) milled around nervously in one of the upstairs meeting rooms overlooking the square, and much to Reynolds' obvious delight he was called to the chair in O'Connor's absence.

After half an hour or so of waiting around, there was a commotion in the street below. This turned out to be a reaction to a messenger from Scotland Yard stoically making his way through the hostile crowd. He was a clerk rather than a peeler, or he was dressed as a civilian at any rate, which probably saved him from a beating. The message he bore was duly reported to Reynolds by the secretary, Mr. Doyle. It stated that the Commissioners of Police were instructed to inform the Chair that the government was agreeable to the petition being presented to the House of Commons, but that no accompanying procession would be allowed to take place, or be permitted to proceed through the streets of the metropolis.

'We have them on the back foot,' said Reynolds triumphantly, 'we must proceed with the procession at any risk. Whatever our masters do or do not allow, practically how can they stop us?'

With powder and shot, I thought, lots of powder and shot.

'We will carry our petition down to the Commons,' he continued, 'after which the procession will continue on to Kennington Common, where we will hold our meeting as planned.'

'Thus rattles the tin kettle at the mad mob's tail,' snorted Ernest Jones, O'Connor's assistant. Jones was another literary man, and also a follower of Marx and Engels. He tended to support physical force, but as was common between Reynolds and most writers, radical or otherwise, there was no love lost. 'And how do you propose we meet the household troops?' he continued. 'This is no mere window breaking expedition, man.'

Reynolds looked hurt, but he held his ground. 'We are for peace,' he said, 'but if the government are indeed for blood, for we all know that they only want the smallest excuse for a bloody slaughter, then by God the cup should be filled for them brimming full, and they should be allowed to drain it to the last dregs.'

He said that well, I thought. There was widespread approval from the floor. The other delegates nodded, even Jones, to give him his due. It would seem that we were for a fight after all. I thought of Trafalgar Square and my heart sank. I wasn't the right sort to die for a cause.

At that moment O'Connor finally arrived and, at a stroke, everything changed. Reynolds retired in silence, and O'Connor took the chair, informing us there assembled that as this was the last morning the Convention would sit before the presentation of the great petition, he wished to make 'a few observations.' The room fell at once into a reverential silence.

'My friends,' he began, in that rich and commanding Southern Irish voice that made you believe his claims to be descended from Celtic warrior kings, 'never forget that our position has always been one of opposition to the British Government. It is therefore quite natural under the present circumstances that this government should place itself in a position of defence. In the same place we would do the same.'

This was a somewhat conciliatory tone for the firebrand who had at once galvanised and divided the original movement by advocating physical force; the man who had done hard time for the cause in York Castle, the founder of the *Northern Star* and the National Land Company. He looked genuinely troubled. Not afeared, but certainly conflicted.

'I have thought long on this matter,' he continued, 'and I have come to the conclusion that in the face of a threat of violence from the government upon our people, it is my responsibility as their leader to persuade our members not to come into direct conflict with the police or the military.'

This was not what any of us expected to hear, and there were several audible sighs that I can only ascribe to disbelief around the room. I, for one, was quite relieved.

'Our brother member Mr. Reynolds is right,' O'Connor went on. 'To the authorities, the slightest provocation would be perceived as sufficient cause for attack. I therefore decided, after much searching of my soul last night, that should the procession be forbidden I would ask our members to abstain from any demonstration while I, myself, would go down to the House of Parliament alone to remonstrate at such a step being taken, and to present our case.'

He paused to let his words sink in. It was Jones who first broke the silence. 'If we back down now,' he said, 'then we lose all credibility as a mass movement.' Several delegates, including Reynolds, nodded in agreement.

'We will do more damage to the cause by persevering with the procession,' said O'Connor, 'whereas by wise moderation we can only strengthen it. This government is weak, should we reinforce it by our own folly? You know as well as I that these blackguards will always prop themselves up by war when they need to distract the populace from reality. Why give them the chance to snatch a bloody victory from the jaws of a peaceful settlement?'

'I have heard it said,' replied Jones, 'that the police have put it about that you are marked out for a bullet should there be any trouble.' He left the implication hanging.

'As are you, Ernest,' said O'Connor.

'Let them try,' said Jones. 'We must fight force with force, like men.'

There was some support for this position from the floor, but O'Connor raised his hand and the room once more fell silent. 'For God's sake,' said he, 'I implore you not to proceed on such a course.'

Jones was not to be gainsaid. 'For once,' he said, 'I find myself in agreement with Reynolds.' (There was some nervous laughter from the floor.) 'Unless we wish to excite the contempt of our enemies and our friends, we must proceed with the procession in the teeth of every prohibition.'

'Hear, hear,' said Reynolds, indicating that enemies can become friends under certain circumstances. These sentiments were once more received with general applause, and a resolution was immediately passed adjourning the meeting to the common, as arranged. O'Connor slumped in his chair, obviously exhausted, but he did not object.

During this discussion two specially constructed ornamental carts had been driven up to the doors of the institution. The vehicle intended for the carriage of the great petition was on four wheels, and drawn by as many huge farm horses, while there was also a long cart in waiting for the delegates and their associates, harnessed to six more monster animals. The latter conveyance contained transverse seats to accommodate the senior Chartists and several representatives of the press, myself included. The gentleman from the *Illustrated London News* was an odd dog, but the quill driver from the *Manchester Guardian* was all right. Our transport was festooned with fluttering banners, each bearing an elaborately embroidered demand from the People's Charter, such as 'Universal Suffrage,' 'Annual Parliaments,' and so forth, while one side of the petition-bearing cart bore the legend 'No Surrender,' the other 'Vox populi vox Dei.'

O'Connor climbed in first, assisted by marshals in rosettes, followed by the other senior delegates, Reynolds, Jones, Harney, McGrath, Clark, Wheeler, and Hunter. The rest of us scrabbled in inelegantly behind them, and the cortège lumbered off amidst loud cheers from the by now huge crowd around the Square. I was reminded of Jack Sheppard on his final journey to Tyburn.

We passed along Goodge Street into Tottenham Court Road, and then travelled the length of the High Street to the National Land Company's office in Bloomsbury, from which five huge bales of paper, comprising the great petition, were brought out by brawny men who were nonetheless struggling like schoolboys under the weight of too many library books. These were secured on the first cart. The scene was more comic than dramatic, but we all cheered and threw our hats, anyway.

Again the cavalcade moved forward, the crowd increasing the train at every step. The windows of the houses in New Bridge Street were filled with spectators, and, amidst much applause, the moving mass took an onward course across Blackfriars Bridge. At this time a detachment of the battalion of Pensioners, under arms and fully accoutred, were observed to have landed at the City Pier, and on reaching the Surrey side of the river, the first display of the civil force appeared, and we saw the uniforms of both the Metropolitan and the City Police.

'Now we'll see some sport,' said the man from the *Illustrated London News*.

The general atmosphere, however, remained carnival, and everything seemed peaceful and well conducted. At the Elephant and Castle, a new mass joined in the rear of those who had followed the train from Fitzroy Square. As I looked back at them, all marching eight abreast like a People's Army, I was amazed by their numbers. It is difficult to estimate such things, but I would calculate that there were not tens but hundreds of thousands in that procession, regardless of what you might have later read in the Tory press.

We reached Kennington Common just before midday, joining up with several thousand more people, already assembled having arrived from their different rendezvous some time previously. I could see members of the Irish Confederation, and the various bodies of the trades of London, each group distinguished by its emblematic banner. The Irish, for example, displayed a splendid green standard emblazoned with the motto 'Erin go bragh.' Our appearance was hailed with loud and continued cheering, and as friends and allies met in one vast throng you could almost believe that the British Working Class Movement had some chance of success. This was as long as you did not look too closely at all the special constables that flanked the crowd, clearly identifiable by their white armbands, many of whom were dressed in the habiliments of working men, clerks and shopkeepers; just the men, in fact, that you would expect to have been supporting our cause. You notice things like that when you're a tailor by trade.

As soon as the carts had come to a stop a senior copper was on hand, conveying a request from the Commissioners of Police to O'Connor that he join them for a private chat at the tavern on the south side of the common, where they had set up shop with the local magistrate.

'It's a little early for a drink,' said O'Connor, raising a laugh, 'but we'd better see what their lordships want.'

He struck off across the common with another delegate, McGrath, in tow, strolling alongside the policeman and chatting. If not for the surrounding crowds, probably around the same in number as the population of a small city, you might have taken the odd delegation for three old friends engaged upon their daily constitutional.

As had happened that morning, when O'Connor had been inexplicably late in arriving, a cry went forth that he had been arrested. Dr. Hunter, speaking from the cart (which had now, as planned, become the stage), set the matter at rest, and in a short time O'Connor and McGrath were observed wending their way back through the crowd, pausing frequently to shake hands or exchange a few words with supporters.

After the customary formalities that always made Chartist meetings, great or small, so byzantine (motions tabled and seconded, chairs appointed, the secretary's speech, and so forth), O'Connor finally presented himself, having previously been in a heated private conference with his fellow delegates at the back of the cart. He stood proudly upon the makeshift stage, smiling amidst the prolonged cheers of the multitude, the slogans of the movement fluttering behind him, and looked every inch the great statesman he was, even when going down in defeat, although we did not know it then.

He worked the crowd for a start, praising them for their fortitude and commitment, before launching into the usual Chartist rhetoric, that liberty is worth living and dying for, and that onward we conquer, backward we fall and all that, concluding with the question, 'Who would be a slave that could be free?'

The cheers were deafening. He then went on to assure all present that he had nothing that he had ever said or done to retract. 'If, indeed, I was to withdraw anything,' he said, 'I would be a most unfit and improper member of a movement such as this.' Another ovation followed of such a length that my reporter's eye started to wander. I noticed for the first time that Reynolds and Jones were both silently weeping.

O'Connor settled the crowd and continued. 'England,' he said, 'has never before seen a day such as this. The people have spoken, and must be heard.' The crowd drowned him out again, and he waited patiently for the applause to die down before continuing. 'I see hundreds of thousands before me today, brothers, sisters, united as one, and I bear with me a petition for reform signed by millions.' He let the word hang for a moment before repeating himself: '*Millions*, my friends, our petition bears no less than five million six hundred thousand signatures, and here today we represent every last one of them.'

If at that moment he had called on us to storm the barricades and take Parliament by force I don't think a man or woman among us would have done anything other than lay down their lives for the cause.

Instead he asked us to peacefully disperse.

This time nobody cheered.

'We have no choice, my dear, brave friends,' he said, his voice catching for the first time. 'The Commissioners of the Metropolitan and City Police have informed me that their officers, supported by the army, have taken possession of all the metropolitan bridges. We cannot therefore pass without significant loss of life on both sides, a situation that I cannot allow.'

Many then called that we should fight and, if necessary, die for the cause, like our brothers and sisters in France. O'Connor did his best to sooth this feeling, offering instead a compromise in which he, as the Executive of the National Chartist Association, would convey the petition to the House of Commons and present it on the members' behalf; to preserve, he concluded, the lives of those who were jeopardised, and so that the cause which was so near and dear to his heart might not be injured.

O'Connor then left the platform, accompanied by considerably less enthusiastic applause that had heralded his arrival. Ernest Jones then addressed the meeting. He said that although he was what was called a physical force Chartist, it was useless for them to engage in a violent confrontation for which they were wholly unprepared.

'Would that this meeting had been held on the other side of the river,' he lamented, as did many, as in that case the bridges would not have needed to be passed. 'As it is,' said he, 'we have achieved a victory, for we are at a meeting which had been forbidden and proclaimed down. Under these circumstances, I trust you all to follow the admirable advice given today by our friend and leader.'

Even though it was unlikely to have been otherwise, Jones' support for O'Connor's position was decisive, I think, in averting a riot. 'If we behave with honour and forbearance this day,' he concluded, 'then our eventual success is certain. The government must recognise the rights of the working classes in England, as they had been compelled to recognise them in France and elsewhere.' This seemed to rouse the assembly, for the cheering regained its former volume once more.

O'Connor then again came forward, and asked the meeting to give him authority now to wait upon Sir George Grey, the Home Secretary, and to tell the right honourable baronet that the people were determined not to come into collision with any armed force, police or military; and that they were resolved to keep the peace inviolate that day. The meeting at once responded to this demand in the affirmative, and O'Connor quit the cart in the company of McGrath. Both men then began walking back in the direction of the tavern turned police station. The crowd parted in silence, some of the members patting O'Connor on the back or shaking his hand, others scowling.

At that moment, Reynolds turned to me and said simply, 'It's over.'

The meeting was then declared to be dissolved at a quarter past one. The five large bundles forming the petition were removed from the carriage and placed in cabs, and taken in charge of the Executive Committee to the House of Commons. The remaining delegates then mounted their carriage, which was dismantled of its trimmings and decorations, and left, followed by the empty cart that had carried the petition.

I could not face the miserable journey home, and elected to remain on the common, with some vague idea of interviewing members of the crowd. In the end I just sat down against a tree and smoked for a while. As if by means necromantic, the huge crowd dispersed before my eyes, shuffling away as if leaving field, mine, or manufactory after a long day, heads down, and mostly lost in their own thoughts. In about an hour not more than a hundred people remained upon the common, and many of these looked to be its usual occupants, boys playing football and bat and trap, women pushing perambulators, men walking dogs. By mid-afternoon a stranger to the day's proceedings would never have guessed, from the appearance of the common, that anything extraordinary had taken place there at all.[28]

CHAPTER XXXIV

When I hear people on both sides of the debate regarding the Third Chartist Petition celebrating the fact that there were no fatalities that day, my response is that there was to my mind one very high profile casualty: the truth. This is hardly a revelation to anyone in either politics or journalism, but it still amazes me how many ordinary people still do not understand how this particular branch of epistemology works.

First, there were the actual numbers in attendance at the Kennington Common meeting. O'Connor claimed there were half a million there if there was a man; twenty thousand said the *Times*; the *Observer* estimated fifty thousand; the *Illustrated London News* cited 'military persons of experience in such computations,' and came up with twenty-three to twenty-five thousand; while the official government statement was fifteen thousand, which would have been piss poor for a provincial cricket match. I, too, have experience in such computations, and in my opinion there were about two hundred thousand of us out that day, which was a huge achievement for the movement, not that it did any good. The government stuck to their figures, and as the memory of the real event faded Londoners began to believe the lying bastards.

Then there was the petition itself. O'Connor claimed it contained five million six hundred thousand signatures, whereas three days later the Commons Committee on Public Petitions reckoned it at just under two million, many of them obviously fake, or so they claimed, with a large number of the autographs consecutively written in the same hand, while many more were those of persons unlikely to have supported the document, such as the Prime Minister, Her Majesty the Queen, and the Doddering Duke himself.

Whether this was true or not, the whole thing had become a farce, *Punch* noting that, 'Had the petition been anything but a hoax, Her Majesty would have been observed at an early hour wending her way towards Kennington Common with seventeen Dukes of Wellington at her side and Sir Robert Peel conspicuous on the cart.'

For my own part, I would say that Kennington Common was and remains an excellent venue for cricket, but an ill-advised place to rally a demonstration intended to march on Parliament, being on the wrong side of the bloody river. As a result, when the authorities called O'Connor's bluff, he could no more get across Blackfriars Bridge without a bloodbath than Lars Porsena and the Legions of Clusium could have strolled across the Pons Sublicius. His capitulation looked like defeat, and the government exploited this failure for all it was worth and quickly won the war of words. The wave had broken and rolled back. Who cared what actually happened?

The only people who did not realise that Chartism was now dead in the water were the Chartists themselves. I interviewed dozens of working class supporters in the wake of the Third Petition, and not a one had a bad word to say about O'Connor. Most, in fact, were quite optimistic, echoing their leader's belief that, one day, justice must come. Mayhew had a radical soul and was quite impressed that I had been on both the Trafalgar Square and Kennington Common demonstrations, but I had to reassure the editor of the *Chronicle*, Andrew Doyle, that I was not one of the delegates before he would give me a job.

I had other concerns that summer anyway. There were far too many new novels coming out that were selling faster than eel pies at a hanging, none of them written by me. I felt my own failure more keenly that year than at any other since my fall from grace at the start of the decade, taking little comfort in the fact that the majority were as tedious and preachy as a Presbyterian service in Hell.

Dombey and Son finally came out in book form in April, and I could avoid reading it no longer. The plot was largely a sermon on the dangers of pride and arrogance, with a strong first act promising more than its development eventually delivered, but for all that the literary execution remained astounding. Reading Dickens was becoming a lot like reading Shakespeare. The stories were not new, the jokes were not funny, and there were interminable diegeses when you wished he would just get on with it, but these things made the writing no less brilliant. You simply could not match him, and although I am equally sure that Thackeray genuinely believed his was the superior talent, it was not.

Thackeray, of course, finally achieved the glory he so desired with the clever but appallingly self-righteous *Vanity Fair*, the resolution of which, he said, was intended to inspire readers to look inward at their own moral deficiencies. He even paused to take another shot at me and Ainsworth, in a section written in mockery of the Flash language called 'The Night Attack,' the supercilious Jesuit boxer.[29] Although he and Dickens were both prize cheese screamers, it was clear that neither had learned their own lessons regarding the value of humility.

There was some very interesting stuff from the mysterious Bell family in circulation as well. 'Ellis Bell' had reinvigorated the old gothic romance in the wonderfully mad *Wuthering Heights*, in which passion knew no class barriers and was as destructive as a hurricane at a regatta (which had certainly always been my experience), whereas 'Currer' seemed to be suggesting in *Jane Eyre* that what middle class women really wanted was to be fucked by the rich. The best of this queer batch, for my money, was *The Tenant of Wildfell Hall* by 'Acton.' The rumour was that all these books were by the same man, yet the styles were obviously very different. From the overall tone, my suspicion was that these books were all written by women.

The worse of the anthem cacklers that year was, I also suspected, another woman. This one was writing anonymously, either at the behest of the publisher, or more likely because of all that 'Separate Spheres' nonsense that probably had Flora Tristan spinning in her grave like a steam-driven jack. The novel in question was *Mary Barton*. This 'Tale of Manchester Life' soon became a literary sensation, purporting as it did to expose the suffering of the industrious classes. The first few chapters might have done so, but the book quickly descended into melodrama. The story of John Barton, who assassinated the son of the local mill owner, was particularly galling. The murder was presented as a Chartist statement, after which Barton was tortured and ultimately destroyed by his own guilt. Reynolds and I had written of many working class characters that had done for their masters, and none of them felt anything but good about it afterwards. Fallen women were also fated to find their reward only in Heaven, much as if they were written by Dickens. The novel expected its audience to at once sympathise with management as well as the workers, and the moral of the story looked to Christian Brotherhood as a solution to social division. No doubt Marx and Engels were kicking themselves upon reading this rabbit catching rubbish, at having neglected to conclude the *Communist Manifesto* with a line about everyone trying to just get along.

Lytton and Ainsworth were still banging away as well, neither appreciating that the historical romance was now almost as dead as Sir Walter Scott. Lytton scratched at the casket with *Harold, the Last of the Saxons*, while Ainsworth published *The Lancashire Witches*, a gothic novel of the old school. Ainsworth's book was doing well, though the serious meditations included upon the persecution of women in the stupid ages might have carried more weight if his heroines had not been presented as real witches who rode on broomsticks and regularly cavorted with the Devil.

I sent him a message of congratulation anyway, and he returned a response that was as charming as it was daft. In addition to appearing genuinely pleased that I had contacted him out of the clear blue sky, he said that upon reading *Wuthering Heights* he fancied that the author might have been me, 'Coming upon us again in a fresh and questionable shape.'

But all these books were in the mainstream of literary publication, and this was not my world. Blotting the skrip and jarring it for Mayhew and Doyle was not so bad though, as long as I did not think too much about financial security or the bestseller lists. I was now on the bottom rung, as far as respectable journalism was concerned, in a position that suited the likes of John Binny, who was young, ambitious and willing to work long hours for a bunter's fee, but a poor place to be at my time of life.

Living hand to mouth without hope was as familiar as my shadow by now though, and at least, as Flora Tristan would have said, I remained true to my class. It was clear to me that these rising bourgeois authors had never toiled around the clock without money for food or drink, dodging the bailiffs and quill driving for a penny a line, so, as far as I was concerned, my soul was the purer. Only Dickens knew what it was to be truly poor, and although he wrote of it endlessly, that life was in reality a long way behind him now, whereas I was still living it in an abysmal and unending recurrence. Ah well, I thought, choak away, the churchyard's near, as they used to say in the Marshalsea.

I was, at least, off the death hunting, although my reputation in that quarter was such that I would still receive the odd tip from an informer hopeful of some sort of a finder's fee. I tended to bat these folk away as politely as I could, but one morning a particularly tenacious three-outer caught me at the office and set Mayhew's antennae all of a quiver. He had covered the cholera outbreak in Bermondsey, and knew the value of corpses in our game, which were as useful to us as they were to the surgeons and resurrection men.

The young fellow had a powerful scent about him that already suggested an intimacy with cadavers, and he addressed me with a familiarity that I found quite distasteful, although it was, as ever, my easy way of communing with these people that made me so indispensable to social investigators like Mayhew.

'It's a good'un, Jack,' said this grimy Hermes with macabre delight, 'I wouldn't bother you otherwise.'

'Where?' I said warily.

'Golden Lane,' said the boy, 'behind St. Luke's.'

Clerkenwell, I thought morosely.

'Your old stamping ground, Jack,' said Mayhew, with a sly grin. This was where I had been recruited by Binny. The old cleverstick was also playing upon the long association between Clerkenwell Green and English radicalism.

I formed my features into what I hoped was an approximation of enthusiasm. 'It's all pubs, printers and prisons there, isn't it?'

'A veritable home from home,' agreed Mayhew.

'I'll get my coat,' I said.

Despite the desire of chroniclers such as Engels, Kay and Mayhew to precisely document the nature of every poor dwelling in the Metropolis, the plain truth of the matter is that when you've seen one London shit-hole you have seen them all. The one to which I was now brought, after a brisk walk through the centre of town in a black rain, was one of those low, dark, basement rooms with stone steps up to the street, in a gloomy house in a court behind the church. Although it was miserably wet, a small crowd had already assembled around the building, because a good death can always brighten up an otherwise dull morning.

Someone had scratched the word 'Witch' into the dark, peeling paint of the door to the apartment in large letters. 'What's that about?' I asked my guide.

'Dunno,' he said, 'I can't read.'

'Of course you can't,' I said. 'Silly me.' I let it go at that. If this had any relevance to the story, if story there was, then I had no doubt that I could get the intelligence from one of the idiots out the front.

The scarred door was shut but it had recently been forced open with some violence, the frame newly splintered around the lock. There was a middle-aged constable stationed outside, waiting upon a doctor to certify the death, but we all knew the drill. I slipped him half a crown, to which he replied, standing away from the door, that he made a point of always keeping on the right side of the press.

My young companion could neither conceal nor contain his excitement. 'I heard there's nothing left of him,' he said enthusiastically.

'Yes,' said the copper slowly, addressing himself to me, 'it's a very nasty business.' He pushed the door open with some effort, its ruined hinges causing it to scrape heavily along the stone floor. 'We was called,' he added, lowering his voice conspiratorially, 'on account of the smell, sir.'

Lovely, I thought.

It was a wretched two room apartment, the first sparsely furnished chamber darkened by layers of waxed paper pasted over broken casements in an ineffectual attempt to keep out the cold. The rain drove against these patches as if they were the skin of some muted funerary drum, and despite the autumnal chill the draft the tiny windows afforded was something of a relief. It stank in there worse than any tannery, and not solely on account of the miasmic vapours of the Fleet, which ran just around the corner under Ray Street. Had I been a stranger to the scene, I would have still known the cause of it at once, for there is nothing so obscenely foul as the stink of a dead human body. The decomposing remains of cow, horse, or even pig on the side of the road are nosegays by comparison, and I had left in haste and was here without a smoke. Mayhew and this urchin had well and truly sandbagged me, and I was quite out of sorts. Going to a death without pocket full of cheap cigars was the act of an utter greenhorn.

The charnel room was behind a tattered curtain. It moved in some invisible draft, or I thought it did, for a huge rat stuck its head out from underneath and regarded the three of us levelly. 'Jesus!' said the boy, backing towards the door but resisting the temptation to bolt.

'Get away with you,' called the copper, ineffectually kicking the air before the beast. The animal had no respect for the law of the land however, and held its ground. I selected a large coal from the grate and hurled it at the floor in front of it with a crack. The triangular head vanished.

'It's in there,' said the constable redundantly.

'So I gathered.'

I braced myself, tied a handkerchief around my nose and mouth like a highwayman in a comic opera, and drew the curtain aside. A legion of rats scampered in all directions and the air became black with blowflies. The atmosphere of the room was solid with corruption, and it took all my journalistic resolve to prevent me from doing the only sensible thing, which would have been to run out of that terrible room and never look back until the air was clean again. Behind me the policemen fired his lantern and passed it to me, explaining that the light should keep the rats back. I noticed that he did not care to enter the room. Once had obviously been more than enough.

The boy stuck his head around the door. 'Bugger me!' he exclaimed, before the receding slap of his bare feet on the flagstones and the distant sound of retching indicated that he, too, had seen his share.

I shone the light on the rough wooden bed that all but filled the room, and upon the human figure under the shuddering cover of rank black fur and loathsome animalculae. I fought back an ocean of nausea and kicked the frame with the flat of my foot as hard as I could. Most of the vermin scattered into the shadows, revealing the partially devoured remains of what appeared, from the vestiges of the garments, to be a male lying atop the foul straw mattress, stained with oily, black blood. The rats had been at that as well. His coarse work trousers had been gnawed to rags, his legs were eaten down to the bones and his belly and bollocks were gone. By the general state of what was left, my guess was that he had been dead about a week, although the room was cold so it might have been longer. In a final, crowning horror, the man's arms were flung across his face, given the impression that he might have still been conscious when the rats had started on him. It didn't bear thinking about.

This ghastly tableau should have been more than sufficient for any death hunter, but not for me. Oh no. I could not tell you why, even now, but I had to see his face.

'Did nobody hear anything?' I asked the copper.

'This is an old building, sir,' he said from the other room. 'The walls are a good foot thick.'

'May I lower his arms?'

He started remonstrating about the medical examination and the integrity of the scene, but I bunged him a couple more bob and he looked the other way, on condition that I return the deceased to his proper position after.

I looked around the room for something to protect my hands, for I only had the one fogle wipe about me, and that was not leaving my air holes. I settled for some ancient newspaper pasted over a crack in the plaster over the doorway, which had a corner up and was easily peeled away because of the dampness of the walls. I idly noted that the page was torn from the *London Journal*.

The exposed parts of the forearms had been got at, and the fingers were mostly gone, but they had served their presumed purpose in protecting the poor devil's face. He was no longer stiff, and using the paper as an insulating agent I gently pushed his hands down where they crossed, while raising the policeman's lamp in my other hand. The absence of flesh on the rest of the corpse made the contorted face doubly grotesque in the flickering lamplight.

The copper ventured into the room out of morbid curiosity, but looked away quickly, swearing. 'Eaten alive by the look of him,' he finally said, 'how horrible.'

The eyes had not yet gone, and they stared past us both and into a hell that even I could not begin to imagine. Though decomposition had set in, the irises still retained their original pigment, which was a deep, crystalline blue. The eyes were not vacant in the manner of most bodies once the occupant has departed, but were wide with horror. Worst of all, there was a strange familiarity about them.

A cold, creeping dread that went well beyond even this vile scene froze my bones, and I began to shake uncontrollably. Fearing I must fall among the rats that were beginning to reassemble on the flagstones, I sat on the edge of the bed, my violent tremors agitating the corpse into the most hideous animation.

'Come away now, sir,' said the copper gently, taking the lamp from my numb hand and attempting to guide me from the bed.

I could not move.

'Jesus Christ,' muttered my companion in exasperation, for it was likely the doctor would be arriving soon.

He grabbed me by the arm and yanked me off the bed. I was still holding the wrists of the corpse so he came too, landing on the floor and dragging me down across his chest, which ruptured as soon as I came into contact with it and painted me in putrefying fluids. Once more the rats scattered.

The copper gave a dreadful oath and pulled me, spewing, to my feet. He shoved me through the doorway into the outer room and, by the sound of it, set about restoring the scene, swearing all the time like a particularly intemperate drill sergeant parading newly recruited soldiers. I struggled out of my pus soaked coat, and sank to the floor shivering, although I felt not the cold, until the policeman returned. He picked up my filthy coat and went through the pockets, pulling out my notebook and my wallet.

'I reckon you owe me for that,' he said, opening my wallet and helping himself to the notes before returning it with about enough change for a cab. He chucked my notebook at me and told me to be sure to write everything up proper like, but to keep him out of it. I nodded glumly and rose unsteadily to my feet.

'Now fuck off,' he said, 'before I arrest you.'

I regained the street, but my legs would take me no further. I leaned against a wall and slid down it into the mud and shit. The sightseers were still milling about, mostly elderly locals and a few sooty children, and they found my predicament most amusing.

'What's up with him?' said a wizened old coal whipper in a flat cap.

'I reckon he's been taken a bit ill,' answered an ancient baby farmer, wraith-like chavs hanging off her skirts.

'If you can't take it, darling,' chimed in a particularly loathsome old brass in a bonnet that looked as if a carthorse had stomped on a chicken, 'then you shouldn't look should you?'

The crowd were still cackling at my expense when the copper appeared at the top of the steps to the basement, looking important and glowering fiercely at the ghoulish onlookers.

'Sling your hooks, the lot of you,' he commanded.

'You can't stop us walking on the street,' said the tart, the irony of her statement escaping her.

'Try me,' said he, staring her down until she scarpered along with the rest. He then walked slowly over to me. 'Are you still here, sir?' he said, quite matter-of-factly, despite our recent adventures. You had to admire the professionalism.

I had not the energy to address him, or even to raise my head. I stared fixedly at the ground and concentrated on not passing out completely. The frozen rain running down my neck was helping.

'Leave him be,' said a faraway female voice. 'Can you not see the poor man's unwell?'

'Raving mad more like,' said the copper.

I looked up. A dark haired young woman wearing a plain, black dress and carrying a basket was looking down at me as if I were a lost child. She held out her hand. 'Come along, sir,' she said, 'let's get you inside and cleaned up, shall we?'

'Bleeding nonsense,' said the copper with a snort.

'There's no need for profanity, constable,' said the woman sternly. The policeman coughed awkwardly but said no more. She collected my coat from the filth, despite my protestations that I did not want it, and led me into the main building.

I followed her up several dingy and narrow flights of stairs in a daze, until we arrived at her lodgings. 'I hope you don't think I make a habit of inviting strange men up to my rooms,' she said.

'Perish the thought,' I agreed, trying to pull myself together for the sake of propriety. She was taking a huge risk, but these Good Samaritans always do. She was neither young nor old, perhaps in her late-twenties, and her features, although pale with want and care, were pleasing and agreeable. She also had the most remarkable eyes, deep and dark, and although her clothes had obviously seen better days she was singularly neat and clean in her appearance. 'I am profoundly grateful for the assistance,' I added. 'I fear I must look a state.'

'You are a bit bedraggled, sir,' she said.

'Jack,' I said.

'As you like, Jack,' said she, 'then you must call me Grace.'

We were still hovering at her door, me leaning on the wall for support, her looking at me nervously, probably wondering why on earth she had brought me up here. She took a chance and opened up. Although the hour could have been no more than eleven it was quite dark in the room. There was a small window, but its proximity to the wall of the adjoining building was such that it might as well have been paned by bricks. She lit a twist of paper from a tinder box, and touched the top of a candle upon a small table. Along with two ancient dining chairs this was the only furniture in the room. I had expected something like this, but what I was not prepared for were the drawings that covered the rough plaster of the walls like the paintings discovered in the ruins of Pompeii. There were recognisable cityscapes, portraits both realistic and grotesque, and fantastic creatures of land, air and sea that seemed animated in the flickering auburn light.

'I mostly do these with charcoal,' she said, as if this explained everything.

'I expect your landlord loves you,' I said.

'We never see him,' she replied. 'An agent collects the rent, and I don't let him past the door.'

'Then I consider myself extremely privileged to have seen such powerful work,' I told her. She smiled shyly, while I swayed like a tree in the wind. Eventually I had to ask if I might sit.

'You do look a bit green around the gills,' she agreed, motioning towards one of the chairs. I fell into it with a sigh. The table was covered with delicate lacework that I had initially taken for a table cloth, as well as various sewing accoutrements.

'You are a seamstress?' I ventured, while she set to lighting a fire and hanging a rusty kettle.

'That's right, sir.'

'I used to be a tailor.'

'What a coincidence,' said she, 'I believe the unfortunate gentleman downstairs was also of that profession.'

My heart started to clatter again and I felt, once more, lightheaded. 'I rather feared he might be,' I said quietly, for it was not the sight of a mere corpse gutted by rats and slugs that troubled me so, even if the damn thing had leaked all over me. I had come into close contact with far worse in my days as a full-time death hunter. It was not a game for the squeamish. The reason for my present distress was that I was increasingly certain that the thing in the basement was the mortal remains of my father, lost for years in life but easily found in death. The irony was almost as hideous as his demise. I had searched for him for years without a sign. I wondered at the chain of random events that had brought us both together now. You could not invent such a tale.

'I assumed you must have known the poor soul from your reaction,' she said. 'Bereavement is a terrible thing.'

I realised then that her dark vestments indicated mourning. 'I'm sorry,' I said uselessly. 'You have lost someone too.'

'My father,' she said, 'a while ago.' She looked lost, momentarily, but recovered her composure. 'I am more concerned for your poor friend just now.'

'Tell me,' I asked, although I did not want to, 'was there anyone else living down there with him?'

'Come to think of it there was,' said she, 'although I have not seen them of late.'

'A man and a woman?' I asked urgently. 'The man about my age, the woman closer to you in years?'

'That's right,' she said, 'his children, I think. A strange pair.'

'How so?' I asked, trying to maintain a calmness in my voice that I did not feel in my heart.

'The woman always wore kid gloves,' she explained, 'whatever the hour or the weather.'

'And the man?'

She looked a little flustered. 'You'll think me silly, Jack, but the man was—' She paused for a moment, searching for the right word. 'Well,' she resumed, 'I don't like to speak ill of my neighbours, but he was just— *creepy*. The way he would look at you.' (I could imagine.) 'There were rumours,' she continued, 'that the woman had the second sight. Some of the more superstitious locals reckoned she was a witch.'

'I saw the door,' I said, though this was news to me if this was, indeed, my sister. 'Do you recall their names?'

She thought for a moment. 'Smith, I think, John and Jane.' (No wonder I could not find them, I thought. Could the pseudonyms have been anymore generic?) 'I do not know the father's name,' she added.

'Joseph,' I said. 'He was my father too.'

'Oh, Jack,' she said gently, 'I am sorry.'

'I lost him,' I said, my voice failing, 'years ago—'

I did not weep then, for I still never cried. Rather I collapsed. Again, my whole body began to shake violently, as if in the thrall of fear or fever, as it had done in that other terrible apartment. The air became dark and foul, and I could no more see or breathe than if filthy smoke had suddenly filled the room. I rubbed my eyes and clawed at my throat in agitation, unable to stand or to speak. My companion obviously interpreted my neurasthenic convulsions as a manly attempt to suppress tears of grief. Without hesitation, she came to me and I felt the warmth of her consoling embrace.

She held me until the attack was over, passing no judgement. Even so, I was thoroughly ashamed, but as my senses were restored a more pressing problem made its presence known. The sawbones, I realised, must have attended by now, and the unclaimed bodies of the poor went straight to the anatomist under law. If I did not act promptly, my father would be dissected by some bastard surgeon in front of a load of feckless medical students. If that damn peeler was still about the place though, he would most likely run me in as soon as I showed my face.

I urgently explained my predicament, and she announced without hesitation that she would go downstairs at once, and make it clear to those in authority that I was the next of kin and that arrangements were being made for the care of the deceased. 'I will send for an undertaker as well,' she promised.

I was forced to explain that I had next to no cash about me, and precious little at home now that bastard copper had rolled me.

'Don't you worry about that either,' she said.

Where have you been all my life? I thought, although it would not have been proper to say so. No one had ever looked out for me before, not like this. I settled for offering my profoundest thanks. I knew not why she would help me, although I suspected, quite wrongly as it turned out, religious enthusiasm, but just then I was happy to take any help I could get. Had I returned to that awful basement there would almost certainly have been a scene.

'You can pay me back later,' she said, preparing to leave. 'Now what is your full name, and where should your father be sent?'

I told her my address.

'Very nice,' she said, 'and the name?'

I told her that too. She paused, standing by the door and fastening her shawl, regarding me quizzically.

'The novelist?'

'Used to be,' I said, 'I'm just a journalist now.'

'Bloody hell,' she said, and then laughed, embarrassed. I knew then she was no anthem cackler. 'And all this time I thought you were in the rag trade.'

'Oh, I am,' I said.

'Stay here,' she said firmly, and then she was gone.

I now found myself with time to spare in the most Spartan of environments. She had made tea, so I took the liberty of helping myself. Although it was a poor substitute for a smoke and a real drink it was at least pleasantly warming. I then applied the rest of the water from the kettle to my dishevelled clothes, with varying degrees of success. The coat I threw on the fire. It was a relatively new garment, by my standards, and I could ill-afford to do this. The smell was appalling, like a burning dog. I had to force the small window and hold the door open in order to ventilate the room, colourfully cursing my impulsive and boneheaded actions as I did so.

This killed about an hour, after which I was left with nought to do for a distraction but investigate the drawings on the walls more closely. She had a graphic style, not dissimilar to the woodcuts and engravings that illustrated popular fiction, including my own, but tempered with the softer tones of grey possible in charcoal. She made much use of shadows to give the drawings depth, and there was a darkness about both imagery and technique that greatly appealed to me. I wondered what she might be capable of with some decent pens and paper, or even oils and canvas. The pictures themselves were both representational and fantastic, the scenes and subjects various, yet the arrangement suggesting some sort of narrative involving a journey by land and sea. In a lighter mood I might have started to weave a story.

I turned my attention next to the lace on the table. It was beautiful, delicate work, and probably paid by the piece. With a stab of guilt, it occurred to me that I was wasting her time, because the life of the common seamstress was one of endless and terrible toil, for a pittance, naturally. Going out on my account would almost certainly cost her what little sleep she would usually allow herself in order to remain on schedule. Seamstresses around here usually worked for an agent, and were paid about sixpence for a sixteen-hour day. (You will have no doubt read Mr. Hood's poem upon the subject.)[30] I felt a mortal shame at my own complaints, as I often did in the face of the true working class experience. Writing, even chaunter culls and low tales, was infinitely preferable to genuine labour, that ceaseless, squalid toil with no more possibility of escape or remission than that of a convicted felon who has just undergone the cramp word.

I told her as much upon her return, without, I hoped, suggesting that her situation was in any way squalid. She made light of it though; honest labourers and artisans always do. My parents were the same.

She sniffed the air like some delicate woodland creature. 'What's that funny smell?' she said.

'I can't smell anything,' I said.

She had returned, hair and outer garments as wet as an otter's pocket, bearing both lunch and favourable news. She had claimed to be a relative acting upon my behalf, which had been good enough for the doctor, who cared not about one stiff pauper more or less, and my father's arrangements had provisionally been made, with the ten bob I had managed to scrap together earlier serving as a down payment with the undertaker. A good man, she had assured me, who had also dealt gently and fairly with her own dear father's interment.

We ate bread and cheese and shared a bottle of beer, which I could tell was an extravagance for her, and talked of many things, confiding recklessly. Her father had been someone once, but he had gone bankrupt when she was a child, and had spent the remainder of his life as a penny scrivener doing the donkey work for accountants who paid even less than the publishers of the penny dreadfuls. I felt for him. He had died the winter last from an inflammation of the lungs. Her mother she did not remember, and she had no surviving siblings. Like me, Grace had known, briefly, a better life. Unlike me, she did not seem to be bitter about its loss. I did not push the point, and I concealed my own darkness, for it would have been far from seemly to discuss such things so early on in an acquaintance, even one as unusually informal as this. Instead we talked about art and music, about which she knew considerably more than I, and of literature and the literary life, which she thought sounded most exciting, which it most certainly was not and still isn't.

The lunchtime conversation was an escape for both of us, but eventually she had to politely indicate that she must work, having fifty floral motifs to embroider upon a shawl before the next morning, in addition to a dozen or so doilies to sew. I had no wish to leave, and as I had helped my mother stitch many a doily when I was a boy I volunteered my services, so that she might at least be relieved of this tedious work and could therefore concentrate on the more demanding task of the shawl. Embroidery of the standard required on a rich client's garment was well beyond my capabilities.

She looked uncertain, and I knew she was calculating whether she dared risk the materials to test me. 'It was my family's trade for years,' I reassured her. 'Please let me do this for you.'

My first piece passed muster, and I was allowed to sit with her and sew through the night, both of us disclosing more and more as the hours slipped pleasantly by. We worked through the dawn, but got it all done. Like her, I was no stranger to impossible deadlines.

So then I had to go. The poor woman was exhausted, and might still snatch an hour or so of sleep before she had to deliver the work.

'May I call on you again?' I asked her, as I regretfully took my leave.

'I would like that, Jack,' she said, her eyes big and bright despite hours of excruciating detail work. I thanked her again, and left, very quietly, so as not to scandalise the neighbours. Once again, I realised, love and death were coming together, unbidden, into my world.

CHAPTER XXXV

I HAD NOT THE resources to send my poor father to lie by my mother, so we buried him in the new cemetery at Tower Hamlets. It was a simple service, just a few secular words over the grave, with only Grace and myself in attendance. The trail of my sister and the one that controlled her was already as cold as the grave in which my father now lay. Yet now, at least, I knew where she had been, that she wore gloves to disguise her ruined hand, and might be connected in some way with the new spirit mediums that were beginning to appear just then. And if not among these people, I reasoned, a 'witch' might find refuge in the older communities of fortune-tellers, faith healers and mystics in and around London. This was a lead I could investigate and follow.

Mayhew forgave me the lack of a story, for I would neither write of my father or my new friend. Instead, I promised to explore the superstitions connected with the denouncement of a modern sorceress. This would allow me to seek out my sister, while also getting paid to research and write about the strange folk who made their living from the occult. He declared this a capital idea, as his series was also intended to explore the 'beliefs' of the urban community, while Reynolds discretely let it be known that he would have it if the *Chronicle* did not. I had explored this world before, first as a ghost breaker for Egan, and later when it thrust itself upon me in the mistaken belief that I was some sort of practising alchemist. (Lytton remains convinced of this to this day.) I therefore still had contacts, although this was very much a moonlight enterprise in both senses of the word, for the gothic theatricals rarely emerged before twilight, and I still had to earn my keep on the more conventional *Labour and the Poor* articles.

I continued to call upon Grace in Golden Lane, which had become locally known as 'Rat's Alley,' where, it was said, only the vermin ate well. She found my tales of séances, rituals and readings terribly exciting, and begged leave to attend some with me. I was far from comfortable drawing her into all this lunacy, even though, as she pointed out, she could identify my sister by sight. She therefore had to content herself with my accounts, several of which she illustrated. I had made a gift of some drawing materials, for the sake of her walls, and she was now perfecting her art at an astounding rate. But all this is a story for another time. I never found my sister, and none of the gypsies and table-tappers that I met ever foresaw the slightest hint of what truly awaited me in the future. They were not even close.

Grace and I would often dine together at her lodgings, and then we would both work in each other's presence late into the night, she sewing and me writing. I would frequently help her with needlework, and she would listen to and comment upon my compositions. Sometimes I would just read to her (she liked ghost stories the best), and often she would sing. It was the most gentle and rewarding of companionships, but neither took it to be more than it was, which was friendship.

It was Grace's agent that unwittingly expanded the parameters of our relationship. I had never met the woman, and Grace was careful not to speak ill of her, but I had already formed my own opinions. Mayhew and I both despised the piecework system and those that exploited it, and we had denounced it in our articles. The agent expected Grace to walk to her shop to deliver the work every morning, only rarely collecting a piece by hand herself if the client was rich enough to warrant the personal touch. Such a visit was arranged one bitter December evening, in order to take possession of an urgent and intricate job that my dear friend had been working on without a break since dawn. She had not told me about this commission, for she did not wish me to worry on her account, and the work was far too elaborate for me to have aided.

She was a sorry state when I arrived, her delicate fingers almost paralysed by the cold and labour, and I confess I remonstrated as to why she had kept the details of this task from me. I could have at least provided food and drink and kept her company.

'I will not keep you from your work during the day,' was her answer.

The job in question was another fine silk shawl, similar in kind to the one she had been making on the day that we met, but this time embroidered with eighty floral motifs. She had calculated on finishing by eight in the evening, which was when I usually arrived with some food, but the hour had struck, as well as the next, before the last stitch was put into the last flower.

The agent was late. This was initially fortuitous, but then increasingly tiresome as the evening progressed, and Grace was soon fit to drop for waiting. I urged her to retire, leaving me to pass the work over, but she would have none of it. We sat by the fire talking and drinking black tea until there came a knock on the door sometime around midnight.

I was herded into the back room and sworn to silence. I had never seen this second room, which was barer than the one downstairs in which my poor father met his terrible end, having nothing in it but an old mattress on the floor and a single blanket. I positioned myself close to the curtain that partitioned both rooms in order to get a good look at Grace's employer, about whom I knew only that she and her husband ran a shop on Finsbury Pavement and that they were intent on expanding the business. The fine cut of her clothes did not disguise the hard face of a ruthless and ambitious dog's wife, a particular cast of countenance that was familiar to me from my fleeting days in London Society. This one may have been part of the mercantile middle classes, but they were nowadays all of a type as far as I was concerned. She had red hair, irregularly dyed so that a parting line of grey roots was visible when she removed her bonnet, and like most ginger-hackled women she was under the mistaken impression that the colour that best suited her was green. She had the dried up, thin features of a woman in her middle years who did not care for much but money.

My initial impressions were confirmed when she opened her mouth. 'A pretty time of night to call me from my hearth,' she said, by way of greeting.

'But you elected to come to me,' said Grace shyly, 'and it is later than the hour we agreed upon,'

'Don't talk back to me, girl,' snapped the woman, snatching the shawl from Grace and examining it by the candle on the work table. I knew it was without a flaw. 'There are fifty or sixty flowers I see,' she said, affecting to be careless of the order.

'Eighty,' said Grace desperately, adding, 'as you instructed.'

'Well, missy,' said the old woman, 'is there so much difference between sixty and eighty?'

I could see the tension in Grace's body from my hiding place. She only shook her head sadly, fearful of contradicting the woman again. The difference between sixty and eighty flowers was a good four hour's work.

'And how much do you expect for this?' demanded the woman.

My blood began to heat, but I had promised to remain out of sight. I attempted to count silently to five-and-twenty in order to calm my spirit. It didn't work.

Grace remained deferential. 'I must leave that entirely to you, ma'am,' she said.

'Oh, you leave it up to me, do you?' said the cold hearted woman, turning the shawl over and scrutinising it at all points. 'Well, it isn't so badly done, for a girl of your age and inexperience.' She produced a tiny purse, and picked at it like some hideous tropical insect at its prey. She selected a single coin, which she offered to Grace. 'I presume this is more than sufficient.'

'Madam,' said Grace, bursting into tears. 'I have worked nearly seventeen hours on that shawl.' She could say no more for sobbing.

'Stop that whimpering, girl,' said the old bitch. 'Take up your money, if you like it, and if you don't then leave it. Only decide one way or another, and make haste!'

Grace took up the sixpence and turned away, drying her eyes with an old piece of cotton waste. Her labours had earned her about a farthing and a half an hour, for an article of clothing that the old woman was probably selling for two or three quid.

'Do you not want any more work?' said the old woman abruptly. Grace was over a barrel, for she had rent to pay, so she meekly turned back towards the uncouth female and accepted another shawl, to embroider in the same manner and for the same price. 'What do you say?' said the old woman.

'Thank you, ma'am,' said Grace with a curtsey.

'That's better,' said the old woman, taking her leave. 'I'll be back for this tomorrow night.'

As soon as I heard her boots on the stair I exploded out of the back room cursing. Grace looked at me dumbly, and then collapsed into my arms, quaking with grief. I stroked her hair and cooed at her like a child while she wailed into my chest. Her swollen fingers let the new job drop to the floor, and I regarded it as I would a rat in a graveyard. Eventually she began to compose herself, so I guided her to a chair and poured more tea. Would that I had something stronger to offer the poor girl, I thought.

We discussed her lot for a while, and of the frustration of having a skilled trade that paid so little for the practitioner and so much for the agents. There was no possibility of an improvement in circumstances. You worked until you dropped. Neither said it, but we each knew that when we could no longer physically labour it would be the street or the workhouse for us both, and an early grave in either event.

'I fear we are but food for the rich, Jack,' she said, 'and of considerably less value than cattle.'

'You are of inestimable value to me,' I told her.

'Oh my dear Jack,' said she, 'I don't know what I would do without you now'

'You know,' I said, choosing my words with care, 'I have a very big house for a man with no family.' She looked at me but said nothing, and, as it so often does, my nerve failed me utterly. 'And a man in my position,' I continued, 'is almost certainly in wont of a housekeeper. Perhaps that might be a position you would consider, for a suitable remuneration of course.'

'As long as I might start before tomorrow night,' said she, laughing for the first time that evening.

'I shall send for your belongings first thing in the morning,' I promised, 'and bollocks to that carroty pated old cow.'

'You can tell you're a writer,' she said, giggling like a convent girl on the gin.

'Bestseller,' I agreed, snuffling with the laughter that is born of acute embarrassment, but also sheer delight. As an old friend had previously told me, many years before, the dice were once more rolling.

*

Before you start judging, I would have been perfectly content to have employed Grace as my housekeeper. It was a philanthropic gesture, I admit. I neither required, approved of, nor could I really afford a domestic, but I felt an affinity with this young woman the like of which I had not known in three decades. It was perhaps because she had been at least in physical proximity to my father and sister, or because we shared a common trade, but Grace felt like family. To be exact, she felt like home. On my word, I harboured no ulterior motives, and although it was an ordinary practice for middle aged men to take younger wives I had always personally felt that it was against nature, which I concede was an odd position given my predilection in youth for women older than myself. But I am not Monsieur Rousseau, so I will probe such sentiments no further.

Grace took her new role extremely seriously, and threw herself into the running of the house, which, she declared upon arrival, was rather too full of spiders. Having cleared out the wildlife, she set about addressing matters of interior design with a similarly urgent idealism. She made many of the fittings herself, until my stark and dusty house, which local children believed to be abandoned and haunted, became positively well-appointed. So good, in fact, was she at domestic management that I was soon persuaded to place the financial reigns of my estate, such as it was, entirely in her hands. I was earning about a hundred a year, which was pitiful, but still exceeded Grace's previous income fivefold. While I was in Bushy Park she was now in Tip Street. As I had only mortgaged half my property, I could just about survive on this sum while meeting the bank payments each month. I could have borrowed against the rest of the house easily enough, which was now worth about a grand (lots of space, good area), but why be poorer to look richer? I had made that mistake once already. When I offered Grace a salary of thirty pounds per annum she told me not to be silly.

I was happy to trust her, for I was terrible with money. Before her stewardship, I wasted most of mine needlessly by dining out every night in preference to cooking for myself, and drinking far too heavily, although I had found myself doing much less of the latter since we had become friends. Reynolds had spotted this quickly, and was now onto me to sign the pledge, citing the well-known example of my old sluicing partner, George Cruikshank, Corinthian Tom himself, who was now fanatically opposed to the sinful waters. He was also against smoking. As I was off the opium I tried to explain to Reynolds that, contrary to his opinion, a cheroot and the occasional small sherry were actually advantageous to my general health, but he was having none of this. I suspected that Grace was also of his part, although she could at least be persuaded to take a glass of wine with a good dinner at the end of the working week.

Grace occupied the rooms on the first storey of the house, while I lived and worked on the second. The kitchen and the parlour on the ground floor we shared, continuing to sit together of an evening in much the same way that we had done in her rooms in Clerkenwell, mostly talking or reading. Sometimes I would forgo the solitude of my study and write downstairs while she read, sketched, or sewed, although now the latter was undertaken for pleasure, or because one or other of us needed something made or repaired. I would not see her sew for sixpence ever again, and we had enough money between us as long as we were careful.

Sometimes she would join me in a glass of something in the evening. I then had to control myself; she tended to start shifting her bob after the first round, and could quickly become quite amorous and flirtatious. I tried to serve her modest measures of wine, or to baptise any spirits, but it did little good, for she was a small woman and a thimble of the good stuff went straight to her head. It went to other parts of her as well. She would hold my gaze in the most disconcerting manner, for her eyes were as dark and mesmeric as those of some nocturnal animal, while the demon drink diluted her pupils until the indecent intention behind them was very clearly communicated indeed. Even the highest class of whores cannot counterfeit a look of such lust. I would fidget and talk too much, and she would move closer and hang dreamily upon my every word, often sitting at my feet by the fire and resting her lovely head on my lap, a galvanic current seeming upon contact to surge through my body. At such moments it was certainly not the wine that made me lightheaded.

If the evening took this kind of turn, I would just keep talking like an idiot until she began to drift, at which point I would get her to her bedroom door and then retire like a gentleman. She would sometimes offer arguments in protest of my retreat; for example that there were precedents in romance for housekeepers and governesses falling in love with their employers, not to mention the widespread practice of masters of houses who took it for granted that sexual favours were included in the job description of any domestic employee that took their fancy.

'I wouldn't like to lose the possibility of a reference,' she said once, cackling in a most unseemly fashion and almost shooting the cat.

'I'm too old for you,' I would mutter, with a similar level of assertiveness and conviction to that which I deployed when dealing with particularly tenacious street sellers.

'I am twenty-five years old!' she announced, as if this indicated a great depth of years and wisdom.

'And I am almost forty,' said I, locking my door behind me.

'We could be like Mr. Keats and Fanny Brawne,' she called after me.

I hope not, I thought.

The Saviour himself could not have resisted such relentless temptation. I lasted about six months before she moved, unopposed, from my spare room to my bed. We were married in the autumn. Reynolds and Dicks were our witnesses, and once again the pitcher that wenteth often to the well gotteth broken at last.

Our son, Joseph, was born the following July, my dear Grace

insisting we named him for my father. She announced this intention quite early on in her pregnancy, claiming that the headaches that plagued her always denoted a boy in her family. I supported her like a qualified rabbit catcher, but in my heart all I could think of was the fate of my poor mother. I knew that Grace knew this too, but she was a brave one and worked hard to keep her anxieties to herself. Thus we planned for our new family, while inwardly I feared the worst. Never have two such hysteric personalities, me by nature, she by condition, so expertly maintained the appearance of sanity.

As it was, it was a relatively straightforward delivery, the final labour lasting no more than five hours. Much to the fingersmith's annoyance, I insisted at being present at the birth, though I recollect very little aside from repeatedly soaking a flannel in a bowl of cold water and applying it to my love's face and forehead. I do on the other hand remember the moment I first beheld our son (with more clarity than Grace as it turned out), his little face knotted with outrage at his violent treatment, and his surprisingly long arms flaying like one of the bruisers of England. At that moment I knew the true meaning of my life, which was to protect this child.

The midwife handed me some warm scissors she had waved over a candle. 'As you're here you can cut the cord,' she said, her tone leaving no room to gainsay.

I squeamishly addressed the rubbery tentacle, and was rewarded with a face full of hot and colourful gore. The woman found this greatly amusing. She obviously liked a bit of slapstick.

CHAPTER XXXVI

NOT LONG AFTER we lost Herbert Briscoe and Sheldon-Bond's horse, we put into Madeira for fresh fruit and water, a significant quantity of supplies having been destroyed during the storm.

Sheldon-Bond had gone as far as to suggest that the stoker had taken advantage of the incident with the unfortunate animal and deserted. This was a theory enthusiastically supported by Speer, the Second Master, on whose watch the man had been lost, and thus far the proposed memorial had been delayed in case there was word of Briscoe in the Savage Islands. The story of the stoker doing a runner for whatever reason and swimming for land certainly calmed the ladies, but those of us who had seen the great fish knew better.[31]

The memory of that grey-backed monster had left me desperately in need of the security of terra firma. The more firmer in fact, the less terror, I always say, so I took a brief stroll around the Porto de Funchal, the streets rocking in a most disagreeable fashion after a month before the mast. It was a torrid and dusty island, which rose in grey layers behind the town like a giant's altar of burnt offerings. I cut my constitutional short, however, after I saw two boys at a market near the quay leading a striped and quivering spider the size of an animated cartwheel loose its rim about on a lead like a dog.

'You don't usually get those so far north,' observed Lakeman when I told him later over lunch, as if that explained everything. 'I must have a look for that myself.'

I would not have put it past him to buy the brute and bring it aboard, so I lied about the exact location.

'My father used to say,' he said, 'that one should never be afraid of anything that cannot fit your head inside its mouth.'

'You didn't see it,' I said sulkily.

'They eat birds you know,' he replied helpfully.

''Tis nought but another of the Lord's wonders, Mr. Vincent,' said Seton, 'something at which to marvel, not despise.'

Wright nodded with exaggerated spirituality, and helped himself to another glass of port.

'Had I been creating the universe,' I said, 'I would not have bothered inventing spiders.'

'Or sharks,' said Salmond, who had not otherwise taken part in this or any other conversation during the course of the meal.

'Or sharks,' I agreed, thinking once more of poor old Herbert Briscoe, as, I assume, was our Captain. That man could swim like a fish with a gold medal, but he had, alas, met something else in the water that could quite comfortably fit his head in its mouth.

Our next port of call was Sierra Leone, or the 'white man's grave' as it was then charmingly known by the military. Why it was considered any more or less dangerous to my race than the rest of the Gold Coast I was not exactly sure, but I assumed that there was a correlation with the repeated destruction of Granville Town, the first 'Province of Freedom.'

While the ship was being coaled, the senior officers went ashore to visit the garrison there and pay their respects to the Governor. Lakeman managed to attach himself to the group via Salmond, and I was also invited in my capacity as an official observer. In periods when there is no mortal peril with which to contend, sea travel is a tedious business and I was grateful for a break in the monotony. It was hideously hot for formal dress though, and even in a pale, summer-weight suit borrowed from Lakeman the walk to the Governor's Residence was punishing. Military men have a tendency to perambulate at marching pace at the best of times, and Lakeman and Seton appeared to be competing.

The white-washed barracks were on top of a hill overlooking Freetown. The soldiers in evidence were all strongly-framed blacks, each man highly disciplined and very well turned out. As we entered the neat but baking courtyard, Lakeman remarked to no one in particular that he fancied if these men were well led they would be equal to a deal of hard fighting.

'Oh, they are,' said a soft, oily looking Caucasian male in military dress, framed in a columned doorway and flicking a long, white horse tail about his face. He was attended by several black men in livery, and clearly the Governor, O'Connor (no relation, I took it, to my old gaffer at the *Northern Star*). For all his affected, casual entry, this was a very powerful man indeed. 'How nice,' he said, approaching our party, 'more guests.' He rightly presumed that Salmond was our Captain, despite his lack of a uniform, and greeted him first, after which he saluted Seton and Wright in turn, following the correct order of rank. Lakeman's private colours foxed him momentarily, and then he greeted him in French, which was a damn good guess. Lakeman then presented me as their illustrious chronicler. 'I am always delighted to welcome the gentlemen of the press,' said the Governor, with that cloying insincerity that one associates with officials in the colonies, and politicians in general. I gave a low bow, not out of respect so much as in anticipation of a rich man's table and something strong and cold to drink, the price of which was some meaningless fawning. Much to my relief we were then invited inside, with the command that we absolutely must join the Governor for dinner.

We were shown to separate room to refresh ourselves, and while, I later gathered, Salmond, Lakeman and Wright inspected the garrison and Seton paid a visit to the local bishop, I enjoyed the comfort and the privacy. I passed a very pleasant afternoon lounging beneath mosquito nets on a huge bed, letting my mind wander and availing myself of the complimentary cigars and a river of gin and tonic. One must be ever vigilant against malaria in foreign climes.

We were expected to dress for dinner. Thankfully, formal attire was provided, because I had thoughtlessly left home without mine, having forgotten that the very foundations of the empire rested upon ties and tails. I assumed the etiquette of the gubernatorial table was also maintained in times of strife, with straight-backed and immaculately presented diners indifferently picking plaster out of the soup during the shelling of the residence by insurgents.

An English servant led me through the complex network of whited corridors, and ushered me into an anteroom to join my party and await the arrival of our host. Salmond, Lakeman and

Wright were engaged in an animated discussion concerning garrison defences, while Seton floated by an ornate bookcase, listlessly leafing through a small, leather-bound book. It was a vulgar piece of furniture, even by the standards of the day, totemic almost, covered as it was in elaborate carvings of aggressive looking mermaids.

Salmond spied me looking at these creatures and moved to my side, leaving Wright in mid-sentence. 'Told you so,' he growled.

I had no desire to revisit this subject, but I was saved by Seton, who replaced the book upon the shelf and gave me a queer look. 'Most colourful, I must say,' he said.

I took him to be referring to the carvings, but then I realised that the shelf upon which he had replaced the book was occupied by the triple-decker first editions of the three novels I had written for Colburn. The subject of Seton's observation was easily identified, as he had imperfectly returned it to its place. It was the final volume of *The Shivering of the Timbers.*

Salmond started to laugh. 'Did you read the part where the witches consume the headless corpse of the virgin sacrifice?' he said.

Seton raised an eyebrow. 'I must have missed that,' he said.

'That was always my favourite scene,' said Salmond. 'Saw things like that myself, when I was a youngster.'

'Yes, Glasgow can be rather rough,' said Seton.

While I fought not to drown upon my apéritif, Salmond regarded the younger officer with the look of a pirate about to strangle a vicar. 'In the Tropics,' he said, very slowly, as if addressing a child or a foreigner. 'Mr. Vincent catches the atmosphere very well.'

'Murderous yet strangely magnetic,' I agreed.

'And were you writing from personal experience?' asked Seton, who I knew for certain had seen considerably more of the world than I ever would or wished to.

'London can be rather rough,' I said.

'So I've heard,' said Seton, directing his gaze between and past both of us towards the door, as if it was suddenly important to check that the exits were clear. 'Oh look,' he said, abstractedly, 'here's our host.'

O'Connor entered in full dress uniform, escorting a handsome woman in her middle years wearing a red satin evening dress that displayed her full figure to fine advantage. They were followed by a small, sallow man in his mid-sixties sporting a carefully trimmed beard.

The rest of the company acted as men usually do in the presence of a stunning woman, even one who would not be seeing fifty again. They simpered about her as the host presented his guests of honour, who were, he explained, visiting the Gold Coast from England on a fact-finding tour of the region. I doubted that my companions read the Society columns, but I had recognised the celebrity couple at once, and not just from their likenesses in the papers. We had met before, although I had seemingly made little impression.

When she got to me the lady declared herself to be utterly charmed to make my acquaintance, and as she offered a bejewelled hand I confess a certain sting of desire at the sight, sound and scent of her. She was recently married to the austere and sour faced older man, a Member of Parliament, who, said the Governor, was strongly tipped to be the next Foreign Secretary. (If the Tories get in, I thought.) The man scowled at the indiscretion, and then made light of it, but you could tell he had wanted us to know. We were all suitably and politely impressed, although when I was seated next to the Captain at the unfashionable end of the table, he took the opportunity to whisper to me that this pair was hardly Victoria and bloody Albert.

Even though there were several of my books about the place, the man affected to have no idea who I was, although he was perfunctorily polite. Like most politicians, he fastened onto the most important person at the gathering, and that was O'Connor. They had travelled down on the *Harbinger*, he said, and had been staying at the Governor's residence while the woman recovered from a slight fever. It was hoped that Salmond might find a berth for them so that they could continue their journey to the Cape. Otherwise, they must wait for *HMS Styx*, which was expected in a few days.

The mention of the *Styx* was what swayed Salmond, for there was a great rivalry between our Captain and his opposite number on that ship, and they competed to make the best time to the Cape.

Conveying a soon-to-be senior member of the next Cabinet would certainly not hurt Salmond socially or professionally, but I never received the impression that he cared much for such things, especially from the English. It would, however, certainly be one in the eye for the captain of the *Styx*. Lakeman immediately volunteered to give up his stateroom, and he and Salmond returned to the ship later that evening to make the necessary arrangements. The rest of us passed the night at the Governor's residence.

It had been an awkward evening, especially after the departure of Salmond and Lakeman. Neither Wright nor, especially, Seton were raconteurs, and the senior guests had no desire to converse with me, or I them. It was therefore a profound relief to escape to the peace of my private room. I was escorted there by one of the maids who had attended at dinner, a small African girl with large, frightened eyes, who had been skittish and clumsy whenever she served the illustrious guests. I tried to coax the reason out of her but she would only shake her head and stare at the floor.

'I'm sorry,' I said uselessly, for I had a pretty keen idea of what had happened to her. They had done it to me as well.

CHAPTER XXXVII

I HAD LOST one family but gained another. As soon as my boy started kicking away we had made friends, and I would read to this little fish for hours long before we formally met. If he was too energetic, and Grace was suffering from his exertions, he could be calmed, as could she, by an application of Wordsworth and Coleridge, my father's copy of *Lyrical Ballads* having lost none of its magic. If he was still for long enough to cause us concern, then I found that he could be roused by Dickens, whether from strong like or dislike I cannot say.

When he was born, I called upon my experiences as my sister's keeper all those years ago and threw myself with pleasure into this new life of wonder and toil. Before her pregnancy, Grace had started drawing for Reynolds' publications, and Dicks had been teaching her to engrave. There was no more reason for her to stop doing this now Joseph had arrived than there was for me to abandon writing, especially as she could potentially bring in as much money with her work as I could with mine. I remained a very lowly reporter, no more than an uncredited assistant, and if I had possessed more sense and less pride I would have suggested we establish a tailoring shop. We therefore quickly fell into a system by which one worked while the other looked after Joseph.

I could feel my spirit slowly healing. No longer did I obsess over the whereabouts of my sister, or rail at Grimstone's immoral activities when his name came up in the press. Even the nightmares about my father were becoming less severe. I would look at my new and unexpected family, and all the rest could wait upon Saint Geoffrey's Day.

What I did worry about was Joseph's likely station in life with a failure for a father. Grace forbad the use of the word about the house, but I knew what I was. 'You are a good man and a wonderful father,' she would say, 'and I did not marry you for your money.'

'You'd have been a damn fool if you had,' said I, but despite being rich in love this was still not accepted as legal tender. I had worried about money my entire life, and was hardly likely to change now. I was desperate not to raise my child in poverty, although, again, Grace would patiently explain that we were far from destitute, especially if our present circumstances were measured against our pasts. She yet retained the hopefulness of youth, whereas I had a much keener sense of how easy it was to change economic classes for the worse. Dickens' parents had been educated and middle class, and that had not saved them.

In order to protect my family's future security, I needed to make some serious money, preferably enough to repay the mortgage. It was clear this was not going to happen if I continued to tick along writing for Mayhew. To make matters worse, Mayhew's relationship with Doyle was becoming increasingly abrasive, and he claimed that he was being politically censored. I would once have taken arms at his side against the management without a second thought, calling for industrial action and urging the printers to man the barricades, but I now had more than my own skin to worry about.

The argument was about the Corn Laws in any event, and I never could make my mind up about that issue one way or the other. It was a dispute between land owners and factory owners as far as I could see, and the working man was likely to remain under a halfpenny planet whether or not the damn things were repealed. Bollocks to the balance of trade, I thought. But if Mayhew went out at the 'paper, most likely so would I. The thought of losing another job was almost as terrible as the thought of losing my family, and the first outcome could well lead to the second. Grace's growing talent as an illustrator was not enough on its own to protect us from the debt spiral. Somehow, I had to regain some of my former station. The only means I had at my disposal was to try and write my way back, and that was always going to be a very long shot indeed.

I talked many of these matters over with Reynolds, and although he could always provide me with a little work he was far from a wealthy man himself, and thus unlikely to make me so again. 'We learn wisdom from failure much more than from success,' he would say, having some regard for the philosophy of Samuel Smiles. My own experience, however, showed up the popular doctrine of 'Self Help' for the myth that it was. I had raised myself by dint of self-education from poverty to social eminence and prosperity, and I was still boned, having hit the unseen yet unbreakable barrier that keeps working men and women from gaining the upper levels of society, like a bird flying into a window. One word from a rich man had been enough to destroy me.

I was not inclined to go cap in hand to Ainsworth or Dickens. *Ainsworth's Magazine* was a disaster, while I did not see myself as a likely contributor to *Household Words*, even if I did have something on its distinguished editor. I would have never heard the end of it from Reynolds, either. And thus I drifted; wasting time, getting older, and waiting desperately for something to turn up.

When Mayhew finally and inevitably resigned from the *Chronicle*, he asked me to go with him. After considering all the options, I decided to decline. I had done this for Reynolds, and not come off the better for it. I had also started to lose faith in *Labour and the Poor* as a worthwhile social enterprise. There was far too much attention paid, in my view, to the groups that Mayhew had categorised as the 'Street Folk' and 'Those That Will Not Work.' He may have dressed it all up in statistics and personal testimonies, but Mayhew's articles were every bit as sensational as *Life in London* and *The Mysteries of London*, much of the ink spilt concerning prostitutes, thieves, and beggars. At least in *The Mysteries of London* we had remained true to our politics (alongside all the sex and violence), as well as taking on the evils in all sections of society. And if you look you will see that we had also included dramatic monologues years before Mayhew.

I still had a deal of respect for Mayhew, don't get me wrong, and we parted on good terms. He was an excellent journalist, and had also brought me a little further in from the cold. I dared not go freelance again though, not with a wife and child to support. As I had jammed my foot firmly in the door of the *Chronicle*, I decided to give it a kick. No one told me what was happening, but I was not going to go quietly. Having now nothing to do at the 'paper while still inhabiting a desk, I made a polite nuisance of myself until I was finally summonsed to the top floor.

Like all busy men, Andrew Doyle did not beat about the bush. 'Well, Mr. Vincent,' said he, surveying me from behind a desk as broad as the deck of a ship, 'whatever shall we do with you?'

I am not good at interviews. To be honest I resent them, especially when conducted by newspapermen no more experienced than I. They know who I am, and I think they enjoy making me beg, secretly wishing all the time that it was Dickens or Thackeray squirming in the chair instead. Fortunately for me, Doyle valued loyalty, and he knew a good thing when he saw it. He had lost Mayhew, but I was just as practised, and he could have me for a fraction of the price. I was hardly likely to rock the boat with my background, and my notoriety might even shift some copy. The Newgate scandal had not done Ainsworth's sales any harm.

'You have stuck by us, Jack,' he said, 'and we will stick by you. I have need of a good man just now, and your famously protean abilities would suit the job perfectly.'

'What do you mean by "protean abilities" exactly?' I asked him.

'How do you feel about soldiers, Jack?' said Doyle. Like all journalists he always answered question for question.

This was difficult to answer. I detested the officer class on point of principle, but I equally possessed that common male mix of awe, respect and fear for the bloody backs in the ranks. It was not their fault that they defended the interests of the elite, and I no more thought ill of them than I did most coppers. I had interviewed several for Mayhew, the poor, maimed bastards who had been pensioned off on a penny a day (if they were lucky), and I knew that the majority of common soldiers took the shilling rather than starve. Like most things in the life of the labouring classes, it was purely a matter of survival.

'Officers or other ranks?' I asked him cautiously.

'All of them,' said he, with a knowing smile. We both knew I was a subversive bastard.

'I have nothing but respect for Her Majesty's Armed Forces,' I said. If there was a steady wage in it, I thought, I was happy to support our boys in red.

'And who could not?' he said. 'Now let me tell you what I need you to do—'

It was a lousy job, but he had me over a barrel. He could have very easily cancelled my contract. It was temporary and pertained only to Mayhew's project. Recent events in Afghanistan and Africa, as well as the growing public anxieties about Russia, he explained, had made his readership very interested in all matters military. He already had war and foreign correspondents, but Mayhew's work had suggested another approach, whereby a representative sample of all classes of the army might be interviewed and documented.

'It's a new angle,' he told me enthusiastically, 'and it'll catch the competition on the hop if we do it right.'

My protean abilities were thus explained. I was naturally between classes. I had a reputation for getting on with common people, while I could also hold my own with the officers, who in those days were still mostly supplied by the aristocracy. If your son was too dull-witted to be a politician or a diplomat, or too dissolute for the clergy, then you stuck him in the army or the navy. Doyle had connections in the Admiralty, and was confident he could get me on a troopship. There I would interview members of all ranks, as well as the navy boys, and report back under the byline of 'Our Special Correspondent.' He hinted that if I pulled this off then there might be a permanent post in it.

'With your reputation for sea stories you'd be in your element,' he said, eyes all a gleam at his fine idea. 'What say you, Jack? Can you do it? Are you game?'

'I'll have to talk to my wife,' I told him.

It was a hard sell. Grace was not happy, but she understood. It was an opportunity to make some real money again, and perhaps to finally achieve some sort of security for the family. We both knew without saying that I still sought professional redemption as well. She was worried, as was to be expected, but Doyle had assured me that there would be no danger, and that the new iron ships were a great improvement on the wooden, relatively rat free and fireproof. Had I known what I know now, I would have told him to shove his special correspondency up his arse and instead gladly taken a job cleaning the spittoons at The Horn of Plenty. But it is always easy to be a prophet facing backwards. At the time, I was a little apprehensive of the journey, but only in terms of the necessary discomfort and privations of sea travel. I knew I could do the job well enough, and while too old to be excited I remained fundamentally grateful to the gods of writing for a serious second chance. The trouble with dealing with deities, though, is that the price is always high. It was going to kill me to be separated from my wife and child.

And so it was that just after our third Christmas as a family, in the foul winter that concluded 1851, I found myself alone and freezing in a coach headed for Portsmouth and my present berth on Her Majesty's Troopship *Birkenhead*, bound for the warmer climes of Africa, and from there straight into Hell and History. All of them places I had no desire to go.

BOOK THREE

- Shark Alley -

CHAPTER XXXVIII

Away from the ship the air was close and humid, and the great net under which I lay combined with the night sounds of nature did not reassure. Yet these factors alone had not banished sleep. I had much to consider.

I was therefore wide awake when I heard someone at my door. I had long since pawned my pocket watch, but judging by the stillness of the house and the level of darkness in the room it was a couple of hours before dawn. As far as I am concerned a knock at the door in the small hours always means trouble, and my body tensed in anticipation of fight or flight. It was a gentle tap, but insistent, and my caller was thus, I soon concluded, unlikely to be easily deterred by my indifference. It occurred to me that it might be the pretty young servant from earlier, emboldened enough to confide while the rest of the household slumbered. There was no accompanying hue and cry, so the residence was neither afire or under attack, and the bailiffs of London, although tenacious, were unlikely to have followed me all the way to Sierra Leone. It was a feminine knock I was sure, having, as I did, an ear for such things. I cursed quietly, lit a candle, then made myself decent and opened the door.

'You needn't have dressed for me,' said Mina, the woman from dinner and my lover of old, for an instant bridging those fourteen frozen years between us with that demure half-smile of hers. The effect was, however, fleeting; I was not prepared to trust her or her latest husband any further than I could comfortably expectorate a fair-sized rodent.

The visit was not completely unexpected, but was for all that as unwelcome as a religious canvasser. She was wearing a long silk nightgown ill-suited to the climate, and she had unfastened the matching pastel wrap to reveal far too much of her dewy and perfumed skin. Moving beyond the memory of this woman had been one of those long hard roads out of Hell, like the pains of opium withdrawal or getting off the drink, and in common with my other destructive addictions I had never been truly free of her influence. The cold shock that I had experienced when I first saw her on the Governor's arm returned, and it was an effort not to visibly tremble in nervous agitation.

I had no intention of giving her any such satisfaction. 'You've remembered who I am now then?' I said frostily, barring her way like one of Drake's marines. At dinner she had behaved as if we had never met before that evening. By the fish course I had acquired the mind of a murderer.

She looked at me with those wide and dark eyes of hers and said, 'I never for a moment forgot you, Jack.'

I was determined to have none of her. 'What do you want, Mina?' I said.

'I want to talk to you, Jack,' she said, 'there is so much I need to tell you.'

'You're fourteen years too late. Please go away.'

'Let me in, Jack,' she said, 'you know you want to.'

I hesitated and in that moment she was past me and in like a cat. She went straight to my bed and sat boldly upon it, arranging her wrap so that I might see her clearly, and crossing her legs to reveal high boots of soft white leather. She would have just turned fifty-four, and the years had been very kind. Her pale skin had been touched by the African sun but still looked as smooth as ever, although she was thinner about the face, her cheekbones more pronounced. There were a few more lines about her eyes than I remembered, and she was allowing her long hair, which she had let down, to turn naturally grey. She had largely retained her figure, and if her hips were slightly more fleshy and her breasts a little broader what did it matter? None of these changes made her any less magnificent than the last time I had stared into those goddess eyes in love. She was as beautiful and alluring as ever, like some terrible drug.

'Give a girl a drink,' she said, carelessly.

I maintained my composure and found and fired a cigar, before serving us both large gins. Then I sat upon a wicker chair, which I slid away from the bed, and waited for what must come. I did not offer her a smoke. I needed all of them.

She regarded me imperiously. 'You're looking well,' she finally said.

'As are you,' I conceded.

'I do my best,' said she. 'You know me. I always show a man what he wants to see.'

'What happened to Mr. Garwood?' I said, for the man she travelled with, although not unknown to me, was certainly not the husband I recollected.

'A shooting accident, poor dear,' she said. (Of course it was, I thought.) Were this a play she would have dabbed an eye at this point. 'I was a mess after that, Jack,' she continued, 'and John was kind to me.'

'Small world,' I said. 'Does John remember me, too?'

You will by now have guessed the identity of her new husband, the rising politician. Mina was Mrs. Grimstone. The two architects of my emotional and professional destruction had been placed in my path again, together and halfway around the world from where we were all supposed to be. I would say that the odds against such a mad coincidence would make even the most reckless gambler cringe. Even Dickens would have not tried that one on in a story.

Ah well, I thought, he who has one enemy will meet him everywhere.

'He hates you, Jack,' she said, her expression suddenly not so self-assured. 'If he knew I was here he would destroy us both.'

'You had better make yourself scarce, then,' I suggested.

'Not until we've talked,' she said, with a familiar and casual authority that had once, briefly, made me feel so safe.

'You make a lovely couple,' I said, 'very well matched.'

'Don't sneer, dear, it doesn't suit you,' she said, putting me in my place again. 'It's all a façade, though,' she continued, in a more notionally earnest tone, 'could you not tell?'

'Clairvoyance doesn't run in my side of the family.'

It was the old script, but she put me through it anyway. 'It is a political marriage, Jack. I wanted security, and he required a Society wife.' She leaned forward, letting the wrap fall from her shoulders. I tried not to look at a very familiar collection of delicate freckles. 'His tastes are somewhat different to mine.'

'I can imagine,' I said, 'what did he do to that maid, by the way?'

'I don't have the faintest idea what you're talking about,' she answered quickly. 'We lead entirely separate lives in that regard.' She moved a little nearer to the edge of the bed, and therefore me. 'I'm very lonely,' she said.

'I'm sorry,' I said, 'but I can't help you. Under the present circumstances I can't see that friendship between us is a possibility, so please leave me alone.'

Her eyes flashed, briefly, and then became yielding and wanton. 'I read all your books,' she said softly. 'That woman, in *The Death Hunter*—'

'Millie.'

'Yes, Millie. That was me, wasn't it?'

'You flatter yourself.'

'And so do you,' she said, returning the blow. 'The couple in that book made love the way we used to.'

Needless to say, she was absolutely right. The whole book had been about her, or a version of her, the plot an allegory of our time together, all that pointless passion leading to an inevitable betrayal. 'You're not like Millie,' I lied.

'How am I not like Millie?' she demanded with incandescent eyes.

'You're worse,' I said, lighting another cheroot and slumping in my chair. I had not the stamina for such heightened emotions these days.

Her countenance became soft, sad and self-deprecating. She leaned forward and took my hands. 'I really hurt you, didn't I, Jack?'

'Yes,' I said. My eyes were stinging; it must have been the cigar smoke. I pulled my hands away and shoved my chair back even further.

'You still think me an over-privileged, upper class bitch,' she said quietly. I think I might have called her that the last time I saw her. I was shamed by the recollection. Neither of us had covered ourselves in glory that day.

'I'm sorry.'

She moved close again. 'Why are you sorry, Jack?'

'I was a fool and I prig,' I confessed, recklessly dropping my guard. Cruikshank was right, women do make me stupid. 'I did not accept our relationship for what it truly was, and just enjoy it on its own terms. I was young. I was out of my depth.'

Her voice was an intense whisper: 'And?' she said.

'I fell in love with you.'

She took my hands again and moved to kiss me. 'I fell in love with you, too, Jack,' she said, her breath hot and sweet with gin.

But I did not love her now. I sprung from my chair as if burned and pushed her from me. She moved once more to embrace me and I backed away, trying to keep the furniture between us. Eventually she returned to the bed, this time lying back, arms open and legs exposed. 'I want you, Jack,' she said, 'I wanted you from the second I saw you tonight. Look me in the eye and tell me you did not feel the same.'

I looked her in the eye. 'I'm married,' I said, 'very happily.'

'Ah yes,' she said, sitting up, her body less open now, 'the seamstress, the common girl.'

'Artist.'

'If you say so, dear.'

'And she's a finer woman than you'll ever be,' said I, 'for all your airs and graces. I have no desire to discuss my family with you though, so, again, please just go away.'

She made no attempt to move. Feeling far from chivalrous after the slight against Grace, I seized her quite roughly by the arms and heaved her up. 'Good boy!' she cried, breathing heavily, 'that's more like it.'

I steered her, kicking and swearing, towards the door. She squirmed and heaved beneath my hands, and denounced me as a talentless hack, a drug addict, an atheist, a drunk and a poltroon, all accusations that I would have been hard pressed to refute at the best of times. I was stronger than her though, at least physically, and I managed to get her through the door. Thankfully, no one appeared to have heard the altercation.

'You brute,' she said, panting and petulant. 'I'll say you tried to rape me.'

She would, too, but I was expecting a move such as this and was prepared. 'How would you explain your presence here,' I countered, 'all *décolletage*? Even your foul spouse would have trouble making that charge hold.' I collected her forgotten wrap from the bed and handed it to her. 'For the sake of propriety,' I suggested, moderating my tone as much as I was able, 'let us all just try to be civil. I will keep myself to myself, and when we reach the Cape we can go our separate ways.'

'Propriety does not become you, Jack,' she said artfully, 'and a ship is a very small place.'

'Believe me,' I said, ignoring her provocation, 'if I did not have a job of work to do I would remain here and buy a passage on the *Styx* just to be free of the pair of you.'

I must have finally appeared convincing, for although she countered by calling me a bastard and an ineffectual little man, she at that point withdrew, comically clattering away on those preposterous heels.

I returned to my bed, which was still warm, and did the only sensible thing under the circumstances, which was to finish off the gin. But it didn't help. I could not sleep, and at dawn I paid a fisherman to take me across to the ship, in order that I might avoid an awkward trip in the *Birkenhead* cutter in close proximity to Mr. and Mrs. Grimstone. There was not much consolation to be found in sneaking back early, though, like some darkman's budge. Lakeman was giving up his cabin and they were to be berthed right next door to me, like monsters evaded in a nightmare which turn out to be waiting for you up ahead every time.

As a child, I had often imagined myself the hero of my mother's fairy tales, aided in my adventures by magical helpers. This had become a necessary fantasy in the Marshalsea, where I would often yearn for oriental genies to swoop down upon Euripides' crane like unravelling gods to set me free. I had not thought of these childish daydreams for years, but I suddenly remembered them now. Had some djinn appeared that morning and offered me my heart's desire,

I would have wished without hesitation to just go home. No treasure was required. I longed only for my family, and to be as far away as possible from old lovers, and other enemies.

CHAPTER XXXIX

After Sierra Leone, my life on board the *Birkenhead* became darkly comedic, as I tried as hard to avoid the company of Mina as she did to seek out mine. Our previous quarrel was, it would seem, to be overlooked. Her husband and I, meanwhile, continued to pretend that we had never met before, until the strain at the Captain's table eventually became such that I started taking hardtack and cocoa with the soldiers.

The change in the soldiers under Seton's rigorous training regime was nothing short of astounding, especially when compared to the sorry shower on the square at Spike Island a mere month and a half before. Since the nadir of the storm, the men had learned to take a pride in their appearance and personal hygiene, and each regimental contingent, no matter how small, seemed now much more of a bonded unit, well drilled and highly disciplined. Regardless of the heat, above or below decks, one never now saw a top button undone or a helmet off, and it was clear that the majority of these transformed men bore a genuine respect for their superiors, especially Seton. He continued to visit the troop decks daily, always pausing to speak with individual soldiers, who he would always address by name, either because he was genuinely kind and paternalistic, or because, unlike most of his peers, he understood the value of compassionate leadership. No man was flogged on that voyage, yet, against the conventional wisdom of the day, the behaviour of the soldiers was impeccable and morale was good. As everyone trained together, some of this new shine had also transferred to Lakeman's rangers, who were now, like the redcoats, as neat, tough and organised as a Spartan legion.

I was also in somewhat better trim myself. I wish I could say it was the famously medicinal qualities of the sea air, but my renewed vigour and clearness of mind was largely down to enforced abstinence. I had no access to laudanum, nothing to drink in my quarters, and I had voluntarily cut myself off from the Captain's free grog. I was even smoking less, for I had to ration what tobacco Lakeman donated. I had gained a healthy equatorial tan, and there was not an ounce of fat upon me. I am not vain by nature, but I had noticed the changes in a cheval glass when I roomed at the Governor's residence, and the man in the mirror had been quite a shock. Aside from a few more lines about the face, which made my visage quite windswept and interesting, I looked much as I had in the good days before the fall, when I was the toast of literary London and the world was mine for the asking. Perhaps Mina had seen this in me as well, or perhaps I was merely as embellished by memory as was she.

Grimstone had not aged as well as his wife or I, and bore all the marks of a physically and morally corrupt life. His hair was a thin and dirty grey, licked back across a spotted and scrofulous skull, while eyes dead as dangerous fish were sunk deep in their sockets and framed by a livid lattice of blocked pores and broken veins most prominent about his pinched and pointed nose. His beard was well trimmed but stained by God knows what, his teeth looked unnatural, and although he dressed well his frame remained rat-like and skeletal. I felt quite sick in his presence. Beyond my natural revulsion, there was also a deep sense of frustration, not founded so much upon his treatment of myself and my family, but because this agent of darkness had fooled, and continued to fool, so many. I feared that this type of man very much personified the new spirit of the age: the *pater familias*, captain of industry, and politician, spouting pious platitudes in public while robbing his workers and tenants blind, and then raping the maid or visiting a child brothel after church and the family dinner on Sunday.

Grimstone was still affecting a vague military background, and this was accepted without question by the other officers on board, the same men who had been so sceptical of Lakeman's foreign credentials. Wright claimed that he had noticed the bearing of an officer of the old school as soon as he had clapped eyes upon him, and the company soon took to addressing him as 'Captain,' making him much more part of the club than Lakeman or myself.

This supposedly heroic past was the foundation upon which much of his reputation was based, but when I had investigated him in the early-40s it was notable how vague he was on and off the record, downplaying while strongly implying an involvement in the Hundred Days.

One night, after the ladies left the table, I had taken it upon myself to ask him outright.

'Well, one doesn't like to boast,' said he, as cool as ever, 'I simply did my duty, just as the fine officers here assembled do theirs.'

Wright was positively luminous with pride and Seton seemed quite choked, the way they usually were when the Queen was toasted at the end of the evening.

Salmond was not so easily distracted by patriotism, especially from an Englishman, and as an officer by warrant he was not in the club either. He was of the same generation as Grimstone as well, so less inclined to deference. 'I'm still not clear concerning which regiment you served with,' said he, doing my job for me.

'Let's just say I played my part in the Great Game,' said Grimstone, 'and leave it be at that, for I am not at liberty to discuss the matter further.'

This was checkmate, because the necessarily clandestine work of a spy meant that it was impossible to verify one way or another and would, further, be very bad form to attempt to do so, as it could put several Intelligence officers in peril and compromise the security of the nation.

Salmond, however, was not so easily deterred. 'But that would be against the Russians,' he continued, 'and I rather received the impression from the newspapers that you gained your laurels against the French.'

I could have kissed the seditious old bastard.

Grimstone parried well; you could see why he was such a powerful politician. 'But we are all friends now,' he said, glancing significantly at Lakeman, who was formally of the French military and half-frog himself. Lakeman smiled and casually raised his glass. 'Besides,' Grimstone went on, 'the Russians continue to threaten the empire.'

'Hear, hear,' said Wright.

Salmond finally let it go. 'We'll be stopping over at St. Helena,' he said. 'I expect you'll want to pay your respects.'

'Most certainly,' said Grimstone, before claiming some fatigue as a result of the 'old wound' that, although unspecified, had engendered his early retirement from the service, and calling for the final toast.

I decided then to withdraw from this trying nightly ritual, especially after the look Grimstone gave me when he left the table, but I equally resolved to get on the landing party at St. Helena.

Lakeman guessed immediately that we had some sort of history, having made the obvious connection with the arrival of the Grimstones and my self-imposed exile from the Captain's table. He, too, had banished himself to the troop decks, having given up his berth for the couple, and we continued to regularly socialise down among the mercenaries and the foot wabblers. I told him enough of my story for context, and my suspicion that the intelligence that had ruined me could only have come from Mina, although he was less inclined to speak ill of a lady. He was obviously sweet on her; she had that effect on men, especially young ones. I considered trying to warn him off, but he would not have listened and I had come to value his friendship.

I think he was a little jealous of my previous involvement. 'She must have been a fine looking woman back then, you dog!' said he. 'And she's still in good condition now.'

'The memory is bitter-sweet,' I told him, 'mostly bitter.'

'Dog,' he said. 'She still seems quite taken by you, though.'

'How do you mean?' I inquired innocently.

'Oh come on, man! Her eyes never leave you, surely you must have noticed?'

'Unlike Mrs. Grimstone,' I said, 'I am very happily married, and wish to remain so.'

'You wouldn't mind if I had a gallop at her then, old chap?' said he.

I resisted the immediate temptation to call him a dog. 'She is hardly mine to give away,' I said, for I have always been uncomfortable with such patriarchal assumptions of ownership. All the women with whom I had been intimate were considerably more in control than was I. 'But I can assure you it would cause me no concern if the two of you were to become close. Just watch out for the husband, he's much more dangerous than he appears.'

'If a man had treated me the way he has you,' he said, suddenly serious, 'I should have to kill him.'

'Don't think I didn't consider it back then,' I confessed, 'but I'm a writer not a soldier. I wouldn't have got anywhere near the man and they'd have still hanged me for trying.'

'Fair point,' Lakeman generously conceded. 'You'll just have to shove him over the side when nobody's looking.'

'I'll bear that in mind,' I said.

'Unless he gets you first,' he replied, rising to return to his duties.

*

Mina soon joined the creative writing group that I had established for the ladies. Here we discussed the practice and philosophy of literary form, and they shared their leaden and inexpert prose and, sometimes, God help me, poetry. I had never really taught my art in this way before, and now understood more about the challenges Seton faced with his recruits, although they were making more progress towards being soldiers than my students were to becoming writers. Only Mrs. Metford displayed any real talent. She was slowly crafting a fantastic story founded upon a favourite Celtic myth from her youth concerning a water spirit in love with a young Irish cailin, a kind of gothic and inverted 'Den lille havfrue.' I liked this little story and was keen to know how it would end. I doubted she would want to publish, but if she did I was confident Reynolds would run it.

As to the rest of my students, I frequently returned to the sage advice of Dr. Johnson on the editorial process: 'Read over your compositions, and wherever you meet with a passage which you think is particularly fine, strike it out.'

The literary ladies, who were upper-middle class at best, and mostly, like young Mrs. Metford, not even that, were delighted to receive the patronage of a Society doyenne. In return Mina regaled them with a long anecdote about our days in the Blessington circle.

'She's dead now, poor dear,' she concluded, brushing away an imaginary tear.

'Yes,' I agreed, 'and buried under a pyramid I believe, so nothing too ostentatious.'

'Dear d'Orsay designed it,' she said.

'I'm sure he visits it often.'

I was allowed the wardroom for two hours on Tuesday and Thursday mornings, and we all sat around the long table like students at a university seminar, with me the lecturer. That must be an easy life, I thought, if you can get your foot in the door. But it went without saying then as now that working class fellows like myself need not apply. I had done a bit of private tutoring though, as Mina reminded me after the other students had left.

'Do you not miss it, Jack?' she said boldly, sitting upon the table and leaning back on her long arms in a most provocative manner, 'wasn't it the best you've ever had?'

'You don't really expect a gentleman to answer such a question, do you?' I said.

She laughed at me archly. 'Oh Jack, you were never a gentleman, that's what I loved about you.'

'Well a lot of Mayfair nuns and rich dog's wives fantasise about a romp with a working man,' said I, determined to be offended, 'and as I recall, you discarded me afterwards without compunction.'

She either missed or ignored the insult. 'And what a fool I was,' she said, with apparent sincerity, damn the woman. 'You were certainly the best I ever had.'

'It was a long time ago, Mina, let it go.'

'So you keep saying,' she said, 'but it was not so long ago when I was last alone in your bedroom.'

'That was unsolicited and unseemly, Mina, and an encounter, like this one, that I could have well done without.'

She would not concede the final word, and remained as vicious as ever. 'Is your little shop girl as game as I?' she said.

'I'll want no other until the day I die,' said I.

'Oh, Jack,' she said, rising and moving towards the door at last. 'You don't really want to get on the wrong side of me again, do you?'

I let her go without an answer, and continued to count the hours until I could get off that bloody boat. The irony would have greatly tickled the lost and depraved gods of the Greeks and the Romans, who would have no doubt intervened, if they were not doing so already. While Mina flung herself at me like a Drury Lane Vestal, I was very likely the only man on board who did not want to have her.

What my body and soul craved, my lack, my need, remained firmly and unambivalently located in my little house in London. I ached to wake up next to my wife, rise quietly, start a fire and make a brew, as I always did at home, and then rouse my son and bring him into us. We would drink our tea in bed and Joseph would explain one of his simple yet largely incomprehensible dreams, as he did, very seriously, every morning. New and wonderful words were forming all the time, and in his tiny interior world fact, fantasy and experience knew no boundaries, and merged alchemically together in his little mind, so that trains were really dragons that, if not kept in careful check, would eat all our apples. While my present situation with the *Chronicle* was not without potential merit, no amount of money, I had long since realised, was worth a single day spent without my family.

And as for the dubious charms of women like Mina, my only regret was that I had wasted so much of my precious time on them in the past. As far as I am concerned you only go around the once in this life, and, contrary to the common belief, once you're dead you're fucking dead.

*

We moved a little closer to the end of the line when we docked at St. Helena a very long weekend later, tying up on the second Monday of February and the thirty-third day since we left Ireland. If we kept to Salmond's estimated time of arrival, we would get where we were going in sixteen days.

It was not difficult to once more attach myself to the landing party. And while Lancers, Highlanders, Rifles, and Rangers assisted the bluejackets in loading yet more water and coal, the senior officers, in the company of Lakeman, Grimstone and I, sauntered up a dusty volcanic path to Longwood House, the residence in which Napoleon had met his end.

The house and the island had reverted to the Company after Boney kicked his bucket and his entourage disbanded. It was now a crown colony, although from the state of the place you would not think it so. The bored civil servant who gave us the tuppeny tour kept muttering about budget cuts as if that explained everything, although the house looked not so much neglected as completely abandoned. The small garden in which the Little General had spent so many weary hours trying to dig away the cankering bitterness of defeat and exile was choked with weeds and scarred with poultry shit, while the small, unplastered and half-rafted room in which he had breathed his last was packed with broken agricultural tools. By the time we entered the adjoining chamber, in which he had discussed with Montholon how kingdoms were won and lost, I was having real difficulty controlling the impulse to laugh out loud. The room was full of brooding chickens.

The mood elsewhere in the room was sombre. Everyone seemed quite embarrassed, except Lakeman, who was plainly furious at the lack of respect. 'Posterity will lay this woeful wreck to England's charge,' he said, genuinely horrified and struggling to moderate his tone. The garden, in particular, had really unsettled him. 'How can this pitiful plot of earth,' he complained, 'scarce larger than a Cockney's flower bed, be all that remained to him who had given realms away?'

'It certainly puts power in perspective,' said Salmond.

Lakeman was quite wild about the eyes. 'It is too much perspective, sir,' he said, his voice rising with unnatural excitement, 'the contrast is too great. Something is very wrong with this.'

'Imperious Caesar, dead and turned to clay, might stop a hole to keep the wind away,' muttered Seton.

I nodded in mute agreement. I had been thinking along similar lines myself. *Look upon my works, Ye mighty, and despair.*

Lakeman turned on him. 'How could your people shut away the greatest military commander of all time in these damp, wretched rooms?' he demanded. 'My God, sir, you put him living into his own tomb.'

'My people?' said Seton, confused.

'I speak as an officer of France, sir. He was the best of us all.'

'Well, he wasn't so great that he couldn't be bested by the Iron Duke, and good men like Captain Grimstone here,' said Wright.

Grimstone looked uncomfortable, and appeared unable to hold Lakeman's gaze. The latter was now staring venomously at him, as, presumably, both a representative of all the armies of the Seventh Coalition, and of the parliament that had, effectively, condemned the Emperor of the French. He did not speak.

'Horrible weather and the fortuitous arrival of Kraut reinforcements do not constitute tactical genius on the part of the British,' said Lakeman, 'now if you gentleman will excuse me, I must attend to my men.' He gave a perfunctory bow and left.

'Bloody foreigners,' muttered Wright after him.

It was clear that Lakeman had lost all the stock he had gained since Spike Island at a stroke. 'Exile is obviously a habit of the French,' said Grimstone, and everyone except me shared in his laughter, including the poultry. 'Are you not joining your friend, Mr. Vincent?' he asked, when the general merriment had subsided.

'I like it here,' I told him.

'As do I,' said he. The rest of the company regarded him with exaggerated ears, waiting upon an anecdote or two concerning the final defeat of the French, in which he was widely rumoured to have taken part, and which he was supposedly revisiting here. Back home, much of Grimstone's standing in business and politics rested upon his status as a wounded veteran of Waterloo.

It was Wright who prompted him to speak. 'My God, but it must have been something to have fought with Wellington,' he said, with a genuine and sober admiration that was unlikely to be easily misdirected.

'It was an honour,' said Grimstone, clearly choosing his words with care, 'although I was under Maitland and saw precious little of the Duke.'

'You were with the men who broke the Imperial Guard,' whispered Wright reverently. 'Who were you with, the 52nd?'

Seton, Salmond and I looked on with great curiosity. Wright's knowledge of military history was formidable.

'I was attached to the 30th,' Grimstone finally admitted, 'partially disbanded now, sadly.'

'A fine regiment,' said Seton.

'There are none on board, I suppose?' inquired Grimstone casually.

'One tends to associate them with India rather than Africa nowadays,' said Wright.

'Of course,' said Grimstone, visibly relaxing. He then delivered a very clear account of the closing overs of the great battle, of the attack of the Immortals after the fall of La Haye Sainte, and the merciless volley fire and final bayonet charge of Maitland's Foot Guards that routed them, before Adam's Light Brigade finished the job. 'La Garde meurt, elle ne se rend pas,' he concluded, which I'm sure Lakeman would have loved had he been in attendance.[32]

I will not reproduce the account here, as this narrative of the battle is well known and widely reported elsewhere. The old king, I have heard, told the story so many times that he eventually came to believe that he had fought there himself.

CHAPTER XL

JUDGING FROM THE sounds of love emanating from the cabin next door upon my return, Lakeman had come up with a novel way of avenging the Horse Thief of Berlin. I knew it was him, for he had a distinct laugh and a voice that certainly travelled, while Mina still boomed like a bittern at the height of her passions. It was a cry not easily forgotten, so I was pretty certain he was not at clicket with the maid. Lakeman did not strike me as the type to copulate outside his social class.

In a music hall attempt to alert my friend to the impending return of the husband, I commenced to clatter about my cabin, coughing loudly.

'Are you having a fit?' he demanded, thumping upon the connecting bulkhead. I could hear Mina laughing. He nonetheless took heed, for I soon heard the cabin door slam and all was quiet next door after that.

Despite my best efforts, I bumped into Mina and her maid on the main deck later that afternoon, shortly after we left the island, for Salmond did not wish to let the *Styx* catch up to him. She was wearing an extravagant dress of white silk and taffeta with an enormous bustle, and sporting a giant, veiled bonnet to keep the sun at bay.

'Twenty times around the deck is a mile,' she said cheerily, raising her curtains. 'I like to keep myself in trim.'

'You certainly look quite invigorated,' I agreed.

She leaned in close so that the maid could not hear and whispered, 'I was thinking of you the whole time,' before twirling away like a giant, demented meringue, with the maid scuttling after her. Clearly Lakeman's arrival on the field of play was to give me no relief, even though, as far as I was concerned, he was welcome to her.

As I had carried a torch for that woman for several years, you may wonder at my indifference, doubly so given what I have told elsewhere of my early life and indiscretions. A godless man must either take every pleasure life offers as it comes, I used to believe, or live to repent having not done so at the end. This is not such a wicked or reckless philosophy to adopt when there is neither God nor Devil above or beneath you, assuming there are other checks and balances in place moderating your behaviour and therefore keeping you alive and out of prison. I was in possession of a reasonably functioning moral compass, no more deviated than the one presently directing the ship, and I always felt that Pascal's Wager would have benefitted from a third choice before I bet my life upon it. I had nevertheless more recently come to appreciate that living 'authentically,' as Mr. Kierkegaard had put it, did not mean entering into amorous congress with everything in sight, and, further, that this tendency in my younger self was no different to the constant need for strong drink and various other forms of *pharmakeia*. I also suspect that a doctor of either philosophy or medicine specialising in the physiology of the human mind would likely add the compulsion to write to the above list, because I was certainly not turning a profit. Whether this need to lose myself by a variety of means can be ascribed to my childhood, or was simply in my nature, I cannot say, but after becoming a literary success I was damned to excess either way, for celebrity tends to breed hedonism, as does its loss.

Yet beyond all this wool gathering (a hazard of my occupation), the simple truth was that I would have died before I betrayed my wife and son. A man should be loyal to a family that loves him, and, especially in a case such as mine, eternally grateful. They were the light at the end of my sorry little tunnel. Grace was not a jealous woman, or a particularly pious one, but for reasons that she had not disclosed but I suspected were connected to some past trauma, the thought of infidelity appalled her. The slightest suggestion of it would be the end of our marriage. Similarly, I did not want destructive forces like Mina and Grimstone anywhere near my family, any more than I would have courted the friendship of he who had killed, or caused to be killed, my father, and no doubt still corrupted my poor sister.

You should also know by now that if I had acted upon Mina's

advances I would have confessed in these pages, for my intention in these memoirs is to give an honest account of myself, for I still value truth even if God is dead.

I could not for the life of me fathom Mina's true motives, and the alternative interpretations upon which my mind increasingly turned were all equally alarming. For her, our little fling had been a mere fire of straw at best, extinguished by her own hand fourteen years since, and her current endeavours to rekindle our relationship were as inexplicable as they were blatant. There was no sign she saw any impediment in my marriage or her own, or in seducing Lakeman on a whim and then applying the act to me in spirit. It was almost as if she were casting a spell of magical correspondence. Otherwise, I surmised, her intention had been to make me jealous. Either way, the woman was clearly barking, and dangerously fixated upon me. There had always been a touch of the vampyr about Mina, after all.

The more rational scenarios were only marginally less disturbing. Mina might be playing out some sort of vendetta against her husband, viewing me as a likely antagonist given our histories; or, worse, she might be following his directions. The cold, familiar dread from the old days came upon me with this final realisation, which seemed much more plausible than a doomed quest to regain a love long lost. The latter contingency was more of a romantic, male affectation anyway, and somewhat out of date. Mina was hardly Young Werther, and I was not so vain as to believe myself a likely subject for such devotion, not that I wished it. As I stood there on the deck, bathed in warm sunlight, I considered Grimstone's reach and shivered in fear not fever. Whatever Mina's reason or reasons, this demented pursuit could have been the plot of an erotic novel purchased under the counter at a Wych Street bookshop (it could even have been one of mine), and I was well aware that such stories did not end well.

Just as Mina no doubt studied my onboard routine, I observed hers, and this intelligence allowed me some freedom of movement about the ship, for whatever she did in the evening after dining, she did in the privacy of her cabin. I could therefore move between the troop decks and my quarters unmolested, and enjoy the cooler air of the evening over a cigar while idly watching the alien stars, before retiring to my cabin to write. Often I would not encounter another living soul on the main deck between changes of the watch, and these moments of unconfined solitude in such a usually crowded environment were extremely sacred, like the hours before dawn at the Marshalsea a lifetime ago.

I therefore felt most aggrieved one evening to observe a lone male figure by the rail in front of the port paddle-box, looking out to sea. It was a still, clear night, and I could see him quite clearly under the light of a gibbous moon and the brass lanterns slung between the masts. From the civilian evening dress, posture, and the general cut of his jib, I was certain this was Grimstone.

The ceaseless churning of the huge paddle-wheel would have disguised my approach, for he showed no sign that he marked my presence, and as I froze, Lakeman's words from our conversation the previous week returned to me. *You'll just have to shove him over the side when nobody's looking.*

I looked fore and aft, my spit turned suddenly to ash and my heart racing, and wondered if I really had it in me to do it. It was after midnight, there was no one about, and the lookouts and officers of the watch on the poop and fo'c'sle would be looking out not inward. The rail was not a high one, the water below was cold and dark, and we knew that there were still sharks following us, quietly waiting. Every piece of refuse dumped over the side became a boiling frenzy when it hit the water. If a man went over the side, even on a moonlit night such as this, and if the fall, the paddles, or the water did not get him before a boat could be dropped, the sea lawyers surely would. I looked about me once more, and began to quietly approach the man many already predicted would be Prime Minister one day.

When I was within striking distance, he spoke without turning. 'My wife,' he said, 'fears the ocean at night.' I stopped like a criminal caught in a watchman's light, unsure whether to fight or flee. 'Mr. Vincent,' he added, just so I knew that he had me bang to rights.

'I rather like it myself,' I managed in reply, my delivery as awkward as the most amateur and provincial of thespians.

'As do I,' said he, turning at last to look me in the eye and leaning precariously against the rail. 'But I fear that you do not like me so much.'

He did not strike me as the kind of man who would believe an enemy who declared otherwise, so I did not. 'No,' I said, 'I don't.'

He held my gaze in silence until I eventually averted my eyes, as if presenting an application for parochial relief before the parish beadle. 'Political differences?' he finally asked.

'Something like that,' I said.

I was more than a little confused. Although I had been prepared for almost anything, I had not anticipated charm. Mina had said that he hated me, but her behaviour appeared increasingly delusional. Was it possible that he really had no idea who I was? I supposed that I was fairly if not utterly insignificant to one such as he, and of no more need of memory than any other animalcule kicked aside or casually crushed. I had built this man in my mind to resemble the Adversary himself, whereas he no more knew me than had my poor father when last we met. I was not even a ghost.

He reached inside his jacket and withdrew a large leather cigar case, before producing a match from an outside pocket. It was a warm night and his buttons were undone. As he raised his hands to light up I could see the hilt of a large pistol in some sort of holster beneath his left arm.

He noticed that I had noticed, and to my horror he unslung the long weapon and held it up between us like some great black phallus of death. 'Colt Walker,' he said proudly, '.44 caliber ball, six round single action revolver.' Like most enthusiasts, he was disposed to lecture. 'Twice the power of an ordinary pistol,' he explained. 'If you as much as clipped a man with this beauty you'd have his arm clean off,' he concluded, with a disquieting chuckle.

I agreed that it was most impressive. 'I saw the display at the Crystal Palace,' I added.

He suggested I have a closer look and handed it to me, stock first, before I could make an excuse. The barrel was nine or ten inches long and damn thing weighed a good five pounds. It occurred to me that if you missed your target you could always beat his brains out with it. 'So much better than those clumsy things from Birmingham.' he continued. 'A man in my position has enemies, you see, Mr. Vincent, and I prefer to take care of myself.'

'So I see,' I said, carefully returning the gun.

'I'm not one for bodyguards, at least not these days,' he said, replacing the portable cannon in its holster. 'Besides, servants always know far too much about one, do you not find?'

'I hadn't really thought about it,' I confessed.

He realised that he had neglected to offer me a cigar, and insisted I take one. It was a 'Prince of Wales,' and probably the finest leaf I had ever smoked in my life.

'My wife seems quite taken with you,' he said, in a perfectly reasonable tone in every way appropriate to two gentlemen in conversation, 'but then she has always been rather Bohemian in her outlook.'

'She's in one of my writing classes,' I said, aware that my voice remained strained and nervous. I coughed in a pointless attempt to clear my throat.

'Is she good?'

'I'm sorry?'

'Is she a good writer?'

'Above average,' I lied. In fact she wrote not a word in my class. She mostly either stared at me in a most disconcerting manner, or distracted the group with anecdotes about how she, Dickens and I were all such good friends.

'I must ask her to read me one of her compositions some time,' he said. I agreed that he should and attempted to bid him goodnight, but he would not let me go. 'How is your own work progressing?' he asked instead.

'I am reasonably pleased with it,' I said, guardedly. I had dropped off a packet of articles at St. Helena that would by now be wending their leisurely way to the *Chronicle*, alongside a serious of carefully worded letters to my wife. 'But the real work will begin up country,' I added, for I fancied he feared I had written of his monologue in Longwood House, which I had not. I was still evaluating.

'Yes,' he said, 'I suppose it will.'

'I am charged with writing about the common soldier in action, after all,' I added.

'You must give me a puff as well if you can bear it, old man,' he said mischievously. 'I like to keep on the right side of the press.'

'Well don't we all?' I agreed.

He laughed and flicked the remainder of his cigar over the side. I watched the orange spot disappear into the blackness. 'Good night, Mr Vincent, sleep well,' he said, finally taking his leave. At least he did not expect us to walk to our respective cabins in each other's company.

'Jesus step-dancing Christ,' I whispered, slumping against the rail as if suddenly invertebrate. If I had many more encounters of this character, I thought, I would likely never sleep again.

The midnight meeting unsettled me deeply, and not for the usual emotional reasons connected with even the idea, let alone the presence, of John Grimstone M.P. For the first time in my life I began to doubt my own hatred. Was it possible, I conjectured, that my childhood memories were unreliable? Perhaps my father and I were no more than commonplace failures, with nobody to blame but ourselves. He was always a poor businessman, and even more helpless without my mother, while in youth I had been impulsive, reckless and arrogant. I began to wonder if the man I had seen in The Fiddler's Elbow all those years ago had even been Grimstone, my subsequent social and professional downfall a mere coincidence. The press had been gunning for me since the Newgate Panic, and I had certainly left my flanks exposed on numerous occasions. With my blood cleaner than it had been for years, I realised with a clarity more sickening than any intoxicant or its aftermath that this whole elaborate conspiracy by which I obsessively justified every setback in my life could have been a fantasy; a series of patterns and connections that existed only as a false narrative within my own deluded consciousness, like a bad melodrama. That such a powerful man would prosecute a vendetta against a humble tailor, let alone his descendants, suddenly appeared ludicrous. The thought that I might actually have murdered him had me retching over the rail.

As I knew sleep to be an impossibility, I paced the deck like some unquiet sea spirit until the passengers began to rouse. Only then did I retire to my cabin in a state of fear and self-loathing, pausing only to ask Davis, the Second Master, to convey a message to Seton that I had a fever and that, with regret, I must cancel my classes that day. I took to my bunk and smoked until my lungs ached, reading constantly in order that my own thoughts might be driven from my mind by those of others.

I was therefore in no condition for a visit from Mina, who was troubled by my absence from the creative writing group, and who refused to leave until I let her in.

She was, as usual, quite overdressed, this time in blue silk. 'My God, Jack,' she said as soon as I opened the door, 'you look terrible.' She breezed into my cabin and started tidying, opening the porthole to dispel the layers of cigar smoke. 'You don't look after yourself, Jack,' she said, 'that's always been your problem. What you need is a good woman.'

'I have a good woman.'

'Then where is she?' she demanded. 'She clearly doesn't care for you at all.'

'She's taking care of our boy and I'm fine,' I said weakly. 'It's just a slight fever, a touch of the sea sickness, nothing more.'

'Nonsense,' she said, guiding me back to my bunk, 'you could be seriously ill. I shall fetch the surgeon.'

'Please don't,' I pleaded. 'I need rest, that's all, if you could just leave me to sleep—'

'Very well,' she said, 'but when you are feeling better we must talk. I fear my husband suspects.'

I felt a sudden sense of leaden oppression in my chest that was, I supposed, quite independent of the symptoms of heavy smoking. 'Suspects what, exactly?' I said slowly.

'Our affair,' she said, quite prosaically, sitting on the end corner of my bunk in a most familiar manner. 'I hear you were talking about me last night,' she continued.

I got up and tried to look imposing by standing over her, but I had never got the better of her fourteen years ago and was thus unlikely to start now. Her response was to start fiddling with the buttons on my trousers. I knocked her hands away and retreated. 'For God's sake, Mina, we were talking about writing.'

'Don't you dare lie to me, Jack Vincent,' she said. 'John has not the slightest interest in such things.'

'Listen to me,' I said, as firmly as I was able under the circumstances. 'There is nothing to suspect, at least not involving me. Captain Lakeman, on the other hand, is another matter.'

Without warning she slapped me hard across the face. 'You blackguard,' she hissed. 'How could you accuse me of such a thing, after all we've been to each other.'

I tried again. 'Whatever we were to each other is long dead, and you know as well as I that we have done nothing since. Now stop this nonsense before you do us both serious harm, I implore you.'

But she was now completely impervious to reason. 'I wonder what my husband will have to say about that,' she said, with a disturbing calm, 'or that little shop girl of yours.'

At that point, the rusty shackle that mostly held my anger in check snapped. I flew at her cursing, my arms waving in semaphoric agitation, a sure sign that I had lost all mastery of my emotions. 'Don't you dare to threaten my family, you demented old hag!' I bellowed, effectively loading the gun and handing it back to her.

She backed away in obvious fear, despite my tactical blunder, and I knew that in her mind I had already physically assaulted her. 'You beast!' she cried, looking her age for a moment as she retreated to the door, still watching me warily.

I stood stock-still, shaking with rage and trying to regain some sort of composure. Whether in ecstasy or anger, I do not like to lose control, at least not these days. There are some things in one's nature that are best left locked away.

Mina did not speak either, but instead began to circle back towards me in a strangely simian crouch, her eyes locked with mine in a most unsettling manner, until we stood face to face. Her silent gaze was so discomforting that I attempted to look away, but every time I turned my head or body she shifted her position to remain in front of me, staring. I tried to talk to her but in response she locked her arms about my neck and positively ground her lips against mine, driving her tongue into my mouth in a gesture as violent as it was baffling. I pushed her from me, horrified.

'Get away!' I cried. 'Get out!'

She moved not an inch, and continued to watch me like an animal while I finished my tantrum. She then became once more human, but none the less disquieting for all that.

'Nobody turns me down,' she said imperiously. 'Are you some sort of sodomite?' At that moment it occurred to me that, unlike the rest of us, Mina had probably never faced rejection and was struggling to cope. There were no doubt other anxieties in play as well, age, perhaps, or simply the humiliation of a refusal from a common man, but she looked genuinely perplexed. 'Explain yourself,' she demanded, in that same regal tone.

I considered the question for a moment, before formulating an appropriate reply. 'It's because I married for love not profit, you stupid bitch,' I told her.

It was the honest answer, though not the prudent one; I cannot deny that the look on her face was worth the provocation.

She became once more discomposed. 'Liar!' she cried. 'Degenerate!' I could live with that, but then she added, 'I will make it my mission to call upon your poor wife upon my return to England, and to expose you for the adulterous scoundrel that you are.'

Despite my best mental exertions, I once more lost control of my temper, to the point that just then I would have gladly seen her dead. I communicated these sentiments to her in a manner that must have convinced, for she finally held her tongue.

'Enjoy your descent into monomania,' I said, by way of a farewell, seizing the moment to show her the door, which she slammed in my face with a force that would have sent the older seamen cowering for cover in fear of chain or grape.

I stared at the door cursing under my breath, lighting another cheroot with palsied hands. I wondered if it was feasible to hide in my cabin feigning illness until we came to Simon's Bay the next day, where I assumed the pair of them would disembark for the Cape Colony. This thought was hardly of itself a relief. Even if she decided it was unwise to antagonise her husband and thus jeopardise her financial security, I was in no doubt that one day Mina was going to contact my wife and poison our family with her madness and lies. Stalking lunatics always do. It would be my word against hers, and Mina could be very persuasive.

I really had not the stamina to go through another crisis and then have all the trouble of putting myself back together again. Such personal reconstructions became more difficult and tiresome with age. Only the thought of my wife and son stopped me putting myself over the side of the ship then and there to avoid the bother of it all. If there was another way out of this nightmare, the path was invisible to my eyes. It was a bad bargain either way, and the thought that once again I was destined to lose everything drove me to my knees. I slid down the cool bulkhead to the floor, head in hands, in possession of the certain knowledge that there were no such things as miracles. I would not be saved, neither from Mina's inner darkness or my own.

CHAPTER XLI

OUR CAPTAIN WAS almost as good as his word, and although he did not quite match his best time ever to the Cape, we docked at Simon's Bay on the 23rd of the month, a Monday, after forty-seven days at sea. I could have well done without those extra two days, I reflected, as I stood on the main deck and regarded the rocky coastline with considerable relief. I was weak after two nights without sleep, my body running on a poisonous mixture of nicotine, caffeine, and a bottle of some sort of potcheen that I had illicitly purchased from the ship's cook. It tasted like gin mixed in a bathtub recently vacated by an incontinent ape, but it got you there. Well, it got you somewhere, and if the creature did not blind or kill you, then the old moonraker swore that his potion's pleasurable effects could be enjoyed once more the following morning, purely by drinking water. I had followed his advice, and was presently experiencing what I can only describe as drink induced visions. Select members of the ship's complement were to my eyes bathed in a queer blue light, Salmond, Seton, Metford and Granger among them. The effect was peculiar, yet oddly calming.

I had returned to wearing my dark English clothes as lack of sleep had made me cold, although the morning was more than clement. In comparison to the gleaming ship and the equally pristine soldiers standing at attention on deck I must have appeared in quite a sorry state, greasy, unshaven, and no doubt positively wild about the eyes. Salmond and Seton, on the other hand, both knew how to make an entrance. The ship had been scrubbed and polished from stem to stern, and Salmond rode it in from the poop like Odysseus upon his shield, while Seton, in full-dress uniform with a sword at his side, proudly paraded his troops on deck for the Simon's Town locals who had turned up to cheer us in from the quayside. It was a tableau that would no doubt have brought a tear to Victoria's eye.

As ever, Salmond was in no mood to hang about. Like me, he

had a wife and family in England to whom he was eager to return, and there was also the race with the *Styx* to be won. As soon as those passengers who were not going all the way disembarked, he therefore immediately prepared the ship once more for sea. Among those going ashore I marked Lieutenant Fairtlough of the 12th Foot, who I had not seen since Portsmouth, and Freshfield, the ship's clerk, both of whom were down with the fever, and my best student, Mrs. Metford, whose brief honeymoon was now emphatically at an end. She was to be left to the mercy of Cape Colony Society, while her young husband would continue with us to Algoa Bay, and from there join his regiment on the frontier. The short story she had begun in my composition class remained unfinished. Nine passengers bound for Port Elizabeth also came aboard, a woman with four children, three soldiers, and a civilian male servant. Much to my chagrin, during all this coming and going, I could not but notice that my neighbours in the adjoining cabin did not appear to be disembarking as planned.

It took forty-eight hours of around the clock loading to satisfy the ship's insatiable hunger for coal. Having born witness to the taking on of provisions several times by this point, I did not feel the need to observe in the name of accurate reportage. Instead, I slipped away to walk the barren coastline in order to clear my head, careless of whatever wildlife I might encounter along the way, and turning down Drake's offer of a marine escort.

A couple of miles to the south of the bay, I came to a sheltered beach lost between two natural walls of huge granite boulders. The spot was so peaceful it might have been the surface of the moon, and the healing solitude gave me the chance to work uninterrupted. Mina's harassment, my own crisis of identity, lack of sleep and a general derangement of the senses notwithstanding, I had never missed a deadline in my life and was not about to start now.

I was well provisioned, and as ever had my writing materials about me. As long as I remained the only living soul upon the sand, I thought, I should be able to generate enough copy to dispatch from Simon's Town and thus fulfil the terms of my employment. I therefore managed to produce an adequate account of the visit to St. Helena, smoothing out the friction between Lakeman and the other officers, and omitting Grimstone's monologue completely. Although I was still uncertain how to take the man after our recent encounter, I remained certain that he was no war hero and had no intention of presenting him as such in print. Even if our relationship was not quite as fatal as I had previously believed, he was still a Tory after all. I had also discreetly pointed him out to Jeffries on deck when the occasion arose, and asked if he recalled Grimstone fighting with the Suffolks at Waterloo. He did not, and although this would have been a gift to my former self, I was genuinely unsure of what to do with this intelligence.

'Ask to see his medal,' Jeffries had advised, but I thought it best to let sleeping dogs lie on that point, at least for the time being.[33]

I longed to talk the matter through with my wife, but there was half a world between us. All I had was the written word, an imperfect medium at the best of times, and these were the worst. As the sun was still relatively high, and the prospect of returning to the ship less than inviting, I remained on my private beach, took a late lunch and set about composing a long letter to Grace, feeling strangely compelled to write all those things that a man should say to his wife but never does. If I left this at the naval mail office in the morning, she would receive it sometime in May, while I was still God knows where up country. I prayed to the old gods of the sea that this missive should find Grace, Joseph, and, indeed, myself safe and well, and while resting my eyes and daydreaming about my family, the whispering of the waves and the warmth of the white sand soothed me into much needed slumber.

I awoke in the darkness before dawn and instinctively knew that I was not alone. I silently cursed my weak and reckless stupidity, which was most likely about to get me killed. The figure I saw further down the beach, crouched by a driftwood fire and casually driving the point of a long-handled weapon repeatedly into the sand, was clearly not on our side.

The sea always sounds louder in the dark. It was a typical sub-tropical void of a night, and the fire illuminated nether the ocean before the stranger or the brush and the mountains behind and beyond. There was only the crashing of the black waves and the music of the grass, and I prayed that I, too, was lost in the shadow of the great rock beneath which I had slept. There was no more than twenty yards between us, but fortunately the man was looking away from me and out to sea. I could see him quite clearly in the firelight. He was naked save for a loincloth, his skin insect black across muscles like those of a dancer, and when he stood and shook his loose limbs his tall, lithe physique radiated strength and power. I was unarmed, and there was not a cat in hell's chance that I could take him down with anything other than the kind of six-toothed revolver that Grimstone carried; probably not even then, for he looked as fleet as quicksilver.

The man returned his attention to his weapon, and appeared to regard his features in the highly polished blade. I remained motionless in the darkness, debating internally the prudence of continuing to play hide and seek in the hope that he would just go away, or attempting to quietly escape before the sun rose, at which point I was almost certainly dead. While I thus fret, the ocean breathed sharply and it became suddenly cold. He must have felt it too, for he moved closer to his fire. Behind us, out in the scrub, something died violently, presumably a small mammal taken by some sort of nocturnal predator. Whether the awful accompanying shriek that cut off so abruptly was uttered by hunter or prey, it communicated a further chill to my already numbing bones. In response, so it seemed, the man took out a sharpening stone, spat on it, and began to hone the blade of his knife.

If I had learned anything from keeping company with soldiers, it was that in a crisis a bad decision was better than none at all. I therefore gathered up my papers with excruciating care and made my move. Keeping to the shadows, I tried for the dune path back to the bay in a low crouch, walking as one does in a nightmare.

He heard me almost immediately, and his eyes swiftly found me out. He pointed his long knife towards me, his arm outstretched accusingly, and bellowed a word I did not know but which was clearly a command to stop. I knew I had no defense against the man, and not a prayer of outrunning him, so I collapsed upon the sand, staring at him dumbly and awaiting the unimaginable agony that a death by that evil blade promised. But death did not come. The man did not approach me. Instead, he motioned with his assegai that I should remain where I was. I did as I was told and sat back down, facing him across the sand.

Dawn came early, and I could soon see his face. He looked younger than I had thought; his features quite adolescent, he nonetheless had the look of a soldier about him. I had no idea what to do, and my ludicrous attempts to communicate in English, French, German, and Latin were all met with the indifference they deserved. Feeling foolish, I absentmindedly reached into my coat for a smoke. The soldier tensed, and I waved my cigar about like an idiot in order to reassure him it was harmless. I was suddenly aware of the acute need to feed my lungs and thus had no intention of throwing away my last gasper. I also felt far from out of the woods, and considered a final smoke a small price to ask of the universe. I was clearly not perceived as the slightest threat, for I was allowed to light up unmolested. The tobacco did its work and my pulse settled. I continued to watch the soldier cautiously, but inside I was away with my son, observing him with utter delight as he strode purposefully about the downstairs rooms of our house, discoursing unintelligibly about this and that, and investigating or discarding the toys that we had made him.

I was returned to reality by the young soldier, who gave a jaw breaking yawn, shook the tiredness from his long limbs, and threw the last of the wood upon the fire. He rose silently to his full, willowy height, stepped out of his loose garment and turned towards the sea, naked but for the long knife, as if deliberately displaying his sleek, ebony, and quite beautiful body to the water itself, or perhaps something in it. Whether this was done proudly or defiantly I could not tell. Then he began to sing, a slow, haunting lament that seemed to me to tell a story, although I'll be damned if I could say what about. As he sang, the sun rose on the horizon, its rays forming an aureate path of light beyond the surf. Still singing, the soldier walked out to join it.

The crashing waves tried to push him back, but he was a rock. I looked on, bewitched by this strange ritual. Finally, he was clear of the breakers, and was able to wade out beyond the deafening surf and stand, quite comfortably, waste deep in the cool, clear morning water. Singing softly and keeping a good hold on his knife, he raised his free left hand, open as if in greeting, and then bought it down swiftly, slapping the water with a crack. He repeated this movement, building up a rhythm that pulsed away from him in ripples across the silken surface and out into the darkness beyond where the shallows dropped away into the lightless abyss of the open ocean. The soldier beat the water as he would a drum, and he watched, and he waited, as did I.

Out in the darkness, something heard, or rather felt, the soldier's call, and turned towards the shore. I could not tell you how, but the soldier knew and so did I. You could feel the change in the sea and the air, the silence, the dread. He stopped hitting the water, shielded his eyes from the glare of the sun, now well risen, and scanned the foamless blue before him.

The shark was a big one, maybe as long as two men, and closing fast. The soldier did not move, did not flinch, as he saw the great grey back of the beast break the surface in its killing run, dorsal and tail slicing through air and water. He stood his ground and gripped the handle of his knife as the monster fish's ugly triangular head broke the water, dead eyes rolling over white, and mouth gaping in a disgusting ecstasy of anticipation. At the last second the soldier deftly side-stepped, plunging his knife into the animal's side with both hands. The shock of the impact must have been tremendous, but the soldier braced himself as his bare feet slid along the ocean floor, leaning forward and standing firm as the great fish tore past him. The monster's momentum carried it along the blade, which must have been as keen as a razor, ripping it open from its jagged gills to its huge tail and spilling its oily guts into the water as it thundered towards the breakers, unaware of its own death. It seemed to go on forever, but the soldier held on. As the great tail thrashed past his hands, the boy heaved on the hilt of his knife and yanked it out of the body of the shark, turning his head and watching the huge dorsal fin moving away from him in a crimson wake, slower now, less steady. He hurriedly sluiced his blade in the water, gripped it in his teeth and swam after his prey through its own blood, breaking stroke periodically to raise his head and risk a look. The great fish was rolling on its dirty white side in the pink foam of the breaking waves, its mortal wound facing the sky, black blood and water licking obscenely around its gaping mouth. It was a flat, dark grey, like the silent deep in which it had formerly ruled, with a belly as white as death and nothing.

The soldier swam more steadily now, knowing that he had won. He rose up from the water and walked towards the shark. He had cut the fish along the uneven line on its hide where the white of its belly merged with the grey of its upper body. The gaping slit yawned horribly as the bloodless fish rolled uselessly in the shallows, its mouth slowly moving as if trying to speak. Cautiously, the soldier approached the huge head, watching the single black eye watching him, and wary of the jaws.

I should have been running while my captor was otherwise engaged, but I was completely transfixed by the scene. As I yet looked on, the soldier raised his knife and drove it deeply into the top of the creature's skull, between dinosaur eyes, and into its brain. He twisted the blade savagely and the shark shuddered, whatever lived behind those empty eyes finally leaving. The soldier grabbed its enormous, rough tail and began dragging it onshore. The fish appeared too heavy for one man to land, but he used the animal's remaining buoyancy to get it as far into the shallows as he could. He fell, gasping, beside his conquest in a few inches of murky water, and patted its unlovely head with an affectionate hand. Beyond the surf, grey dorsal and tail fins moved through the rapidly dispersing blood cloud. The soldier called out to them in triumph and waved his knife above his head, before he set about cutting and knocking out several of the animal's evil and twisted teeth.

After collecting his trophies as best he could, he pushed the carcass back into the sea, and returned to the fire, ignoring me and wrapping the teeth carefully in a square of red cloth. He then walked back to the ocean and rinsed his knife again, watching the dead thing twitch in the boiling scarlet foam as its brothers and sisters took it apart. Soon there would be nothing left, I thought, as I have heard that these animals are too ancient and strange to be held together with bones. The soldier raised his knife, shook the salt water off it and once more looked at his face in the mirror of the blade. He studied his reflection seriously for a moment, and then he smiled at his other self before gazing once more out across the sea. He shaded his eyes and watched the dead shark until the water closed over it, then, laughing, he turned and walked slowly back towards the fire, and to me.

*

It was Lakeman's view that I had witnessed some sort of rite of passage, based upon my estimate of the shark killer's age, and it frustrated him that I could not recall any physical markings or other adornments that might have indicated a specific tribe.

'There are many ways for a boy to enter manhood and become a warrior,' he said, as we killed a bottle of brandy that he had been considerate enough to bring to my cabin that evening, having learned of my recent adventure. 'And I have heard of many cultures that believe that the spirit of an animal chooses to join your soul when you are born.'

'A bit like Plato's dæmon,' I said.

'Well this poor bugger's was certainly a demon,' said he, laughing. 'And my guess was that he had to take its life to prove himself, yes, but to also make it physically part of him. Did he take any trophies?'

'Both ears and the tail.'

'Be serious, for once, you bloody commoner.'

'The teeth,' I said, with a shudder, 'he knocked out a load of its teeth.'

'Well there you go,' said Lakeman, helping himself to another huge balloon of bingo. 'Those teeth'll be hung around his neck by now. I shall keep my eye out for him when I'm up country.'

'He killed one of those white sharks with nothing but his wits and a dirty great knife,' I said. 'I never want to see him again. He might not be so forgiving next time.'

'And he let you watch,' said Lakeman, 'and then let you go.

Now why the deuce was that?'

It was generally agreed on board that I had 'tipped the Dublin packet' that morning, which meant that I had had a very narrow escape indeed. The tribal identity of the man remained a mystery, but it was the opinion of Wright and Seton that he was undoubtedly a 'hostile,' given his actions and appearance. I had been debriefed in Seton's cabin, with the Captain in attendance. When I asked why the enemy should be so close to Simon's Town, as there appeared to be only one, Salmond had replied that if a man had a mind to catch a white shark in the surf, then these were the waters in which to do it. They were teeming with the blighters, he explained, as they came to the Cape to feed off the seals, those cheerful, barking water-dogs that looked like creatures of the land but swam like fish.

There's your bloody mermaids, I thought.

'We're not far off the Bay of Geese here, Mr. Vincent,' Salmond had added, by way of dubious clarification.

'That doesn't sound too bad,' I replied flippantly, missing his meaning completely as geography had never been my strong suit.

Then he fixed me with his glittering eye and said, 'Also known as Danger Point.' He did not even pause for me to ask why, and this time his explication was unambiguous. 'On account of its sunken rocks,' said he, with a ghoulish relish, 'suffocating weeds, violent surf, and vicious fish.'

'That place is truly Satan's aquarium,' agreed Wright.

'They call it "Shark Alley" hereabouts,' said Salmond.[34]

'Fair enough,' said I. 'That would certainly explain the unorthodox fisherman's presence.'

'We pass through it,' said Salmond, ignoring my last remark, 'on the way to our final destination.'

All in all, it had been a very trying day, and my encounter with the mysterious native remained a confusing experience. After he had dispatched the devil fish, he had returned to his fire, dressed, organized his possessions and left. He had paused only to address me, in a manner that I could not understand, for several minutes. At first his tone was quite heartfelt, but he became agitated towards the end of his speech, facing me and shouting like a Whitechapel street-fighter. I raised my hands in the universal gesture of the man who does not want any trouble and backed away slowly. He looked at me with obvious contempt, and reached into a small leather pouch that hung about his neck. He then came close in again, and deft as a dummy hunter knapping a reader he held up his hand and blew a palm full of ash into my face. While I brushed the foul stuff away, having instinctively closed my eyes and mouth as soon as the hand came up, he said something unintelligible but clearly far from complimentary, and strode off muttering to himself like a drunken Methodist. As soon as he was out of sight I legged it back to the ship.

I have no idea why he spared me, unless it was my job to report what I had seen in order to strike fear into the hearts of his enemies. I had suggested this to Moran earlier that evening, to which he confidently responded that just because the bloody heathen could stop a shark it did not mean that he could not stop a bullet. I had conceded that this was a fair point, but wondered privately what such warriors could do while our soldiers were busy reloading. Otherwise, in a scenario I preferred not to consider, I had become part of the ritual. The shark killer's parting act had felt and sounded disturbingly like a curse. This strange encounter had, however, certainly put my other problems in perspective. When Mina came rapping at my cabin door later that evening expressing concern, as I knew she would, I told her in no uncertain terms to fuck off and thereafter ignored her. Life, I had been forcibly reminded that morning, was simply far too short.

We were by then well under weigh again. Salmond had received his orders from Commodore Wyvill, the Naval Commander at the Cape, which were to proceed with all possible haste to Algoa Bay and Buffalo Mouth, wherever they were, to land the drafts of the different regiments and to ensure that an urgent government dispatch was placed into the hand of Sir Harry Smith, who was believed to be somewhere in the Waterkloof Mountains. Mr. Grimstone and his wife also remained with us, in order, it was said, that he might speak with Smith personally. The rumour was that Smith was to be relieved of his command. I heard from Lakeman that Grimstone had urged Mina to disembark at Simon's Town, but that she had refused.

Wednesday evening was fine and calm with smooth water, and it was a reassurance to have the coast ever in view to port after almost two months of Open Ocean. As it was to be our final night on board I took one last meal on the troop deck with Moran and Jeffries, before brandy and cigars with Lakeman. We spoke late into the night, and he finally retired some time after one. I felt not in the least tired, and as the night was pleasant I decided to take one last turn around the upper deck before I got my head down. I paused for a final smoke at my preferred spot by the port paddle-box, and watched the occasional comforting light glinting on the shadowy shore. The great sidewheels plunged relentlessly into the dark water below, bearing us across False Bay and onwards towards Danger Point.

CHAPTER XLII

I COULD NOT sleep, and was thus still up on deck when four bells was called, the sea and sky fused in darkness. The night had remained clear and calm, and so gentle was the running that we might as well have been steaming through the luminiferous aether of outer space.

I was chatting with Drake on the fo'c'sle when the ship struck something sharp about three miles offshore. We had been moving at around eight and a half knots, and, as it always must be with the journey of life, we had come to a very sudden stop. The impact sent Drake sprawling one way across the deck and me the other, almost going over the rail. The ship's inertia kept her grinding forward, and we heard the terrible and unmistakable screech of cold iron tearing and the fatal roar of seawater flooding in under pressure below. Then the *Birkenhead* came to a shuddering stop, the deck tilting horribly.

'What the fucking hell was that?' demanded Drake, a crack briefly showing in his legendarily cool façade.

The enquiry was evidently rhetorical. Although there was a certain incredulity about the initial shock, it was more than obvious what had just happened. An icy fist of fear rammed its way down my throat. We had hit a hidden rock or a reef, and were most likely going down for the bow was already pointing crazily at the stars. I helped Drake to his feet and we made our way to the poop, slipping and sliding as if struggling down a steep hill. We were desperate to find out what was happening, although the ugly angle of the deck could tell only one tale.

We blundered into Salmond on the top deck, wearing nothing but a dressing gown. Like me, he had obviously been drinking that night, but he seemed sober enough now. Seton and Wright were not far behind, dressing as they came, and we all ran to the poop. There, we found the terrified helmsman fighting the wheel and Davis, the Duty Officer, sitting upon the deck vacantly with blood pouring from a wound on his head.

'Where are we?' bellowed Salmond, 'and what have we hit?'

In the flickering light of wildly swinging lanterns Davis' face took on the hue of a corpse. His voice seemed to come from somewhere else, an immeasurable distance away. 'I don't know, sir,' he said quietly, 'we were steering sou'-sou'-east-half-east as instructed, and our bearings are all correct.'

'But where are we, damn it?' said Salmond.

'Danger Point,' whispered Davis, drifting away and saying no more.

Salmond shook him by the shoulders. 'Wake up, man,' he said. 'What is our situation?'

Seton knelt by Davis and checked his pulse. He looked up at the Captain and shook his head. Davis had quite clearly gone.

Salmond looked as suddenly pale as the departed Second Master. 'What is the hour?' he asked abstractedly.

'Just after two,' replied Seton.

Salmond grabbed a telescope that was attached to the wooden wall of the poop awning by means of spring clips and swept the shore with the glass. 'Something is very wrong,' he whispered.

'Indeed,' said Seton, standing and buttoning his shirt. In his haste to reach the Bridge he had neglected his tunic and out of uniform he had the look of a Romantic poet. I noticed he was, however, wearing his sabre, and wondered if he had expected pirates.

How wrong things were became quickly apparent as men in various states of undress began to struggle out of tight hatches and bulkhead doors onto the deck beneath the poop shouting and swearing. Drake spied a familiar face and called down to him, 'Private Moran, to me!'

Moran scrambled up the steps to the poop and did his best to come to attention on the listing boards. He was one of the few men on deck in uniform.

'Report,' said Drake. Moran was shaking, and being in the presence of the senior naval and military officers on board was not helping his nerves. I tried to look reassuring, but he did not acknowledge me. 'Come along, son,' said Drake kindly.

Moran sniffed loudly. 'The lower troop deck,' he said, a catch in his voice that could easily have prefaced a sob.

'What about it, man?' demanded Salmond.

'It's gone, sir,' said Moran, 'flooded. I was on sentry, sir, otherwise I'd have drowned with the rest.'

'My God,' said Seton. 'How many were sleeping there?' he asked, turning to Wright.

'A hundred and fifty on the lower deck,' said Wright.

'There are others still trapped, sir,' said Moran, forgetting protocol and speaking without being spoken to, 'and the water's still coming in.'

Other officers, army and navy, were now arriving breathlessly, while the surviving NCOs took charge of the soldiers. Lakeman and his people were not among them. Even then, in all that destruction and chaos, it was difficult to accept that he had gone, probably in his hammock with the rest of his lads, drowning in the darkness. Not a good way to go.

'Then we are sinking,' said Seton, addressing the Captain with admirable calm.

Salmond, too, seemed to have composed himself. 'There are watertight compartments,' he said, 'we may yet survive this.'

'But perhaps,' replied Seton, 'we should prepare for the worst. There are, after all, civilians on board.'

This straightforward exchange restored us to our senses. The entire scene could not have been longer than a couple of minutes, but until that instant it had been as timeless as a dream.

Salmond turned to Brodie, who had materialised on the poop and was covering Davis with his coat, and gave the orders to stop all engines and drop the small anchor in the hope that the ship could be kept from slipping off the rocks and into deeper waters, thereby buying some time for those still below. The engine room telegraph was still working, which offered a modicum of hope. If the engine room was not flooded then it was possible that the watertight compartments were holding, although my spirits sank once more when I recalled how many of those inner bulkheads had doorless holes cut in them to accommodate the traffic of large groups of soldiers.

Salmond then dispatched Speer, the surviving Second Master, to assess the damage below decks, and Hare, the Master's Assistant, to the engine room. 'Be precise in your observations,' he said, 'but for the love of God be quick.' Next he asked Drake to find some marines and then bring all the civilian passengers up on deck. Finally, Brodie was told to assemble a detail and lower the boats, just in case they were needed.

The implication of the Captain's final instruction was awful, but also something of a relief. The thought of entering these waters had me as terrified as a prisoner of the Inquisition, and not for fear of drowning. I had seen what was down there, waiting. I knew that there were eight boats in all. There were two gigs on the fore part of the ship, and a long pinnace amidships between paddle-boxes, both of which were covered by large boats which served as cowls; two cutters hung on davits on the quarterdeck, and a small dinghy dangled over the stern. Not enough, I realised, even after subtracting the men on the lower troop deck.

Seton was also issuing orders. He called his junior officers around him and impressed on them the necessity of preserving order and silence among the men. He then directed Wright to take and have executed any orders from Salmond, who promptly requested that sixty men be put on the chain pumps on the lower afterdeck, and told off in three reliefs. Wright delegated this to Giradot; a further sixty men were put on to the tackles of the paddle-box boats under Cornet Rolt, and Sheldon-Bond was instructed to put the horses over the side. The rest of the soldiers were assembled by drum call on the main deck as they fought their way up from below. I watched the young officers calling the fittest men to them, and glimpsed Jeffries among Rolt's party.

Then Wright turned his attention to me. 'Mr. Vincent,' said he, 'if you would be so kind as to join the ladies.' And thus was I politely but firmly ordered off the command deck. He told Moran to look after me, and then go and join his mates on the main deck. 'And be quick about it,' he said.

We left together, me leading the way down the steps to the quarterdeck. Moran grabbed my shoulders from behind as soon as we were out of sight. 'It's now or never, Jack,' said he, in sibilant excitement.

I am the antichrist, I thought, will you deny me?

'What's "now or never"?' I asked, although I had a pretty shrewd idea.

'The magazine,' he said, in an urgent whisper. 'They'll be no one fool enough to be guarding it now.'

'They'll be no one alive,' said I, 'the hold's long flooded if the troop decks have gone.'

'Look about you,' he said artfully. 'The bow's out of the water, and we know the engine room's still dry. A tasty pair of sneaksmen would be in and out as quick as throwing a crab, and whose to know for it'll all go to the bottom soon enough. A victimless crime, Jack, that's what it would be.'

'Go back down there?' I said. 'You're insane.'

'I'm poor,' he said, 'that's what I am, always have been.' He came in close to my face to make his point, 'And I'm fucking sick of it,' he concluded.

'So am I,' I replied, for I must not have been as sober as I had formally believed.

'Good man,' he said, 'for I can't do this without you.'

*

It was not difficult to slip back inside claiming to bear an urgent message for the Chief Engineer, although several haggard survivors from the upper deck castigated us for going the wrong way.

'There's nothing back there, you feckin' fools,' said a huge, half-dressed Irishmen shoving his way through weaker men towards an open hatch. 'They're all of them feckin' dead.'

'Appreciated,' said Moran coolly, 'but duty still calls.'

'Yeah, duty,' I mumbled, squeezing with some difficulty past the great, ginger-hackled giant and the tide of humanity that bore him, in the half light of the lamps, along the gangway. If he were trying to save us, I thought, he could have moderated his tone. Courtesy should cost nothing, even in the face of certain death.

'And how did you get out?' called Moran back to the Irishman over his shoulder, 'on the backs of your mates I'll be bound.' But he had long gone by then. 'That's what I did,' Moran said more quietly.

Time was wasting. I patted him on the back, which for working class men is the equivalent of at least six months of spiritual counselling, and bade him keep moving. 'When the cards are down,' I told him, 'there is no shame in saving yourself.'

'Sure enough,' he said, recovering quickly, thank God, for if he had turned French on me at that moment then I was surely doomed. 'Grab a light, Jack, and then let's fuck this dog.'

'Charming,' I said, unhooking the fullest oil lamp I could find from the bulkhead and following him into the darkness.

We were, of course, essentially retracing our steps from our first meeting all those weeks ago, in which we had become hopelessly lost on the lower decks. Since those early days we had become as adept as moles at navigating the tight, barely-lit passageways. Only then the gangways had not been quite so dark, or at such an unnaturally steep and twisted incline, causing you to dodge unsecured equipment as it clattered past. Neither were we accustomed to the unrelenting rattle of the chain pumps, nor the constant creaking and cracking of the hull as it was subjected to elemental stresses never calculated by marine architects. These eerie sounds were periodically punctuated by unidentified but powerful percussive blows from above, as if of buildings collapsing.

'That'll probably be the funnel going over,' remarked Moran, as if the latest muffled concussion was of no more significance than a dray horse breaking wind in a side street.

I marvelled at his self-control. It had scared the atheist right out of me, and even though so low in the belly of the beast, we could still hear the shrill sound of steam venting above, as if the ship in her death throes was screaming.

'Then there's not much time,' I said, mouth dry, but still pressing on.

I was driven by avarice, for sure, desperation I would have said, but also that ridiculous optimism, even in the most dire of circumstances, that will not allow you to accept the inevitability of your impending demise. Having lived an entire life based upon morbid fancy, I was utterly in denial of the fact that my number was well and truly up.

Those dark passages had equally never before echoed with the desperate cries of the men still trapped in the troop decks behind us, the ones not killed outright, but cursed to wait against buckled bulkheads as the waters slowly rose, with absolutely no hope of escape; that anguished howling and banging at doors that would never open again, like the sound of wolves going mad in a pit. Neither my companion nor I was brave or foolish enough to suggest trying to go back and help. That part of the ship was already underwater, and the wailing and hammering did not last for long.

'Lord have mercy upon them,' I found myself saying, although I had not the right.

'And may they be in Heaven half an hour before the Devil knows they're dead,' agreed Moran, offering a much more practical prayer than my own, and continuing to drag himself forward up the newly formed mountain path of iron that perversely led to the hold and thus the magazine.

I followed close behind. It was like traversing one of Piranesi's 'Imaginary Prisons,' for we had to make our way up in order to go down.

We circumnavigated the great engine room as unobtrusively as we were able. It was still occupied and seemingly operational. A stoker spotted us, but he was hardly likely to question our reason for being below decks, which was that we were charged with releasing the guards in the hold. Moran retained his uniform and weapon, and thus looked reasonably official, and as everyone knew a marine would stand to attention while he drowned unless an officer gave him leave to swim for it, no one was likely to doubt us. My presence was not remarked upon, and as I vaguely knew the man I can only assume that he thought I was covering the story down to the bones.

'What's the news from the helm?' asked the stoker, hopefully.

'Bad,' I said.

The hold was on the other side of the engine room, and mercifully still dry underfoot. Many of the ship's stores had broken free, and great crates slid about on the thirty-odd degree gradient, creating a nightmarish and constantly shifting maze that we had to navigate in order to locate the magazine. We were, however, aided in our design by quite clear sounds of violent occupation from that side of the hold. Fearful of extinguishing our lights, we covered the glasses as best we could with cloth torn from our shirts and peered cautiously around the final crate.

The short, low corridor to the magazine in which we had once passed the time of day with two of Drake's implacable leathernecks was still clearly lit, and much against our original calculations the guards were still in place, although they appeared unconscious. From inside the magazine came the sound of desperate fighting.

Someone had obviously beaten us to it, and I was for cutting our losses. Moran was having none of it. 'I've not come so far to turn back now, Jack,' he said, 'now get your dander up and hook it!'

'After you,' I said.

He gave the marines a cursory check, but they were both quite dead. One had been shot through the chest and by the state of him looked to have drowned on his own blood. The other was missing an eye, most likely taken out when the blade that had obviously pierced his brain was removed.

'Good kill,' breathed Moran, reverentially. This was not a side I had seen before, and it was most disconcerting.

Whoever was in the magazine was putting up a better fight, presumably for not being taken unawares. I opened the door a crack and squinted. The scene was illuminated by an overturned lamp alarmingly close to some powder and resting by an overturned strongbox that had shed its gold. On the slanting deck two big men were locked in a terminal embrace, their clothes in disarray, hands around each other's throats, eyes popping with strain and pure, animal hatred. They were grotesquely underlit as they careened about the small room, but I could still make them out. It was Barker and Granger, finally finishing the fight begun back on Spike Island all those weeks ago.

Our unannounced arrival tipped the balance, for Granger saw me and was, for a second, distracted. He must have relaxed his grip a minute amount in consequence, and this was enough for Barker to knock his arms away and deliver a devastating uppercut. Granger went flying and hit the deck insensible, and then Barker was on him, a long knife suddenly in his hand, his arm raised to strike.

His mistake was in ignoring us as insignificant. In an instant I had brained him from behind with a gold bar, and as he reeled around cursing Moran shot him. At such close range, the force of the ball blew him off Granger like a shot from a cannon. He slumped against a heavy crate and moved no more. We paid him no further heed.

Granger was still unconscious, so we righted the lamp and set about robbing the place, gathering the small gold bars that had spilled out on the deck and stuffing them into boots and pockets. Moran emptied out his pack and filled that too, and then Lieutenant Granger began to revive so we made ourselves respectable.

Granger sat up, rubbing his jaw and wincing. Moran gave him some water. 'I came down to get the guards,' said the young officer, 'but they were dead, murdered, and that blackguard was raiding the strongboxes.'

'He'll not raid no more,' said Moran.

I had moved in to hear him speak, and Granger was therefore able to grab my hand. 'You saved my life, you bloody Chartist,' said he, trying to smile with his broken mouth, 'I'll not forget it.'

I decided not to reply that I was sure he would have done the same for me, while there was still some ambiguity. Like Sheldon-Bond, Granger had never disguised his contempt for my profession and politics, while I was almost equally damned by my association with Lakeman.

We picked him up between us and got an arm around each shoulder, before we began our tortuous descent, now hampered by the awkward weight of all that gold, as well as the still useless legs of the young subaltern, who had once more passed out. We dragged him back to the engine room and managed to revive him with brandy and water donated by Whyham, the Chief Engineer, still at his post with his crew until ordered otherwise, the boilers still stoked.

'Did you not find the marines?' said the man with whom we had spoken on the way through the first time.

'Both dead,' I told him.

'Oh,' he said.

Now Granger was restored to his senses and thus able to walk, we made for the ladders to the upper decks, and the relative safety of the topside, where hopefully by now the boats had been lowered. As I climbed beneath the soldiers, a sensation that had been troubling me, but which I had not consciously identified, began to make its presence more concrete. There were two gold bars stretching my inside top pocket, which were forced against my chest uncomfortably every time they snagged on the rung of the ladder. This sharp discomfort would have been cheap at the price, had I not at that moment realised that the reason I had room in that particular pocket was that it was otherwise empty. This was the pocket in which I always carried my father's copy of *Lyrical Ballads*, my magic book, which I could now see, quite clearly in my mind's eye, carelessly left upon my bunk where I had been reading it before Lakeman had visited earlier that fateful evening.

The last time I cried off the drink and the drugs, I remember falling into such a terrible depression that I knew not what to do with myself. I was on ragged edge all of the time, but despite various, often genuinely dreadful happenstances in my professional and public life in that period, what finally caused me to break down was something that was, in context, laughably trivial. I awoke one morning, I recall quite clearly, to discover that I had neglected to put the cat out the evening before, and that he had dislodged a manuscript from my desk, spread it unevenly across the study floor, and then spectacularly evacuated upon it. I mention that incident, as the feeling of blind, hopeless rage and despair I felt then, and which knocked me straight off the wagon, was very much the equal of that which I experienced upon the realisation that I had left my father's little book behind, proving the old seafaring adage that you should never take anything aboard a ship that you are not prepared to lose.

Still on the ladder, I made this point colourfully and at considerable length.

'Steady on, old man,' said Granger.

I gained the lower deck, pacing and ranting, my companions no doubt surmising some sort of nervous breakdown, which may well have been the case. I was beside myself. Whatever the danger, I had to retrieve my book. I communicated this to Moran, who was less than impressed.

'Buy another one,' he said.

'But I need this one,' I said, part of me knowing full well that I was being ridiculous, but nonetheless unable to control my rising sense of panic.

'What on earth for?' said Granger 'Is a blasted book worth your life, man?'

'I cannot write without it,' I said hopelessly. There was no time to debate the matter further. With a lunatic resolve, I was compelled to return to my cabin. 'Go,' I told them. 'I promise I will not be far behind.'

'I'll come with you,' offered Moran, but it was clear from Granger's deathly pallor as he slumped against the bulkhead for support that he still required assistance.

I offered him my hand. 'Take the Lieutenant and go. I'll not be a minute.'

He looked far from convinced. 'She'll not last much longer, Jack.'

'I know,' I said. 'So no more talk, my friend. Just bugger off the pair of you.' Then giving him no more chance to convince me otherwise, I struck out for the stern cabins as briskly as I was able.

'Think of your wife and son, Jack,' he called after me, the bastard.

'It is because of them that I go,' I countered.

'It is because of yourself, you fucking eejit,' I heard him growl, and then his light vanished and he and Granger were gone.

CHAPTER XLIII

THE CIVILIAN CABINS were forward on the upper deck, which was not as yet flooding. After my recent adventures, I was hopeful that this particular errand would be a breeze by comparison. I would recover my book, climb the steps to the main deck like a rat up a drainpipe, and then catch the first lifeboat off this damned widow-maker.

The slanting corridors were eerily deserted yet still lighted, and it was strange to imagine walking these so casually with Lakeman the previous evening. This was now a very different environment, and cold fingers of fear stroked my hair and urged me to be gone from this sepulchral place. When I reached my cabin, I was dismayed to find it partially destroyed, the door forced outward off its hinges, and the berth itself compressed by some monstrous pressure from above. Presumably, as Moran had surmised, something very heavy had fallen on the main deck and crushed the one beneath at this point. The ceiling of my now former residence had partially collapsed, but these ironclads were damn sturdy, so although the cabin was now less than half its original height, it remained otherwise intact save for the disarray attendant on the initial impact and the listing of the ship. My bunk was still in one piece, and my book was like as not on or near it. I peered through the door paralysed with indecision, before finally crawling into the devastated cabin, pushing my lamp ahead of me. Above my head, the low ceiling began to creak.

Swearing, I reached my bunk and began frantically searching the covers. The book was not there. I next explored the floor as well as I was able, and this time my labours were rewarded for I found my book undamaged in a corner in a muddle of clothes and personal items. I retrieved it hastily, along with an oilcloth sou'wester that I could never bring myself to wear, and slid out on my belly like a reptile. Only then did I consider rescuing my great leather coat, but a moan of tortured metal from within quickly dissuaded me. I had been lucky so far, and I knew it. Why tempt fate further, I thought. Back in the relative safety of the corridor, I used my teeth to start a tear in the oilcloth, which I then ripped into a rough square in which I wrapped my book in case of water damage, although God forbid I was actually going to get my feet wet. At that stage I yet retained a naive faith in the skills of our Captain and the security of the boats. For someone who had made a career out of writing of pirates, I knew precious little of the reality of shipwrecks.

The door to the cabin next to mine was fastened, but as I passed it I heard the unmistakable sounds of human occupation from within, in the form of muffled voices that just carried above the clatter of loose debris and unfastened equipment above, the crashing of the sea, and the sorrowful groans of the hull. Once more polluting the air with profanity, I tried the door, which appeared unlocked but was nevertheless jammed shut. Inside, the voices became more agitated. I put my shoulder to the door and managed to shift it a few inches, after which I drove it inwards with a couple of robust kicks.

'My darling Jack,' said Mina from the shadows, 'I knew you would come for me.' Her voice lacked its usual theatrical projection, and instead sounded small and distant.

I felt those fingers of fear again. No one should have been down there by then. The marines had been evacuating the women and children before Moran and I had snuck away about our nefarious business a good quarter of an hour before. If we really were sinking, then they should have been the first into the cutters. It suddenly occurred to me that I might also have missed the lifeboats, and it was all I could do to avoid being violently sick in sheer terror.

I held up my light and peered into the dark cabin. For the most part, it appeared not as demolished as mine, with the exception of the ceiling panels along our adjoining wall, which had obviously come down when my cabin was partially flattened. It was under this jagged triangle of solid wreckage that Mina lay, attended by her terrified maid, her legs beneath a ceiling plate attached to what appeared to be a huge iron lintel that had swung down at one end. Grimstone was nowhere to be seen. I bade the maid take my light and surveyed the scene, whispering pointless and soothing platitudes that seemed to calm Mina. She was deadly pale and drifting in and out of consciousness; her face serene in sleep one moment, as young as when I had first known her, and then, upon waking, suddenly aged, a pained mask mirroring her future features after ten or twenty more years of life. Although she was a threat to my family, I could not leave her like this.

The maid, whose name I ascertained was Clara, said that they had all been roused by the initial collision, and that the master and mistress were in the process of hastily dressing in order to go up on deck when the cabin had fallen in. Grimstone had promptly fled, leaving her alone with her injured mistress. At first she had been too scared to do anything other than cower in the corner praying, but when Mina revived she had ordered her to go for help. Before she could do so a further impact from above had warped the bulkhead just enough to jam the door, imprisoning them both.

'Have you tried to move her?' I asked the maid.

'It's too heavy, sir,' she said, weeping in fear and frustration and indicating the girder, which on closer investigation was embedded firmly in the cabin floor.

I tried getting my arms around it anyway, but the damn thing might as well have been riveted in place at either end, and so absolutely resistant was it to my exertions that I did not even disturb Mina. We then tried together, with no more success than before. There was nothing for it but to go for help.

We were debating how best to go about this, and whether or not Clara should remain with Mina or accompany me, for she confessed she was too afraid to make for the main deck in the dark on her own, when we felt the engines start. The vibrations were enough to cause Mina great distress, although after initially crying out she bore it with a level of stoicism I doubted I could have matched, breathing rapidly through the pain, which must have been terrible.

'Hold on,' I told her, 'this means the damage is not as bad as it looked.'

She gripped my hand until it hurt and stared at me silently with the eyes of an animal.

'Thank God,' said the maid.

Were there a Supreme Being making some sense of the universe he was either otherwise engaged just then or was, when all was said and done, as vindictive as the God of Abraham. I was knocked on my arse as the ship lurched drunkenly, freeing herself with a dreadful screech. Mina screamed too, long and loud, and when I had recovered my footing and retrieved the lamp (which had flown from Clara's hands as she also went over but had mercifully not been extinguished), I saw for the first time her blood around the iron.

We were now once more upon something approaching an even keel, and the cabin had righted itself. Clara set about trying to make her mistress as comfortable as possible again, and I checked the wreckage that trapped her in the hope that something might have moved. It had not. Then the ship struck again, much more violently than in the first instance, throwing us once more to the deck. Almost immediately came the same terrible tearing sound that I had first heard with Drake up on deck, amplified a hundredfold now that I was within the hull. This was at once followed by the unmistakable thunder of tons of water pouring into the stricken ship.

'It appears you spoke too soon, Jack,' said Mina, and I swear she started laughing.

Then a muffled detonation rocked the ship, presumably caused by seawater reaching the great boilers. The immediate and accompanying cessation of the familiar vibrations running through the deck was a silent but emphatic statement that the engines were now quite dead.

The thunder, however, did not end, and when I stuck my head out of the cabin doorway I could hear the rush of water flooding all the decks beneath, watertight compartments be damned. Soon it would reach us.

I could not fathom what had just happened. Only the Captain could have given the word, assuming he yet lived, but God alone knew why; some final, desperate roll of the dice perhaps, intended to get us off the rocks and stable enough to safely abandon ship. Whatever lie behind that fateful decision though, it was clear that it had doomed the ship. The only small mercy was that, miraculously, the previous list remained corrected and the deck was relatively level. While trying to conceal my growing sense of panic from the ladies, I redoubled my efforts to free Mina, bracing my back against the fallen girder and heaving against the bulkhead with my feet. This was utterly ineffectual, so I then tried to find something about the cabin sturdy enough to act as some sort of lever or pivot, but nothing served there so I set to kicking the iron as hard as I could on the off chance it might come loose until Mina begged me to stop. It was hopeless.

'Go,' she said, 'and get help if you can.' The thunder was getting closer now, and neither Clara nor I spoke. 'And if you cannot find help,' Mina continued slowly, 'then save yourselves.'

'Mistress!' said Clara, collapsing by Mina's side and sobbing.

Mina stroked her hair affectionately and then bade her sit up straight. She removed a ring from her right hand and pressed it into the palm of the weeping girl. 'I wish I had more about me to offer you for such good and faithful service,' she said, smiling. 'Now let me have a word with Jack.'

I knelt beside her. 'Mina,' I said, helplessly.

She grasped my hand again, and pulled herself as upright as she could upon her elbows. The effort of moving told upon her face, and when she spoke it was in a whisper. I bowed my head to hear her better.

'Jack,' she said, 'I'm sorry.' I began to answer but she put a finger to my lips. 'Let me speak,' she said. 'There's not much time.' I nodded and held my peace. 'It's about John,' she continued, 'and why he hates you so much. It was your mother, Jack. He was a friend of her brother, before the last French war, and he was besotted. But when he plighted his troth she turned him down flat. "No prospects," she said. So he went out into the world to make something of himself, and what did he find upon his return? Although he was now a rich man, the love of his life had married a common tailor.' She paused for breath, and then gave a little chuckle. 'And to make matters worse, my dear Jack, you apparently look just like him.'

'That's true,' I said, smiling despite myself.

'Love makes us do stupid and awful things,' she said.

I took her hand without thinking and squeezed it futilely. It was already bloodless and cold. 'But also wonderful things,' I said.

She neither affirmed nor denied, but let go of my hand and started fiddling about with another ring. 'Take this,' she said, closing my fingers around it until it hurt, 'and remember me.'

Even after all those years I recognised the ring, it had belonged to her mother. 'I can't take this,' I said.

'Nonsense,' said she, 'give it to that pretty young wife of yours. I won't be needing it where I'm going, and anyway I owe you.'

'You don't owe me anything.'

'I do, dearest Jack,' she said. 'Now take the damn ring.' (I acquiesced and placed it on my little finger.) 'It was me that betrayed you,' she continued. 'I told John about the prison and he used the intelligence to ruin you.'

'I know,' I said, 'don't worry.'

'But you didn't give up,' she continued, determined in her penitence, 'and now here you are, still fighting to be more than you are. My folly was that I learned to live with my own hopelessness.' She leaned back then, and I carefully helped her to lie down. 'I can't feel my legs, Jack,' she said quietly.

'Sleep, now,' I said, uselessly, 'it'll be over soon.' Water was trickling through the doorway but I don't think she felt it.

Suddenly she lifted her head once more. 'You'll tell my boys what happened?' she said insistently.

'You can tell them yourself,' I told her.

'Swear!' she demanded, so I crossed my heart and that seemed to placate her. There was now water all around us, and she swirled her hand through the growing puddle. 'Clara!' she called.

'Ma'am?' said the servant, and in a gesture at once poignant and absurd she curtseyed.

'It's time to go,' said Mina, 'and take this reprobate with you.' Clara again began to cry. 'Look after her, Jack,' I was ordered.

'You have my word.'

'Good boy,' she said. Her hair was now loose in the water, and she raised her head again. 'Do you think it will hurt, Jack?' she said, sounding suddenly childlike.

I've always assumed that things that kill you generally do, but instead I said, 'I've heard it's very peaceful, like drifting off to sleep.'

'That's good,' she said, laying back as if in a bath.

I leaned in and kissed her gently on the cheek. She smiled and tried to raise herself again but the water was moving faster than her now. I held her up as long as I could. Her hands found mine and then the water closed over her. In the shadows Clara was convulsed with great, wracking sobs. I held on to Mina as she started to writhe and thrash horribly beneath the suffocating water. After an eternity she finally stopped moving and I let her go. It had not looked in the slightest bit peaceful to me.

CHAPTER XLIV

The choice was to move or die, so I grabbed the hand of the horrified servant and dragged her out of the cabin, waist deep in frozen water. She was still in a nightdress and could move easily. Had she been dressed in one of those ridiculous crinoline bustles she would most likely have drowned before we got ten feet, proving that those American women who advocated 'rational costume' undoubtedly had a point. The gold I secretly carried slowed me down, but after what I had been through to acquire it I had no intention of ditching it now.

We bounced and waded along the corridor, which was thankfully still mostly lit by high hanging lamps and remained remarkably level, until we came to a ladder that led to the upper and main decks. I sent the girl up first, but I was right behind her. The rising water carried bodies with it. I could see the engineer and the stoker with whom I had recently conversed swinging limply by the ladder where it vanished into the dark water, as if trying to gain a rung. I harried Clara with stern words and injunctions against looking down.

The upper deck had that same melancholy emptiness as the berth deck, and if not for the frantic activity we could now hear above I would have thought the ship deserted. It was still dry but we did not tarry. This time I went ahead in order to lift the heavy iron hatch, but when I reached the top of the ladder the damn thing would not move. I realised with a sickening dread that the hatches had been battened down, presumably in a desperate attempt to trap air within the hull and postpone the inevitable long enough to complete the evacuation. There was no way to open the thing from the inside. I could have howled with frustration. To die now, after escaping the hold and the cabin deck was the most bitter of ironies, and all for a bloody book, a thing of nothing more than ink and paper. Moran and Granger had been right, I realised. What in God's name had I been thinking? I could have petulantly cast it from me at that point, but needless to say I did no such thing.

'What is it?' said the girl below me. 'Why do you hesitate?'

I pulled myself together as best I could, and resisted the urge to start punching the hatch and swearing. Somewhere inside me a tiny spark of reason advised me not to break my hand.

'We need to find another way out,' I told her, but the water was already flowing through the hatch beneath us. We were out of time.

Her response was to start screaming for help, which seemed as good a strategy as any under the circumstances. Perhaps someone above might hear us. I took a gold bar from my pocket and commenced to hammer upon the hatch with all my will.

'Come on, you bastards!' I shouted, my arm soon beginning to palsy.

Clara had already screamed herself hoarse. As I continued to tap feebly, I was answered by a rap from above. I responded in kind, and was rewarded with a new sound, a scraping and clattering, accompanied by the kind of profanity that only a mariner can muster.

At once the hatch was thrown back, and I was stung by the cold night air. It was the sweetest sensation I had ever known. 'You took your fucking time,' I said, as large hands seized hold of my arms and dragged me through the hole. My lifeless fingers, meanwhile, dropped the gold bar, and I heard a splash below as my plunder became a hundred and fifty quid lighter. Cheap at the price, I thought.

'Give a man a bleedin' chance,' said Seaman Bewhill, the duck fucker himself, looking down at me indignantly while I lie on the deck like a bag full of hammers, laughing.

He shrugged his shoulders, and then gently guided Clara through the hatchway, after which he slammed it shut and immediately set to work upon the bolts.

'God bless you, sir,' she said.

The salt night air soon restored me to my senses. It was infused with smoke from the rockets that someone was firing into the night sky to signal our distress, and another, more mysterious perfume, which was at once familiar yet enigmatic. This second scent at first confused me, until I beheld the full extent of the carnage topside in the cold light of the waning moon and the blue flashes of the Congreves. This was the smell known to all true death hunters: fear and blood.

Moran had been correct in his supposition concerning the funnel. It had come down on the pinnace and the starboard paddle-box, evidently before the team working to free the boat had done their work. I could see its splintered remnants scattered about the crumpled smokestack, fused with what could only have been mashed human remains. I could also see quite clearly from my position amidships that only five of the eight lifeboats were missing from their stations, and a quick look to port told a sorry story. The other paddle-box boat was hanging uselessly against the side of the ship by its tackle at the bow, while there was a gig in the water by the ship, but capsized.

A horrible screeching announced that the horses were being put overboard, and I could see the Lancers and about half a dozen redcoats trying to blindfold the terrified animals in preparation to go over the side. In contrast to this violence, there was a great body of men on the quarterdeck, as silent as shadows. Most were not properly attired, and some were virtually naked, but scattered among them were the uniforms of common soldiers, and I spotted several familiar faces in the ranks, including Moran, although there were many gaps within the crowd. I did not see Jeffries, and I saw him no more that night. He had survived Napoleon, the plague, and the slavers of Mauritius, but his luck, it would seem, had finally deserted him. Many of the men were clearly in distress and were supported by comrades, and I could see Drake walking among them, as if on parade, dressing a line or stopping to speak. A few had retained their arms, but most had not. These were clearly the survivors from the troop decks, those not on the pumps or boat stations. Ordered to stay silent and still they were doing just that, no matter how wet, cold and terrified. I had the curious thought that they were a much more orderly group now than they had been during embarkation or the field day. I saw none of Lakemen's men among them. Salmond, Seton and Wright, along with a couple of junior officers and a drummer boy, were still on the poop. Inexplicably, Seton had drawn his sword.

'Come on,' said Bewhill, 'or you'll miss the last boat.' He took Clara's hand gently and led us across the slippery deck, now littered with broken spars and tangled rigging. The masts above us remained otherwise intact, despite the undeniable fact that the ship was now beginning to roll badly. 'They got off one gig and two cutters, I know of,' said Bewhill, breathlessly, as we walked, 'maybe the dinghy as well, for the women and the children.'

'What happened to the rest?' I said, not that it mattered. It was plainly too late to do anything now. While this young man was saving our lives he must have known that he, along with the rest of the remaining crew and military personnel, was already dead. Three miles from shore without a boat in Shark Alley did not bear contemplation.

'Rusted,' he said, 'we couldn't get the bloody bolts out.'

He led us to the poop awning, where the civilian passengers had been assembled. By the look of it most of the women and children had already been evacuated. We soon joined the end of a line of wailing women at the starboard gangway, several of whom had husbands on board they were loath to abandon. They were being firmly moved along by Lucas and Kilkeary of the 3rd, and assisted into the cutter below by two marines. Richards, the young Master's Assistant was in the boat and appeared to be the officer in charge. It was clear the cutter was already dangerously overcrowded, and Richards was desperately moving people around to redistribute the weight. Seaman Bewhill had left us to it, and Clara and I did not speak. When Richards called from below that he could take only two more, we were thankfully all that were left. Clara climbed down first, and I followed, gingerly taking my place next to her among the bodies in the base of the boat, which rocked like a ladder in a gale while the black water slapped at its sides.

Just then, a voice from above cried, 'Hold!' It was Sheldon-Bond, carrying two young children, one under each arm and both so traumatised that they did not resist at all. 'I found these two hiding among the straw bales,' said the young Lancer. 'Can you take them?'

'Not a chance,' Richards called up emphatically, before looking suddenly mortified at his own response. 'We'll not stand another body,' he explained, 'not even a little one. It would kill us all.' This last remark was enough to set several women to crying again, but none claimed the children.

'The thing of it is,' whispered a woman next to me conspiratorially, Mrs. Secker, I think, 'is that other folk's children ain't *our* children.'

I looked around me just to confirm my initial impression, which was that I was the only man on board save for the marines, who were the oarsmen, and Richards. I don't know if it was the thought of my son being thus so easily condemned in, God forbid, a similar situation, or simply the desire to get away from that old bitch Secker before I drowned her, but I suddenly found myself rising uneasily.

'I was the last in,' I said, 'so I'd better be first out.'

Clara cried out and grabbed my arm. I took her hand and placed the ring that Mina had given me in her palm, closing her fingers around it with my own. 'Take this,' I said, 'for luck.' Then, ignoring her entreaties, I made my way carefully to the scramble-net and thus back to the ship.

Bond's charges, a boy and a girl, were unfamiliar to me. Neither was more than four years old. He insisted on shaking my hand after he pulled me up and we both gently passed the children down to the marines in the cutter. 'Good show,' he said, his voice clogged with boyish emotion.

'You too, old man,' I replied, outwardly getting into the spirit of the things in order to stop myself screaming. If the silly sod had not found those kids hiding among the horse pens I would have been away free and clear.

'God bless you all,' called Richards from the cutter, and then his oarsmen began to slowly pull away to join the other lifeboats standing off far enough to avoid the coming vortex as the ship went down.

'What do we do now?' I asked Bond.

He gave a mirthless laugh. 'We die, my dear chap,' he said, turning and making his way back towards the few remaining horses. I noticed Lakeman's mount, Élise, was still among them and felt suddenly sick. I vomited over the side and then sat down with my back to the rail, snorting in a most vulgar manner.

'Stop shooting the cat, Vincent!' cried a sailor I did not know but who evidently knew me, 'and make yourself useful.'

He had black hair, piercing dark eyes and a prominent chin, and his clothes were quite archaic, in a maritime kind of way, like a pirate in a nautical melodrama. Just as quickly as he had appeared he was gone. The strange thing was that, upon reflection, I realised that he looked exactly as I had always imagined my old hero from *The Shivering of the Timbers*, Bannockburn.

I briefly considered this contingency and then put the foolishness from my mind. 'Preposterous!' said I, to no one in particular, after which, as a condemned man is usually allowed a smoke, I made for the poop in the hope that I might scrounge a cigar off one of the officers.

Wright obliged, God bless him, and as no one ordered me off the poop this time I loitered near the officers, who had now been joined by Giradot and Dr. Bowen, smoking hungrily, as the third act began.

'Glad to see you're still with us, Mr. Vincent,' said Seton, still holding his sword.

I wondered if he fancied himself William Wallace. 'Are we charging?' I asked facetiously, my mask of gentility not so much slipping as flying from my face. What did I care? I was about to die horribly.

Seton let the remark pass. He regarded the sword in his hand like some alien object, the purpose of which he could not quite divine, before shyly returning it to its scabbard. 'I thought I might need it,' he said, which was not, in itself an explanation, but then he continued, 'I feared that the men might try for the boats, but not a one of them broke rank.'

'They do you credit, sir,' I said, ashamed of making sport of him.

'And so do you, my friend,' he replied, with a trace of a smile. 'We heard of your part in saving Lieutenant Granger.'

'Did he make it out?' I asked, for I realised that although I had seen Moran there was no sign of Granger.

'He remonstrated a great deal,' said Seton, 'but I put him on a boat. He could barely stand.' There was an irony in all this that I refrained to mention, for the disgraced Lieutenant Granger would no doubt have much preferred to make the ultimate sacrifice along with the rest of us.

He asked after the Grimstones, as he was concerned, he said, that he had not seen them in all the confusion. I briefly informed him of the details surrounding the death of Mina, concluding that, in my opinion, if Grimstone had only gone for help in the first place then there had been more than enough time to save her.

'Good God,' said Seton, 'what a cad. Let us hope the spineless cur has also perished, and saved parliament another scandal.'

'If anyone lives to tell the tale,' I said with a shrug. 'If he's escaped then he can make up any story he likes back in England, for dead heroes do not speak once the battle is over.'

'Then we must take care that one of us lives, Mr. Vincent,' he said. 'Can you swim?'

'Not really,' I said. 'Can you?'

'Alas, no,' he said, gazing past me and out to sea for a moment, before excusing himself to issue his final order, which was that the remaining soldiers should move to the poop, which was higher.

The drummer beat assembly, and Drake brought the soldiers aft, about two hundred at a guess. Once again they fell in silently, although the word came from Booth of the 73rd (who had just relieved Giradot and his gang), that the men on the chain pumps preferred to remain at their post. Seton nodded, and dismissed the messenger with that same nervous half-smile he had given me.

Water was flowing from the hatches and sweeping across the main decks now, and we were clearly going down in the next couple of minutes. I stood there, trying to contemplate my own death, but I could not believe that this was the end, despite overwhelming evidence to the contrary. So many had already died that night, one of them in my arms. I wish I could tell you that I had some kind of sublime vision, that the meaning of my life revealed itself to me, or even that I wept or shook. The simple truth is that like the rest left behind I just stood there waiting.

Suddenly there was a commotion at the other end of the ship, by the hatch that led to the pump room. Like everyone else, I imagine, I assumed that the hands at the pumps had called it a night, but then I heard voice I knew well triumphantly shouting.

'We've made it, my boys!' cried Lakeman, wet, bloodied, and naked to the waist; larger than life as always, but evidently still corporeal. No spirit, I thought, could possibly be that loud.

He emerged from the hatchway imperiously, leading his rangers. I stared, transfixed, and soon lost count. There were about fifty in all, I estimated, including three of the four officers. Like Seton's soldiers, many were in night clothes, undergarments, or simply wrapped in blankets, and from the state of them I guessed that none would ever have to stick their face in a fire to see what Hell was like. Only the enigmatic Graves was absent, as he always had been as far as I was concerned, for we had never exchanged so much as a word. Given what I had heard of his religious convictions, he was no doubt delighted to have joined his saviour ahead of the rush.

Sheldon-Bond was still fiddling about with the more obstreperous horses, including Élise. Lakeman positively sprinted towards him, hurdling wreckage like a Head Boy on Prize Day, until he reached his beloved mount. Bond looked across to Seton for guidance, and the returned gesture indicated that if Lakeman wished to die with his horse then that was perfectly agreeable. Bond admitted defeat, and joined our party. The rangers followed the beat of the drum, and stoically joined the other soldiers on the poop, as if sleepwalking. The officers all shook hands.

Lakeman trotted Élise to the poop awning and left her standing by the mast, before climbing to the crowded deck and, after a quick exchange with Seton, coming over to me. I talked Wright out of another cigar and a long match, to which he graciously replied that he did not expect that he would need more than one. I handed it to Lakeman and struck the match with my thumbnail.

'I always wished I could do that,' he said, with a look that briefly revealed the child within.

Seton gave the word that the men might smoke and matches began to flair around the deck, with those that had pipes and cheroots passing them around to those that had not, everyone taking a drag before handing the precious leaf to the man next to him.

Lakeman's officers were in a tight huddle with Lucas and Giradot, no doubt relating their adventures, so I turned to my friend. 'What happened?' I said.

He took a long, grateful pull on the cigar, inhaling rather than tasting the smoke, as was I, for the additional narcotic effects of doing so. 'I was asleep in my hammock,' he said, 'dreaming of mermaids or some such nonsense, and the next thing I knew I was swimming in freezing water. It took me a moment to comprehend that I was actually awake. Everyone was shouting and thrashing about, and you couldn't see a damn thing of course—' He trailed off for a moment, smoking. 'Are there no boats?' he finally asked.

'Not anymore,' I said.

'Bugger.'

'So what happened next?' I asked him, suddenly desperate to hear one last story.

'Well,' he replied, laughing, 'then we drowned.'

Before I could interrogate Lakeman further, the ship finally succumbed to the weight of water upon her. With a terrible wail of rending iron and an almighty crash, her bow, from which Lakemen and his men had lately emerged, broke clear away at the foremast and disappeared beneath the waves with a sound like steam venting, taking Booth and the sixty men at the pumps with it to the bottom. The ship lurched forward on the rock that still held her, the stern lifting violently and knocking the bulk of us off our feet. Those not nimble, quick-witted, or otherwise able enough to grab onto something or someone followed the wreckage into the water. Their desperate cries for assistance that would never come were heartrending, and, may God forgive me, it was a mercy when they ceased.

The shock was too much for Salmond. He lurched to his feet and shoved his way past the other dazed officers. Cursing loudly, he climbed the steps of the mizzen, until he was about the height of a man above us. Clinging to the base of the mast, with his long beard wild and his dressing gown flapping about him he took on the appearance of an Old Testament prophet.

What motivated him to act thus I do not know. I can only conjecture that he knew that the game was up, and in his own way was trying to help, for he shouted, 'Save yourselves! All those who can swim, jump overboard and make for the boats.' Seton was on his feet looking up at him in horror, and I found myself aware of nothing but the Captain's words, despite the call of the waves and the dying voice of the ship. 'That,' he concluded, quieter now, 'is your only hope of salvation.' He slumped on the steps, suddenly spent, repeating his final point several times in a whisper. Then he called for a report from Brodie, and had to be told that the Master of the ship had been lost when the bow broke. 'Oh,' he said, vacantly.

Of the eighteen officers of the *Birkenhead* crew, I could now see only Speer, the Second Master, and the engineers Renwick and Barber, all standing by their broken commander. Like the endgame of a chess match, pieces were rapidly disappearing from the board.

The soldiers fidgeted uneasily, no doubt wondering if they should break ranks and try for it. I saw Seton's right hand return to the hilt of his sword. He made sure he stood where the majority could see him and raised his free hand as if halting a carriage. The growing murmur among the soldiers immediately ceased, and their leader, this son of the manse, the man who had trained them all, began to speak.

'You will swamp the boats containing the women and the children,' he said, in that resonant highland voice of his, that one heard, only occasionally, upon parade, but which let all know that he was in deadly earnest. 'I implore you not to do this thing,' he continued, 'and I ask you all to stand fast.'

Ask, I minded, for he did not order it so. The last of his officers, Wright, Lucas, and Giradot, moved forward, echoing the request.

'Stand fast.'

'Aye, lads, hold you hard,' said Drake.

The moment was mesmeric, magic, mythic. I cannot truly say what on earth it was, for although all must have yearned to make for a boat, to go on living, to just go home, see their loved ones again, sit by an open fire, eat a Sunday roast, get drunk with old friends, or make love again (I know I did), not a single man jack of them so much as moved a muscle.

'God bless you all,' said Seton.

The last of the rangers were not inclined to face death quite so passively, although they stopped short of Salmond's suggestion. Instead they began gathering and tearing up anything that might float, and casting it over the side. I saw spars, benches, barrels, bales of hay, stable doors, and what looked like the Captain's table all going over.

Lakeman looked on proudly. 'Those boys are born survivors,' he said.

'How do we survive this, Stephen?' I asked him. 'Can we survive this?'

'We can have a bloody good go.'

I felt I should tell him about my recent tussle with Barker, casting myself in the role of the disoriented civilian lost below darkened decks. The story lost a lot of its lustre if I admitted that I was down there with exactly the same criminal intent as the defeated antagonist, even if there was something poetic about the symmetry.

'That's a rum do,' said Lakeman, 'are you certain that he's dead?'

'Moran shot him,' I said, 'he looked pretty dead to me.'

'But did you check the body?' he said, clearly disconcerted. I suspected he was already aware of what a dangerous bastard Barker was when he recruited him. I knew from experience that men like that can be very useful when there's bad work to be done, but only if you have them under control, which Lakeman never really had.

'The ship could have gone at any moment,' I told him. 'We just grabbed the lieutenant and bolted.' That part at least was true.

'For future reference, old chap,' he said, as if offering advice on my forward defensive stroke, 'always put one in the brain, just to be on the safe side.'

I assured him that if I ever found myself in a similar position again, I would make sure that I did just that.

'Good man,' he said.

In a dark coincidence, it was at that moment that a single gunshot rang out, the sound as unmistakable as it was incongruous within the present symphony of rolling destruction playing upon what was left of our hull. Someone was shouting and we all looked about us, our eyes searching for the smoke of the discharge. As I was close to the officers, I soon located the origin of the blast. Salmond had found a pistol, or perhaps he had been in possession of it all along, stuffed in a pyjama pocket for the same reason that Seton had strapped on his sword. In either event, because of the weight of guilt upon him, the expectation of a painful death by water, or to avoid the inevitable court martial, our Captain had chosen his own form of escape. He had taken the barrel of the gun between his teeth, and then blown the entire back of his head away. There was now only a mask, with the face intact, but nothing left behind it. His brain, skull, and hair were all gone, painting the steps where he had sat, while his mouth still exhaled smoke as if it were a cigar in his lifeless hand and not a heavy cap and ball revolver. I knew he had sucked upon the thing, for there were teeth quite clearly embedded in the base of the mast like pearls. Speer was kneeling beside him, evidently in distress, while the engineers hovered nervously in the wings until someone had the good taste to lay the man on the deck and cover what was left of the top half of him with a tunic.

'That's it,' said Lakeman. He took a long drag on his cigar, then, clamping it between his teeth he jumped off the poop onto the watery deck below with a splash. He climbed upon his horse's bare back, and from this position he hallooed his men. 'Rangers!' he cried.

'Aye!' they bellowed back.

'Are you game for another adventure, boys?' said Lakeman.

Again his men responded in the affirmative.

'For peril?'

Once more they raucously agreed.

'For death?' he said, with the gleam of madness in his eye.

His men were not quite so sure this time, but there was still a murmur of general agreement.

Now level with the poop again, Lakeman caught my eye and winked before once more addressing his men. The army officers and soldiers, meanwhile, looked on in silent fascination, as did I.

'The shore is that way,' said he, pointing to the north. 'I will see you all there.' And with that he grabbed Élise's mane with both hands, and dug his bare ankles into her flanks. Thus spurred, the horse launched herself off the starboard gangway and into the awful nowhere. Lakeman's men let out a cheer as one, and began to follow him over the side.

I had not the courage to go with them.

'Barbarian,' said Sheldon-Bond, but he had missed the point. The lifeboats were all holding off to port; Lakemen had sent all his men in the opposite direction.

Still Seton's soldiers stood fast. I tried to locate Moran, but I could no longer see him in the ranks, and was not sure if he had gone over with the bow. The officers were talking and shaking hands, bidding one another farewell, and some, including Seton, were obviously praying. Someone somewhere in the ranks began to sing 'Guide me, O thou great Redeemer,' and soon everyone had joined in. Each was in his own key, but nonetheless as one voice they sang.

I had written enough sea stories to know that the end was nigh, and that if I failed to follow Lakeman now then the ship would take me down with her, with little chance of divine intervention landing me safe on Canaan's side. Childhood horrors that I had thus far endeavoured to deny began to swim up from the depths of my soul, and I could not move. Part of me nevertheless recognised the absurdity of my paralysis, for there was no question that I was going into the water one way or another. Better, surely, I argued against myself, to meet your end defiantly rather than just waiting around, as if Death was the omnibus from King's Cross to Piccadilly. I was no hero, and I could hold no line, although neither, seemingly, was I capable of putting one foot in front of the other. I had not swum in thirty-five years, and the monsters I feared had grown much in that time.

I leaned hopelessly against the rail and pulled desperately on the remnants of my cigar, looking past the carnage and the terrible void that was the sea at night, trying to focus upon my family in the eye of my mind. At first I saw only my own death, but then, miraculously, I saw Grace, first a mere apparition, but then quite clearly, standing at the door to our home. Joseph was by his mother's side, one hand in hers, the other beckoning me to get a shift on, as he so often did, for time moves at a different pace when you are two.

'Come on, Daddy,' I seemed to hear him say, as he often did when I was slow to rise of a morning. I understood then that if there was the remotest chance that I might see my wife and child again then it was worth any trial, however terrible the price of failure.

As nervous as a virgin in a brothel, I climbed down to the main deck, which was now awash with very cold water, and cast my eyes about for anything that might float. I was rewarded by a broken spar that must have either been missed by the rangers or had just come down, for the mast was dropping strange and heavy fruit as if it were falling from the sky, and this had done for several men not quick enough off the main deck. It was the size of a small tree trunk, splintered at one end, and it had not quite floated free of the surrounding clutter. When I tried to move it, a face came into view in the shallow water, bleached by death and moonlight. It was Seaman Bewhill, the man who had saved me at the hatch, freed too late. The shock of recognition caused me to jump backwards, landing on my arse in about a foot of water, blaspheming profusely.

'If you want the Lord to smile upon you in this time of trouble,' said a Cockney voice behind me, 'then you'll have to show more respect than that.' It was Moran, this *deus ex machina*, sent to save me by Colour Sergeant Drake, who could see that I was far too useless to take care of myself. He quickly managed to separate the spar from its victim, working fast as much, I suspect, to avoid being called back to the ranks as he was to escape the coming catastrophe. 'All we have to do,' he advised, 'is stay alive till morning.' Thus was his thesis as plain as it was profound, and who was I to argue? We were close to land, he explained, and even if we got no further than the rocks that lined the coastline like teeth and made the landing of any small craft a lethal proposition, we could wait it out, safe from sea and sharks, until a rescue ship arrived, which he was confident would happen within twelve to twenty-four hours. 'We can do this, Jack,' he promised.

'What should we do if we see a shark?' I asked him.

'Say three Hail Marys and four Our Fathers.'

Working together, we steered the spar to the gap in the rail at the gangway that had recently accommodated Lakeman's leap of faith, letting the water draw it off the ship, and us with it. It was immediately apparent that we both carried far too much weight, especially my companion. He clung desperately to one end of the spar, exhibiting no natural buoyancy whatsoever, his backpack, laden with a small fortune in gold, straining against his shoulders as he fought to keep his mouth out of the water. I was fairing little better. The sea had already sucked off both of my boots, which cost me another heavy toll for each contained two small gold bars, and my jacket, its pockets full of gold, was trying to kill me as if it, itself, were a drowning man, heedless of the life of his saviour. It was cold, and I wanted that outer garment, so with one arm locked around the spar I emptied my pockets, and became once more a poor man.

Thus released, I began to kick us away from the ship as best I could, the sea supporting me gently now, like a newborn babe. I begged Moran to unfasten the rucksack and let it sink, but he was having none of it, and continued his struggle with the damn thing until even in the pale, pre-dawn light I could see that he was exhausted.

We were advantaged though, in that the current carried us, and we were soon, I hoped, a reasonable distance from the ship, a hundred and fifty yards or so at a guess. I could still see the lamps about the poop burning, and the indistinct faces of many of the men that remained upon her, either out of bravery, resignation, or purely because they could think of nothing else to do but follow Seton's final request to stand fast. It was a calm night, and their voices travelled easily to us, still singing, this time 'Abide with Me.' I stared at the shadow of the ship, entranced, until the stern lights suddenly flew upwards and disappeared, as, with a devil's roar, she finally broke her back on the rock and went down like lead. We were close enough to hear the awful screams of the dying, and the desperate calls of those who now, like us, were fighting for their lives in the water. It was hard to decide which group was the more fortunate.

I turned back to Moran to speak, but he had gone. I looked about me frantically, but I could see no sign of him on the smooth, rolling surface, and I shouted in vain until my voice cracked with dehydration and despair. The night tide swelled and momentarily lifted me a little closer to God, and then back into Lucifer's cold embrace. As far as I could tell from the fading cries in the darkness, I was near no other survivors. In fact, I seemed to be drifting further away from the wreck, although its position was now impossible to ascertain, as was any sense of distance or, indeed, direction. Lakeman's people were long gone as well, and I could see neither land nor lifeboats, despite the light of the moon. With a creeping dread I knew then that I was alone in Shark Alley, and I had not the slightest idea which way to kick, if I dared move my legs at all.

CHAPTER XLV

One of the many disadvantages attendant on being cursed with a human consciousness is that when one is desirous not to dwell upon a particular subject the mind will think of nothing else. Alone and adrift in that ink-dark water in the hours before dawn, I was haunted by one such dominant and ceaseless meditation.

In vain I laboured to suppress it by examining a fanciful internal ledger in which I entered the recent events of my life, the point of which was to reassure myself that the balance of my account thus far could be reasonably assessed as in credit, indeed positively in the black. It was an idea I had nicked from *Robinson Crusoe*, although to be fair Defoe had pinched if from a Protestant tract. In terms of assets, income, and equity, I reasoned, I was still in full possession of my mortal existence, when so many around me had just been deprived of theirs. Admittedly I was no longer any great shakes as a swimmer, having assiduously avoided the practice since the fateful encounter with the monstrous pike in my childhood, but I was managing to maintain a good hold on the spar and could thus keep my head above water. On the other hand, the muscles in my neck and shoulders were beginning to protest, which was something of a liability. It was therefore possible that I might become so weak that I could no longer hold on, which would constitute a major expense. One had to be prepared for anything in such a fluid market.

I was aware that we had been close to land when the ship struck, and there was some comfort in that too, although I could not make out the coastline against the night sky. Having escaped the lethal traps of the lower decks and the actual sinking of the ship when so many had drowned, I should have been guardedly optimistic, but the more I tried to positively envisage being saved, either by boat or somehow getting ashore myself, the more I thought instead of the great grey fish that I knew to inhabit these waters. It was not the memory of the gaping, jagged smiles of these ancient creatures that tormented me so much as the vacant stare of those soulless black eyes. When one is in Hell, it is judicious, after all, to expect demons.

There were other admittedly less pressing issues upon which I might usefully reflect. The loss of Moran, who I counted a friend, weighed heavily upon me, the only scant consolation that he was most likely drowned by his own avarice rather than taken by a shark. I meant no judgement against the man by this. When I was his age I would have been just as reckless and as fatally stubborn. My thought was instead that in the ledger of horrible death (a second mental book of account that kept intruding upon the first), drowning, although clearly deeply unpleasant, did not seem quite so horrendous as being suddenly consumed alive by a silent and spectral sea monster. I grieved for Salmond too, whom I had liked, although it seemed probable that he was the author of the disaster, and for all the other good men that had died that night. At least the Captain's end had been a swift one. I hoped that Seton and his men had escaped the wreck, but in my heart of hearts I very much doubted that many had.

Now that I had time to think, a process largely suspended during the destruction of the ship and the scramble to survive her, there was also Mina to consider, how she had died, but also what she had told me.

For most of my life I had felt as if I were trapped within a serial romance, and not a very good one at that. I was borne along by the momentum of the plot, with no more idea of its design than a soldier on a battlefield knows the mind of his general, unable to predict the resolution, and with no way of flicking forward to the final chapter. Mina's intelligence, which I doubted I would ever have learned had she not known she was dying, explained much of the narrative in which I lived, if it were true. It was, at bottom, equally in her interest, albeit posthumously, to light my fuse and then point me at her husband, whose desertion had murdered her. Even so, her story had about it a certain veracity when applied to the facts that I did have. Did my father know, I wondered? Had my mother ever told him? Not for the first time, I realised how little I knew of my parents' lives before my own, despite all the much-loved family anecdotes. Nonetheless, for the second time in my life, I had something on my enemy. Not the treatment of my family, mind, for no one would care about them, but for his cowardly abandonment of his wife. Yet even if I survived the present ordeal, I thought it unlikely that I would ever be allowed to expose him. I would no doubt return to England to discover that I had sabotaged the ship, probably as part of an elaborate satanic rite. At least now was I released from my previous state of confusion, and could go back to simply hating the bastard.

I started to hear voices in the darkness, distant, often indistinct, and impossible to identify, but surely real. I at first hoped that these random utterances might indicate a boat in the area, but I could hear enough to soon determine that the speakers were in the same situation as I, if not worse, so I kept quiet for I doubted my float could accommodate many more. There was an almost Bouzingo poetic to this ethereal chorus, an irregular and unmetered antistrophic in which pain and fear debated duty and faith in a fractured discourse, punctuated by piercing and unnerving shrieks, with different speakers and distinct accents drifting in and out of the range of my hearing, like voices from a dream.[35] The last thing I heard was someone singing 'The Rose of Allendale,' becoming quieter, then a whisper, and then nothing, as if we all of us were drifting through the endless void of space, moving ever in opposite directions. There was also, periodically, a distant yet growing thunder, although no rain came, and I fancied these sightless sounds must be waves crashing upon the rocks that lined the coast. But despite my rational interpretation, I was soon flinching with each new concussion, like a soldier under a prolonged bombardment, the irregularity of the mysterious explosions only increasing my already keenly developed sense of unease. I have always possessed a deep mistrust of nature.

I recalled that the African warrior I had seen on the beach had summoned a monster by agitating the water, and resolved to do as little of that as possibly myself. Fortunately, my arms were quite strong, at least for a quill driver, and I was fitter than I had any right to be given my lifestyle. I had inherited my father's yeoman strength by sheer luck, for my mother had been a delicate woman, forever ill, as if cursed by a bad fairy at her christening. Ironically, the voyage had been of great benefit to my health, bringing me to a state of enforced sobriety in a way that willpower never had. In short, all this sea air had done me the world of good, at least up to now.

Something brushed against my leg and I kicked out in horror. I managed to keep one arm wrapped around the spar, while with a dread-filled right hand I explored myself beneath the water, expecting warm blood and sharp bone where flesh once was. I was intact. I attempted to calm myself with controlled breathing; a trick an incarcerated street singer once taught me in the Marshalsea to overcome nerves during public readings. It was nothing, I told myself repeatedly, a bit of seaweed, nothing more. Eventually, the thud of my heart began to fade, although a little ditty had now come unbidden into my thoughts to replace the beat of my body's panic, where it lodged itself with the tenacity of a barnacle up the back passage. This was courtesy of my father's love of a particular rhyme, which my dark muse had re-written to suit the occasion: *Like one that in a lonesome sea doth feel a little grim, because he knows a frightful fiend doth close behind him swim.*

Bloody Coleridge.

Something bumped against me again and I recoiled once more in terror. I saw only a vague, dark shape in the water to my left, which I stared at as one might a clown encountered on an unlit street after midnight, drawing my legs up beneath me and trying to remain perfectly still. Instead of the desired effect, I started to tremble uncontrollably.

Then the shape spoke. 'Who's there?' it said. The voice was quiet and hesitant, muted by fear and exhaustion, but undoubtedly that of Metford, the young ensign who had married the Irish girl in Cork a few weeks before.

'Jesus Christ!' I cried, gripped with a hysterical desire to laugh. 'You scared the shit out of me.'

'I'm frightfully sorry,' he said, as if apologising to a housemaster. When all was said and done, none of the junior officers were far removed from their schoolboy selves, although for most, I reflected sadly, this was as old as they were going to get. For them, the army was merely an extension of public school, with the houses become regiments. You could tell from their leadership style where they had been in the savage hierarchy. Giradot had Head Boy written all over him, Sheldon-Bond was a bully, Rolt was a swot, and Metford, like Granger, was definitely a fag. The absurdity of our situation seemed to have eluded him, given his admittedly admirable commitment to good manners, even in adversity, and it had seemingly not occurred to him that I might have been a common soldier. (Sheldon-Bond would probably have had me flogged for swearing.) 'I've been swimming,' he said absentmindedly, 'for such a *long* time.'

I could see his face now, the boyish features aged in a deathly moonlit portrait, like one visited by his own future shade. He was treading water as if sleepwalking and I gently guided him to the spar. 'Hang on to this, old fellow,' I said, 'if you can manage it.'

'Thank you,' he said, letting the spar carry his weight and resting his head upon the hard wood contentedly, as if it were a nursery pillow. He did not seem to know nor care who I might be, soldier, seaman, or civilian, officer or foot slogger. If I let him fall asleep, he was dead.

'Try to stay awake, old chap,' I said, guiltily, reaching over and shaking his shoulder. 'It'll be light soon, and then we'll see what's what.'

He raised his head slowly and once more dreamily apologised. 'What happened to the ship?' he asked after a moment.

'When did you go into the water?'

'I was with Rolt and some others, on the quarterdeck,' he said, 'trying to free up one of the gigs. We got it loose but the tackle broke while we were still lowering away, and we all fell. Then the boat came down on top of us. I think it hit me on the leg. I don't know what happened to the others.'

I told him what I had seen, and who I was.

'Oh how I wish I had been there at the end,' he said wistfully, transported by the glory of it all. 'To have witnessed such a thing, to have been part of it.'

I resisted the temptation to reply that I would have cheerfully exchanged multiple Florentine kisses with the giant spider I had seen in Madeira just to avoid the experience. Instead I tried to reassure him that he had more than earned his place, for his somnambulistic demeanour suggested that he might well be making the supreme sacrifice himself quite soon if we did not get out of the water.

'This is a club in which all of us are members,' I told him, 'and it sounds to me as if you did your bit admirably.'

He thought about this for a moment, drifting in and out. 'This is a story that people are going to tell,' he finally said. 'You'll tell them, Jack, won't you? You'll tell them I was part of it. You'll tell my Mary.'

'You'll tell her yourself,' I countered.

He smiled weakly, but appeared far from convinced. 'But to have been there,' he said, quietly, before suddenly becoming quite agitated and crying out, 'Angustam amice pauperiem pati robustus acri militia puer!'

I presumed he had memorised these lines at Sandhurst. 'Dulce et decorum est pro patria mori,' I replied mechanically, my heart not really in it.[36]

'You know it, Jack!' he said, as pleased as a puppy.

'Well, we're not all barbarians in Fleet Street,' I said. I could see that final act of courage the way that he did, but I could not for the life of me understand it. I had spent a lot of time with those mostly very young men, and I knew full well that the majority were not battle hardened troops but nervous, half-starved boys, most of them not even English, who had known nothing of the army two months before, and belonged to a dozen different regiments. 'Why did they stand?' I finally asked him. 'This wasn't an enemy on a battlefield, this was certain death. Why face it so stoically? Not a man broke rank, except for the one ordered to help me.'

'That's what it is to be a soldier,' he said simply.

He began to doze again, and I called out until he opened his eyes. Protecting him was becoming a way in which I could avoid thinking about my own vulnerability. I remembered hearing that shipwrecked mariners with families were much more likely to survive than those without, so I urged him to think of his pretty young wife, sang the praises of my own, and spoke to him of the rewards of fatherhood. When my tongue cleaved to my palate for want of water and that final cigar, I would swill seawater around my mouth and then spit it back out as if treating a toothache in order to maintain the conversation. Despite a hammering, thirst-induced headache, I remembered enough of my own sea stories to know better than to swallow.

'All we have to do,' I assured him, 'is keep our wits about us until dawn. Then we can strike out for the shore.'

I dare not risk kicking out in the darkness, for fear of attracting something nasty, especially when I still knew not which direction to take. I had no idea how to navigate under African stars, and could easily propel us further out to sea in error. And although my companion could remember his Horace from military school, he confessed that he was, 'Quite out of sorts this evening,' and could not recollect his training in basic night orientation.

Something splashed, quite near us, from time to time, and although it was most likely just small fish jumping, each sound increased my general agitation. As a fisherman, I knew that little fish jumped when the big ones were around.

'Why don't we get going?' I casually suggested. 'I think I see the shadow of the mountains over there.' I nodded towards an imaginary coastline. My white lie seemed to perk up Metford, but when he tried to kick in unison with me nothing happened, and my exertions thus spun me and the spar around his axis in a near perfect circle.

'I say,' he said, 'my leg has gone a bit stiff. That bally boat must have really given it a clout.'

I decided that I better investigate, and pulled myself along the spar until I was next to him. 'Do you mind if I take a look?' I asked him.

'If you think it'll help,' he said cheerfully. 'It's the right one.'

Typically, I was on the wrong side, which meant I had to swim around him. I did so inelegantly, with all the assurance of a man on a precipice in a gale, grabbing the spar once more in panic and relief.

'Steady on, old man,' said Metford.

'I hate bloody swimming,' I confessed.

'Whatever for?' he said. 'I find it most invigorating myself.' He realised what he had just said and gave a shy little laugh. I delivered a manly pat on the back and shook my head, smiling despite myself. It was something of a relief to be in this predicament with such a likable young man. His general air of untroubled positivity had no doubt been a powerful factor in attracting Mary.

There was no point trying to look at the leg by starlight, so I carefully explored it with one hand, while clinging onto the spar for all I was worth with the other. My attempt at swimming had told me that without a float I would probably sink even faster than the ship.

Something was very wrong. Metford's leg was bent at the most alarming and unnatural angle below the knee, and with a sickening start I soon felt what could only be bone protruding from his bare shin. The cold or the shock must have numbed him, for the salt water was surely eating corrosively into the torn flesh. I thought about the trail of blood that he was leaving and felt suddenly sick.

'Try not to worry,' I said, gulping back my fear dryly, 'but I think it's broken.'

'Oh dear,' he said, reaching down, 'is it bad?'

I grabbed his hand before he could discover just how bad and replaced it on the spar. 'It's a clean break,' I lied, 'but I think I should try to splint it.'

'If you think it best,' he said.

I had no way of setting his leg, and nothing to splint it with anyway, but what I had in mind was a cross between a patch and a light tourniquet. I bade him hold onto me while I set about my work, for I needed both my hands. Fortunately, most of Metford's uniform was intact, which gave me a stout leather belt to play with, so I tied his leg off above the knee, and then tore the tail off my shirt to bandage the break as best I could, sewing it in place by touch using my running repair kit of button thread wrapped tightly around a pair of needles always stuck behind my left lapel. He was too far gone to even wince, but he thanked me very sincerely when I was done. We spoke in whispers, a compromise on my part for I feared my companion would slip into an endless sleep if we stopped talking, despite the obvious dangers inherent in making a noise in these waters. While noting the absurdity of the act, I carefully replaced my sewing things when I was done.

'How on earth did you manage to swim with a dicky leg?' I asked him, because there was still enough of the journalist left in me to deplore a loose end, and because I had to keep him awake.

'Well, one doesn't like to blow one's own trumpet,' he said, 'but they used to call me the old fashioned Olympian at school. I can basically swim like a fish.'

'That's good to know,' I said. 'I'd certainly strike you a medal myself if I could, son.'

The sky was now taking on a lighter, predawn hew in the east, which at least gave us a bearing, for all the good it did as I doubted even the old fashioned Olympian was much use now, and it was unlikely that I could move us both very far on my own. I nervously scanned the expanding blue horizon, eyes hard as pebbles with concentration. We appeared to have drifted far away from the wreck and the coastline, for there was nothing to see around us but the grey flatness of open water welded to the lightening sky. There was no sign of any boats, or any other survivors.

'I say,' said Metford, 'is that a mountain?'

'Where?'

'Over there,' he said, pointing to the east.

'That's the wrong direction for land,' I said, trying to make light of my concerns by adding a flippant remark about drifting to Australia. I could not see anything.

'There!' he said, this time looking more to the north.

'I can't see anything,' I said, truthfully, although I could feel something in my bones, like one that in a lonesome sea—

'There!' he cried again, becoming quite agitated, and once more gesturing to the east. 'It's big, whatever it is,' he added.

I was not sure at this point whether he was excited and expecting rescue, or as frightened as I was. 'All right,' I said, regarding him steadily, 'what did you see?'

'I don't know for sure,' he said, not meeting my gaze but instead looking over my left shoulder. 'There, look!'

I spun around fast enough to catch a fleeting shadow on the

water that was there for a heartbeat and then gone the next, so fast that the tail of my eye barely registered its passing.

'Did you see it?' he said.

'I'm not sure,' I told him, reviewing the image in my mind's eye and concluding that yes, I probably did see something, although identity, scale and distance were all impossible to gauge.

'Was it a sail?' asked Metford hopefully.

'I don't think so,' I said, drawing my legs up instinctively. 'I think we better stay quiet and keep still.'

'Oh,' said Metford. He looked around uneasily, and then took a long breath. 'Probably nothing though, 'ay?' he said.

'Yeah,' I agreed, without conviction. 'I expect it was just a seal, or a dolphin perhaps, minding its own business and not at all troubled by us.'

'Yes,' said Metford, 'definitely a dolphin.'

I said no more upon the subject, but inwardly retained the eldritch feeling that we were somehow under observation. But we saw nothing more after that but the waves upon the water, and as the dawn light spread we began to relax and discuss our options. Metford was for trying for north, where, however far we might have drifted, we would be heading towards land. 'If anyone's searching yet,' he said, 'it's going to be along the coast.'

That made sense, but I was unsure how we could kick against the current with his leg in the state that it was. He insisted that now it was daylight I could patch him up a bit better, then, he said, if we positioned ourselves either side of the spar, pointing its tip landward like an arrow, he could probably swim with his left arm and leg. Having been captain of his school swimming team, among various other athletic achievements that he listed with some pride by way of an argument, he reckoned his half-body stroke would about balance me at full tilt.

'No offense,' he said.

I assured him that none was taken. I was still less than keen on flailing about in the water. I was equally aware, however, now I knew our situation, that if we continued to aimlessly drift we would likely be dead by the following dawn, if not before, from exposure or dehydration, if we were lucky. I was therefore willing to take his lead, having no better strategy to contribute myself, while holding out little hope of rescue if we remained as we were, purposeless and lost on this rolling iron landscape.

Having survived the chill of the night, Metford seemed a lot more cogent than he had been a few hours before, although his leg was now clearly paining him a great deal. Perhaps, like me, the shadow in the water had brought him to his senses; or, possibly, also like myself, he had simply decided not to die. We both, after all, had family we could not afford to let down.

The first task was to make Metford's ruined leg as comfortable as possible. Unfortunately, he could now feel it. I left my improvised bandage alone but removed the belt. Using his tunic, I fashioned a kind of padded cocoon about his lower leg, which again I sewed together, before wrapping the belt around it for added rigidity. It must have been agony for him, but he made not a sound until I tied off the belt. He turned as pale as a ghost, but soon gained mastery of his pain with remarkable self-control for one so young. We then arranged ourselves as he had suggested, and found that we could, indeed, move forward. Gently paddling, and keeping the rising sun to our right, we struck out for the invisible shore.

After about half an hour at this pace I suddenly felt a wave of pressure from beneath us that lifted our float in the water and then gently lowered it down again. Panic rippled through my body, my gut urging my limbs to paddle faster, while another inner voice told me to keep very still. Although I had previously exhibited a calmness of spirit under pressure that night of which I would never have hitherto believed myself capable, I knew that this was to be one trial too far. I managed, just, to keep myself from sobbing out loud, but my breathing became rapid and ragged.

'What was that?' said Metford. He stuck his face in the water and scanned the blackness below, while I tried to cover all points on the compass on the surface at the same time.

My body was rigid with frozen fear and my mind was screaming, but I saw absolutely nothing above the waves. I breathed deeply to calm myself, although I continued to tremble quite violently on occasion. Some bastard is walking on my grave, I thought, or swimming over it.

Metford raised his head, breathing fast. 'It's a shark,' he said, 'a big one.'

'Oh, bollocks.'

'Quite,' agreed, Metford.

We huddled together, praying that in combination with our float our silhouette would appear large enough to discourage the animal. We desperately watched the water, starting with fright and cursing whenever the jagged dorsal fin and crescent tail momentarily broke the surface. The damn thing was clearly circling us, at a radius of about ten yards. Every time the fin sunk beneath the waves one or other of us would thrust his head under the water to try to keep track of the great fish, which could be seen moving quite leisurely around us. Periodically, it would slip into the darkness beyond our fields of vision, only to appear from an entirely different direction a few moments later, just as we were daring to think that it had lost interest and moved away. Suspended in the water where the sunlight still penetrated, it floated like some awful phantom, the long, counter-shaded body supporting a cavernous maw that should belong to no animal alive in this day and age, marine or otherwise. It was shockingly primitive, just a swimming mouth, ancient and terrible. My previous encounters with its kind had not prepared me for the horror of actually sharing the water with one. The more firma, I remembered grimly, the less terror.

Eventually it went away. We searched the water above and below until our eyes burned, but there was no sign of the shark. It would seem, God willing, that we were big and unfamiliar enough to trigger a note of caution in its rudimental, prehistoric mind.

'We need to keep going,' Metford finally said.

This was in itself a frightening prospect, but at least it would get us away from the shark, which was last seen swimming out to sea about twenty feet down. We once more began to kick apprehensively towards the north, looking around all the time but saying nothing.

The sky was draped with clouds the colour of damaged skin, linked by delicate threads of white, like bandages. Behind these strange curtains shone a bloodshot glow, peering through every rift as the sun rose above the clouds, which thickened until the firmament once more faded.

'Nice day,' said Metford. Without his tunic, he matched the colours of sea and sky, which were a washed out and variegated grey, like a rain spattered daguerreotype.

I was still formulating a reply when the shark hit us. The attack came so fast that I barely realised what had happened until it had gone again. It came in from Metford's side, the great grey back of the thing arching through the water at incredible speed, with a hundred stinking rows of flint-like teeth beneath glimpsed so fast that I did not immediately realize that it had attacked the spar and not one of us. The float was jerked out of our hands and down, leaving us both shaking in the rippling water, Metford breathing very rapidly, his eyes darting about wildly, me swearing loudly.

We both jumped out of our skins when the spar resurfaced about twenty feet in front of us. 'Jesus Christ!' I shouted.

'There's no need for profanity, Jack,' said Metford, treading water by my side. 'We might be meeting our Lord and Saviour quite soon.'

'I'm beginning to think that if there is a God,' I replied testily, struggling to stay afloat and wondering if I should bother, 'then he's a vicious bastard and I have no desire to make his acquaintance.'

'Jack,' said Metford, 'for shame.' But this was not the moment for a theological debate. The shark had not returned and we needed the float, which bobbed innocently in front of us but was clearly drifting in the opposite direction. Metford realised this too, and apologetically explained that he didn't think he could swim over to it with only one leg functioning.

A tremendous effort of will was required to move away from my companion, but I could hardly drag him with me so I struck out cautiously for the spar using my clumsy breaststroke.

It took an age to reach the thing, but eventually I was able to throw my trembling hands around it and rest. I looked back towards Metford and waved, indicating that I was going to get my second wind and then paddle back towards him. He was in mid-reply when that terrible fin broke the surface behind him, moving at a blurring speed. He must have seen the horror in my face, or perhaps he sensed the monster behind him, for he turned just as it was on him, driving him beneath the water in an instant.

I stared at the spot where he had been in shock. There was no sign of him, no blood, nothing. He was just gone. I managed to crawl onto the spar, wrapping my arms and legs around it obscenely, and trying to keep the reassuringly solid wood beneath me. I was shaking uncontrollably, and the damn thing kept rolling so that I had no choice but to drop back into the water, my legs tucked in and aching, my arms locked around the float, and my head jerking around like a bird in distress. My salted eyes searched the sea in panic.

An appalling eternity later, Metford somehow clawed his way back to the surface, gasping for air about thirty feet in front of me, the water already turning crimson around his thrashing form. He was screaming. 'Jack! Jack! My good leg's gone, Jack! It took my bloody leg!'

Paralysed with horror, I watched as the sea around him became a giant mouth as the shark hit him from below, breaching like Leviathan, its pectoral fins resembling vast, white wings. It seemed to go on forever, Metford's upper body moving feebly in the huge jaws offering an unwanted sense of scale. He looked like a doll in its savage grip, and as its tail cleared the water my guess was that it was a good twenty feet in length. Metford had just enough time left to call out his wife's name before the great fish spun and crashed back into the water spraying blood and spume. I knew then the source of the explosions I had heard in the darkness after the ship went down. Each one had been a life lost so terribly.

This time there was no return to the surface. The water where Metford had come up and then been taken was oily with blood, and my only thought was to get away from that awful spot as quickly as I was able. Perhaps it would be satiated. Perhaps it would leave me alone. I took a quick bearing. Thankfully, the spreading blood cloud was behind me as I looked towards what I hoped was the right direction for land. I began to kick away as if the Devil himself were upon my tail, although of course what likely pursued me was a deal older and a damn sight worse. Needless to say I did not look back.

I continued flat out until my lungs were shredded and my legs lead, and then I kicked out some more. I was sure I was moving north, but no land came into view. It was hopeless.

I thought of my family in despair. My son would never know me, and soon his pre- and paralinguistic perceptions of me would be lost forever, while my poor dear wife would never know my fate. They would bury an empty coffin, perhaps containing the old *Fraser's* portrait and a couple of my books (that is what I would have done in a story). What would they do without me, I wondered miserably? Grace could not maintain the mortgage, and I doubted Dickens would come to her aid. His secret would go to this watery grave with me, and he would most likely consider himself released of all obligations. I prayed that Reynolds would be able to help her, and that she would never find out about Shark Alley.

A low, slim object in the water ahead completed my sense of abject desolation. I stopped paddling and rested, waiting.

CHAPTER XLVI

I REGARDED THE dark shape in the water with loathing. If it was the same animal that had killed Metford, it had overtaken me unawares and was now not hunting me so much as simply waiting for me to join it, like the first guest to arrive at a restaurant. It was the insouciance of the beast that outraged the most at that point, above and beyond its previous, murderous stalking and the subsequent slaughter of my companion. I imagined its fixed and unnatural grin, and realised that it had been laughing at me all along. Left with nothing but language, I unleashed a stream of obscenities in its direction that would have shocked a dockyard bunter, making my point, at length, until my parched throat surrendered and I could do no more than gurgle that I hoped the bastard would choke on me.

'Stop shouting and save your strength,' the shark called back, turning its great bulk towards me. It had a surprisingly refined accent, I noted, very upper class.

I was in no mood to be put in my place by a fish, however well spoken, and on the contrary remained determined that if this was to be the death of the Death Hunter, as it surely was, then I was not going to go quietly.

'Shove it up your arse,' said I, once more finding my voice, 'and fuck off while you're doing it.'

'Are you injured?' said the fish, coming closer now, but moving quite slowly.

It occurred to me at this juncture that I might possibly have misinterpreted the situation. This would have been far from the first time I had done so, after all. As my wife once put it, I do have a tendency to grab the wrong end of the stick and then start beating about the bush with it. Just as poor Metford had seen sails for fins earlier that dreadful day, I had mistaken the *Birkenhead's* dinghy for a shark.

'Sorry,' I said, still projecting my voice, but now somewhat sheepishly, 'it's been a bit of a bad morning.'

'Is that you, Jack?' said a male voice from the boat. 'Hold on, old man, and we'll come and get you.'

Alongside the profound sensations of relief and embarrassment that now flooded through my veins, I suddenly felt acutely vulnerable. I began to kick out towards the boat, for one second less in the water was now worth more to me than a pension. I drove the spar before me frantically, quickly closing the gap between myself and the small craft. I was soon close enough to see half a dozen or so figures in it, men and women, and clearly identify Lieutenant Granger at the prow. Then something sharp grabbed my leg and pulled me under.

The attack was so fast that I barely even understood what was happening to me. I clung onto the spar stubbornly, as if it might yet save me, dimly aware of the huge body of the animal displacing the water at great speed, and of the daylight receding above me to be replaced by the unimaginable pressure of a terrible, suffocating darkness. If I felt anything conscious it was not fear so much as frustration; to have been so close to rescue and to still be consumed alive, like my poor father before me, was infuriating. Angry blood pounded in my ringing ears, and my smoker's lungs were soon bursting for release. Then, as death by water was infinitely preferable to a giant maw packed with carving knives, I gave in and let myself drown.

I have heard the new Spiritualists speak of an otherworld they call 'Summerland,' a place of peace where everything you hold dear is preserved, and of a bright, beckoning light that your spirit follows when your body dies. I had always assumed this secular version of a heaven populated by benevolent, table-tapping ghosts to be utter bollocks. Yet, while my body convulsed in its death throes, my soul, or at least my mind, vacated the prison of the flesh, and regarded my predicament perfectly calmly from a quiet, external point of vantage, as if watching a play. I could see the great fish quite clearly, its thickly muscled body illuminated by a mysterious source of light from above, and my flimsy carcass flailing about its enormous head, my right leg caught in its teeth below the knee. My arms were still locked about the broken spar, my eyes were bulging with horror and asphyxia, and my mouth was moving, apparently still complaining.

While I watched my own death serenely, my wife and son came to join me. It seemed entirely natural that they should be there, and I took Grace's hands and kissed her, as if in greeting upon her return from a routine domestic errand. After I embraced my wife, I gathered my little boy into my arms, as I always did after we had been apart, even if only for a few hours. I snuggled my face in his thick, blond hair and inhaled his delicate bouquet, the most perfect of drugs. He turned his little face towards me in turn, and gave me a smile that could melt iron, the look of my mother about his eyes.

'I've missed you both so much,' I told them.

'But we've only been to the market,' said Grace.

'Silly Daddy,' agreed Joseph.

As it was our habit to tell each other stories, I set about relating my recent adventures to my son, although taking a mental blue pencil to all the death and horror, and doing it like a fairy tale involving sea serpents, which I hoped would satisfy his present taste for dragons and other mythic monsters. But Joseph, like his father, was possessed of a restless, imaginative nature, and we rarely got all the way through a story. This present tale was no exception, and he soon wished to be free of me in order to run around. I hung onto him in sport as he wriggled and squirmed to be free of me, bucking and kicking and laughing. I held onto him harder, becoming slightly aggrieved, as I really wished to reach the end of the story, just for once, and he twisted in my arms like a cat in a canal. Still I clung on, amazed at the strength of my boy, who was not yet three years old, until he finally cried out in a most exasperated tone and wrenched himself free of me. Then the spar broke the surface, and it was back to reality for dear dead Dad.

I looked around, coughing and spluttering, barely cognisant of my escape. The shark had let go of me, or taken off my leg, and the spar, thus released, had shot to the surface, dragging me along with it. I had come up about thirty feet away from the boat, and Granger was already swimming towards me. The surrounding water was reddening, but I was sure the shark no longer had hold of me. I dare not investigate my leg, and kept hold of the spar instead lest I sink once more.

Granger was a powerful swimmer, and he was soon at my side, gently prising my fingers from the float. 'Come on, old chap,' he said kindly, 'I've got you.' He put an arm around me and bade me lay back while he swam on his side, pulling me along with him until he got us to the boat, a tiny skiff with a single oarsman. 'Hell of a night, 'ay?' he said, grinning in a fashion that might have been either valiant or insane.

I was still gasping for air, but I finally managed to thank him.

He blew some water out of his mouth and winced, Barker having badly split his lip, and gave me a manly pat on the shoulder. 'You've already treated me more than in kind,' he said.

'It's not the same,' said I, 'you have no idea—' Then a powerful fear came upon me, the same sense of exigency that I had felt when I had first awaited rescue. 'We should get out of the water now,' I said urgently, 'because it's going to come back.'

'It's all right, Jack,' he said, supporting me while the oarsman kept the boat steady and the other man pulled me up. I flopped among the passengers' legs, most of which appeared to be female, and noted with profound relief that I was still in possession of my own, and the foot that went with it.

Thank Christ, I thought, at which point my attention returned to my more immediate saviour. I became instantly alert. Granger was still in the water.

'Get him out!' I screamed at the man who wasn't rowing, climbing to my knees and looking back desperately over the side. I could move well enough, but there was a dull pain in my ankle, curiously like a toothache.

'Calm yourself, sir,' said the seaman sternly.

Inwardly I ignited, but I managed to moderate my tone. 'I'm just saying that we need to get Mr. Granger out of the water,' I replied steadily.

'Just leave all that to the professionals, sir,' said the seaman. I ignored him and kept my eyes on the water.

Finally, Granger got his hands on the gunwale and heaved himself up as if climbing out of a public bath. 'Perhaps if you have another boy,' he said to me, half out of the water, 'you might name him after me.' Then he laughed and added, 'Just don't put me in one of your bloody awful books.'

'But I don't know your first name,' I said, but before he could answer, the carving knives flashed again and in the blink of an eye he was gone, a look of horror on his face indicating a clear recognition of his fate as he was pulled under.

A woman screamed behind me, and there was general panic in the boat, which rocked in a most alarming fashion. The seamen bellowed at the passengers to stop moving. I tried to talk to the man in charge but it was clear that he thought me hysterical, for he ordered me to compose myself in the most uncompromising terms.

'It lets you go,' I tried to tell him, desperately scanning the swirling water. 'Keep looking,' I pleaded. 'It lets you go first. It doesn't kill you straight away. It lets you go—' But this time it did no such thing; there was not even any blood. Eventually I stopped searching and collapsed in a pool of blood and water in the bottom of the boat.

'He redeemed himself,' said the oarsman, who must have known the story of Granger's humiliation on Spike Island.

'Shut up, you stupid cunt,' I told him, suddenly furious and heedless of prevailing social boundaries. Granger was a brave man, and had no need to prove himself. What use is reputation, I thought bleakly, if you're fucking dead?

'It is clear,' he replied shakily, 'that you are not a gentleman.' That was true enough, but I was largely past caring just then.

The rest of the ashen faced survivors were looking down upon me in shock. The little boat was packed to the gunwales, and dangerously overloaded. The oarsman, who was presently glaring at me like a scalded cock, was Wilkins, the Captain's cook, and the officer in charge was Hare, one of the Master's Assistants. He was a young man, younger even than Granger, and why Salmond had put him in charge of a lifeboat, even such a small one, was a mystery. There were two women which I vaguely recognised but could not name. The younger of the two was pale and drawn with mousey hair, and in possession of a greatly disgruntled baby, so small and new that it was likely one of those born on the ship. The other woman was older, darker and larger, and cradling a pallid and unconscious young man that looked like Duffy, one of the Ship's Boys. I was pretty sure she had been one of the three women who had cared for the expectant mothers during the storm. There were also a couple of younger girls, twins of eleven or twelve, who I took to be the daughters of the older woman. And behind these two silent and shaking children, at the stern of the narrow boat, sat Mina.

It was definitely her, as large as life, in that same meringue of a dress and ridiculous veiled bonnet she had been wearing after she first shagged Lakeman at St. Helena. I wondered if anyone else could see her, or if perhaps I had died after all. It appeared I had not, for the young officer was speaking to me, saying something about my leg. I looked down with some trepidation, but as I had first thought I appeared to be intact, although bleeding quite copiously. This was causing my fellow travellers considerable alarm, although all were seemingly too squeamish to assist. I tried appealing to Mina but, being dead, she ignored me. I bit my lip, fought back the bile, and then examined the wound, presuming the apparition to be some sort of hallucination brought about by my injuries.

'Is it bad?' inquired Hare, refraining to look too closely himself.

It was far from good, but equally it could have been considerably worse. Remarkably, my foot had survived the encounter unscathed; my remaining toes were unharmed, and given that I was still alive I concluded that whatever arteries were down there had also escaped serious damage. I recalled that the creature's grip had been surprisingly gentle, almost exploratory rather than aggressive, and by the look of things it was the release not the bite that had wounded me, as my calf and shin were dragged across its rows of razors. It had basically flayed my lower leg, the skin hanging off the muscles of my calf and shankbone, and sheeted about my ankle like the hide of a Catholic martyr. As soon as I realised that these ugly rags were part of me and not my clothes my head spun, and it was only the accompanying pain, suddenly as intense as a full thickness burn, that prevented me fainting on the spot. The vitriolic saltwater had at least kept the torn flesh clean, and I knew exactly what I had to do if I wanted to save my leg. I was still in possession of needle and thread, and had sewn up a fair few fighters in my days at the Fancy. I gingerly tore away the bottom of my trouser leg and, biting upon a rolled up piece of bloody serge as if kissing the gunner's daughter, I set about stitching myself back together again.

When I had done the work, the woman taking care of young Duffy obliged me with some silk from the bottom of her dress and I bandaged my leg tightly. I would say that the limb was wooden, inasmuch as the muscles were palpably stiffening, but that would not adequately define the accompanying agony. Suffice it to say that if my lower leg felt like wood, it was firewood. Nonetheless, I was still surprisingly mobile under the circumstances. It was possible that I had learned something from Metford's example, or perhaps I was just stubborn. Either way, I willed my body to keep going. You can only know pain, after all, if you yet live.

'Tout est pour le mieux,' I said, but nobody got it.[37]

They had water, and better still rum, and when I was restored to something loosely resembling human form I was thoroughly interrogated about the fate of the ship and my own escape. I told them all that I knew and had experienced. Hare and Wilkins looked quite bilious by the end of my account.

'Did you see Corporal MacGlashan of the Argyllshires?' the older woman said. It was clear that she had been bursting to ask me this since she had given me the bandage. The girls looked on hopefully. MacGlashan was obviously her husband and their father. She had a gentle border accent, and a hard face softened by deep brown eyes.

I had indeed seen MacGlashan, for I knew the majority of the NCOs through my interviews. He was in the last detachment at the chain pumps. My hesitation gave the game away as unequivocally as if I had just come out and said it, and she slumped against her girls, all of them shaking with grief.

'It was quick,' I said ineffectually, making matters even worse. The woman with the baby glared at me as if I had killed the man myself.

'I should have stayed,' wailed Mrs. MacGlashan.

'He'd have wanted you and the children safe, Lorna,' said the woman with the baby.

I felt it was now my turn to ask some questions of the bluejackets, particularly why in God's name they had not landed the women, children, and wounded, and returned to the wreck, where a good three hundred men had gone into the water some six hours before.

Hare protested that the coastline was far too wild to land the dinghy, which would have been torn up in the surf, and in any event his orders had been to stand off the wreck in order that soldiers not swamp the boat and thus doom the civilians.

'Mr Granger was in complete agreement,' he said, which to be honest I doubted given Granger's prompt action when he saw me in the water. They had, he continued to explain, spotted a ship in the distance, possibly a whaler, and had struck out after it in the hope of raising the alarm and getting help for the men in the water. It had not seen them, they had not been able to catch it, and now they were lost.

I tried to persuade Hare to head for the shore, but he was adamant that we were now in the shipping lanes and the best strategy was thus to sit tight and wait for rescue. I confess I became quite heated, but he shouted me down in the end and I was banished to the back of the boat, where Mina still sat silently.

The spectre was incredibly solid, but if anyone was to have a powerful essence, I reasoned, it was going to be her. She had to be a phantom; had I not just watched, in fact *held* her as she expired? Although a life-long gothicist by profession and inclination, I had never before believed in, let alone witnessed, a full body apparition, however much my fancy may have yearned for such phenomena to be authentic. I was thus ill-equipped for a genuine encounter with the realm ethereal, and despite spending more time that was healthy among mediums in search of my sister, I was unsure of how best to approach the situation. In the end I decided to just try talking to it.

'I'm so sorry,' I said.

'Shut up,' she replied, in a rather waspish tone.

I looked around to see if anyone else had heard, but no one

was paying us the slightest attention. Just me, then, I thought, which made a perverse kind of sense. Visitants did not, as a rule, reveal themselves to any but the select few, or so I had been told, only I had never before deemed it possible. Until that moment, ghosts, to my mind, were always the stuff of stories, delusions or confidence tricks. I had on the other hand attended enough séances to know that direct communication was deemed a major breakthrough, and as anyone who knows me will tell you, I never know when to shut up.

'I managed to save Clara,' I thus told the shade, hoping that this intelligence might afford her some consolation.

Alas, it did not. 'Fuck the fucking maid,' she said petulantly.

She was obviously still adjusting to her new condition, and a touch out of sorts in consequence. This would explain why she was still loitering near living survivors of the ship in preference to taking her place in the celestial city.

'Are you in limbo?' I asked her, for I had read that some spirits are cursed to walk the earth. I had also heard that some do not realise they have died and need help to move on. 'Go into the light,' I said, in a sonorous tone, as I understood that was the right advice to offer under such distressing circumstances.

She turned on me quite aggressively then, and in a sibilant voice from beyond the veil demanded, 'Why couldn't you just fucking die?'

I briefly considered sharing my views on the essentially random nature of the universe, but it seemed in poor taste to do so. We cannot all be winners, after all. I was only just then beginning to comprehend my own survival, and there was a sense of accompanying exhilaration that was potentially embarrassing in the present situation. 'Well,' I said, 'a miss is as good as a mile, I always say.'

'You little shit,' she said, suddenly lunging for my throat with her parchment claws.

I tussled briefly with the revenant, soon getting the better of it. The clothes felt surprisingly real, and the mass contained therein quite corporeal, like a table-rapper caught cheating. I pinned its arms at its side, and when it ceased to struggle I steeled myself and quickly pulled back the veil. Mina had a beard.

'Good God almighty!' exclaimed the young officer. 'What manner of trickery is this?'

'You blackguard,' said the cook.

'Poltroon,' said Mrs. MacGlashan, fetching the ghost a solid clout with her portmanteau.

'Nice dress, John' said I, releasing my grip, for it was Mr. not Mrs. Grimstone with whom I conversed, escaped from the wreck by nefarious and dishonourable means, while the true owner of the meringue had been abandoned to a hideous end.

He removed the bonnet and remained seated next to me, fuming. The woman with the baby spat at him. He looked to me with desperate eyes. 'It was the old intelligence training,' he said imploringly, 'you tell 'em, Jack.'

I kept silent. It was all rather awkward, truth be told.

'I have despatches for Sir Harry Smith,' he continued, addressing the other passengers and crew, more his old self. 'I had to get through at any cost. My training just took over. The Great Game, you know? Jack'll tell you—'

'You left your wife,' I said flatly. 'She didn't make it.'

'Well obviously I'm sorry for that,' he said, wrong-footed. He must have thought she had been saved with the other women.

'She died in my arms,' I said.

'My poor Mina,' he said, bringing all his political acumen to the fore and affecting to grieve, his head in his hands.

'Yeah, poor Mina,' I said. 'You're a public figure, for God's sake. They would have got you off safely.'

He looked up, and the tears looked quite authentic. He must be a demon in the house, I thought. 'Seton thought me a soldier,' he said hopelessly, 'he would have asked me to stand.'

'You're no soldier,' I said, before making my way to the front of the boat.

'Throw the bastard over the side,' said Mrs. MacGlashan.

'Feed him to the sharks,' said the woman with the baby. The two seamen looked inclined to agree, and took on a conspicuously menacing air.

'Jack?' said Grimstone, in a very little voice.

'Leave him,' I said. 'We have a more pressing concern.'

'Is that a sail?' said Hare, shielding his eyes with the flat of his hand.

'No,' I said.

The shark had returned, and was circling the boat.

'I wonder,' I said, politely addressing the woman with the baby, 'if you might keep the little chap quiet.'

The baby, in blue so I was assuming male, had been crying on and off ever since I had arrived on board. Being stoic by nature, and a parent myself, I had largely ignored him. I had my own problems, as did he, and I could hardly blame him for protesting in the only way he could at such disagreeable, and, for him, incomprehensible circumstances. The altercation with Grimstone had now set him off again, and I had an unpleasant feeling that the noise was attracting the shark. If it was the same one that had grabbed me and taken Granger, then this was not a big enough boat. The mother rocked the child, but he remained inconsolable. I knew the feeling.

'Please just feed him,' I said.

'In front of everyone?' she said, horrified.

'Time is an issue,' I said, as patiently as I was able, 'perhaps Mrs. MacGlashan can cover you.' The older woman offered the mother a long woollen shawl, and she draped it across the baby, adjusting her garments awkwardly beneath it. The gentlemen all looked away, and the baby went quiet. The shark slipped soundlessly beneath the waves.

No one spoke, and we all nervously watched the surface of the water. The girls were whimpering, but their mother managed to quiet them. I held my breath. Please God, not again, I thought.

It hit us from below, causing the boat to lurch crazily and Wilkins to lose an oar. The women all screamed, and the baby started crying again. 'Mother of God,' said Grimstone, 'we're sinking.'

'Check!' shouted Hare, and he and I dropped to the base of the boat, exploring for damage. There was a little water, but I was confident that it was the remains of what had come in with me. The fragile hull seemed secure, at least for now.

'We need to get out of here,' I told him quietly, while we were still crawling about in the bottom of the boat.

'Agreed,' said he, standing.

Once more there was no sign of the animal. 'Do you think it's the same one?' Mrs MacGlashan asked me.

'I hope not,' I said.

The oar was drifting quite a way away now, but Wilkins managed to use its companion to reach it, as if paddling a canoe. No one was inclined to put their hands in the water to assist his progress, although we had seen no more of the shark. The water was smooth and dark, and the lost oar barely moved upon its surface. Wilkins shipped the oar he did have, and then reached out to retrieve the other. As he did so, the boat rocked violently. I feared he would be pitched out, but instead he fell back into the boat, his right arm, shoulder and head gone, the rest of him flailing spastically, the hole in the top of him spraying blood like a fountain. You would not think we had so much blood in us. Everyone was screaming, and the boat was beginning to roll alarmingly as the passengers attempted to get away from the animated corpse while also avoiding the gunwales. This part of Wilkins remained ignorant of its own death and was jerking around wildly, perhaps searching for its head. I had seen so much horror in the last few hours that I was becoming quite inured, so while Hare cowered with the rest I took hold of Wilkins's legs and heaved him over the side, pushing the body away from us with our remaining oar. When the fish raised its huge head to have a go at this one I hit it on the snout as hard as I could and it sunk beneath the waves with a hiss. It soon set about Wilkins's remains, which jerked a couple of times in the water and then disappeared, the blood cloud vanishing before my eyes as the ocean dispersed it to nothing.

The boat by contrast was full of blood. We were covered in it, not merely painted but soaked. 'Oh my God,' Hare was saying, over and over to himself, tears cutting a track down the filth on his face. Grimstone had become a dragged up parody of the Whore of Babylon, Mina's white dress now dyed a deep arterial red, and the women were frantically wiping their faces, which did nothing but smear the gore around more grotesquely. I could feel the sticky mess on my skin and hair, and smell that peculiar scent of iron and sugar that went with it. My mouth flooded with saliva and I vomited where I sat, fearful of sticking my own head over the side. This set the twins off, and soon the stench of sickness added to our diabolical funk. The baby, meanwhile, seemed unbothered, and was licking the blood from his little hands, while Duffy remained unconscious and even more blissfully oblivious than the infant.

Grimstone struggled out of the dress and threw it over the side. He was wearing a flannel nightshirt underneath with a frock coat thrown over it, the bottom already fringed with Wilkins's blood. The dress sunk far too quickly, and appeared rather to have been pulled down.

Hare curled up on the bottom of the boat, crying. 'We need to go, now!' I told him, but he took no heed of me and wrapped himself up more the tighter, no longer aware of the puddle of blood in which he lay. Everyone else, including Grimstone, was looking at me.

'What shall we do, Jack?' he said, as if I was now the expert on the doings of sharks and boats by virtue either of recent events or my old books upon the sea.

It seemed sensible to keep away from the sides, so I directed everyone to huddle in the centre of the boat, back to back. Hare I left where he was, tucked in the bow, with Duffy lain down next to him. He had received a head wound when the *Birkenhead* had struck and had been evacuated with Granger. From the dried blood in his hair and his dreadful pallor it did not look good, but he might have been the luckiest among us all. I realised that I needed to row with the single oar as Wilkins had done, so I had to persuade everyone else to move back to give me room. Grimstone I put at the stern, which he was far from pleased about.

'Just watch the fucking water,' I told him.

I started to paddle cautiously, as I had seen Wilkins do, sweeping the oar either side of me in turn. I had to sit quite far forward to be able to reach both ways, and my arms were soon burning, but at least we appeared to be moving. Paradoxically, I had ceased to notice the pain in my leg. I had no real idea of direction; I just wished to be away from where we were. No one spoke, or even caught one another's eye. All simply watched and waited.

Hours passed without further incident, but there was still no sign of land. I was trying to use the sun to navigate, but it was overhead by now and of little help. No one else on the boat had anymore idea of how to take a bearing than I, except for Hare, who was in shock and of no more practical service than the catatonic Duffy. Our only real hope was to blunder into a ship before nightfall.

It was clear that morale was in the cesspit, so I suggested a song. They all looked at me as if I had proposed an orgy but I persevered, belting out a half-remembered pirate song from the Newgate Calendars that I had later knocked off myself—

> 'Oh, my name is William Kidd,
> As I sailed, as I sailed,
> My name is William Kidd.
> Yes, my name is William Kidd,
> And God's laws I did forbid,
> And most wickedly I did!
> As I sailed, as I sailed—'

It was a good song, but probably not the right one for that moment. At least I remembered to stop before the verse about throwing prisoners to the sharks. My dreadful baritone achieved the desired motivational effect nevertheless, for one of the twins began to bleat out a popular ballad before I had a chance to sing anything else. The ladies soon joined in, all chanting something sweet about a gypsy in a sycamore glade.

We passed the early afternoon singing robustly, although Grimstone refused to lift his voice to the heavens with the rest of us, and as the sun moved west I was able to make a guess at a heading, hopeful that no one had noticed that I had been rowing out to sea in error for the last hour or so. We still had drinking water, but the lack of any other provisions was starting to tell, and even the foul state of the boat and our clothing did not deter the twins from professing their hunger on an increasingly regular basis. I had to rest frequently, but Grimstone would not paddle, claiming he was too weak to do so. I suspected that he feared to be any closer to the water, and his caution was born out when the oar was suddenly yanked out of my hands, almost taking me with it. This signalled the return of out travelling companion, which swam around the boat with the oar sticking out of the water as if the animal was breathing through a giant straw. Then, with an audible crunch, it bit down and snapped the paddle off, before disappearing beneath the waves. The jagged shaft that remained, turning in the water, might perhaps have furnished a weapon, but I was damned if I was going to reach for the bastard.

The women began to whimper, and I think I heard Grimstone quietly praying. A moment later the monstrous head slammed into the bow, its jaws closing on the wood and shaking violently. I clung onto the gunwales, unable to tear my eyes from those of the beast, and around me everyone started to scream again. Hare jumped up with a start, and before I could stop him he got his arms under Duffy and heaved him out of the boat. The shark let go, and helped itself to Duffy, tearing into him while he continued to float on the surface, no more than five feet away. Fortunately, he never awoke.

'I'm sorry,' said Hare, weeping and pulling at his hair and pacing about, rocking the boat far too much.

'Fucking sit down!' I yelled, but still he kept wobbling about. Eventually I punched him in the face and knocked him on his arse.

'Jesus Mary and Joseph,' said Mrs. MacGlashan.

'What have you done?' said the woman with the baby.

'I'm sorry,' Hare said again, in a wailing tone that made you hate him even more. It was not his fault though, I have come to realise; any of us could have cracked.

'We'll deal with him later,' I said. 'Just stay together and don't move.' I had nothing else to offer except empty promises, but I made them anyway. 'Someone will come,' I told them. 'Sooner or later, someone will come.' I knew, of course, that we were doomed, but giving our fate a name just then would have achieved nothing useful. The most humane thing I could have done for those women and their children at that moment would have been to recover the broken oar and then finish them off with it quickly.

The boat shuddered again. The animal clearly meant to sink us. I could not quite bring myself to believe there was a malevolent intelligence at work, so I decided that Wilkins's blood, which infused the woodwork, was the attraction. Any mammalian predator could smell and track blood, and I suspected that this hunter was just the same.

I made my way over to Grimstone, who was hunched aft, looking utterly defeated. I sat down beside him and appealed with my eyes for any sort of strategy, but before we could exchange a word Mrs. MacGlashan cried out suddenly. I turned to see the dorsal fin and tail had surfaced about twenty yards in front of us and was moving towards the boat. It struck us head on with tremendous power, pushing the bow sideways and sending Hare flying forward into the water. I saw him bobbing about for a second, looking confused, and then he disappeared, pulled straight down without a sound.

'For God's sake,' said Mrs. MacGlashan, 'how much more can it eat?'

I decided that was a question best left unanswered, and after the initial shock of another fatality had subsided enough for something approaching rational thought to re-emerge, I asked Grimstone if he had any ideas.

'Hare was on the right track,' he whispered, 'but without the oars we can't capitalise on it.'

Thus spoke one of nature's true survivors. He would pitch any one of us out to buy himself a few more moments of life, including the baby. 'The only difference between you and that shark,' I replied, 'is that he's not lately been wearing a dress and a pretty bonnet.'

'Oh, do grow up,' he said, but when I rose to escape his company and join the ladies he took my arm, indicating that he felt there was more to discuss. 'We can't get away,' he said, keeping his voice low, 'but if we play our cards right, perhaps we can hold out until we're spotted. There must be boats searching by now.'

'I'm listening,' I said.

'When it's feeding,' he said, 'it's not interested in the boat. So let's keep it fed.'

'You can't be serious,' I said, appalled.

'Oh, I am,' said he, 'deathly serious.' He let his coat fall open enough to reveal the hilt of his revolver. It had never occurred to me that he would have had time to arm himself when the ship was going down. 'We could have a little fun too,' he said conspiratorially, nodding towards the women, huddling terrified in the middle of the boat. 'No one would know,' he continued. 'I know you like the older girls, Jack, so you could take Lorna and I'll have the other one. She's a handsome woman, and you could have her any way you liked. We could share the other two, then chuck 'em over the side one by one to keep the fish busy.' He slowly unholstered the gun, keeping it hidden under his coat. 'They can't argue with this,' he said, 'and we could last a fair few hours that way, I reckon. What do you say?'

I sat back for a moment, affecting to think about it. I smiled in acquiescence, and he responded in kind, which gave me the split second I required to swing my forehead down onto the bridge of his nose as hard as I could without him seeing it coming. His mistake had been to hold the revolver away from me, and by the time he thought to bring it up I had both my hands on his wrist. He was not a strong man, his arms weak for lack of honest labour, and I soon gained possession of the pistol. I slammed it into the side of his head and he slumped down, blood gushing from his smashed nose. Mrs. MacGlashan was yelling at us to stop fighting, but I told her in no uncertain terms to sit down and shut up. Keeping the gun in my right hand I hoisted the semi-conscious Grimstone up with my left and hung his head and shoulders over the side of the boat, using the weight of my body to hold him down.

'Dear God, Mr. Vincent, what are you doing?' cried Mrs. MacGlashan, fortuitously resisting the temptation to leap on my back and start pulling my hair.

'This piece of devil's shit wants to rape you and then feed you to the shark,' I told her, 'now for heaven's sake madam, please leave me be.'

Mrs. MacGlashan sat back down.

Grimstone was beginning to realise his predicament. 'Jack, Jack,' he was saying, his voice thick and uneven, 'what are you doing, Jack?'

I held him firmly and let his blood fall into the black water. His eyes told me he knew exactly what I was doing, and he squirmed beneath me trying to get away. I moved as if in a dream, but I knew the shark was coming, and whether or not it got Grimstone meant nothing to me.

I felt it before I saw it, and I pulled the old lecher back into the boat at the last moment, much more by luck than judgement. I threw him behind me as the animal's huge head exploded out of the water, the jaws grinning obscenely as it bit down on the top of the transom. God bless British craftsmanship, for the woodwork held as if made of iron. The shark kept its grip, shaking its unlovely head from side to side and staring into my soul with its lifeless black eyes, a dead man still on its breath. It was either stuck, or this was an attempt to drag the boat under and get us all into the water. The monster's mouth was almost as wide as the boat, its body twice as long, while its squat, pointed snout hung over the transom, serrated teeth sawing as if independent of the jaw.

'Stop laughing, damn you!' I cried, sprawling across the cold grey head. It was like throwing myself onto a large wet rock. Most of my body was still in the boat, and I was well enough balanced to slide around on the rough, scarred leather of its skin without flying off while it did its best to dislodge me.

Believe it or not, I had a plan. I placed the barrel of the pistol in the centre of its huge head, pointing straight down, at the spot, I prayed, where I had seen the African hunter deliver the *coup de grace*. I was by now so sick of the bastard that my anger had overwritten my fear, or perhaps I was purely motivated by a kind of suicidal despair, a desire for nothing more than the ordeal to be over, one way or the other. In truth, I knew not then and to this day I remain none the bloody wiser. The animal bucked but it could not bite me, and in its lust to have me it chewed the transom even harder and did not release the boat. I clung onto its giant skull and laboriously emptied the pistol into its brain, cocking and firing until the gun was empty. I then fell back into the boat on top of the prostrate Grimstone.

The centre of its head was a gory pulp, but still the shark held on. Its great body whipped from side to side and threatened to capsize us, and I thought for a moment that it meant to take us all with it. With no more ammunition, I was reduced to desperately pistol whipping its hog-like nose while screaming at it to fuck off. The wood finally gave with a tremendous crack, and the head slid beneath the waves, leaving an enormous crescent bite in the top of the transom.

It did not rise again.

'Bloody hell,' said Mrs. MacGlashan.

I staggered over to her and collapsed onto the rough seat by her side, my hand throbbing almost as much as my leg. The other woman and the twins were regarding me in silent amazement. Mrs. MacGlashan caught my eye and I found myself laughing. She joined in, and was soon followed by the others, aside from Grimstone, who was still lying at our feet sulking.

'What'll we do with him?' said Mrs. MacGlashan, finally.

'Put him over the side,' said one of her girls.

'Yeah,' said the other, 'drown him and feed him to the fish.'

The woman with the baby said nothing, but nodded her head in assent. All the women looked at me. A moment before it would have been so easy to have done exactly what they proposed. But I was now myself again, and no more capable of killing him than I had been when I saw him alone on the deck of the *Birkenhead*. The weight of taking a human life in cold blood was always going to be too much for me to bear, whether he deserved it or not.

I shook my head. 'Leave him,' I said, 'but tie him up because he's still dangerous.'

'You wouldn't dare,' said Grimstone, from the bottom of the boat.

Such ingratitude, I thought. This was the second time that day I had saved his life by talking the others out of killing him, and the third if you counted not feeding him to the shark myself.

Mrs. MacGlashan obliged, using yet more strips from the bottom of her supremely versatile skirts, and pulling the knots tight with savage pleasure. Grimstone was still half in a daze and powerless to resist, and she was a big woman as well. I searched him for cap and shell and was rewarded with enough loose ammunition to reload the pistol.

'You'll be hearing from my lawyers,' he said.

'What do we do now?' said Mrs. MacGlashan, disregarding him.

'If this was one of his pathetic sea stories,' muttered Grimstone, 'it'd be time to start eating each other.'

'If you say one more word,' I told him, I'll fucking shoot you.' When he said I wouldn't dare, I put one over his head, just to show that I was not fooling around. He shut up after that. 'Now,' I said, returning my attention to the ladies. 'Have we got any rum left?'

We drifted, unmolested, until the following day, huddling together for warmth and telling stories through the night. I tried very hard to banish the memory of the phantom helmsman and his charges drifting forever south, awaiting a rescue that would never come.

In the afternoon of the second day we saw a sail on the horizon, which, as it came closer, remained a sail still. We attracted attention to ourselves by emptying the pistol into the sky. It was another British Navy steamer, the *Rhadamanthus*, searching for the last lost children of the *Birkenhead*, and by dusk we were safe in her maternal embrace and heading back to Simon's Bay. Once again, I had lived to tell the tale.

CHAPTER XLVII

THE REMAINING NARRATIVE of that terrible night belongs to others. In addition to Hare's tiny command, three other boats were got away from the ship, the two cutters and a small, four-oared gig. The first cutter was crewed by Robbie Richards, another young Master's Assistant, and an Able-Seaman name of George Till. The second had a three-man crew under the charge of Able-Seaman John Lewis. I do not know the two seamen who manned the gig. Richards' boat carried the majority of the women and children, while Lewis and his people hauled as many survivors out of the water as they could before being forced to pull away for fear of being swamped. Lewis saved thirty-two men in total, while eight got on board the gig, including Culhane, the surgeon, and Renwick, the engineer.

About two hundred and fifty men went into the water.

Sheldon-Bond was one of the lucky ones. He had somehow got hold of a Mackintosh life-preserver at the last minute, and this saved him from the vortex. He survived the night, although two soldiers who were swimming with him, the enigmatic Lavery and Quinn, inseparable to the end, were both taken by sharks. The strangulating seaweed that fringed the coastline like a deadly net almost did for Bond though, but, more by luck than judgement he later confessed, he hit upon a landing place after about three hours in the water. Giradot and a small group of men were clinging to some floating wreckage in the surf nearby, and Bond guided them in. This time he also managed to save his horse, newly purchased and loaded at the Cape, which had made it safely to shore along with several other mounts; his orderly, Private Dodd, was never heard of again.

The steadfast Colour Sergeant Drake, meanwhile, had used a piece of decking plank for a float. He saw Cornet Rolt struggling in the water, and was able to paddle over to the young Lancer, who had been badly injured by the falling boat that had broken Metford's leg. He dragged Rolt up onto the plank and held on to him, but they were swept against a rock and the wood broke apart. Rolt was too weak to save himself. Drake then swam for the wreck, as the maintopmast and topsail-yard remained above water. He joined the forty-odd men who were already desperately clinging to the rigging, many of whom would ultimately drop from their frail supports through exhaustion, the fortunate among them drowning before the sharks got to them.

Captain Wright also escaped the death of the ship. He took possession of a broken section of deck, and using only this most basic of rafts he saved fourteen men. This group got ashore at Danger Point, and soon joined up with other survivors scattered along the coast. Wright organised these men and, as they were in the middle of God's own nowhere, they did what soldiers do and marched out, eventually finding help at a farm at Sandford Cove, twenty or so miles away. Corporal Butler, of the 12th Lancers, who had once granted me a very candid interview, got in on a straw bale and joined up with Wright. Of the other NCOs I came to know while interviewing the men, Corporal Smith of the 12th was, like me, saved by a spar, and found his way to land despite a near encounter with a shark; Isiah Teale of the 6th was saved by the maintopmast, and Bernard Kilkeary of the 73rd was picked up by Lewis' cutter. Seton's Corporals, Laird and Matheson, both perished. Giradot's friend, Ensign Lucas, succeeded in swimming ashore unaided, while Staff Surgeon Bowen was also saved by Lewis. Along with Sheldon-Bond, Giradot, and Wright, they were the only army officers to keep their lives that night.

Lakeman and Élise survived, with several of his people, although numbers are difficult to verify as many of them promptly deserted. Legend has it that Lakemen was on horseback the whole time he was in the water. The precise fate of Major Seton is to this day unknown, and it is presumed that he went down with the ship.

While Hare's boat became separated from the group, ultimately charging off on a fool's errand that found me rather than salvation, the other three initially tried to land in the dark. But their oars repeatedly became entangled in the choking seaweed, while the savage swell kept throwing them back. Richards' boat was damaged during one of these attempts, and as it was too treacherous to swim for it, especially for the women and children, the decision was made to return to open water in the hope of finding a safer place to land further along the coast.

Soon after the failed landing, the crew in Lewis' cutter saw a man moving in the water, clearly exhausted and close to death. Lewis was fearful of adding any more weight to the already perilously overloaded boat, but Ensign Russell of the 74th, Seton's right hand man, insisted that the survivor be taken on board. Russell took the man's place, although he had not been long out of the water himself, and within five minutes a shark took him.[38]

A sail was sighted at dawn, although all attempts to signal the ship, a medium sized schooner, failed, and she soon changed course and began to move out of sight. Dr. Culhane, on the gig, suggested that the group's best hope was to transfer the strongest men to his boat, which was the smallest and the fastest, and then make for the schooner, just as Hare had tried for the whaler. The slower cutters followed, but Culhane failed to catch up. Rather than rejoin the group, Culhane then convinced his oarsmen to pull for the shore instead. They landed at Port D'Urban, about fifteen miles from the wreck, in the late afternoon. Culhane then talked a horse out of a bemused shopkeeper, and rode a hundred-odd miles across hard country to Cape Town to raise the alarm. He arrived about twenty-four hours later, by which point all survivors had either long made their own landings, been rescued, or died.

'Presque tous les hommes meurent de leurs remèdes,' Giradot later remarked of this escapade, 'et non pas de leurs maladies.'[39]

Culhane was the first to alert the Naval Command at the Cape, and Wyvill on the *Castor* dispatched *HMS Rhadamanthus* to the wreck. The ship that Culhane could not reach was the British schooner, *Lioness*, which had subsequently tacked again and started moving back towards the cutters, this time spotting the boats and taking everyone off before lunch. The *Lioness* then made for the wreck, and rescued the men who had been strong enough to hold onto the mast through the night and morning, including Colour

Sergeant Drake. The rescuing seamen told dreadful tales of body parts and mutilated corpses littering the sea for miles around the wreck, often with pale shapes beneath them, feeding.

The *Lioness* rescued a hundred and sixteen survivors from the cutters and the rigging. She rendezvoused with the *Rhadamanthus*, and as there was no wind the steamer towed the schooner into Simon's Bay before returning to continue the search; first locating our boat on the Friday, and then Wright's party, which included Lakeman, the following morning. It was by then three days since the ship had gone down, and Bunce, the Commander of the *Rhadamanthus*, was satisfied that he had done enough and that there were no more survivors to be found. He therefore set course for his anchorage at the Cape.

The *Rhadamanthus* was another iron paddle-steamer, and although she was not the *Birkenhead's* sister ship, she was an eerie double, so similar in design that the wreck might have been her shadow in the water. When I saw her approaching, I was just about far gone enough from shock, dehydration, sunstroke, and general exposure to see the *Birkenhead* risen to claim us, and I found the strangely familiar decks and corridors most disconcerting once I was safely aboard. Only then did I check the condition of my father's book, which had inevitably turned to porridge in my pocket. I mourned its passing, but no longer felt the panic at its loss that I had on the night of the catastrophe. I had a new story to tell.

The women got a cabin, as did Grimstone, who had the sense to keep his mouth shut after we released him, explaining to our rescuers that he had lost his senses and required physical restraint. (He later sent me a message, via a steward, requesting the return of his pistol, but I pretended that I had lost it over the side.) I was spirited away to the sick bay, where surgeons pawed me about and made jokes about tailors sewing themselves up. Such witticisms aside, I was in surprisingly fine fettle, all things considered. The salt water had burned my skin like acid, but it had cleaned my wound as well. My stitching was also neater than that of many a saw bones, and Mrs. MacGlashan, being the wife of an old soldier, knew how to tie a good field dressing. My leg was still stiff and on fire, but there was no sign of infection, or much discernible damage to muscle or tendon. I could just about walk on it, so they bound me up again, loaned me a walking stick and a pair of sea boots, and sent me on my way to create more room for those less fortunate than I, of whom there were many. I thus declined the offer of an analgesic, and hobbled off in search of a drink instead.

Although civilians and officers were accommodated below, the decks were crowded with common soldiers and seamen from the *Birkenhead*, wrapped in blankets, shaking, smoking, and sipping endless mugs of cocoa. I limped around searching for a familiar face. I came across a few of Moran's mates, but no one had seen him or Jeffries and all presumed them lost. Eventually Lakeman found me, and steered me to a berth with the other officers, who were crammed into a cabin not unlike the one I had occupied on the *Birkenhead.* Lucas and Sheldon-Bond were off somewhere doing something with horses, Bowen was occupying the bunk, and Wright and Giradot were sitting on the floor. When I arrived they all started to applaud, then I was suddenly surrounded and having my hand pumped, my back slapped and all those things that middle class men do in order to express the right kind of affection. Lakeman shoved a flagon of rum into my hand, and I took a damn long pull on it I can tell you.

'You did a man's work out there, by God!' said Wright. 'I told you there was a soldier in there somewhere.'

I shook my head shyly, and tried to sit on the floor. Bowen was having none of this, and insisted I take the bunk. I perched on its edge, and bade him sit back down for God's sake.

'We expect a full statement of the case,' said Lakeman, and all looked on expectantly.

I was informed that accounts around the ship differed wildly. In one version popular with the soldiers, for example, I dived down the shark's throat, knife between my teeth, and then cut my way out of its gut clutching a baby, while in my personal favourite, I subdued the beast with my fists, then fashioned a bridle out of hastily woven ladies' undergarments and rode it to shore. The most fantastic tale of all, of course, was the one nobody else paid much mind, which was the blind luck of being released from the monster's jaws relatively unscathed in the first place. I can only presume that I was not considered worth eating, or that the buoyancy of the spar to which I clung so tenaciously was too much of an inconvenience, and that it required less energy to let go than to take off my foot. Who can know the mind of such an alien creature?

I played it all down in the present company (although I confess I have dined out on this tale many times since), and we swapped survival stories while killing the rum. Wright and Giradot were furious about the people in charge of the boats, with a particular resentment directed towards Culhane. Wright had come ashore quite safely in a small cove east of Danger Point, and believed that it could have been used as a landing site to safely shuttle back and forth to the wreck, had there been a boat available.

'Had Culhane's boat remained by the wreck, or even returned after landing up the coast,' he said, 'nearly every man on the driftwood between the wreck and the shore might have been saved. They could've been picked off the spars and wood when they were outside the seaweed which stopped them coming in, and then landed at the cove. That damn boat could've made forty or fifty trips between daylight and dark, but what does that idiot do? He leaves the boat and the oarsmen, and *rides* to the Cape.'

'A lot of good men died because of him,' agreed Giradot.

This was an argument that was quickly picked up by the 'papers, so I will not waste words on it here, other than to say that whenever a British institution such as the army or navy suffers a particularly spectacular disaster a scapegoat quickly emerges, as if terrible acts of God or the random injustices of existence can be so easily explained or averted. Culhane did not sink the ship, probably neither did Salmond, or the poor bastard at the helm that night. It was simply an escalating catalogue of unforeseen failures. Perhaps we should blame Laird's shipyard for not providing enough lifeboats in the original design, or the men who painted the release pins closed, or the salt of the sea that rusted them shut and useless. Surely the Admiralty idiot who ordered holes cut in the bulkheads between watertight compartments deserves some rebuke?

I liked Culhane, and from what I knew of him I would say that he did what he thought was right at the time, fatigued and under terrible stress, which was to try for immediate help. When that was not forthcoming, he did the next best thing, and raised the alarm in a country that had no train or telegraph to send the message quickly. At least his actions caused the *Rhadamanthus* to be dispatched, and it was that fine ship that plucked me from a watery grave. There was no telling Wright or Giradot though. They would have had Culhane flogged over a cannon if they could. I think that was how they grieved.[40]

We arrived back at the Cape a week after we had left, and the longest week I have ever lived. After all the rolls were called, and copies of the ship's manifest checked and cross-referenced, the final tally of survivors was two hundred and seven, from a total of six hundred and forty-three souls known to have been on board when the ship struck. With the exception of Mina, all the women and children were saved. Of the two hundred and fifty or so men who went into the water, only a hundred and twenty-five came out, the sea and the sharks took the rest. Some of them went quietly, facing death like a lover or a traveller returning home, some went in prayer, and some of them were still fighting as they sank beneath the fatal waves. They were all of them better men than I, and may they rest in peace.

The surviving soldiers were soon shipped off to rejoin their respective regiments up country, but I did not go with them. I was in no fit state to carry on my duties for the *Chronicle*, and even had I been able to walk unaided, the desire to return to my family with all speed and then never leave them again was much stronger than my work ethic. Sod the money, I thought. There was also, inevitably, to be a court martial in England, even though all the senior naval officers were dead, and I was one of those called as a witness. It was time to go home.

*

Before I left I called upon Mrs. Metford. She was a guest at the residence of another officer's family, and when I presented myself at the house a servant discreetly directed me to a small church a few streets away. It was a plain colonial building of white wood, with more of the barn about it than hallowed ground, and exactly the type of exterior design that Pugin had moaned about. Yet the air inside was cool and still, and the décor medieval enough to please the Pope, so it was as close to home as young Mary Metford from Galway was likely to get in Cape Town.

I found her alone and praying. She was greatly changed, like a figure that had stepped out from behind a mirror, her widow's weeds more lightless than her shadow, her countenance as pale as quicklime. I had not the slightest idea what to say to her, so I sat beside her in silent contemplation until she spoke, still facing the altar.

'You were with Lawrence,' she said, 'at the end.' This was not a question but a statement of fact, and I wondered what else she had been told about that night.

'Yes.'

'Did he suffer?'

'It was as sudden as it was peaceful,' I lied, 'he would not have felt a thing.'

She turned to me then, and I saw in her sleepless eyes the need for a resolution that I did not feel able to offer. The truth would have only given the poor girl nightmares. 'A soldier I did not know came to the house,' she said. 'He told me that Lawrence had been very brave and was lost at sea, but he couldn't, or wouldn't say anymore.'

From the description she gave I guessed that she had seen Fairtlough. 'Did he tell you I was with your husband in the water?' I said.

'No,' she said, 'Lawrence did.'

The atmosphere became yet cooler, as a whisper from another world intruded into this one, like the final breath of a corpse. 'He visited me that night,' she said, 'the night they say the ship went down.'

I nodded carefully, not daring to interrupt.

'He came to my room,' she went on, 'and he loved me.' She hesitated then, and looked away. I gently bid her continue. 'He told me he had been with you,' she said. 'Then he became agitated around dawn and said he must not stay any longer. I was worried that he was absent without leave on my account and I let him go. A few days later the soldier came and I knew that my Lawrence had drowned.'

She must have been dreaming, I thought, but the coincidence was disconcerting nonetheless. A terrible wave of melancholy rolled over me, formed upon an ocean of sadness in which the tragic Metford and his helpless young wife forever drifted. It was a great effort to speak from the depth of such suffocating darkness.

'I believe I would have perished without him,' I eventually said, fighting my way to the surface.

As I uttered these words, I realised the ineluctable certainty of the statement. Metford had as much saved my life as Granger, and both had died in my stead for their trouble.

She began to weep quietly, and I took her hands in mine. 'His last words were of you,' I told her. That much, at least, was true.

'Thank you,' she said. 'I will see him again, I know.' I nodded, having nothing else to say, and left her to her grief. As I walked slowly back to my hotel, it occurred to me that perhaps I had learned how her story about the selkie who loved the Irish girl had ended after all.

I took my leave of Africa a couple of days later, having seen very little of the country and far too much of its oceans. I left a letter with a navy liaison to send to Grace, and joined the surviving ship's officers and crew on board the naval corvette *HMS Amazon*, along with the women who had lost their men and therefore had no more reason to follow the camps. Lakeman was there to see me off. He was already recruiting a new company of rangers, and seemed in very positive spirits. I gathered his equipment had been very heavily insured.

Before we parted he reached into his borrowed blue jacket and took out a small, glistening object which he passed to me reverently. 'They found this stuck in your boat,' he explained. I examined the cold hard thing in my hand. It was a sharp, oddly triangular tooth, serrated like a fighting knife, and about the length of an iron arrowhead. 'Both ears and the tail,' he said, shaking me warmly by the hand for the last time.

He had not been summonsed back to England with the rest of us. The Admiralty, it would seem, had no wish to speak to him in person, which, he told me, suited him just dandy. 'I don't want to speak to them, either,' he had said.

He was already preparing to travel up country. I bade him keep his head down, although I knew by know that he'd do no such thing.

'We will meet again, sharker!' said he, with an enthusiastic grin, and then he was away, quickly lost in the frenzied activity of the quayside as our ship prepared for sail.

CHAPTER XLVIII

Without a calamity, an account of a long sea voyage is a bore. Suffice it to say that it was a trial to once more board a ship, and I fretted at every pitch and roll until I was off the damn thing. I largely avoided the society of others, and I passed much of my time writing in my cabin or pacing the deck with the aid of a stick in order to strengthen my leg. I was, however, party to enough discussions with fellow survivors to add my assent to the collective decision to draw a veil over the Captain's suicide. This was done out of respect for his memory, for he remained much loved by his crew, such as it now was, and also to protect the reputation of his wife and son. During the voyage I was ably attended by the ship's surgeon, and my leg healed well, although the scar was an ugly one. The passage home took longer than the journey out but felt shorter, probably because it was non-stop, and we arrived at Spithead at the end of April, after which we were all rushed to Portsmouth with indecent haste in order to testify before the court martial. In accordance with official naval policy, every surviving crew member was to be put on trial.

No wonder Salmond shot himself, I thought.

I was deposited in a drab seafront boarding house (without a bar), and told by a bad tempered marine to present myself at Her Majesty's Warship *Victory* at an ungodly hour the following morning. I thought at first that he was having a laugh, but he assured me that he was perfectly serious. I dashed off a couple of lines to my wife, and gave a houseboy a shilling to put the letter in the post, before limping off to the nearest public house.

My group was not the first to bring the news of the disaster to England. Grimstone had already travelled back independently on the mail ship *Propontis*, along with Freshfield, the ship's clerk, who had had the fine fortune to disembark at Simon's Bay with Fairtlough because of fever. These men arrived three weeks before the rest of us, and thus the legend was beginning to form by the time I saw a 'paper, although neither of these men had witnessed the ship's final moments. It was sickening to read of Grimstone's deeds of derring-do with sharks and shipwrecks, while there was nary a word about yours truly. He had effectively stolen my story.

I returned to my lodgings in a foul humour, drunk and muttering. A woman stopped me by the gate. 'Leave me be, love,' I told her, 'I'm a happily married man.'

'I'm glad to hear it,' said a familiar voice.

I regarded the woman more closely in the misty gaslight. 'Are you real?' I said.

'For heaven's sake, Jack,' she replied. 'How much have you had to drink?'

And so was the third and most significant reunion of this narrative affected. No one had thought to tell Grace that I was among the living, and the letter I had assumed dispatched from Simon's Town was either never sent or lost in the post. She had thus left Joseph in the able care of Reynolds and his wife, and taken it upon herself to travel down to Portsmouth to discover my fate. Her enquiries had led her to this address, only to find me elsewhere. The landlady refused to let a strange woman into my room, so she had been loitering among the geraniums ever since. Fortunately, the rain had held off.

She was dressed in a fetching configuration of dark silks that showed off her figure to great advantage. 'You should wear black more often,' I said.

'I'm in mourning, you dunce,' she said, throwing her arms about me and laughing and sobbing at the same time. I felt her tears on my face as I savoured the heady warmth of my love's embrace, until a passerby coughed loudly to indicate that such a public display of affection was most unseemly, especially in the provinces.

We reluctantly released each other and I steered her inside. It was difficult to gauge who was less stable, and my newly acquired walking stick clearly upset her. I was not so crippled though, and I therefore did the only sensible thing under the circumstances, which was to take her straight to bed.

Afterwards, we talked until dawn, with Grace becoming more horrified with every twist of my tale. She cried again when she saw the bite on my leg, but I raised a smile by suggesting that scars on a man could be viewed as attractive. In my turn, I wanted to know everything that I had missed at home, despite her protestations that this was hardly an interesting story by comparison. I disagreed, and pressed her for domestic details. She was still illustrating *The Mysteries of the Court* for Reynolds, drawing after she put Joseph to bed. He remained a good sleeper, although he had been unsettled for the first week or so I was away. I was reassured that our little man was in rude health, and now talking in elementary sentences, unless frustrated or elated, in which case he reverted to the language of monkeys. He remained fascinated by the printed page, said Grace, and although far too young to read he attached his own interpretations to the text. I often featured in these readings, frequently sharing my son's strange little narratives with his other principle preoccupation, dragons.

I told her then of my strange underwater vision. 'Your love brought me back,' I said, which is what I should have told her the moment I saw her. This set her once more wailing like a widow at a melodrama, and I held her again and thus pursued the substance of the subject by other and better means.

Eventually we had to stop fooling around and face the day, at which point, over breakfast, Grace felt able to let a little of the outside world intrude. 'The most disagreeable man visited me the other day,' she announced.

'Was he selling something?' I said, attacking another round of limp toast before it dissolved on me.

'I'm not sure,' she said. 'He turned up at the door claiming to be some sort of agent, I presumed literary. He got quite shirty when I wouldn't let him in.'

'That's my girl,' I said. 'What did he want?'

'It was very curious,' she said. 'He would not give a name, but said he was in a position to offer me a tax free sum of five thousand pounds for exclusive rights to your story. But when I asked him what story he had in mind, which publisher he represented, or if he knew what had happened to you, he became evasive to the point of discourtesy.'

From her description I did not know him. 'Five grand sounds a bit queer,' I said. 'Even Dickens doesn't earn that for a book, besides which, deals from agents and publishers that sound too good to be true are usually just that.'

'I didn't know what to think,' she said, 'and to be honest I got quite upset about the whole thing. As far as I knew you'd probably been lost at sea. I told him I needed time to consider his offer and shut the door on him. He opened the letterbox and said he'd be back. Then I took Joseph and myself over to Reynolds.'

'What did he say?'

'He said it would depend upon the story, and that I should not write you off until I saw the box going into the hole.'

'Quite right,' said I, pursuing the matter no further.

Unsolicited offers of ridiculous sums of cash were always catchpenny schemes and the trickery of coiners, and I had more pressing affairs to which to attend just then, specifically my appearance at the show trial of the ship's survivors. The press were already baying for Culhane's blood, and since my involvement in the Newgate and Bible scandals ten years or so before that level of public outrage had always particularly unnerved me. Like shit, vitriol, and smallpox, it was best to never get any on you.

The court was not open to civilian observers, be they wives or journalists, but Grace walked me to the harbour anyway. The gates of the great naval base were already heaving with reporters, who swarmed about us demanding names and details.

'If you don't know this man,' bellowed a deep Northern baritone from the rear of the crowd, 'then you've none of you any business calling yourselves newspapermen.'

We all turned to identify the source of these comments. They originated from a large, ruddy, and bullet headed man in possession of oddly Napoleonic features beneath short, receding curls which might once have been ginger. He was dressed in a storm coat and topper, and in his mid-sixties at a guess. Although he looked like a coachman, he exuded natural authority.

'He looks loosely familiar,' I said to Grace.

'He certainly does,' she said. 'He was the fellow who offered me all that money.'

The man approached us, shoving the quill drivers out of the way as if they were leprous beggars. 'Jack,' he said warmly, doffing his hat and offering his hand. 'It's been a dog's age.'

'Thirty-odd years,' I agreed, the scales having fallen from my eyes. I did not accept his hand.

'But I've watched your progress with considerable interest,' he replied, beaming at Grace with small, animal teeth as he spoke. 'He was but a boy the last time we met,' he told her, in the manner of an enthusiastic relative returned from a long sojourn abroad.

'I was fourteen to be precise, Mr. O'Neil,' I said flatly, 'the year you sent me to prison.'

He waved his arms dismissively, as if I had accused him of some trifling childhood slight. 'For shame, Jack,' he said, 'I did nothing of the sort. The matter was between my employer and your father, and you and I were merely unfortunate intermediaries. But look what you've achieved, man! I'd venture to say that that stint inside was the very making of you.' I began to formulate an outraged reply, but I could not get a word past the man. 'And you could achieve even more,' he was saying, 'if you'd just hear me out.'

I had distantly wondered what had happened to O'Neil when Grimstone had once more thrust his life before my face, but I had not bothered to enquire. I had assumed that he had long since been left behind, hopefully with a knife in his back or some sort of terminal illness. There were already more than enough past demons made flesh on that accursed boat without evoking his name as well. Clearly he was still attached to the corporation, and I thus required no visionary powers to predict the substance of his present purpose. He was set on telling me anyway though, and insisted we all adjoin to his unmarked coach for some privacy.

The journalists surged around us, but seemed not to know who O'Neil was, any more than they did us. 'I prefer to keep a low profile these days,' he explained.

'Cut to Hecuba,' said I, as we used to say in the theatre. 'I'm due on the *Victory* in ten minutes.'

'You're a man after my own heart,' he said. 'Time wasters need not apply, 'ay?'

I shuddered at the thought of any notional similarity between us. 'Something like that,' I said.

He made his pitch without further chatter. 'I represent certain interests,' he began, 'who would prefer certain aspects of their part in the recent tragedy to be, shall we say, kept out of the limelight.'

'I thought you might,' I said.

'And these certain interests,' he continued, 'would be prepared to pay handsomely in order to facilitate this preference.'

'I read the 'papers,' I said. 'It seems to me that your lord and master has come off rather well in the court of public opinion already.'

O'Neil dropped the mask of amiability for an instant, and regarded me with obvious hostility. 'You misunderstand, Jack,' he said. 'He is not the master of me. The gentleman in question is more of a figurehead, a non-executive director.' Then the performance resumed, with me still stuck in the cheap seats. 'You're a hero now, Jack,' he said, 'no one wants to take that away from you. All we ask is that you tell your tale in such a way that the reputation of the gentleman whom I represent remains intact.'

'What about the other witnesses?'

'They are being attended to,' he said ominously, 'besides which, who cares for the opinions of servants and the wives of common soldiers? You can spin the story right, Jack, that's what you do.'

'What are you offering?'

'Five thousand, as I told your good lady wife,' he said. 'That's more than generous.'

'Would you go to ten?'

'I might be persuaded.'

'I'll think on it,' I said, opening the cab door.

O'Neil placed a light but restraining hand on my arm. 'Don't think on it too long,' he said.

Beyond the hungry pack of Grub Street's finest, the gates were now opening. I saw my chance, and concluded the interview, taking Grace's arm and dragging her through the gate, calling to the bemused marine guards that we were both *Birkenhead* witnesses.

'What are we going to do, Jack?' said Grace, when we finally came to a halt somewhere quiet.

'God knows,' I said.

'You know,' she said, 'ten thousand pounds could set us up for life.'

'For what they're asking it'd be cheap at the price,' I said sadly. 'I value my soul a deal higher than a lousy ten grand, and that's if they're playing us straight, which is highly unlikely.'

'Mr. O'Neil seemed quite genuine, and anyway, my love, you're an atheist, you don't have a soul,' she temperately replied.

'My self-respect then,' I said, a little irritably. 'Besides which, I've seen these men deploy the charm before. It's as insidious as a child's imaginary friend that turns out to be the devil. The only reason they're trying to buy my silence is that when the story breaks I'll be too high-profile to knock off quietly. Grimstone tried to have me killed once before, and when that failed he ruined me as completely as he had done my parents. I had something on him then, too, remember?'

'That's true,' she conceded. She knew the story well enough. She took my hands in hers and looked at me with so much love in her eyes that it was difficult to hold her gaze, like observing the sun through a telescope. 'I will support whatever you choose to do, my love,' she said.

And she always did. 'Thank you,' I said, kissing her lightly on the lips.

'Now what are we going to do, Jack?'

'God knows,' I said.

CHAPTER XLIX

I HAD TO leave Grace with the marines at the gate. I explained that she was being hounded by journalists, and they agreed to hide her in the guard room and then conduct her to an alternative exit. I knew she could hold her own with leathernecks, hacks, and sinister men of business, but it was still with a deal of reluctance on both sides that we parted, agreeing to meet back at the boarding house later.

When I found it, the *Victory* had the same air as the Tower of London before the recent restorations started, that of a national treasure inexplicably neglected. That was always the trouble with Victoria's new order; no real sense of history, despite all the pomp, and absolutely no style. I have since read accounts of the *Birkenhead* court martial that assume its cultural significance based on the location, but the reality at the time was that although the Admiralty had stopped short of scrapping Nelson's flagship, it was no more than a tatty depot ship, and a cheap and convenient space in which to conduct the proceedings. I nonetheless paid my silent respects to the ghosts of Ushant, Capes Spartel and St. Vincent, and, of course, Trafalgar when I came aboard, now having some modest idea of what they must have been through.

I was conducted without much ceremony to an uncomfortable chair at the back of the improvised courtroom in the great cabin on the upper gun deck, which the likes of Keppel, Cromwell, and Nelson had once called home. I was informed by a clerk that I was unlikely to be called in this session, but that I was free to observe as long as I agreed to divulge nothing of what I saw and heard to the outside world for the duration of the trial. I was the only journalist present, and I found myself part of a relatively small and seemingly quite privileged audience, mostly comprised of nervous looking *Birkenhead* veterans, all male.

The Court convened shortly after I arrived, Rear-Admiral Henry

Prescott presiding, attended by two retired naval officers and nine active, including Martin, the present Captain of the *Victory*. Sir George Greetham, the Deputy Judge Advocate of the Fleet, was there to minute and to advise on Navy Regulations, and it was he who explained the substance of the proceedings to those of us there present.

'As there are no surviving senior officers who can answer charges concerning the actual loss of the ship,' said Greetham, in a resonant but local accent, 'the Court can only hear evidence concerning the behaviour of survivors, and to seek to determine the cause of the disaster.'

Effectively, this was to be a court of inquiry. The hearing, he continued, was to be conducted in three separate parts: the first would examine the crew of Richards' cutter; the next would combine an examination of Lewis' crew with those on the gig commandeered by Culhane; and the final session would deal with the events on my boat, designated 'Boat Number Four.' Various apologies for absence were then read out, including one from the Right Honourable John Grimstone M.P., who cited nervous exhaustion as a result of the wreck and grief at the loss of his dear wife.

Richards and his crew were led in as prisoners. Nine survivors from the other boats appeared in turn as witnesses, largely setting the scene leading up to the wreck and subsequent evacuation. Among the notable witnesses that day were Seaman Tom Cuffin, who was at the helm when the ship struck, and Drake, Lewis, Renwick, and Culhane. No army or civilian survivors from Richards' cutter were called, and I saw none in the Court. In every case the examination was much the same. Each witness was placed under oath and then asked his name, rank and duties. After this, each had to state his whereabouts on the ship prior to the impact, and then to give his own account of the loss of the ship as he had perceived and experienced it. Each witness was then questioned in detail by the Court, with prisoners also allowed to stick an oar in if so desired. Finally, the prisoners were sworn in and similarly interrogated.

These examinations were made public soon after the trial and I see no reason to reproduce them here.[41] It was established that the ship's chronometers were accurate, but that the ship had not been swung at Portsmouth, Cork or the Cape to ascertain the deviation of the compass. It was further suggested that Salmond had hugged the coast too closely, and that his decision to give the back turn when already aground had been disastrous. By lunchtime, it was apparent that the late Captain was going to carry the can for not sailing defensively enough in treacherous waters. Richards, by comparison, had exercised much more reasonable caution in assessing the surf running on the shore to be too dangerous to attempt a landing. All the witnesses were of the opinion that this had been the correct judgement, and that he and his crew had done everything in their power to save as many as possible from the wreck.

The key question that morning, and asked of every witness, was: 'Do you know of any cause of complaint against Mr. Richards, or the seamen now on trial, in regard to the loss of the ship?'

In each case the witness replied without hesitation that he did not, and by six o'clock Richards and his crew had all effectively been acquitted.

The *Victory* must have been leaking from the top, because there was a full account of the first day's proceedings in several local and national newspapers the next morning, including my own. I had kept completely silent on the doings of the Court, but the anonymous piece in the *Chronicle* caused me considerable embarrassment. I received a dressing down, thankfully in private, from the Deputy Judge Advocate, because I have one of those guilty faces. I had been avoiding O'Neil's lurking coach, and had done nought but go straight back to a deplorable dinner at the boarding house and an early night with my wife. I was on my own now though, Grace having left for London on an early train in order to attend to Joseph.

When Doctor Culhane took the stand in defence of Richards, it had been apparent that he was positively bursting to offer an account of his own actions and the reasons thereof. He was given no opportunity to do so until the second day, when he and the remaining survivors of the ship's crew were examined. It was a large group, but it was clear that Culhane was the principal defendant, albeit unofficially. Other than the surgeon, the only interesting prisoners were John Lewis, who had commanded the second cutter, Renwick, the engineer, and John Archibald, the gunner, who had been responsible for firing off the distress rockets I had seen when Clara and I had been saved by Seaman Bewhill.

Renwick gave a harrowing account of the final moments in the engine room. He described the terrible sound of tearing iron after the Captain ordered the back turn, and how all the engineers and stokers watched in silent horror as the starboard bilge plates tore like newspaper and the sea exploded inward, killing all but Renwick and the other assistant engineer, Ben Barber, who somehow managed to fight their way to the ladder.

'What do you believe would have been the case, had the back turn not been made?' Renwick was asked.

'I believe that the framework of the vessel would have remained intact for some time,' he replied, 'sufficiently so to have got the paddle-box boats out clear.'

Archibald, the gunner (third class), was a shy and unassuming young man, and he gave a faltering account of his actions that night, seemingly unaware of his own gallantry. He had fired one of the ship's only guns ceaselessly in the hope of attracting attention from the shore, and when he ran out of ammunition he tried for the magazine, by that point underwater. Undeterred, he remembered some blue lights and rockets stored near the Captain's cabin. He had retrieved these and climbed onto the port paddle-box to fire them all off, before joining Brodie's team in trying to release the boat. Archibald was washed overboard with Brodie when the ship's bow broke, and he had fought to save the badly wounded Master by hanging on to him with one arm while clinging to some floating wreckage with the other. He struggled to remain composed as he described Brodie dying as he held him. I would have given him a medal and a pension personally, not put him on trial. By the sound of it, Archibald spent more time alone among the sharks than any of us. He got in on a piece of wreckage with Barber, and Wilson, the Boatswain's Mate.

Lewis followed, and he described lightening his boat by jettisoning everything not required to keep it afloat and moving in order to get as many survivors out of the water as possible. He confirmed Richards' account of the lack of a safe landing point, saying that it was impossible to land by night or day. He also established a clear chronology for the events leading up to Culhane's gig giving up the chase for the *Lioness* and making for land, and the schooner's subsequent change of tack and fortuitous sighting of the two cutters. He told the shocked courtroom the tragic tale of Ensign Russell, and concluded by stating his belief that all in charge of the boats had taken the best means of saving the greatest number of lives.

Finally, Culhane was examined. He began with a lengthy statement describing the wreck and the events on the poop in much more detail than the other witnesses, and thereby giving a clear account of Salmond's actions (*sans* his suicide, as we had all agreed), and the bravery of Seton and his men. He then explained how he had gone into the water with the rest and how he had swum about half a mile to Lewis' boat.

It was clear from the questioning, which was at times quite hostile, that Culhane had actually been acting in a triumvirate with Richards and Lewis up until the point that they could no longer physically communicate because of the distances involved.

'Did Mr. Richards give the order that you should pull for the shore in the event that you did not catch up to the ship?' asked Martin of the *Victory*.

'He did not,' conceded the doctor. 'But we had all agreed,' he hastily continued, 'upon initially joining up about half a mile from the wreck, that we could do no good but much harm by returning before we had landed those already in the boats. As this proved impossible, as the other witnesses have already confirmed, the only hope was to try for a landing further along the coast, and to raise the alarm in that way. When we saw a ship in the distance, it was agreed that the best hope for all on the boats, and any survivors at the wreck, was for my party to make for it at all speed.'

'Was there perfect unanimity in the gig among the officers and men as to the mode of proceeding?' asked Martin.

'Very much so,' said Culhane.

'So the operation was a complete success,' said Martin.

'I would say so, yes,' replied Culhane.

'Only the patient died.'

'I beg your pardon?' said Culhane, his face reddening.

'No further questions,' said Martin.

Subsequent witnesses who had made their own way to the shore were all pointedly asked, 'Did you think that the ship was abandoned by the boats while they might have rendered any assistance?' No one affirmed this position, but not all of them denied it either. Several answered neutrally, along the lines that they could not say having not seen any boats. Nevertheless, all who were asked if they had any misconduct to allege against any of the prisoners answered in the negative, and once again all those who stood accused were exonerated, including Culhane. So despite the feelings of several members of the military (all of whom were still in Africa so unable to express an opinion in person), no one had thus far been hung out to dry, at least by the Royal Navy.

Being in much need of fresh air and exercise after two days in court, I took a chance and decided to walk back to my lodgings. I got about halfway before O'Neil's coach glided alongside me and the window slid down.

'Have you had time to make a decision yet, Jack?' said Grimstone's man, still sporting the false face of artificial amiability.

'I'm still thinking on it,' I replied.

'Would fifteen thousand accelerate your mental processes at all?' said he.

'It might,' I agreed.

'Then I will expect you to do the right thing on the morrow,' he said, as if the deal was done, before tapping the roof of the coach with his cane and clattering away.

I waited and watched until he was out of sight, swearing quietly, then strode off in the opposite direction.

I needed Grace, and passed a tense and fitful night without her, arriving at the *Victory* the next morning ill-prepared for what must follow. Fortunately, I was granted a reprieve in the form of a very long lecture on the swinging of the ship by one William Madge, Master of the *Victory*, and not a man gifted at coming to the point. There had already been so much conjecture regarding the recklessness of Salmond's course that an expert witness was really just there to blot the skrip, which he did, at considerable length, concluding that had there been the slightest swell or current that night (which there was), he would not have taken that course.

'A prudent captain,' he suggested, 'would have taken his vessel sixty or so miles out to sea before retiring, then changing course eastward at first light and steaming parallel to, but still well off, the coast. Why this was not the case though, I cannot say, for the compasses would have had to be out by as much as forty-five degrees for such a blatant mistake to occur accidently, and they had by all accounts been functioning perfectly well when the ship steamed into Simon's Bay two days before.'

His final analysis was human error.

This left just half a day to me, but after lunch it was not I who was sworn in but a surprise witness. John Grimstone M.P. was, it would seem, greatly recovered and raring to testify. As I looked at him standing there my arms and legs went numb. He caught my eye and smiled that rodent grin of his; presumably comfortable in our mutual perjury, and keen to demonstrate to anyone observing the bond between us that can only have come of true adversity shared and survived. I resisted the animal desire to run screaming from the court, and dejectedly took my seat.

CHAPTER L

BEING A POLITICIAN, and therefore deeply enamoured with the sound of his own voice, Grimstone spoke even more than Culhane and Madge combined, monopolising the Court for much of the afternoon session. It was a very fine story. In his opening statement he spoke, at length, of his struggle to save his trapped and injured wife, before finally admitting defeat and wading through rising waters to get help. He made no mention of the maid, Clara, as he described rallying several marines about him (all now conveniently deceased), only to discover upon his return that the cabin decks were now flooded.

'I was too late,' he said, with a catch in his voice that could not but fail to move all there assembled.

He also described his tireless efforts to aid at the pumps, and then on freeing the boats, before finally joining Seton and his men at the call of the drums and standing fast as the ship went down. As he had been nowhere near the ship by that point, and had never gotten so much as a foot wet, it was a pretty fair account, laced together as it was from the reports of real eyewitness, myself principal among them. The Court was then treated to his various heroics in saving drowning soldiers, including the injured Lieutenant Granger, before finally being picked up by Hare's boat, snatched from the very jaws of a mighty killer shark. I then received a cursory mention, although I took no real part in Grimstone's version of events, and was relegated to an unspeaking role alongside the women and children. The navy boys died much as they had in real life, but the ladies and myself were delivered by Grimstone's resolve and natural seamanship. He stopped short of claiming my kill, suggesting instead, in a somewhat muddled account, that we had all driven the shark away by shouting and punching. After we were spared, he said, by the grace of God and a couple of good right hooks, he had spied the *Rhadamanthus* on the horizon and attracted her attention by waving his shirt. He concluded that his faith had kept him strong, and he thanked the Almighty for allowing him to save the children.

A murmur of approval rippled around the room, except in my environs. As a civilian, I had no right to ask a question, and in following this stirring recitation I was going to sound like the plagiarist if I actually spoke the truth. I was beginning to wish that I had just taken the money and run. There was no sign of another survivor from Hare's boat to contradict Grimstone and corroborate my story, should I dare to tell it, and without another credible gainsayer to back me up he would again assume the laurels of others and use the publicity to further his political ambitious. As the 'Hero of the *Birkenhead*,' a term that some 'papers were already applying, for military disasters always require heroes, I could see this scabrous rat in Downing Street by the end of the year.

Grimstone fielded a few questions from the Court easily, mostly minor details, politely enquired, before Nathaniel Claverly, the retired Captain of the *Indefatigable*, took the lead. Until that moment, my private impression of Claverly had been fairly irreverent. He was an old man, bald, with shrewd eyes, no teeth, and a short, white beard. He also had several bits missing, and with his wooden leg and hook for a hand, the overall impression was that of an elderly cat curled around a hat stand.

'I know a thing or two about sharks,' said he, cupping his hook in his good left hand for dramatic effect. 'They do not normally quit after they've attached themselves to an open boat.'

'As I said, we drove it away,' replied Grimstone coolly.

'Could you be a little more precise?' said Claverly.

'Yes, please do,' said Prescott. 'The navy is always very keen to learn how sharks might be repelled. Such intelligence may well save lives in the future.'

For the first time that afternoon Grimstone looked a little flustered. 'Well,' he said, 'we hit it with an oar.'

'I thought the oars had already been lost,' said Claverly.

'We must have beaten it with our bare hands then.'

'How?' said Claverly. 'Did you lean over the gunwales?'

'Its head was in the boat,' said Grimstone defensively.

'Then you're very lucky to be alive,' said Claverly. 'Did the ladies thump the animal as well?'

There were a few chuckles about the courtroom.

'Yes,' said Grimstone. 'I mean no. They just shouted, I think, I kept them back.'

'That was very brave,' said Claverly. 'So, you're belting this shark. Where did you hit it, exactly?'

'On the nose,' said Grimstone.

'And did Mr. Vincent join in?'

Good question, I thought.

'I can't remember,' said Grimstone. 'Probably.' He appealed to the rest of the Court with a winsome smile. 'It all happened very quickly,' he said apologetically, 'the heat of battle and all that.'

Claverly then sought me out with mischievous eyes, and promptly broke all the rules that the Deputy Judge Advocate had explained on the first day by addressing me directly. 'Mr. Vincent,' he cried, 'can you shed any light?'

Quick as a flash, before anyone had a chance to shut me up, I replied, 'I jumped on its head, sir, and then I shot it until it died.'

'Good man!' roared Claverly. 'I knew it didn't just bugger off!'

Grimstone reacted as if he had just swallowed a stinging insect whilst bestride a velocipede and had to be given water. Prescott leaned over to Claverly and began to whisper frantically, presumably pointing out that I had not been sworn in. But in the game we were playing, Grimstone and I, points of order and legal precedents were really of no account. As they used to say in the Prize Ring, I had just got a good one in.

It was almost six by now, and Prescott had no choice but to adjourn. He apologised for the breech of protocol, and ordered the Court to disregard my statement. 'If there are no further questions for Mr. Grimstone,' he said wearily, 'the Court will examine Mr. Vincent correctly in the morning.'

I had no desire to hang around, and I flew out of the courtroom as soon as the gavel was banged. I made for the gangplank at full speed, with the intention of losing myself in some random inn in Gosport in order that I might avoid any threats or entreaties from

O'Neil, who was doubtless lurking somewhere close. I moved with stealth and haste, and hid myself among mariners in a charming seafront barrel house until the small hours. After that, I found a thre'penny back slum full of rum gaggers, dingy Christians, and whores resting between clients and large gins. I fit right in, and passed the remainder of the night in their company.

I turned up at the base the next morning smelling so foul that the marines had to let me wash in the guardroom. Although it was very early in the misty morning, the main gate was already filthy with journalists, all of them after an exclusive statement.

'Who killed the shark, Jack?' called one.

'Where'd you get the gun?' cried another.

'Did Grimstone stand?' said a third I recognised from the radical press.

Aided by the marines, I fought my way through the hacking hoards, explaining repeatedly that I had no comment to make at this time.

When I was safely on the other side of the gate, hosed down and drinking cocoa in the guardroom, the marines showed me some early editions. By questioning the veracity of such a well-known witness, I discovered I had furnished the press with a good many headlines of the most startling character. The substance of the coverage was that the court martial was now not so much about the fate of the ship, which had largely already been decided, but between Grimstone and myself. There was a lot of money changing hands on who had really bested the shark, the marines told me, but I was not the favourite.

I was still drunk from the night before, so possessed of more bravado than any sane and sober man in my position should have been. 'Bet heavily on me, my lads,' I advised, 'and never tell me the odds.'

'And why should we do that?' said a leatherneck corporal.

I fudged around in my pockets until I found the shark's tooth. 'Because I am telling the truth,' said I, holding the nasty thing up between my thumb and forefinger.

They all cheered and pronounced me a trump and a fine fellow when I left.

I felt considerably less cocksure when I arrived at the courtroom. Grimstone was now accompanied by O'Neil, and a well-dressed companion who had London lawyer written all over him. I had no one in my corner, and I was acutely aware that I was the social inferior and the rank outsider. All the same, I had made up my mind to tell my side of the story, and O'Neil could shove his money up Grimstone's bony arse.

I declined to make a long statement, but gave a reasonable summary of the events I have already related in these pages: of saving Granger, and failing to save Mina, Moran and Metford; my rescue, in turn, by Granger, his subsequent demise, and our relentless pursuit by the shark. I described how I killed it, although not how or why I used Grimstone as bait. All in all, he came out better than he deserved, but he no longer looked the hero of the tale.

Granville Loch of the *Winchester* led the questioning. He was a young, ambitious officer, clearly out to make a name for himself. I just hoped he was willing to do it at Grimstone's expense and not mine. He was, as the official transcript of his opening questions (a copy of which I still possess) clearly demonstrates—

Captain Loch: You say you tried to help Mrs. Grimstone?
Mr. Vincent: Yes.
Captain Loch: Was Mr. Grimstone in evidence?
Mr. Vincent: He was not.
Captain Loch: Do you think he had gone to get help?
Mr. Vincent: No.
Captain Loch: Why?
Mr. Vincent: Because his wife told me he had left her.
Captain Loch: Is it possible that he returned with help after you had left?
Mr. Vincent: No.
Captain Loch: You seem very sure.
Mr. Vincent: Mr. Grimstone was on the first boat to get away. Major Seton told me he had put Lieutenant Granger on that boat because he was injured. It was got off while I was still below. Mr. Richards' cutter was still boarding when I came up on deck.

Captain Loch: How do you know that?
Mr. Vincent: Because I was the last man to board it.
Captain Loch: Then how was it that you subsequently went into the water?
Mr. Vincent: I gave up my seat.
Gasps of surprise are heard around the courtroom. Captain Loch looks taken aback, and the Rt. Hon. Mr. Grimstone M.P. appears startled.
Captain Loch: Why would you do that?'
Mr. Vincent: Because Cornet Bond discovered a couple of children still on the ship. The lifeboat was already overloaded. Someone had to get out in order to save them.
Captain Loch: Were you asked or ordered to give up your place?
Mr. Vincent: I did so voluntarily. Mr. Richards can confirm this.
Captain Claverly: Good show!
Rear-Admiral Prescott waves him silent, but there are definite murmurs of agreement from the floor.
Captain Loch: *Clears throat.* I see. Then did you see Mr. Grimstone on deck at all?
Mr. Vincent: I did not.
Captain Loch: But he could have helped at the pumps, or on the boats, as he said, while you were below?
Mr. Vincent: I don't think so.
Captain Loch: Why?
Mr. Vincent: Because he said that he went for help first, but that it was too late. He never came back to the cabins.
Captain Loch: How do you know that?
Mr. Vincent: Because I was with Mina, I mean Mrs. Grimstone, when she died. Her maid and I were the last people from those cabins up on deck before the hatches were sealed.
Captain Chads of the Excellent *enters the examination.*
Captain Chads: Perhaps Mr. Grimstone's memory of events is cloudy. Is it possible he is simply mistaken in his chronology?
Mr. Vincent: That is possible, but I doubt he was on the pumps.
Captain Chads: Why is that?
Mr. Vincent appears to be deep in thought, and is silent for several

seconds.

Mr. Vincent: Because when I met him in the lifeboat he was wearing a dress. That would be bound to have got in the way.

'Shame!' is whispered around the courtroom.

Mr. Lastly, Mr. Grimstone's lawyer, springs to his feet.

Mr. Lastly: Objection!

Rear-Admiral Prescott: This isn't the Old Bailey, sir. Please be silent.

Mr. Lastly pales, and silently sits back down.

Needless to say, the final point was the beautiful irony of this entire exchange. We were both civilian witnesses at a naval enquiry, and therefore under no legal duress whatsoever. But outside, Grimstone was facing a more deadly assize: a trial by the newspapers—just as I once had, at his instigation. From his countenance, Grimstone was painfully aware of his situation, for he appeared suddenly seasick, despite the calmness of our moorings.

Loch followed my lead. 'Did you see Mr. Grimstone stand with Major Seton and his men?' he asked me.

'No,' I said.

'Did he kill the shark that attacked your boat?'

'No.'

'Who did?'

'I did.'

'And how exactly did you go about doing that?'

'As I said yesterday,' I said, 'I shot it in the head repeatedly.'

'Are you in the habit of carrying guns, Mr. Vincent?' asked Chads.

'It belonged to Mr. Grimstone,' I replied.

'So Mr. Grimstone helped you kill the shark?' said Chads.

'No,' I said, and left it at that.

'Can you prove any of this?' said Chads sceptically.

In response, I placed my right foot on my chair and raised my trouser leg like a Mason (which no doubt helped my case as well), revealing the livid scarring, lost tissue, and the marks of hundreds of stitches below my knee. 'This happened when the shark got me,' I told him, and as it had worked so well with the marines, I once more produced the ugly incisor, holding it aloft like Excalibur in the form of a penknife. 'And then I got the shark,' I added, with a perfect sense of dramatic timing, if I do say so myself. 'When our boat was examined,' I further explained, 'this tooth was found stuck in the transom. It was passed on to me as a trophy.'

'Well done, lad!' cried Claverly, and the whole courtroom erupted around me, with men on their feet clapping and whistling. Prescott ineffectually called for order, until he finally threw in the towel and adjourned for lunch.

Claverly wobbled over to me and started talking enthusiastically about the time a shark took his hand when he was wrecked off the Azores. He then tapped his artificial leg with his hook. 'This was shot off on this very vessel,' he said, and then he was off— These were grand stories, and their telling saved me from my enemies. I stuck close and listened attentively, and let the old captain slowly guide me out of the courtroom and onto the quarterdeck, where we shared a cigar and a tot of rum from a flask concealed in the base of his hook, which is not the sort of thing you see every day.

This pleasant reverie was not a long one, and O'Neil was on my tail soon enough. Directly Claverly wandered away he came over, all smiles as ever. 'Your cheap theatrics won't fool anyone,' he said sweetly, no doubt looking to any that observed as if he was complementing me on my choice of necktie that morning.

'I thought it went down rather well,' I replied.

'You know it's just your word against ours,' he continued. 'The story of a respected businessman and Member of Parliament against that of an embittered hack: a liar, a failure and a drunk, with an axe to grind against an honest public servant. That's what they'll say, you know.'

'Thank you for summing that up so succinctly,' I said.

'You're no hero, Jack,' said O'Neil. 'You know it and I know it. You'll be easy enough to rebut in the afternoon session, after which we'll sue you till you have nought left to give but the skin off your back, and then we'll sue you for that as well.'

He was absolutely right, blast his eyes. I had very little defence against what was coming, and no real resources with which to fight. But back in that courtroom it had felt so satisfying to drop Grimstone right in it, just for once, just for a while. With any luck, word had already reached the reporters at the main gate, in which case I would make the afternoon editions. I consoled myself with the thought that although most people never have to worry about public opinion, politicians care about little else.

'I think we might start with that mortgage of yours,' he said, before leaving me to reflect upon the error of my ways.

'The funny thing about facing death,' I called after him defiantly, 'is that you care much less about money afterwards. If your guv'nor wasn't such a coward, he'd have known that.'

That was far from true in practice, at least in my case, but you have to admit that it sounded good. Words, as ever, were all I had. They had certainly carried though, for everyone around us had stopped talking and was staring at me.

'Humbug!' said O'Neil, breaking the silence and stomping off in the direction of the courtroom.

Grimstone had recovered in the recess and was holding his nerve. He would not have been as successful as he had been for so long if he could not, and when the Court reconvened he caught my eye and swiftly drew his finger across his throat like a knife.

That's the thing with melodramatic villains, I thought, they're so predictable. I gave him a cheery wave and took my seat. When your ship is in flames, it is best to ram something big.

Prescott entered last and we all stood. He looked troubled as he addressed the Court. 'In order to resolve the most distressing dissonance regarding accounts of the behaviour of certain parties on the lifeboat designated "Number Four",' he began, 'the Deputy Judge Advocate and myself have decided to accept the testimony of some additional witnesses recently made known to us.'

I could see Grimstone's lawyer was dying to object, but, as had already been demonstrated, in a court martial he was well out of his depth. He turned the most pleasing shade of puce though, and started to scribble down notes furiously. I felt like joining him in this reassuring act, for I had no more idea of what to expect than did he, and when the first new witness was called, no idea what I would hear either.

It was Clara, looking nervous and wane. If O'Neil had paid her off, I was as good as dead. I tried to catch her eye in order to shame her into giving an accurate account, but I need not have been concerned. Her testimony was short, not particularly articulate, but utterly damning as far as Grimstone was concerned.

She wept as she essentially corroborated everything I had said. 'I owe Mr. Vincent my life,' she concluded, 'and if the master had only got help as soon as he ran off, I'm sure the mistress would be here today as well.'

No one bothered to ask any questions.

As a mere servant, Clara alone could have been undermined, but she was then followed by Mrs. MacGlashan, dressed in black and thinner than I remembered. Again my story was confirmed. She even went as far as to explain that she had been offered money to keep silent.

'Some people,' she said, glaring at Grimstone with the wrath of the Eve Titan herself, 'cannot be bought.'

'Hear! Hear!' someone muttered behind me.

One of her twin daughters was sworn in next. It would seem that the girl had heard everything Grimstone had said at the end, even though she did not fully comprehend its meaning. In a line that was afterwards quoted in every 'paper in London, she summed up her statement by saying, 'The nasty man wanted to hurt us, but the nice man wouldn't let him.'

At that point I looked over to Grimstone, and enjoyed drawing my finger across my throat in return.

And thus the evidence concerning the lifeboat designated 'Number Four' was emphatically concluded in my favour. Whatever Grimstone might do to me, I had killed his career in that courtroom as surely as the bastard had killed my parents and damn near destroyed me. I just hoped my wife would understand when my fine principles got us turned out on the street.

I need not have worried on the latter account. I soon discovered that it was Grace who had found Clara in London and telegraphed Mrs. MacGlashan in Argyle, convincing both to testify, while

Grove, still the family lawyer, had persuaded Prescott and Greetham to allow them to appear.

The Court was then cleared, and the officers retired for deliberation. I contrived to lose myself on the *Victory*, exploring the cockpit on the orlop deck where Nelson had breathed his last, a ball through his spine, poor bastard.

After an hour or so, a bell was rung to call us back to our seats, and the Judge Advocate read out the findings of the Court. 'From the unfortunate circumstances of the Master commanding, and the principle officers of the ship, having perished,' he began, 'the Court feel that it was in the highest degree difficult, and that it might be unjust to pass censure upon the deceased, whose motives for keeping so near the shore cannot be explained; but they must record their opinion that this fatal loss was owing to the course having been calculated to keep the land in close proximity. If such be the case, they still trusted that they were not precluded from speaking with praise of the departed, for the coolness displayed in the moment of extreme peril, and for the laudable anxiety shown for the safety of the women and children to the exclusion of all selfish consideration.'

So, as had always been on the cards, Salmond, and, to a certain degree, all of his senior officers were held to account, while at the same time at least partially redeemed for their professionalism, not to say heroism in many cases, after the ship struck. Given the monumental nature of the original blunder, this was as good as Salmond's ghost was likely to get.[42]

'In respect of the prisoners tried under the authority of this court martial,' Greetham continued, 'for the loss of the said ship *Birkenhead*, and for their conduct consequently thereto, the Court was of the opinion that no blame was imputable to them. But on the contrary, the Court saw reason to admire and applaud the steadiness shown by all in the most trying circumstances, and the conduct of those who were first on the boats, and who, to the best of their judgement, made every exertion for the rescue of that portion of the crew and passengers who remained upon the wreck; and did adjudge all surviving officers and crew tried under the authority of the above mentioned order to be fully acquitted.'

And that was that. Finally, I could go home. I hung around long enough to thank Clara and Mrs. MacGlashan, then allowed Grace and Grove to lead me out of the base. Grimstone and his party positively fled from the courtroom, and were no doubt pursued by a swarm of journalists, for the boys around the gate had thinned out considerably by the time we reached them. A few tried to get a line out of me, but I just told them that justice had been served and that they could read all about it in the *Chronicle.*

Reynolds was waiting in a coach outside the gate, through the window of which peered a cheeky little face. 'Come on, Daddy!' said Joseph, as if we had parted company no later than that morning, rather than four very long months ago.

*

Back in London, I first honoured my promise to Mina and visited her children. Her eldest son now resided at her first husband's house in Mayfair, and much to my discomfort we met in the library where I once courted his mother. Clara had insisted on returning the second ring, arguing that the gift was to me. I didn't want the bloody thing, so I gave it to the son along with my story. He listened with horror, and denounced his step-father as a scoundrel and a blackguard. When we parted, he shook my hand warmly.

'You are a good friend to this family,' he said.

I had returned to the capital something like a hero. My moral slate was not, perhaps, polished to gleaming, but it had certainly been buffed up a bit as far as the gentlemen of the press were concerned, including the Tories, who knew that even their most aggressive propaganda could not save their man now.

It is well known that no party is more ruthless than the Conservatives when it comes to the sacrifice of senior figures, and Grimstone was forced into an immediate resignation of his seat on health grounds within days of the court martial. You will now find nary a mention of him in histories of the Earl of Derby's government, which came to power shortly thereafter, so utter was his removal from the annals of the party. His board of directors were of a similar mind, and he was swiftly deposed as the chairman of his own company in a boardroom coup orchestrated by O'Neil. That night he returned to his house in Belgrave Square, sunk a bottle of brandy, called for a bath, and then slit his throat with a straight razor. He left no message, save the dreadful hieroglyphics sprayed across the chamber in his own vital fluids. When asked about this on the record, I spoke of a deeply troubled man and sympathised with his family. In private I hoped he felt my hand on the blade as it did its work.

Ours was a diverting little subplot, and it certainly did my reputation no harm, but the press forgot us soon enough. The real story belonged to Seton and his men, who, by their collective action, had turned a senseless and easily averted catastrophe into something tragic and noble. It was thus in the interests of the Crown to focus upon them, rather than the reasons why. The army does not like disasters, any more than the navy, and it is something of a classic move in these situations for the parties concerned to invoke the rhetoric of Agincourt, of the iron courage of our island nation against overwhelming odds, what Mr. Carlyle has called 'a wrappage of traditions.' In such a narrative, Seton's soldiers easily became martyrs, who defended the nation's honour and the empire as surely on that deck as if they stood in battle or siege.

The politicians on both sides of the house were similarly keen to deflect attention away from their spectacularly fallen member, a base coward who left the ranks, and was careless enough to be caught out by a servant, a soldier's widow, and a penny-a-liner. Ironically, however, as a participant observer I was ideally placed to tell the tale. Doyle had honoured my contract in full, considering my eyewitness account of the wreck to be of considerably more value than the original brief. He also offered me a permanent job as a special correspondent travelling with the military, suggesting that the Eastern Question would likely demand a loud answer from the British Lion very soon. I was in no hurry to leave my family again though, so I graciously declined, citing the need for rest and recuperation and playing up my injuries for all they were worth. I never saw myself as a war correspondent, besides which Jesus Christ himself could not have persuaded me to set my good foot on a pleasure boat on the Thames, let alone another bloody troop carrier.

I also had some unfinished business in London that urgently acquired attention.

The army were wary enough of me, as a known radical, to send some shadowy, semi-official representations to Doyle urging my restraint. They need not have worried. I already knew the drill, and had been successfully writing within its ancient, unrecorded and utterly binding regulations since my piece on the Graveyard Rangers. More importantly, though, whatever I may have believed, or thought I knew, about soldiers, seaman and their officers when I began my journey, I was now resolved to do the men of the *Birkenhead* proud. This was not a commitment I made for the sake of the army, navy, or the government, or even for my own self-interest, but for Salmond, Seton, Granger, Metford, Moran, Bewhill, and the rest. I had admittedly discussed my options with Reynolds and Grace, but in my heart of hearts I had always known, ever since I saw the sails of the *Rhadamanthus* on the horizon and knew I would live, that what was going to endure about this story was the legend.

My account was therefore not as candid as this present narrative. But, having said that, there was not so much to abridge or conceal, even back then, aside from Salmond's suicide, Hare's breakdown (which had been downplayed by the court martial anyway, as he was not there to defend himself), and, obviously, my part in the robbery of the magazine. I did not disguise Mina's death in my reports either. This would have been pointless given my testimony at the court martial, but the official version quickly became that not one woman or child was lost. So, in the end, Mina was not as important to Society as she supposed.

The only other fact not widely reported at the time was that most of the soldiers on deck that night were in nightshirts and blankets, and many of those who successfully swam to shore did so bollock naked. I knew that clothes did not make a true warrior's death, but I had come to know and respect Seton, and he would have been appalled to have been remembered standing to attention in his shirtsleeves. I therefore dressed all officers and men in uniform, and those that survived never got round to contradicting me. As with the field day on Spike Island, I reported what I saw, just not all of it. It was simply a matter of basic *narratologie*.

So whether or not most of the officers were fops, snobs, glorified clerks, or insane, and their men often liars, thieves, drunks, and blackguards, I saw them all out in style, because, once in a while, for all our numerous faults as individuals, a nation, and a race, we do something selfless and wonderful. Whatever you may hear, one way or the other, and however the story may be spun, whatever interest may be served in its telling, not one Englishman, Irishman or Scotsman broke ranks that night. And even if I know not why, I know what I saw, and you cannot take that away from them. Perhaps they were all simply doing what we all do, and following someone, for those men loved Seton like a father at the end. Or maybe it was just stoic resignation; the majority of the common soldiers, especially the Irish, had lived lives so miserable that the only way to negotiate them was to endure. Many have argued since that it was a collective Christian act of Golgothan sacrifice. Others see it as proof of genuine human altruism. While, to old soldiers everywhere, it is a testament to military discipline, the unquestioning obedience of a soldier to his orders, whatever the consequences.

In all honesty, I do not presume to understand, and I doubt many of those involved did either. In a moment of extreme crisis, when there was no time for thought, just action, a decision was made and agreed that the men on board would give their lives for the women and children, rather than risk even the possibility of overloading and capsizing the lifeboats. I have no time for authority myself, I fear unquestioning cultural conformity, and I do not believe in God, but I went along with it with the rest. I have been asked why, many times since, and the best I have ever managed to reply is that it seemed the right thing to do.

I hope that the tone I struck in my reports at the time was respectful but not overly sentimental. I admit I imposed a plot on reality, as we so often do, and I worked upon it as if polishing a rough diamond. But I was also mindful to temper all that rousing gallantry with enough of the real for the readers to understand the tenacity, the practicality, and blind luck it took just to stay alive that night. That, too, is what it is to be a soldier.

I cannot deny that I did well by these articles, and more work quickly followed, as did invitations to dine with people from whom I had not heard in years, including Dickens and Thackeray. The latter was greatly inspired by the valour so casually exhibited on the *Birkenhead*, and he wrote about it several times, although he always downplayed my part in proceedings. I think he was a little jealous, for how can a man truly know anything about himself if he has never lived through his own death?

It was good to be working again, instead of scrabbling desperately around the periphery of serious publishing. We remained far from financially secure, though, despite my partially rehabilitated reputation. I often wondered if I should have just taken Grimstone's money and kept my head down and my mouth shut, especially when the mortgage payments were due. But I was one of those strange and damaged human beings (an author) who required approval from complete strangers over material wealth, so I was not so unhappy at the way the cards had fallen, and my wife knew me well enough to understand. O'Neil never made good his threat to ruin me; in fact, I think that once his share price recovered he came to realise that I had done him something of a favour. In any event, he left us alone. I locked Grimstone's gun away, hung the shark's tooth around my neck for luck, and went back to freelancing.

The story finally ended some months after my return, when two packages were delivered to me via the *Morning Chronicle*. One was from Lakeman's London tailor, who had been commissioned to replace the ranger uniforms lost on the *Birkenhead*, and was directed to send me one of the new leather storm coats. The second was postmarked Cape Town. It was quite small and inexplicably heavy, and my first thought was that Lakeman had sent me another souvenir. The package contained a wooden cigar box, inside which there were two carefully wrapped gold bars and an unsigned handwritten note that said, 'Make sure you don't throw these ones away.'

These could only have come from Moran, there was no other explanation. Somehow the old cross-cove had cheated his death that night, the same as I, and had managed to keep a tight hold on his loot into the bargain. On reflection, it all made perfect sense. In addition to acquiring the gold, Moran had to escape the army, and he had done so by counterfeiting his own death, with me his witness. While I was transfixed by the ship going down, he had quietly swum away, the crafty bastard. It really was quite brilliant.

'I've earned this,' I told Grace.

After some negotiation she looked the other way, and I realised almost three hundred pounds on the gold from an angling cove I knew in Saffron Hill. Along with my fee from Doyle, this was more than sufficient to clear our mortgage, with enough coin left over to fund a project that had lately become very dear to me.

As I recovered with my family, and reflected upon all those in my life that I had lost or left behind, there was one face that haunted me above all others. It was time to find my sister.

THE END OF THE FIRST VOLUME

APPENDIX
Finding Jack Vincent

As a child growing up in the 1970s, I possessed a passion for morbid nineteenth century popular literature. I had inherited this trait from my mother, a Catholic turned Spiritualist with a taste for gothic film and fiction. I was thus always dimly aware of the name 'Jack Vincent' through the cheap paperback anthologies of out-of-copyright horror stories which I sought out compulsively in second hand shops and jumble sales. These I demolished with a similar enthusiasm to *House of Hammer* magazines, and Saturday night double features on BBC 2 that twinned black-and-white expressionist melodramas from Universal and MGM with lurid, Technicolor horror from Amicus, Hammer, and American International.

Vincent was always a ghost back then though, more likely to be mentioned in passing than actually quoted in New English Library books on the Gothic such as *The Frankenstein Files* or *The Dracula Scrapbook* (both edited by Peter Haining), and completely absent from my *Pelican History of Victorian Literature.* There was, however, one short story by Vincent that re-occurred in several collections, either in the company of Regency tales of terror, mostly from *Blackwood's* and the *London Magazine*, or, occasionally, alongside better known literary authors such as Poe, Dickens, and Le Fanu. This story was 'The Shivering of the Timbers,' a surprisingly lively, imaginative and violent ghost story that seemed to me to anticipate popular but controversial twentieth century horror fiction, such as EC comics and the so-called 'video nasties' that were then in the process of being banned in Britain.

'The Shivering of the Timbers' really put the hook in me, and I searched in vain for anything else by this author. It was clear to me that this text was conceptually and structurally out of place with its contemporaries, while sophisticated enough to suggest that the author surely must have written more than this one story. What I realise now is that the old pulp anthologies tended to feed off one another, so if Herbert van Thal included it in a *Pan Book of Horror Stories* then it would be recycled in other miscellanies. The story appears, for example, in the *Daggers of the Mind* collection edited by August Derleth, Peter Haining's *Regency Tales of Horror and Romance*, Sarah Ravencroft's *Lost Tales of Terror*, and the *Everyman Book of English Ghost Stories.* It even turns up in Alfred Hitchcock's *Stories My Mother Told Me Not to Read.* I carried this story with me to university, where I read, unsurprisingly, nineteenth century literature. I subsequently even managed to get a paper out of it for the *Legacies of Walpole* conference at Strawberry Hill, but by then I had given up ever finding another tale by Jack Vincent. It is notable that even Google Books and Project Gutenberg remain bereft to this day.

This insubstantial shade acquired a more definite shape in the course of my doctoral research into the life and works of that other great lost Victorian novelist, William Harrison Ainsworth. I had discovered Ainsworth as a kid in much the same way as Vincent, through a magical find in an antiquarian bookshop, in this case an illustrated edition of *Rookwood.* While researching Ainsworth, I began to notice references to Vincent, especially in contemporary journalism around the period of the so-called 'Newgate Controversy,' a moral panic at the end of the 1830s concerning the supposedly pernicious effects of 'criminal romances' on young, working class male readers which dragged in Ainsworth (ruining his serious literary reputation), Edward Bulwer-Lytton, and even Dickens. Probably because of his Chartist affiliations, Vincent's novels were considered particularly dangerous, and so those that went on to dictate nineteenth century literary history, men like John Forster, R.H. Horne, and the formidable Charles Wentworth Dilke, appeared to have been especially diligent in eradicating all trace of Vincent from Victorian culture.

I came across him again when I read Ainsworth's unpublished letters, which were held in the Local Studies Unit of Manchester Central Library as part of the James Crossley Papers. Crossley, a Manchester solicitor, amateur historian and literary dilettante, was Ainsworth's closest friend, and he had retained a vast amount of private correspondence, including not just letters from Ainsworth that mention Vincent, but letters to and from Vincent himself. It is clear that he and Ainsworth were intimately acquainted, and that Ainsworth, unlike Dickens, had been prepared to retain the friendship, perhaps because he felt himself similarly ill-used by former friends in literary London. From these letters I was able to piece together some sort of publication history for Vincent, now forced to write under a series of aliases and pseudonyms because of his scandalised reputation. He therefore appears in my biography of Ainsworth, *The Life and Works of the Lancashire Novelist*, but still as something of a footnote.

I relocated to Japan a couple of years after my doctorate was conferred in 2000, spending three years as an associate-professor of English and American literature at the University of Fukui. I returned to the UK ten years ago, taking a post in literature and creative writing at my old *alma mater*, the University of East Anglia. It was during this period that I commenced a new research project with a view to a book on the jobbing writers of the early-to-mid-nineteenth century, the hack journalists and penny-a-liners who ground away at the wheel of fortune for years, earning just enough to survive, but never achieving the recognition of their literary contemporaries. But the business of life intervened, as it so often does, and the book remained unfinished for several years, during which time I married and had a child, and the needs of my new family led to a decision to leave academia in favour of publishing.

I nonetheless continued to tinker with my book, publishing extracts in journals and speaking at academic conferences, and I eventually secured an independent research grant which bought me the time I needed to once more focus on this project. It was during this period, just over three years ago, that I was fortunate enough to make the acquaintance of the eccentric and remarkable collector Horace Frome, a long retired rag-and-bone man who would nowadays be referred to as a 'hoarder.' Mr. Frome's small terraced house was packed from floor to ceiling in every room with stacks of late Georgian and Victorian periodicals, as well as an impressive amount of newspapers and books from those periods, old and worn and yellow, much like Mr. Frome. This collection was begun from clearance auctions during the Blitz, and continued to expand throughout Mr. Frome's professional life and into his retirement. His dream had been to write a comprehensive history of Industrial Britain, and he believed these papers to be essential primary source material. He continued to save daily editions of several contemporary tabloids and broadsheets, and was eventually killed when he was trapped under a collapsed pile of *Daily Mails*, dying of a combination of dehydration and suffocation. Not, as Jack Vincent would say, a good way to go.

I first met Mr. Frome at an auction of Victorian furniture and bric-a-brac at which we had both good-naturedly bid against each other for a tea chest full of *New Monthly Magazines*. Mr. Frome won the auction, but he seemed to want the ear and understanding of a fellow antiquarian, and he therefore invited me to view his treasured archives at home. His collection was not what I expected. The house was in a terrible state; the papers unsorted, and in varying states of preservation, from surprisingly well-kept to destroyed by damp, mould and vermin. Mr. Frome was obviously not in the best of health, and I urged him to let me assist in cataloguing this maze-like private library. As my field of research was different to his own he saw no harm in sharing this invaluable resource (as he still believed he would one day finish his great project), as long as I was willing to voluntarily aid him in its organisation. He also tapped me for a significant amount of my research grant for a fee. We laboured together for the last six months of his life, until his hoard finally killed him. I pleaded with the local authority to let me continue to work through the papers, but this wonderful, if rat infested private archive was deemed a fire and a health hazard, and carted away to the local incinerator.

Mr. Frome had no known family and died intestate, so I saved what I could around the council workmen, bribing them to look the other way while I filled my car with random books and periodicals as they filled their skips. In the final, frantic stages of this rescue, I came upon a battered suitcase underneath a mummified cat that contained a jigsaw of musty shoeboxes. Each of these, on inspection, held several hundred delicate pages of closely handwritten manuscript. Intrigued, I ditched my spare wheel, jammed the suitcase into the boot and made good my escape.

I like to imagine that I was destined to find this suitcase. Its contents, I soon discovered, were the letters, short stories, novels and, most astonishingly of all, the extended memoirs of Jack Vincent. Given their position in the paper strata, my guess is that they were purchased early on by Mr. Frome, probably during the war. It took quite a few weeks to arrange the boxes into some kind of order, as the memoirs, although in several volumes, were not dated or numbered, and I had to work out their chronological position based upon content and context. It soon became clear from contemporary cultural references that Vincent began writing his memoirs in parallel with his fiction in the middle part of the century, before continuing the process retrospectively in later life. Several of the manuscripts are dedicated 'To My Wife and Son,' and it is my belief that Vincent, who married a woman much younger than himself and became a father in middle age, wanted to explain himself as much as possible to his family (particularly the boy) in the event of his death quite early on in his child's life, especially given his relationship with his own father, as documented in the first volume of memoirs. The language is confessional, but also much less formal and restrained than would be expected in print during that period. Vincent had a serial writer's gift for narrative structure, however, and the memoirs do read very much like his novels, only in a style that sometimes anticipates the naturalism of the early-Modernists as much as it is more conventionally Victorian.

Once reasonably satisfied that I had located the first volume, I set about transcribing and editing, a process that has taken much of the last three years to complete around my other professional and family commitments. I am confident that this volume is the first, because it deals in detail with Vincent's own childhood, and, as previous stated in the Explanatory Note that prefaces the present edition, I am convinced of the veracity of these documents. I have now applied for further funding, and it is my intention to continue to bring Vincent's life and stories to the attention of the twenty-first century reading public, in the true spirit of the original penny-a-liners.

S.J.C.

NOTES

1 '2 bore' was the largest caliber shoulder rifle ever manufactured, and was used mostly by the British in Africa and India for hunting big game. The rifle was loaded with black powder, and was known for its discharge of thick smoke and excessive recoil. 'The recoil was so terrific,' wrote Sir Samuel White Baker of a similar weapon, 'that I spun around like a weathercock in a hurricane.'

2 The poet and critic Richard Hengist Horne (1802 – 1884) was then a sub-editor of Dickens' *Household Words*. He was the author of the influential collection of critical essays *A New Spirit of the Age* (1844), in which Dickens was praised at the expense of several of his popular rivals, including Jack and his old friend William Harrison Ainsworth. John Forster (1812 – 1876) was Dickens' best friend and later biographer. At this point in time he was the editor of the *Examiner*, in which he had frequently attacked Jack's writing as socially dangerous.

3 Scott's epic poem *Marmion; A Tale of Flodden Field* was published by Archibald Constable in 1808. Jack is referring to Canto II: XXXIII.

4 James Henry Leigh Hunt (1784 – 1859) was a radical English poet and journalist, and a close friend of Hazlitt, Keats, and Shelley. He was the editor of the *Examiner* between 1808 and 1817, the *Reflector* (1810 – 1811), and the *Indicator* (1819 – 1821). The character of Harold Skimpole in Dickens' *Bleak House* is rather uncharitably based upon him.

5 Alongside his rival Mrs. Ann Radcliffe, Matthew Gregory 'Monk' Lewis (1775 – 1818) was the most influential gothic writer of his age, best known for *The Monk: A Romance* (1796). William Beckford (1760 – 1844) was the author of the gothic novel *Vathek* (1786); Dr. Nathan Drake (1766 – 1836) wrote gothic tales in the journal *Literary Hours* from 1798 to 1804; and Francis Lathom (1777 – 1832) was a novelist and dramatist from Norwich whose gothic romance *The Midnight Bell* (1798) is cited by name in Jane Austen's satire of the form, *Northanger Abbey.* 'The Conclave of Corpses' (AKA 'The Monk of Horror') was an anonymous plagiarism of Lewis that appeared in the chapbook *Tales of the Crypt* in 1798. *The Midnight Groan; or The Spectre of the Chapel: Involving An Exposure of the Horrible Secrets of the Nocturnal Assembly* was another anonymous chapbook published by T & R Hughes in 1808. 'The Dance of the Dead' (c.1810), also unsigned, was equally inspired by Lewis, and taken from a Silesian folk tale not a million miles from the story of the Pied Piper of Hamlin. Scott's 'Narrative of a Fatal Event' appeared in *Blackwood's Edinburgh Magazine* III (12), (March 1818), under the signature of 'Tweedside.' 'Extracts from Gosschen's Diary' was written by John Wilson and published in *Blackwood's* III (17), (August 1818). Daniel Keyte Sandford's 'A Night in the Catacombs' appeared in *Blackwood's* IV (19), (October 1818). 'The Vampyre' was published in the April 1819 issue of the *New Monthly Magazine* as 'A Tale by Lord Byron,' but it was actually the work of his personal physician, John Polidori; and Hunt's 'A Tale for a Chimney Corner' appeared in the *Indicator* in 1819. I have not been able to identify 'The Early Grave,' but I suspect that Jack is thinking of John Galt's 'The Buried Alive,' in which case his memory is playing him false, as this story was not published in *Blackwood's* until October 1821.

6 John Gibson Lockhart (1794 – 1854) was a Scots advocate and writer, known in his early career at *Blackwood's* for his savage attacks of the so-called 'Cockney School of Poetry,' in which he included Leigh Hunt, William Hazlitt, Coleridge, and Keats. He is most remembered today for his seven volume biography of his father-in-law, Sir Walter Scott. 'Wet with the blood of the Cockneys' was how fellow writer William Maginn described Lockhart in *Blackwood's* X (9), (February 1821), in response to the duel in which the liberal editor and publisher John Scott was killed. Jack's summary of the duel and Jonathan Henry Christie's subsequent acquittal matches contemporary accounts.

7 The All Max was a 'Flash Ken' (or low drinking house) in East Smithfield, its name a mockery of the high citadel of the Regency social season, Almack's Assembly Rooms of St. James's.

8 Harriette Wilson *née* Dubouche (1786 – 1845) was a Regency courtesan whose scandalous memoirs appeared in 1825. Harriette requested a payment of £200 from each of her lovers if they wished to remain anonymous. When her publisher contacted Arthur Wellesley, 1st Duke of Wellington, His Grace replied (so legend has it, in blood red ink), 'Publish, and be damned!' Victorian literary critics tended to denounce these memoirs as obscene, and they were frequently evoked in critiques of contemporary popular authors as a comparative example of rank filth from a more primitive age (often conflated with Egan's *Life in London*).

9 When Cruikshank died it was discovered that he had fathered eleven illegitimate children with a former servant, Adelaide Attree, who lived close to the family home in North London.

10 Isaac 'Ikey' Solomon (c.1787 – 1850), sometimes mis-called 'Solomons' in the broadsheets of the time, was a highly successful and flamboyant criminal. Because of his profession and ethnicity (he was an East End Jew), he was almost certainly the model for the character of Fagin in Dickens' *Oliver Twist.*

11 This is a reference to the notorious 'Gill's Hill Tragedy' of 1823, in which the boxing promoter John Thurtell (and his accomplices Joseph Hunt and William Probert) brutally murdered the solicitor William Weare over a gambling debt. Thurtell was the son of a former mayor of Norwich, and a regular at the Fancy. George Borrow records meeting him in the early-1820s in his memoir *Lavengro* (1851), and he also appears as 'Tom Turtle' in 'The Fight' (1822) by William Hazlitt. Egan interviewed Thurtell in prison and subsequently wrote two broadsheet accounts of the case.

12 Seton travelled under the rank of Major, and is referred to by that title in contemporary documentation, but his promotion to Lieutenant-Colonel, although not published in the *Gazette* until January 16, had taken effect from the previous November. Seton was the replacement for Lieutenant-Colonel John Fordyce, the previous commander of the 74th, who was killed in action in Africa. It would seem that modesty prevented Seton from assuming his new rank before he arrived at his Cape command. In the original manuscript Jack refers to Seton variously as both 'Major' and 'Colonel,' but to avoid confusion I have standardised the references to Major.

13 The Basuto (Sotho or Basotho) Nation was formed of ancient Bantu clans united through the diplomatic and strategic acumen of King Moshoeshoe I (c.1786 – 1870). Threatened by Zulu expansion and European migration throughout the 19th century, the Basuto fought the British in three colonial wars between 1834 and 1853. Moshoeshoe finally accepted peace terms from Sir George Cathcart, Sir Harry Smith's successor as commander of British Armed Forces at the Cape, after the inconclusive Battle of Berea in December 1852. Lakeman is here referring to three embarrassing British defeats in South Africa, although citing Somerset's failure at the Battles of Burns Hill and Hobbes Drift in April 1847 (which, like Jack, I take to be his implication) is rather slanted given that Somerset went on to win a decisive victory at the Battle of Guanga in June. It is surprising, in fact, that none of the British officers present during this discussion raised the latter point. The 'Warden Line' (named after Major Henry Douglas Warden) was the uneasy border established between the British territories of the Orange and Vaal Rivers and the Basuto Nation in 1851. As the British had drawn up this border, it naturally favoured them, claiming the fertile Caledon River Valley. The cold war again became hot, and British forces were defeated by Moshoeshoe at the battle of Viervoet on June 30, 1851. Somerset and Smith were still skirmishing with this elusive and clever enemy at the time of this conversation, and the *Birkenhead* was indeed carrying reinforcements.

14 Although few close to him knew the truth, Dickens' father, John, had gone to the Marshalsea in February, 1824, owing £40.10/, his mother and younger siblings following in April. Just twelve years old, Dickens was taken out of school and sent to work at Warren's Blacking Warehouse, a factory owned by a maternal relative. John Dickens was released after three months, but the family remained poor and Charles was forced to continue working at the factory. Despite concealing his origins, they constantly surface in Dickens' fiction. He sent Mr. Pickwick to the Fleet debtors' prison, in an uncharacteristically bleak section of the otherwise essentially comic novel, Mr. Micawber to the Marshalsea, and his alter ego, David Copperfield, to 'Murdstone and Grinby's Wine Warehouse.' *Little Dorritt* (1857) returns to the Marshalsea, and the novel is predominantly set in the prison; the protagonist of the title, Amy Dorritt, is born there, just as Jack's sister, Sarah, was widely presumed to have been by other inmates.

15 John Mitchel (1815 – 1875) was an Irish nationalist and political journalist. He was charged under the new Treason Felony Act of 1848 for 'seditious libels' and sentenced to be transported for fourteen years. He was subsequently moved from the penal colony at Bermuda (where Jack places him) to Van Diemen's Land (modern-day Tasmania), from which he escaped to New York in 1853. He there established the radical Irish nationalist newspaper *The Citizen,* and in 1854 published his *Jail Journal* documenting his period as a prisoner of the British, including his time at Spike Island.

16 The 'Nimrod Club series' was *The Posthumous Papers of the Pickwick Club*, inaugurated when the publishers Chapman & Hall approached Dickens in the spring of 1836 with a view to him providing the text for a serial about a gentlemen's sporting club based around Robert Seymour's humorous illustrations. Seymour, down on his luck and in need of a hit, had in mind a monthly illustrated serial specifically modelled on Egan's *Life in London*, which still remained the benchmark for such writing, as can be seen immediately from the original subtitle: *Containing a Faithful Record of the Perambulations, Perils, Travels, Adventures, and Sporting Transactions of the Corresponding Members.* Dickens and Seymour did not see eye-to-eye on the direction of the project, and the notoriously sensitive, near-bankrupt artist committed suicide after revising the illustrations for the second issue (Dickens had rejected the originals).

17 Ainsworth and Cruikshank publicly supported these unlicensed theatrical adaptations of their work, whereas Dickens, in general, loathed it when it happened to him. Forster relates the following anecdote in his *Life of Dickens*: 'I was with him at a representation of his *Oliver Twist* the following month [December 1838] at the Surrey Theatre, when in the middle of the first scene he laid himself down upon the floor in a corner of the box and never rose from it until the drop-scene fell.'

18 This article appeared in the *Athenaeum Journal of English and Foreign Literature, Science, and the Fine Arts*, 626 (October 26, 1839). As this is effectively an editorial within a literary review, it is possible that the author may indeed have been, as Jack conjectures, Charles Wentworth Dilke, the editor from 1830 to 1846.

19 The so-called 'Bedchamber crisis' arose when the Whig Prime Minister Lord Melbourne resigned in May, 1839, and Queen Victoria invited Robert Peel to form a minority government. Peel notionally accepted, but only on the condition that Victoria dismissed several of her personal attendants, or 'Ladies of the Bedchamber,' on the grounds that they were married or otherwise related to prominent Whig politicians and that, he argued, a monarch should not be seen to favour a party in opposition. Victoria refused, and Peel did not form a government. Melbourne was persuaded to remain Prime Minister until he was defeated by Peel in the general election of 1841, after which the Whig Ladies of the Bedchamber were quietly replaced by Conservatives.

20 The poet and journalist Samuel Laman Blanchard (1804 – 1845) was then the editor of *George Cruikshank's Omnibus*, before moving to the *Examiner* in 1841; like Ainsworth and Jack, his literary reputation has not endured, despite his contemporary popularity. The Church of England clergyman Richard Harris Barham (1788 –1845) was a novelist and humorous poet who wrote under the pseudonym 'Thomas Ingoldsby.' He is best known for *The Ingoldsby Legends* – a series of mock-medieval ballads and ghost stories that appeared first in *Bentley's Miscellany* and later in the *New Monthly Magazine*, originally illustrated by John Leech and George Cruikshank. The wit of Barham's verse and its lively anapaestic structure anticipates the work of W.S. Gilbert later in the century.

21 'Condition of England' (or 'Industrial') novels collectively represented an attempt to address, or at least explore, working class life during the Industrial Revolution. The 'Condition of England question' was originally posed by Thomas Carlyle in the first chapter of *Chartism* (1839), which begins: 'A feeling very generally exists that the disposition and condition of the Working Classes is a rather ominous matter at present; that something ought to be said, something ought to be done, in regard to it.' Examples of the literary form in print when Jack was considering his lecture included *Coningsby, or The New Generation* (1844), and *Sybil, or The Two Nations* (1845), both by Benjamin Disraeli; Elizabeth Gaskell's *Mary Barton: A Tale of Manchester Life* (1848); *Shirley* (1849) by Charlotte Brontë; and *Alton Locke: Tailor and Poet* (1850) by Charles Kingsley. Dickens' *Hard Times* was not published until 1854.

22 Tristan later wrote in her *London Journal* that she was accompanied on her evening expeditions by 'two men armed with canes.' She does not identify her bodyguards, but the present memoir would suggest that she was referring to Jack and Hetherington.

23 In Chapter LVIII of *The Mysteries of London*, the Resurrection Man breaks into Buckingham Palace with the intention of stealing the plate, sending the diminutive pot-boy Henry Holford in first to open a window much as Dickens' Bill Sikes attempts to use Oliver Twist. Holford explores the palace, and conceals himself beneath a sofa in the Sculpture Gallery, from where he observes Victoria (now sitting above him) discussing affairs of state with Melbourne and Palmerstone. 'Her bust was magnificent, and her figure good,' notes the narrator, 'in spite of the lowness of her stature.' In Chapter LIX, entitled 'The Royal Lovers,' Holford locates and then sits upon the throne of England, and later eavesdrops on a *tête-à-tête* between Victoria and Albert. In the following chapter, Holford overhears two ladies in waiting discussing the royal bloodline. 'The entire family of George the Third has inherited the seeds of disease – physical and mental,' says one. 'Maladies of that kind are hereditary,' agrees the other. When Holford does not immediately return from the Palace, the Resurrection Man goes in after him; by then his accomplice has become so obsessed with the royal couple that he subsequently attempts to assassinate Prince Albert. This episode would appear to be founded upon two real events: the pot-boy Edward Oxford taking a shot at the royal couple on Constitution Hill, and Edmund Jones breaking into the Palace, where, he reportedly said, 'I sat upon the throne, saw the Queen and heard the Princess Royal squall.'

24 George Henry Borrow (1803 – 1881) was a novelist and life writer best known for his memoirs of his time among the Romani, *Lavengro: The Scholar, the Gypsy, the Priest* (1851), and *The Romany Rye* (1857). Borrow was born in East Dereham, Norfolk, an area possessed of a prominent regional accent which Jack would have shared as a boy, also growing up in East Anglia. From this reference, it seems likely that Borrow and Jack were acquainted.

25 The 1st Battalion of the 27th (Enniskillen) Regiment of Foot fought at Waterloo as part of General Lambert's 10th Brigade in the 6th Division. After the French captured La Haye Sainte, they brought up several cannon and shelled the British line at close range. The 700-odd strong 1st Battalion was deployed in square on the Ohain road, 300 yards from the French guns. By the end of the day there were barely 200 men left standing. Many eyewitnesses reported the regularity of the fallen, still maintaining the square.

26 Jeffries is presumably here referring to Maurice Quill, the Assistant-Surgeon of the 31st Regiment of Foot during the French Wars, and one of the unsung pioneers of antiseptic medicine.

27 'Our destiny is frequently met in the very paths we take to avoid it.' La Fontaine, *Fables*, Book VIII (1678–1679), 16, 'The Horoscope.'

28 Jack's description of the Kennington Common rally tallies quite closely with other contemporary reports, for example those in the *Manchester Guardian*, the *Illustrated London News*, the *Northern Star*, and R.G. Gammage's *History of the Chartist Movement, 1837-1854* (1854); although, as he later notes, estimates of the size of the crowd varied wildly.

29 'The Night Attack' was originally a false beginning to Chapter Six of *Vanity Fair*, in which the author considers whether or not he should proceed in the style of 'the genteel, or in the romantic, or in the facetious manner.' 'Fancy,' he finally announces, 'this chapter having been headed...'

> THE NIGHT ATTACK
>
> The night was dark and wild – the clouds black – black – ink-black. The wild wind tore the chimney-pots from the roofs of the old houses, and sent the tiles whirling and crashing through the desolate streets. No soul braved that tempest – the watchmen shrank into their boxes, whither the searching rain followed them where the

> crashing thunderbolt fell and destroyed them – one had so been slain opposite the Foundling. A scorched gabardine, a shivered lantern, a staff rent in twain by the flash, were all that remained of stout Will Steadfast. A hackney-coachman had been blown off his coachbox, in Southampton Row – and whither? But the whirlwind tells no tidings of its victim, save his parting scream as he is borne onwards! Horrible night! It was dark, pitch dark; no moon. No, no. No moon. Not a star. Not a little feeble, twinkling, solitary star. There had been one at early evening, but he showed his face, shuddering, for a moment in the black heaven, and then retreated back.
>
> One, two, three! It is the signal that Black Vizard had agreed on.
>
> 'Mofy! is that your snum?' said a voice from the area. 'I'll gully the dag and bimbole the clicky in a snuffkin.'
>
> 'Nuffle your clod, and beladle your glumbanions,' said Vizard, with a dreadful oath. 'This way, men; if they screak, out with your snickers and slick! Look to the pewter room, Blowser. You, Mark, to the old gaff's mobus box! and I,' added he, in a lower but more horrible voice, 'I will look to Amelia!'
>
> There was a dead silence.
>
> 'Ha!' said Vizard, 'was that the click of a pistol?'

When Thackeray revised the novel in 1853, this passage was omitted, and remained absent in all subsequent editions, the author considering it no longer relevant as a contemporary satire.

30 Jack is referring to 'The Song of the Shirt' by Thomas Hood. The poem was published anonymously in the 1843 Christmas number of *Punch*, and lyrically documented the terrible working conditions and relentless cycle of poverty suffered by many seamstresses.

31 The story that Briscoe's disappearance was voluntary seems to have stuck. In 1902, William Butler, the corporal from the 12th Lancers with whom Jack had conversed on the subject of officers (see Chapter 30), told the journalist W.M. Nightingale that he recalled that a stoker from the *Birkenhead* 'swam ashore to desert.'

32 Legend has it that when the last square of the Old Guard was surrounded at Waterloo and invited to surrender, the soldiers chose, instead, honourable annihilation, their commander, General Count Etienne Cambronne, returning the cry, 'La Garde meurt, elle ne se rend pas!' ('The Guard dies, it does not surrender!') Cambronne was subsequently taken prisoner by Colonel Sir Hugh Halkett, leading some of his contemporaries to suggest an alternative slogan: 'Cambronne se rend, il ne muert pas.' ('Cambronne surrenders, he does not die.')

33 The 'Waterloo Medal' was the first British campaign medal awarded to all soldiers present in a military action, in this case any man who fought at Ligny, Quatre Bras and/or the Battle of Waterloo. The obverse bears the profile of the Prince Regent, while the reverse depicts Victory seated with 'Wellington' inscribed above the figure, and 'Waterloo June 15 1815' below. The medal was silver, and 39,000 were awarded, recipients being described as 'Waterloo Men.'

34 The Bay of Geese (Afrikaans: 'Gansbaai') on the Western Cape is famous for its dense population of Great White Sharks. 'Shark Alley' is a name nowadays commonly applied to the narrow channel of water running between Dyer Island and Geyser Rock, about five miles offshore south of Gansbaai, Geyser Rock being home to a large colony of Cape Fur Seals which the sharks hunt. As far as I am aware, this is the first recorded use of the term 'Shark Alley,' although Salmond seems to be using it to describe the Danger Point peninsula as a whole.

35 The Bouzingo were a group of highly experimental artists and writers active in Paris in the 1830s and 40s that practiced an extreme and eccentric form of Romanticism. In many ways the Bouzingo anticipated the early-Modernist *avant-garde* of the late-19th and early-20th centuries, most notably da da and Surrealism, and André Breton cites their influence in the first Surrealist Manifesto. They were also known variously as 'Le Petit Cénacle' (a more playful version of the 'Cénacle' literary group), 'Les Tartares,' 'Les Frénétiques,' and 'Les Jeunes-France.' Leading members included Gérard de Nerval (Gérard Labrunie), Théophile Gautier, Petrus Borel, and Xavier Forneret, and it is likely that Jack has Nerval's poetry in mind here. The group's reputation for radical bohemianism and their status as a refuge from bourgeois society would have appealed to Jack, and it is likely that he was involved with them during his self-imposed exile in Europe in the early-1840s (see Chapter 27).

36 Metford and Jack are quoting the Horacian ode III.2 on virtue, in which Horace extols endurance, valour, and patriotism. The ode begins: 'Angustam amice pauperiem pati robustus acri militia puer' ('To suffer hardness with good cheer/In sternest school of warfare bred/Our youth should learn'). Jack offers the famous line from the same poem in reply, 'Dulce et decorum est pro patria mori' ('What joy, for fatherland to die!').

37 'Tout est pour le mieux' ('All is for the best') is the optimistic mantra of Professor Pangloss in Voltaire's *Candide* (1759), quoting Gottfried Leibniz's famous refutation of the philosophical 'problem of evil' as a barrier to the logical proof of the existence of God; the problem being how to account for all the suffering and injustice in the world if God is omnipotent, omniscient, and supremely good. Since God is omnipotent, omniscient, and supremely good, argued Leibnitz in *Essays on the Goodness of God, the Freedom of Man and the Origin of Evil* (1710), and since God chose to create this world out of all possibilities, this world must by definition also be good, and in fact must be the 'best of all possible worlds.' Pangloss is a strict adherent to Leibnitz's theodicy, and Voltaire sends him up something rotten.

38 The maritime artist Thomas M. Hemy, known for his painting 'The Wreck of the Birkenhead' (1893), also depicted the sacrifice of Ensign Russell, which he later described in his memoir of 1926, *Deep Sea Days: The Chronicles of a Sailor and Sea Painter*:

> When my painting of 'The Wreck of the *Birkenhead*' was on exhibition at Bristol in 1893 it led to my getting into touch with one of the survivors of that disaster, and obtaining a story of it which I am able to give here for the first time.
>
> Mr. Coffin [*sic*] was at the wheel when the ill-fated vessel struck the rocks off Danger Point in 1852, and witnessed the troops fall into line on the deck by order of the officer; everything being done as at a formal parade.
>
> Mr. Coffin was coxswain of one of the cutters and the boat of which

> he was in charge, with its freight of women and children, was the first to leave the ship. He was afraid to keep too near on account of the swell that lashed around her, but managed to pick up several other survivors. He verified an incident which I had introduced into my picture on hearing the detailed stories of other survivors with whom I had been in personal touch while the picture was in progress. It related to a young officer, Ensign Russell, who gave up his place in a boat to make room for a soldier rescued from drowning, probably the husband of one of the women in the boat. When the picture was first exhibited there was much discussion about this 'melodramatic incident,' but Mr. Coffin verified it fully, and said that when the ensign jumped out of the boat, he was immediately dragged down by sharks.

This painting remains in the possession of the Russell family, and at time of writing it is held at the Regimental Museum of the Royal Highland Fusiliers in Glasgow.

39 'Nearly all men die of their remedies, and not of their illnesses.' Moliere, *Le Malade Imaginaire* (1673), Act III, scene iii.

40 Captain Wright made this point quite forcibly in his initial report of the disaster to the Cape Town Commandant, Lieutenant-Colonel Ingelby:

> Had that boat remained about the wreck, or returned after landing the assistant-surgeon on Danger Point – about which there was no difficulty – I am quite confident that nearly every man of the 200 who were on the drift-wood might have been saved.

He further reiterated this position in his second statement to Commodore Christopher Wyvill, written on the same day, March 1, 1852:

> I cannot express how much the loss of this boat was felt, and had it returned after landing Dr. Culhane I have no hesitation in saying that nearly every man of the two hundred (about) who were on the drift wood between the wreck and the shore must have been saved.

Lieutenant Giradot expressed a similar opinion in a private letter to his father shortly after the wreck, writing that, 'a great many more might have been saved but the boats that we got down deserted us.' Fifty years later he still bore the grudge, writing of the press reports commemorating the anniversary of the disaster, 'The only boat that did not stay by the ship was that Dr. Culhane was in, which went away; had it remained until it was light, it might have saved many lives.'

41 Jack is presumably referring to contemporary press reports, but extracts from the court martial can be read in *A Deathless Story: The 'Birkenhead' and its Heroes* by A.C. Addison and W.H. Matthews (1906), and several of these are reproduced in *Stand Fast* by David Bevan (2nd ed 1998), presently the definitive history of the disaster.

42 It is notable that there is no record of Salmond's suicide, as witnessed by Jack, in the official documentation, which is an indication of the esteem in which he was held by his crew, who to a man clearly kept their secret to the grave. In the letter to his widow from Admiralty House in Simon's Bay dated March 2, 1852, the captain is listed among the '400 souls who drowned,' while one unidentified survivor (possibly Dr. Bowen) was widely reported to have said that, 'I saw him swimming from the sternpost of the ship to a portion of the forecastle deck which was floating about twenty yards from the main body of the wreck. Something struck him on the back of the head, and he never rose again.' Addison and Matthews describe this as 'Captain Salmond's pathetic end,' quoting Alexander Pope's Prologue to Addison's *Tragedy of Cato* (1713):

A brave man struggling in the storms of fate
And greatly falling with a falling state.

ACKNOWLEDGEMENTS

This project has grown out of so many years of research that it would be impractical to cite every source. That said, there are some books to which I feel particularly indebted, most notably *A Deathless Story: The 'Birkenhead' and its Heroes* by A.C. Addison and W.H. Matthews, *Stand Fast* by David Bevan, *The Birkenhead Drill* by Douglas W. Phillips, and Peter Ackroyd's wonderful biography of Dickens. I also owe a debt of gratitude to Professor Anne Humpherys and Professor Louis James for their work on G.W.M. Reynolds, an ongoing and fascinating piece of cultural retrieval. I would like to thank Professor Roger Sales for his inspirational teaching on the Victorian underworld and for reading an early draft, Professor William Hughes for his tireless support of my academic writing, and Professor Victor Sage, who led me to the serious study of gothic literature all those years ago. Warmest regards as well to Ashley Stokes for all his encouragement, Anne Shilton, who also acted as a beta reader, and all our friends at Green Door. Finally, and most importantly, all the thanks and love in the world go to my dear wife, Rachael, who has not only supported this project at every stage but who also designed and illustrated the book and its online platforms, and acted as my copy-editor. Thanks babe, I couldn't have done it without you.

Printed in Great Britain
by Amazon

39479248R00324